THE MOLLIE McGHIE COZY MYSTERIES

BOOKS 1–3

ELLEN JACOBSON

CONTENTS

Murder at the Marina

Book #1

THE CREW

MOLLIE MCGHIE—Wanted diamonds for her anniversary, got a dilapidated sailboat instead. Focused on getting a promotion at work, investigating mysterious events at the marina, and getting rid of the unwanted boat.

SCOOTER MCGHIE—Needs to up his game in the gift-giving department. Recently sold his business. Now has way too much time on his hands to devote to his midlife crisis—a sailing obsession.

NANCY AND NED SCHNEIDER—Owners of the Palm Tree Marina. Nancy runs a tight ship, keeping everyone on their toes. Ned is easy-going and has a soft spot for cats.

KATY AND SAM—Nancy and Ned's grandchildren. Seven-year-old Katy takes sailing lessons, while her younger brother tags along.

CAPTAIN DAN—Local boat broker. A Texan native, Captain Dan uses his dubious southern charm to try to woo the ladies.

PENNY CHADWICK—Also from Texas, Penny lives aboard her boat at the marina and teaches sailing classes.

SANDY AND JACK HOLT—Had hoped to be enjoying their retirement by now. Instead, Jack runs a small business from their boat, while Sandy struggles with health issues.

MRS. MOTO—Sandy and Jack's cat, a Japanese bobtail. A talkative calico with black markings on her face that resemble eyeglasses.

ALEJANDRA LOPEZ—A young waitress at the Sailor's Corner Cafe. Saving up her money in the hopes of opening up a nail salon one day.

BEN MORETTI—A wannabe pirate often found drinking beer. Struggles to make ends meet. Picks up odd jobs at the marina.

MR. AND MRS. DIAMOND—Mollie isn't sure what their real names are, but she's dubbed them "the Diamonds" on account of the wife's sparkly diamond necklace.

LOLA—A curvaceous, flirtatious redhead and Mollie's rival for a promotion at work.

BRIAN MORRISON—Works with Mollie. Impervious to Lola's charms and rooting for Mollie to get the promotion.

CHIEF DALTON AND OFFICER MOORE—Local law enforcement officers who investigate the murder at the marina. Mollie is fascinated by the chief's eyebrows.

WAYNE GRIMM AND FRED ROLLINS—Two local hooligans who are often found at the Tipsy Pirate bar.

TONY DUBLONSKI—Manager of Melvin's Marine Emporium.

TIFFANY AND CHAD—Two teenagers who work at Melvin's part-time.

CHAPTER 1
SURPRISE!

WHAT WOULD YOU DO IF YOU found out your husband was having an affair? Would you:

- (a) be understanding—he's just going through a midlife crisis;
- (b) throw your glass of champagne in his face and storm out of the restaurant;
- (c) tell him about the new love of your life—Sven, your Swedish masseur; or
- (d) order an extra-large piece of chocolate cake?

You can cross (a) off the list—believe me, I wasn't in a very understanding mood. And (b) is out too. Why would I waste a perfectly good glass of champagne? Of course it's not (c)—what kind of girl do you take me for? The correct answer is obviously (d), chocolate. Lots and lots of chocolate, washed down with lots and lots of champagne.

You know what made matters worse? He told me about her during our ten-year anniversary dinner. You're supposed to get diamonds after ten years, not your husband's confession about his torrid love affair with some hussy named Marjorie Jane. And, as if that weren't bad enough, it turned out that she was a redhead! I mean, Lucille Ball is great, but certain other redheads really made my blood boil.

There we were, dining at my new favorite seafood restaurant, Chez Poisson, when Scooter reached across the table, took my hand in his, and rubbed it softly. This was the moment I had been waiting for. Any minute now, he was going to reach into his jacket pocket and present me with a velvet jewelry box containing some lovely little thing encrusted with diamonds.

Instead, he pulled his cell phone out of his pocket. "You know how much I love you, don't you, Mollie?" I nodded, wondering why he was holding his phone. Maybe it was going to magically turn into a diamond bracelet. I kept my eyes on it, just in case.

He pressed a button, looked at the screen, and smiled. "Well, it turns out I've fallen in love with another pretty lady too. Her name is Marjorie Jane." He glanced at me and chuckled. "Not that anyone could replace you, of course, but Marjorie Jane is pretty special."

I was stunned. My husband, in love with another woman. And not only in love with another woman, but casually announcing it over dinner as if I'd be okay with it. I think I would have been less surprised if Scooter's phone had turned into a diamond bracelet than I was by his confession.

"Wait until you see these shots of her," Scooter said. He adjusted his tortoiseshell glasses, then swiped his finger across the screen on his phone, gazing at picture after picture of the new love of his life. "She has the sleekest lines. You won't believe how she moves through the water." He got a dreamy expression in his dark brown eyes. "You can really see her red coloring shimmering in this one."

Now I was starting to get angry. There he was, ogling photos of this red-haired hussy in her bathing suit, swimming in the water. I bet it wasn't a one-piece suit either, but one of those skimpy bikinis that left nothing to the imagination.

I leaned back in my chair, ran my fingers through my frizzy, mousy-brown hair, and stared at my empty crystal champagne flute. I really needed a refill. And where was the cake I had ordered earlier?

As I scanned the restaurant for the waiter, my eyes were drawn to a young couple sitting by a window overlooking the water. She toyed with her wedding ring while the waiter refilled her wine glass. I heard the young man tell his wife to close her eyes. He got up from the table and walked behind her. He pulled a small velvet box out of his jacket pocket, opened it, and removed a necklace. Brushing her long, black hair to the side, he gently placed it around her neck. She opened her eyes and squealed as she looked down and saw—yes, you guessed it—a diamond pendant sparkling on a delicate gold chain. I bet they hadn't been married for even a year and he was already giving her diamonds.

Our waiter bustled up to the table, interrupting my thoughts about sparkly diamonds and unfaithful husbands. "Voilà, madame," he said, putting a dessert plate down in front of me with a flourish.

"You call this big?" I pointed at a tiny slice of chocolate cake. Sure, it was beautiful, artfully arranged on a rectangular white plate with a drizzle of raspberry sauce and crushed hazelnuts sprinkled in the shape of a heart, but it was positively microscopic in size. "I specifically asked for the largest piece of chocolate cake you have. Can't you see that this is an emergency?"

I thrust the plate into the waiter's hands. "Take this back to the kitchen and add at least three more slices before you come back." As he started to walk away, I grabbed his arm. "How about a couple of scoops of chocolate ice cream while you're at it?"

I looked over at Scooter. He had been oblivious to the whole chocolate cake fiasco. I took the opportunity to switch my empty champagne glass with his full one. He didn't even notice.

"You're drooling all over your phone!" I said sharply.

Oops, that might have been a bit too loud. The young woman with the diamond necklace turned and stared at me. My mother would have been telling me to use my indoor voice right about then. She'd probably also have had something to say about ordering chocolate cake and what it could do to my waistline.

Just then my phone beeped. I pulled it out of my beaded evening bag. Yep, right on cue—a text from my mother.

What did Scooter get you for your anniversary this year? Something with diamonds?

I sighed. How was I going to explain Marjorie Jane to her? She had never been that crazy about Scooter to begin with. Probably best to get straight to the point. It was easier that way.

No diamonds, just a redheaded midlife crisis named Marjorie Jane.

I saw the waiter coming back to the table with a heaping plate of chocolate cake and enough ice cream piled on top to guarantee a healthy tip. My phone kept beeping. No doubt my mother wanting to know more about the other woman in Scooter's life. I tucked the phone back into my purse. Chocolate deserves one's undivided attention.

"Sir, can I get you anything else? Some more coffee, perhaps?" the waiter asked. Scooter barely glanced up from his phone. "No, thank you. I'm fine," he mumbled.

Who sits and stares at pictures of their mistress during an anniversary dinner with their wife? I could feel the muscles in my neck tense up. Too bad Sven wasn't around to work out the knots. Maybe that would have gotten Mr. Oblivious's attention—the sight of a cute, young, blond guy massaging my neck. Nah, probably not. He was so wrapped up in Marjorie Jane that he wouldn't have even noticed Sven.

I felt my eyes tear up, which I didn't like one bit. I pride myself on not breaking down every time something goes wrong. I took a deep breath. *You're in control.* I crumpled up my linen napkin and placed it next to my dessert plate, which sadly only had crumbs left on it, took aim, and kicked Scooter under the table. I was wearing very pointy shoes. That got his attention.

"So, did you think you could just find another woman and I'd be okay with it?"

He looked at me with surprise. "What are you talking about, my little sweet potato? What other woman?"

"Are you serious? You've been staring at pictures of her for the last half hour." I was proud of myself for using my indoor voice this time. "Sure, I know men have midlife crises, but they usually get a sports car or a toupee or something like that. But no, you had to go and get yourself a mistress. And a redhead at that!"

Scooter's brow furrowed. "But Marjorie Jane isn't my mistress. She's a sailboat. I'm buying her for you as an anniversary present."

I put my champagne flute down. "What? An anniversary present? A sailboat?" This wasn't making any sense. I wondered if he had had too much champagne to drink, but I think it was possible I had finished off the entire bottle myself. Normally, I would guess that's why my head had started to hurt, but let's be realistic—my husband was talking gibberish. Who buys their wife a sailboat as an anniversary present?

"Yes, a sailboat. See, she's gorgeous." He passed me his phone. "Look at those classic lines, those teak decks, the red hull, and the white-and-gold trim. Snazzy, huh?"

He leaned over the table and squeezed my hand. "I've arranged for us to meet the boat broker at the marina tomorrow so that you can see her. I know you're going to love her as much as I do."

I was so flabbergasted I didn't say anything. Trust me, that's highly unusual. I've typically got a lot to say. All of it very interesting, I might add, and none of it about sailboats.

I didn't talk to Scooter as we left the restaurant.

I didn't talk to Scooter on the car ride home.

I didn't talk to Scooter when we got home.

I didn't talk to Scooter when we went to bed.

A normal guy would have figured out by this point that he was getting the silent treatment. Nope, not Mr. Clueless. He was so wrapped up in his daydreams about Marjorie Jane that he didn't even notice.

Marjorie Jane was seriously getting on my nerves. Something was going to have to be done about her.

CHAPTER 2
THE RED-HAIRED HUSSY

I STARTED TALKING TO SCOOTER again in the morning, but that was only because he asked me if I wanted a mocha. I need caffeine to function, preferably caffeine that's made by someone else.

I could have just nodded in response to his question, but I noticed that he wasn't putting nearly enough chocolate syrup into my cup. After the events of last night, I deserved an extra chocolaty start to the day. This required words.

"Scooter, why are you skimping on the chocolate?"

He turned and smiled. "Sorry, I was lost in thought about *Marjorie Jane*." He stirred in a few more spoonfuls.

I put my head in my hands. I couldn't believe it. *Marjorie Jane* was even getting in the way of my morning mocha.

Scooter tapped me on the shoulder, placed the steaming cup on the counter in front of me, and gave me a kiss on my forehead. I took a sip and sighed. It was delicious. That man sure could make a tasty mocha. It was almost hard to stay mad at him.

He sat on the barstool next to mine with a bowl of Froot Loops. Just like I can't start my day without caffeine, Scooter can't start his day without cereal. He prefers it to be full of brightly colored, sugary nuggets that crunch loudly when you eat them, disturbing those of us who prefer to quietly sip our mochas.

As he munched away, Scooter sorted through a pile of mail. He passed some catalogs and bills to me, then pulled out a magazine that had a picture of a couple of geeky-looking guys underneath a headline declaring them the winners of this year's telecommunications technology innovation award.

"Why do they keep sending me this?" He clenched the magazine in his hands. "The last thing I want to be reminded of is these two idiots. The only reason they're on the cover is because of my research." He tossed the magazine across the counter, pulled his bowl toward him, and pushed the rest of his Froot Loops back and forth with his spoon.

I reached over and squeezed his arm. He gave me a half-hearted smile. Ever since he had been forced to sell his stake in the high-tech telecommunications business that he had founded with the two geeks in question, he hadn't been himself. Sure, he had made enough on the sale that he didn't have to work again, but he was struggling to figure out what to do next with his life, especially as he was only in his forties. Although the gray that had begun to appear in his dark-brown hair made him look distinguished, it was probably due to stress.

I pulled out one of his sailing magazines from the stack. "Here, why don't you read this instead? That should cheer you up."

He leafed through the pages for a few minutes, then seized my hand. "Thanks for being so understanding. I'm sorry if I've been a real pain to live with lately."

"It's okay. You've been going through a rough patch."

He put the magazine down and slurped up the last of the milk in his bowl. "What do you say we head over to the marina after I take a quick shower?"

I shrugged. Might as well get it over with. Maybe I could talk some sense into him about the boat once I saw what I was up against. "Sure, as long as you make me another mocha for the road."

* * *

"Are you excited to meet *Marjorie Jane*?" Scooter asked as he pulled into the marina parking lot.

"Sure, as excited as that time the dentist told me I was doing an excellent job flossing my teeth." I gave him a big grin to prove my point. "See, good dental hygiene does pay off."

"Why do I think you're being a tad sarcastic?"

"Sarcastic? Me? Never. No, I'm dying to meet this red-haired hussy of yours."

I stepped out of the car and closed the door. It might have sounded like I slammed the door, but I swear that's just the acoustics you get when you're near the water. Sound carries farther over water; at least that's what I think my science teacher said back in high school.

While I reminisced about my struggles getting a passing grade in physics class, Scooter was busy grabbing a navy-blue tote bag out of the back. It had a picture of a sailboat with "Let Your Dreams Set Sail" printed underneath. No doubt he had bought it at one of those boat shows he was always going to.

"What's in the bag?"

"You'll see. It's a surprise."

"You know I don't like surprises."

"Sure you do. Remember how thrilled you were last night when I surprised you with *Marjorie Jane*?" He bent down and gave me a quick peck on the cheek before hurrying down the path.

"You really are dense sometimes, aren't you?" I shouted after him as I tried to catch up.

Scooter sure can move fast when he's focused on something. And by focused, I mean obsessed. He has two modes of operating—fixated on something 24/7 or completely disinterested.

His interest in sailing had started a couple of years ago when he had gone on a weekend charter trip with some buddies. After that, he spent countless hours looking at sailing websites, leafing through glossy boat magazines, and reading books on rather dull subjects like diesel engine maintenance and repair.

I had hoped it was just another one of his temporary preoccupations, like the time he decided he was going to learn to make Ethiopian food. He bought all sorts of unusual ingredients, scorched several pots and pans, and couldn't speak for days after adding too much hot pepper to a chicken dish and burning his mouth. After one final failed attempt at making an Ethiopian spice blend, he lost interest and ordered pizza for dinner instead.

I should have realized that his fixation with sailing was a lot more serious. Buying a sailboat was probably a good clue. Maybe that's what a midlife crisis was—an obsession gone wrong.

When he arrived at the boardwalk, he turned and wiggled his finger at me. "Come on, my little sweet potato. This is no time to dawdle. We're due to meet the boat broker soon."

I certainly wasn't dawdling. Okay, maybe a little. I really wasn't in any hurry to see *Marjorie Jane*. But my short, stubby legs could never keep up with his long ones. He had been a star basketball player in college, and it was his speed running up and down the court that had earned him the nickname "Scooter." I glared at him. He caught my meaning.

"Sorry about that." He clutched my hand and gave it a squeeze. "It's just that I'm so excited to see my new girl."

I glared at him again. My patented knock-it-off-or-you'll-suffer-serious-retribution glare. The last time I'd given him a glare like that, I hid his Froot Loops and he had to eat oatmeal every day for breakfast for a week instead. Oh, how he'd suffered.

He gave my hand another squeeze and quickly said, "Of course, *you're* my best girl, Mollie. No one could take your place."

When Scooter calls me by my first name instead of a silly pet name, then you know he's serious. Or worried he might be served more oatmeal.

"All right. We better get a move on if we're going to meet this boat broker of yours," I said. I tried to see what was in the tote bag he was carrying.

"Hey, no peeking." He switched the bag to his other hand and walked down the boardwalk to a creaky dock that had seen better days. He pointed to a sign that said B Dock. "She's just down here. There are three other main docks: A Dock, C Dock, and D Dock."

"Do you think they hired external consultants to come up with those clever names? Probably the same team that came up with the name Palm Tree Marina on account of all the palm trees. And let me guess, they came up with the name Coconut Cove on account of all the coconuts floating in the water?"

Scooter suppressed a smile. "There's also a fuel dock and a dinghy dock. And yes, before you ask, they have clever names too

—Fuel Dock and Dinghy Dock." He pointed at the boats bobbing in the water near the breakwall. "People who keep their boats in the mooring field use their dinghies to get back and forth to shore, and have a special dock to tie up at. And the fuel dock is—"

I held up my hand. "Let me guess. The fuel dock is where you get fuel."

"You're catching on quick. Do you want to know about the boatyard?"

"Not really."

"Of course you do. If you need to do repairs or maintenance to your boat, you have it hauled out and taken there to work on it."

"Fascinating."

I gingerly stepped along the dock, avoiding planks that looked like they were missing nails. It reminded me of that kids' game where you avoided stepping on cracks so that you wouldn't break your mother's back. Except, in this case, I wasn't worried about my mom as much as I was worried about one of the planks breaking and tumbling me into the water. Sure, I like splashing around in the water, but only in pools and hot tubs. I find the chlorination in the water reassuring—it's a sign that humans are in charge and that you're less likely to find scary critters, like sharks and alligators, lurking about. When it comes to the ocean, you're on your own. You never know what sea monsters might be waiting for you. I'm not a very strong swimmer, so I'd much prefer to fight off someone trying to steal my lounge chair by the pool than fend off a great white or a gator.

We had only moved to Florida a few months ago, so worries about sharks and alligators were pretty new to me. When Scooter's uncle passed away and left him his cottage in Coconut Cove, a small tourist town on the Gulf Coast, we decided it would be a good opportunity to make a fresh start, away from reminders of Scooter's old business and former partners.

Across from the marina, stairs led down to a sandy beach. I watched some tourists wading in the water, a dog carrying a large piece of driftwood to his owner, and a couple of kids flying colorful kites. Maybe I could convince Scooter to go for a stroll after we were done looking at this boat of his.

After successfully navigating the rest of the dock, I saw him standing in front of a red wooden boat. He stared at it rapturously, his mouth hanging open.

I grabbed a tissue out of my purse. "Here," I said. "You're drooling again."

He wiped the corner of his mouth. "She's so beautiful!"

I'm not sure "beautiful" was the word I would have used. Paint was flaking off the side. The teak decks looked like they had seen better days. And to top things off, the name *Marjorie Jane* was written in an ostentatious, flowery gold script on the front of the boat. "Tacky" is the word that came to mind, not "beautiful."

I was all set to explain exactly what the difference between beautiful and tacky was when Scooter gazed at me with those dark brown eyes of his.

We used to have a chocolate Labrador dog with the same exact eyes when I was a kid. One day, he came bounding up to me with my Barbie doll in his mouth, dropped it at my feet, wagged his tail, and looked at me with his soulful eyes. Sure, Barbie was missing a leg and covered in dirt, but how could I stay mad at a dog who oozed so much cuteness? It was the same with Scooter, except this was a boat and not a mangled doll.

"How much did you pay for this thing?" I asked. "She looks like she should have sunk to the bottom a long time ago."

"I've only put down a deposit," Scooter said. "That's why we're meeting the boat broker. To sign the papers and finalize the deal."

"You mean you can get out of this?" I asked hopefully.

Scooter didn't answer my question. He had a faraway look in his eyes as he caressed the side of the boat. Either he was lost in daydreams about sailing or he was deliberately ignoring me. I wasn't sure which was worse. I hated it when he pretended he couldn't hear me, but daydreaming about a boat, of all things—especially this boat—really took the cake.

He rubbed his hands together. "Come on, let me show you the cockpit. Imagine relaxing there at night over one of those tropical cocktails you're fond of. Sounds romantic, doesn't it?"

It's true. I do like tropical cocktails. Especially when they're served in coconuts with tiny umbrellas. But I wasn't sure you needed a boat to enjoy coconut drinks. They had these beach bars that did the trick just fine.

Scooter slipped off his shoes, then jumped athletically up from the dock onto the teak deck, as though he were going for a slam dunk. He ducked under the red canvas shading the cockpit from the sun and sat behind the steering wheel, grinning from ear to ear. He looked like a lovesick teenager.

He patted the seat next to him. "Hop on up. But first, take off your flip-flops. You should never wear shoes on a boat."

I placed my sandals on the dock next to his shoes and tried to pull myself up onto the deck. I didn't get very far. Stupid short legs.

Scooter whistled some sort of sea shanty while he pretended to steer the boat. At least I thought it was a sea shanty. It might have been the latest girl-group song we'd heard on the radio on the drive over to the marina. Either way, it was annoying.

"Are you coming or what?" he asked as he spun the wheel from side to side.

"Exactly how am I supposed to get up there?" I said, putting my hands on my hips. "The boat is like twenty feet above the dock here and I'm only five feet tall."

He peered down. "Math never was your strong suit, was it? It's only a few feet, not twenty." He pointed at a twisted metal cable that ran from the mast to the deck. "Just grab onto that and hoist yourself up." Then he went back to steering the boat and whistling away to himself.

After several attempts, I eventually managed to scramble on board, holding on for dear life. I teetered precariously on the edge, trying to figure out how I was going to get my legs over the lines that ran around the boat. "Hey, Scooter, mind giving a girl a hand here?" I asked.

He stepped out of the cockpit. "See, I knew you could do it. You're going to love being on a sailboat. It's great exercise, isn't it, climbing up and over things?" He held onto my hand. "Now, just put one leg over the lifelines here. That's good. Now the other one."

The boat rocked back and forth as a powerboat sped past *Marjorie Jane* and headed toward the inlet, which led out of the marina and into the deeper waters of Sunshine Bay. I clung to

Scooter so that I wouldn't lose my balance and land back on the dock. The last thing I wanted was to have to climb back up again.

"Welcome aboard *Marjorie Jane*," he said as he clasped my waist and gave me a kiss. "This is the greatest day ever. My very own sailboat that I get to share with my best girl."

When he let go of me, I nearly lost my balance again. I clutched the lines I had just climbed over. "What did you call these again?"

"Lifelines. They keep you from falling off the boat and into the water. They can save your life, so to speak."

I thought about all the potential sea monsters circling below, just waiting to gobble me up. I tugged on the lifelines. "These feel kind of loose. If I fell against them, they'd just give way. Shouldn't they be tighter than this?"

"Nah, they seem fine to me. Don't worry. You're not going to fall in the water. Sailing is perfectly safe." Scooter sat back down behind the wheel.

I climbed into the cockpit, stepping on tattered white cushions with a red starfish pattern. "These are in pretty bad shape."

"That's just cosmetic stuff. You have to look past that and see the beauty that lies underneath. Besides, that's why we're getting *Marjorie Jane* at such a bargain price."

"And what exactly is a bargain when it comes to sailboats?" I asked as I sat at the other end of the cockpit.

"She's a steal," he said evasively. "Captain Dan says we're lucky that we snapped her up before anyone else did."

I had a feeling I wasn't going to get a straight answer. I reached out and touched the wooden boards at the entryway to the boat. Red paint flaked off on my hands.

"That's the companionway," Scooter said. "You push back the hatch and pull out those washboards to get into the boat. I know you can't wait to see down below. Captain Dan will be here any minute to unlock her."

I picked up a broken padlock from the cushion next to me. "You mean this lock? I think someone may have used bolt cutters on this."

Scooter narrowed his eyes. "Bolt cutters. Of course you'd know it was bolt cutters."

"Do we have to go into that again? It was just that one time," I said quickly. "Besides, there's a bigger issue here. Who broke into the boat and why? There's much nicer boats to break into around here than this piece of junk." I looked around the dock at the fancy powerboats and well-maintained sailboats nearby.

Scooter elbowed me out of the way. "Let me see that," he said, grabbing the padlock. He turned it over in his hands. "Looks like you're right. This was cut. That's definitely your area of expertise, isn't it?"

"Focus, Scooter, focus. The past is the past. More importantly, do you think anyone's still down there?" I asked.

"Move over," he said. He slowly pushed back the hatch and peeked down into the cabin.

"Do you see anyone?" I asked.

He put a finger to his lips. "Shh. I'm going to check it out. You stay here and keep quiet." He pulled the washboards out, setting them down gently on the cockpit floor. He carefully climbed down the ladder.

"I can't see anything with your big head in the way. Can you move over to the side?" I asked, trying to peer down below.

"What part of keep quiet didn't you understand?" he whispered. "Just stay there. I'm going to try to find the light switch."

I heard a lot of banging and a few swear words followed by a loud exclamation. "Ouch, that hurt!"

"Scooter, are you okay?" I asked.

"I'm fine. I just banged my foot on something."

"What was it?"

"How would I know?" He sounded grumpy. "It's dark down here. I can't see a thing."

I reached into my purse, pulled out a flashlight, and pointed it down the companionway. There were cushions and clothes scattered everywhere, cans of food piled haphazardly on a table in the center of the cabin, cupboard doors hanging open, and books strewn about.

"There's the light switch," Scooter said as he turned an overhead fixture on. The place looked even worse when illuminated.

Scooter sat on one of the couches, bent down, and rubbed his left foot. I quickly climbed down the ladder and rushed over to him. "Is your foot okay?"

"It'll be fine. I stubbed my toe on that winch handle over there." He pointed at a large metal object next to the ladder.

"Did you say *witch* handle? Are you saying this boat is haunted?" I picked up the long metal object. "What do witches do with these? Wave them over their heads and cast magic spells to ensure good fishing?"

"No, not witch, *winch*. You insert the handle into the winch to grind the sails in. You know that metal drum you tripped over getting into the cockpit? That's a winch." He must have seen the confused look on my face. "Never mind. I'll show you how it works later. Here, give it to me." I passed the handle to him, being careful not to step on an overturned toolbox.

Scooter examined it closely. "It appears to be brand new. But the size is all wrong for our boat. This handle is way too big for the winches on *Marjorie Jane*."

"How is it you know the sizes of the winch handles on this boat but you don't know what shoe size I wear?"

"What are you talking about? I bought you fuzzy bunny slippers a few years ago for your birthday."

I rolled my eyes. "Yeah, I remember. That's why I started leaving sticky notes on your desk for you with gift suggestions."

"Oh, is that what those were?" he asked with a smirk on his face.

"Yes, and if you'll recall, there wasn't a note that said dilapidated sailboat on it."

"Trust me, *Marjorie Jane* will look great once she's all tidied up. Why don't you go check out the rest of the boat while I clear up this mess?" He pointed toward a tiny hallway running along one side of the boat. "That's the kitchen. Or, as we sailors like to say, the galley. Just imagine yourself whipping up some tasty treats in there for us."

I watched in surprise as Scooter began putting books back on the shelves and cans into cupboards. At home, he usually left stuff all over the place and I picked up after him. This stupid boat inspired tidiness in Scooter, whereas I had failed miserably in my efforts to domesticate him. Just another reason to despise *Marjorie Jane*.

I sighed and walked into the galley area. I could see why they called it a galley. A space as small as this certainly didn't deserve to be called a kitchen. There was barely enough room to turn around. The stove and oven were tiny, the counter was practically nonexistent, and there wasn't a fridge to be seen.

"How are you supposed to survive on this thing without a fridge?" I asked Scooter.

"There's a fridge." He pointed at where I was leaning on the countertop. "Right there, underneath your hand."

I glanced down, and sure enough there was a tiny, hinged door on the top of the counter. I pulled it open and stared into something that appeared to be the size of a small cooler you'd take on picnics. As I was puzzling over this, I heard a man call out, "Ahoy, is anyone there? Permission to come aboard?"

Scooter poked his head up the companionway. "Hey there, Captain Dan. Come on down." He chuckled. "Although I'm not sure I can give you permission to come aboard. *Marjorie Jane* isn't our boat yet."

"Don't you worry. This pretty lady will be all yours once we sign these papers and you hand me a check," Captain Dan said in a slow Texas drawl. I admired his agility as he made his way down into the cabin. He made climbing down a ladder seem easy. He was wearing a denim shirt with mother-of-pearl buttons tucked into well-pressed jeans. My eyes were drawn to his shiny red cowboy boots and an even shinier belt buckle in the shape of an anchor. I looked up, expecting to see a cowboy hat. Instead, the boat broker had a navy-blue captain's hat perched on top of his head. He had neatly trimmed salt-and-pepper hair and a bushy beard and moustache. Something about him was familiar, but I couldn't figure out what it was.

Captain Dan shook Scooter's hand heartily while he surveyed the cabin. "My, oh my, what happened here, li'l pardner?"

"Oh, it's nothing," Scooter said.

"Nothing?" I said in disbelief. "It isn't nothing. It looks like someone cut through the padlock, broke in, and was searching for something."

Captain Dan turned, stared at me, and gave a low whistle. "Now, let me see here. This must be the missus. Whew-whee, you sure are one lucky fella, Scooter. She's got more curves than a barrel of snakes. And what color are those lovely eyes? It's hard to tell in this light, but they sure are sparkling."

I was pretty sure the sparkle in my eyes was due to my surprise about how corny this guy was. "They're hazel."

Scooter wrapped his arm around my waist possessively. "This is my wife, Mollie. But you better not talk about snakes around her. She had a run-in with one a while back."

"Okay, no more talk about snakes," Captain Dan said. "Well now, missy, have you seen the rest of the boat?"

"Not yet. There are more important things to worry about, like who broke into the boat and why."

"Oh, that? That's nothing, probably just some of the high school kids on a dare. I wouldn't worry your pretty little head about it, Mrs. McGhie. Now, why don't you have a look back here at the aft cabin." The captain slapped Scooter on the shoulder. "We menfolk are gonna sort out the paperwork."

Scooter grinned. He seemed to be having fun watching my reaction to Captain Dan's patronizing comment about my pretty little head. Not that I didn't like being told that my head was pretty. Given the perpetual frizzy state of my mousy-brown hair, it didn't happen very often. But somehow I didn't think Captain Dan was complimenting my efforts at trying to tame my unruly locks with hair straighteners.

"Go on," Scooter said. "The aft cabin will be our bedroom. You're going to love it. It's really spacious."

"Aft?"

"Just walk through the galley to the back of the boat. That's what 'aft' means—toward the back or the stern."

I thought about giving the boat broker a piece of my mind but decided I might as well see if the burglars had rifled through the aft cabin too. I wasn't buying his explanation that a bunch of high school kids had broken in on a dare. How many teenagers carry around bolt cutters?

Scooter called after me, "Make sure you duck your head."

"Too late," I said as my head smacked into a low ceiling. After making my way through a tiny door suitable for Hobbits, I found myself in a cabin with a full-size bed against one wall and a small seating area against the other. What I didn't see were any walk-in closets or dressers. Yet another thing to add to the list of complaints about *Marjorie Jane*.

The cabin was neat and tidy. Nothing was out of place. Had the intruders found what they were looking for in the main cabin, or had they been disturbed before they could search this part of the boat?

I made my way back through the galley, remembering to duck my head this time. I could have sworn I felt someone swat me on the butt as I inched into the main cabin. Captain Dan winked at me.

Unaware of the captain's flirtations, Mr. Oblivious glanced at me and said, "There, doesn't it look better?" The cushions were back in place and all the items that had been strewn about the cabin were piled on one of the couches.

"I guess so. But it is a bit dark in here," I said. I pointed at the small windows set high up on the cabin walls. "Maybe we could replace those with some large picture windows to let in more light. And I bet a light-colored wallpaper would do wonders for those walls. All this dark wood makes the place feel so old-fashioned, kind of like the paneled den my dad had in the basement."

Scooter's eyes got wide. "Wallpaper...picture windows...," he sputtered.

Captain Dan chuckled. "Never mind about that just now, missy. Why don't you have a look at the V-berth? Scooter, go on, show her the V-berth."

Scooter opened up a door at the front of the boat and showed me a room that was shaped like the letter V. Yep, V-berth—another highly original name. The room was taken up by a large raised platform topped with dark-green cushions. I bent down to get a better look at the pattern, when I realized that it wasn't a pattern at all—it was mildew. Gross. There were two floor-to-ceiling cupboards flanking each side of the berth. I didn't dare open them for fear of what bacterial cultures I might find growing inside.

As I was brushing a cobweb away from my face, I heard Captain Dan whispering to Scooter, "Let the ladies have their way when it comes to decorating. Your life will be so much more peaceful."

"But picture windows, wallpaper..." He was still sputtering.

"Y'all will have plenty of time to figure that all out. Maybe we should go ahead and sign these papers now."

"Captain Dan, what exactly do these papers say?" I asked as I closed the door to the V-berth.

"You know, standard stuff. Just a few signatures and a couple of initials, then this gorgeous little lady will belong to y'all," Captain Dan replied. He sat and put a folder on the table.

"Scooter, don't you think we should talk about this a bit more?"

Captain Dan opened up the folder and pulled out a stack of papers. "Well, little lady, I wouldn't take too long. There's a couple who are flying down from New York City tomorrow to see the boat and the phone's been ringing off the hook. Lots of other people are interested in *Marjorie Jane*. If you don't snap her up now, I can't guarantee she'll still be parked here on the lot. Um, I mean *docked* at the marina."

Scooter looked through the papers and then up at me with those cute little puppy-dog eyes. Okay, maybe he did need a new hobby to lift him out of his funk, but I wasn't sure a boat was the best solution. Especially this dilapidated one.

Captain Dan handed Scooter a pen. "And, it's a heck of a price. You won't find a better price on a boat like this anywhere. Captain Dan has the best deals in town, guaranteed!"

Scooter hesitated. "I don't think we can let this slip out of our fingers. You know we have the money from the sale of the business and from my uncle's estate. Besides, I think it would be a nice way to honor my uncle's memory. He always did enjoy sailing."

It was true; we did have some money in the bank, and his uncle always did talk fondly about his days sailing in the Caribbean. I suppose if you were going to have a midlife crisis, a sailboat was better than a bad toupee or a sports car.

I sighed. "I guess it's okay."

Scooter grinned from ear to ear. "It's going to be great. Just imagine us out there on the water with dolphins frolicking alongside *Marjorie Jane*. Just the two of us."

The way he was talking about *Marjorie Jane*, it was more like the three of us. But who's counting?

"Fine. While you two do the paperwork, I'm going to go outside for some fresh air. It's so stuffy in here." I looked around the cabin again. "I really think some picture windows that we can open up to get a breeze in here would do a world of good."

Scooter turned red and sputtered again. I wondered what it was about windows that got him so worked up. Captain Dan distracted him by pointing to a spot that needed to be initialed.

While Scooter was leafing through the paperwork, Captain Dan leaned back and looked me up and down. I was getting a little tired of how he leered at me. And Mr. Oblivious continued to be, well, oblivious. I knew his rather nerdy powers of concentration were what made him so successful in his line of work, but sometimes I wished he were able to pay attention to more than one thing at a time. Maybe it was a good thing we were getting this paperwork over and done with so we wouldn't have to deal with Captain Dan much longer. And what made him so special that he could wear cowboy boots on the boat, but I wasn't allowed to wear my flip-flops?

"Come on by the patio later, around four," Captain Dan said. "The marina hosts a barbecue every Friday. They'll provide the hamburgers and hot dogs. All you have to do is bring a side dish or a dessert to share. It'll be a good chance to meet some of the other cowboys and cowgirls who have boats here."

"We'll bring dessert," I said quickly. I always bring dessert to potlucks. Usually brownies. That way I know there's going to be something decent to eat. One time somebody convinced me to bring a salad. Well, that turned out to be a colossal mistake. There were salads of every kind, but no brownies. Not even any chocolate chip cookies. No desserts at all. The worst potluck ever.

I grabbed my purse off the table. "Since I don't have time to go back to the cottage and make brownies, I'm going to see what I can find in town and meet you back here at the marina."

"Sure thing," Scooter said while he continued signing papers and handing them back to Captain Dan. "Why don't you pick up a bottle of wine while you're out so we can celebrate?"

I looked around the cabin and sighed. I wasn't sure one bottle of wine was enough to help me come to terms with the arrival of *Marjorie Jane* in our lives.

* * *

I didn't know how to get back off the boat without breaking a leg or, at the very least, spraining an ankle. *Okay, just do everything in reverse.* Somehow, I managed to get both of my legs over the lifelines and was hanging on for dear life when a cat jumped up onto the boat, dashed past me, leaped back onto the dock, and darted off. I was so startled that I let go of the lifelines and ended up landing smack on my butt on the dock. Splinters in your butt are very awkward.

"Are you all right, sugar?"

I looked up and saw a woman, probably in her midthirties, staring down at me with concern. She was wearing a pink baseball hat with a long blonde ponytail pulled through the back and sporting a pink-and-white-striped T-shirt and pink shorts. Even her sneakers were pink. If I had to go out on a limb, I'd say pink was her favorite color.

I'm not a big fan of pink. Don't get me wrong—I like girly things, like facials and diamonds. But pink? Ugh.

She held out her hand—bright pink nail polish, of course—and helped me to my feet. I stood and heard a rip as my jeans caught on one of the rusty nails sticking out of the dock. Great. Just what I needed. Splinters in my butt, a rip in my jeans, and a stupid sailboat as an anniversary present. Could the day get any better?

"They really need to do something about fixing these docks. Someone could get seriously hurt one of these days," she said. She had a sweet-sounding drawl that was far more pleasant on the ears than Captain Dan's.

"Yeah, don't I know it," I said, brushing dirt off my rear end. "My name's Mollie McGhie, by the way."

"And I'm Penny Chadwick." She pointed at *Marjorie Jane*, who gently bobbed up and down in the water as if she didn't have a care in the world. And why should she? She had just suckered someone into buying her. "What were you doing on *Marjorie Jane*?" she asked.

"My husband decided to buy her for me as an anniversary present."

She furrowed her brow. "He bought *this* boat for you?"

"Exactly!" I said. "Who buys their wife a boat for their anniversary when everyone knows diamonds are a girl's best friend?"

"Well, diamonds are nice," she agreed. "But what I meant was, why did he buy *this* particular boat, especially when there are so many nicer ones available on the market?"

"Honestly, I have no idea. I guess when Captain Dan told him what a bargain it was and that there were lots of other people interested in her, he figured it was too good of a deal to pass up. Plus, he's been wanting a boat for a while and when our anniversary came up, it probably seemed like the perfect excuse to take the plunge."

"Did Captain Dan really say other people were interested in the boat?" She bit her bottom lip. "Did you sign any papers yet?"

I hesitated for a moment and then said, "My husband is signing them now."

A loud cheer erupted from *Marjorie Jane*. I heard Scooter yell, "Whoo-hoo! I own a boat!"

I sighed. "I guess he's finished signing them now." Penny continued chewing on her lower lip and looked at *Marjorie Jane*. My stomach started to churn. "Why, what's wrong?"

"I don't know if I should say," she said.

"Please, you have me worried. What's the deal with this boat?" I asked. "My husband can be impulsive at times. I really would like to know what he's gotten himself into this time."

"Well, you have to wonder why the previous owners are in such a big hurry to get rid of her. They've priced the boat to sell quickly."

"Where are they now? Maybe I can talk to them and find out what's going on."

"Easier said than done. After they sailed the boat over here from Texas a few days ago, they skipped town right away. From what I understand, they gave Captain Dan power of attorney to sell the boat. I guess that's what he's doing now with your husband—completing a bill of sale and transferring the title over to his name on their behalf."

"But why did they leave town? Why didn't they complete the sale themselves?"

Penny shrugged. "Who knows?" Then she smiled slyly. "Wait until Ned and Nancy hear about this!"

"Who are Ned and Nancy?"

"The Schneiders? You haven't met them yet?" I shook my head. "Oh, well, they own the marina. They were already pissed at Captain Dan about the previous owners. They're going to be livid when they find out that he helped them by selling their boat."

"Why would they be so mad?"

"When they brought *Marjorie Jane* into the marina, they rammed into one of the docks, causing a lot of damage. Captain Dan told them not to worry, that they were good for the money. They believed him and didn't get a deposit or credit card details. Then the owners left in a hurry, leaving a big unpaid bill behind, which they blame Captain Dan for."

I rubbed my temples. I could feel a headache coming on.

"Hey, it'll be okay," she said. "I'm sure your husband knows what he's doing. Has he restored a boat before?"

I laughed. "Scooter? Restore a boat? Not that I know of."

"I'm sure he's an experienced sailor, at least. He must know a lot about boats."

"He used to sail on Lake Erie when he was a kid, but that's quite a while ago now. Does that count?"

She tilted her head to one side. "I suppose he might be a little rusty. And what about you? Do you have much experience on boats?"

I shook my head. "No. *Marjorie Jane* is the first sailboat I've ever been on."

"Goodness gracious," she said. She paced back and forth on the dock. "Listen, sugar, there's no way Captain Dan will let you out of this deal. I've known him for a while and with him, all sales are final." She paused for a moment. "But considering you and your husband's lack of sailing experience, not to mention lack of experience restoring older boats, I might be able to do you a favor and take her off your hands. I was thinking of getting another boat anyway. I always thought fixing a boat up would be fun. *Marjorie Jane* might be too much for the two of you to cope with."

"Really?" I said enthusiastically. "I'd love to get rid of this piece of junk."

She smiled. "Well, talk it over with your husband and let me know what you think. I run the sailing school here at the marina. You can find me on my boat, *Pretty in Pink*, on D Dock or just ask for me at the marina office."

"You have no idea how much I appreciate your help. I'll give it a while before I talk with him about it. I think he's a little too excited right now to see reason." I reached into my bag and grabbed my phone. "Before you leave, let me take a picture of you with what hopefully will be your new boat, and not ours." Penny stepped over to the front of the boat and smiled while I snapped a photo.

"Hope to see you later, Mollie," she said over her shoulder as she walked down the dock.

I turned, looked at *Marjorie Jane* for what I hoped was the last time, and went in search of brownies. And wine. Scooter thought the wine would be for celebrating getting *Marjorie Jane*. I hoped it would be for celebrating getting rid of her.

CHAPTER 3
MY LITTLE SWEET POTATO

AS I MADE MY WAY BACK down the dock, I tried to figure out the best way to convince Scooter that we should sell *Marjorie Jane* to Penny. Once he had his heart set on something, it was hard to get him to change his mind. I thought about pointing out all the things that were wrong with the boat and what a huge project it would be to restore her. Nope, that probably wouldn't work. Scooter is one of those guys who loves the idea of fixing things up. Unfortunately, he's not one of those guys who's good at fixing things up. Just ask me about the time he tried to install a garage door opener at our old house. On second thought, don't. I ended up having to park on the street for almost a year. It's possible I might still be a little bitter about that.

I reached the end of the dock and stepped onto the brick patio area in the center of the marina. It really was a lovely spot. People were sitting at tables underneath large umbrellas. Some were chatting, others were reading, and a family with small children was enjoying ice-cream cones.

At the back of the patio, nestled among some palm trees, were a few buildings painted in the bright, cheerful colors common in this part of Florida. I was pondering which was my favorite color when my phone beeped, alerting me to yet another text from my mom. She must have sent a dozen last night wanting to know who *Marjorie Jane* was and asking why Scooter was too cheap to get me diamonds for our anniversary.

I really didn't want to deal with responding to her just then. My mom doesn't get the whole concept of texting and the fact that it's supposed to be a quick, shorthand way of communicating. One time I texted LOL to her. She was perplexed for a week. I figured it was easier to send her a picture of *Marjorie Jane*. No words. No chance of getting drawn into a long round of back-and-forth texts. I attached the picture, clicked Send, and chucked my phone back into my purse.

Enough thinking about Scooter, *Marjorie Jane*, and my mom. I really needed to get focused on my mission at hand—brownies. Normally, I bake my own award-winning, gooey, quadruple-chocolate brownies, but I didn't have enough time to make them before the barbecue. I decided to pop into the marina office and see if they knew of a good bakery in town.

The office was located in a small two-story wooden building. The white trim and shutters were freshly painted and contrasted nicely with the bright yellow clapboards. As I stopped to admire the colorful flower beds in front of the office, the screen door flew open and a ball of fur streaked past me, followed closely by a woman brandishing a broom.

"If I see you in here again, you'll be sorry, you mangy cat!" she yelled, waving the broom back and forth for emphasis. I jumped back quickly to avoid getting clobbered. Unfortunately, I stepped straight into the flower bed, crushing some purple impatiens under my flip-flop.

"Look what you did," she said, shaking her fist. She stared at the flower bed in dismay. "I just planted those, and now they're ruined!"

She glared at me over the top of her reading glasses without saying a word. I figured she was in her late fifties or early sixties, based on the wrinkles around her eyes and her laugh lines. Although in her case, I suspect they were more like frown lines. Unpleasant reminders of childhood popped into my head. My mom was the master of long, uncomfortable, silent stare-downs. Ultimately, I would confess to whatever it was that she thought I was guilty of, like polishing off the cookies she had been saving for her bridge group. Not that I ever did anything like that as a child, mind you. As the stare-down continued, I began to think that my mom was just an amateur compared to this woman.

I wasn't sure what made me more uncomfortable—her piercing blue eyes peeking out from underneath her immaculately coiffed hair, or how tightly she was gripping the broom handle. I averted my gaze and noticed she was wearing white capri pants and a navy-blue polo shirt with the Palm Tree Marina logo embroidered on it. A name tag that said "Nancy, Office Manager," was pinned underneath.

I'd read somewhere that if you use a person's first name it defuses the tension. "This sure is a nice place you have here, Nancy," I said. She continued to glare at me while increasing her death grip on the broom. I wondered who was going to crack first, the broom handle or me. Probably me.

I decided to try a new tack. "Your cat's awfully cute. What's its name?" People love it when you ask about their pets.

"That is *not* my cat," she said. "Cats don't have any business being here at the marina. Next time I see the owner of that vile creature, I'm going to give her a piece of my mind." Her eyes narrowed as she saw the mangled impatiens.

"Um, sorry about the flowers, Nancy. I was just trying to get out of the way and stumbled. I'm a bit of a klutz."

She relaxed her grip on the broom slightly. "Humph. Well, accidents happen. Especially if you're klutzy." She inspected me up and down, pausing when she saw the rip in my jeans.

I put my hand over the tear, trying to cover it up from her disapproving look. "Like I said, I'm klutzy. I ripped my jeans getting off our boat."

"Your boat? What's your boat's name? I don't think I've seen you around here before," Nancy said, tightening her grip on the broom again. I didn't think the broom was going to live to see another day. "Did you dock here without getting permission first?"

"No, the boat was already here," I stammered. "We just bought her from Captain Dan. She's the red boat on B Dock."

"You don't mean that floating monstrosity, *Marjorie Jane*, do you?" I nodded, both in agreement to her question and with her assessment of *Marjorie Jane* as a monstrosity.

Nancy started to sweep the area around the flower bed furiously. "That man, I swear, he's always up to something. I'm going to wring his neck when I see him," she muttered.

"What do you mean, he's always up to something?" I darted out of the way as Nancy swept the dirt back into the flower bed. She ignored me and kept sweeping.

I tried again. "Listen, I just met a woman named Penny who told me that *Marjorie Jane* isn't in the best shape. I'm worried that my husband bought a lemon. Do you think it's possible that Captain Dan pulled a fast one on us?"

Nancy snorted. "Whatever deal you made with Captain Dan is between you and him. I don't want any part of it."

"Well, can you at least tell me a little bit about him? Scooter—that's my husband—doesn't really think things through before he buys something. He even bought a case of Elmer's glue once because it was on sale. I asked him what he thought we were going to do with that many bottles of glue. He was at a loss for an answer but was still convinced it was a great deal. I'm worried that this is another one of his rash decisions. People have taken advantage of him before. I'd hate to think Captain Dan did the same thing."

Nancy stopped sweeping and looked at me with concern. "Oh, you poor thing. I know all about foolish husbands." She paused before adding, "To be honest, I don't really know too much about Captain Dan. He moved down to Coconut Cove about a year ago and opened a boat brokerage business at the marina. We lease him space for his office, and he keeps some of the boats he's selling here at the marina. It's purely a business arrangement."

She leaned the broom on the wall next to the office door. "Now, why don't you come inside with me, and we'll get you registered as *Marjorie Jane*'s new owners."

I wasn't convinced that Nancy didn't know more about Captain Dan, but I was relieved that she had finally let go of the broom. I followed her into the office, wiping my feet on the mat by the door first.

Nancy sat behind a counter, adjusted her reading glasses, and tapped away on the computer keyboard. "It will be just a minute while I pull up the records, dear."

I thought I saw a faint smile when she called me "dear." Maybe she wasn't so scary after all. Turned out it was a short-lived feeling.

"You didn't track dirt into here, did you?" she barked, peeking over the counter at the gleaming pine floor.

I gulped. "No, I wiped my feet on the mat."

"Good. We like to run a tidy ship. Being neat is a good thing, wouldn't you agree?"

"Of course," I said, while I thought about the fact that I hadn't made the bed this morning and that the sink was full of dirty dishes.

I looked around the room while she worked away on the computer. The wall behind Nancy was painted turquoise and had framed photographs of dolphins, tropical fish, and seashells on display. Nancy looked up from the computer. "Those are for sale if you're interested. My daughter took them. We also have some guidebooks and nautical charts by the door. Those might come in handy, considering you just bought a boat."

I walked over to the shelves stocked with cereal, cans of soup, crackers, and other basic groceries that boaters might need. As I contemplated the mystery of canned artichoke hearts, the screen door opened.

Nancy pursed her lips and glared at the entryway. "Is that you, Ned? Don't just stand there letting all the flies in. Get in here and close that door."

A man wearing a matching navy-blue Palm Tree Marina polo shirt tucked into neatly pressed khaki pants entered and quickly shut the door. "What happened to the flower bed?" he asked tentatively, running his fingers through his gray hair.

Nancy pointed at me. "That's what happened."

He looked over at me and gave me a warm smile before turning back to Nancy, who was picking some papers off the printer. She stapled the pages together so firmly that I thought the stapler might break. She put the papers down and waved the hunk of metal at Ned angrily. "Her husband just bought that old boat, *Marjorie Jane*. Can you believe Captain Dan went and did that behind our back?"

Ned stepped back to avoid being hit by the stapler. Nancy certainly had a way with office equipment and cleaning supplies. He rubbed his chin for a few moments. "But maybe that's a good thing. We won't have the hassle of trying to track down and deal with the previous owners any—"

Nancy slammed the stapler down on the counter, cutting him off. "Never you mind about that. Shouldn't you be setting up the tables for the barbecue?"

Ned took that as his cue to leave, nodded at me, and scurried out the door.

"I've got your paperwork for you." Nancy motioned me over to the counter and explained the monthly rates and marina rules and regulations. She became quite animated when she got to section 8.1—pets must be on leashes at all times. I discreetly moved the stapler a safe distance away and filled in my details while Nancy quickly fired questions at me. "You don't have a pet, do you? You do have a credit card, don't you? Do you have loud parties at night?" I must have answered yes and no correctly, because she eventually handed me a copy of the papers and a credit card receipt.

As I opened the door, I noticed Ned setting up a folding table next to the grill, which reminded me that I needed to get brownies. I looked back at Nancy, who was busily tapping her perfectly manicured pink nails, each adorned with a white starfish, on the computer keyboard.

"Do you happen to know a good bakery around here?" I asked.

"Try Penelope's Sugar Shack. It's just off Main Street. Big purple awning. You can't miss it." She stared at the screen door, which I had left partially ajar. "Hurry up now and close the door on your way out. The last thing we need is more flies in here," she said as she whacked one unfortunate victim on the counter. I'm surprised flies even dared to come into the office when Nancy was on duty. I don't think I would unless I had to.

As I walked across the patio, I noticed the cat that Nancy had chased out of the office sitting on top of one of the tables. Ned was scratching behind its ears to the accompaniment of a loud purr. He caught my eye and motioned me over.

"Listen, don't mind my wife. Her bark is worse than her bite. It's just that she's very, well, how should I put it…"

"Organized?" I offered.

"Yes, that's a good description for it—organized."

I actually thought scary was a better description, but organized seemed more polite. The cat nudged Ned's hand, reminding him that his primary duty should be ear-scratching, not chatting with people.

"Sorry about that, Mrs. Moto," Ned said. "Only a few more scratches, then I have to get back to work."

"Mrs. Moto is an interesting-looking cat." I stroked her white fur while she purred approvingly. "I love the black rings around her eyes. And her black-and-orange patches remind me of a calico cat I used to have when I was growing up. Except my cat had a fluffy white tail, while this one doesn't have much of a tail at all."

"That's because she's a Japanese bobtail. I think it's kind of cute, like a rabbit's tail." Mrs. Moto meowed in agreement. "She's such a sweet cat. Aren't you, Mrs. Moto?" Ned gave the cat one last scratch on her head, picked her up, and set her on the patio. "Time for you to run along now before Nancy catches you out here."

Ned turned to me. "Do me a favor, will you? Don't let Nancy know that you saw me out here petting Mrs. Moto. I think she gets jealous when I pay attention to her."

"No problem. Your secret is safe with me."

I watched the calico scamper down the dock while Ned returned to setting up tables on the patio. My phone beeped. Another text from my mom.

I thought you said Marjorie Jane was a redhead. She has blonde hair in the picture you sent.

I checked the picture. Sure enough, Penny was in the corner at the front of the boat. She must have thought that Penny was *Marjorie Jane.* I sent her a quick text before heading over to Penelope's Sugar Shack.

That's Penny. Gotta go. Need brownies.

* * *

By the time I got back to the marina, the barbecue had already started. I put my box of brownies down on one of the tables. I saw lots of different types of salads, but no desserts. People sure were going to be glad I stopped by the bakery.

I saw Scooter walking down the dock toward the patio. I waved at him but he didn't notice. He kept stopping and admiring each one of the sailboats along the way. It was bad enough that he'd paid more attention to *Marjorie Jane* than to me, but now he was paying more attention to all sorts of other sailboats as well. He was so lost in his daydreams that he bumped into me at the end of the dock.

"There you are. I was wondering what happened to you. Great news—I finished signing all the paperwork, and *Marjorie Jane* is officially ours!" He grinned. It was a cute grin, and I really hated to crush his spirit, but he needed to know about Penny's offer.

"I know. I heard you cheering earlier when I was speaking with this lady named Penny. She seems to think Captain Dan did a number on us. *Marjorie Jane* needs a lot of work. She's a major fixer-upper. It might be a little too much for us, don't you think?"

"Penny, you said? She doesn't happen to be the sailing school instructor, does she?"

"Yes, that's her. Why?"

"Captain Dan warned me about her. He said she's been dying to get her hands on *Marjorie Jane* and will say or do anything to warn prospective buyers off."

"But she sounded quite sincere and she even offered to buy the boat off us."

"Well, there you go then. I bet she would offer a really low price and we'd lose money on the deal. No, I trust Captain Dan. Everything is going to be fine, you'll see." Scooter glanced at the patio. "There he is now. Let's go say hi. I'm sure he'll put your mind at ease."

Captain Dan waved us over. "Glad you could make it!" He turned to the couple standing next to him. "Let me introduce you. This here is Scooter and Mollie McGhie. They're the proud new owners of *Marjorie Jane*. And this here is Jack Holt. Just look at those freckles on him. He looks like he swallowed a quarter and broke out in pennies." Captain Dan playfully punched Jack in the arm as though they were best buddies.

Jack pulled up the sleeve of his brightly colored Hawaiian shirt and rubbed his arm before shaking hands with us. "Why would you buy *Marjorie Jane*?" he asked in disbelief. He took the words right out of my mouth. Why would anyone buy that boat? Or any boat, for that matter.

Scooter beamed. "I bet you're jealous, Jack, that I snapped her up. Captain Dan's been telling me that his phone has been ringing off the hook with people wanting to buy her."

Jack raised his eyebrows at the bearded man. "Your phone's been ringing off the hook?"

Captain Dan nodded. "Sure has. Captain Dan is the number one boat broker in all of Coconut Cove." He inched over to the woman standing next to Jack, draped his arm around her shoulder, and winked. "Isn't that right, sweetheart?"

Jack stared at him. "That's my wife, Sandy." I wasn't sure if he was introducing her to us or reminding Captain Dan whose wife she was. Sandy brushed her curly, silver hair behind her ears and smiled at us.

The captain gave Sandy's shoulder a squeeze and looked over at us. "She's as cute as a calico kitten, isn't she?" Sandy blushed, unaware that her husband's stare had turned into a glare. She looked at Captain Dan wistfully when he took his arm off her shoulder.

He reached into a cooler, pulled out a couple of beers, and offered one to Scooter. "Anyone else want one?"

A young man tapped Captain Dan on the shoulder. He had a scruffy beard and long, greasy, brown hair tied back in a ponytail. When I saw the tattered shorts he was wearing, I self-consciously put my hand over the tear in my jeans, wishing I had been able to change before the barbecue. But while I was embarrassed by my ripped clothing, he seemed unfazed. I wondered if wearing a bright orange T-shirt that said "Trust Me, I'm a Pirate" and a leather cord with a skull-and-crossbones pendant around your neck was the latest in sailor chic. I really hoped not, because I didn't think it was a look that Scooter could pull off.

"I'll take one of those," he said, holding out a rather grimy-looking hand.

"I can always count on you to show up when there's free beer." Captain Dan sneered as he handed him a bottle. "This is Ben Moretti. He lives on a sailboat out on one of the mooring balls. It's cheaper out there than getting a slip on the docks. You're always trying to save a buck, aren't you, Ben?"

Ben took a large swig of beer. "You know good and well why I'm broke." He nodded at us, pushed past the captain, and walked toward the barbecue.

Our boat broker shook his head. "Well, somebody's a little touchy, aren't they? Oh, I see Nancy and Ned over there. I need to have a word with them. I'll catch y'all later."

Sandy gazed after Captain Dan longingly. Jack grabbed her by the elbow. "It looks like the hamburgers and hot dogs are done. Why don't we go over and get some food, Sandy?"

Sandy pulled her arm away from Jack and took mine instead. "Sure thing. Mollie and I will meet you guys over at the barbecue."

* * *

After loading my plate up with a cheeseburger and all the fixings, I checked out the buffet table, where everyone had placed their contributions. I bypassed the healthy-looking salads, opting instead for a large helping of baked beans and some corn on the cob. I snagged a brownie while I was at it too.

Captain Dan sidled up to me. "You sure are a sweet little thing, just like those brownies. Go on and pass me one of those, darlin'."

I reluctantly put one on his plate. "Are you originally from Texas, Captain Dan?"

"Sure am. Texan, through and through."

"You look so familiar. Did you ever spend time in Cleveland? Scooter and I lived there before we moved down here. Maybe we ran into each other up there?"

"Nope, never been to Cleveland."

"What brought you to Coconut Cove?"

"Um...I just wanted a change of scenery." He winked at me. "I heard the ladies are real purty out here."

I was officially creeped out. I changed the subject. "Have you always been a boat broker? It seems like an interesting job." It didn't really seem that interesting, but one thing I've learned in my line of work is that people love to talk about themselves and what they do.

"I've always been in sales," Captain Dan said. He hesitated, then pointed across the patio. "Look, the gang's got a table over there." While he hurried off, I put another brownie on my plate.

* * *

"There's my little sweet potato." Scooter pulled out a chair next to him for me.

Sandy cocked her head. "Sweet potato?"

"I think Scooter has a hard time remembering my name," I said. "He's always calling me these strange pet names. Lately, they've all been related to vegetables, which is odd because Scooter isn't really a big fan of vegetables."

Scooter pointed at his plate. "That's not fair. I've got some baked beans right here. Those are vegetables, aren't they?"

"I guess. But I really meant vegetables like broccoli and cauliflower. Like the ones on that list your doctor gave to you."

Scooter shuddered at hearing the names of two of the vegetables he'd least like to make an appearance on his dinner plate. He scooped up some of the baked beans. "Yum, these are delicious. I wonder who made these."

Sandy beamed. "I did. I'm glad you like them."

I took a bite and had to agree. "They're fantastic. What's your secret, Sandy?"

"It's an old family recipe. The trick is to add a touch of cocoa powder and some maple syrup. I bring them to all the potlucks we go to. They're always a big hit."

"I can see why. Everything's better with chocolate in it." I batted Scooter's fork out of the way when he tried to get the last of the baked beans on my plate. "Hands off, buster. These are all mine."

As I finished off the rest of my beans, I heard my phone buzzing. My boss, Brian Morrison, had sent me an email. I quickly scanned it between bites of my cheeseburger.

"Scooter, you'll never believe this! Brian says they're down to two candidates for the promotion at work. It's between me and Lola."

Scooter furrowed his brow. "Work? Promotion? What are you talking about?"

I clenched my phone and glared at him. "How can you say that? I've told you a million times that I'm up for a promotion."

Sandy leaned over. "I know what you mean about having to constantly repeat yourself. Jack doesn't listen to a word I say."

Scooter's brow was still furrowed. If he kept this up, he was going to get a headache. "I always listen to what you say, Mollie. But since you don't have a job, how can you be up for a promotion at work?"

I looked at Sandy. "See, he called me by my name, rather than a vegetable. He knows he's in trouble." Then I turned to Scooter. "You know good and well that I have a job. I do important work for FAROUT."

Scooter leaned back in his chair. "Oh, that. I thought you meant a real job."

"You know what I was thinking I'd start making you for breakfast, Scooter?" I asked. "Oatmeal with broccoli and cauliflower on it."

Scooter blanched. "How about if we just stick to Froot Loops? I don't want you to go to any trouble making a fancy breakfast for me." He quickly added, "Of course the work you do for FAROUT is a real job."

Jack pushed his plate aside. "Well, at least your wife has a job. I can't remember the last time Sandy worked for a living."

Sandy glared at Jack. The way she held her plastic fork made me think she was considering stabbing him in the hand. She scooped up some baked beans instead. Wise choice. When your husband is annoying, my philosophy is to eat chocolate. Or in this case, baked beans with cocoa in them.

Captain Dan held up his bottle of beer. "You know what we need? A little toast. Here's to Scooter and Mollie on the purchase of their new boat."

Scooter looked cautiously at me and raised his bottle. Sandy and I raised our wine glasses while Jack stared off into the distance.

Our boat broker nudged Jack. "What's wrong with you? You look as mean as a mama wasp. Come on, let's congratulate these fine folks." Jack grudgingly raised his bottle.

After a few minutes of silent eating and drinking, Captain Dan leaned back and rubbed his belly. "That sure was some good grub, and the company wasn't half-bad either." Sandy gave a sudden yelp and fidgeted in her chair. I could have sworn that the captain had put his hand on her knee under the table. He pushed back his chair, stood, and looked at some kids building sandcastles on the beach.

"Scooter, why don't you take your missus out for a sunset stroll on the beach. Y'all can get a good view of the marina from there. While you're off doing that, I'm going to pop by *Marjorie Jane* and leave a little boat-warming present for you on board."

Scooter got up from the table. "That's awful nice of you." He reached into his pocket. "I found another padlock on the boat. Here's a spare key for it."

Captain Dan took the key, then shook Scooter's hand heartily. He nodded at the rest of us. "Have a good night, y'all."

As he ambled across the patio, I saw Penny come up and grab his arm. Captain Dan stopped and tried to remove her hand. She tightened her grip on his arm and spoke to him in an agitated manner. Whatever she was saying appeared to be making him angry. His eyes narrowed and he pushed her away from him. The others at the table were busy talking about injector valves on diesel engines, which was not a conversation I wanted to be a part of. I decided it was time to do a little bit of investigating.

"Here, why don't I throw all of this in the trash," I offered, gathering up the paper plates, utensils, and cups.

"Thanks," Scooter said absentmindedly, and turned back to his conversation with Jack and Sandy.

I headed toward the trash can and hid behind some potted palm trees so I could listen to Captain Dan and Penny's conversation.

"You promised me that we'd be partners in the boat

brokerage," Penny said.

"I never did any such thing," Captain Dan said.

"Yes, you did. And you owe me, especially after I lost all that money I put into your last business."

"It was an investment. Sometimes you win and sometimes you lose. If you can't stand the heat, you should get out of the kitchen, as my mama always said." He folded his arms across his chest. "You knew when you put that money up that it was a risk."

"You told me it was a sure thing. Otherwise, I would have never given you the money."

"Well, I don't know what to tell you, darlin'. It's not my problem, is it?"

"I'm going to make it your problem. You better watch your back, Bob. It isn't just me who's livid. Ned and Nancy are pretty hot under the collar. And wait until those new marks of yours find out what you sold them."

He shook Penny by the shoulders. "You better not say anything, you hear me?" He pushed her back, turned, and stormed off. Penny chewed on her nails while she watched him walk away.

I was left with two questions—why did Penny call Captain Dan "Bob," and who were these new marks she was referring to?

CHAPTER 4
UNEXPLAINED LIGHTS

WHEN I GOT BACK TO THE table, Scooter, Jack, and Sandy were engrossed in conversation. "You wouldn't believe it—there was oil everywhere, even on Sandy's T-shirt and hair!" Jack chuckled. "Yep, those were the good old days, weren't they, honey?"

He leaned over to Sandy, smiled softly, and rubbed her hand. Sandy looked at him in surprise, then pulled her hand away. Jack's smile faded, and his eyes got steely.

"But those days were a long time ago," Jack said bitterly. Sandy blushed while Scooter did his best to pretend that things weren't incredibly uncomfortable.

"So, Scooter, what about that stroll on the beach?" I asked.

He looked at me with relief. "Yes. That would be great."

"See you guys tomorrow," Scooter said as we walked toward the boardwalk.

I glanced back and saw Jack staring angrily off into space while Sandy rubbed her hands together anxiously.

"What was that about?" I asked.

"I'm not sure. One minute we were talking about changing oil filters and the next minute they were, well, you saw it."

"Do you think there's something going on between Sandy and Captain Dan?"

"What?" Scooter asked incredulously.

"Didn't you see how Captain Dan kept flirting with Sandy? I even think he had his hand on her knee at one point during dinner."

"I think you're reading things wrong. Before you came back to the table, Jack was telling me that he and Sandy were high school sweethearts. They've been married for over thirty years."

"Just because you've been married a long time doesn't mean you're happy."

Scooter puzzled over this while we walked down the wooden steps from the boardwalk that led to the beach. "I can't imagine not being as happily married to you after thirty years as I am now. These past ten years have been wonderful." He added with a smirk, "Even if you do hog the covers at night."

"That's not true! *You* steal them during the night and wake me up. All I'm doing is getting back my rightful share."

"Anyway, we won't need covers once we sail *Marjorie Jane* to the tropics. It'll be too warm at night."

"Let's not get ahead of ourselves. I'm still not convinced that we should keep this boat. Do you really think we're cut out to be boat owners?"

"Of course we are. It'll be fun—something we can do together. Don't let Penny mess with your head."

"I don't know. There's something fishy going on between Penny and Captain Dan. I happened to overhear them talking, and based on that conversation, I think our boat broker is a pretty shady character."

"You *happened* to overhear? Isn't that another way of saying you eavesdropped?" Scooter asked. "Kind of like the time you told me you *happened* to open a padlock without a key while you were holding bolt cutters in your hand?"

I shook my head. "How else was I supposed to get into the storage shed behind that grumpy old man's house? You knew as well as I did that he stole my bike and locked it up in there. The police didn't take me seriously, so I had to take matters into my own hands. And I was right, wasn't I? My bike was there. Honestly, are you ever going to let that go?"

Scooter laughed. "Probably not. You're too cute when you get all worked up."

"Humph. Anyway, Penny was complaining angrily to Captain Dan about how he had conned her out of some money and—get this—she called him Bob. I don't think Dan is his real name!"

"Sure it is. He gave me a business card." Scooter fished in his wallet and handed it to me. "See? Right there. Captain Dan Thomas. There's even a little anchor logo next to his name that proves he's a certified captain."

"Uh, yeah. You do know anyone can get business cards printed up, don't you? And how do you know he's a certified captain anyway? How does this prove anything? Besides, he wore those cowboy boots of his on the boat. I thought you told me you always had to take your shoes off. Wouldn't a legitimate boat broker know that?"

Scooter chewed on his lower lip. "Um, I'm not sure what that was about. It's a bit strange, but I'm sure he had a good reason. Maybe they're orthopedic cowboy boots?"

I decided not to press Scooter on Captain Dan or *Marjorie Jane*. I needed to figure out another approach to get him to sell her.

I slipped off my flip-flops and walked down the beach, relishing the feel of the warm sand between my toes. The sun was beginning to set, its waning light glistening on the water between the boats moored in the cove.

After a few minutes, Scooter caught up with me and handed me a sand dollar. "I thought you might like this for your collection."

I tucked it into my purse. I'd started collecting seashells when we moved to Florida. I'd found a number of pretty specimens, but this was my first sand dollar.

"I think your shells are going to look great on the boat. You should start thinking about how you want to decorate. A nautical theme might be nice. But no picture windows or wallpaper, right?"

As far as I was concerned, my seashell collection was staying right where it was—in a basket by our bed at our cottage. I was about to make that clear when I noticed red and green lights flashing on the water and moving toward the far end of the beach.

Scooter was walking along the beach, his eyes downcast,

scanning for more shells. I ran over to him and grasped his arm. "Do you see that?" By the time he looked up, the lights had vanished.

"See what?"

"Those lights. They were there for a few seconds, and now they're gone. I wonder if it was a—"

Scooter put his finger on my lips. "No, it wasn't what you think it was."

"It was. I swear it was. After all, I've got a lot of experience with this kind of thing because of my work with FAROUT."

Scooter rolled his eyes at the mention of FAROUT.

"Stop with the eye-rolling. I wish you'd take my work more seriously."

"But it's not work. It's some organization you volunteer for. You don't even get paid for all the hours you put into it."

"Just because I don't get paid doesn't mean I don't do important work." I stomped my foot on the ground for emphasis. Unfortunately, the emphasis part of it didn't work. I just ended up kicking sand everywhere.

"I know, I know," Scooter said soothingly after he wiped sand off his shorts. "Your work is important. I should take it more seriously. I really do hope you get that promotion. You deserve it far more than Lola." He took my hand. "Come on, let's find a place to sit for a while."

As we walked down the beach, I kept glancing over my shoulder to see if the lights reappeared. If they were what I thought they were, then the Palm Tree Marina and Coconut Cove could make the national news.

* * *

Later that night, as we walked across the patio toward the dock, I stopped to check the buffet table. Sure enough, all the brownies I'd brought were gone, but there were plenty of salads left. We waved good-night to a couple of stragglers who were having a nightcap before heading back to their boats. I saw Mrs. Moto chasing a lizard near one of the palm trees. After she trapped it under a paw, she looked at me and meowed. "Good girl," I said.

"You sure are cute, aren't you, with those black markings around your eyes?"

We turned down the dock toward *Marjorie Jane*'s berth. I tripped over an empty beer bottle and grabbed Scooter's arm to steady myself. The bottle reminded me of how angry Ben had been at Captain Dan, although not angry enough to refuse an offer of a free beer. I wondered why Ben was so short of money. Had the Texan conned him like he had Penny?

By the time I reached the boat, Scooter was already in the cockpit. "Can you hand me a flashlight?" he asked as he pushed back the hatch. "It looks like Captain Dan didn't lock up the boat. I want to have a look around here and see if I can find the padlock."

I reached into my purse and found the flashlight tucked beside the sand dollar and other shells we had collected on the beach. I climbed onto the boat and handed it to him. "Do you think someone broke in again?"

Scooter shook his head. "No. You heard what Captain Dan said. That was probably just some kids. I don't think they'd come here twice. Captain Dan probably forgot to put the padlock back on." He pointed the flashlight around the interior of the boat while I climbed down the ladder into the main cabin.

"Be careful. There's something on the floor there next to your foot. Don't trip on it."

I squinted in the dark. "Isn't that one of those winch handles you were showing me earlier?"

Scooter poked his head down. "I think so. Hang on a minute; I can't see very well from up here."

While Scooter made his way down the ladder, I turned on the overhead light. Nothing happened. I moved over to the galley and tried the light in there. Nothing again.

"One more reason to sell *Marjorie Jane*. The lights don't work."

Scooter rolled his eyes. Or at least I think he rolled his eyes. It was hard to tell in the dark.

"Here, I'll trade you," I said as I handed him the winch handle and plucked the flashlight out of his hand. As I pointed the light around the main cabin, I noticed a pool of liquid on the floor near the V-berth. I walked over and pulled open the door. That's when

I saw a foot hanging off the mildew-patterned cushions. And not just any foot, but a foot wearing a red cowboy boot.

"Uh, Scooter. We've got another problem."

"Don't worry about the lights. I'm sure it will be an easy fix," he said while he examined the winch handle.

"This is a far bigger problem. I found Captain Dan in the V-berth—and I think he's dead."

CHAPTER 5
EMERGENCY CHOCOLATE

"DID YOU JUST SAY CAPTAIN DAN is dead? Are you sure?" Scooter asked as he stepped toward me, clutching the winch handle in his hand.

"Of course I'm sure," I said.

"But how do you know?"

"Just trust me on this. You really don't want me to describe what I saw." Scooter took a few more cautious steps. I pointed the flashlight down on the floor near the V-berth. "Watch out—you're going to get blood on your shoes."

"Blood?" he asked in a shaky voice.

I shined the flashlight directly at Scooter. He just stood there with his mouth open, staring in horror at the floor. "I think that might be blood on the winch handle too," I said.

He gasped and dropped the handle on the table. He was never very good with blood. Every time Scooter cut his finger, he would close his eyes and scream for me to bandage it up quickly so he didn't have to see the blood. Don't even get me started on the time he cut open his forehead and needed stitches.

"Why don't you go sit down on the couch? I'll call the police." I dug my cell phone out of my purse and dialed 911. While I was talking to the dispatcher, I pointed the light at Scooter. He was looking rather pale. I ended the call and sat next to him. "They'll be here in just a few minutes. In the meantime, we're supposed to sit tight."

I pulled a Hershey's bar out of my purse and broke off a piece. "Here, have some. It'll make you feel better." I always keep a supply of chocolate handy for emergencies. Scooter nodded, ate the chocolate, then put his head between his hands. I squeezed his arm and passed him a few more pieces of chocolate.

"It'll be okay, Scooter. Why don't I get you something to drink?" I cautiously made my way back to the galley to get a bottle of water. Waving the flashlight from side to side, I hoped I wouldn't run across any more unpleasant surprises. I stopped in my tracks when the narrow beam of light illuminated a shiny object on the floor. Praying it wasn't something else covered in blood, I bent down and shined the flashlight directly on it. To my relief, it was just a pink fingernail. I picked it up to examine it more closely.

"Hello, is anyone down there? This is the police," a loud voice boomed.

"Yes, we're down here with the body." I looked at Scooter, worried he might faint at the mention of a body. He stared into space blankly and held out his hand for more chocolate.

"All right, ma'am. We're coming on board. Step aside."

It's not easy to step aside in a boat. I squeezed as far into the galley as I could, while a burly man climbed down the ladder, followed by a petite woman carrying a large black plastic case. The man said briskly, "Sir, ma'am, I'm Chief Dalton and this is Officer Moore. Officer Moore is going to have a look around while I ask you some questions." He reached up and flicked the overhead light on.

"I thought the lights weren't working," Scooter said. I think he had been hoping they still didn't work. He closed his eyes so he could avoid looking at the blood on the floor and on the winch handle.

Officer Moore stepped into the galley and set the case on the counter. "We noticed your shore power cord had been disconnected, so we plugged it back in."

Chief Dalton asked us what we knew about Captain Dan and why he was on our boat, our whereabouts prior to discovering the body, and when and why we'd purchased *Marjorie Jane.* I told him about the break-in earlier and Captain Dan's theory that it had been high school kids. He scribbled down notes while Officer Moore took photographs.

Once he was done questioning us, he told us to wait on the patio while they examined the boat and removed the body.

* * *

Scooter slumped into a chair and I passed him the rest of the chocolate. While he scraped every last morsel from the wrapper, I looked around the patio, wondering if someone who had been at the barbecue earlier in the night had killed Captain Dan.

A small crowd had gathered, watching the police go back and forth between the parking lot and B Dock. Sandy and Jack stood at the edge of the group. Sandy appeared agitated, pulling on Jack's arm and whispering something in his ear. Everyone gasped as two officers wheeled a gurney with a body bag on it past them.

Sandy hurried over to us, Jack in tow. "Did you see that?" she asked, pulling up a chair next to mine. "I wonder if Mr. Kennedy had a heart attack. Did you know he's in his late eighties and still living aboard his boat? He's been having heart problems for years."

"No, I don't think it was Mr. Kennedy," I said, glancing at Scooter to see how he was holding up. He was searching through my purse, presumably looking for more chocolate. I leaned over to Sandy and whispered, "Captain Dan was murdered on our boat."

Sandy shrieked, "Captain Dan was murdered? Are you sure?" Everyone on the patio turned and stared at her.

Scooter dumped the contents of my purse on the table and pawed through them. "Where's the rest of the chocolate?" he muttered.

Sandy tugged Jack's arm. "Did you hear that? Captain Dan is dead."

Jack looked at her quietly for a few moments. "It's not really a great loss, is it?" He walked over to the boardwalk and gazed blankly out at the water.

The color drained from Sandy's face as she wiped away tears. She probably could use some chocolate too. Clearly, I wasn't prepared for a chocolate emergency of this magnitude.

Ned and Nancy pushed through the crowd and walked over to us. They looked like they had just woken up. Nancy was wearing a fleece robe cinched tightly over her nightgown. Ned had a matching robe over striped pajamas.

Nancy eyed the police officers milling around the patio. "Is it true that Captain Dan was found murdered on your boat? At this time of night?" she asked, peering over her reading glasses. I had a feeling she thought murders should be scheduled ahead of time at a more convenient hour. The way she was staring at me, I wondered if she was going to make a citizen's arrest for disturbing the peace, or rather disturbing *her* peace.

"It's true. I found him in the V-berth."

Nancy frowned and made tsk-tsk sounds. Ned looked woozy. He grabbed onto the back of a chair to steady himself.

Chief Dalton marched toward us, followed by Officer Moore, who was still carrying the black case.

"Mr. and Mrs. Schneider," Chief Dalton said. He pulled a notebook out of his pocket. It wasn't a question, but Ned and Nancy nodded while the chief scribbled something down. "A Daniel Robert Smith was found dead aboard a boat named *Marjorie Jane*." More nodding. "I understand Mr. Smith was a boat broker at the marina." Ned and Nancy continued to nod. I was beginning to like Chief Dalton's effect on Nancy.

The burly man flipped over a page in his notebook. "Is it true that the two of you had an argument with Mr. Smith earlier in the evening?"

Nancy stopped nodding. "Now, just you wait a minute here, mister," she said, jabbing the chief in his stomach with her long nails. The stout man looked down at her hand. She jabbed him again. "The people you should be talking to are them." She stopped jabbing his stomach and pointed at us. I pulled back in my chair, worried she might poke me in the eye with her fingernail. "They bought *Marjorie Jane* from Captain Dan, realized after the fact that they got conned, and then 'discovered' his body on their boat." She used her fingers to make air quotes around the word "discovered," then jabbed Chief Dalton in the stomach again for emphasis.

Ned seized Nancy by the shoulder and pulled her back. "Hang on there a minute, honey. There's no need to get worked up. The police chief is just doing his job." He looked over at the beleaguered man. "Maybe we could continue this inside our office?"

Chief Dalton snapped his notebook shut. "That sounds fine, sir. While we're at it, we'll need you to make a list of everyone who was at the marina tonight."

Ned nodded while Nancy glared at me.

The chief pointed at the marina office. "After the two of you." Before following them, he looked at us. "I'm afraid you won't be able to get back onto your boat until sometime tomorrow. Why don't you head home for the night? We'll follow up with you in the morning with any additional questions we may have." Scooter appeared relieved. He didn't want to get back on a boat covered in blood anytime soon.

Then it hit me. This was our way out. There was no way that Scooter was going to want to keep *Marjorie Jane* after this. He'd have to agree to sell her to Penny now, although selling a boat that someone had been murdered on might not be so easy. I thought about this while I put everything back in my purse that Scooter had dumped out.

Sandy snagged a pack of tissues off the table before I could put them away. "Do you mind?"

"No, they're all yours." She wiped her eyes and then blew her nose. "I just can't believe he's dead."

Jack wandered back to the table. "Come on, Sandy. The police said it's okay for us to head back to our boat." He walked down the dock without waiting for her.

Sandy got up and gave me a hug. "Thanks for being so understanding, Mollie."

I hugged her back. "I'll come by tomorrow and check to see how you're doing." I silently cursed Jack for ignoring

Sandy. His wife was falling to pieces and he didn't seem to care. Then again, he didn't really seem to care that Captain Dan had been murdered either.

* * *

The next morning, Chief Dalton called and asked us to come to the police station. As we drove down Main Street, I pointed at Penelope's Sugar Shack. "That's where I bought the brownies for the potluck yesterday. They were good, weren't they? Captain Dan had a couple of them. That's the kind of last supper I'd like to have."

Scooter gripped the steering wheel tightly while he pulled up in front of the police station. It was painted bright blue and had flower baskets hanging from the windowsills, like the rest of the buildings on Main Street. It almost felt cheerful until I remembered why we were there.

Officer Moore greeted us and ushered us into the chief's office. After exchanging a few pleasantries, we tried to make ourselves comfortable in the hard wooden chairs in front of his desk. He reached into a cardboard box and pulled out a large plastic bag. He placed it on the desk with a thud. Inside the bag, I saw the winch handle that had killed Captain Dan. It was still covered in blood.

Scooter pushed his chair back. I reached into my purse, grabbed a bag of Peanut M&M'S, and passed them to him.

Chief Dalton looked at Scooter popping M&M'S rapidly into his mouth and raised his right eyebrow. "What can you tell me about this winch handle?" he asked, raising his eyebrow even higher.

I hadn't really noticed with all the commotion and the dim lighting yesterday, but he had the bushiest eyebrows I had ever seen in my life. They were fascinating in a strange sort of way, conjuring up visions of two dark, fuzzy caterpillars playing tug-of-war on his forehead.

Scooter crumpled up the empty M&M'S bag and tossed it in the trash can. "Is that the winch handle that, um, you know..."

"Killed Captain Dan?"

Scooter shifted in his seat and nodded.

"It is," Chief Dalton said. "What can you tell me about it?"

"It isn't ours. I mean, it doesn't belong to *Marjorie Jane.*"

"Go on."

"Well, *Marjorie Jane* came with two winch handles. I saw them both when I did the original inventory with Captain Dan a few days ago. This isn't one of them. It's designed to fit a much larger winch."

"So you're saying that you had never seen this before last night."

"Yes, that's correct. I mean no, that's not correct." Scooter took a deep breath. "What I mean to say is that we did see this handle earlier in the evening. Mollie almost tripped over it. But it wasn't covered in..." Scooter clenched the sides of the chair.

"Blood?" Chief Dalton offered.

Scooter nodded.

"And you, Mrs. McGhie. Had you ever seen this winch handle before last night?"

I snorted. "Are you kidding me? I hadn't even seen *Marjorie Jane* before yesterday, when Scooter signed the papers to buy her, let alone any of her winch handles."

Chief Dalton raised his other eyebrow. "You mean to say you bought a boat without seeing it first?"

Scooter smiled. "It was a surprise. I bought *Marjorie Jane* as an anniversary present for Mollie. I took her over to see her for the first time yesterday afternoon, then signed the papers to buy her."

"Wow, that's some anniversary present. You must really like sailing, Mrs. McGhie."

I snorted again. "I've never been sailing before in my life."

The burly man looked at me in surprise, then at Scooter in disbelief. He picked up the winch handle and put it back in the cardboard box. Scooter breathed a sigh of relief now that it was out of sight.

"Tell me again, where were the two of you between six and eight last night?"

"We were walking along the beach," Scooter said nervously.

"That's a long walk."

Scooter gulped. "Well, we did sit for a while and talk."

"What did you talk about?"

"Oh, you know, this and that." Scooter took his glasses off and rubbed his eyes. "I've been going through a tough time lately with work stuff. We were talking about plans for the future, that kind of thing."

The chief chewed on his pen for a moment. "Did anyone see you?"

Scooter looked questioningly at me. "I'm not sure. I didn't notice anyone. Did you, Mollie?"

I shook my head. "I don't think so, but it was dark out once the sun went down. It would have been hard to see anyone." I tried to recall the details of our walk, then remembered that I had seen something important. "But there were these bright red and green flashing lights out on the water. I think they might have been a—"

Scooter interrupted. "Chief Dalton is asking if we saw any people, not if you saw any flashing lights."

The chief wrote something down on a piece of paper and tucked it into a file folder. "I'll need to go over the documents of sale."

"Wait a minute," I said excitedly. "Maybe the sale didn't go through because Captain Dan died. Maybe we don't actually own *Marjorie Jane*."

The chief thumbed through a pile of papers. "From what I can see here, it all looks legitimate. I'm afraid you're the owners of the boat."

"Does Mollie need to stay for this? I was the one who signed the paperwork," Scooter said.

"She can go, if she wants."

I grabbed my purse. "Great. I told Sandy I would check in on her this morning. You go through those papers, Scooter. Maybe you can find a loophole to get us out of this sale, while you're at it. I'll meet you at the marina later."

As I walked toward the door, I turned to Chief Dalton and asked, "Who's on your suspect list?"

He seemed taken aback by my question. I could tell by the twitching of his eyebrows. They were enough to frighten small children, let alone murder suspects. "I'm afraid I can't share that with you. It's confidential."

"You know, I'm an investigative reporter. I've got a knack for getting people to open up and admit things they don't want to talk about. I bet I could help you out by chatting with some of the folks at the marina. There did seem to be a number of them that held a grudge against Captain Dan."

Chief Dalton raised both of his eyebrows and gave me a faint smile. "That's okay, ma'am. I think we've got it covered."

"Fine," I said. "Scooter, want to walk me out?"

He nodded and walked with me to the lobby. "What was that back there about being an investigative reporter?"

"Okay, I might have exaggerated a bit. I'm not technically one yet, but I'm sure I'm going to get the job."

"Are you talking about this thing with FAROUT?"

"Of course," I said with a frown. "How many times do I have to tell you about this? It's between Lola and me. You remember Lola, don't you? That obnoxious redhead who wore those very tiny skirts at the FAROUT convention in Texas last year?"

"Oh, her," Scooter said with a faraway look. "Who could forget her?"

Yeah, of course he couldn't forget her. She had had Scooter and every other guy at the convention wrapped around her little finger.

"Scooter, snap out of it! Back to business. I'm going to go to the marina and start questioning people. Once you're done here, you're going to stop by Penelope's Sugar Shack and pick up a couple more of those brownies and meet me back at the marina."

"Sure thing. Brownies and then the marina." He leaned down and gave me a kiss on the forehead. "Don't worry about Lola. I'm sure you're a shoo-in for the job." I was pleased that he was referring to my work as a job now, and not a volunteer position. "But do me a favor and don't get in Chief Dalton's way. And for goodness' sake, don't tell him about FAROUT and your theory about those red and green lights." I pulled away from Scooter, and he quickly added, "It's just that I don't think he'll understand —it's not that I don't believe you."

"Fine. Whatever," I said as I stomped across the lobby and out the door.

* * *

One of the advantages of living in a small town is that you can walk everywhere. As I made my way toward the marina, I breathed in the salty air and breathed out my irritation with Scooter. I knew he tried to believe in the work I did, but it was hard for people to accept the truth sometimes, especially when no one talked about it. That was one of FAROUT's missions—to raise awareness and make people more comfortable sharing their stories.

When I got to the marina, I popped in the office to find out where Jack and Sandy's boat was located. Fortunately, Ned was staffing the desk. He told me that I could find them on C Dock, then asked me how I was holding up. You would think that a little of Ned's compassion would have rubbed off on Nancy after so many years of marriage.

We talked for a few minutes about what it was like to find a body, then I headed to Jack and Sandy's boat. As I walked down the dock, I ran into Penny. She was wearing another all-pink outfit. Pink tank top, pink shorts, and another pink hat.

"Can you believe what happened to Captain Dan?" I asked her.

"It's terrible to think he's gone, isn't it?" Penny started chewing her nails. Her manicure looked terrible. Half of her nails were long, shiny, and pink. The other half were short and ragged. She looked at me. "Is it true that you found him on *Marjorie Jane*?"

"Yes. In the V-berth."

Penny shuddered and continued mangling her nails. I thought about giving her a hug, but she didn't seem like the hugging type. I pointed at her hand. "My mom does that when she gets nervous." Penny quickly put her hands in her pockets.

"It's a bad habit. Besides, short nails are better for sailing. Otherwise, you end up breaking them." She stared down at the dock absentmindedly and mumbled something that sounded like "poor Bob."

"What was that you said?" I asked.

Penny looked up at me sharply. "Nothing. Just saying that I need to get going. I've got a sailing class starting in a few minutes." She hurried down the dock, leaving me to wonder if she was referring to Captain Dan as Bob, like she had when I'd overheard them arguing at the barbecue.

I remembered the pink fingernail that I had found on the boat when I'd discovered Captain Dan's body. When the police had come on board they'd startled me, and I'd completely forgotten to tell them about it. I'd have to figure out what I did with it and give it to Chief Dalton. It could be an important clue. Both Penny and Nancy had been sporting pink manicures. Could one of them have been on our boat?

I pondered this as I made my way to *Island Time*, Jack and Sandy's boat. I saw her halfway down the dock. Jack and Sandy were in front of her, arguing.

"How can you say that, Jack?" Sandy said. "You're the one who should be careful. After all, I heard it was a large winch handle that was the murder weapon."

Jack clenched his fists. "I had nothing to do with it, Sandy. But I can't say that I'm not glad he's gone. He's caused enough trouble for us financially and otherwise."

He stormed off, ignoring me as I tried to say hello.

Sandy waved me over. "Sorry you had to see that. I think this murder has stressed out all of us. Come on aboard and I'll fix us some coffee."

"Will Jack be joining us?" I asked as I followed her down into the boat.

"No. He has to take care of some business matters." Sandy put a kettle on the stove and pulled out a French press from the cupboard.

"What kind of business is he in? I thought the two of you were retired?"

"Oh, we are, but you know how it is. Retirement savings only go so far, and we've had some financial difficulties. Jack has been making extra money buying and selling used marine equipment, like outboard motors, replacement parts, that kind of thing."

"Does he also sell winch handles?"

Sandy shrugged. "I guess so." She pulled a container of milk out of the fridge and scooped some coffee into the press. "I try to stay out of his business, except for helping with the bookkeeping. He gets mad whenever I ask him anything about it. After so many years of marriage, I've learned to bite my tongue. You know what I mean, don't you?"

"I think Scooter would be surprised if I ever started biting my tongue."

Sandy smiled. "Go on, have a seat. It won't be long."

I sat down on one of the couches and was admiring the embroidered throw cushions when a calico cat jumped onto my lap, turned around a couple of times, and then settled down on my legs.

"Sorry about that," Sandy said. "I hope you don't mind cats. That's Mrs. Moto."

I scratched Mrs. Moto behind the ears. "I know you, don't I?" I explained to Sandy, "She jumped onto our boat yesterday, and then I saw her again later at the marina office. Nancy was chasing her away with a broom."

"Oh, Nancy hates cats." Sandy held up a cup of steaming coffee. "How do you take yours?"

"Milk and sugar, please." Mrs. Moto perked up at the word "milk." "Do you like milk too?" The calico responded with a loud yowl, which I took to mean "Yes, please."

"She's not allowed to have milk. Vet's orders." Sandy passed me a cup of coffee and placed hers on the table. She sat next to me and started to sniffle. "I don't know what I'm going to do with her when we sell the boat. They won't let us have cats at the condo we're moving into."

"You're selling your boat?"

"Yes, Captain Dan was going to list her for us. Now we've got to find another boat broker and a home for Mrs. Moto." Sandy's sniffles turned into a loud crying noise. "I've put notices up everywhere, but no one wants her. I hate the idea of having to take her to a shelter."

The Japanese bobtail rubbed up against my hand, demanding that I scratch under her chin. I hated the idea of her going to a shelter as well.

I took a sip of my coffee while she dried her eyes. "Why exactly are you moving?"

"We can't afford to keep the boat and our condo. We'd been renting out the condo, but the tenants just left. We thought about selling it and staying on the boat, but to be honest, we're getting too old for all the work involved in boat ownership. So we decided to move into the condo and sell the boat. Things have been tight, so any money we can get for the boat would be a big help."

Sandy groaned and rubbed her temples with her fingers. "Feels like I've got another one of my headaches coming on."

"Oh, no! Can I get you anything?"

"Would you mind? There's a bottle on the counter in the head." I must have looked confused. "The head is what we call the bathroom. Just down the passageway before the aft cabin."

I nudged Mrs. Moto. She moved over to Sandy's lap and purred while I went in search of the head. I peeked in and saw Sandy's pill bottle. As I picked it up, I noticed a white pillowcase in the sink covered in red spots.

I came back out and handed Sandy the bottle. Her hands shook as she swallowed two pills with her coffee. While she sat back and rubbed her neck, I saw bruises on the back of her arms. "Sandy, what happened to your arms?"

She lowered them. "Those marks? Oh, I don't know. I'm always getting bruises and cuts and I don't remember how." She pointed down at her legs, which were covered in small cuts and deep-purple bruises. "Like these ones here. No idea how they happened."

"I saw the pillowcase in the bathroom—I mean, head. Was that blood on there?"

"Yes, I must have gotten a nosebleed during the night. It happens from time to time. I'm just glad I was able to sleep last night. Sometimes, it's hard to fall asleep and stay asleep. I'm constantly having nightmares. Did you know that last night I dreamed someone was operating on me in a dark metal room? Must be the financial stress. And worrying about finding Mrs. Moto a new home." She frowned and stroked the cat's glossy fur.

When I sat back down on the couch, the calico ran over, plopped next to me, and rolled over on her back.

"She must really like you," Sandy said wistfully. "She rarely does that for anyone. Go on, rub her belly. She loves that."

Mrs. Moto really did love having her belly rubbed. Her purring grew so loud that I could barely hear what Sandy was saying. "If you can't find anyone to take her, maybe I can talk Scooter into letting us adopt her," I offered impulsively.

"That would be fantastic," Sandy said. She hesitated and then added, "Maybe this is too much to ask, but Jack and I are running up to the condo later today. It's north of here, about four hours away. We'll be away overnight, possibly two nights. Maybe you could look in on her and feed her while we're gone?"

"Sure, I'd love to."

"You're a lifesaver," Sandy said. "I had originally asked Penny if she'd take care of her, but she told me last night that she wouldn't be able to."

"What time did you see her at?" I asked.

"Oh, I don't know. I went for a walk before going to bed and saw her sitting out on the patio. She seemed really distracted." Sandy lowered her voice. "Between you and me, I think she and Captain Dan had a thing going on. I heard a rumor that she even moved up here from Texas to be with him."

"Really? I didn't think she was all that sweet on him. I overheard them last night arguing about the boat brokerage. It sounded like she had invested money in his last business, and he'd promised to make her a partner in the boat brokerage." I quickly added, "Not that I was eavesdropping or anything."

"Hmm. That's interesting. I saw them fighting last week too. I couldn't hear what they were saying and just assumed it was a lovers' quarrel, but maybe it was more than that," Sandy said. "Do you think she could have had anything to do with Captain Dan's murder? I mean, I hate to think that anyone we know is a murderer, but you can never tell about people, can you?"

While I reflected on this, Mrs. Moto decided that I wasn't paying enough attention to her. She jumped onto the floor and chased after a toy mouse.

"When we spoke with Chief Dalton this morning, he said Captain Dan had been murdered between six and eight o'clock." Mrs. Moto dropped the toy mouse at my feet and was delighted when I threw it on the other couch for her to chase. "What time did you see Penny at?"

"It was probably around six thirty, maybe a little earlier. We left the barbecue around six and headed back to the boat. I'm not sure about the time, but it was probably fifteen minutes later that I went out for a walk. I needed a break from Jack and a few minutes to clear my head."

"Where exactly did you run into Penny?"

"On the patio. She was sitting there, biting her nails and looking at something on her computer."

"What was she looking at?"

"I'm not sure. When she saw me, she turned her computer off and put it away quickly in her laptop bag. I probably talked to her for about five minutes, and then I headed up to the trail that leads around the cove. There's a nice lookout there with a park bench."

"When did you go back to your boat?"

"Oh, not too much later. I was probably back by eight." She paused. "When I came back to the marina after my walk, I saw Penny walking down from B Dock—you know, the dock where you keep *Marjorie Jane*." She shook her head. "It's all probably a coincidence. I can't imagine Penny was involved in anything like that."

Mrs. Moto meowed loudly, jumped onto my lap, and deposited her toy mouse. I told her what a good cat she was. She seemed pleased with herself.

I thought about Penny and Captain Dan's argument. Was it possible Sandy was right, and the two of them were involved? If that were the case, why was he flirting with Sandy? And why did he look so familiar?

"I can't figure out why Captain Dan seems—I mean, seemed—so familiar," I said. Sandy winced at the reminder that Captain Dan was dead. "I keep thinking to myself that I've seen him someplace before. Has he always been a boat broker?"

"I'm not sure. I suppose so. I don't think you just become a boat broker overnight. It's not like just anyone can sell boats." Sandy rubbed her temples again. "It would appear that my pills aren't taking care of this headache. I think I'm going to lie down for a bit if that's okay."

"Of course," I said. "Is there anything else I can get you?"

"No, I just need to rest in a dark room." She hesitated. "So, you're sure you're okay to look after Mrs. Moto?"

"Not a problem," I reassured her.

"Okay, Nancy has a key to our boat at the office, and I'll leave a note with some instructions with her later today. We'll be leaving later this afternoon. I'm really not looking forward to the long car ride with this headache."

I couldn't imagine the car ride with Jack would be very pleasant, headache or not, given their fight, but decided to keep that thought to myself. Their relationship certainly was a puzzler. Last night, Jack had alternated between hot and cold with Sandy. Maybe he was just jealous of Captain Dan's flirtations, but maybe it was more than that.

CHAPTER 6
FLYSWATTER

I WAS HALFWAY DOWN THE dock when I realized I hadn't checked my phone since the previous night. My phone's always stuck somewhere down at the bottom of my purse, and half the time I don't hear it go off, something that annoys my mom to no end. She hates it when I don't reply right away and then sends a million more texts asking where I am as some sort of punishment.

Yep, there were a million texts from my mom. Most of them said things like, *Where are you? Why are you ignoring your mother? and Why don't you ever check your phone? I could be dead for all you know.* I'm not sure how she could be texting me if she were dead, but knowing my mom, she'd find a way. I scrolled back to her original message.

Who's Penny? What happened to Marjorie Jane? Did he ditch her already? Has Scooter moved on to another bimbo?

As usual, she had gotten it all wrong. I thought about explaining that Scooter was stuck on a sailboat, not on another woman, but that would require a lengthy conversation, one I wasn't really up to dealing with just now. After her latest divorce, she tended to think the worst of men, including Scooter.

Nothing's going on, I texted back, hoping that would be the end of it.

Her response was quick. Almost like she had her phone glued to her hand. *Don't be so sure. Where there's smoke, there's fire.* Just as I started to respond, she followed up with another one. *Why did it take you so long to reply to my original text? You know I worry.*

I typed a response as quickly as I could. *Things have been crazy. Someone was murdered. I'll call later.* For some reason, she didn't respond right away. Maybe the battery on her phone died. As I was waiting for her inevitable response, I saw Jack walking toward me pulling a cart. I quickly popped my phone into my purse and rushed over to speak with him.

"Hey, Jack," I said. He looked like he wanted to avoid me, but I stepped in front of him and blocked his path. "I'm so glad I ran into you. When I was visiting with Sandy earlier, she wasn't feeling well. I left so she can try to get some sleep."

Jack rolled his eyes. "Another one of her headaches, isn't it?" I was surprised by the bitterness in his voice. "She always seems to get one whenever there's work to be done. I told her that I need to get these parts inventoried and priced right away. She promised she'd help enter everything into the computer. Now what am I supposed to do?"

I thought he might start by offering to give Sandy a foot rub. Scooter always does that for me when I have a headache. Jack didn't appear very receptive to my suggestion, so I decided to change tack. "You know, I'm awfully worried about Sandy. Not only does she have a really bad headache, but she also has all sorts of cuts and bruises on her. She told me she had a nosebleed last night as well."

"If she wasn't so clumsy, then she wouldn't have all those cuts and bruises, would she?" he asked angrily. "You don't see me complaining every time I get a little boo-boo."

"But it sounds like more than that. She also said she has a hard time falling asleep and staying asleep."

"Well, she's always been that way. Terrible insomnia and waking up in the middle of the night screaming. Even sleepwalking sometimes."

"Sleepwalking?"

"Yeah, I can't tell you how many times I've woken up late at night and discovered she's disappeared. I go out and find her walking along the docks in the dark. I'm worried that one of these times she's going to fall in the water." His expression softened. "It wasn't always like this. We've been married for over thirty years. At first, things were great; she slept like a baby." He smiled gently at the memories. "But over the past few years, it's gotten worse."

"What do you think caused things to change?"

"I don't know. It was probably right around the time we moved onto the boat. Must have been around four years ago. She said it was the lights that kept her from sleeping well. She began sleepwalking a lot more."

"What lights are you talking about?" I asked. "Bright white lights shining in your cabin?"

Jack furrowed his brow. "You mean like moonlight?"

"Not exactly."

"Well, the moon can shine brightly, but it's more the lights here at the marina that bother her. There's also the fishing boats that are coming and going at all hours. Sandy did get some drapes made for the cabin that block out a lot of the light, but she's still sleepwalking."

"Maybe your trip will be a chance for her to relax," I said.

"What trip?"

"Sandy said that you were going to head up to the condo and that you'd be away for a day or two. She asked me to look after your cat."

"We're not going anywhere. I don't know where she comes up with these things. Besides, it's *her* cat, not mine." He looked down at his cart. "I should get going. I've got a lot of work to do, and it sounds like I'll be doing it all on my own."

I peered at the cart. I didn't recognize anything except for one item. "Is that a winch handle?"

"It is. I bought a bunch of them from a salvage dealer."

"Did you know that the murder weapon was a winch handle?" I asked, regarding Jack carefully.

Jack fidgeted with the cart. "I might have heard that. But I'm sure it wasn't one of mine."

"How can you be so sure?"

"I keep a careful inventory of everything I buy and sell. I know for a fact that all of my winch handles are accounted for."

"Sounds like something the police will be interested in."

"Excuse me, sir. We need to have a word with you."

I turned and saw Chief Dalton standing behind me. "Speak of the devil," I said.

He looked at me and scowled. "Your husband is on the patio, Mrs. McGhie. Perhaps you want to join him?"

"Definitely. He should have some brownies for me."

* * *

After grabbing a brownie from Scooter, I walked down to the beach and called Brian Morrison at FAROUT headquarters. I filled him in on my interviews with Sandy and Jack.

"I'm sure of it, Brian. She's got all the signs. Her husband said she sleepwalks at night. There's been many times he's found her walking along the docks in her nightgown. He's been afraid that one of these nights she's going to fall in the water and drown. I also found a pillowcase with blood on it in the bathroom. I asked her about it, and she said that she had a nosebleed the night before."

"Hang on a minute, Mollie. Let me make sure I've checked off all the boxes on the official checklist. Okay, that's two indicators—sleepwalking and nosebleeds. What else do you have?"

"She has unexplained marks on her body. Cuts and bruises on her legs and arms. When I asked her about it, she said she can't remember how she got them. And, get this, she said they weren't there the previous night. She claims she must have bumped into something, but I don't think that's what it was."

I heard Brian scratching down notes. "Let's see. That's one more indicator—unexplained marks."

"Her husband mentioned that Sandy was complaining about bright lights shining into their boat at night. He tried to pass it off as moonlight and fishing boats, but he could be in denial or trying to cover things up."

"Good, lights," Brian said. "That's another indicator."

"And it's not just Sandy who's been seeing lights. When Scooter and I were out walking on the beach last night, I saw flashing red and green lights on the water."

"Oh, now that's interesting. Did you get any video?"

"No, they were gone too quickly. I'll have to get back out there one night and see if they reappear."

"Okay, but please tell me you'll be careful. I'd hate to think of anything happening to you."

"Don't you worry about me. I took your safety course last year, remember?"

"I do. You were my star pupil. Now, what about her dreams? Did she mention anything unusual?"

"She sure did. I was saving the best for last. She says she has frequent nightmares. Last night she even dreamed that she was having a medical procedure in a dark metal room."

"Wow, this is amazing, Mollie. I'd have to agree with you. This is a clear-cut case of alien abduction. You write this up in a report, send it to the board of directors, and you're a shoo-in to be the Federation for Alien Research, Outreach, and UFO Tracking's investigative reporter! There's nothing that Lola can do to top this."

After hanging up with Brian, I celebrated by eating my brownie. Not only was I going to beat out that vile redhead, but I was also going to use all my investigative skills to figure out who killed Captain Dan.

* * *

I was in such a good mood after my call, I practically skipped up the steps from the beach to the boardwalk. Scooter was flipping through some magazines at one of the patio tables. I sneaked up behind him, put my hands over his eyes, and said, "Guess who?"

"Is that my little kohlrabi?" he asked as he pulled me onto his lap.

"What happened to 'sweet potato'? I don't know that I want to be your little kohlrabi. They're a really weird-looking vegetable."

"Your wish is my command, my little sweet potato."

"What are you looking at there?"

"Oh, it's a fascinating article on holding tanks. Doing something about our holding tank is on our project list. I was thinking that instead of a marine toilet, we might want to go with a composting toilet and get rid of the holding tank completely. What do you think?"

"I don't need to think about toilets. That's what plumbers are for." I opened up the box from Penelope's Sugar Shack. "What happened to the rest of the brownies?"

"Guilty," Scooter said as he snagged another magazine from the stack.

"Darn. I was hoping to nab another celebratory brownie."

"What are you celebrating?"

I slipped off Scooter's lap. "Long story. I'll fill you in later. Suffice it to say, Lola is history."

* * *

Maybe one brownie was enough. Did I really need more celebratory chocolaty treats? Of course I did. I had a lot to celebrate. Besides, if I bought a chocolate bar at the marina store, it would give me a chance to question Nancy and Ned about Captain Dan's murder.

A bell rang as I opened the screen door. Nancy stepped out of the back room, holding a couple of large cans. "Hurry up, close that door. You're letting flies in." I shut it behind me, but not fast enough for Nancy. "Now look what you've done! There's a fly next to my computer. Grab that flyswatter and get it."

"Um, I don't see one."

Nancy pointed at the counter. "There. Right there. Are you blind?" All I saw were some large bars of chocolate next to a display of fishing lures.

Nancy marched up to the counter, slammed the cans down, reached behind a vase of flowers, and pulled out a flyswatter. I stepped back. I had a feeling she could turn a flyswatter into a deadly weapon—not just against flies, but also against people who didn't close screen doors quickly enough.

"There. Got it," Nancy said with satisfaction. She tucked the swatter back behind the vase and straightened up some brochures that had gone askew when she whacked the fly. "Good thing you're here," she said gruffly. "You forgot to sign one of the forms yesterday."

"I signed everything you asked me to. Maybe you forgot to give it to me."

Nancy pursed her lips. "I run a tight ship here. If you didn't sign something, it's because you forgot to, not because I didn't give it to you to sign. Are we clear?"

She didn't wait for my answer. After placing the cans on a shelf, she walked behind the counter, adjusted her glasses, and pulled out a stack of papers from a file cabinet. She thumbed through them while I looked at the chocolate bars.

"Those are homemade by a gal who lives in one of the old fishing cottages on Harbor Street," Nancy said without looking up. "She makes all kinds. The dark chocolate butterscotch crunch is popular with the tourists."

Who was I to argue with tourists? I placed a bar next to the cash register.

"Here you go. Put your initials here and sign at the bottom." Nancy tapped her fingers impatiently on the counter while I scanned the form. The click-clack of her nails was distracting me from the finer points of what to do in the event of a fuel or oil spill.

"Nice nails, Nancy," I said. "The navy-blue color matches your shirt perfectly. And I really like the tiny white anchors on each tip. Where do you get them done?"

Nancy stretched out her hands and admired the artwork. "I do them myself. It's my Friday night ritual. I sit down in front of the television, watch my favorite shows, and give myself a manicure."

"You painted on those anchors yourself? I would have thought you'd need a nail salon to get that done."

Nancy warmed up to the subject. "I'll let you in on a little secret. They're press-on nails. They're so simple to use. And if one falls off, you just press another one on." She looked down at my short, unpolished nails with disdain. "You might want to think about doing the same."

I took out my wallet to distract her from my nails. "How much do I owe you for the chocolate?"

After giving me my change, Nancy pushed the chocolate bar toward me. "Aren't you going to try some of it now? You might like it so much that you'll want to buy another one."

You don't have to ask me twice to eat chocolate. I tore open the wrapper and popped a square in my mouth. "Oh, that's delicious. I might need another bar."

Nancy watched as I broke another piece off. She reminded me of one of those cats that would stare at your tuna sandwich, slowly inching forward until it could steal a hunk off your plate. I was worried Nancy was going to grab the chocolate bar and stab my hand in the process with her nails. "Here, do you want—" She snatched the square out of my fingers before I could finish my sentence.

The situation reminded me that I might be kitty-sitting Mrs. Moto sometime in the future when Sandy and Jack rescheduled their trip. "Do you have any cat treats?"

The question brought a scowl to Nancy's face. "Of course I don't have any cat treats," she snapped. "What does this look like, some sort of pet store?"

I handed her another square of chocolate. Somehow, she managed to keep scowling even while eating chocolate. I didn't think that was possible.

"Nancy, I have a few questions."

"Electricity and water are included in the monthly slip fee," she said. "If you need quarters for the washing machine and dryer, come see me."

"Good to know, but what I really wanted to ask was what you thought about Captain Dan's murder. You know everyone at the marina. Who do you think could have done it?"

"That sounds like a question you should be asking Chief Dalton, not me." I waved a square of chocolate in front of her as an enticement. She seized it and shrugged. "Could have been anybody. He didn't have a lot of friends, and he sure made a lot of enemies."

"You and Ned had some issues with him, didn't you? I'm sure the chief has asked you where you were between six and eight."

Nancy took the chocolate bar from me and broke off not one, but two squares. "Like I said, I was doing my nails last night. Ned and I were both in our apartment all night."

I pulled the chocolate bar toward me. "Captain Dan sure was a real smooth talker, wasn't he? I mean, look at Scooter. He managed to talk him into buying *Marjorie Jane*. I'm sure he pulled the wool over lots of people's eyes."

"Well, that's true. He sure suckered Jack in once." I nodded encouragingly and pushed the bar back to her. She took another square. "He sold him a whole bunch of anchor chain. Convinced him it was stainless steel, the best money could buy. Turns out it was a bunch of junk. Most of it was rusted out. It wasn't worth anything. Boy, Jack sure was mad. Captain Dan refused to give him his money back. He said that he sold the chain as is, and that Jack knew what he was getting into."

"Do you think that's all Jack was mad about? It looked like Captain Dan was awfully flirtatious with Sandy at the barbecue last night."

"He was like that with all the women. I bet Sandy played that up to make Jack jealous. They've been having difficulties for a few years."

I thought about this while I savored some more chocolate. "You could be right. Sandy mentioned that she thought Captain Dan and Penny were an item. Did you know anything about that?"

"When Penny first moved up here from Texas, they seemed to get along well, but then it was like things went sour between them. Can't quite picture them romantically involved."

"Maybe things got real sour. I heard them arguing last night, and Sandy said she saw them have a big fight last week."

"Well, they did have a pretty big argument a couple of days ago. I could see them waving their arms. But I couldn't hear anything."

So much for that line of questioning. Just then Ben opened the door. He headed to the coolers in the back, grabbed a six-pack of beer and a bag of potato chips, and put them on the counter.

Nancy shook her head. "I can't give you any more credit, Ben. You've got to pay in cash from now on."

Ben pulled out his wallet and thrust a few bills at Nancy. "Don't worry, I've got the money for both this and for what I already owe you."

While he was collecting his change from Nancy, I noticed that his wallet was crammed full of bills. Several even looked like hundreds. He snapped his wallet shut and stuck it back in the pocket of his cutoff jean shorts. He nodded at both of us and walked outside to the patio.

"Nice to see Ben has some money for a change," Nancy said, shutting the cash drawer firmly.

I went to corral the last square of chocolate, but it was gone. Nancy wiped chocolate off her fingers with a napkin, crumpled up the bright-pink wrapper, and threw both in the trash. "Want another one?"

After giving Nancy money for another dark chocolate butterscotch crunch bar, I was tucking it into my purse when the wrapper caught my eye. I turned to Nancy. "Weren't your nails pink yesterday before you redid your manicure?"

Nancy peered at me over her glasses. "Were they? I don't remember. Close the door. You're going to let flies in."

* * *

Ben waved me over when I came out of the office. He held up a can of beer. "Want one?"

"Uh, no thanks. It's a little early for me."

He chuckled. "It's always five o'clock somewhere."

"Have you seen Scooter?" I asked.

"He went up to Melvin's Marine Emporium to get a catalog," he said after taking a sip of beer.

I noticed Ben was wearing another pirate-themed T-shirt. This one let me know that drinking rum before noon made you a pirate. I had the feeling this was Ben's personal motto. He drained his can, then patted the chair next to him. "Come on, have a seat. I could use the company."

"I guess the events of last night have hit everyone hard," I said, assuming that was the reason he was cracking open another beer. "I still can't believe Captain Dan was murdered on our boat." I pulled out a chocolate bar from my purse. "Want some?"

"No thanks," he said, much to my relief. "Not sure chocolate goes all that well with beer."

I almost unwrapped the bar, but decided I should save it for later in case there were any other chocolate emergencies. "You know, I've talked to a few people, and it doesn't sound like too many folks are broken up by Captain Dan's death," I said, reluctantly tucking the chocolate back in my purse. "I was surprised. I thought the marina would be a tight-knit community. What about you? Were you and Captain Dan on friendly terms?"

Ben's eyes widened. "What exactly are you implying? I didn't have anything to do with his death. Not that I could have anyway."

"Why's that?" I asked, noticing Ben reaching for a third beer. I thought about the brownie and chocolate I'd eaten earlier. I guess we all have our own vices.

"I keep my boat out in the mooring field. You need a dinghy to get back and forth from your boat to the marina. When I headed back to my boat after the barbecue, my outboard engine was acting up. It ended up dying on me. I was lucky to have made it back to my boat, especially as I didn't have any oars on board." He added sheepishly, "I dropped them in the water last week. I wasn't able to get the motor fixed until this morning, when Jack came out to help me."

"I didn't see you leave the barbecue. What time did you head back to your boat?"

"I don't know. I guess around six-thirty. I don't really pay much attention to things like that."

"Wouldn't it be easier to get a slip rather than have to go back and forth on your dinghy?"

"It would, but the rates are practically double. I've been out of work for a while and things are getting tight."

I thought about all the money I had seen in Ben's wallet. It didn't seem like things were too tight. "What kind of work do you do, when you're not out pirating?"

Ben smiled. "Pirating would be more fun, but it doesn't pay as well. I work on boats. I'd been doing some work for Captain Dan. He bought old boats, fixed them up, and sold them, but that didn't work out."

It sounded like all those home improvement shows I liked to watch. "Have you ever put picture windows in a boat? I was thinking that's just what we need to brighten up *Marjorie Jane*. It's really dark down below."

"Picture windows?" he asked with disbelief. Then he laughed.

"Oh, I get it—you're pulling my leg." I decided not to mention the wallpaper. Ben's eyes lit up. "Hey, are you guys looking to have anything done on your boat? It sure does need a lot of work, doesn't it?"

What was I doing thinking about making improvements to *Marjorie Jane* like picture windows and wallpaper? Someone had been murdered on the boat. We needed to get rid of her, not fix her up. Obviously I wasn't thinking clearly.

Just as I was about to tell Ben that I wanted to sell the boat, Ned walked over to the table and pointed at the empty beer cans. "Where'd you get the money for the beer? Next month's mooring fees are going to be due soon."

Ben raised his can in a mock toast to Ned. "No, it won't be a problem. I already settled up with Nancy for last month, and I've got stuff in the pipeline. I picked up a few gigs at the Tipsy Pirate. Plus, Scooter and Mollie might hire me to do some work on their boat." He tried to high-five me, but fortunately Mrs. Moto jumped onto my lap and saved me from inadvertently committing us to having Ben work on a boat I hoped to sell.

"Well, hello there, you pretty little thing," I said.

"Don't let Nancy see that cat," Ned cautioned. As he walked toward the office, he said over his shoulder, "You better not be joking about coming up with that money, Ben."

Ben reached over and gave the calico a scratch on her head. She purred loudly in response. "She's a sweet cat, isn't she? Did you know Jack and Sandy are selling their boat and looking for a new home for her? She seems to like you. Maybe you should take her. She's a great boat cat."

Mrs. Moto looked at me and blinked slowly. I think she was trying to tell me something. What she didn't know was that it wasn't me she had to convince. It was Scooter. I turned back to Ben. "Yes, Sandy told me that earlier over coffee. I was surprised that they listed their boat with Captain Dan. Jack didn't act all that friendly toward him."

"That's true. Jack didn't want to use Captain Dan, but when he heard that he'd managed to offload *Marjorie Jane* onto you and Scooter, he had second thoughts. He figured if Captain Dan could sell that boat, he could sell anything." Ben started putting his empty cans into a plastic bag.

"He did seem like a smooth-talking salesman. He sure fooled Scooter."

Ben turned bright red. "Um, that's not what I meant. I meant to say Jack was impressed that Captain Dan sold *Marjorie Jane* so quickly, not that he pulled one over on Scooter."

He got up and grabbed the plastic bag. "Uh...gotta go, Mollie. You'll talk to Scooter about working on your boat, won't you?"

"Wait, Ben. You forgot a full one."

"You can have it," he shouted as he ran over to the dinghy dock.

Hmm. Ben giving away beer? Such a difference from yesterday, when he was happy to take a free beer from Captain Dan.

CHAPTER 7
NOSEBLEEDS

"THANK YOU, SIR," I HEARD someone say behind me. "We'll be in touch if we need any more information." I turned and saw Chief Dalton ushering a man out of the lounge next to the office. He caught sight of me, walked back inside, and shut the door. He wasn't going to get away from me that easily.

I seized my purse and Ben's beer and pushed the door open. Mrs. Moto ran in and jumped on the windowsill. The chief wasn't anywhere to be seen. He was stealthier than I would have guessed. There was a kitchenette at the back of the lounge. I decided to tuck Ben's beer in the fridge and give it back to him later. I turned to close the door and saw the chief standing behind it rubbing his nose.

"Oh, there you are," I said. "What are you doing hiding back there?"

"I went to get my briefcase off the table when you smacked into me with the door." At least, I think that's what he said. It's hard to understand someone when they're pressing a napkin to their face.

"Is your nose bleeding?"

"Yes," he said. He arched one of his bushy eyebrows, then the other. Good. He still had full range of movement of the furry caterpillars adorning his forehead. He couldn't be too badly hurt.

"You should really sit down," I said. He raised his eyebrows again. "You might be more comfortable sitting while I give you my report."

He furrowed his brow as though he didn't understand what I was saying. Blood loss will do that to you.

"You know, my report on the investigation." I sat in one of the comfy lounge chairs in front of the big-screen television. Chief Dalton continued to stand near the door. "Plus, I have evidence for you. Something I found on *Marjorie Jane* last night." Finally, he came over and sat in a chair.

"Evidence?" he asked as he pressed another napkin to his nose.

I reached into my purse and pulled out a plastic bag containing the pink fingernail. I had even labeled the bag with a description of where I had discovered the evidence at the crime scene. Chief Dalton was sure to be impressed by my professionalism. "Right before you arrived at our boat, I found this on the floor," I said proudly.

The burly man continued to press a napkin to his nose with one hand and took the bag in his other.

Mrs. Moto streaked across the room, jumped onto the chief's chair, pawed at him, and meowed loudly. He dropped the bag in surprise.

"Is that your cat?" he asked as he tried to push her off. Mrs. Moto pawed at him again, this time with her claws extended. Chief Dalton backed down. Smart move.

"No, she belongs to Jack and Sandy. I should probably start with them first."

"Start with them first?"

"Yes, I've got quite a lot to report."

The chief picked the evidence up off the floor, sighed, and sat back in his chair. "Go on."

"I interviewed Sandy this morning. Have you interviewed her yet?" He was too busy trying to keep Mrs. Moto away from the fingernail to respond. I continued. "Well, if you have, you're probably as concerned as I am. Not just about the murder, but about the abduction."

Chief Dalton looked at me with surprise. "Abduction? We haven't had any reports of an abduction."

"Oh, that's interesting. No other reports of bright lights, unexplained bruises, that sort of thing?"

"What exactly are you talking about, Mrs. McGhie?"

"The classic signs of abduction, such as sleepwalking and strange dreams. Nosebleeds, like yours." He looked confused. "Don't you guys get training in this?"

"Come again?"

"Alien abduction. What else could I be talking about?"

Just when I didn't think the chief could raise his eyebrows any higher, he managed to. "Mrs. McGhie, we're investigating a murder here, not an alien abduction. You don't honestly believe in that sort of thing, do you?"

He got up, threw the napkins in the trash, and put the plastic bag with the fingernail in his briefcase. Mrs. Moto padded over to him and meowed loudly. He ignored her. "Now, where exactly did you find this fingernail?"

"In the galley. Did you notice the color? It's bright pink. Two women had bright pink manicures yesterday—Penny, the sailing school instructor, and Nancy, the owner of the marina. Both of them had reason to be angry with Captain Dan. He cheated them out of money. My theory is that one of them came on our boat last night, whacked him with the winch handle, and somehow lost one of their nails in the process."

"Why don't you leave the murder investigation to the professionals, and we'll leave the alien abduction investigation to the amateurs." He snapped his briefcase shut and left.

Mrs. Moto ran to the door and meowed loudly. She really didn't miss that infuriating man, did she? I opened the door. She walked across the patio toward the beach, stopping now and then to look back at me as though she wanted me to follow her.

* * *

While Sandy's cat chased seagulls on the beach, I sat on a piece of driftwood and thought about what the chief had said. I couldn't believe he had called me an amateur! It was bad enough that

Scooter pooh-poohed what I did for a living—well, not exactly for a living, but you know what I mean—but now Chief Dalton was dismissing me too. You would think a professional law enforcement officer would take alien abduction more seriously.

That was the problem. Individuals who come forward with their accounts aren't taken seriously. As a result, people don't put two and two together when it comes to recognizing the signs of alien abduction. People like Sandy. Chances were she didn't even realize what had happened to her. I needed to figure out a way to help her process her experience and come to terms with it.

I got out a notebook from my purse. It was time to start a to-do list:

1) Type up the notes from my interview with Sandy and write a report on her abduction for FAROUT's board of directors
2) Type up the notes from my interviews with Jack, Nancy, and Ben
3) Buy more chocolate
4) Figure out how to get Scooter on board with adopting Mrs. Moto
5) Figure out how to convince Scooter that we should sell *Marjorie Jane*
6) Solve Captain Dan's murder

I underlined the last item and put a couple of exclamation points after it. I imagined the expression on Chief Dalton's face when I solved the murder before he did. It would be almost as sweet as seeing the one on Lola's face when I was promoted to the investigative reporter role over her.

As I was daydreaming about my promotion, Scooter called out, "There you are, my little bok choy." I wrinkled my nose. "Okay, I take it that's a no to bok choy."

He took a seat next to me. "I was just at Melvin's Marine Emporium looking at stuff we're going to need for *Marjorie Jane*. I know how much you like catalogs, so I brought one back for you."

I leafed through the glossy pages. "Um, Scooter, the catalogs I normally look at have things like sweaters and shoes in them. I don't know what anything is in here. Like this," I said, pointing at a strange rubber item.

Scooter leaned over and looked at the picture. "Oh, that's a joker valve. You need to replace them in marine toilets periodically. I've heard it's a really nasty job. One more reason to go with a composting toilet instead, don't you think?"

"Is there anything in here that's less gross and more interesting?"

Scooter turned to a page with pictures of inflatable dinghies. "We're going to need one of these."

"Wow, those are expensive."

"Yep, you know what they say BOAT stands for—Break Out Another Thousand, or in this case, several thousand."

"Don't you need an outboard motor for a dinghy too?"

Scooter laughed. "That's the spirit. See, you're really getting into boating."

"I was talking to Ben earlier and he said that his outboard died last night. I guess that's his alibi for Captain Dan's murder. He couldn't have come to shore during the time Captain Dan was killed because his engine wasn't working. Jack went out this morning to help him fix it."

Scooter shuddered at the mention of the murder. He collected himself and smiled. "Yeah, that's the problem with boats. Everything breaks sooner or later." I wasn't sure why he was smiling. Who in the world likes it when things break? "Except the good news is that when stuff on our boat breaks, we'll be in exotic locations. We can fix things in the morning and then go for a swim in the afternoon."

"I don't know, Scooter. It all sounds really expensive. Just look at the prices on some of these things."

"See, it's a good thing we got such a deal on *Marjorie Jane*."

"But it's not much of a deal if we have to fix lots of things on her, is it? Everyone I talk to seems to think Captain Dan sold us a lemon."

"Nah, they're just jealous. We got a great deal that they missed out on."

"But are you sure you want to keep *Marjorie Jane* after someone was murdered on board?"

Scooter clasped his hands together tightly and took a deep breath. "To be honest, last night I started to have second thoughts, but what better way to honor Captain Dan's memory than by fixing her up?"

I could think of plenty of better ways to honor Captain Dan's memory, none of which involved fixing up a boat.

"What's that cat doing over there?" Scooter asked. Mrs. Moto was fishing her paw underneath a small overturned wooden boat on the beach. After a few tries, she managed to get the object out, then pounced on it. She tossed it in the air a few times, then came bounding over to us holding it in her mouth. She dropped it at my feet and meowed.

"Good kitty," I said. "What did you bring me?" I reached down and picked up a crumpled piece of paper.

I smoothed it out. "It looks like an IOU." I squinted at the torn paper. "Is that Ben's name on it?"

"Let me have a look at that," Scooter said. After examining it, he handed it back to me. "I can't really make anything out. It's probably nothing. I'm sure stuff washes up on the beach all the time." I folded it carefully and tucked it into my purse.

Scooter slapped his knees with his hands. "I can't believe I forgot to tell you the good news. I saw Chief Dalton on my way down to the beach. He said we're free to go back on board *Marjorie Jane*. They've cleaned everything up." He hesitated and looked a little woozy. "But there is one big issue. There are blood stains on the floor. I'm not sure I really want to see that."

"I think I have a solution to that. There's only one problem," I said, pointing at the mooring field. "We need to get out there."

* * *

We decided to walk back to the marina and see if anyone could give us a ride out to Ben's boat. I kept my eyes on the beach in search of seashells to add to my collection, while Mrs. Moto trailed behind me, keeping the seagulls in check.

I was picking through a pile of shells when Scooter stumbled into me, knocking me down. "Sorry about that," he said as he helped me up. "I was so caught up watching the racing that I didn't notice where I was going."

I held my hand over my eyes to minimize the glare of the sun bouncing off the water. I could see half a dozen small boats weaving through the bay, adjusting their sails as they changed direction.

"What are those?" I asked. "I didn't know they could make sailboats so small."

"They're Optimist dinghies. Kids use them to learn how to sail." He shouted encouragement to the girl who was in the lead. "I wish I had done something like that when I was their age," he said wistfully.

We watched as the tiny boats zipped back and forth, followed by a small pink speedboat. "Hey, I think that's Penny out there," I said, wondering what in Penny's life wasn't pink.

"Makes sense. She's the sailing instructor."

Mrs. Moto dropped something at my feet, and then twined herself around my legs.

"What did you bring me now, Mrs. Moto? Oh, that's a pretty one." I rubbed sand off the small green seashell.

"How do you know that cat's name?" Scooter asked suspiciously.

"Oh, she belongs to Jack and Sandy." I gave Scooter a bright smile. "They're looking for someone to adopt her."

Scooter frowned as the calico played with his shoelaces. He pulled his foot away. "Why don't they want to keep her? She's really adorable." By adorable, I think he meant annoying.

"They need to sell their boat and their condo association doesn't allow pets." I watched as Mrs. Moto tried to untie his laces again. I suspect she thought Scooter pulling his feet away was part of the game. "You know, I feel bad for Sandy. They've got financial problems, and their marriage seems on shaky ground. And on top of all that she has to deal with what they did to her."

"They?"

I pointed at the sky. "You know, them. I'm writing a report on her abduction for FAROUT."

"Sandy, an alien abductee? I doubt it." He laughed. "Heck, there's probably a bigger chance that she's the murderer."

"Murder? No, I don't think Sandy could have done that. She's in too much of a fragile state. The woman can barely function with her insomnia, headaches, nightmares, and sleepwalking." I picked Mrs. Moto up before Scooter lost patience with her. "My money is on Penny or Nancy. That pink fingernail I found in the galley could belong to one of them." Scooter looked at me quizzically. "Oh, yeah. I guess I forgot to tell you about that. Don't take it personally. Chief Dalton didn't know about it either until today. Both Penny and Nancy had pink manicures the day of the murder, which means one of them must have been on *Marjorie Jane* that night and killed Captain Dan."

Scooter flinched at the mention of murder but held it together. It was probably being in close proximity to Mrs. Moto. Cats have a calming effect on people. "But couldn't that fingernail have been there before?" he asked.

"Remember how you cleaned up the boat after the break-in?" Scooter nodded while keeping a wary eye on the Japanese bobtail. "You didn't see it then, did you?"

"No, I don't think so." He thought about it for a few minutes. "But still, I can't picture it, especially Nancy. She's an older lady. Could she really have had the strength to, you know—"

I interjected quickly before Scooter had to utter the word "murder." "You need to spend more time with Nancy. She's got a serious temper, and given the way I've seen her brandish brooms, staplers, and cans, I don't doubt that she could wield a winch handle if she were angry enough. She's definitely got motive. And so does Penny. Captain Dan cheated them, just like he cheated Jack."

"What did he do to Jack?"

"Sold him some worthless anchor chain."

"So maybe it was Jack," Scooter said. Then he added quickly, "I'm just kidding. Jack seems like a stand-up guy. I'm sure it wasn't him."

"Maybe I need to talk with him some more," I mused. "I did see him with a cart full of marine equipment earlier, including a large winch handle."

Mrs. Moto suddenly yowled, jumped out of my arms, and ran toward the water. I looked over to see what had her so excited. "Scooter, did that boat just capsize?" I asked in shock.

"Yep. That happens." He saw the concerned expression on my face. "They'll be okay." We watched as a boy righted the small boat and climbed back on board.

I breathed a big sigh of relief. "Falling out of a boat would be my worst nightmare."

"Don't worry. That will never happen to you."

* * *

We watched the end of the race, cheering along with the families who were gathered on the beach. The children brought their dinghies on shore, stowed their gear, and teased each other about who was a better sailor. Penny gathered the children and parents around her, debriefing them on the morning's activities, and giving them instructions for the following week's class.

"Come on, let's go over and talk to Penny," I said. "Maybe she can take us out to see Ben on that fancy pink boat of hers."

"That was an exciting race," Scooter said to her. "Those kids are fearless."

"They sure are," Penny agreed. "Teaching the children's course is one of my favorite parts of being a sailing instructor. They're so eager to learn." She turned to me. "What about you, Mollie? You're going to need to learn how to sail now that you're a boat owner. I do ladies' lessons every Thursday. I find women have more confidence learning sailing skills when their husbands aren't around." She glanced at Scooter. "No offense."

"None taken." Scooter put his arm around my shoulder. "I think it would be a great idea. Let's sign you up."

Penny was giving us the details when the young girl who had won the race came bounding up wearing a polka dot swimsuit with an octopus on it. She wore her light-brown hair in two braids, and her green eyes sparkled. "Can you believe I won, Miss Penny?"

"Of course I can, Katy. You've been working really hard, and you had a great race."

"I just wish my grandparents could have been here to see it," Katy said. Her eyes got big. "Someone was killed at the marina last night. Grandma and Grandpa have been busy with police and reporters all morning."

My ears perked up at the mention of reporters. Was someone trying to steal my story about Sandy's abduction? Was it about the mysterious lights I saw?

Penny tugged at the girl's braids gently. "It's okay, Katy. They'll be able to watch you next week. Maybe you'll even win again."

Katy grinned, showing off two gaps in her front teeth. I wondered how much the Tooth Fairy was paying out these days. I use my credit and debit cards for practically everything and never have any cash on hand. Does the Tooth Fairy have the same problem?

She hugged Penny good-bye and ran up the stairs from the beach to the boardwalk. "Katy is Ned and Nancy's granddaughter," Penny said. "She's a regular little mermaid. She's only seven years old, but she's taken to sailing quickly."

"I didn't realize Ned and Nancy had grandkids," I said, watching as Katy stopped to scratch Mrs. Moto on the head.

"They raised their kids in Coconut Cove. Their sons moved away, but their daughter and her husband settled here and had two kids—Katy and her younger brother, Sam." Penny adjusted her hot-pink baseball hat. "If Katy can learn to sail, then you can too. Unless, of course, you want to sell that dilapidated sailboat of yours. I'm still interested in taking her off your hands."

"Thanks for the offer, but we're committed to fixing her up and sailing her off into the sunset," Scooter said.

"You're gonna need to do a lot of work to her," Penny said. "That's a big job for just two people."

Why was she looking at me? Did she think I was going to work on that boat with Scooter? Time to get that idea out of her head, and more importantly, out of Scooter's head. "Ben mentioned that he was looking for work. He might be a good person to help Scooter."

"That's not a bad idea," Penny said thoughtfully. "When he isn't drinking beer, Ben's actually a good worker. He knows tons about boats."

"Well, the first thing we need to get him to do is remove the stains from the floor," I said.

"Stains?" Penny asked.

"You know, from the, um..."

"Oh, stains. Gotcha."

"We were actually hoping you might be able to give us a lift out to Ben's boat to tell him that he's hired."

"Sure, no problem." She pointed at her pink speedboat, which was anchored a few feet from the shore. "Hop on in."

* * *

I was still wringing out my skirt, which had gotten soaked getting into Penny's boat, along with the rest of me, when we pulled up to Ben's boat. I didn't think it was possible to find a boat that looked worse than *Marjorie Jane*, but Ben had achieved that dubious honor. What appeared to have been blue paint at one time was chipped and faded, the canvas was ripped, and the decks were long overdue for some varnish. I could just about make out the name, *Poseidon's Saber*, next to a carving of a scantily clad mermaid.

Penny knocked on the side of the boat. "Ben, are you there? It's me, Penny, along with Scooter and Mollie from *Marjorie Jane*."

I heard some banging, followed by a few salty phrases that any pirate would be proud to have in his vocabulary. Ben came up on deck, stretching his arms. "Sorry about that. I was having a bit of a nap down below." He grabbed a rope from Penny and tied off her boat to the side. "Come on aboard," he said, pointing at a rickety ladder.

I wasn't too sure that I wanted to climb up that. "Maybe I should just wait here," I suggested.

"Nonsense," Scooter said. "It'll be a good chance to check out another sailboat and get ideas for *Marjorie Jane*. Climb on up." He held the ladder steady while I cautiously made my ascent.

"How's it going, Mollie?" Ben said, offering me his hand and helping me up on deck. "Long time, no see. To what do I owe the pleasure of this visit?"

"I talked with Scooter and we want to hire you to do some work on the boat."

After agreeing to an hourly rate, Ben said, "This calls for a celebration." He shoved aside an old guitar and a pile of rags and motioned for us to sit down. "Who wants a soda?"

Obviously, Ben didn't realize that celebrations involved

chocolate, not a can of warm generic cola.

Scooter took him up on his offer and popped open a can. "How long have you had this boat?"

"I bought her earlier this year from Captain Dan. You should have seen what she looked like before I got my hands on her. Boy, was she a wreck."

"She used to be owned by that old guy, didn't she?" Penny asked.

"Yep, a real old salt. He circumnavigated the globe on this boat. I'm hoping to do the same thing." He combed his fingers through his hair, then pulled it back into a ponytail. "But it'll be a while yet before I can get her off this mooring ball. She needs a new engine and a million other things." He slapped Scooter on the knee. "Working for you is sure going to help a lot. I'm gonna save up my money, point *Poseidon's Saber* toward the Caribbean, and never come back."

"You'd sail down there all by yourself?" I asked.

Ben sighed. "I guess so. It's really hard to find a woman who wants to live aboard a boat and share the sailing dream." He punched Scooter in the arm. "You're a lucky fellow. Not every guy has a wife who's willing to sell everything, move aboard a boat, and sail around the world."

My jaw dropped. Selling everything and sailing around the world was news to me. Scooter's midlife crisis was taking on new proportions.

Scooter patted my arm. "One step at a time, Ben. First, we need to get *Marjorie Jane* fixed up. When do you think you'd be able to start work?"

Ben's eyes lit up. "How about later this afternoon?"

"Sounds good. The first thing we have to do is some cleaning." I noticed Scooter didn't mention exactly what needed to be cleaned up. "The boat's in a bit of disarray given what happened last night."

"Oh, yeah, the murder. Do the police have any idea who did it?"

"Not yet," Scooter said. "I think they've been interviewing everyone today. Hopefully, they'll solve the case soon, and we can all move on with our lives."

"Did they interview you, Penny?" I asked.

"Bright and early this morning," she replied.

"I bet they asked you the usual questions, like what you were doing at the time of Captain Dan's murder."

"They did."

I was hoping for a little more information. Fortunately, we'd received training on questioning techniques for reluctant interviewees from FAROUT. I tried again. "What exactly were you doing at the time of Captain Dan's murder?"

Penny looked flustered. "I was on my boat reading a book about old whaling captains and their crews. Did you know some of the captains took their wives with them on trips that lasted for years?"

I wasn't going to be sidetracked. "Were you all alone?"

"Yes, they were alone. No other women on the ship," Penny said. "Can you imagine raising children on a whaling ship?"

No, I couldn't. I couldn't imagine raising children at all, let alone on a boat. Now, a cat, on the other hand—that was something I could imagine. Just the right level of responsibility for me to deal with.

I mentally shook myself. Somehow, Penny had managed to distract me. I was thinking about cats instead of Captain Dan's murder. I was determined to get an answer to my question. "No, I meant were *you* alone?"

"Yes," she said, frowning.

"So no one can vouch for you, Penny?"

Penny began to look irritated. "Not everyone lives with a husband or partner like you do, Mollie."

"No, that's not what I meant," I said quickly, realizing that my blunt questions weren't having the desired effect. I've been told that subtlety is not my strong suit. "All I meant was that they asked us about our alibis and who could vouch for us. I was just curious if they asked you similar questions. I wasn't sure if you had someone special in your life."

Ben inched closer to Penny. "I guess we're in the same boat. I don't have anyone special. You don't have anyone special. Neither of us has anyone to back up our alibis."

Penny moved closer to me and farther from Ben. "Maybe we

should do something to change that. Whaddya say we hit up happy hour tonight at the Tipsy Pirate?"

"Sorry, sugar, but I've got plans tonight," Penny said.

Ben slumped on the bench. "Sure, I understand," he said slowly.

Penny stood and clapped her hands together. "All right. Let's get this show on the road and head back to the marina. I've got a million things to do this afternoon before my date."

This time, I managed to stay dry, which made the boat ride more enjoyable. The gentle breeze and clear blue water didn't hurt either. During the trip back, I remembered that Sandy had said that she had seen Penny at the marina on the night of the murder. Why did Penny say she was on her boat alone? Something wasn't adding up.

CHAPTER 8
TO-DO LISTS

AFTER PENNY DROPPED US OFF at the marina dinghy dock, we walked into town to the Sailor's Corner Cafe for a late lunch. It was popular with locals and tourists alike, and we were lucky to get a table. We had been coming here regularly since our move to Coconut Cove. I always thought the nautical decorations were cute, but now that we owned a sailboat, I looked at the old steering wheels, oars, ship's bells, and anchors dotted around with more interest.

I noticed the young couple I had seen at our anniversary dinner holding hands in a booth. The sunlight from the window made the diamond necklace he had given her that night sparkle brightly. "Aww. Aren't they sweet?" I said. "Look at how in love they are. I really like her necklace, don't you?"

Scooter glanced over at them. "It's okay." He put his menu down. "That reminds me—you have to stop trying to fix people up."

"What are you talking about? Who was I trying to fix up?"

"Penny and Ben."

"You've got to be kidding me. They are the least likely couple I can think of. She doesn't exactly seem like the type to go for an unemployed pirate wannabe."

"Then what were you doing asking all those questions about their alibis and pointing out that they're both single?"

"That's all I was doing—checking on their alibis. I'm done trying to fix people up. Remember what happened with your sister?"

"She's still not speaking to me." He picked his menu back up. "What are you going to get?"

"I can't decide. I'm torn between the Pirate's Platter or a BLT."

Scooter's eyes followed a waitress who was bearing two large sundaes on her tray. "You should probably go for the BLT so you save room for dessert."

"Good call. The BLT it is."

Scooter waved the waitress over to our table. "We're ready to order, Alejandra."

Alejandra Lopez was one of the reasons we kept coming back to the Sailor's Corner Cafe. I envied her silky, black hair, which she wore in a French braid while at work, and her youthful energy. I certainly wouldn't have been able to put the hours in that she did, always with a big smile on her face.

After we placed our order, she asked, "Is it true that Captain Dan was killed on your boat?"

"Unfortunately, he was," I said.

"¡*Oh, Dios mío!* Are you doing okay?"

"We're trying not to think about it," Scooter said.

"You poor things. How awful." She scooped up our menus and tucked her pad and pen in her apron pocket. "Captain Dan used to come in here quite a bit. He always got the same thing—the Fisherman's Combo." She bent down and said in a low voice, "Between you and me, for all of his boasting about how great of a salesman he was and how much money he made, he sure was a lousy tipper. He used to try to hit on me too. Like I'd be interested in somebody like him." She gave us a smile. "Anyway, enough about him. I'll be back with your meals in a jiff."

After we polished off our sandwiches and hot fudge sundaes—complete with extra sprinkles and whipped cream—I got out my notebook. "We should probably make a list of what needs to be done on *Marjorie Jane*." I really shouldn't have been encouraging Scooter's midlife crisis, but I figured that if he was going to have one, I might as well make sure it was organized.

"You do love making lists, don't you?" Scooter said. It was true. I do love to-do lists. It's the doing stuff on the to-do lists that I don't like so much.

"So where should we start?" I asked.

"First, we should probably do a full inventory of everything that's on the boat. After they found that winch handle, it makes me wonder what else is on there that we don't know about." I was proud of Scooter. He didn't look like he was going to pass out at the mention of the winch handle. I think the hot fudge sundae had had a fortifying effect. "Although there's so much stuff crammed in the lockers, it could take a while," he warned.

I wrote down "inventory" on the list with "VBT" next to it. "VBT" stands for Very Boring Task. I like to categorize my to-do lists by how interesting the items are. That way I have a better sense of how to prioritize my time.

We continued our discussion about the list, and I added a number of other items with various codes such as "EBT" (Extremely Boring Task), "NTWL" (Need to Win the Lottery First), and "AAAC" (Avoid at All Costs).

While I was trying to figure out how to code the installation of a composting toilet, I heard the squeal of children behind me. I turned and saw Nancy walking toward our table with Katy and another child in tow. Katy saw me and waved. "Grandma, they saw me sailing today," she yelled. She tugged on Nancy's hand and pulled her toward us. "Tell my grandma what a great job I did sailing today."

"She did a wonderful job," Scooter said. "And who's this?" He pointed at the boy standing shyly behind Katy.

"This is Sam, my little brother," Katy said enthusiastically. "I'm going to teach him how to sail! But first, we're going to have lunch!"

Nancy smiled and patted Katy on the head. She seemed a lot less grumpy when surrounded by her grandchildren.

"Where's Ned? Isn't he joining you for lunch?" I asked.

Before Nancy could answer, Katy shouted, "The police took him in for questioning!"

"Is everything okay, Nancy?" Scooter asked with concern. "I

thought they had spoken with you both already."

"Everything's fine. It's all routine. All right, children, let's grab a table and get some lunch," she said as she ushered them to the back of the restaurant.

"I wonder what that's all about," I said.

"I don't know, but it doesn't sound routine to me at all."

"Nancy told me that both of them were at their apartment watching television while she did her nails. But now I'm wondering if Ned was there the whole time. After we pay the check, let's go back and see what we can find out."

* * *

After lunch, we met Ben back at the marina. While he and Scooter went to start work on *Marjorie Jane*, I headed to the lounge to type up my report on Sandy's abduction. The air conditioning was going full blast, which was a nice relief from the hot, humid afternoon weather. Looking at the gray clouds forming overhead, I figured we were due for the usual afternoon showers. Sitting inside on one of the comfy chairs with my laptop seemed like a good idea.

I kicked off my flip-flops and stretched out my legs on the ottoman. After opening my laptop, I had the funny feeling that someone was staring at me. I looked around but didn't see anyone. I poked behind the drapes, just in case someone was hiding there. You never know. Puzzled, I walked past the bookshelves to peek out the window. Then I heard a loud meow from above. There was Mrs. Moto, perched on a pile of sailing manuals on the bookshelf. She blinked at me a few times, then jumped down and rubbed herself against my legs. I picked her up, had a quick cuddle, and deposited her on the coffee table. Just as I settled back into my chair and got my laptop situated, the calico plopped down next to me and wiggled her way between my right leg and the side of the armchair. She started kneading my leg and purring loudly. After a few minutes, she put her head down and settled in for a nap.

I positioned my hands on the keyboard just like Mrs. Purdy had taught us at school—my index fingers poised above the *f* and *j* keys—and waited for inspiration. I waited some more. And some more. I stroked Mrs. Moto's soft fur for a few minutes, then hovered my hands over the keyboard, ready to write the report that was going to propel my career forward. Nothing. Absolutely nothing. This must be what they called writer's block.

I took a break and checked email. Brian Morrison had sent me a note marked urgent.

You'd better hurry up and submit your report. I heard a rumor that Lola has uncovered a major government conspiracy that might top your alien abduction case. I think you're the best candidate for the investigative reporter job, so please send your report in today, if possible. I'll put in a good word for you with the board of directors.

The mere thought of Lola motivated me to get cracking. I clicked away at the keyboard furiously, documenting Sandy's abduction in detail. From time to time, Mrs. Moto would open her eyes and demand to be scratched. I'm pretty sure aliens never abducted cats. They were far too demanding as test subjects.

As I was trying to write a scintillating conclusion, Ned walked in carrying a bucket full of cleaning supplies.

"How did she get in here again?" he asked. The Japanese bobtail peeked over the side of the armchair to look at him. She gave him the feline equivalent of a shrug and nestled back down to continue her nap. "Don't let Nancy see her," he warned.

"Don't worry, I'd be the last person to rat out Mrs. Moto," I said. "We saw Nancy and your grandkids at the Sailor's Corner Cafe earlier. They said the police were questioning you some more."

"Oh, that was nothing. Just routine." He pulled a rag from his bucket. "They all got back about ten minutes ago. The grandkids are helping Nancy out in the store this afternoon while their mom's running errands. By helping, I mean eating all the chocolate."

"Not only are they adorable, but they have their priorities straight," I said with a smile. "We saw Katy racing earlier today. I can't get over how good of a sailor she is for her age."

"She begged her parents for months for sailing lessons," Ned said as he started dusting and polishing the furniture. "She's loving it. Between you and me, Penny says that Katy is her best student." Ned glowed with pride. "I bet she'll even make the Olympic sailing team when she's older."

"Did you ever race?" I asked.

"I sure did. Every weekend I would be out there competing. My favorite part was the annual Coconut Cove regatta. We usually beat everyone else." Ned pointed at his knees. "These days, I don't move around as easily. I had both of these replaced a couple of years ago. Between that and my arthritis, my racing days are over."

"It looks like you keep busy around here."

"I do. It's the kind of job where you're never really off duty. We live in an apartment upstairs and have to be on call in case anything happens. But we enjoy it. It keeps us close to the water and involved in the sailing community. It's a close-knit group of sailors here in the area, as you've probably gathered."

"It must have been a real shock to everyone when Captain Dan was murdered."

Ned hesitated. "Of course. Anytime anyone is murdered it's a real shock."

"The memorial service should be packed with everyone from the marina." Ned suddenly became very engrossed in some dust bunnies near the window. I tried again. "Wasn't Captain Dan popular around here?"

Ned weighed up the question before answering. "Well, let's just say he didn't really endear himself in the short time he lived here. There are more than a few people who were cheated by him in one way or another, ourselves included."

"I heard he vouched for the previous owners of *Marjorie Jane*, which left you guys in the lurch with unpaid bills. Was it more than that?"

"It might have been," Ned said evasively. "What are you working on there?" he asked, pointing to my computer.

"It's a report for work. I'm actually really excited about it. It might even get picked up by newspapers nationally. It's a big story!"

Ned sat down in the other armchair. "Really? What's it about?"

Before I could tell Ned what had happened to Sandy, the door burst open, and Katy and Sam ran in. "Look what we got!" Katy shouted, holding out her hands. Sam ran up next to her and held out his hands eagerly too.

"Well, would you look at that!" Ned said, peering at Katy's and Sam's yo-yos. "What did you do to talk grandma into getting those?"

"We promised we wouldn't tell anyone what she said to Jack. She said it was a secret and that we couldn't tell anyone about it, not even you."

"Oh, is that right?" Ned pressed his lips together. "I'll tell you what—why don't we go back to the store to see grandma? Maybe she'll tell me her secret and give me one of those yo-yos so I don't tell anyone either."

"Oh, grandpa, don't be silly. These are just for kids," Katy said.

"Yeah, grandpa, you're a grown-up, not a kid," Sam added.

"Grandpa is being silly, isn't he?" Katy asked me. The calico hopped over to the coffee table, trying to get a glimpse of the yo-yos. "Don't be silly, Mrs. Moto," Katy said. "These aren't for cats either."

Sam laughed. "Yeah, Mrs. Moto, you're a cat, not a kid."

Ned got up from his chair. "Come on, kids, let's go next door and see grandma." He picked up his bucket of cleaning supplies, and the three of them left the lounge. Katy and Sam looked excited. Ned looked concerned.

* * *

After Ned and the kids left, I typed away for another hour, finished up my report, gathered my courage, and hit Send. Considering all that work, I figured I deserved a treat.

As I went to grab my purse, Mrs. Moto reached over and stuck her paw inside. She pulled out the piece of paper she had brought to me earlier on the beach and dropped it on my lap. I think she was trying to tell me something. I had another look at the IOU and wondered how big Ben's money problems were. I tucked it back in my bag and said thank you to Mrs. Moto for reminding me about it by way of a few scratches on her belly.

Sandy's cat followed me out of the lounge, but when I entered the marina office, she wisely scurried away. I quickly shut the screen door behind me, but not quickly enough. Nancy glared at me and got out her flyswatter. Hoping to avoid being mistaken for a fly, I hurried over to the back, where Katy and Sam were playing with their yo-yos.

"Is there any chocolate left? Or have you two munchkins eaten it all?" I asked.

"We want more chocolate!" Katy screamed.

"Yeah, more chocolate!" Sam agreed.

"You've had plenty of chocolate," Nancy said. "Maybe it's time for some apples instead?" Katy and Sam stared at her like she had developed some sort of dementia and went back to playing with their yo-yos.

"Their mother is going to be thrilled when she picks them up with all that sugar running through their system. But that's what grandmothers are for," Nancy said as she smiled fondly at her grandchildren.

Ned poked his head out of the back room. "Nancy, can you give me a hand with this?" She helped him carry out some heavy-looking boxes and stacked them next to the counter.

"It looks like this job keeps you fit," I said.

"I make an effort to stay in shape," Nancy said as she opened up one of the boxes and began stocking the shelves. "I go for a walk every morning on the beach, and I lift some light weights as well. That's the only way I can keep up with those two."

"Are there any more of those dark chocolate butterscotch crunch bars left?" I asked.

"Are we out already? I wonder how that happened?" Nancy smiled at Katy and Sam. "Let me just finish this, and I'll go in the back and get some more."

While I waited, I studied a display of sailing books by the door. I picked up one on cruising in the Bahamas and flipped through it. The glossy photos of sandy beaches, colorful fish, and picturesque towns almost had me thinking that this sailing thing might be okay.

The screen door opened, interrupting my daydreams of tropical cocktails. That young couple—whom I had started to think of as Mr. and Mrs. Diamond—seemed to be following me around. First at our anniversary dinner, then at lunch, and now here.

"Hi there," Ned said, looking up from the computer. "You're the folks out on the catamaran, aren't you? How can I help you?"

"We're not normally ones to complain, but there was someone speeding through the mooring field last night. I was worried he was going to ram into our boat," Mr. Diamond said. His wife nodded while she toyed with her diamond necklace.

"Could you make out who it was?" Ned asked.

"No, I didn't recognize him. I did see him anchor his boat on the far side of the beach and meet up with a couple of guys. It's probably no big deal, but we thought you should know."

"Well, I appreciate you letting me know. Folks shouldn't be driving through there like that. About what time was it, do you reckon?"

"Sweetie, what time was that at?" he asked.

Mrs. Diamond thought about it for a few seconds. "A little after we got back to our boat from the barbecue. Maybe seven."

Mr. Diamond and Ned continued to chat about reckless drivers, both on land and water, while Mrs. Diamond grabbed some milk and eggs from the cooler. As she walked past me, she pointed at the book I was reading. "Are you thinking of going to the Bahamas?" she asked. "If you are, that's a wonderful cruising guide. We'd definitely recommend it. It's got lots of useful information about anchorages, things to do in the area, and good charts."

"I don't even know how to sail," I said. "I can't even begin to imagine going to the Bahamas except on a cruise ship."

Ned overheard us and chuckled. "Can you believe she doesn't know how to sail, and her husband just bought her a boat for their anniversary?"

"Wow, that's some present," she said. "Sailing must be something you've always wanted to do."

"Let's just say that it's something my husband is interested in," I replied tersely, staring at her necklace. I closed the book firmly and put it back on the shelf. While Ned was ringing their sale up, Nancy placed a stack of chocolate bars on the counter.

Katy and Sam looked up from their yo-yos and screamed in unison, "Chocolate!"

Ned peeked out the window. "I see your mom walking this way. Let's go show her your new toys." As they rushed out the door, followed by Nancy, Ned said, "That was a close call. They sure can go through a lot of chocolate."

I handed a bar to Ned to ring up. "It's never too early to learn good taste."

"Well, I suppose. I don't really have a sweet tooth myself."

"Good, more chocolate for the rest of us." I glanced around to make sure Nancy was still outside. "Did you find out what Jack and Nancy discussed?"

"Oh, that was nothing. Kids exaggerate." He sat down and peered intently at the computer. "I better get this inventory done before Nancy gets back. You know how she is."

* * *

I sat at one of the patio tables and checked my phone for emails. I managed to resist sampling the chocolate, despite the anxious feeling I had in the pit of my stomach over the report I had submitted. Was it good enough to beat out Lola? No email from Brian, but plenty of texts from my mom.

Murder!! What murder??

Where are you? Is it safe to be there?

Why haven't you responded? If you don't text me back, I'm going to call the local police to check on you.

Yikes. I hoped she hadn't contacted the police. I could only imagine the acrobatics Chief Dalton's eyebrows would perform if he had to field a phone call from my mother. I looked at my watch and realized I was late getting back to the boat. I sent a quick text to let her know everything was okay.

Don't worry. I'm fine. I'm hot on the trail of the killer. Gotta go.

As I got up, I noticed a copy of the local newspaper on a nearby table. I picked it up and scanned the headlines. Sure enough, Captain Dan's murder was the lead story. His picture still looked familiar, but I couldn't place how I knew him. I tucked the paper into my bag and walked down the dock, trying to figure out how I would have known a boat broker, when I'd known nothing about boats until recently.

* * *

"Ahoy, is anyone there?" I called out when I got to *Marjorie Jane*. I figured if we owned a boat, I might as well start getting used to talking like a sailor.

"We're down here," Scooter replied. "Wait until you see what we found."

I climbed down the ladder, wondering if they had found a tasteful diamond brooch.

Scooter was jumping up and down with excitement. Well, not exactly jumping. When you're a six-foot-tall man and the ceiling height is only six foot two, jumping up and down can be dangerous. It was more like extremely enthusiastic hopping.

"Hold out your hands and close your eyes," Scooter said, finally coming to a standstill. Close my eyes? Hold out my hands? Maybe it really was a diamond brooch.

Scooter placed a flat, metallic object in my hands. It seemed kind of large and heavy for a brooch. I didn't feel anything that could be diamonds on the outside. Wait a minute—maybe this was a gift box, and the brooch was inside. I opened my eyes. Hmm...if this was a gift box, it looked an awful lot like an old compass.

"Isn't it amazing?" Ben asked. "Just look at the filigree work. And check out the etching of a whale on the other side. You don't see too many of these, do you?"

No, I had to agree. You don't see too many old compasses with whales on them. Then again, you don't see too many diamond brooches either. At least, I don't.

Ben blathered away for what felt like ages on the finer points of antique compasses. Scooter nodded and did that weird hopping thing again.

"Whoa, fellas. Calm down and take a deep breath. Where did you find this?"

"In the V-berth. It was behind a hidden panel under one of the storage lockers, wrapped in bubble wrap," Ben said. "I found it after I cleaned up the blood stains from the floor."

I checked out the floor. Not a trace of blood left. I glanced at Scooter. He looked pale. "Don't worry, we can put a throw rug or something over that spot. It'll be like it never even happened," I said. He looked unconvinced.

Ben, oblivious to Scooter's discomfort, motioned to me. "Come on over here, Mollie. Stand where the blood stains were and you can see better. Now, look where the floor meets the bottom of the berth. You can just about make the secret panel out near that wood trim." I saw a faint outline. Ben reached down, pushed on the corner, and the panel opened up. "The compass was right in there!"

While I inspected the secret compartment, Scooter picked up a magazine from the table. "We found a copy of *Nautical Antiquities* magazine in there too." He turned to a page marked with a paper clip. "There's an article on an antique compass that's identical to the one we found. You'll never believe how much it's worth."

Scooter named an outrageous sum. He was right. I didn't believe him. I grabbed the magazine and had a look for myself to make sure he hadn't inadvertently added a few zeros where they didn't belong. He hadn't. "Wow, that's some serious money," I said. "There's got to be a connection between the compass and Captain Dan's murder."

Ben held up the compass. "Imagine, someone bashing you over the head with a winch handle for this."

By this point, Scooter looked like he was in dire need of chocolate. I pointed at my purse. He pawed through the contents, clearly relieved when he found a dark chocolate butterscotch crunch bar.

While Scooter snarfed down chocolate and got some color back in his face, Ben and I tossed around ideas about the murder.

"But if someone killed Captain Dan for the compass, why didn't they get it out of the compartment after he was dead?" I asked.

"Maybe they didn't know how to open the compartment," Ben replied. "You've got to press on it just right for the door to open. Maybe they didn't even know about the compartment."

"Maybe they didn't even know about the compass," I suggested. "It could have been an entirely different motive, like revenge. A lot of people were mad at Captain Dan because he cheated them, including yourself."

Ben stiffened. "Yeah, he owed me for some work I did for him that he never paid me for. But like I told you before, I was stuck on my boat the whole night 'cause the engine on my dinghy didn't work." He exhaled slowly, then handed me the compass. "What do you want to do with this? It was found on your boat, so finders keepers, right?"

I glanced over at Scooter. He appeared to be doing better, probably due to the fact that there was a supply of chocolate at hand. He looked at the antiques magazine and sighed. "It sure is worth a lot of money. But we should give it to Chief Dalton. It could be related to the, you know, the..."

"Investigation?" I prompted. Scooter nodded. "I think you're right. How about if I go drop this off at the police station, give the chief an update, and pick up a pizza for dinner? It's late, and I'm sure you two have worked up quite an appetite. Meet you back on the patio in an hour?"

* * *

I decided to walk into town to drop off the compass and pick up the pizza rather than drive. I needed to work off some of the chocolate-related calories I had accumulated so that I could replace them with pizza calories. Sandy had told me about a path that ran through a wooded area along the beach and ended up behind Penelope's Sugar Shack.

As I trudged along the path, wishing I had worn sneakers instead of flip-flops, I heard arguing on the beach. I couldn't see who it was through the brush, but one of the voices sounded familiar. I pushed my way through the prickly shrubs growing among the palm trees. As I slowly inched forward, I stubbed my big toe on one of the coconuts littering the ground. I yelped in pain, cursing my sandals.

"What was that?" the familiar voice asked.

I peeked through the leaves, trying to get a glimpse of the speaker. Unfortunately, the man with the familiar voice had his back to me.

"Probably just a raccoon or a wild boar," grumbled a man with a dark crew cut. "If you're going to get spooked by some critters, then you're really not cut out for this." I looked around nervously for raccoons and wild boar. Sandy hadn't mentioned anything about encountering dangerous wildlife when she'd recommended this trail.

An older man with silver hair and a beard was standing next to crew-cut guy. He was holding a coconut, which he tossed between his hands forcefully. "Where's our money?" he demanded.

The man with the familiar voice held his hands up. "Like I told you fellows, I don't have it."

The man with the beard continued to slam the coconut back and forth between his hands. "That wasn't our deal. We delivered the goods, and now we want our money."

"I'll get it to you," he stammered. "It's just that with what's happened here at the marina, it's going to take some time to unload everything."

Crew-cut guy grabbed him by his collar. "You've got one more day. You remember what happened to the last guy who double-crossed us, don't you?" He turned to his bearded friend. "Come on, let's get out of here." They strode down the beach, got into a speedboat, and took off.

The man with the familiar voice put his head in his hands and started to shake. Then he drew a deep breath and turned to pick up a backpack off the ground. When I saw his face, I gasped. What was he doing here? What was he doing with those scary-looking guys?

I slowly backed up toward the path, trying not to make any noise, but then I tripped over a coconut, stumbled, and cried out in pain.

"Who's there?" he shouted as he pushed his way through the brush.

* * *

"Mollie, are you okay?" I opened my eyes and rubbed my head. It felt sore.

"Is that you, Scooter? What am I doing here on the ground?" I tried to get up.

"Just stay right there. The ambulance is on its way. Let's get you checked out first before you make any sudden movements."

"What time is it? I forgot to get the pizza!"

"I can't believe you're worried about the pizza," Scooter chuckled as he stroked my forehead. His expression sobered. "I'm so glad you're okay. When Sandy told me she found you lying here, I was so worried. What would I do without you?"

"Sandy found me?"

"Yes, she went out for a walk and came across you. Looks like you got hit in the head with a coconut and it knocked you out."

My head was throbbing. I reached up and felt my forehead. Scooter took my hand and kissed the back of it. "I think you're going to have a pretty spectacular lump," he said.

"I guess there isn't any blood."

"Why do you say that?"

"You're not eating any chocolate."

Scooter smiled. "Here come the EMTs. They'll get you to the hospital, and I'll meet you there."

As they started to wheel me down the path, I suddenly recalled something. "Scooter, wait! I remember what happened. It wasn't a coconut—it was Jack."

CHAPTER 9
PRETTY IN PINK

"OTHER THAN A NASTY BUMP on her head, your wife will be fine," the doctor said as she scribbled some notes on my chart. "Just keep an eye on her for the next twenty-four hours to make sure she's okay."

"Are you sure I should be the one monitoring her?" Scooter asked. "I'm not that good with medical stuff."

"He really isn't," I agreed.

"Oh, you'll be fine. It's just a minor head wound. There wasn't even any bleeding." Scooter didn't look convinced.

The doctor handed me a prescription for pain medicine. "You're probably going to have a nasty headache. If it gets any worse, come straight back in. Otherwise, make a follow-up appointment with your regular doctor for next week." She patted me on the arm and walked out the door briskly.

Scooter slumped into a plastic chair by the side of the bed and breathed a sigh of relief. "I don't know what I would have done if anything had happened to you."

"I'm fine. It's just a bump on my head." I rubbed my forehead. Was it my imagination or had the bump gotten even bigger in the past five minutes? I shivered as I thought about how Jack had grabbed me as I'd tried to run away. "Have they arrested Jack yet for assaulting me?"

Scooter frowned. "Maybe we should have the doctor examine you again. You were hit by a coconut falling from a tree. Apparently, it happens more often than you'd think."

"I know what I saw. I overheard Jack arguing with two men on the beach. They said if he didn't pay them what he owed them, he'd end up just like the last guy. You know who the last guy is, don't you? Captain Dan!"

Scooter pushed himself out of his chair, then paced around the room. "You think those guys killed Captain Dan?"

"They were scary guys," I said. "The way they threatened Jack, I wouldn't put it past them to be killers."

Scooter got out his cell phone, dialed the police station, and explained what I had overheard. "Someone will be here soon to take your statement."

I texted my mom to let her know that I was in the hospital. Oddly, she didn't text back right away. It must have been bridge night with the girls. My stomach grumbled, telling me that I hadn't had dinner. I wondered what they had done with our pizza when I didn't pick it up. While I was contemplating the fate of unclaimed pizzas, Chief Dalton turned up.

"What's this I hear about you being hit on the head by a coconut?" he asked.

"It wasn't a coconut," I said. "Jack Holt did this."

He raised one of his eyebrows. "Why don't we start from the beginning." He took out his notebook and a pen. "I understand Mrs. Holt found you unconscious in the woods with a coconut beside you. Is that correct?"

"Well, since I was unconscious at the time, I can't be sure, but that's what they tell me," I said testily. My stomach grumbled loudly. The chief's eyebrows twitched.

"What were you doing right before the coconut fell on you?"

I seized my purse and searched for something edible inside. All I found were several empty chocolate bar wrappers and a packet of breath mints, which wasn't really going to cut it. I desperately needed pizza. "Let's cut to the chase, Chief. I overheard Jack and two men talking on the beach. Jack owed them money for some presumably stolen goods, and they threatened him if he didn't pay up. Jack caught me eavesdropping, shoved me, and bashed me in the head." I chewed on a breath mint. "If you haven't done so already, you should get out there and arrest Jack and those other two guys."

The burly man tapped his notebook with his pen thoughtfully. "What did these guys look like?" After I provided a description of crew-cut guy and his bearded friend, he jotted down a few notes. "I think I know who you're talking about, Mrs. McGhie. Don't worry, we'll have a word with them." He closed his notebook and put it in his jacket pocket.

"Great, but what about Jack? He's the one who tried to kill me."

"I spoke with Mr. and Mrs. Holt in the waiting room earlier. Mr. Holt was on his boat all evening. His wife was there as well, until she went for her walk and found you. So I'm afraid that you couldn't have possibly seen him on the beach. Maybe it was someone else you saw—that is, if you saw anyone at all. People with head injuries often have fuzzy memories."

"I know what I saw."

Chief Dalton pursed his lips. "Well, maybe it's not a fuzzy memory as much as an, ahem, overactive imagination." I glared at him, but that made the throbbing in my head worse. He looked at the floor and suppressed a smile. "It's just that you've mentioned alien abduction before. You're probably one of those creative types. My ex-wife is like that. She does watercolors. She paints fairies sitting on flowers. Weirdest-looking pictures. But what's even weirder is that she claims the fairies actually talk to her." He turned to Scooter, looking for support. "She even said that they lived in our garden—can you believe that?" Scooter wisely declined to comment.

The nurse came in with my discharge paperwork, which I hastily signed. "If you can't be of any help, Chief, I'll just have to take things into my own hands." I grabbed my purse. "Come on, Scooter, let's get our pizza."

It turns out they don't throw your pizza away, even if it takes you hours to collect it. Good thing I like cold pizza.

* * *

The next morning, I had leftover pizza with some painkillers for breakfast, followed by a strong cup of coffee. Scooter had a bowl of Froot Loops. After I spent ten minutes convincing him that my head was fine, we headed off to Melvin's Marine Emporium.

Scooter had a long list of items he swore we needed for the boat. He had a much shorter second list of items he wanted for the boat. I was pretty sure that a lot of the items on list number one could easily be moved to list number two.

When we walked through the door, we were cheerfully greeted by a gangly teenager with a bad case of acne. "Ahoy there, sailors! Welcome to Melvin's Marine Emporium. My name's Chad. How can I help you today?"

After I confiscated the nice-to-have list, Scooter handed Chad the need-to-have-right-now list. "We just bought a sailboat, and we want to get her outfitted. Our boat broker said this was the best marine store in town."

"You've come to the right place. Melvin's Marine Emporium is your one-stop shop for all your boating needs." Chad paused to admonish a girl with perfect, glowing skin who looked to be about his age. "Tiffany, the winches don't go on that shelf—they go over there." She scowled at him. He turned back to us and said importantly, "I have to keep on top of the staff. I'm the shift supervisor, you know." I had the feeling that if Chad asked her to prom, she'd turn him down flat.

Chad scanned the list. "Why don't we start with anchor chain?" We followed him to the back of the store, where large sections of chain were on display. "Over here, we have our stainless steel chain, over here is galvanized, and this stuff over here—well, you wouldn't be interested in this; it's just cheap chain." While Scooter and the boy discussed the merits of stainless versus galvanized, I had a look at the price tags.

"It costs this much for a foot of chain?" I asked incredulously. "How much chain do we need?" Scooter rattled off a figure, and I did a quick calculation in my head. Okay, it wasn't that quick of a calculation. I cheated and used the calculator on my phone. Wow, for that price, I could have had a very nice diamond necklace.

Somehow it didn't seem fair that *Marjorie Jane* was going to be the only one with a sparkly chain.

Boredom set in as the two guys debated anchoring techniques. I wandered around the store, thinking Melvin could probably jazz up his displays of bilge pumps and marine toilets. I came to a section with flags from various countries. Finally, something interesting. As I was trying to decide which nation had the prettiest flag, I spied Jack walking toward the manager's office.

I put down a Bahamian flag, darted around the corner, and hid behind a display of sunglasses. Jack stood in the door, clenching his car keys.

"I can give you a good deal," he said.

"I don't care how good of a deal it is," replied another man with a high-pitched, squeaky voice. "I can't afford to get caught moving that stuff for you."

"But you used to deal with Captain Dan all the time."

"That was different."

"Different how? Now that he's gone, I'm taking over the business. And I'm telling you, I can keep you stocked with everything you need at rock-bottom prices."

"Maybe after things cool down with the murder investigation. Why don't you come back next week and we can talk about it more then?"

"But I need the money now!"

"What do I look like? Your personal ATM? Get lost."

Jack turned abruptly and stormed toward the exit, pushing Tiffany out of the way in the process.

I hurried back to the anchor chain section and pulled Scooter aside. "I just saw Jack," I whispered. "He was trying to sell stolen goods to the store manager. Captain Dan was part of it all before he got killed."

"Are you sure it was Jack?" Scooter asked. "Maybe we should get the doctor to check your head out again."

"It's not my head that needs to be checked out, it's Jack who needs to be checked out."

Chad waved Scooter over. "Did you see that all our electronics are on sale?" My husband's eyes lit up.

I sighed. "Go on, have a look. Why don't you meet me at the marina later? Just promise me not to go overboard buying stuff."

"Scout's honor," Scooter said. "As long as you promise to stay out of this murder investigation. You've got to take care of yourself."

I crossed my fingers behind my back. "Promise." Then I headed off to confront Sandy on why she lied about Jack's whereabouts last night.

* * *

As I walked through the marina parking lot, I heard a horn. I turned and saw Penny pulling into a spot in a pink convertible.

"Mollie, perfect timing," she said as she hopped out and locked up her car. "Why don't you come with me to my boat, and I'll loan you an introductory sailing book."

"Sure," I replied, pushing my sunglasses back on my head.

"What happened?" She pointed at the big bump on my forehead.

I hesitated. I wasn't sure how close she was to Jack and Sandy. What if she thought I was imagining things like everyone else did?

"Mollie, did you hear me?" she asked.

"Sorry, yes, I heard you. I got hit in the head last night when I was out walking on the trail by the beach."

"Are you okay?"

"I'm fine. The doctor said there was nothing wrong, other than this bruise and the lump on my forehead."

"I bet it was one of those coconuts, wasn't it? Someone else got hit by one of them last year."

I decided to come clean. I figured seeing how Penny reacted could be useful. "It wasn't a coconut. It was Jack."

She stared blankly at me. "Jack hit you in the head with a coconut?"

"He grabbed me, then pushed me, and must have hit me in the head with something. It all happened so fast. But it was definitely Jack, and it was definitely deliberate." I took a deep breath. "You see, I overheard him talking to two guys on the beach. They were

110

threatening him. If he didn't pay them the money he owed them, then things weren't going to go so well for him."

"You're kidding," Penny said. "Aren't you?"

"Do you think I'd kid about this?" I asked, indicating my forehead. "No, it was Jack all right. You know him pretty well, don't you?"

"I wouldn't say I know him well, but since we all live on our boats at the marina, I certainly see him and Sandy often enough."

"What do you think he's involved in?"

Penny shook her head. "I can't picture him being involved in anything. Are you sure it was Jack who attacked you?"

"It was definitely him." I shook my head angrily. That was a mistake. My headache was coming back. "For some reason, Sandy is covering for him. She says he was with her at the time. Chief Dalton thinks I made the whole thing up, and I don't think Scooter believes me either."

"Your own husband doesn't believe you? That's awful. I used to have a boyfriend like that. He never believed me about anything. Lying, cheating jerk!" Penny said.

"No, I think you've got Scooter all wrong. He's not like that at all. Sure, he tends to get obsessed about things, like *Marjorie Jane*, and not always pay attention to what I'm working on. But he'd never cheat on me or lie to me." I sat down on the hood of the car next to Penny's.

"Well, you're lucky then," Penny said, lost in her own thoughts. "I was there for this guy through thick and thin and believed in him, even when no one else would. I even..."

"You even did what?"

"Nothing, never mind," Penny said firmly.

We both sat lost in our thoughts for a few moments. "So what ended up happening with your boyfriend? Are you still together?"

Penny gave a wry chuckle. "No, we're not together. For a while there I thought we were going to get back together, but it didn't work out. And it's definitely never going to happen now." She stood and said, "Well, what about that sailing book?"

While we walked to her boat, Penny told me about her sailing experience. Like Katy, she had begun sailing as a kid. When she was a teenager, she had saved up her money and bought her own sailboat. After college, she crewed on boats in the Caribbean, helping less experienced owners learn how to manage their boats and sail properly. It wasn't long before she realized that she could get paid for teaching people how to sail. She got her certification and had been a sailing instructor ever since—first in Texas and now here in Florida.

I started to ask Penny how she knew Captain Dan in Texas, but she interrupted me by pointing proudly at her boat.

"Here she is: *Pretty in Pink*, my baby," Penny said with pride.

"Wow, I didn't know you could get pink canvas for a boat," I said, marveling at the liberal use of pink all over the boat.

"You can get pink anything these days," Penny said with a smile. "I've even written to several manufacturers of sailing clothing to ask them to make ladies' versions of their clothes in pink. You know, one day, I might even start my own ladies' sailing clothing and accessories line," she confided. "Everything would be in shades of pink."

I was speechless, but luckily Penny went down below before I could come up with a reply.

While she was gone, I checked my phone. A text from my mother, no surprise.

The hospital?! What's wrong?!

There were a number of other texts along that line. I ignored them for now. Probably a bad idea, but I was feeling reckless.

Penny hopped down to the dock, holding a book in her hand. "Here you go. Why don't you read the first couple of chapters and then we can talk through it later? You should also plan to join our ladies' sailing lesson on Thursday. Meet here at the boat at eleven."

As I took the book from Penny, I looked at her chewed-off nails. "Penny, I meant to ask you about your nails. You had such a lovely manicure when I first met you. Long pink nails."

"Oh, yeah. I don't normally go in for that sort of thing. Nancy had me over to her place for a girls' wine-and-nails night. Do you know Alejandra from the Sailor's Corner Cafe?" I nodded, trying to imagine Nancy hosting any sort of party without snarling at her guests. "She brought over all of these press-on nails for us to look at. She's a trained nail artist, you know. She's only waitressing until she can save up enough money to open her own nail salon. Alejandra is such a sweet girl, so I agreed to be her guinea pig."

"Did Chief Dalton tell you what I found at the murder scene?" Penny furrowed her brow. "A pink fingernail."

She smiled. "Oh, that. Yes, he told me about that. It wasn't mine. I ended up taking my nails off right after I saw you that day." She choked up but continued. "The day after the murder."

"So you weren't on *Marjorie Jane* that night?"

"Of course not." She tapped the book. "First two chapters, right?" She waved at someone docking their boat. "I better go help them. See you Thursday."

* * *

When I got to the end of Penny's dock, I saw Jack walking across the patio toward the parking lot carrying a tote bag. It reminded me that Scooter had said he had a surprise for me in the navy-blue tote bag of his. I'd have to remember to ask him about it later, but now was my chance to speak with Sandy while Jack was away. I hurried down C Dock to their boat. Sandy was sitting in the cockpit holding a book, but instead of reading it, she was staring blankly off into space. I tapped on the side of the boat to get her attention.

"Mollie, how are you?" she said. "We waited at the hospital to see how you were, but you must have left without us spotting you. Come on aboard and I'll make some coffee. I even have some chocolate chip cookies from Penelope's Sugar Shack to go with it."

At the mention of cookies, I felt my anxiety levels abate. She seemed happy to see me, despite the fact that her husband had assaulted me the night before. I sat in the cockpit while Sandy brewed the coffee. I picked up the romance novel she was reading: *Revenge of the Jilted Lover*. Not really my cup of tea.

She passed up the cookies and two mugs of coffee. "That bump on your head looks just awful," she said, settling back against the cushions. "A tourist got hit by a coconut last year. They should put signs up warning people about the dangers of falling coconuts."

I put down my coffee cup. "But I wasn't hit by a coconut. I thought the police talked to you about this."

She waved her hand at me. "They asked us about it last night. You really must have been delirious when you came to, saying that Jack was responsible. A concussion can do that, you know. Those coconuts sure are dangerous."

"But it wasn't a coconut."

"Of course it was. When I found you on the trail, there was a coconut next to your head."

"Maybe it was the coconut that Jack used to hit me on the head with," I said, gripping my coffee cup tightly.

"Are you sure they should have let you out of the hospital so soon?" she asked in a soothing voice. "You might still be experiencing some—what do they call them—delusions?"

"It wasn't a delusion, Sandy. I saw Jack on the beach with two guys. I think he's involved in some sort of criminal activity. I overheard their conversation, and when Jack caught me, he assaulted me. That's what happened. It wasn't any delusion."

"No, that can't be. Jack was with me all night, and he was still on the boat when I went for my regular evening walk. When I found you, no one else was around."

"Maybe you're the one who's suffering from delusions!" I snapped. I took a deep breath. That had probably been a bit harsh. I squeezed Sandy's hand. "It's just that you told me about the issues you and Jack have been having. You also mentioned your other symptoms, like your cuts and bruises." Sandy slumped in her seat. "How can you be sure Jack was really here with you? After all, you said that sometimes you have episodes where you don't remember what happened."

"I said Jack's innocent! He was here all night with me. He couldn't have done it!" Sandy shouted as she rubbed her temples. "See what you did. My headache has come back. I'm not supposed to get into stressful situations." She glared at me. "I think it's about time you left, don't you?" She stormed down below while I sheepishly climbed off the boat.

How could I have treated her like that? As a member of FAROUT, I was supposed to support those who suffered from the trauma of being abducted. I'd badgered poor Sandy and made things worse. Lola would have done a better job of managing this situation, I thought to myself bitterly. I might as well tell Brian that he should take me out of the running for the investigative reporter job.

I went back to the patio, sat at one of the tables, took a deep breath, and typed up an email.

Just wanted to check in and see what you thought of my report. I know it's not very good. The more I think about it, the more I realize that I'm not cut out for this job. I just made a mess of a follow-up interview with the subject. You should probably go ahead and tell the board of directors to give the job to Lola. I'll understand.

I hit Send, then leaned back in my chair and watched the boats slowly swinging back and forth on their mooring balls, while wondering if I should keep pursuing the murder investigation or give up on that too.

CHAPTER 10
WEEVILS

CHOCOLATE. I NEEDED CHOCOLATE TO help me figure out what to do. A lot of chocolate. I started to worry that Nancy and Ned might run low on their supply of dark chocolate butterscotch crunch. They probably hadn't counted on me being their biggest customer, no doubt followed closely by Katy and Sam.

As I walked across the patio to the office, I saw Mr. and Mrs. Diamond sitting at a table looking at some nautical charts and guidebooks. Probably their next adventure, I imagined. They seemed so carefree and happy together. Maybe that would be Scooter and me one day. Sipping on tropical drinks without a care in the world and making plans to sail *Marjorie Jane* to an exotic island.

Hopefully, Mr. and Mrs. Diamond wouldn't end up like Jack and Sandy: a criminal mastermind and an alien abductee. Although, having seen Jack in action, it was probably more like a wannabe criminal mastermind.

I swung open the screen door and walked straight over to the display of chocolate bars on the counter.

"Aren't you forgetting something?" Nancy asked, picking up her flyswatter.

"Oops, sorry about that," I said, quickly closing the door. I grabbed a bar and passed it to her.

"How do you manage to stay so slim eating all this chocolate?" she asked.

"Scooter eats his fair share, especially lately. He really doesn't handle things like blood and murder very well. Giving him some chocolate helps to calm his nerves."

"Sounds reasonable," Nancy agreed. She looked at my forehead. I was beginning to feel like some sort of unicorn with this thing sticking out of my head, a curiosity that everyone wanted to inspect. "That's a real beauty," she said. "Have you been putting any cream on it to help bring down the inflammation and speed up the healing process?"

"No, the only thing the doctor gave me was some painkillers. Personally, I find that chocolate works better than the pills." I wondered why she hadn't asked me how I got the lump. Then I realized that in a community as small as the marina, there probably weren't any secrets she didn't already know. I sighed while Nancy rang the chocolate up. She probably thought I'd imagined Jack attacking me too. Of course, she'd take his side. I was just the new chick on the block, or the dock in this case.

After she handed me my chocolate and my change, she reached into a drawer behind her and pulled out a tube of ointment. "Why don't you try this?" she asked. "It's something I concocted. I make herbal remedies using the plants that my daughter grows in her garden. It'll help soothe your head and bring down some of that swelling."

I was torn. I wanted to rip open the chocolate bar, but Nancy was being so nice that I thought I should take a look at the ointment. Greed lost. Politeness won. "What's in it?"

Nancy rattled off a whole list of things I'd never heard of, presumably the Latin names of plants. "There's nothing in there that can harm you. Go on, take it and give it a try. Let me know how it works. I'm always looking for feedback on what people think of my remedies."

I shrugged. It couldn't hurt. "How much do I owe you?"

"Nothing. It's my gift. It's the least I can do after what happened to you."

"So...what did you hear about what happened to me?" I asked cautiously.

Nancy replied just as cautiously. "I heard some conflicting stories. Everyone seems to think you got hit by a coconut. It does happen from time to time, but..."

"But what?"

"But I also heard that Jack attacked you." She fiddled with the brochures on the counter. "Is that true? Did Jack attack you?"

"You're the first person to think that might be what happened," I said as I unwrapped the chocolate bar and broke off two squares. I handed one to Nancy and kept the other for myself. "Everyone else thinks I imagined it."

She looked at me in silence while she ate her chocolate. Then she leaned over and lowered her voice. "Just between you and me, Jack has a bit of a temper. Lately, he's had a lot on his mind, so—"

She was interrupted by the door swinging open as Katy and Sam ran into the store. "Grandma, grandma!" they screamed. "Can we have some candy?" Nancy smiled and handed each of them a lollipop. Katy unwrapped hers while she said hi to me. Sam dove straight into his lollipop, ignoring me completely. I could relate. There were days when I just wanted to eat candy without having to go through all the social niceties.

It was apparent that Nancy was too caught up with the grandkids to tell me any more about Jack. I went outside and sat on the patio. Mrs. Moto spotted me and ran over. I bet she believed me about Jack. Or she didn't care. It didn't really matter. Either way, she jumped on my lap and started purring. Who doesn't love a purring cat when they're feeling a bit down? She seemed offended when I told her she couldn't have any chocolate, even after I explained to her that it was poisonous to cats. Fortunately, all was forgiven when I gave her the empty wrapper to play with.

* * *

While Mrs. Moto batted the crumpled paper back and forth, I looked through the book Penny had loaned me. It was full of chapters on topics like "dead reckoning" and "points of sail." To be honest, it all seemed rather dull. Toward the end of the book was a chapter entitled "Cooking on Board." This was more my kind of thing.

I spent the next hour happily reading about how to store grains so you didn't get weevils in them (use lots of bay leaves), keeping things (like cheese) in your bilge so they stay cool, 101 uses for your pressure cooker (clearly something I'd have to invest in), and recipes that were easy to make when you were underway. There was even a recipe for brownies.

I put the book down on the table and thought about everything that was involved in cooking on a boat in a tiny galley. Mrs. Moto knocked the wrapper off the table, stared at it for a few moments, then stared at me for a few moments. When I made no effort to pick it up off the ground, she lay on the book and closed her eyes. Clearly, all that playing had tuckered her out.

While the calico slept, I put my feet up on the chair across from me and thought about Captain Dan's murder and Jack's attack on me. I might have dozed off too. Next thing I knew, I heard a loud crash and someone screaming, "Put her in reverse, quick!"

I opened my eyes and saw Ned run out of the office to help a frantic-looking couple who were trying to tie up their boat to the fuel dock. "New boat owners," he muttered as he rushed past. He glanced back at me. "You better not let Nancy see that cat!" I think there had been a chapter in my book about how to dock a boat. That might be a good one to read.

The noise had disturbed Mrs. Moto from her slumber. She stretched and nudged at my hand, indicating exactly where she needed to be scratched. Once all of her itchy spots were tended to, she sniffed at the book, then poked between the pages with her paws.

"Be careful, Mrs. Moto," I said, trying to pull the book away from her. She batted my hand away, persisted in her labors, and eventually extracted a folded piece of paper.

"What's that?" I asked. I picked up the chocolate bar wrapper from the ground and gave it to her in exchange for her discovery. I unfolded it and smoothed it out on the table. It was a sales invoice for a car made out to Penny from a place called Cowboy Bob's Automotive Ranch, dated a couple of years ago. Could that be where she'd bought her pink convertible? If so, she'd gotten a heck of a deal on it. I guess Cowboy Bob could do amazing deals because he had such a big inventory. I knew that because it said so right under his logo.

I looked at the address for Cowboy Bob's Automotive Ranch with surprise. It was located in the same city in Texas where FAROUT was headquartered. I wondered if Brian was familiar with the place. Imagine what a coincidence it would be if Brian and Penny knew each other. Maybe Penny knew about FAROUT and was even a member. I thought about how great it would be to have a fellow believer to speak with. If that were the case, she would be able to help me out with Sandy's case.

While I tucked the paper into my purse, Mrs. Moto jumped off the table and ran down to the beach. Not one minute later, Nancy came out of the office and yelled to Ned, "Did you get those folks docked okay?"

"Yep, they're all tied off. Just going to fill them up with diesel and water, and then I'll be back in to help."

* * *

While I was napping, Scooter had texted to say that he and Ben were working on the boat, installing one of the new toys he had purchased at Melvin's Marine Emporium. Calypso music was blaring from the speakers when I got there. It brought back memories of the island where Scooter and I had honeymooned. It was the kind of music that made you want to kick off your shoes and dance on the beach.

Scooter and Ben were on deck, surrounded by toolboxes. Their heads were stuck in what Scooter called an "anchor locker," where the anchor chain was stored. I thought of it more as *Marjorie Jane*'s jewelry box. After all, Scooter was planning on buying a lot of expensive, sparkly chain to store in there. I could make out some swearing from inside. I guess the guys weren't exactly in a festive, dancing kind of mood.

"How's it going?" I yelled over the music. Scooter startled and bumped his head against the side of the anchor locker. He sat up and grimaced as he rubbed his head. "Oh, you poor thing." I rushed over and looked at his forehead. "I think you're going to have a bump there. Hey, we'll be matching!"

Scooter looked dubious about the merits of matching bumps. At least his would be hidden underneath his dark hair. "Ouch, that hurts," he said as he got to his feet.

"Maybe we can have a contest to see who has the biggest bump and who keeps theirs the longest."

"No thanks," he said. "Do you have any ibuprofen? I'm in agony." I fished a bottle out of my purse. It was a good thing he couldn't see the tiny cut on his head and the streak of blood. If he could, he'd need far more than some over-the-counter pain relievers.

"Why don't you go down below and take a couple of these?" I handed him the bottle. "While you're at it, you might want to get a wet washcloth and wipe the blood off your forehead."

Scooter moaned. "Blood? There's blood?"

"Just a little bit. You'll be fine. I'll be down in a minute. I want to see what you and Ben have been up to first."

Ben put down a screwdriver and gestured for me to look inside the anchor locker. I set my purse on the deck and peered inside. "We're installing a windlass."

"A wind-what?"

"It's an electric windlass. It raises and lowers the anchor for you so you don't have to do it yourself. I'd love to have one of these on my boat," he said as he stroked the metal contraption. "But at least I'm young and fit." He flexed his biceps. "So I can pull up my own anchor and chain by myself." When he saw the look on my face, he added, "No offense, Mollie, but you're a tiny lady and I'm guessing you don't work out." Hmm. Was it that obvious? "Scooter could probably manage just fine, but you both are getting up in age, and sometimes it's easier for older folks to use an electric windlass."

I didn't like where this conversation was going. Sure, Scooter was a bit older than me, and he had an unnatural fear of blood, but he was still fit and strong. I'm sure that he could lift the anchor up manually. I glanced down at my arms. Maybe it wouldn't hurt to start hitting the gym.

"I'm having Scooter help me as I work on things so that he learns how everything operates. You should join in too. It can't hurt to have everyone on the crew be able to fix stuff."

"When my car breaks, I take it to the garage. Why would I want to fix things when the boat breaks?"

"Well, a lot of people hire folks to fix stuff for them, which is great for me. Keeps me in beer money, but there'll be a day when you're sailing somewhere, and you're all alone. Then who are you going to get to fix stuff then?"

Good question. I wasn't sure I liked the obvious answer. "I should probably go check on Scooter."

"Hope his head's okay. I've just got a few things to finish up here, and then I'll head off for the evening."

* * *

After reassuring Scooter that his forehead was fine, we decided to sit in the cockpit and have sundowners. Scooter had to explain what they were, but once he did, it made sense—a drink that you had while the sun went down. This was the kind of boating tradition I could really get into.

It was a pleasant evening, which was a relief after the hot, sticky day. A cool breeze blew off the water, causing the palm trees to sway gently. We sipped on our gin and tonics and watched the dolphins play in the bay. Scooter sighed with contentment. "This is what it's all about. This is why I bought *Marjorie Jane* for you. Moments like this. Relaxing in the cockpit, sipping on a sundowner with my best girl."

It was almost enough to make me forget that having a sailboat had never been at the top of my wish list, let alone having a sailboat that someone had been murdered on. I took another sip of my gin and tonic and tried to focus on the gorgeous sunset instead.

Unfortunately, the peace and quiet were shattered by the sound of a dinghy going by. "Scooter, look—that's Jack!" I watched as he pointed his dinghy toward the far end of the beach, where I had overheard him the previous night. "He's going back to that same spot. I wonder if he's going to meet those guys again. Do you think he managed to find the money he owes them?"

"That reminds me," Scooter said. "I forgot to tell you that Chief Dalton called earlier. He checked out those two guys you saw at the beach. Their names are Fred Rollins and Wayne Grimm. They've both been in trouble with the law before, but they couldn't have been involved in Captain Dan's...you know..." His voice trailed off. He took a sip of his drink and continued. "They both have an alibi for that night. Lots of people can confirm that they were at the Tipsy Pirate the whole night."

I thought about this. "So that must mean he believed me when I said I saw them on the beach."

"Well, he did say he had an obligation to follow up all potential leads. He also reiterated the fact that Jack had an alibi for the night of your accident as well." He hesitated. "The chief wanted me to mention to you again that people do get hit on the head from time to time by coconuts."

The thought of his coconut theory and those bushy eyebrows made me fume. I drained the rest of my drink. "Why don't you fix me another one, Scooter?"

A few minutes later, Scooter handed me a fresh drink, along with a bowl of pretzels. "What are you thinking about, my little sweet potato?"

"I'm trying to work through all the suspects in Captain Dan's... you know." I scooped up some pretzels. "If the crew-cut guy and his bearded friend didn't...you know...then who did?" Scooter looked relieved that I'd managed to avoid saying "murder" and "kill" out loud. "Let's see, we have five potential suspects—Sandy, Jack, Ned, Nancy, and Penny."

"What about Ben?" Scooter asked as he pulled the pretzel bowl toward him.

"He's a possibility."

"I was just kidding. I can't imagine Ben being involved. Heck, I can't imagine any of them being involved."

"Well, I can. Some more than others. Take Jack, for example. We know he's mixed up in selling stolen marine equipment, which he got from Captain Dan. It sounds like the deal went sour, and maybe that's why he...you know." Scooter appeared unconvinced. "And don't forget, Captain Dan cheated him before on some anchor chain."

"I don't know. Is that really enough to make you want to...you know...?"

"Well, if it wasn't over money, maybe it was over love. You saw how Captain Dan was flirting with Sandy. Jealousy is a powerful motive."

"That's true. I wouldn't like it if anyone flirted with you," Scooter said, kissing my hand with a flourish. "What about Sandy? Does she know about Jack's illegal operation?"

"That's a good question. I'll have to follow up with her." I took a sip of my drink. "That is, if I can get her to talk to me again." Scooter looked at me questioningly. "Don't ask. Let's just say, I'm probably not cut out to be an investigative reporter."

I stared off into space, reflecting on the trauma I'd caused Sandy with my thoughtless questioning. "Earth to Mollie," Scooter said. "Tell me about your other suspects."

"Well, there's Ned and Nancy."

Scooter scoffed. "They're a bit older, probably in their late fifties. I can't picture either of them hitting Captain Dan over the head with a winch handle with enough force to kill him. Especially Nancy. She's a tiny thing. I know you said she has a temper, but still." Scooter gasped when he realized what he had said. He took a large gulp of his drink.

"I thought that at first about Nancy, but then I saw her lifting heavy boxes at the store, and I know she exercises regularly. As for Ned, even though he's had knee replacements and has some arthritis, he's still in really good shape as well, what with working outside and helping out with boats."

"Okay, so maybe they were fit enough, but why?" he asked.

"They blamed Captain Dan when the previous owners of *Marjorie Jane* stuck them with an unpaid bill."

"Sure, but is that reason enough to murder someone? It's not like that would help them get their money back."

"True. But Nancy implied that there might be more to their grudge than just that. And don't forget about the pink fingernail I found by the galley. Nancy was wearing pink press-on nails the day of the murder. She could have been on our boat that night."

"What about Sandy? Was she wearing press-on nails too?"

"No, her nails are neatly manicured, but she wasn't wearing any nail polish that day. I think I would rule her out because she's so sickly, what with her headaches and poor sleeping. But if she were angry enough and had adrenaline running through her system, then maybe she could have done it."

"What does she have to be angry about?"

"Captain Dan cheated Jack out of a lot of money. And they're already having financial difficulties. What if the fact that they have to sell their boat and move back to their condo pushed her over the edge?"

"I suppose."

"But, like we talked about before, it's more likely that it was the other way around and Jack did it."

"What about Penny?"

"Penny also had a pink manicure the day of the murder. The fingernail could be hers as well as Nancy's. And don't forget, I overheard Penny arguing with Captain Dan about how he cheated her out of some money." There were two pretzels left in the bowl. I took one and offered Scooter the other. "They knew each other before in Texas. I can't figure out why Penny is lying about that. She claims she didn't meet him until she moved up here."

I went down below and grabbed the bag of pretzels from the galley. Sometimes it's nice to put snacks in decorative serving bowls, but then you have to keep refilling them. Eating directly from the bag is so much more efficient. I shoved a few pretzels in my mouth and passed the bag to Scooter.

"Did you know that Penny's car is pink? I'm sure the inside of her boat is completely pink too." He smiled. He knew how I felt about pink.

"So why wasn't Ben on your list?" Scooter asked, passing the bag back to me.

"Oh, I don't know. He seems so goofy. I can't imagine him being serious enough to, you know..."

"He was pretty serious the night of the barbecue," Scooter

reminded me. "Remember how he got into it with Captain Dan?"

"That's true," I said. "But he did say his outboard was broken that night, so how could he get back to the marina?"

"Why didn't he row?" Scooter asked.

"He said he dropped his oars in the water. See what I mean about goofy? I also can't quite figure out his financial situation. One minute he's complaining about being broke; the next minute I see him with a wad of cash. Where did he get the money from? Maybe he did find a way to get back to the marina that night, after all. Did he steal the money from Captain Dan, after he offed him?" I thought about the scrap of paper Mrs. Moto had brought to me on the beach. "Don't forget that IOU with what looked like Ben's name on it. Did he owe money to someone, and was it enough to drive him to murder?"

Scooter put his glass down. "How about if we talk about more cheerful subjects for a while? Do you have any more chocolate left?"

"Sorry, you're out of luck. But I've still got some breath mints." I looked around the cockpit. "What did I do with my purse, anyway? Have you seen it?"

"Nope, I haven't touched it."

"Let's see, I gave you some ibuprofen, then you went down below. Ben showed me the windlass that you're installing...that's it! I set my purse down by the anchor locker." I walked up to the bow.

As I was on my way back to the cockpit, I remembered the compass. "Scooter, you know what I didn't do yesterday? Give the compass to Chief Dalton."

"Well, that's understandable, what with getting hit on the head. We can drop it off tomorrow."

I searched through my bag, unzipping all the compartments. "It's not here!"

"Of course it is."

"No, seriously, it's gone."

"You probably left it back at the house," Scooter said distractedly as he watched one of the dolphins leap into the air. "You've got so much crammed into that thing that the compass could be anywhere and you wouldn't know it."

"I know my purse inside and out. I know exactly how many chocolate bars I have in it at all times, whether I have any change, and if I have a valuable compass inside. It was there and now it's gone, and the only person who could have taken it was Ben."

CHAPTER 11
DISNEYLAND

SCOOTER AND I HAD A BIT of a lively debate the next morning on the subject of Ben. He was convinced that I had taken the compass out of my purse the night we came back from the hospital and that it was lying around somewhere in the house. I was convinced that the compass had been in my purse when I left it by the anchor locker. The only reasonable explanation I had for its disappearance was that Ben had taken it. Scooter suggested that aliens might have abducted the compass.

I'm pretty sure he was being sarcastic. Personally, I think sarcasm is an unfair debating technique, especially before I've had my second mocha. I retaliated by eating some of Scooter's precious Froot Loops for breakfast when he wasn't looking.

In the end, we agreed that since I didn't have any proof that Ben had stolen the compass, we'd still have Ben work on the boat, provided Scooter kept a close eye on him. We also agreed that Scooter owed me a foot rub. It's possible he might not remember that last part of the agreement because he was upstairs getting dressed when it was discussed.

Scooter suggested that I meet up with them later, as while two was company, three was a crowd, especially on a thirty-eight-foot boat with stuff strewn all around the place. I wasn't hard to persuade. The thought of two guys working in a confined space without air conditioning in this hot, muggy weather sounded like a recipe for a real stink-fest.

While the guys toiled away on the boat, I headed to the marina lounge. I sat in one of the comfy chairs, got out my laptop, and connected to the marina Wi-Fi. I heard a scratching sound at the door. I ignored it. It got louder. I continued to ignore it. Then the yowling started. I tried to ignore it but had to give up. I reluctantly got up and let Mrs. Moto in. She jumped on my chair, rolled on her back, and meowed insistently until I rubbed her belly.

Finally, I picked her up, sat down, and set her next to me. I logged into my email account and scanned through my messages. My heart skipped a beat when I saw one from Brian Morrison with the subject line, "Watch Out for Lola!"

Watching out for Lola kind of goes without saying. She's someone who would stick a knife in your back, then ask you if you wanted her autograph while she wiped your blood off the blade. Lola fancies herself as something of a celebrity. She's been an extra on a number of science fiction shows, as well as movies that have gone straight to DVD. She usually plays an alien, although she's very picky about which aliens she'll portray. She refuses to wear any prosthetics, wigs, or makeup that conceals her long, red hair, her big, blue eyes, or her curvaceous figure. The casting directors are more than happy to agree to her demands.

I first met Lola five years ago when I attended the FAROUT convention in Texas. She was working at the registration desk, although "working" is a bit of an exaggeration. She was surrounded by a number of nerdy-looking guys, twirling her hair and regaling them with stories of her latest role as Xandra, a sexy alien princess from the outer moon of a planet in a galaxy far, far away. Thankfully, her character didn't have any speaking lines and was killed in the first scene by a large lizard-like creature with two heads. Not that that deterred her fans.

Eventually, I tired of watching her flirt and the guys drool in response. I pushed my way through the nerds, grabbed my badge, and eagerly went to attend my first session on "Signs You've Been Abducted by Aliens." Who knew that session would lead to where

I was today—vying with Lola for the investigative reporter job? I sighed and opened Brian's email.

Bad news. Lola submitted her report and it's a doozy. She claims to have evidence of a government cover-up of a UFO landing next to Space Mountain in Disneyland. She states that the government is hiding the evidence inside Sleeping Beauty Castle. She has interviews with some Disneyland employees who've seen the spaceship (their identities are protected, of course) and she has photographs taken with a hidden camera (they're blurry, but you can make out what appears to be aliens in the background). The board of directors is very impressed. I think they're going to recommend that Lola be appointed as the new investigative reporter.

Of course they were going to appoint Lola. Not only did she have the scoop of the century, all four members of the board were also members of Lola's fan club.

I think Mrs. Moto sensed how upset I was. She reached up, batted me on my chin with her paw, and meowed softly. I stroked her back while I tried to figure out what I could do to make sure Lola didn't succeed. Getting a career as a sexy alien extra didn't seem like a viable option in the time I had left before the next board meeting.

Somehow, I had to convince Sandy to speak with me—not only about Jack's illegal sideline, but also about her alien abduction. Maybe I could get her to recall details about the spaceship and what the aliens did to her. It probably couldn't compete with Lola's Disneyland exposé, but it was worth a shot.

Considering the way Sandy had reacted the last time I saw her, I needed to find an opening that would make her want to chat. Mrs. Moto looked at me and meowed. That was it! Sandy had a soft spot for her cat. I'd ask her about taking care of Mrs. Moto when they went out of town, then slowly work the conversation around to Jack and to her abduction.

* * *

Before I tackled Sandy, I stopped by the Sailor's Corner Cafe to pick up some lunch for the guys.

"Hi, there," Alejandra said over her shoulder as she walked

past me carrying a tray laden with chocolate shakes. "I'll be right with you."

I picked up a menu from the counter and looked at today's specials. The Captain's Chili sounded good, as did the Boatswain's Burger. But what sounded even better was one of those shakes.

Alejandra set her tray down on the counter. "Are you here on your own today?"

"Just picking up some lunch to take back to the boat."

She whipped out her pad and pen. "What'll it be?"

"I'll take three of the Boatswain's Burgers with fries."

"No problem. Anything else?"

"How about a chocolate shake while I'm waiting?"

The young woman smiled. "Coming right up."

I sat on a stool at the counter and watched as she scooped dark chocolate ice cream into a blender, then added some full-fat milk along with a generous dollop of thick chocolate syrup. A few minutes later she set the milkshake in front of me. "Here you go."

I murmured my thanks between sips. Alejandra sat on a stool next to me, slipped off her sandals, and flexed her feet back and forth. I noticed her toenails were painted with purple-and-silver stripes. "It must be hard to run around on your feet all day," I said, conscious that the only thing my toenails had going for them was a lack of fungus.

"It is, but people tip well, especially the tourists," she said. "Every penny I save means I'm one step closer to opening my own nail salon."

"How did you get into doing nails?"

"During high school, my best friend and I would get together on Sunday nights to do our homework. When we were done, we'd reward ourselves by giving each other manicures." Alejandra looked at her fingernails, which coordinated with her toes. "We had so much fun. When I graduated, I didn't know what I wanted to do with my life, so I found a job waitressing here. I got lots of compliments on my nails, and I thought to myself, here's something I love to do that I could make a living at. I finished nail-technician training, and I'm taking some small-business classes at the community college. Now all I have to do is win the lottery so I can open my nail salon."

A woman at one of the tables waved at Alejandra. "Excuse me for a sec, *chica*," she said, grabbing her tray and bustling over to help. I continued sipping my shake while she refilled ice teas and sodas. After she was done, she came back and perched on one of the stools.

"What about your nails, Mollie? Have you ever thought of having a manicure?"

I looked down at my hands. Although I didn't bite my nails, they weren't much to look at. I kept them short and pretty much ignored them. "I've never really had a manicure."

"Really?" she asked. "Never?"

"Hard to believe, I know. It seems like a lot of work, especially when I see people with full-on nails like Nancy."

"Nancy is very particular about her nails," Alejandra said. "She's actually been one of my biggest supporters, always encouraging me about the nail salon. We get together occasionally for girls' nights. We try out the latest nail products over a few glasses of wine. Lately, she's been into press-on nails. They're really easy to do."

The waitress dashed off to take care of another customer, while I reflected on the state of my cuticles. She pointed out a few of the town's attractions on a souvenir map, then came back to the counter with a smile. "You must have gotten a good tip," I said.

"I'll say," she said, tucking some bills into the pocket of her apron. "Those are the kind of customers I like."

"Did you know I found a press-on fingernail on *Marjorie Jane* the night Captain Dan was murdered?"

"You did?" Alejandra asked while she rolled up silverware into paper napkins. "What did it look like?"

"It was pink with a white starfish on it." I thought about it for a minute. "You know, I'm surprised that Chief Dalton didn't ask you about it. You must be the local expert on nails."

Alejandra laughed. "Wouldn't that be funny—being an expert witness on nails."

"Well, you'd probably know what kind it was, where it was bought, and who in town had similar nails."

"I don't know about that. But it would be interesting to have a look at it. I wonder whose it was."

I took another sip of my shake. The straw made that disappointing slurping noise that lets you know you're nearing the bottom of the glass. I twirled my straw and said, "The day of the murder, I noticed that Penny's nails were identical to the one I found. At least I think they were. I tried to get a look the next day, but she had destroyed her manicure. She chews her nails by the way." Alejandra made a tsk-tsk sound. "Nancy also had a similar manicure. Maybe the nail belonged to one of them."

"You know, Penny and Nancy did have identical manicures. Those pink press-on nails were ones that I brought over to Nancy's last week for the girls' nights. Penny's eyes lit up when she saw the pink color. But what would either of them be doing on your boat?"

"That's a very good question," I said.

* * *

After an uncomfortable lunch with Scooter and Ben—I still wasn't convinced that Ben hadn't been responsible for the missing compass—I decided it was time to summon up my courage and go see Sandy. I hoped Jack wasn't on the boat. The last thing I wanted was to run into him again. I rubbed the lump on my head. It was slowly going down, but it still ached a little bit. The bigger issue was that I was having a hard time coordinating its blue-and-purple color to my outfits. Imagine having to coordinate all your outfits to your manicure as well.

I took a deep breath as I walked over to Jack and Sandy's boat. As I got closer, I saw them standing on the dock. "Just stay out of it," Jack said. "It's none of your business!"

"But it is my business," Sandy replied, her voice trembling. "How could it not be my business? You sunk all our money into this venture and look what's happened as a result. We're broke, we have to sell our boat, and—worst of all—we have to give up Mrs. Moto."

"Is that all you're worried about—the cat?" he replied with venom. "You pay more attention to it than to me."

"That's not true."

"No, you're right; it isn't true. You pay more attention to him than to me. Or at least you did. Now that he's gone, all you can think about is the stupid cat and money."

As Sandy started sobbing, I felt something rub against my leg. I looked down and there was Mrs. Moto staring up at me. I scooped her into my arms. "Don't worry, kitty. It'll be okay." She began playing with my earrings, so I guess she was feeling better. Although I don't do my nails, I always wear earrings. We each do girly in our own way, I guess.

As I was cuddling Mrs. Moto, Jack stormed past. He was in such a huff, I don't even think he noticed me. I walked up to Sandy and handed her cat to her.

"Where have you been?" she asked, drying her tears on the soft fur. "I've been searching for you everywhere." She turned to me and sniffled. "Thanks for bringing her back."

"I saw you and Jack arguing," I said. "I thought you could use a cat cuddle."

Sandy smiled. "You're right. Mrs. Moto is the only good thing in my life right now."

"What were you fighting about?"

"I've been trying to help with his business records. I've spent hours entering data into spreadsheets. Next thing you know, he's yelling at me, saying I did it all wrong. But I didn't. I matched everything up with his notes and invoices."

"What does he think you did wrong?" I asked.

"You know how he buys and sells marine equipment? I enter what items he's bought, the quantity, and how much he paid in one spreadsheet. Then in another, I enter what items he's sold, the quantity, and how much he's sold them for. That way I can calculate any profit that's been made." She shook her head. "Who am I kidding? There hasn't been any profit in a long time. It's been all losses."

"I don't know—it sounds like you're pretty organized." I actually didn't have a clue if she was organized or not. Data entry and spreadsheets mystified me. I preferred the written word to crunching numbers. "So what exactly was the problem?"

"I know he ordered twelve bicolor lights, but he says he never bought any at all. But I have a receipt saying that he sold them to some guy. So how could he have sold something he never bought in the first place? I just don't get it."

"What are bicolor lights?" I asked. Mrs. Moto meowed. I guess she was curious too.

"They're navigational lights you have on your boat at night. The port-side lights are red and the starboard lights are green. That way when you encounter another boat in the dark, you can tell by their lights what direction they're going in. Keeps you from crashing into each other."

Red and green lights—not the most fascinating topic, unless it involved decorating a Christmas tree. Mrs. Moto yawned. I was more polite and stifled mine.

Sandy set the calico down on the dock. "I'm so glad you came by, Mollie. Sometimes it's hard not having anyone to talk to."

I looked at Sandy's eyes. Not only were they bloodshot, but she had dark circles underneath them. "You look tired. How have you been sleeping lately?"

"More of the same. Jack tells me he caught me sleepwalking again last night." She shrugged. "I don't remember a thing, but he says he found me trying to climb into one of the dinghies."

"Yikes!" I said. "That could have been dangerous if you'd fallen in the water."

"That's what Jack says. Somehow he managed to guide me back onto the boat and into bed without me being aware of it." She rubbed her eyes. "He's been trying to get me to take sleeping pills at night, hoping they'll knock me out and keep me from sleepwalking."

That sounded dangerous to me. Who knew what was in those things? "Did you talk to your doctor about it?"

"No," she said. "Besides, we can't really afford to go to the doctor these days." I wondered how they could afford the sleeping pills and where Jack got them.

Sandy yawned. "You look like you could use a nap."

"That's probably a good idea." She rubbed her temples. "I feel another one of my headaches coming on again." She picked up Mrs. Moto. "Why don't you come snuggle with me?" The Japanese bobtail didn't look like she would object to a nap. "Was there anything else, Mollie? Or did you just come to drop the cat off?"

I decided to show more sensitivity than I had yesterday and not press her about the abduction. "No, that was it. Dropping Mrs. Moto off." As Sandy was getting on board her boat, I added, "I guess there is one other thing. Why did you and Jack decide not to go out of town? I meant to ask you before, but I completely forgot about it after Captain Dan's murder."

As soon as I mentioned Captain Dan, Sandy turned white and steadied herself by holding onto the side of her boat. "That was Jack. His business plans changed. He said he had to be here at the marina. I didn't ask any questions. Sorry that I didn't let you know about the change of plans."

"That's okay," I said. She was breathing rapidly, and sweat was beading on her brow. "Sandy, you really don't look good. Are you sure you're all right to be here on your own?"

"I'll be fine. It's the headache. I just need to lie down." She squeezed Mrs. Moto tightly. "Come on, time for our nap." The cat squirmed, jumped out of her arms, and tore down the dock. Sandy frowned, then went down below.

I wished I had been able to ask her more questions. There was more going on than simple alien abduction here, but what it was I wasn't sure. What I was sure of was that as soon as I got to the bottom of it, the story would completely wipe Lola's Disneyland scoop off the map.

* * *

As I was walking back to *Marjorie Jane*, I saw Jack come toward me, wearing another gaudy Hawaiian shirt. I tried to duck behind one of the palm trees, but the problem with palm trees is that their trunks are much narrower than my hips. There's really no place to hide.

"Is that you, Mollie?" Jack called out.

I reluctantly came out from behind the tree and glanced around to see if there were any witnesses in case he decided to assault me again. "Did you want to check and see how I'm doing?" I asked sarcastically.

He came closer and looked at my forehead. "That's a nasty lump. There was a tourist who got hit by a coconut last year. He had a bad lump on his head too, but I think yours is larger. It looks pretty painful."

"It wasn't a coconut and you know it, Jack," I said as I backed up a few steps.

"What do you mean?" he replied. "Sandy found you on the trail with a coconut lying next to your head."

I scouted around to see if there was anything I could use to defend myself if things turned ugly. The only thing I saw were coconuts strewn at the bottom of the palm tree. I picked one up.

"See what I mean, Mollie? Those things are heavy. One of those falling from a tree could easily knock a person out."

"Just stay away, Jack," I said.

"Mollie, what's wrong with you?"

"What's wrong with me? What's wrong with you? You're the one who hit me on the head!"

"What! Are you crazy? I did no such thing." He advanced toward me. I held up my coconut. "Loss of memory can happen when you've had a head injury. I'm sure they explained that at the hospital."

"Just stop lying, Jack. You can't walk all over me like you do to your wife!"

"My wife? Why are you bringing up Sandy? She doesn't have anything to do with this. She's the one who found you. She probably even saved your life."

"I was just over at your boat speaking with her. She's really upset. Not to mention really sick. I heard you yelling at her. How could you do that to a sick woman?" I shifted the coconut in my hands. They really were heavy. "Can you imagine what it would do to her if she knew what you were up to?"

"What in the world are you talking about?"

"When you realized that I saw you with those two hooligans, Fred Rollins and Wayne Grimm, and heard what it was you were up to, you panicked." Jack looked surprised at the mention of crew-cut guy and his bearded friend's names. "You tried to kill me because I discovered you were involved in something illegal. Isn't that right?"

"You're crazy. Just like Sandy. What are you talking about? I'm not involved in anything illegal."

"Oh yeah, then what were those two guys doing on the beach saying that you owed them money?"

"I don't owe anyone money."

"I don't believe you. I think you're up to your eyeballs in debt. I even heard you talking with someone at Melvin's Marine Emporium trying to sell him some stuff. Probably stuff you're trying to fence."

Jack's eyes turned cold. "Well, aren't you a little eavesdropper? Fine, yes, you caught me. I was trying to sell some stuff to Tony. Some stuff from the boat that we won't need anymore now that we're selling her. You've got quite the overactive imagination, you know. I can't imagine how Scooter puts up with it."

"Well, at least we're happily married."

"So are we." Jack frowned. "Why would you think we weren't?"

"I heard you two arguing, and Sandy says that things haven't been great between you two."

Jack looked down at the ground. "Sandy and I have been married for over thirty years. We've had our ups and downs like any other couple. And I'll admit, our financial difficulties have put a strain on our relationship, but we're working through it. Plus, as you pointed out, Sandy hasn't been physically well for quite some time. Her doctor has tried all sorts of things, but we haven't been able to come up with a treatment plan that works yet."

Things didn't add up. Sandy had said they couldn't afford a doctor, yet Jack said she was seeing one. Maybe all this talk about Sandy's treatment plan was just a ruse to play on my sympathies and make me forget about the assault.

I was about to tell Jack exactly that when Chief Dalton walked up. He looked at the coconut in my hands, raised an eyebrow, and asked, "Is everything okay here?"

"Did you know that this man"—I pointed at Jack with my coconut—"is still claiming that he didn't strike me over the head!"

"But I didn't!"

"Oh yeah, then how did I end up with this?" I said, pointing at my head with one hand and trying to balance the coconut in the other. Both the chief and Jack ignored my bump and stared at the coconut.

I almost threw the coconut at them in exasperation. "Just keep him away from me!"

Chief Dalton turned to Jack. "I was actually looking for you, sir. Would you mind coming down to the police station to answer a few questions."

"Questions? Questions about what?"

"Why don't I explain it to you down at the station?" His tone and manner made it seem like it wasn't an invitation.

"Fine, fine," Jack said. "But I've got a lot going on. I don't have much time for this sort of thing."

"Come along, then," the big man said as he ushered Jack down the path. I saw Mrs. Moto peek around a palm tree and hiss at Jack as he walked past her. Can't say I blamed her.

* * *

Scooter and Ben were determined to install something to do with the navigational lights before they called it quits for the night. They were so focused on the task at hand that they didn't even want dinner. My stomach doesn't let me get away with skipping meals. It lets me know in no uncertain terms that it needs to be fed every few hours.

I pulled Scooter aside, reminded him to keep an eye on Ben, and headed into town to find something to eat.

My earlier encounter with Jack had me on edge, so just to be safe, I took a sturdy flashlight with me. I figured it would come in handy not only to light my way, but also to fight back if needed. I thought about tucking a coconut in my purse too, but it didn't fit.

I walked along the boardwalk and paused at the dinghy dock. There were only two dinghies tied up, one of which belonged to Ben. The skull-and-crossbones sticker on the side made it easy to identify. His dinghy was covered in lots of patches. How long would it hold air before it deflated?

A Styrofoam cooler was floating in the water. Similar ones were used by fishing boat crews to transport fresh fish to the local restaurants. My flashlight kept cutting in and out as I walked to the edge of the dock to get a closer look. I opened it up, pulled out both batteries, and reinserted them, giving it a sharp tap as I closed the lid. I bent down to try to grab the cooler before it floated out to sea.

That's one of the reasons that we don't get more alien visitors. They're appalled by all the litter we have floating in the water and the damage we've done to the environment. I figured it was the least I could do, sparing the ocean from one more unnecessary piece of debris.

Fortunately, there was a nylon handle attached to the cooler, which I was able to reach by lying down on my stomach. I pulled it out of the water and set it on the dock. The cooler was taped shut with duct tape, which of course made me want to see what was inside.

I looked in my purse to see if I could find anything that could cut the cooler open. I didn't find a handy pocketknife, but I did find a bag of M&M'S. I munched on a few while I thought about my options. Then I had a horrifying thought. How was it I didn't know I had M&M'S in my purse? After the whole Ben-compass incident, I'd sworn to Scooter up and down that I knew the contents of my purse inside and out. I wasn't about to admit to him that I'd been wrong, so I decided to destroy the evidence by finishing the rest of them.

As I popped the last candy morsel in my mouth, I saw something out of the corner of my eye floating between the two dinghies. Probably another cooler. I aimed the flashlight toward it. It flashed in and out, then cut out, but not before I caught sight of a Hawaiian shirt. It wasn't a cooler—it was a body.

I grabbed an oar out of one of the dinghies and pulled the body toward me. As I held onto his shirt collar, it didn't take long to realize that the man was dead. And even without my flashlight working, it also didn't take long to figure out that it was Jack.

CHAPTER 12
LITTLE GREEN MEN

I WISHED I HAD MORE M&M'S. Why didn't I save them for a real emergency, like this? I got out my phone and dialed 911. The dispatcher said that Chief Dalton would be out right away and not to interfere with the crime scene, like last time. Yes, she actually said that.

While I waited for the chief and his bushy eyebrows to arrive, I took another look at Jack's body floating in the water. I wondered what had happened. Had he fallen into the water and accidentally drowned? Or had something more sinister occurred?

Then I thought about Sandy. How would she cope when she heard about her husband? Despite their difficulties, they'd been married for many years and it would be a huge shock. It didn't help that Sandy was dealing with so many physical ailments either. And somewhere lingering in her subconscious was the knowledge that she'd been abducted by aliens. Many people didn't remember or want to remember their experiences, but when they had a big enough shock, it all came flooding to the surface. I'd have to look out for her.

"Mrs. McGhie, what a surprise to find you here. You seem to specialize in finding bodies." Chief Dalton raised both of his eyebrows. "That makes two bodies in just four days, doesn't it?"

His math was correct. I guess the ability to be able to do simple arithmetic was an important skill for police officers. That's probably why I never joined the force. I struggle with math. I'm also scared of guns.

"It looks like that's Jack Holt from what I can see," I said, ignoring his comment about the number of bodies I'd found to date.

He eyed me suspiciously. "And why would you say that? From his position in the water, you can't see his face. Unless you tampered with the crime scene. Is that what you did? Or perhaps you had something to do with how he got in the water. Is that the case?"

"Me?" I spluttered. "I didn't have anything to do with Jack's death. I just happened to be out for a walk when I saw him floating in the water."

"Then why do you think it's Mr. Holt?"

"From his shirt," I said. "I saw him wearing that same Hawaiian shirt earlier today when I was speaking with him. You were there—you saw it too. You must have had a good look at it when you were questioning him at the police station." I watched Chief Dalton's eyebrows do contortions. "What was that about, anyway? Did you finally get him to confess that he hit me over the head?"

"That's police business, completely unrelated to alien abductions," he said with a smirk. We watched as the EMTs lifted the body out of the water. "In any event, I have to admit you were right. It is Jack Holt."

I noticed a nasty lump on Jack's head. There seemed to be a lot of those going around these days. Maybe he hit his head when he fell into the water, or maybe somebody hit him over the head before throwing him into the water.

As the EMTs removed Jack's body, Scooter and Ben came rushing up.

"What happened?" Scooter asked.

"They found Jack floating in the water."

"They?" Scooter asked dubiously.

"Well, okay, by 'they,' I mean me," I said. "I was walking down to the dinghy dock when I noticed that Styrofoam container floating next to the dinghies. I pulled it out and tried to open it. That's when I saw a body floating nearby."

Scooter clutched his chest and turned pale. "You're not kidding, are you? Jack's really dead?"

"He is," I said, giving him a hug. Ben put his hands over his mouth for a few moments. Then he took a deep breath. "He was a nice guy. Always willing to lend a hand." He knelt down near the container. "I wonder what's inside?" he asked as he tried to pry the lid off. "Maybe it's beer. We could all probably use one about now."

"Hands off that, sir," Chief Dalton said as he came up behind Ben. He shifted his gaze to me. "You weren't going to try to hide this from me like you hid that fingernail the other day?"

"I didn't hide the fingernail. I just forgot about it," I said. "There's a big difference. And I was going to tell you about this. I just haven't had a chance. Besides, you should be grateful I pulled it out of the water, otherwise Jack's body might not have been discovered until the morning. It might have floated out to sea when the tide changed."

I was proud of myself for remembering about the tidal flow in the local waters. Scooter looked at me with pride too. Or maybe that was surprise.

"What might have floated out with the tide?" Nancy asked, sneaking up behind us with Ned in tow.

"Jack," I said.

"Jack? What are you talking about?" Ned asked.

"I found him floating in the water." I looked at their confused faces. "He's dead."

Ned gasped. "Jack...are you sure?" His eyes welled up. "I need to get out of here."

Nancy squeezed his arm. "Do you want me to come with you?"

"No, I just need a few minutes to myself."

Nancy watched him walk away, then looked at me. "That makes two bodies you've found, doesn't it?" Great, another math whiz. I guess simple arithmetic is important if you're a small-business owner too.

"That's not really the point, is it, Nancy? The question is whether or not it was a murder."

Nancy muttered, "That's all we need. Another murder at the marina. This really isn't the kind of publicity that's going to help us attract new customers."

By this point, Scooter had a glazed expression in his eyes and was noticeably unsteady. He pointed at something on the dock. "Is that what I think it is?" he asked.

Chief Dalton reached down and picked it up. "It's just an M&M'S bag, sir."

Scooter stared hopefully at it. "Are there any left?"

Nancy pushed Scooter aside. "Well, Chief, was it murder or not?" she asked impatiently.

"That's not for me to say. That's for the coroner to determine. Hopefully we'll know more tomorrow. In the meantime, I'll need to speak with everyone, just like last time. We'll also need to notify his wife."

"I'll come with you," Nancy said. "She'll probably need someone to support her when she hears the bad news."

"Fine. Why don't you go with Officer Moore? After you're finished there, I'll have a word with you and your husband." He turned to me. "Now, shall we start with you?"

* * *

Scooter had a minor meltdown the next morning when he went to pour some Froot Loops into his bowl only to find there weren't any left. He looked at me accusingly. I suggested that aliens might have abducted his candy-colored, crunchy nuggets. After agreeing to disagree on the cause of the disappearing cereal, we headed to the Sailor's Corner Cafe for breakfast.

"Did you hear what happened at the marina last night?" Alejandra asked as we walked in the door. "There was another murder!"

"How do you know it was a murder?" Scooter asked.

"I overheard a couple of the police officers talking. They always come in here in the morning before their shift starts. While I was cashing them out I heard one of them say that a man had been struck with a heavy object, and then his body had been dumped in the water." She showed us to our table, handed us our menus, and said, "You know, I can't decide if all these murders are good for business or bad." She pointed to the crowded dining room. "We've been slammed with customers all morning and that's all they're talking about."

"They're probably looking for a side of gossip with their coffee," Scooter said as he pulled my chair out for me.

"Speaking of coffee," I said as I sat down.

"Coming right up." Alejandra grabbed a pot from the counter.

"So, what do you know about what happened?" she asked as she filled our cups up.

"Well, Mollie was the one who found the body," Scooter said as he passed me a couple of sugar packets.

"You were?" Alejandra gasped. "Wait a minute, wasn't it you who found Captain Dan when he was murdered, *chica*?" I nodded. "Wow, that makes, what…"

"Yes, yes, I know. Two bodies in four days," I said. "Can I get a short stack of blueberry pancakes and a couple of strips of bacon?"

"And I'll have a Western omelet with home fries," Scooter said as he handed Alejandra our menus.

"Why do they call them Western omelets?" I mused as I sipped my coffee. "I know they have ham, green bell pepper, and onion in them, but what makes that Western?"

"Maybe the chefs wear tiny cowboy hats when they make them," Scooter said. "I remember the best Western omelet I ever had was at the little hole-in-the-wall place we ate at in Texas when we were there for your FAROUT convention. Do you remember that place?"

"I do. They had great French toast." I stirred some more sugar into my coffee. It was feeling like a three-pack morning. "Those are the best kinds of places. The ones you just happen to run across. If we hadn't stopped at that drugstore next door, we would have never found it."

"It was right across from that place with the funny name, wasn't it?" Scooter asked.

"Oh yeah, that used-car lot we made fun of. What was it called again?"

Scooter shook his head. "I can't remember. Something corny."

He held out his cup for a refill as Alejandra passed by.

"Your order will be right up," she said. "More coffee for you, Mollie?"

"Sure, why not? It was a long night. I'm struggling to wake up this morning."

As Alejandra filled my cup, she asked, "Who do you think did it?"

"Well, I have my suspicions," I said. The young woman leaned forward. "I saw Jack arguing with two guys on the beach the other night. That's the night I got this." I pointed at my forehead. My lump was going down, but you could still see it.

"Right, that's when the coconut hit you," she said. "I'm always telling the tourists to be careful of falling coconuts."

"It wasn't a—never mind. Anyway, I think Jack was into something dodgy. He was fencing stolen goods and he owed these guys money."

"Now, you don't know that for sure," Scooter said. "Let the police do their investigation."

A bell dinged from the kitchen. Alejandra said, "That's probably your order." As she placed our plates in front of us, Nancy, Katy, and Sam walked through the door.

Katy skipped up to us, followed by her brother. "Hi! Guess what grandma is getting us?" she asked.

"More chocolate?" I ventured.

"No, silly. It's too early in the morning for chocolate!" Katy said.

"Chocolate!" Sam shouted.

I tried again. "A kitten?"

"No, it's not a kitten," Katy said. "Grandma doesn't like kittens."

"Kittens!" Sam cried.

"You're really a terrible guesser," Katy said. "But I'll give you one more chance."

I thought long and hard about it. "Okay, let me see. Your grandma is going to get you an alligator."

Katy and Sam burst into giggles. "No, it's not an alligator," Katy said. "Grandma is going to get us cocoa for breakfast. And since we've been good this morning, we get to have extra marshmallows in it."

"Cocoa!" Sam shouted.

Nancy smiled behind them. "Come on, kids, our table's free. Go sit down, and I'm sure Alejandra will bring you your cocoa straight away." She watched as they ran over to the table. "I let them have cocoa every time we go out for breakfast. I can't figure out why they think it's such a treat. But the promise of extra marshmallows does seem to produce better behavior."

"Hey, whatever works," Scooter said.

"How long were the police there last night?" I asked.

"Thankfully, not as late as last time. Because it happened during the week, there were fewer people around for them to have to question."

"Alejandra was telling us that it was a murder, not an accident." I took a sip of coffee. "Have you heard anything about it?"

"Chief Dalton called this morning and said it could be homicide. It probably happened not too long before you found him, Mollie. Wasn't that around seven-thirty?"

Goose bumps covered my arms. "About then," I said, wrapping my arms around myself.

"Well, someone saw Jack earlier, around six."

"Do you know what happened?" I asked.

"Someone hit him over the head. Then he either fell or was pushed in the water. Who would do such a thing? And why? Sure, Jack had his faults, but he was a nice man. Ned is just devastated. He and Jack have been friends for years." Katy and Sam started to have a pretend sword fight with their knives. "I better go over there and break things up."

Scooter glanced over at the kids and smiled, then asked, "Before you go, Nancy, how's Sandy doing?"

"Not great. She ended up breaking down in hysterics. Pretty understandable. They took her to the hospital for the night and sedated her."

* * *

When I arrived at the hospital, I ran into the doctor who had treated me in the ER. "Hello there, Mrs. McGhie. Is everything okay? Have you been experiencing any side effects from the bump to your head? Those coconuts sure can be nasty."

"It wasn't a coconut," I said under my breath.

The doctor examined my forehead. "It looks like it's healing nicely. You were lucky the coconut didn't hit you harder. So, why are you here?"

"There was another murder at the marina last night, and the victim's wife was taken here. I wanted to check and see how she's doing. I don't think she has any family in the area, and we became close over the past few days. I figured maybe I could help."

"I'm sure she'll appreciate the company. The volunteers at the front desk can let you know where her room is." She smiled. "Be sure to stay clear of palm trees from now on. I don't want to see you back in here for another coconut-related injury."

"It wasn't a coconut," I muttered under my breath as she walked away.

One of the volunteers printed out a visitor badge, circled Sandy's room on a map, and pointed me to the elevators. I pressed the button to the third floor and tried to decide if I should tell Sandy's doctor about her abduction. I knew that most medical professionals scoffed at the idea of alien abduction, but not all of them. Maybe Sandy's doctor was more open-minded.

The door to her room was open. I poked my head in. "Knock, knock."

Sandy looked up from the magazine she was reading and said, "Mollie, is that you? What a nice surprise."

"How are you doing?" I asked as I sat in the chair next to her bed. "I saw Nancy earlier this morning, and she said they admitted you last night."

Sandy put her magazine down and reached out for my hand. "It means the world to me that you came. I can't believe I broke down the way I did last night. They ended up sedating me. It's just so embarrassing."

"Nonsense. It isn't embarrassing at all. I would have reacted the same way if it had been Scooter. Jack was your husband, after all. It's a devastating blow to lose him, especially like that."

"What do you mean, like that?" she asked, looking confused.

"Nothing," I said hurriedly. "I didn't mean anything by it. Have the police been by to see you yet this morning?"

"No, but the nurse said that they'll be coming by soon. Why?"

"Oh, no reason. I'm sure they just want to give you an update on the case."

"What case? Jack's death was an accident. There isn't any case, is there?" I eyed the call button next to Sandy's bed and was debating whether or not to buzz it when she started sobbing. I passed her the box of tissues. "I'm sorry, Mollie, I just need a moment. It's so much to take in."

"Of course. I understand. Can I get you anything?"

"A glass of water would be nice," she said between sniffles. "There's a pitcher over there on that table." She handed me her magazine. "Here, can you put that over there too?"

While I was filling up her water glass, I glanced at the cover. It was one of those tabloid publications that they sell at grocery checkout lines. This one had a ridiculous headline about a UFO crash-landing in a small town in North Dakota. Apparently, the residents had taken a liking to the little green men and were sheltering them inside one of the local churches. Who would believe something like that? Publications like this gave reputable organizations like FAROUT a bad name.

But still, if Sandy was reading this, maybe that meant that she was a believer. Perhaps the memories she had been repressing were beginning to surface.

Sandy interrupted my thoughts. "Mollie, could I get that water from you?"

"Oh, I'm sorry," I said, passing her the cup. "I got distracted looking at your magazine."

"That piece of trash? It was already here, otherwise I wouldn't be caught dead reading something like that. Did you see the headline about aliens in North Dakota? What kind of people believe things like that?"

I sat back in the chair deflated, clutching the magazine in my hand.

"You can have that if you want," Sandy said.

"No, that's all right." I heard a light tapping on the door.

"Mrs. Holt, it's Chief Dalton and Officer Moore. Can we come in?"

"Of course," Sandy said, settling back into her pillows. She looked pale.

"Are you okay, Sandy?" I asked. "Do you want me to get the nurse? You know, you don't need to talk to the police just yet if you aren't up to it."

"Mrs. McGhie, what a surprise to see you here," the chief said, his eyebrows twitching.

"I'm just looking out for Sandy," I said.

He looked at the magazine in my hand. "Do you write for them?" he asked. "I'm sure they've got some great stories about alien abductions in there."

"No, I don't," I said. I tossed the magazine into the garbage can. "Sandy, if you're sure you're okay to talk to the police, I'll get going now."

Sandy reached out and grabbed my hand. "Would you mind staying? I'd feel a lot better if I had a friend here. If that's okay, officers?"

Chief Dalton reluctantly agreed. "Ma'am, I'm sorry to have to tell you this, but your husband was murdered."

Sandy gasped and clutched my hand harder. She had a strong grip. "Murdered? Are you sure?"

"Yes, we're sure. The coroner found—"

Sandy interrupted. "No, please don't tell me the details. I can't bear to think about it." She clenched my hand even tighter. Then she sobbed loudly. My hand was really starting to hurt, and although I hated to see her cry, I was kind of glad, because that meant she needed both of her hands to wipe away her tears and blow her nose.

"Do you want me to call a nurse?" the burly man asked kindly.

"No, I'll be fine. Could I have another glass of water, though?" Officer Moore filled her glass up, while the chief got out his notebook.

"If you're sure you're okay, I just have a few questions. Do you have any idea who might have done this?"

"No, of course not. Why would anyone want Jack dead?" Sandy

asked. "Everyone loved him. He's lived here all his life and has lots of friends."

"I understand he was having some financial difficulties. Is that true?"

Sandy squeezed her crumpled-up tissues in her hand. Better the tissues than my hand. Finally, she replied with a tight voice. "Yes, he was having financial issues. But it wasn't his fault. He got in over his head and then, when Captain Dan swindled him, he didn't know what to do. Ned was nice enough to loan him some money, but it wasn't enough to settle his debts. It was causing him a lot of stress." She took a sip of water. "Do you think it's possible it wasn't murder, but suicide?" she asked with a trembling voice. "Maybe the stress drove him to..." She began sobbing again.

A nurse came rushing in. "Is everything okay here?"

"We were just asking Mrs. Holt a few questions," Chief Dalton said apologetically.

"Well, you're upsetting her," the nurse replied. "I'll have to ask you to leave. You too," he said, nodding to me.

As I was walking out of Sandy's room, she called out. "Mollie, will you look after Mrs. Moto? Nancy has a key to our boat in the office."

* * *

I unlocked Jack and Sandy's boat and made my way down below. After digging through a few lockers, I eventually found where Sandy stored the cat food. Just as I was pulling back the lid of a can of Fisherman's Delight, I felt a set of claws digging into my leg, and a furry face looked up at me expectantly. I scooped out the contents of the can into a dish and set it on the floor. I have to say, Fisherman's Delight certainly didn't smell delightful, but that didn't seem to be stopping Mrs. Moto.

The Japanese bobtail finished her meal, jumped up on the couch, and washed behind her ears. I poked around in the cabinets until I found where Sandy hid the cookies. I made myself some coffee, grabbed a couple of cookies, and sat down next to her. She sniffed at the snacks but decided they weren't nearly as delightful as Fisherman's Delight. She curled up on my lap for a post-lunch nap.

I might have taken a bit of a nap too.

Both of us were woken up by the sound of a couple trying to dock their boat. When we heard a loud thud, Mrs. Moto ran into the aft cabin. I took this as an opportunity to check out the rest of Jack and Sandy's boat. Although I guess it was just Sandy's boat now.

"Here, kitty, kitty," I cried out as I made my way to the rear. It was a similar setup to our boat—a bed against one side with a love seat running along the other side. What they had, which we didn't, was a large closet with a set of drawers next to it. They also had a small sink beside their bed, which seemed strange. I rarely have the desire to get up in the middle of the night to wash my face, but maybe it's a thing for people who live on sailboats.

I couldn't see Mrs. Moto anywhere, so I sat on the bed and peered out the hatch. I have to admit, the view of palm trees swaying in the breeze overhead was pretty special. I lay down to get a closer look. There was definitely some high thread count going on here. The sheets were soft and silky. I might have had another nap. When I woke up again, I found the calico nestled against me.

I glanced at the clock. How had it gotten so late? Had Scooter noticed how long I had been missing? Or had he been so caught up in boat projects that he hadn't even given my absence a second thought? Both the cat and I had a quick stretch, although hers was far more impressive than mine. If I had attempted what she did, I would have pulled muscles in my body that I didn't even know existed.

After stretching, Mrs. Moto leaped to the floor and stuck her paw into the gap of one of the opened drawers. After a few attempts, she snagged something, dragged it out, and meowed loudly. I picked it up and turned it over. It was a blurry photograph of two people sitting on the hood of a car in what appeared to be a car dealership. I rubbed my eyes and inspected it more closely. The woman had long, blonde hair and was wearing a pink blouse belted over a pair of jeans. The man next to her had a large cowboy hat, cowboy boots, and a three-piece suit that looked like it was made out of some sort of horrible man-made fabric. They had their arms around each other, smiling broadly into the camera.

I looked at Mrs. Moto. "How did a picture of Penny and Captain Dan get into that drawer?" She blinked at me a few times and meowed. I don't think she knew or cared.

CHAPTER 13
BELLY BUTTON LINT

I WASN'T SURE WHAT TO do with the picture. Should I confront Penny? After all, she'd told me that she didn't know Captain Dan prior to moving to Florida, yet according to the date stamp, this picture had been taken a few years before that. But if I did ask her about it, would she tell me the truth?

Amid all these questions, my stomach growled, alerting me to the fact that two cookies and a cup of coffee weren't really going to cut it for lunch. I tucked the picture in my purse, filled up Mrs. Moto's water bowl, gave her a quick cuddle, and headed to the boat to see if the guys were interested in fish-and-chips.

My head was reeling with thoughts of cowboys, cookies, and Penny's poor taste in men when I ran into Ben.

"Weren't you on *Marjorie Jane* with Scooter?" I asked.

"We needed a socket wrench, so I ran back to my boat to grab one," he said, holding up a tool bag. "Scooter doesn't really have a good set of tools, does he?"

"No idea."

"Might be something to think about with the holidays coming up," Ben said. "People always want tools as presents."

"Just like people want sailboats for their anniversary?" I asked.

Ben smiled. "Exactly. Your husband is awesome! I'd love to

find a woman who would be thrilled to get a sailboat as a present, like you were," he said wistfully. "But there's so few women out there who are single, let alone who enjoy sailing."

"It must be tough. I think the only single woman I've met at the marina is Penny."

"Oh, she's amazing. She's smart, she's gorgeous, she's got her own boat, and she's a great sailor. Between you and me, I actually asked her out once. Couldn't believe I got up the nerve, but I'd had a few beers and I thought, what the heck, all she can do is say no."

"So she said yes?" If you had asked me before I'd found that picture, I would have thought there was no way Penny would date an unemployed pirate wannabe. But seeing her with her arm around Captain Dan put a new perspective on things. Maybe she had said yes.

"No, she said no," Ben said, looking down at the dock. "It was kind of embarrassing the next day."

"Why'd she turn you down?"

"She said she had recently broken up with a guy and hadn't gotten over him yet."

"Was he someone you know? Someone from around here?"

"She wouldn't say. She got real evasive. The only thing she did say was that he was an older guy who had swept her off her feet. It might have been a guy back when she lived in Texas. She said that they had been in business together, a business she'd invested heavily in, but when it had started to lose money, he'd dumped her. She thought maybe he had liked her just for her money. She comes from a wealthy family, you know. Talking about it got her really upset, so I dropped it."

"Captain Dan was from Texas, wasn't he?"

"Yeah, he was."

"Do you think they knew each other there? Maybe he was the guy that she was involved with?"

"Captain Dan?" Ben asked incredulously. "I can't see it. That dude was such a jerk. Penny is too nice of a girl to have ever gotten mixed up with someone like him."

I was debating whether or not to show Ben the picture when Scooter walked up. "I was wondering where you got to," he said to

Ben with a wink. "Now I know—you've been chatting up my wife."

Ben flushed. "It wasn't like that at all. It just took longer than I thought. My outboard engine died on me again. Jack helped me last time, and now that he's—you know—no longer with us, I had to try to fix it myself. He knew engines inside and out." Ben shifted his tool bag. "Anyway, I got the socket wrench. Wanna head back to *Marjorie Jane* and see if we can get that bolt out?"

"I'll catch up with you in a few minutes," Scooter said.

Ben mumbled good-bye to me and left without making eye contact. Once he was out of earshot, I punched Scooter in the arm. "Why did you go and tease him? You've totally embarrassed him."

Scooter scoffed. "He knows I was only kidding. It's not like he's one of those creepy guys always flirting with other men's wives."

"Speaking of creepy guys, look what I found on Jack and Sandy's boat."

My husband frowned. "How's she doing?"

"Not great. She's still at the hospital. It was just awful." I smiled. "But there was one bright spot to the visit."

"What's that?"

"Chief Dalton started pestering her with questions and got kicked out by the nurse. You should have seen the look on his smug face."

Scooter pulled me close. "I can't imagine what I'd do if I ever lost you."

"Oh, you'd be fine, provided you had enough chocolate to get you through the mourning period."

He chuckled. "The problem is that you always hide the chocolate. You'll have to leave a note with instructions on where I can find it."

"Enough about chocolate," I said. "You have to see this. It's Captain Dan and Penny."

"Are you sure?" He held the photo at arm's length. "I can't really see all that well without my glasses."

"I'd lay money on it. Or chocolate."

"But why would there be a picture of Captain Dan and Penny on Jack and Sandy's boat? That doesn't make any sense."

"I don't know. There are a lot of things that don't make sense." I put the photo back in my purse and headed off to pick up lunch.

* * *

After a delightfully greasy lunch of fish-and-chips, I decided to bite the bullet and see what I could get out of Penny regarding her relationship with Captain Dan. She was sitting on the deck of her boat with her legs hanging over the edge, polishing a metal railing.

"That looks like hard work," I said.

"Owning a boat isn't for the fainthearted," Penny replied, putting down her cloth. "There's always something that needs to be fixed, installed, or maintained. Like this stainless steel. You have to keep it polished to prevent rust. That's one of the things I like about living on a boat. I've always got a project to work on. It keeps me busy."

"That's probably a good thing, given everything that's been happening at the marina. Jack murdered and Captain Dan before that. I saw Sandy in the hospital this morning, and she's devastated by the loss of her husband. I wonder if Captain Dan had a special lady in his life?" I watched Penny carefully to see what her reaction was.

Penny picked her cloth back up and began polishing furiously. "Not that I know of."

"That's a shame. He seemed like such an outgoing guy. I'm surprised he wasn't dating anyone." Penny didn't respond. I tried again. "You know, I can picture the two of you together. You both like boats and sailing. I thought you guys would have been a good match."

"A love of boats and sailing isn't all it's cracked up to be," Penny said bitterly. "You'd think that would be enough to keep a man interested, but no, it isn't. Trust me. Never date a sailor. They'll cheat on you and lie to you."

"You think Captain Dan was a cheater and a liar?" I asked cautiously.

"I only know what I told you before. Ned and Nancy lost a lot of money when the previous owners of *Marjorie Jane* skipped town, and they blame Captain Dan for it."

"I also heard that Jack wasn't all that fond of him."

Penny reluctantly agreed. "That's true."

"You know, at first I thought Jack might have been the one who killed Captain Dan, but then he was killed."

"Jack kill Captain Dan? Why did you think that?"

"The two of them were involved in selling stolen marine equipment. Things went sour with the deal. Jack was angry about it, maybe angry enough to kill. Plus, he did this to me." I pointed at my head.

"I thought that was a coconut."

"No, Jack hit me on the head."

"Are you sure?"

"I'm positive. It was Jack. But since Jack's dead, who would have reason to kill both him and Captain Dan?"

"No idea. And to be honest, I have other things to worry about, like my sailing school."

"You moved here from Texas, right?"

"I did."

"Captain Dan moved here from Texas too, didn't he?"

"What are you getting at?"

"I was just curious if you knew him when you lived in Texas. You might be able to give some background information to the police to help them figure out who would have a motive to kill him."

"Sorry, I can't help them. I didn't know him there. You know, Texas is a big state. There are a lot of people who come from Texas," she said wryly.

"That's true. I just thought that maybe the sailing community was relatively small and that you two had met through that somehow."

Penny relaxed a little bit. "It is a small community, but I never ran across him before I came here. Honestly, I'm glad I didn't. He's a sleazeball. Did you notice how he flirts with all the women?"

"I saw him chatting Sandy up at the barbecue. I figured it was harmless, although Jack looked irritated. I thought that might have played into his motive for killing Captain Dan as well."

"I can see that. He had a reputation for going after married women."

"You don't think he and Sandy ever, you know..."

Penny bit her lip. "I wouldn't put it past him." She stood,

picking up her rag and a bottle of polish. "I've got to finish the rest of this. I'll see you tomorrow for the ladies' sailing class. Wear clothes you don't mind getting wet and shoes that won't mark the deck, and bring your PFD." She walked to the other side of the deck and resumed polishing.

I was left not only wondering why Penny continued to lie, but also what a PFD was.

* * *

What did we do before Google? When you want to know the answers to questions you're too embarrassed to ask anyone, like "Why is there lint in my belly button?" or "What's a PFD?" Google is there for you. So I made a plan of action. Step one: stop at the marina office for more chocolate. Step two: go to the marina lounge for Wi-Fi.

Fortunately, Nancy wasn't sitting behind the counter when I entered the office. I'm pretty sure a couple of flies followed me in. I looked at the rack where the chocolate bars were usually kept. Nothing. This was disconcerting. How was I supposed to execute step one of my plan?

Nancy came out of the back room carrying cans of soda. "Where's all the chocolate?" I asked.

"It's all gone," she said. She set the box down and opened it with a pair of scissors.

"What do you mean, gone?"

She paused and held up the scissors in a way that made me regret my question. "A group of boats spent the night at the marina and bought the rest of the chocolate. They also cleaned us out of soda and chips. Big spenders—they're the kind of boaters we like to see here."

"But you have some more in the back, don't you?" I asked, keeping a careful eye on the scissors.

"Nope, that was the last of it."

"But what am I supposed to do now?"

"Live without."

Not the answer I was hoping for. Oh well, if I couldn't get chocolate, maybe I could get Nancy's thoughts on the picture of

Captain Dan and Penny. "Here, get a load of this. Don't these folks look familiar to you?"

Nancy took the picture, walked to the counter, and put her reading glasses on. I watched with relief as she placed the scissors down next to the computer. "I don't think so. Like that guy's cowboy hat, though. Ned would look good in a hat. I've been trying to convince him to wear a baseball cap with the marina logo on it."

What was it with women and guys in cowboy hats? "Have a closer look," I said, tapping my finger on the photo.

"No, can't say that they're familiar. Friends of yours?"

"Don't you think they look just like Penny and Captain Dan?" I blurted out.

"Well, the woman does have long, blonde hair like Penny. I guess it could be her. But it's hard to see the man's face underneath that hat. Where did you get this?"

"Oh, I found it lying around," I said, sidestepping the question. "I think this picture was taken in Texas. See the sign in the corner that says 'Lone Star Plaza'? If that's the case, then Penny and Captain Dan knew each other before they moved to Florida."

"But they didn't. They met here."

"Are you sure? How do you know?"

"Penny told me. It's probably just a couple of people who look like them. There are a lot of gals with hair like that." She passed the picture back to me. "Check back in tomorrow. We might have more chocolate then," she said gruffly.

* * *

I sat down in what I was coming to think of as "my chair" in the marina lounge and pulled out my laptop. The car invoice, originally tucked away in Penny's sailing book, fluttered out with it. It was a run-of-the-mill invoice, but something about it niggled away at me. I read the dealership address again—Cowboy Bob's Automotive Ranch, located at the Lone Star Plaza. That was it! I pulled out the photo and squinted at the sign next to Captain Dan and Penny, which read Lone Star Plaza. Penny had referred to Captain Dan as Bob the night of the barbecue. Was it possible they were one and the same?

I decided to add a third step to my plan of action—learn more about Cowboy Bob's Automotive Ranch. But first I was going to find out once and for all the answer to the belly button lint question. I fired up my laptop and did a quick check of my email. Big mistake. There at the top of my inbox was an email from Brian Morrison.

I'm so sorry to have to tell you this, but the board of directors has decided to give the investigative reporter job to Lola. If it had been up to me, I would have selected you, and in fact, I argued strongly for your case at the board meeting, but to no avail. The board is convinced that the publicity generated by Lola's scoop on the Disneyland alien cover-up will advance FAROUT's cause with the general public.

I needed something to distract me from thinking about Lola. Googling about belly button lint wasn't going to cut it. I reached for the TV remote and flicked through the channels. As I was deliberating between a home improvement show and an old black-and-white movie, Ned walked into the lounge carrying his cleaning supplies.

He set his bucket down. "Ooh, *The Thin Man*. That's a great one. I didn't know you liked old films."

"I didn't until I met Scooter. He loves classic movies like this."

Ned perched on the arm of the other chair. "My favorite scene is coming up, where Nick and Nora throw a dinner party for all the suspects. They make investigating a murder look like fun. It's too bad Nancy isn't here. She loves this movie too. Although if she caught me slacking off instead of cleaning, that'd be another story."

While he polished the bookshelves, he kept peeking at the screen, chiming in with trivia about the stars and director. He was telling me about the fox terrier that starred in the film when the door flew open, and Chief Dalton and Officer Moore marched in, followed by Nancy.

Nancy was tugging at the big man's arm. "I'm telling you, he didn't have anything to do with this! You can't do this!"

The chief removed her hand from his arm, raised an eyebrow, and motioned to Officer Moore to escort Nancy outside. "Sir, I'm afraid you'll have to come with us," he said.

"Do you have more questions for me?" Ned asked, while watching Nancy gesticulate wildly at Officer Moore outside. "I thought I answered everything yesterday."

"I'm afraid you're under arrest." I quickly turned off the TV while Ned stared at him in shock. Chief Dalton handcuffed him, read him his rights, and then ushered him out of the lounge.

As I went out onto the patio, I saw the police leading Ned up to the parking lot and the waiting squad car. Nancy was wringing her hands in despair.

"What happened?" I asked.

"I don't know," she said. She sat on one of the patio chairs and rocked back and forth. "They came into the office and started asking me all these questions about Jack and Ned's business dealings. They mentioned the money Ned had loaned Jack, and then the next thing I know, they're arresting him for Jack's murder. Jack and Ned were friends. There's no way Ned would kill him. He doesn't have a mean bone in his body. He can't even hurt the flies that buzz around the office." She saw Mrs. Moto walking off in the distance. "He even has a soft spot for that mangy cat."

"Was Ned involved in Jack's business?" I asked gently.

"No, of course not. We've got plenty to keep ourselves busy with here at the marina without getting mixed up in other business ventures."

"Then why do the police think he was?"

"That's the thing that doesn't make any sense. When they were going through Jack's computer, they found an inventory of the boat equipment Jack bought and sold, and Ned's name was listed as a seller. They claim Ned sold Jack used boat equipment on credit, and that when Jack didn't pay him on time he got angry and killed him."

I thought about this for a moment. "There has to be more to it than that. Couldn't that inventory have been falsified?"

"It has to have been. Sure, Ned loaned Jack money, but it was a loan, pure and simple. He never sold Jack any boat parts."

"Do they think this has anything to do with Captain Dan's murder?"

Nancy put her head in her hands. "I don't know. The police didn't say anything about Captain Dan." She raised her head. "But their murders have to be connected. There must be someone who wanted both Jack and Captain Dan dead and it certainly wasn't Ned. I don't know what to do, Mollie."

"Well, the first thing you should do is call a lawyer." She got up wearily. Ned's arrest had sapped all her usual feistiness out of her. While there were times I wished for a kinder, gentler Nancy, this wasn't the way I would have wanted it to happen. I watched Nancy walk slowly toward the office and pondered Ned's arrest. Could he have really killed Jack? Could he have really killed Captain Dan, and if so, why? Were the two murders connected?

CHAPTER 14
DATING SCOUNDRELS

AFTER THE SHOCK OF NED'S arrest, I decided to go back to Melvin's and find out more about Jack's illegal dealings. Maybe I could discover a connection to Ned.

"Welcome to Melvin's Marine Emporium," Chad said with his usual perkiness. "How can I help you today?"

"I'd like to speak with the manager," I said.

"Tiffany, buzz Mr. Dublonski and ask him to come speak with this lady," Chad said. Tiffany rolled her eyes and put down the stack of T-shirts she had been folding. She walked over to the cash register, picked up the phone that was right next to Chad's elbow, and buzzed the manager. Chad pointed at the T-shirts. "Those aren't going to fold themselves, are they?" Tiffany looked like she wanted to strangle him. Can't say I blamed her.

A few minutes later, a man in his midthirties wearing a rumpled blue suit and shiny black shoes approached me. "Welcome to Melvin's Marine Emporium," he said in a high-pitched, squeaky voice as he shook my hand. "How can I help you today?"

"I don't know if you've heard about the recent tragedies at the marina," I said, wrestling my hand back with difficulty. His grip was almost as strong as Sandy's.

"Tragedies?" he asked. "I heard about Captain Dan. Losing him was a real blow to the local sailing community. He also brought a lot of business to our store."

"He did?"

"Sure. Every time he sold a boat, he helped the new owners make up a list of equipment they needed and pointed them our way."

"I suppose he got a commission."

"A little one, sure, but that's normal in our line of work. Plus, we gave the customers a discount if they spent over a certain amount."

"We bought our boat from Captain Dan."

"You did?" he said. "Did he help you put together a list as well? If you have it handy, I can go through it with you and get you all set up. What's the name of your boat?"

"*Marjorie Jane.*"

"*Marjorie Jane.* Isn't that the one that..." his voice trailed off.

"Yes, that's where Captain Dan was killed."

"Oh, that's terrible."

"I found the body."

Mr. Dublonski put his hand over his mouth. "Oh, dear. What a shock that must have been," he squeaked.

"It wasn't pleasant, that's for sure. Did you know he was killed with a winch handle?"

"Yes, the police mentioned it."

"The police? Did they question you? Did the winch handle come from your store?"

"Of course not," he said in shock. "It was just routine questioning. They wanted to know if I could identify the make and model of the handle. It isn't one that we normally keep in stock."

"Ah, so you're a marine equipment expert witness."

Mr. Dublonski looked pleased with that description. "I guess you could say that."

"So you know everything there is to know about boats, right?"

"I know a bit, yes."

"And you know about all the boat equipment being sold in town?"

"Of course. Wait, what do you mean?"

"You knew Jack, didn't you?" He looked at me blankly. "Jack Holt, the other man who was killed at the marina."

"Oh, him. Yes, he was a customer here. Everyone at the marina is a customer, really."

"Did you know he was murdered? I found his body too."

Mr. Dublonski gasped. "Another murder? This won't be good for business." He took a long look at me. "Wait a minute. That means you found..." I gave him some time to do the calculation in his head. "Two bodies. That's got to be some sort of record."

"Jack was more than a customer, wasn't he?" I asked, trying to guide him back to the topic at hand.

"No, just a customer. He came in from time to time."

"Before he died, Jack told me that he was in business with you." Okay, he hadn't exactly told me that, but I wasn't really in the mood to confess to eavesdropping outside Mr. Dublonski's office.

"In business with Jack? I don't know why he would have told you that. I don't even know what kind of business he was in."

"He was a used marine parts dealer. He told me that you were one of the people he sold parts to."

"I think you must have misunderstood. We only buy marine parts from reputable suppliers. We assure our customers that everything they buy from us is high quality. We don't sell anything used here."

"Maybe he told you the items he was selling were brand new."

"I still wouldn't have bought from him. How could I be sure things were brand new unless they came from the manufacturer or a reputable supplier?"

"Well, that's odd. Maybe it wasn't Jack you dealt with directly, but his two colleagues—Fred Rollins and Wayne Grimm."

Mr. Dublonski scratched his head in an unconvincing manner. "Nope, doesn't ring any bells." He pointed to a part of the store devoid of customers. "Oh, I see some folks over there who need my help," he said as he dashed back to his office.

While I was thinking about Mr. Dublonski's evasiveness, I looked at the clothing display. All the women's items were in various shades of pink. Pale pink, salmon pink, bubblegum pink, fluorescent pink—you name it, any kind of pink you could ever want. Penny must love shopping here.

I picked up a rain jacket on display and tried to figure out if it would be best described as ballet-slipper pink or blush pink. Chad tapped me on the shoulder. "That's one of our biggest sellers. All the ladies love it, especially the color."

I held it up against me. "Do you have my size in navy blue or hunter green?"

"No, only our men's jackets come in those colors. We might have a pastel-blue version in the back," he offered.

"I'll think about it," I said. I poked through the racks. "I was just speaking with your manager about Jack Holt."

"Oh yes, Mr. Holt. He comes in here all the time."

"He's a good customer?" I asked.

Chad thought about it. "No, I'm not sure he was a customer so much as a supplier. I often saw him at the loading dock delivering boxes to the store." He picked up a fuchsia T-shirt. "How about this?"

I shook my head. "No thanks, I'm not really in the market for any shirts today."

"Well, I'll leave you to your browsing. Please let me know if I can be of any further help."

"You've no idea how helpful you've been already," I said.

* * *

As I waved good-bye to Chad, I spotted crew-cut guy and his bearded friend driving a blue pickup truck covered with a tarp. They pulled into Melvin's Marine Emporium and drove through the parking lot around to the rear of the store. I hightailed it back there and hid behind a dumpster.

Crew-cut guy hopped out of the truck, stopped to tie one of his sneakers, then adjusted one of the straps holding the tarp down. After exchanging a few words with crew-cut guy through the window, bearded guy got out of the truck and walked to the door next to the loading dock, his flip-flops slapping loudly on the asphalt. He tried to open it, but it appeared to be locked. He dug his cell phone out of his pocket and called someone, gesturing angrily as he spoke. After a few minutes, the door by the loading dock was opened by none other than Mr. Dublonski. All three of them entered the building, leaving me free to check out the back of the pickup truck.

I untied the strap and pulled back the tarp to see what was underneath. There was a whole bunch of equipment, most of which I couldn't identify. I did see a couple of familiar things, including two winch handles, both of which were smaller than the one that had killed Captain Dan.

I crept around to the passenger side of the truck, opened the door, and poked in the glove compartment. Other than a map of Texas, I didn't find anything interesting. My stomach grumbled when I saw a bag from Alligator Chuck's BBQ Joint on the floor. Ribs were sounding like a real contender for dinner.

"What do you expect us to do with all this?" I heard a man ask. "You're the one who told us to set the whole thing up. You can't back out now."

I quietly closed the passenger door and crouched down next to the truck. I saw three pairs of shoes standing beside the loading dock—Mr. Dublonski's shiny, black shoes, crew-cut guy's sneakers, and his friend's flip-flops. If they walked toward the truck, they would see me. I looked over at the dumpster. It was in direct line of sight of the loading dock. Not an option.

My stomach grumbled again. Something about ribs. I told it to shut up so I could hear what the guys were saying.

"It wasn't my idea." I recognized Mr. Dublonski's high-pitched, squeaky voice. "Captain Dan and Jack organized this. And now that they're gone, I'm wiping my hands of the whole business. I've got enough trouble with the police coming around asking questions."

"You can handle the police," either crew-cut guy or his friend said. It was hard to tell just by looking at their shoes.

"It's more trouble than it's worth. Plus, I had some nosy lady in here just now asking questions about what Jack was up to."

"Nosy lady?"

"Yeah, some broad Captain Dan sold a boat to," Mr. Dublonski said. "I didn't catch her name, but her boat is called *Marjorie Jane*."

"Maybe that's her name."

"No, that's the boat name. I remember him telling me about her. That's the one they brought the stuff over from Texas on."

"Oh, I remember now. We helped the owners of the boat unload it last week and put the stuff in the warehouse. That boat was a mess. It's in such bad condition that I'm surprised it made it over here in one piece. If I ever own a boat, it'll be a brand-new fishing boat. I'd call it *Reel Nauti.*"

"Well, you're never going to get the chance, are you, if you end up in jail?" Mr. Dublonski said, rocking back and forth on his shiny, black shoes. "And that's what's going to happen if you don't get yourselves and your truck out of here."

"Sure, we'll do that. You just have to take the stuff we've got back there and pay us what you owe us."

"I'll do no such thing! Listen, you guys do what I say. You don't want to end up like Captain Dan and Jack, do you?"

"Hah, like you had anything to do with that. You don't have the guts to off anyone."

"Oh yeah, are you saying you guys knocked them off?"

"It wasn't us. Besides, we have an alibi for both murders. And they sure were good alibis too. Curves in all the right places, if you know what I mean. We met them at the Tipsy Pirate."

"Well, if you guys didn't do it and I didn't do it, who murdered Captain Dan and Jack?"

"Who cares? I know I don't. They ended up eating into our profits and your profit too. Come on, admit it. You liked the money."

"Fine, but we can't do this now. Why don't you guys lay low for a while, and I'll give you a call once things get quieter here?"

One pair of shoes walked back to the building while the other two pairs headed my way. I took my chances and ran for it.

"Hey, who's that?"

"Get her! It's probably that nosy lady from *Marjorie Jane.*"

My heart pounded as I ran around to the front of the building. Just as I was about to collapse, someone grabbed my arm. "Are you all right?" I looked up and saw Tiffany staring at me with concern.

"I'm fine," I said as I gasped for breath. I glanced behind me. The two men glared at me. I guess they figured they couldn't make a scene in front of a witness. "What are you doing out here?" I asked.

"I just quit my job. I've had enough of Chad acting all superior. Can you believe he still had the nerve to ask me out?"

Actually, I could believe it. I could also believe I hadn't seen the last of crew-cut guy and his bearded friend.

* * *

After hearing more about Tiffany's teenage dramas, I walked a few blocks to the police station. Even though it had only been a few hours since they arrested Ned, it felt like ages since I had last seen Chief Dalton's bushy eyebrows in action.

The receptionist did a double take when I told her my name. "Oh, the chief's told me about you."

"That must be because the first murder took place on our boat," I said.

She hesitated for a moment. "Yes, that must be it."

"Any chance he can squeeze me in for a few minutes?"

"Can't promise anything, but I'll see what I can do."

While I waited, I looked at the bulletin board. Next to some Most Wanted posters was a takeout menu for Alligator Chuck's BBQ Joint. It had a five-dollar-off coupon on the bottom. I took it off the bulletin board and stuffed it in my purse. We were definitely having ribs for dinner.

I heard a distinctive voice in the hallway behind the reception area. "You didn't tell her I was here, did you?" Even though I couldn't see him, I could picture him raising his eyebrows.

I took that as my cue that he was free to see me now. I poked my head into the hallway. "There you are," I said as I steered him toward his office. As he walked by the receptionist, he said, "See what I mean?"

He sat at his desk and shuffled a few file folders back and forth. "Mrs. McGhie, I've got a lot to do."

"Then I'll make it quick. How's the investigation into Captain Dan's and Jack's murders going? Why did you arrest Ned?"

The chief stared at me quietly for a few moments, then

shuffled his folders again. I took this to mean that he didn't have an update.

"Okay, then, why don't I start? Remember those two guys who were talking with Jack at the beach that night when he hit me over the head?"

He raised an eyebrow. "I thought we had established that a coconut hit you over the head."

"No, we didn't. It was Jack! Why doesn't anyone believe me? Listening to what everyone says, you would think all the coconuts in this town were intent on harming humans at an alarming rate. You should probably put up flashing neon warning signs."

He raised his other eyebrow.

"I was just at Melvin's Marine Emporium and I saw them talking to the manager, Mr. Dublonski. Well, I didn't exactly see them talking, but I saw their shoes talking." He raised both his eyebrows this time. No wonder he had so many wrinkles on his forehead. "Remember how I told you they were all mixed up in something? Well, now I have proof."

"Proof?" There went those caterpillars again.

"Yes, proof. I heard the three of them talking about how they worked it. Captain Dan loaded up stolen marine equipment on *Marjorie Jane* in Texas. The previous owners sailed her to Florida. Then they took off and left *Marjorie Jane* behind. Crew-cut guy and his bearded friend—"

"Who?" Chief Dalton asked.

"You know. Fred Rollins and Wayne Grimm. One of them has a crew-cut and one of them has a beard. I have no idea which one is Fred and which one is Wayne."

"How much longer is this going to take?"

"Let me finish. Once they got to Florida, they helped the previous owners of *Marjorie Jane* unload the stuff and hide it in a warehouse. Jack was going to sell it all to Mr. Dublonski, who would then turn around, pass it off as brand-new equipment, and sell it to unsuspecting customers. Jack was supposed to get the money from Mr. Dublonski and give crew-cut guy and his friend their cut. When Mr. Dublonski refused to buy it, Jack was in a pickle. Those two guys were expecting to be paid for their share, but he didn't have it. They threatened him and then you know what happened next."

The chief sat back in his chair and stared at the ceiling. "Both Fred and Wayne have alibis for the night Mr. Holt was killed."

"I know. They were at the Tipsy Pirate chatting up some girls." Chief Dalton nodded ever so slightly. "And they were at the Tipsy Pirate the night Captain Dan was murdered too." He looked at me and nodded again. "And I think Mr. Dublonski has an alibi too." More nodding. "But even if they didn't kill Jack and Captain Dan, they sure were happy about it. It meant they didn't have to deal with any middlemen anymore. They got the rest of the stuff out of the warehouse, took it over to Melvin's, and tried to get Mr. Dublonski to take it. He said he couldn't do anything until the murder investigation cooled down."

"And how do you know all this?"

"I overheard them at the loading dock behind Melvin's."

"Overheard them?"

"It really doesn't matter, does it? The important thing is that you need to investigate this."

He sighed. "I'm just going to cut to the chase because it's probably the fastest way to get you out of here. We've known about this little operation for some time. It's not the first time these guys have done this. We're investigating, and we should be able to make some arrests soon."

"That's good to hear. Now, since we can rule crew-cut guy, his bearded friend, and Mr. Dublonski out of the picture, the question is, who did murder Captain Dan and Jack? It sure wasn't Ned."

Chief Dalton was lifting that eyebrow when the receptionist poked her head in the door. "Sir, we need you urgently in the conference room."

Just my luck. I was sure the chief had just been about to open up to me about the case.

* * *

There were two things I couldn't forget to pick up on my way home: Scooter from our boat and ribs from Alligator Chuck's. I was so hungry I almost collected my husband second, but he was the one with the cash. The smell of the barbecue was intoxicating on the ride back, but I managed to restrain myself from ripping open the container until we were inside the house.

After washing the last of the sticky barbecue sauce off my hands, I turned on my laptop, sat on one of the kitchen stools, and got back to my action plan. First up, I found out more than I'd ever wanted to know about belly button lint. Then I did a search for Cowboy Bob's Automotive Ranch. I came up with several hits. One was for the car dealership, one was for a consumer affairs site, and the last one was for a dating site.

I clicked on the dealership site first. The top of the page had a banner that read, "Cowboy Bob's Automotive Ranch—You Won't Wrangle a Better Deal Anywhere Else." Underneath was a picture of a large car lot. When I tried to click on the section labeled "Find Out More," I got a message that said, "Sorry, but we're out of business."

After hitting that dead end, I debated whether to check out the consumer affairs site or the dating site. Curiosity made me click on the link for Dating Scoundrels. Turns out it wasn't a dating site. It was a site warning women about scoundrels who'd tried to con women they'd met on matchmaking sites. There were pages and pages of pictures of men, each with a caption underneath detailing his name, occupation, and dating scoundrel crime, such as "married," "gold digger," or "cheater." I scrolled through a few pages until I saw Captain Dan's face staring at me. Or should I say, Bob Kincaid, owner of Cowboy Bob's Automotive Ranch and gold digger? And guess who reported him? None other than Penny Chadwick. Bingo.

Next, I clicked on the consumer affairs site. As I was reading about consumer fraud and protection, Scooter entered the kitchen. He opened the freezer and got out a tub of double-chocolate ice cream. As he walked over to the cupboard where we keep the bowls, he glanced at my laptop. "Consumer affairs? What's that all about? Are you filing a complaint?"

"Not exactly. It's more like I'm investigating a complaint. I found proof that Captain Dan did own a used-car dealership in Texas." I clicked over to Cowboy Bob's website and showed it to Scooter. "They went out of business, but the name of the dealership and logo match the car invoice I found in that sailing book Penny loaned me." I grabbed my purse and pulled out the sales invoice. "See, it's an exact match."

"Okay, they're the same." He put two bowls on the counter. "But what does that have to do with Captain Dan?"

I clicked over to the Dating Scoundrels site and showed him the picture. "See, that's Captain Dan right there, listed as the owner of Cowboy Bob's Automotive Ranch."

"But that doesn't say Captain Dan. It says Bob Kincaid."

"It's him. Look closely. You can't deny they're exactly alike."

"Lots of people look like other people. Maybe it's just a coincidence."

"Or maybe he changed his name because he got into trouble. That's where the consumer affairs site comes in. There's gotta be something on here that implicates Captain Dan."

Scooter scooped ice cream into the bowls. "Here it is. A report on Cowboy Bob's Automotive Ranch, owned by Daniel Robert Smith, who goes by the alias of Bob Kincaid." I tapped my fingers on the counter. "Aha! That's it. I knew I had seen Captain Dan before. Remember that place we had lunch at in Texas? You know, the one with the Western omelets that was across the street from a used-car lot? It was Cowboy Bob's Automotive Ranch. There was a huge billboard next to it with his face plastered on it. That's why he looked so familiar!"

Scooter handed me a bowl and smiled. "You're quite the investigative reporter."

"No, I'm not," I said glumly. "I heard from Brian. Lola got the job."

Scooter gave me a kiss, and then handed me his bowl of ice cream. "Looks like you might need this one too." And that's the secret to a successful relationship—knowing when your partner needs extra chocolate.

CHAPTER 15
MR. AND MRS. DIAMOND

THE NEXT MORNING, SANDY WAS discharged from the hospital. I popped by her boat to check on her, bringing a box of assorted pastries fresh out of the oven from Penelope's Sugar Shack. I had my eye on the one *pain au chocolat* in the box. I knew it was selfish on my part, but I really hoped that Sandy was the kind of hostess who offered a cup of freshly brewed coffee and allowed her guest to have first dibs on the pastries. If she wasn't, I'd have to create a distraction and snatch it before she did.

When I got to Sandy's boat, I realized that in the state she was in, she probably wouldn't have noticed or cared if I took the pain au chocolat. She was sitting in the cockpit staring into space. I waved the pastries in front of her. No response. Even the smell of chocolate wafting from the box wasn't enough to get her attention.

She finally noticed me and motioned for me to join her. She looked at the box. "Is that for me?" I nodded. "That's sweet of you, but I just don't have an appetite. I couldn't eat a thing."

"How about a cup of coffee, then? I could make you one," I offered.

"Sure, that'd be nice," she said with a vacant stare. I placed the box next to her and went down below to put the kettle on. After the water came to a boil, I poured it over the grounds in the French press and set it aside to brew for a few minutes.

"Sandy, do you want cream or sugar in your coffee?" She mumbled some sort of reply. I couldn't make out what she said. I stuck my head up into the cockpit and repeated the question. That's when I noticed that she was covered in little flaky pieces of pastry.

She wiped away some chocolate from the side of her mouth and said, "Just cream, please. I think I already ate enough sugar in this pain au chocolat. It was delicious!"

Lesson learned—never leave a box of pastries unattended, even if the other person claims they don't have an appetite. I passed Sandy a cup of coffee and then quickly plucked out a blueberry muffin before Sandy laid waste to that too. "What did the doctor say?" I asked in between bites of muffin.

"She said I was fine to go home," Sandy said. "When I explained that I lived on a sailboat, she was surprised, but it's my home, you know. I love living on the water and being able to take my floating house with me wherever I go. I really hated being in the hospital. It's good to be back in familiar surroundings."

"Are you still going to sell the boat and move into the condo?" I asked.

"I don't know," Sandy said. Her eyes welled up with tears. "I'll have to talk to our lawyer and accountant first and get a handle on exactly how much money Jack wasted away. When we first got married, he seemed like such a go-getter. I thought for sure he'd be a successful businessman, but everything he touched turned sour." She reached into the box and grabbed a blackberry Danish.

"Look at me," she said, tearing bits off the Danish angrily. "I've got nothing to show for our life together. I should have divorced Jack when I had the chance. If I had, then things would have been different. I could have started over with someone else." She dried her eyes with one of the napkins that Penelope had provided. "Would you mind making me another cup of coffee, dear?" she asked as she held out her empty mug.

I nabbed a glazed donut on my way to the galley. It was tasty, just not as tasty as a pain au chocolat.

"While you're down there, can you get the bottle of pills out of my purse for me?" Sandy asked as she burst into tears. "The doctor gave me some antidepressant tablets. I should probably take one."

I was surprised by her comments about Jack. I knew they'd had troubles, but I didn't realize how bitter Sandy had been about her marriage. It made me realize how lucky I was to have Scooter.

While the coffee brewed, I spotted Sandy's purse on the table and opened it. It was amazing how much stuff she managed to cram in there. I pulled out an eyeglass case, her wallet, a packet of tissues, a hairbrush, a makeup bag, a romance novel, and chewing gum. Finally, at the very bottom, I found a bottle of pills from the hospital pharmacy.

After plunging the coffee, I poured a glass of water and handed Sandy the bottle along with it. "Thanks. I don't think I'm supposed to take these on an empty stomach. Good thing you brought those pastries," she said. "It was really thoughtful of you."

"So what did you think about Ned's arrest?" I asked. "Do you really think he could have killed both Captain Dan and Jack?"

"It's hard to believe, isn't it?" Sandy said. "We've known them for years. Jack and Ned used to race sailboats together. But I guess you never really know someone, do you?"

"But if Jack and Ned were such good friends, why would Ned have killed him?"

Sandy hesitated and then said, "Well, now that he's dead, I guess there's no harm in telling you. Besides, the police are already aware. You know Jack's business selling marine goods? Well, turns out that he was selling stolen goods. He knew some guys who would break into boats that were unoccupied, steal things, and then give them to Jack to fence. Jack would then sell them to unsuspecting people and get a cut of the profit."

"How long had this been going on?" I asked, keeping to myself what I already knew about Jack's illegal activities.

"I can't be sure. Jack started his marine equipment business four years ago after he lost his job. He pretended he hadn't been fired and told everyone he had taken early retirement. At first, he had high hopes for his new business, and I did too. I thought it was going to be the answer to our financial problems. We both were so excited about it initially. But after the first year, it was apparent that he wasn't making much money. We squeaked by for another year, then things picked up and he began bringing home more money. Not enough to let us keep both the boat and our condo, but enough that we could get by. I think that was when he'd started fencing stolen goods."

"Did you realize that right away?" I asked.

"No, it took me a while to even be suspicious, but I finally found proof. You know how I do the bookkeeping for Jack?" I nodded while I listened to my stomach make very unladylike noises. Perhaps two pastries on top of the big rib dinner I had had the night before was a bad combo.

"Well, at first the bookkeeping was straightforward." She took a sip of coffee. "He'd give me receipts from people who he'd bought equipment from. I think I told you before how I'd enter them into a spreadsheet, then enter sales invoices when he sold something. All was good and well but then things changed. He'd just tell me what amounts to enter. He said that he had misplaced the receipts and invoices, but he knew what all the transactions were."

"But wouldn't that get him in trouble with the IRS if he were ever audited?"

"That's exactly what I said, but he told me to mind my own business. That's when things got really bad between us. It was really hard because, to be honest, I didn't have anyone to talk about it with. I still wasn't sure what was going on, but I knew something wasn't right."

"That must have been so hard not to have anyone to confide in."

"Well, there was one person I could talk to, for a while at least." She twisted her wedding ring nervously. "Then I found out..."

"What did you find out?" I prompted.

"Nothing important," Sandy said. "Anyway, it turns out he couldn't be trusted either."

"When did you know something was wrong?"

"A couple of days ago. Jack's cell phone rang and I picked it up. A guy was on the line, but he didn't even wait to see if it was Jack who had answered the phone. He started screaming that if Jack didn't come up with the money he owed, he was going to make sure the police got wind of what he was up to and that he'd take the fall for everything. I ended up confronting Jack about it that night, and he didn't deny it. I kept quiet about it, but once he was killed, I told the police what I knew."

"I still don't understand how Ned was involved."

"I'm not sure. All I can think of is that it had to do with the previous owners of *Marjorie Jane*. They blamed Captain Dan for what had happened with them."

"Okay, maybe Ned might have had a motive to kill Captain Dan, but Jack?"

"Ned's always been a straight shooter. He probably threatened to turn Jack in, there was a struggle, and Ned accidentally killed Jack."

I thought about this while I finished my coffee. "So you don't think it was murder, just accidental homicide?"

"I hope that's the case, for Nancy's sake," she said. "Oh, no, look who's coming." Sandy pointed at Penny, who waved while making her way down the dock. She was closely followed by Mrs. Moto, who meowed loudly when she reached the boat. "She's got some nerve, showing her face," Sandy whispered.

"Hi there," Penny said as she scooped the Japanese bobtail up and put her on the deck. "I thought I'd check in and see how you're doing, Sandy."

Sandy gave her a brittle smile. "I'm just fine, Penny. I see you found my cat. I was looking for her everywhere this morning. She must have sneaked off the boat when I wasn't watching."

Penny scratched behind her ears. "She's such a lovely cat. I bet she missed you while you were in the hospital."

Sandy reached out her hand. "Here, Mrs. Moto, come say hello to mama." The cat stared at her, then jumped in my lap and purred. Sandy looked crestfallen.

"Penny, we were just talking about Ned's arrest," I said. "It seems hard to believe he could have been responsible for Jack's death. What do you think?"

Sandy turned and scowled at me. She grabbed the coffee cups. "I better go wash these out."

After Sandy was down below, Penny whispered to me, "How's she actually holding up?"

"Okay, I think."

"She doesn't really think Ned killed Jack, does she?"

"Well, she thinks it could have been an accident," I said. I decided not to share what Sandy had told me about Jack's shady business.

"Well, if that's the case, why would they have arrested Ned?" Penny asked.

"That's a good question. Unless the police got it wrong. In a small town like this, they probably don't have to deal with murders very often. Maybe they made a mistake."

"I can't imagine Chief Dalton admitting the police made a mistake, can you?" Penny asked. "Although, going up against Nancy—that took guts on his part. She's a pretty tough lady."

"I don't know. This may be too much, even for her. I should go check on her later," I said.

"I'm sure she'd appreciate that. I've gotta skedaddle. I'm helping a young couple check out a couple of boats for sale. Say good-bye to Sandy for me."

Sandy popped her head out of the companionway. "Is she gone?"

"She just left. I should probably get going too," I said.

"Oh, no, you don't have to leave. It's nice having the company. It's just Penny I don't want to talk to."

"Why's that?" I debated whether or not to mention the picture I'd found of Penny and Captain Dan the night before. "I thought everyone got along with Penny."

"I used to think she was all right, but then I found out something about her that changed my mind." When I gave her a questioning look, she shook her head and said, "Never mind. I don't want to spread gossip. Just suffice to say that she isn't somebody you should trust."

I was starting to get a bad feeling about my sailing lesson. But then again, Sandy might be overreacting. After all, her husband had just been killed, and that had to have been a shock, no matter what difficulties they were having. Plus, the alien abduction experience wouldn't be helping matters either.

"What do you mean, you wouldn't trust her? Is she dangerous?"

"She's definitely the backstabbing type." Sandy thought about this for a few minutes. "Backstabbers can become dangerous when they don't get what they want."

"But is she the type to bash your head in with a winch handle?" I asked.

"Poor Dan," Sandy said, evading the question. "What a horrible way to go." She put her hand on the side of her head. "I think I'm getting another one of my headaches."

"Why don't you go lie down? I need to get going anyway and find a PFD, whatever that is."

"I think I will. Come on, Mrs. Moto, want to go take a nap with mama?" The calico stared at Sandy, then jumped off the boat and ran down the dock.

*　*　*

Although I'm sure I earned plenty of good-calorie karma from sharing the box of pastries with Sandy, I figured it couldn't hurt to go for a walk on the beach to burn off any residual calories that hadn't gotten the message about my good deeds. I kicked off my flip-flops and scrunched my toes in the sand. As I walked along the water, I saw Mr. and Mrs. Diamond wading. I sat on a piece of driftwood and watched them splash each other playfully. Mrs. Diamond's pendant glistened as the sun's rays bounced off it. They walked toward me hand in hand, giggling at some private joke.

"Sorry, were you sitting here?" I asked when I noticed a straw bag with water bottles, sunglasses, and towels propped up against the driftwood.

Mrs. Diamond picked up the towels, handed one to Mr. Diamond, and wrapped the other around her waist. "Not at all, there's plenty of room for everyone," she said, sitting next to me. "I've seen you around before, haven't I?"

"Yep, at the marina office." I decided not to mention that I had originally seen them at Chez Poisson. I really wasn't in the mood to hear about their romantic dinner or tell them about my less-than-romantic dinner that night.

"That's right," she said. "Isn't the water great? So refreshing on a hot day like today."

"I've had so much going on that I haven't really had a chance to go swimming lately." I watched the waves crashing on the beach. "Although I do get a little nervous swimming in the ocean. I'm not a very strong swimmer."

Mrs. Diamond pulled out her sunglasses and put them on. "I'm a real water baby. If I could, I'd swim in the ocean every day. We were just away for a couple of days at a marine biology conference." She pointed at Mr. Diamond. "He's a marine biologist, specializes in sea turtles. Sometimes I think I'm a sea turtle too, I'm in the water so much."

"So you weren't here for all the drama, then," I said.

Mr. Diamond pulled a water bottle out of the bag. "What drama?" he asked as he twisted the cap off.

"Jack Holt was killed on Monday night. I found him floating by the dinghy dock."

Mrs. Diamond gasped. "We know him. We were talking to him about buying a used outboard motor for our dinghy, weren't we, sweetie?" Mr. Diamond nodded. "I can't believe you found the body. How horrible," she said, patting my arm.

Mr. Diamond looked at me curiously. "Weren't you the lady who found Captain Dan as well?"

"Yes, that was me. I found him on our boat."

"So that means you found two bodies." He shook his head in amazement. "That must be some kind of record."

"Not exactly the kind of record I'd like to have," I said. I decided to change the subject. "You know Ned Schneider, the owner of the marina? They arrested him for Jack's murder. They might also be charging him with Captain Dan's murder."

"Ned? I don't know anything about the night that Captain Dan was murdered, but we saw Ned on Monday night, didn't we, sweetie?" Mrs. Diamond said. "We went for a swim and then had a picnic on the beach. He was sitting right here on this driftwood the entire time we were here."

"What time was that at?" I asked.

"We were here from about seven to ten. It was all his idea,"

Mrs. Diamond said as she squeezed Mr. Diamond's hand. "It was so romantic. A full moon, warm night, no rain. My sweetie had a picnic basket, wine, candles—the works."

Mr. Diamond really was setting high standards in the romance department for the rest of the guys at the marina. A diamond necklace and a romantic picnic dinner. I was going to have to introduce him to Scooter.

"Nancy told me that Ned doesn't have an alibi for the night of Jack's murder. She was at her daughter's house that night. While she was gone, he went for a walk on the beach. He said he didn't see anyone and no one's come forward to say they saw him."

"Well, we did wave at him when we walked by that night, but he was just staring out into space, oblivious. Wasn't he?" Mrs. Diamond asked her husband. Mr. Diamond agreed.

"We need to sort this out," Mrs. Diamond said. "He's such a sweet guy." She pulled out her cell phone. After a quick conversation, she said, "Chief Dalton is going to come talk to us."

* * *

The next morning, I sat on the patio with the sailing book Penny had loaned me, doing some last-minute studying. My first lesson began in a couple of hours, and I still didn't know what a PFD was. Mrs. Moto helpfully jumped on the table and lay on the book. She stretched out on her back, obscuring the section on man-overboard drills.

While I scratched the calico's belly, Ned came out of the office carrying a broom and dustpan. He started sweeping the patio, slowly making his way over to where I was sitting. He put the broom down and smiled at Mrs. Moto. "You better not let Nancy catch that cat out here."

I returned Ned's smile. "It's so nice to see you back here!"

"It's good to be back," Ned said, sitting in one of the chairs and scratching behind Mrs. Moto's ears.

"What exactly is it that Nancy has against her? She's as sweet as can be."

"It isn't this one specifically as much as it's all cats and dogs. She doesn't like how they roll around on the beach and then deposit sand everywhere. She's a bit of a stickler for everything being neat and tidy." He pointed at his broom. "Whenever I say I'm all caught up on things, she manages to find something for me that needs to be cleaned. To be honest, it's actually kind of nice taking a break from time to time and getting out of the office."

The feline jumped onto Ned's lap. "She likes you," I said. "But you better not let Nancy catch you with cat hair all over you."

"I've got one of those hair-remover rollers in the storage shed. I make sure to clean up all her hair before she catches me. Isn't that right, Mrs. Moto?" he asked.

"I meant to ask Sandy why she named her that. It's a rather unusual name."

"Oh, she didn't name her. I did."

"You did? But I thought she was Sandy's cat."

"She is. But I'm the one who found her late one night yowling on the patio. I think her owners abandoned her, or she jumped off a boat and they left without her. I knew Sandy was feeling down about things, and I thought a cat would cheer her up."

"But why that name?"

"You know how I like old movies?" I nodded, remembering our discussion in the lounge right before the police had arrested him. "Well, some of my favorite movies are the 'Mr. Moto' ones, starring Peter Lorre as a Japanese secret agent. He wears these glasses that kind of remind me of the black circles around Mrs. Moto's eyes." He saw the look of confusion on my face. "I realized after I picked the name that was a she, not a he, hence the Mrs."

"What do you think happened to her tail?" I asked. "Was she in an accident?"

"No, she was born that way. I think I told you she's a Japanese bobtail? Their tail, or lack of tail, is characteristic of the breed. They're also known for being very talkative. Isn't that right, Mrs. Moto?" he asked. She enthusiastically agreed with a loud meow.

"I have to say, it was strange to see a cat without a tail, but I think it suits her," I said.

Ned smiled. "It sure does." Then his face sobered. "You know, Mollie, I wanted to thank you for what you did for me, finding that young couple who could back up my alibi. I can't imagine what I would have done if the police didn't release me. The thought of being locked up and apart from Nancy, our kids, and the grandkids—well, I don't even want to think about it." There was a loud meow. Ned chuckled. "And of course, you too, Mrs. Moto."

"I'm just so glad I was able to help."

The calico yowled, jumped off Ned's lap, and ran toward the beach. I heard the marina office screen door bang shut. "Ned, what are you doing sitting there?" Nancy asked. "That patio isn't going to sweep itself."

"Just having a little chat with Mollie, thanking her for her help. Maybe we should give her one of those chocolate bars to show our appreciation."

"Humph," Nancy said. She narrowed her eyes, then turned and went back into the marina office.

As soon as the screen door closed, Ned stood and rushed toward the storage shed. He quickly used a roller to remove Mrs. Moto's telltale hairs from his clothes.

A few minutes later, Nancy came out and put a chocolate bar in front of me. "Here," she said. "It's a new kind. Dark chocolate mint swirl." She took a deep breath, put her hands on her hips, and said, "Thank you."

***

"Scooter, can you take this? I've got to get going," I said, holding up a paper bag.

"Just a minute," he said. He walked up to the bow of the boat and handed Ben a toolbox. Ben rummaged through it, plucked out a wrench, opened the anchor locker, and started doing whatever it is you do with a wrench. Scooter leaned over the lifelines and grabbed the bag from me. "What's this?" he asked.

"Some sandwiches I picked up from the Sailor's Corner Cafe for you guys to have for your lunch."

Ben stopped what he was doing and set the wrench down beside him. "Thanks, Mollie! You didn't happen to get any brownies as well while you were at it?" he asked with a sly grin.

"Nope, sorry. Maybe next time," I replied, neglecting to mention that I had a dark chocolate mint swirl bar in my purse.

Mrs. Moto had followed me down the dock, and now she jumped up and sat next to Ben. "Make sure you don't feed her any human food. Sandy said it isn't good for her tummy."

"Aren't you going to be joining us for lunch?" Scooter asked.

"No, we're having lunch as part of my sailing class. Unless you think I should stay here instead," I said, half hoping he thought I should cancel the lesson. The section on man-overboard drills in the sailing book had made me slightly nervous.

"That's right," Scooter said. "I forgot about that. No, you should definitely go. You're going to love sailing."

"Hey guys, look what I found," Ben said. He reached into the anchor locker and pulled out a compass. "It's the one we found on *Marjorie Jane* the other day, the one that Scooter said went missing." He sat back on the deck and smiled. "Looks like I've got a streak of good luck going lately. First, I win eight hundred dollars from a scratch-off lottery ticket the other day, then I find this compass that you lost."

"Eight hundred dollars? Wow, that's a lot of money," I said.

"Well, it *was* a lot of money," Ben said sheepishly. "I repaid some money I owed, and I'm afraid I spent the rest at the Tipsy Pirate. Oh well, easy come, easy go."

Scooter set the paper bag down and inspected the compass. "I wonder how that got in there?" Mrs. Moto stuck her paw into the sandwich bag and tried to fish one of the sandwiches out. Scooter seized the bag from her. He looked at the cat, then back at me. "Remember how you left your purse by the anchor locker when we had sundowners? Well, I think I know how the compass might have found its way out of your purse and into the anchor locker." He pointed at the calico. She meowed and twined herself around Scooter's legs. I'd like to say she looked guilty, but we all know she didn't.

* * *

When I got to Penny's boat, I saw Sandy sitting in the cockpit giggling and chatting away with Penny. It appeared that she had gotten over her concerns about the sailing instructor.

"There she is," Sandy said. "We were beginning to wonder if you were going to make it, Mollie."

"Sorry about that. I was speaking with Scooter and Ben about..." I hesitated, not wanting to mention the compass until I'd found out more about it.

Sandy leaned forward. "Speaking with them about what?"

"About Mrs. Moto and how cute she is."

Sandy beamed. She patted the seat next to her. "Come sit beside me, and Penny will show us where we're going on the chart."

"Oh, are you coming with us?" I asked. "I thought this was the ladies' sailing lesson. Don't you know how to sail already?"

"I do, but when I heard Louise and Wanda couldn't make it today—food poisoning, you know—I offered my services to Penny. It'll be easier for her to have a third person aboard." Sandy's eyes sparkled. "You'll be glad I came. Not only did I bring lemonade and shortbread cookies, but I also brought you a PFD to use. I remember you saying you weren't sure if you had one." Sandy held up something that looked like a harness.

"Is that what a PFD is? A life jacket?" I asked. "I always thought they were bright orange and bulky."

Sandy handed it to me. "PFD stands for personal flotation device. If you should fall overboard—not that that would happen," she said with a wink to Penny—"then this will automatically inflate."

I sat next to Sandy and put the PFD on while she explained to me how it operated. While I was buckling it up, Mrs. Moto jumped on the boat, darted over to me, and played with the straps. "Did you follow me?" I asked, pulling the straps out of her way and cinching them tightly.

Sandy went down below to stow the lemonade and cookies. Penny whispered to me, "You don't mind if she comes, do you, sugar? I figured it would do her good to get off her boat and get some fresh air."

"No, that's fine." We listened to Sandy cheerfully singing to herself. "She does seem to be in a better mood than yesterday. I guess those antidepressants are working."

***

Turns out sailing is actually quite a rush. The feel of the salt air on my face and the wind whipping through my hair as we tacked the boat back and forth was exhilarating. Watching dolphins frolic alongside the bow of the boat as we slipped through the water was so mind-blowing that when I reached up and felt how tangled and frizzy my hair had become, I didn't even mind. Of course, I didn't plan on telling Scooter that I liked sailing right away. He can be a nightmare to live with when he thinks he's right. He would feel that he deserved two bowls of Froot Loops for breakfast instead of one.

After a couple of hours, we dropped anchor in a small cove on the north side of the bay for lunch. Penny let me operate the controls for the windlass to lower the anchor. I could see why this might be a useful gadget to have on board *Marjorie Jane*.

"Why don't I go down and get us some lemonade?" Sandy offered.

"Thanks," Penny said. "Can you grab the sandwiches as well?"

"Of course I can, honey," Sandy said. "Anything for you."

Penny and I exchanged glances while Sandy went down below. A few minutes later, she put a plate of sandwiches on the cockpit table and handed us each a glass of lemonade. "You've got really darling glasses, Penny," she said. "I like how each one has a different pattern. I chose the one with the dolphin for you, Mollie, because you enjoyed watching the dolphins so much. And I chose the one with the octopus for you, Penny, because you have your tentacles in everything."

"My tentacles?" Penny asked, taking a sip of her lemonade.

"You know, having your fingers in so many pies. I just don't know how you do it, balancing running your sailing school with your love life."

"I can't say I have much of a love life these days." She took a sip of her lemonade. "Mmm. That's tart, just the way I like it." She drained the glass quickly.

I snagged a ham-and-cheese sandwich and sipped on my lemonade thoughtfully. What had gotten into Sandy? Just yesterday, she had hinted that Penny had some dark secret, but today she was acting as if they were best friends.

"Let me refill that glass for you, Penny," Sandy said. "Better yet, why don't you come down with me, and I'll give you the recipe so you can make some for yourself."

I finished off my sandwich and counted how many were left on the plate. Darn, there weren't enough for everyone to have a second one. Hopefully, Sandy would break out the shortbread cookies soon.

"Penny is going to take care of a few things down below," Sandy said as she came up into the cockpit without any cookies. "The wind has really kicked up. See those waves rolling in? Penny wants you and me to check to make sure the anchor is set properly."

I followed Sandy to the front of the boat, feeling *Pretty in Pink* swing back and forth on the anchor. "Watch out for that boat hook," she said, picking the long metal pole up off the deck. "We don't want you to trip."

Sandy spent a few minutes explaining how to check and make sure the anchor was set properly and why it was so important. "I remember one time, Jack and I were anchored in this very same cove. We had problems setting our anchor, and the next thing we knew, we had dragged and were drifting across the bay toward that rocky shore. Thankfully, we managed to get the engine started in time before we crashed."

After that story, I was reconsidering my newfound love of sailing, but then I saw two dolphins swimming nearby. "Look!" I said, tugging on Sandy's arm. "I wonder if they're the same ones as before."

"Wouldn't it be fun to go swimming with them?" Sandy asked. "Why don't you stand over here and watch them for a while? I'll go check on Penny."

I watched the dolphins leap in and out of the water, wishing I could swim as well as they could. As I leaned against the lifelines to get a closer look, I heard someone come up behind me. I saw the boat hook out of the corner of my eye. It crashed into the side of my head. I tried to steady myself by grabbing onto a lifeline, but the boat hook came down hard on my hand, and I pulled back in pain. Two hands seized me by my shoulders. I lurched forward.

The lifelines snapped. I fell into the water, screaming for help.

When I surfaced, I tried to tread water. Waves crashed into me, making it hard to keep my head above the surface. Why hadn't my PFD automatically inflated? I pulled on the cord to manually inflate it. Nothing happened. I tried to swim back to the boat, but the current was pulling me in the opposite direction. I watched helplessly as someone in the cockpit turned on the engine. The windlass creaked and groaned as it lifted the anchor. I waved my hands frantically over my head so they could see where I was, coughing as I swallowed sea water. Then the boat turned toward Coconut Cove, leaving me drifting out to sea.

CHAPTER 16
KILLER COCONUTS

"MOLLIE, MOLLIE, ARE YOU OKAY?" A dinghy pulled up beside me. I struggled to reply, barely able to keep my head above water. "Here, give me your hand." I reached up and saw Ben looking at me with concern. He pulled me into the dinghy, setting me next to a case of beer, a fishing pole, and a tattered orange life jacket.

"What were you doing in the water?" he asked as he tossed an anchor over the side. He examined my PFD. "What happened here? This isn't inflated. Did you fall off a boat?"

I sat up carefully, wincing as I bumped my shoulder on the fishing pole. "I didn't fall. Someone..." I tried to catch my breath. "Someone tried to kill me."

"Kill you?" Ben asked. He moved the fishing pole out from underneath me.

"Yes, kill me. See this lump on the side of my head? That's from a boat hook."

"That does look pretty nasty," he said. "You sure it wasn't from a coconut?"

"A coconut?" I asked incredulously. "How would I get hit by a coconut here in the middle of the water?"

Ben shrugged. "I don't know. Sometimes I see them floating in the bay."

"But they'd have to fall down from something in order to hit me. Do you see any palm trees floating out here?" I gestured out across the water.

Ben put his hands over his mouth and scanned the horizon. "You're right. I don't know what I was thinking. It's just that... well, it's hard to believe." I started coughing. Ben handed me a water bottle. "Here, have a drink. You look terrible. Let's get you back to the marina."

"Okay, but first we need to alert the authorities. There's a killer on the loose. Do you have one of those walkie-talkie things?"

"You mean a VHF?"

I shrugged. "I'm not sure what they're called."

"I used to, but it doesn't work anymore, and I can't afford to replace it."

"Well, what about your cell phone?"

"Sorry, I don't have it with me. I forgot it on your boat. Scooter had to go back to Melvin's to pick up some supplies, so I decided to take off and do some fishing."

"Okay, no phone and no VHF. Let's turn on the motor and hightail it back to the marina so we can catch this killer."

Ben got the outboard engine started after a few attempts. "Luckily, I managed to get this fixed, Mollie."

"Just hurry, as fast as you can," I said. "We need to make sure they catch the killer before she escapes."

"Are you really sure someone tried to kill you?"

"I am. Someone hit me from behind and shoved me off Penny's boat."

"Are you saying Penny did this?" he asked.

"It was either her or Sandy. They were the only two people on the boat."

I curled up in the bow of the dinghy, listening to the engine sputtering. At the rate we were going, the killer would be long gone by the time we got back. As I struggled to keep my hands from shaking, I wondered what had happened to my PFD.

* * *

The sound of the dinghy hitting the dock alerted me to the fact that we were back at the marina. "Wait here, Mollie," Ben said as he tied it to a cleat. "I'm going to get help."

I struggled to hoist myself out of the dinghy, flopping ungracefully on the dock. I shuddered when I looked over at the small boat, remembering that I'd found Jack's body floating nearby. I tried to sit up but couldn't find the energy to move. I lay on the dock, staring at the seagulls circling overhead. After a few minutes, Ned came running toward me.

"Are you all right?" he asked, bending down and pushing my wet hair out of my eyes. "Ben said he found you in the water off Pirate's Cove."

"Can you help me up?" As Ned pulled me to my feet, I groaned in pain.

He put his arm around my waist to hold me steady. "That's a nasty lump, Mollie. How did that happen?"

"Someone whacked me with a boat hook and then pushed me overboard," I said. I bit my lip. "Did Ben call the police?"

"He didn't mention anything about the police. He just told me you were hurt and went to find Scooter."

"I don't need a doctor—I need you to call the police!" I screamed, my voice cracking with hysteria. Ned stared at me in shock. "I need you to trust me. Please, just call them," I pleaded.

"Okay, I will. Let's just get you settled first." Ned helped me over to the patio. He got out his cell phone and placed the call. As I sank down on a chair, Mrs. Moto ran across the patio, catapulted herself onto my lap, stretched up, and nuzzled my face.

"Hello, you beautiful girl," I said, snuggling her against my neck. She meowed loudly. "Wait a minute—if you're back at the marina, that means *Pretty in Pink* is back." I set the calico on my lap. "Ned, have you seen Penny and Sandy?"

"They docked a little while ago." He looked at me quizzically. "Weren't you on *Pretty in Pink* today for your sailing lesson?" I nodded. "But if that's the case, why did Ben fish you out of the water?"

"The boat hook and being pushed overboard. Ring a bell?"

Ned stroked his chin. "You were serious about that? I just figured you—"

"Imagined it?" I asked. Ned looked chastened. "Never mind. The important thing is to track down Penny and Sandy. Did you see both of them when they docked?"

"Now that you mention it, I just saw Sandy. She said Penny was down below doing something with the engine."

"I have a feeling that something may have happened to Penny, just like it did to Captain Dan and Jack." I shooed Mrs. Moto off my lap and pushed myself up. "Hurry, we've got to get to the boat and make sure Penny is okay."

I stumbled, and Ned held my elbow. "You're in no shape to go anywhere. I see Chief Dalton coming this way. You sit back down, and we'll let him take care of this."

Ned walked over to the chief. I watched as he tried to explain the situation, pointing toward me, then pointing to where *Pretty in Pink* was docked. The burly man seemed unimpressed. Even from a distance, I could see his raised eyebrows. I was about to go over and try to get him to see reason when I saw Sandy dashing across the patio in the direction of the parking lot.

"Hey!" I shouted as she ran past me. Sandy stopped in her tracks and looked at me in shock. "You! What are you doing here? You should be at the bottom of the sea by now." She grabbed my arm and yanked me out of my chair. "Now I'm going to have to find another way to deal with you." Mrs. Moto arched her back and hissed at Sandy. Sandy tried to push her out of the way with her foot, but the cat jumped back too quickly.

I fought to break free of Sandy's grasp, but she dug her fingers into my arm, adding new bruises to the ones she'd given me a short while ago on Penny's boat. I stepped down hard on her foot, pushing her off-balance and causing her to let go of me. I lifted my arm to wave at the chief, but she yanked me back. She wrapped her powerful hands around my neck with a vise-like grip. With a crazed look in her eyes, she squeezed her fingers. I tried to yell for help, but no words came out. As I struggled to breathe, I could feel the world fading away.

Then I felt an abrupt jerk and Sandy's hands were no longer around my neck. I collapsed on the patio, gasping for air. Hearing a gruff voice say, "You're under arrest," I looked up and saw Chief Dalton pulling Sandy back. While the big man handcuffed her,

Ned rushed over and helped me to my feet.

After reading the handcuffed woman her rights, the chief turned to me. "I'm going to need you to come down to the station and tell me what happened. But we'll get you to the hospital first." For a second, I thought I saw a hint of a smile as he raised one of his eyebrows. "Looks like you got hit by a whole bunch of coconuts this time."

I gingerly rubbed my neck. "Feels like it too."

"I'll make sure she gets medical attention," Ned said.

The chief nodded and escorted Sandy toward the parking lot.

"Oh, no! I forgot about Penny," I said frantically. "You have to go check on her."

Ned hesitated. "Are you sure you'll be okay?" I assured him I was fine for the time being. The Japanese bobtail and I watched him hurry down the dock.

Nancy poked her head out of the marina office and peppered me with questions. "What's all the commotion out here? Where's Ned going? He should be cleaning the shower room. What's that mangy cat doing here?"

I smiled, picked up Mrs. Moto, and said sweetly, "Better close that door before you get flies in there."

CHAPTER 17
THE MYSTERIOUS TOTE BAG

THE NEXT DAY, I STOPPED by Penelope's Sugar Shack to pick up a tray of brownies. No, they weren't for me, they were for the barbecue—although one of the brownies did accidentally fall off the tray and into my hand on the way back to the marina, so I had to eat it. It would have been wasteful not to, right?

I have to confess, I did feel guilty about it—not about eating the brownie, but about not baking my own award-winning, gooey, quadruple-chocolate brownies. But really, when you've been investigating not one but two murders and an alien abduction, someone bashes you in the head when you're out for a walk, someone else throws you overboard, you're up for a promotion at work (which gets snatched away from you by that evil, red-headed Lola), and your husband surprises you with a sailboat for your anniversary, there's really not a lot of time left for home baking.

By the time I got to the patio—I needed a few moments to wipe the brownie crumbs off my clothes—the barbecue was in full swing. I watched everyone chatting, laughing, and having a good time, then pulled out my cell phone. My mom had left a number of text messages over the past couple of days, which I hadn't had a chance to read properly. Rather than continue to exchange endless texts trying to correct misunderstandings, I decided to phone her instead. We had a nice talk, once she got over the shock of what had happened to me. I think I even convinced her to come visit and see *Marjorie Jane* for herself.

After promising to call more often, I wandered over to join the crowd. I put the tray of brownies on one of the tables. The smell of the barbecue was heavenly. I couldn't help but check out what Ned was grilling.

"It's one of my specialties—chicken legs marinated in lemon, garlic, Dijon mustard, and olive oil. The secret is to let them marinate for at least twenty-four hours," Ned said as he checked the chicken, turning over pieces to make sure the skin got evenly crisped. "Of course, the other secret is expert grilling, and that's where I come in." He smiled.

"They look delicious," I said. "How long until they're ready?"

"About another five minutes or so."

"I don't know if I'll be able to hold out that long."

"Who put these over here?" Nancy asked, pointing at the tray I had set down.

"Might as well get it over with, and confess to your crime," Ned said. "It'll be easier that way. Trust me."

I held my hand up meekly. "It was me."

Nancy summoned me over. "This table is for side dishes," she said as she pointed to an impressive array of salads. All of them seemed to feature plenty of vegetables prepared in a variety of low-fat dressings. Fortunately, I spotted a dish of potato salad oozing with mayonnaise. "These brownies do not belong on this table. They belong over there, on the dessert table." I muttered my apologies and placed the tray of brownies next to a lonely bowl of fruit salad.

"Come and get it!" Ned yelled out. He placed a big platter of chicken on the table and set aside a few legs for Nancy and himself before the crowd rushed over. While they were fighting over the chicken and salads, I put a brownie on my plate. Then I found a gap in the crowd, made my way to the table with the side dishes, and scooped up some potato salad.

"There you are, my little sweet potato," Scooter said. He held out his plate. "Can you put some of that on mine too? No, not the quinoa salad, the potato salad." He took some napkins and pointed to the far side of the patio, where Penny, Ned, and Nancy were sitting. "The gang's all over at that table. Come on, let's go join them."

As we sat down, Penny looked at my plate and smiled. "I see you got some of my potato salad."

"Did you make this?" I asked as I sampled it. "It's delicious! You make it with plenty of mayonnaise, just the way I like it."

"Oh, that's not mayonnaise. That's tofu that I whipped up in a blender. Tastes like the real thing, doesn't it?"

I put my fork down slowly and grabbed one of my chicken legs. At least this was real chicken and not something made out of tofu. Maybe I was going to have to start bringing coleslaw with extra mayo, plus dessert, to these barbecues.

Ben sat in the chair next to me. Today's T-shirt advised me to keep calm and say "Arr." He appeared relatively neat and tidy. His hair looked like it had been recently shampooed, and his shorts didn't have any holes or stains. "You shaved your beard off," I said as I toyed with the misleading potato salad on my plate.

"What do you think?" he asked. "I thought I'd go with a clean-cut look for my new job."

"Your new job?"

"Didn't you hear? Ned and Nancy hired me to work in the boatyard," he said with a huge grin. "Beer's on me tonight at the Tipsy Pirate."

Nancy leaned over and poked Ben in the ribs with one of her long fingernails. "Don't forget, Ben, it's for a trial period. If you do a good job, then maybe we'll talk about hiring you on a permanent basis."

"I'm going to do a great job, just you wait and see," he said, digging into his baked beans. He set his fork down. "You know, these baked beans are good, but not as good as the ones Sandy made. I still can't believe she tried to kill you, Mollie."

Ned polished off the potato salad on his plate. Clearly, he wasn't averse to tofu being disguised as mayonnaise. "I can't believe Sandy killed Captain Dan and Jack," he said. "I would have never thought she had it in her."

"I still don't get why she did it," Penny said. I noticed she was eating some of the quinoa salad. It probably had tofu in it too.

"Well, it was because of you," I said.

"Me?" Penny put her fork down. "What did she have against me?"

"It all had to do with you and Captain Dan."

"Captain Dan? I don't know what you're talking about," she said. Her eyes began to water. I got a tissue out of my purse and passed it to her.

"It's okay, Penny. It happens to the best of us, falling for the wrong guy," I said. "It wasn't your fault that he conned you. He conned lots of people." Ned, Nancy, and Ben all nodded in agreement.

"But how do you know about Bob—I mean, Dan?" she asked, dabbing at her eyes.

"Who's Bob?" Nancy asked.

"Bob was an alias for Captain Dan. Before he moved to Florida, he had a used-car dealership in Texas called Cowboy Bob's Automotive Ranch. Penny knew Captain Dan back when he was Cowboy Bob. He sold her that pink convertible she has. I'm not sure when or how it happened, but at some point, they became romantically involved."

Penny put down her tissue. "I met him at a bar one night. He was a smooth talker. I fell head over heels in love. My family warned me about him, but I didn't believe them. He asked me to invest money in his car dealership, and I did. I ended up losing every last cent." Nancy patted Penny's arm sympathetically. "Turns out he was conning other women out of money as well. He got in some trouble with the law, so that's when he moved here."

"But why did you follow him up here to Florida if you knew he was no good?" Nancy asked.

"I was curious about that too," Scooter said. "You reported him on that Dating Scoundrels site, didn't you?"

"That's the part that's so embarrassing," Penny said. "He convinced me that everything that happened in Texas was a misunderstanding, and that he wanted me to come to Florida and be his partner in the boat brokerage business. What was I thinking? He was a used-car salesman, for goodness' sake. And I was stupid enough to believe he could make a success of being a boat broker, something he knew nothing about, and that things would work out between us." She put her head in her hands and groaned.

"You weren't the only one who believed him," I said. "Sandy fell for his charms too. That's what started this all. He flirted with her, and she fell for him, hook, line, and sinker. Then she found out about you and him."

"How did she find out about us?" Penny asked.

"I'm not sure, but Mrs. Moto found a picture on Sandy's boat of you and Captain Dan, or Cowboy Bob, in Texas with your arms around each other. Sandy wanted to leave Jack and marry Captain Dan. She was convinced that you were the reason why Captain Dan was hesitating. She didn't like being part of a love triangle."

Scooter looked at me quizzically. "How do you know about Sandy wanting to marry Captain Dan?"

"Oh, I ran into Officer Moore when I was at Penelope's Sugar Shack. She's so much nicer than Chief Dalton. She was at the police station yesterday when I went in to give my statement about what happened on *Pretty in Pink*. We had such a nice chat. Then when I saw her today, I gave her one of the brownies, and she told me all about the case and Sandy's confession."

"What else did you find out?" Scooter asked.

"Yeah, tell us about the murders," Ben said. "Let's hear all the details about how she whacked Captain Dan over the head with that winch handle."

Scooter sat back in his chair and shuddered. I don't think he really wanted to hear all the details. I passed him my brownie. He ate the whole thing in two bites.

"After the barbecue last week, Captain Dan told Sandy in no uncertain terms that he didn't want her leaving Jack, and that they should continue to have an affair behind his back. He needed Jack to help him fence stolen marine equipment, and he certainly didn't want to be tied down to one woman."

I looked over at Penny's hand. "Remember how you were chewing on your nails when you had a fight with Captain Dan at the barbecue?"

"Yeah, but how did you know about that?"

"Never mind," I said. "It's not important. Sandy found one of your press-on fingernails on the patio and picked it up."

"See, I told you it wasn't my fingernail," Nancy said. "What happened after that?"

"She followed him to *Marjorie Jane* when he supposedly went there to leave a boat-warming present for us. They got into a fight, she picked up the winch handle, and...well...you know what happened next. She must have decided to leave the fingernail to implicate Penny."

Everyone thought about this for a few minutes while Nancy cleared the table. When she sat back down, she asked, "What do you mean by Captain Dan *supposedly* going to *Marjorie Jane* to leave a boat-warming present?"

"Oh, that." I nodded at Ben and Scooter. "The guys found an antique compass hidden on *Marjorie Jane*. Turns out Captain Dan had stolen it from some people in Texas and tucked it in a secret compartment before the previous owners of *Marjorie Jane* sailed her over to Florida. He was planning on retrieving it when no one else was around. That's why he said he wanted to leave a boat-warming present for us. But before he could get it, Sandy surprised him, they argued, and then she murdered him."

Scooter blanched at the reference to murder and pointed at my purse. "Do you have any more chocolate in there?"

"No, sorry," I said. "At the rate things have been going, I'll have to start stocking up on a lot more emergency chocolate."

"You sure are." He dumped the contents of my purse on the table. "Maybe there's some in here you forgot about." Scooter sighed. "Nope, nothing." He fiddled with my keys. "So was it high school kids who broke into *Marjorie Jane* originally, or was that Captain Dan?"

"No, Captain Dan had a key. He didn't need to break in. That was Jack. Jack overheard Captain Dan talking on the phone with a prospective buyer for the compass. Jack told Sandy he was going to get to the compass before Captain Dan did, as payback. So he cut the padlock and searched the boat. That's how that large winch handle ended up on the floor. He found it when he was tearing the boat apart. Crew-cut guy and his bearded friend must have left it behind when they unloaded the stolen goods."

"Crew-cut guy and his bearded friend? Who are they?" Ben asked.

"A couple of local bad guys—Fred Rollins and Wayne Grimm. They helped Captain Dan and Jack fence the stolen marine equipment."

"Oh, Fred and Wayne," Ben said. "I know those guys. They hang out at the Tipsy Pirate."

Penny folded her hands together. "Okay, so I understand now why Sandy killed Bob," she said, sniffing slightly. "But why did she kill Jack?"

"Jack and Sandy had been having problems for years," I said. Ned and Nancy nodded. "She couldn't bear to be around him anymore. She blamed him for their money problems. And in her mind, Jack was the reason that things didn't work out with Captain Dan. She snapped that night. When he got back from the police station, they had an argument on the dinghy dock. She hit him over the head with an oar, and he fell into the water. I'm not sure if she meant to kill him or not, but either way, he ended up dead."

Nancy pursed her lips. "She tried to frame Ned for that," she said angrily. She squeezed Ned's hand. "Thankfully, you found that young couple who could vouch for his alibi."

"That's when Sandy really got desperate. She thought I was asking too many questions, so she decided I was going to be her next victim."

Penny shivered. She zipped up her pink jacket. "I'm so sorry about that, Mollie. I should have known what she was up to. I should have checked that PFD she brought for you to use. I had no idea she had taken the cartridges out so it wouldn't inflate."

"It wasn't your fault," I said.

"But it happened on my boat," Penny said. "She even undid the clasps on the lifelines so they'd be loose and you'd fall overboard."

"You can't blame yourself. She put sleeping pills in your lemonade."

Nancy shook her head. "No one is to blame, especially not you. You just put that idea right out of your head. You hear me, Penny?"

Penny nodded, but I had a feeling it would take some time before she could forget the impact Captain Dan and Sandy had had on her life.

"What I want to know is what was in that Styrofoam cooler you found the night Jack was killed," Ben said. "Was it beer?"

"No, Officer Moore told me it was full of illegally caught fish," I said.

Ben reached for another beer. "I've heard rumors that there's been some poaching happening lately."

Ned frowned. "Where did you hear that?"

"At the Tipsy Pirate. Who knows if it's true or not?" After cracking open his bottle of beer, Ben looked at me with a big grin. "Hey, maybe that's what you should investigate next, Mollie—the case of the mysterious fish poachers."

Scooter put his arm around my shoulders. "No way is Mollie getting involved in that. We have enough to keep ourselves busy with all of the boat projects we need to do on *Marjorie Jane*. She won't have time for any more investigations. Isn't that right?"

"Well, there still is the matter of the mysterious green and red lights I saw on the water last week. It could be a—"

Scooter interrupted. "That didn't have anything to do with aliens. I'm sure those were navigation lights on a boat. They use them at night so you know which way other boats are going, and you don't crash into each other."

"Or were they?" I asked. "You'll have to wait until I complete my report for FAROUT."

"Another report?" Scooter asked.

"Yep, turns out Lola faked those pictures at Disneyland. Those weren't aliens hiding in Sleeping Beauty Castle. Those pictures were from the annual staff Halloween party. Some of the guys dressed up as little green men, thinking it would impress Lola. That means the investigative reporter job is all mine now!"

* * *

After the barbecue, Scooter and I went back to *Marjorie Jane* for sundowners. "You wait here in the cockpit. I'll go down and fix us some drinks," I said. I listened to Scooter humming away happily to himself while I cut up a lime for the gin and tonics.

It was nice to see my husband so happy. He had received a call earlier in the day about a potential new business opportunity that had him excited about the future. Hopefully, that meant *Marjorie Jane* wouldn't be occupying all his time anymore. With Scooter busy, I would be able to put my investigative skills to good use unraveling the case of the poached fish, or look for another story to pursue for FAROUT, or just enjoy a well-deserved rest. It would be a nice change from finding dead bodies. But tonight was for celebrating, not thinking about work.

"Here, take these," I said, passing him the glasses and a bowl of potato chips. After he set everything down on the table, I told him to close his eyes. "I've got a surprise for you," I said as I set his present in his lap. "Okay, you can open your eyes."

"But this is a cat," he said.

"Not just any cat. This is your cat—Mrs. Moto. She's my belated anniversary present to you. Remember how you surprised me with *Marjorie Jane*? You told me that I'd love having a sailboat?" Scooter reluctantly nodded while the calico nudged his hand. "Well, now I'm surprising you with your very own cat. See, I even put a ribbon around her neck. You're going to love her."

Scooter sighed. I think he knew that I had beaten him at his own game. "Welcome aboard, Mrs. Moto," he said, scratching under her chin.

"Speaking of surprises, what was in that navy-blue tote bag you had the day you first showed me *Marjorie Jane*? You said it was something for me."

Scooter handed Mrs. Moto to me. "I can't believe I forgot all about that. The bag is somewhere here on the boat." He went down below and searched for a few minutes before coming back up and triumphantly presenting me with the tote bag. "Have a look in there."

I pulled out a couple of sailing magazines, a water bottle, and a sweatshirt. At the very bottom of the bag was a small velvet jewelry box. "Is this what I think it is?" I asked.

"Go on, open it." And there it was, my very own diamond necklace. I took it out of the box and looked at the pendant. "I meant to give this to you on the day we bought *Marjorie Jane*. See the diamond at the top of the lighthouse? It's meant to represent the light that they shine to guide mariners safely into port. Lighthouses are a symbol of the way forward. I can't imagine going forward in life without you by my side," Scooter said as he put the necklace around my neck.

Yeah, he really did say that. Kind of mushy, but sometimes you need a little mushiness. As we sat in the cockpit with Mrs. Moto by our side, watching the sun go down, I realized that I just might be able to get used to this sailing life.

Bodies in the Boatyard

Book #2

THE CREW

MOLLIE MCGHIE—When she isn't investigating murders, Mollie spends her time educating the public about UFOs and alien abduction.

SCOOTER MCGHIE—Mollie's husband. Passionate about boats, he dreams about selling everything and sailing around the world.

MRS. MOTO—Mollie and Scooter's Japanese bobtail cat who has a talent for finding clues.

NANCY AND NED SCHNEIDER—Owners of the Palm Tree Marina.

KATY AND SAM—Nancy and Ned's grandchildren.

PENNY CHADWICK—Runs the local sailing school and boat brokerage.

ALEJANDRA LOPEZ—A young waitress at the Sailor's Corner Cafe.

BEN MORETTI—A wannabe pirate who works at the marina.

CHIEF DALTON AND OFFICER MOORE—Local law enforcement officers.

TIFFANY AND CHAD—Two teenagers who work part-time at Penelope's Sugar Shack and Melvin's Marine Emporium.

ALLIGATOR CHUCK—Mollie and Scooter's neighbor. Owns a local barbecue restaurant.

KEN AND LEILANI CHOI—Young couple living aboard their sailboat in the boatyard. Ken is a marine biologist. Leilani works as a virtual assistant.

NORM AND SUZANNE THOMAS—Norm owns a number of local businesses, including a fishing charter business. Suzanne is a real estate agent.

LIAM THOMAS—Norm's nephew. Works for his uncle's fishing charter business.

XANDER CARLTON—Suzanne's son.

MELVIN ROLLE—Originally from the Bahamas. Owner of the local marine store and a fishing charter business. Mollie and Scooter's neighbor.

DARREN ROLLE—Melvin's nephew. Works for his uncle's fishing charter business.

SIMON—Does volunteer work with Mollie investigating UFOs and alien abduction.

CONNIE AND FIONA—Do volunteer work to protect sea turtles and other marine wildlife.

MABEL—Does volunteer work at sea turtle sanctuary.

HANK AND VIOLET—Snowbirds looking to buy a home in Coconut Cove.

ALAN—Aspiring photojournalist.

CHAPTER 1
MR. OBLIVIOUS

WHAT WOULD YOU DO IF your husband announced over a romantic Valentine's Day dinner that the two of you were going to sell the house, do some extreme downsizing, get rid of all your belongings—including your beloved collection of boots—and move onto a dilapidated sailboat? Would you:

(a) see about arranging for a little "accident" that causes the boat to sink;

(b) suggest downsizing his comic book collection and watch him have a panic attack;

(c) roll your eyes—this isn't the first harebrained scheme your husband has come up with; or

(d) skip the rest of the main course and crack open the gift-wrapped box of chocolates sitting next to you?

I have to confess, it wasn't the first time that (a) had crossed my mind. Ever since Scooter had presented me with a sailboat named *Marjorie Jane* a few months ago for our tenth anniversary, I had been trying to figure out how to get rid of her. She was run down, in need of serious repairs, and was costing us a ton of money. Sometimes I even thought my husband paid more attention to her than to me. But before I resorted to something so drastic, I would need to check our insurance policy and see if we'd be covered if she "mysteriously" sank.

Scooter had an unnatural attachment to his comic books, so (b) was seeming like a real possibility. It would probably put downsizing into perspective if he realized he'd have to give up Batman, Superman, Spider-Man, and Cotton-Candy Man. Okay, I totally made that last one up, but could you imagine how awesome his superhero getup would be? Some sort of fluffy pink wig and a cape made out of white crepe paper. I could just picture him stopping criminals in their tracks by wrapping them in sugary strands of cotton candy while shouting out his trademark line, "I'm going to fluff you up, man!"

I definitely did a bit of (c). Harebrained schemes are par for the course when it comes to Scooter. Like the time he thought building a carport out of straw bales and Popsicle sticks was a good idea. I don't think I'd ever rolled my eyes so much before.

I seriously thought about (d), but my mother had always told me to finish my dinner before I had dessert. Hey, stop laughing out there. Yes, I know I have an unnatural love of chocolate and other sugary treats, but I can show some restraint at times. Like in this case, where I was perfectly happy to finish eating my greasy french fries before opening the box of chocolates.

I nibbled on a few fries while I thought about how to respond to Scooter's announcement.

"Why are you rolling your eyes, Mollie?" he asked while he tried to steal some food off my plate.

I batted his hand away. "Eat your own, mister." I put my arm in front of my dish to act as a defensive barrier. "Why am I rolling my eyes?" I asked. "You casually mention that you want to sell our cute cottage on the beach and move onto *Marjorie Jane*. Did you really think I'd be okay with that?"

Scooter furrowed his brow. "But we've talked about this before."

"No, *you've* talked about wanting to sell the house and sail around the world, but I never said I was on board with the idea."

"Hang on, I don't understand. Just the other day I mentioned getting a real estate agent out to look at the cottage."

"Was I even in the room at the time?"

"What do you mean? Of course you were." He chewed on his lip. "At least, I think you were."

"Sometimes you have entire conversations with people, but it turns out they happen only in your head." I sighed. "I know, you can't help it. That's what I get for marrying one of those introverted, nerdy computer types. You might have a high IQ, but your EQ could use some work."

"EQ?"

"Emotional intelligence. You know, being able to read and understand emotions." He looked perplexed. I squeezed his hand and smiled. "I guess that's why people call you Mr. Oblivious."

He frowned. "Mr. Oblivious? Who calls me that?"

I busied myself putting more ketchup on my plate. When I glanced at Scooter, he was staring at me and drumming his fingers on the picnic table.

"Well?" he asked.

I pointed over at the public docks, where commercial boats tied up to offload their catch, pick up and drop off charter passengers, and wash down their decks. "Hey, a couple of fishing boats are coming in."

"Don't try to change the subject. Now, 'fess up. Who calls me that?"

"Well...Mrs. Moto does."

He snorted. "Mrs. Moto is a cat. She can't talk."

"Of course she can talk. Don't you hear her meowing when you forget to fill up her food bowl? She's saying, 'Hey, Mr. Oblivious, I'm hungry. Snap to it.'"

"I feed her all the time, yet she always seems to be hungry." He smiled. "She even dragged her bowl into the center of the kitchen the other day to get her point across."

Despite his objections to adopting the calico Japanese bobtail a few months ago, I think he'd become rather fond of her, which was probably due to the fact that she had black markings on her face that resembled eyeglasses. Since Scooter was as blind as a bat without his glasses, I suspect he liked seeing someone else always "wearing" a pair as well.

He leaned across the table. "I think *you're* the one who calls me Mr. Oblivious."

I shrugged. "Maybe, but with good reason." I took a sip of my soda. "I mean, come on, buying a boat for our anniversary, knowing that I had never even been on one before—unless you count the log ride at Disney World."

"But you love *Marjorie Jane* now, don't you?"

"Love's a strong word. I love Mrs. Moto and I love you." I untied the red ribbon from the heart-shaped box and peeked inside. "And, of course, I love chocolate."

"Aren't you going to eat the rest of your fish first?"

"Nah, let's take that home for Mrs. Moto. She'll be starving by the time we get back."

I popped one of the chocolates into my mouth. "Mmm... delicious." Scooter stared at me with those dark-brown puppy-dog eyes of his that I have trouble resisting. I pushed the box toward him. "Go on, you can have *one*, provided you agree that we're *not* selling the cottage and that I'm *not* giving up my collection of boots."

Scooter started to take one of the chocolates out. I pulled the box back toward me. "Promise first."

"Okay, I promise," he said, snatching it back and quickly grabbing a cherry-filled one. "But I still don't understand why you have all those boots. We've been living in Florida for almost a year. The only thing I see on your feet lately are flip-flops."

"You never know, it might snow here. You know what they say about climate change."

Scooter laughed. "I'll remind you about that the next time you're complaining about being too hot."

"See, another reason why we shouldn't sell the cottage—air conditioning. All *Marjorie Jane* has going for her is some really disgusting mold growing on her deck."

"Pass me a coconut-filled one," Scooter said. "It seems appropriate, since we live in Coconut Cove."

"No problem. You can have them all." Scooter's eyes lit up. "No, not all the chocolates, just the gross ones. I still can't believe they couldn't come up with a more original name for this town."

"I don't know, the tourists like the name. Plus, it kind of fits, considering how many accidents there are each year with coconuts falling down and injuring people."

I shuddered. "Let's not talk about that. It reminds me of how I was attacked after we first got *Marjorie Jane*. I still can't believe everyone thought it was just a coconut that fell off a tree and hit me on the head."

Scooter slid off his bench and sat next to me on mine. He pushed a lock of my frizzy mousy-brown hair behind my ear, then kissed me on my forehead. "I'd be happy to never talk about that again or the fact that you were almost killed. Swear to me you won't get mixed up investigating any more murders."

"Coconut Cove is a small town. What are the chances that anyone else would get murdered here?"

Scooter put his arm around my shoulders, and we snuggled while watching the moonlight dancing on the water. We had decided to have a low-key Valentine's Day celebration with our picnic of fish-and-chips in the waterfront park. From our vantage point, I could just about make out the mooring field, with boats bobbing gently up and down in the water, and the Palm Tree Marina, where our sailboat was berthed.

Despite the fact that *Marjorie Jane* and I weren't exactly BFFs, I did enjoy watching other boats out on the water and when they came into port. *The Codfather*, a large blue charter fishing boat, had tied up at the dock a few minutes earlier.

A lanky young guy with short red hair and a sunburn to match was busy carrying a cooler over to a fish-processing station, while an older man wearing a floppy hat and long-sleeved shirt helped two couples disembark. One of the women seemed grateful to be on land again.

"Liam, do you mind getting Lisa's backpack from the boat?" the older man asked, his nasal voice ringing out across the waterfront. "She's not feeling well."

"Sure thing, Uncle Norm," he replied.

As he walked back toward *The Codfather*, another charter boat, *Nassau Royale*, inched into the slip next to theirs. It was captained by a short, wiry black man with dark-gray hair. "Hey, Liam, do us a favor and take that line from Darren," he yelled out, pointing to the bow of his boat. His accent reminded me of past vacations in the islands. A young man with dreadlocks, who appeared to be the same age as Liam, was poised to toss the line down to the dock.

Liam scowled. He leaned over the side of his boat, grabbed the backpack off one of the bench seats, then walked up the dock, ignoring the cries from *Nassau Royale*.

The captain shook his head in disbelief. "What is wrong with that boy?"

"Don't worry, I've got it," Darren said. He jumped off the boat, quickly tied the bow line to the cleat on the dock, and secured the stern.

The older man handed him some gear. "Looks like Liam's uncle's bad habits are rubbing off on him. No respect for his elders. No nephew of mine would have an attitude like that. Isn't that right?"

Darren smiled. "Of course not, Uncle Melvin."

"I can't believe he treated you like that. You two are supposed to be friends."

Darren shrugged. "We are, I guess."

"I imagine things have changed since you were in high school." Melvin wiped his brow with a towel. "Help an old man down," he said. Darren pulled the side of the boat closer while his uncle stepped onto the dock.

I nudged Scooter. "Did you hear him call the older man 'Uncle Melvin?'" I whispered. "Do you think he's the same Melvin who runs your favorite store, Melvin's Marine Emporium?"

"Hmm. Could be. Which reminds me, I heard they're having a sale."

"Shush, I want to hear what they're saying."

Scooter poked me in the ribs. "No, you just don't want to talk about spending money on boat equipment."

We watched as Melvin walked to the end of the dock. He pointed at Norm chatting with the two couples. "If he thinks he's going to be the only charter business in town, he's got another thing coming," he said to Darren. "Especially after this morning when he poached *our* customers, getting them to go out on *his* boat instead of ours. He's been trying to sabotage my business ever since I got back from the Bahamas." He rubbed his temples. "It was foolish for us to go out fishing today without any paying customers. We barely caught anything. Think of all that money we spent on diesel. It would have been easier just to pour it down the drain."

"Don't be like that," Darren said. "You needed a break from everything. Besides, it was nice to spend time with my favorite uncle."

The older man smiled. "You're just saying that so you don't have to wash down the boat." He wagged his finger. "But you're still going to."

Norm and Liam waved goodbye to the two couples, handing them a bag full of cleaned and filleted fish. As they made their way back to *The Codfather*, Norm elbowed Melvin in the stomach. Melvin seized him by the arm and shoved him backward, knocking the hat off his head into the water. Norm pulled his arm away and made a fist. His nephew gripped him by the shoulder.

"It's not worth it," Liam said. He pointed over at where Scooter and I were sitting. "Especially with witnesses."

Norm cupped his hand to his mouth and yelled, "Are you enjoying the show? Should I get you some popcorn? How about a couple of drinks?"

I started to hold up my empty soda can, when Scooter snatched it out of my hand. "Knock it off," he whispered. "Don't make him angrier."

After looking at us with daggers in his eyes for a moment, he turned back to Melvin. "I've told you once, and I'll tell you again— don't mess with me or my family. There's only room in this town for one fishing charter business, and it's mine!"

CHAPTER 2
THAT SINKING FEELING

"WE'RE ALMOST THERE," I SAID to the ball of fur perched on my shoulder and meowing loudly into my ear. Scooter turned into the parking lot of the Palm Tree Marina and pulled into a shady spot. I clipped Mrs. Moto's leash onto her harness, opened the car door, and set her gently on the ground. She ran toward the path that led down to the marina, pulling me along with her. You might not think a cat could drag a human behind them, but they're surprisingly strong when single-mindedly focused on their destination or chasing a lizard.

"She's a real marina cat, isn't she?" Scooter asked. "She loves poking around the docks, jumping on boats, chasing seagulls, and begging for treats from the tourists." He nudged me. "I think she'd vote for selling the cottage and moving onto *Marjorie Jane*. If she could talk, that is." The calico twined herself around his legs and made a chirping noise.

I stifled a laugh. "Allow me to translate. She said that she has no intention of downsizing her collection of catnip mice and giving up her air-conditioned house. That makes two against— and only one for—selling the cottage."

Scooter pushed his tortoiseshell glasses up his nose and

glanced down at the leash twisted around his feet. "You women always stick together, don't you?"

After he untangled himself, we walked across the patio, nodding at people sipping on their coffees and enjoying the morning before it became too hot later in the day. Before we'd left for the marina, my husband had thoughtfully made me a mocha with a double shot of espresso, which would keep me going until lunchtime.

Scooter had a lot on his plate lately with work, and as a result, we hadn't been down to see the boat for over a week. This meant that there was some serious boat withdrawal going on—on his part, not mine.

I don't know if you've ever seen someone suffer from this affliction. It's not pretty, trust me. He had given up his beloved Froot Loops and had started eating Cap'n Crunch cereal practically nonstop to lift his nautical spirits. And I had caught him watching sailing videos on his laptop at two o'clock in the morning the other night while he and Mrs. Moto shared a bowl of cereal. He'd take a spoonful, then wait while she lapped up some milk. When I expressed surprise that he was eating from the same dish as the cat, he shrugged and said, "I didn't think she'd mind."

I don't know what was worse—that he had eaten an entire box of Cap'n Crunch in one sitting and would be complaining about a tummy ache the next day or that the YouTube vloggers were so impossibly young and good-looking. Seriously, who looks that gorgeous after they've been on a boat all day? No one, that's who. You inevitably end up with grease stains on your clothes, scrapes, bruises, and sweat dripping everywhere. If anyone tells you that sailing is a glamorous lifestyle, they've clearly never been on a boat. Sadly, I'd become all too well acquainted with the reality of boats over the past few months.

After spending a few minutes standing on the boardwalk and watching the tourists strolling on the beach, Mrs. Moto insisted that we remove her harness and leash. Before we'd adopted her, she had lived on a boat at the marina and had free run of the place. While she reluctantly accepted being restrained elsewhere, she refused to put up with our nonsense here.

She scurried away ahead of us toward B Dock, where we kept *Marjorie Jane*, while we trailed behind her. When the dilapidated sailboat came into sight, my husband let go of my hand, rushed past Mrs. Moto, and had what amounted to a tearful reunion with the other woman in his life. If he could have hugged her, he would have. But since she was thirty-eight feet long, he couldn't quite get his arms all the way around her.

Personally, I didn't get it. All I saw was red paint flaking off the hull, weather-beaten teak decks, and an old, rusty anchor at the bow. You would have thought that—considering all the money we had spent on her to date—she would have looked a lot better by now.

As I was thinking about our latest credit card statement, someone tapped me on the shoulder. "Hey there. I haven't seen you guys in a while." I turned and saw Ben Moretti, a wannabe pirate who lived on a sailboat that rivaled *Marjorie Jane* in the fixer-upper category. "She's sure been missing you," he said, pointing at my nemesis.

"I'd say the feeling is mutual," I said. "At least on Scooter's part. See him fawning over her?"

I tore my eyes away from the scene and looked at Ben. Something was different. Greasy brown hair tied back in a ponytail—check. Ripped khaki shorts—check. Goofy smile—check. Ah, that was it. "New T-shirt?" I asked.

"Yeah. How'd you know?"

"It's clean, and there aren't any holes."

Ben chuckled. "That's true. It's hard to keep things looking brand new when you work in a boatyard. Maybe I should change into something else and save this one for a date."

"Date? Who's the lucky girl?"

Ben gazed down sheepishly at the ground. "No one yet. But there is someone I'm thinking of asking out."

"Well, you might want to think about a different shirt before you do. I'm not sure one that says 'Pirates get all the booty' next to a picture of a scantily clad girl is the way to go."

He glanced down at his shirt and frowned. "Hmm...I hadn't thought about that."

Scooter looked over at Ben. "Just the person I wanted to see! I was over at Melvin's the other day, and I saw they had a sale on tung oil varnish. I wanted to get your thoughts on whether you think that's the right way to go."

While the two of them debated the pros and cons of synthetic wood finishes, I stifled a yawn and kicked my flip-flops off. The last time I had tried to get on the boat wearing them, one of them had fallen off into the water, and I had to scramble to get it out before it drifted out into the bay.

"I'm going to open the hatches up and air this place out," I said. I climbed up onto the boat, adding a new bruise to the collection on my shin. Mrs. Moto executed a graceful leap on board, then stretched out on a tattered cushion in the cockpit. I gave her a quick scratch behind her ears before unlocking the boat.

I cautiously made my way down the narrow ladder into the cabin below and stepped onto the floor, straight into a puddle. This was not good. While I didn't know a lot about boats, I did know one thing—water belonged on the outside of the boat, not the inside.

After turning on the overhead light to see exactly what was going on, I ended up sliding on the floor and landing on my butt with a thud. *Great, now it wasn't just my feet that were wet.*

I ran my fingers through my hair, which I realized was probably a stupid thing to do—who knew what was in that puddle?—and assessed the situation.

There was at least three inches of water above the floorboards. Or maybe it was three centimeters. My mom and I were planning a trip to Canada, and I'd been trying to get the hang of the metric system, but I had to admit that it wasn't going all that well. In any event, there was water everywhere, which wasn't good, no matter what units of measurement you used. Thankfully, she was on a trip in Europe for the next few weeks and didn't know how to use her cell phone over there. Otherwise, she'd have been texting me constantly during the day, as she usually did, so I was glad I didn't have to explain the latest issue with *Marjorie Jane* to her.

As I got to my feet, Mrs. Moto scrambled down the ladder and leaped onto one of the couches. The way she was staring down at the water, it seemed like she expected some fish to swim by any moment now.

I called out to Scooter. "You'd better get down here. We've got a problem." I put my purse on the galley counter, grabbed a dish towel, and wiped my hands.

"I'll be down in a minute, my little panda bear."

I glanced at the water again. "I'm not sure we have a minute."

The boat rocked back and forth in her slip as Scooter climbed aboard. He poked his head down the companionway. "What's going on?"

I pointed at the floor. Scooter gasped, uttered a few curse words that would have made any salty sailor proud, and scrambled down the ladder, splashing water onto Mrs. Moto. She did not seem amused.

"Ben, get down here!" Scooter yelled. "Now!" He put his head between his hands and whimpered.

"Here, sit down next to Mrs. Moto," I said as I led him to the couch. I reached into my purse and pulled out a pack of M&M'S. Scooter doesn't deal well when things get dicey. I've found that having an emergency stash of chocolate comes in handy in circumstances like these. He popped several pieces into his mouth while Ben made his way aboard.

"That's not good," Ben said. He leaned down and flipped a switch on the wall near the galley. "I wonder why the bilge pump isn't coming on."

Scooter crumpled up the empty bag in his hand and looked at Ben with a worried expression. "It isn't?"

Ben fiddled with the switch. "Nope, it isn't. I guess it's one more thing to add to your to-do list."

"Is the boat going to sink?" Scooter asked. He wrapped his arms around himself and rocked back and forth while Ben pulled up an access panel on the floorboards, peered into the bilge, and examined the pump.

"Well, the water doesn't seem to be rising, so that's a good sign." Ben ducked into the passageway and opened up the engine compartment. "It doesn't look like the water has gotten into here, which is a plus."

Scooter held up the empty M&M'S bag with a pleading

expression in his eyes.

"Sorry, I'm out of chocolate," I said, squeezing his shoulder.

Ben walked back into the main cabin. "Maybe your water tanks are leaking. Or maybe it's because of those heavy storms we had last week. Water could be coming in through the deck." He glanced down at the floor. "Tell you what—why don't you taste the water? If it's salty, then you'll know it's coming in from outside the boat. If it's fresh, then you'll know it's not."

Scooter cocked his head at me.

I shook my head. "You've got to be kidding. I'm not going to do that. You do it."

"No way," he said. "Not after I ate all that chocolate." He turned his gaze to Ben.

Ben shrugged, bent down, and stuck his finger in the water. He put it in his mouth. "Can't really tell. Listen, you were saying you needed to do work on the bottom. Why don't you just get the boat hauled out now and take her into the boatyard? That way you can find out for sure what's causing the leak. Give the office a call and see if the Travelift is free. Just make sure you tell them it's an emergency."

"What exactly is a Travelift?" I asked.

"It's a big blue crane-like thing with straps." He paused and rubbed his chin. "I'm really not sure how to describe it. Basically, it lifts boats out of the water and moves them around on land."

"Sounds weird," I said.

"Well, you'll see it soon enough," Ben said.

Scooter got out his phone and had a quick conversation. "Okay, they can pull us out now," he said.

Ben clapped his hands together. "Good. Let's get this baby fired up."

As he and Scooter tried to start the engine, I began to feel pangs of guilt. What if I were responsible for the leak aboard *Marjorie Jane*? After all, just last night I had been thinking about different ways to get rid of her, including having her spring a leak and sink to the bottom of the sea. Did some vindictive mermaids use their ESP to read my thoughts? Did they decide to teach me a lesson by convincing a shark to chew a hole in *Marjorie Jane*'s hull? But, more importantly, would our insurance company pay up if she sank before we could haul her out?

* * *

Thankfully, *Marjorie Jane*'s engine sputtered to life. We hadn't fired up the boat since we'd bought her a few months ago. Come to think of it, there were a lot of things we hadn't done since we'd bought the boat, like take her out of the slip.

"Okay, here goes nothing," Scooter said as he started to reverse the boat.

"Watch out to your port," Ben said frantically as a wood piling came precariously close. "Put it in neutral, quick!"

I shut my eyes and clutched my hands together. While I didn't see the boat hit the piling, I felt the thud. Mrs. Moto yowled and cowered in my lap.

I breathed a sigh of relief as I heard Ben tell Scooter that it seemed like a minor scrape. *What's one more dent? Marjorie Jane already makes us look like trailer trash at the marina with all the marks on her hull. This one will just blend in with the others*, I thought to myself.

"I guess he's a little rusty," Ben said in an effort to calm my nerves. Or maybe it was to calm his nerves. I wasn't sure.

I rubbed my temples. "I'm not sure a little rusty actually covers it. Completely oxidized would be more like it. I don't know when the last time was that Scooter drove a boat. Certainly not in all the time we've been married, and that's been ten years now."

Ben gulped. "Scooter, want me to take over?"

I watched as Scooter gripped the wheel tightly and stared straight ahead. "No, it's okay. It's a straight shot from here to the haul-out area." I think the last thing he wanted to do was admit to Ben that he was in over his head.

As we passed by other boats, people waved at us and yelled out encouragement. "Finally taking *Marjorie Jane* out for her first sail?" "You're going the wrong way—the open water is that way." "Whoa, that was awfully close." "Hey, watch where you're going! You almost hit my stern!"

"It's a shame the first time you're taking *Marjorie Jane* out is because she has a leak," Ben said. He reached down and playfully batted at Mrs. Moto's cute little rabbit-like tail, which was a hallmark of Japanese bobtails. She was so entranced by the other boats that she didn't even notice.

After we passed the dinghy dock and the fuel dock, a blue fishing boat cut in front of us and slipped into the area where they haul boats out.

"Hey, isn't that *The Codfather* from last night?" I asked. "The captain is one of the guys who got into a fight. Can you believe he just cut right in front of us?"

"I'm busy trying to steer the boat," Scooter said. "I can't check to see who that is. But whoever it is, that was a really crappy thing to do."

Ben leaned forward to get a closer look. "Yeah, that's Norm Thomas's boat. It doesn't surprise me in the least. He's such a jerk."

"I recognize him too," I said, pointing at a young sunburned guy with short red hair who was standing on the dock. "He was there last night. Norm is his uncle."

"Yeah, I know him as well. We went to high school together." Ben walked out to the bow and yelled down at Liam. "Hey, man, what's going on? These folks arranged for an emergency haul-out. Tell your uncle he has to wait his turn."

The redhead sneered. "First come, first served." He glanced at *Marjorie Jane* dubiously. "I'm surprised that thing is even floating. I still can't believe anyone would be suckered into buying this excuse for a sailboat."

Scooter looked like steam was coming out of his ears. He gripped the steering wheel so tightly that I thought he might bend the metal. "She's a great boat, bud," he snapped. "She just needs a little TLC. Now get that other boat out of the way, so we can get hauled out before we sink!"

Liam laughed. "Nah, you can wait. That's what bilge pumps are for. Besides, we're running a business. Time is money, you know."

He sauntered over to *The Codfather* and had a few words with his uncle, pointing back at us occasionally. Then he walked over to the Travelift operator and handed him something.

"What was that?" I asked. "Did he just bribe him?"

Ben shook his head. "Nah, I don't think it was a bribe, just a tip. Lots of folks tip those of us who work at the marina." He grinned. "I know I sure like it when it happens. Keeps me in beer."

"Ben, what are we going to do here?" Scooter asked anxiously.

"Hang on a bit. Let me go check down below." After a few minutes, Ben popped his head back up. "It looks okay. The water doesn't seem to be rising. Why don't we tie her off here and wait for them to come haul you out when they're done with Norm's boat?"

"Wait? Why should we have to wait?" I asked. "That Norm guy is really getting on my nerves."

"Well, don't take it personally," Ben said. "He treats everyone that way. He thinks that because he's a successful businessman, he's in charge of the town."

"Can you really make that much money from running a fishing charter business?" Scooter asked. I was relieved to notice that his grip on the wheel had loosened slightly.

"Oh, that's just one of four charter boats he owns. Plus, he has his finger in a lot of other pies in town. That guy is ambitious. If he had his way, he'd own everything in Coconut Cove."

While Ben and I got *Marjorie Jane* tied off, I thought about how Norm had threatened to drive Melvin out of business the previous night. Exactly how far would he go?

* * *

As I walked across the patio, a group of kids tore past me. One of the girls glanced back as she reached the top of the steps, which led down to the beach. "Hi, Miss Mollie! Where's Mrs. Moto?"

"She's on the boat," I said. "I'll tell her you said hi, Katy."

"Can I come visit her later?"

"Of course, anytime." I looked over at the marina office. "But maybe we should keep that between you and me. You know how your grandmother feels about cats."

She giggled and raced down the stairs to catch up with her friends.

I watched as the sailing instructor, Penny Chadwick,

attempted to corral them. "All right, kids, settle down," she yelled with an adorable Texan twang in her voice. The kids bounced up and down while she briefed them on the morning's activities.

My weekly ladies' sailing lessons with Penny were very different—less youthful exuberance and more complaints about muscle aches and knee replacements. Having only recently celebrated my fortieth birthday, my joints were still working adequately, but *Marjorie Jane* seemed to be trying her best to change that. Crawling in and out of confined spaces to fix things and doing yoga-like moves getting on and off the boat were starting to take their toll.

Although we might not have showed it in the same way, I think we had as much fun as the children did. It really was exhilarating to take Penny's boat out into the bay and feel the wind in her sails. While I wasn't very fond of *Marjorie Jane*, I had learned to appreciate the joy of sailing over the past few months.

I took a deep breath and summoned up my courage to face Katy's grandmother. Nancy Schneider and her husband, Ned, owned and managed the marina. They were close to retirement age, but they loved running their own business too much to consider selling it.

While Nancy oversaw day-to-day operations with an iron fist, Ned was more easygoing, the type of guy who couldn't even hurt a fly. Not that flies would get anywhere close to the marina office these days—word had gotten out about Nancy's exceptional talents when it came to wielding a flyswatter.

As I opened the screen door to the office, I saw a sign stuck in the middle of the carefully manicured flower bed that read "Gone Fishing with Norm's Charters." I reached over and spun it around to face the wall. Yes, it was a bit petty, but I should get some credit for not ripping it out of the ground and hurling it in the trash.

"Why is that door ajar? Are you coming in or out?" a shrill voice yelled from inside.

I stepped inside and quickly shut the door behind me. Nancy peered at me over her reading glasses. The look in her intense blue eyes caused me to stop slouching and stand at attention.

"Yes, what can I do for you, Mollie?" She tapped her long,

exquisitely manicured fingernails on the counter. I think she liked the slight intimidation factor her nails had on people. I'd seen large men cower when she jabbed her talons in their direction to emphasize her point. "You haven't jammed quarters in the washing machine, too, have you?" she asked.

"Huh? I have a perfectly good machine at home. Why would I need to do laundry here?" I asked. I felt guilty despite the fact that I hadn't done anything wrong.

A young woman approached the counter. "Nancy, for the last time, I'm really sorry." She tucked her long glossy black hair behind her ears and straightened her shoulders. "But it wasn't my fault that someone gave me a Bahamian quarter. They're the same size. How was I supposed to know it would mess everything up?"

"Well, dear, if it were me, I would look at the coins *before* I put them in the washing machine." She pursed her lips, then added, "But that's just me. I'm sure Mollie would agree, wouldn't you?" I reluctantly nodded. I really didn't want to get caught in a squabble over foreign coins. "You know Leilani, don't you?" Nancy asked.

The woman's glittering necklace caught my eye. "Yes. I've seen you around the marina. You're Mrs. Diamond," I said.

She cocked her head to one side. "No, it's Mrs. Choi, actually. But it feels weird when someone calls me that. I always think they're referring to my mother-in-law instead. Just call me Leilani." She smiled. "I'd shake your hand, but...well..." She held up her right arm, which was encased in a cast that extended above her elbow.

"Ouch. How did that happen?"

Leilani grimaced. "I fell off the ladder trying to get on our boat. Fortunately, I only broke the one arm, but my other one still got pretty banged up." She certainly did have a lot of bruises on her wrist.

I thought about getting on and off *Marjorie Jane* at the dock. Sure, it was a pain, but I wasn't convinced that a ladder would help. When I asked Leilani about it, she smiled.

"No, we've got a ladder because we're on the hard," she said.

"I know what you mean. I'm flabbergasted at how much it costs to have a boat. It seems like everyone is hard up at the marina." I furrowed my brow. "Although I'm not sure how a ladder would help when it comes to paying the credit card bills. Unless, of course, you're talking about climbing the corporate ladder." I shuddered as I remembered my days working as a temp in cubicles for big companies. The thought of spreadsheets, dress codes, and only getting thirty minutes for lunch was enough to make me break out in a cold sweat.

Leilani laughed. "No, we're not hard up," she said. "Our boat is out of the water and on the hard in the boatyard." I didn't have a clue what she was talking about, and I guess my expression must have given me away because she added, "You know how the boats are propped up on jack stands?" I shook my head. "You know the metal stands they place around a boat's keel to keep it from toppling over?"

Nancy gave a dry chuckle. "You'll have to excuse Mollie. She's new to boats."

"Well, there's no way you can get on a boat without a ladder or steps of some kind," Leilani said. "We're on a catamaran, so we don't have as far to climb. Only about five feet, but I'm living proof that you can still do a lot of damage from that distance. Some of the other boats in the boatyard have a ten-foot drop."

"The boatyard can be a dangerous place," Nancy said. She pointed at a series of binders on a shelf behind the counter. "That's why we have so many safety rules and regulations in place. People complain about them. I don't know why they don't realize that they're for their own good."

"Nancy, it wasn't a safety issue. It was pure clumsiness on my part. A dog barked and it startled me. I lost my grip, and well...you know what happened next." Nancy's eyes narrowed. "I'd better go get my clothes out of the dryer," Leilani said hastily.

"That's probably a good idea, dear," Nancy said.

"By the way, who's Mrs. Diamond?" Leilani asked me as she reached out to open the door.

"Oh, that's you. At least, that's what I used to call you, on account of your diamond necklace. I saw your husband give it to you over a romantic dinner at Chez Poisson a few months ago. We were sitting a couple of tables away."

The young woman smiled. "Oh, that was such a magical night. Ken really outdid himself with my birthday present this year." I put my fingers to my own necklace—a lighthouse pendant with a small diamond representing its beacon. Scooter had outdone himself as well when he'd given it to me as a belated anniversary gift. Far better than any dilapidated sailboat.

"Enough talk about jewelry," Nancy snapped. Leilani slipped out the door while I turned back to the counter. "Why exactly are you here?" she demanded.

"It's about our emergency haul-out," I said. "What happened? Scooter called, told you about the leak, and arranged to get lifted out of the water and taken to the boatyard. But when we got there, Norm cut in front of us, and they hauled him out instead."

Nancy seemed puzzled. "What emergency haul-out? This is the first I'm hearing about it. I'm in charge of the schedule and any exceptions."

"But Scooter said he talked to you."

"Are you saying I forgot a conversation with your husband?"

"It doesn't really matter. The important thing is to get *Marjorie Jane* out of the water before she sinks. Now, when can we—"

The door swung open and Ned rushed in, dripping wet. "Mollie, there you are," he said, gasping for breath. "I'm so sorry about what happened. It's all my fault. I was heading down to tell the guys at the Travelift about your emergency when I tripped and fell in the water." He pulled a cell phone out of his pocket. "I tried to call, but I'm afraid this didn't survive."

"What were you doing making haul-out arrangements?" Nancy asked.

"The phone rang. You were in the back," Ned said as he wrung out his shirt.

"Are you okay?" I asked.

"I think so," he said. "Probably just a few bruises and scrapes."

Nancy reached under the counter and pulled out a rag. "Here, wipe yourself off," she said gruffly. "Then you should go upstairs and change out of those clothes."

As Ned tried to get water out of his ear, Nancy made a call to the Travelift crew. "Okay, they can haul you out in about a half hour. You're lucky. We only have one spot left in the boatyard." She handed me a form and a pen. "Fill this out."

"Can't this wait, Nancy?" I asked. "I really want to go back and give Scooter an update."

"It will just take a minute." She eyed Ned. "If this had been filled out before someone arranged for an emergency haul-out, you wouldn't be in this situation."

Ned threw the rag on the counter. "You and your organization, Nancy. I'm getting sick to death of it." He stormed out of the office, the screen door slamming behind him, leaving me wondering what had happened to the normally mild-mannered Ned.

* * *

"Are you sure those straps are strong enough to hold *Marjorie Jane*?" I asked. "She must weigh a ton."

"Eleven and three-quarters, to be exact," Scooter said.

"You're such a nerd."

My dorky husband smiled as he cleaned his glasses with a cloth. "You didn't seem to complain when we won fifty dollars at that pub trivia contest. And all because I knew that *Isotelus trilobite* is Ohio's official state fossil."

I shrugged. "Okay, so it comes in handy from time to time." I watched as the operator, who was sitting in a cab attached to the side of the large marine hoist, pulled on some levers. *Marjorie Jane* slowly rose out of the water, then dangled in the middle of a large metal frame. "But seriously, what would happen if the straps did break?"

Scooter ran his fingers through his hair. "I don't even want to think about it. We've had enough bad luck today." He looked around. "Where's Mrs. Moto?"

"Ben's got her. He'll meet us in the boatyard."

The operator reversed the Travelift, backing onto a concrete pad. He hopped out of the cab and grabbed a power washer. "This is going to take a while," he said. "See all these barnacles? When's the last time you cleaned the bottom?"

"We just bought her a few months ago. This will be the first time we've done it," Scooter said.

After quite a bit of blasting with water and scraping by hand, the operator stepped back and surveyed his work. "That'll have to do. Looks like you've got a lot of work ahead of you. Most of the bottom paint is gone, and these might be blisters here." He chuckled. "Reckon you'll be spending a long time in the boatyard."

Before he climbed back into the cab, I collared him. "Exactly what happened earlier with *The Codfather*?"

"Whaddya mean?"

"Norm pulled in front of us. We told his nephew that we had a leak and needed to get hauled out, but he acted like he couldn't care less. Didn't you hear us yelling at you that we had an emergency? Then right after that, Liam had a few words with you, maybe slipped you a little something, and next thing you know, they're getting hauled out and not us."

He pulled his arm away. "Listen, lady. I don't know what you're implying, but it was a scheduling snafu. Take it up with Nancy."

"Just let it go," Scooter said. "Come on, let's walk behind and make sure nothing happens." We watched as the Travelift slowly made its way down the road, *Marjorie Jane* swaying gently in the slings as the operator turned into the boatyard.

There were around twenty boats arranged in a U shape around a workshop in the center, all propped up with metal stands and wooden blocks. It looked precarious, to say the least. One stiff breeze coming through this place and I could imagine them all toppling over like dominoes.

My heart sank when I realized the Travelift was headed toward the only empty space in the yard, right between a catamaran named *Mana Kai* and my archenemy, *The Codfather*. After the operator and his assistant positioned *Marjorie Jane* in her spot and propped her up off the ground on jack stands, they unfastened the straps and left us to our own devices.

"Hey, you're that broad who believes in little green men, aren't you?" a nasally voice called out. I glanced up and saw Norm leaning over the side of his boat holding a beer can. "What's the name of your boat, *ET*?" The obnoxious man snickered at his own joke, took a big swig, then burped loudly. He pointed at Scooter. "Want one?" he asked, holding up his can.

"No, I'm good," Scooter said. "Besides, we've got a lot of work to do."

Norm guffawed. "You can say that again. *ET* doesn't look like she'll be flying off into outer space anytime soon."

"Her name isn't *ET*," I said indignantly. "It's *Marjorie Jane*. And she's a fine boat." No one was allowed to say disparaging things about our boat except me.

"How would you know? Women don't have any place on boats. They're bad luck." He added with a smirk, "Unless, of course, they're paying customers. But that's where I draw the line. Women certainly shouldn't be in the boatyard. They don't have a clue about how to fix anything on a boat."

"I have just as much right to be on this boat as my husband does. And I can fix anything that he can."

"Oh yeah? Are you going to be the one who paints the bottom?" he asked doubtfully.

"I am. It's my project."

Scooter's mouth fell open. I had been doing my best to avoid boat projects ever since we'd got this wreck. Now here I was volunteering to lead one. I stepped back and stared at *Marjorie Jane*. I had never seen her out of the water before. The bottom half looked massive. I hadn't painted anything since kindergarten, and that was with finger paints. How in the world was I going to manage this?

"Hah, I don't think you'll last two hours." Norm crushed his empty beer can with one hand, then tossed it on the ground. "Make that two minutes."

"Well, I will. You'll see."

"Want to make a little wager?"

Scooter whispered in my ear, "That's enough, Mollie, you've made your point."

I put my fingers on his lips to shush him, then turned back to Norm. "Sure," I said. "If I paint this bottom, then you have to name your boat *ET*."

"You're on. And if you lose, you have to paint the bottom of my boat."

"Deal."

Norm grinned. "See those paint cans down there under my boat? You'll need those when you lose." He pulled his phone out of his pocket. "Guess I'll call Liam and tell him he can cross the bottom paint job off his list."

"That's one guy you don't want to make angry," a voice said behind us. I turned and saw Leilani struggling to carry a laundry bag with one hand.

"Here, let me help you with that," Scooter said. He took the bag from her. "Where to?"

"Right here," she said, pointing at the catamaran. "Looks like we're neighbors. Did I hear that right? You made a bet with Norm about bottom painting?"

I put my head in my hands. "I guess so. Sometimes I'm a little..."

"Impulsive?" Scooter suggested gently. He glanced at Leilani and smiled. "Sometimes it gets her in trouble, but it is one of her best qualities. It's probably why we have so much fun together."

I walked over and picked up a paint can. "These are heavy."

"Twenty-three pounds, to be exact," Scooter said. "The anti-fouling chemicals they add to the paint to keep stuff from growing on the bottom add about nine pounds. So a can of that is much heavier than your average house paint."

"You're just hoping that will come up in a trivia contest, aren't you?" I asked with a smile.

"Not only are they heavy, they're also expensive," Leilani said. "They're having a sale at Melvin's right now. You might want to get some before the price goes back up."

"Why don't I take this bag up onto your boat? It's going to be hard enough for you to climb up with that cast as it is," Scooter offered.

"Oh, you don't need to worry about that. I see my husband over there. He can take care of it." I looked over and saw a young man with dark hair carrying a briefcase. "He just got back from giving a lecture about sea turtle nesting patterns at the community college." She looked at him proudly. "Ken's a marine biologist. We met right after he finished his PhD." She waved at him with her good arm, then frowned. "I wonder what's going on."

Her husband had set his briefcase on the ground and was standing stiffly while a young man with dreadlocks gripped his shoulder and whispered something in his ear.

"Hey, isn't that one of the guys from last night?" I asked Scooter.

"Yeah, I think so."

"Do you know Darren?" Leilani asked.

"No, we haven't been formally introduced," I said.

"He's normally a nice guy. I'm not sure what's gotten into him," she said. She watched anxiously as Darren jabbed her husband in the chest. He gave Ken a mock salute, then walked toward the entrance to the boatyard. Ken clenched his fists, then caught sight of Leilani. He gave her a weak smile before picking up his briefcase and coming to join us.

"What was that about?" Leilani asked after giving him a kiss.

"Nothing," he said.

"It didn't look like nothing."

"Babe, don't worry—" Ken's phone beeped. I watched the color drain from his face as he read a text message. He shoved the phone back into his pocket. "It's nothing," he said with a note of finality.

But I wasn't so sure it was nothing, especially when I spied Darren standing by the workshop, holding his phone, watching Ken, and looking very pleased with himself.

CHAPTER 3
THE DATING GAME

MRS. MOTO PADDED ALONGSIDE ME as we made our way down the boardwalk at the marina. When we neared the stairs that led down to the beach, she stopped, crouched down, and slowly inched toward the top step.

"I bet you want to go and harass those seagulls, don't you?"

She gazed up at me and made a chirping noise.

"Okay, but don't stay too long. Otherwise, you'll miss out on all the bits of hamburgers and hot dogs that people 'accidentally' drop on the ground for you."

She meowed in agreement, then sneaked down the stairs. Both the calico and I looked forward to the potluck and barbecue that the marina hosted every Friday night. Ned and Nancy provided the meat, and everyone else brought a side dish or dessert to share. I walked toward the buffet table, occasionally pausing to chat with some of the friends we'd made since owning *Marjorie Jane*.

"Humph. Store-bought brownies again?" Nancy asked, noticing the distinctive purple box from Penelope's Sugar Shack I was holding. She shook her head and gave me one of her patent-pending tsk-tsk sounds. "You have crumbs on your shirt, dear."

I looked down at my top and saw a chocolate chip precariously balanced on my collar. If there hadn't been any witnesses, I probably would have plucked it off and popped it into my mouth. No point wasting perfectly good chocolate.

Nancy interrupted my thoughts about how to discreetly rescue the chocolate morsel. "How many brownies did you eat on the way to the marina this time?"

"I don't know what you're talking about," I said, brushing the crumbs off my shirt and saying a silent farewell to the chocolate chip as it fell to the ground.

"Last week, Penelope told me you bought two dozen brownies. When I opened the box, there were only twenty inside. That means four were unaccounted for."

"Wow, you've got some impressive math skills, Nancy. Must come in handy when you're counting up all the quarters from the washing machines and dryers." I gave her an appraising look. "How do I know *you* didn't make off with the missing brownies? Everyone knows how much you love chocolate."

"Don't change the subject, dear," she said. As I started to place the box on the table, Nancy pointed at the bowls of pasta salad, coleslaw, and baked beans. "You know the rules. Only side dishes on this table. Desserts go over there. We wouldn't want cross-contamination, would we?"

"As much as I hate to say it, Nancy, I'm on the same page as you when it comes to this. Brownies and vegetables don't go together."

As I put the box on the appropriate table, Nancy said, "For someone who's always bragging about her homemade quadruple-chocolate brownies, you never seem to bring any."

"I just haven't had time to bake lately," I said. "I've been so busy with work since I've been promoted to investigative reporter."

"Ooh, did I hear that right? Are you really a reporter?" Leilani asked as she gingerly set a colorful straw tote bag down at the end of the table.

"It's not what you think, dear," Nancy said. "She doesn't work for a TV station or newspaper. It's with some strange organization. What's it called again, FLAKEOUT?"

I sighed. Although I had become used to people making fun of my career, sometimes their derision was hard to take. "No, it's FAROUT—the Federation for Alien Research, Outreach, and UFO Tracking."

Leilani's eyes lit up. "That sounds fascinating. What kinds of things do you investigate?"

Nancy rolled her eyes. "Why don't you two talk about that somewhere else? I need to get everything organized." She pointed at Leilani's bag. "I assume this is for the potluck?"

Leilani nodded and tried to unzip it with her bruised left hand. "Here, let me," Nancy said. She opened the bag, pulled out a large plastic container, and placed it next to the coleslaw. "How did you manage to carry this down here with just one arm? Why didn't that husband of yours help?" She put her hands on her hips. "I don't know what's with your generation. No sense of chivalry."

Leilani looked down at her cast. "He offered, but I told him I could manage." She pointed over in the direction of the barbecue. "Besides, he's busy helping Ned with the grill." She smiled. "Your hubby is such a sweetheart. I saw him doting on Mrs. Moto earlier. That's something he has in common with Ken—they're both animal lovers."

Nancy pursed her lips. "Well, if Ned knew what was good for him, he'd spend less time with mangy creatures like that cat and more time concentrating on the marina. He was ten minutes late getting the grill set up."

"Relax, Nancy. No one will mind. We're all here to have a good time," I said. "Besides, it's not like there's a firm schedule for these types of things."

"Of course there is." She pulled a small notepad out of the pocket of her neatly pressed Bermuda shorts. "According to this, I'm five minutes behind getting the buffet table set up. Now shoo, and let me get on with it."

Leilani and I managed to keep from bursting out laughing until we were out of earshot. After we stopped giggling, she said, "Now, tell me all about your job."

"I investigate UFO sightings, alien encounters, that sort of thing. You know, we actually had a case of alien abduction here at the marina when we first bought *Marjorie Jane*."

Leilani's eyes lit up. "I heard about that. Wasn't that all part of the mur—"

I spied Scooter from the corner of my eye and interrupted before she could utter the word "murder." My husband gets a little squeamish when it comes to stuff like this. Even the mere mention of homicides, blood, or corpses can drive him headlong into a bag of chocolate.

"Yes, that's the one. Unfortunately, I wasn't able to prove definitively that the abduction took place. I'm also in charge of community outreach." I swallowed. "I actually have to give my first public lecture next week. I'm so nervous. I've never done anything like that before."

Leilani smiled. "You seem so confident to me. I'm sure you'll be great."

Scooter came up behind me and put his hands on my shoulders. "What will you be great at?" he asked.

"My talk next week."

"Of course you'll be great. You've been practicing for days. I only wish I didn't have that conference call scheduled so I could go."

"I wish you could come too," I said. "I could use the moral support."

"I'll go," Leilani offered.

"Perfect. Now you'll have a friendly face in the audience." Scooter pointed at a table. "Come over and join us. Penny is telling me stories about sailing in bad weather, and Alejandra seems to be…well…wishing she weren't the center of attention. She might need our help to change the topic of conversation."

We had become fond of Alejandra Lopez during our time in Coconut Cove. Not only was the young woman our favorite waitress at the Sailor's Corner Cafe but she had also been sharing family recipes with us and giving us cooking tips.

As we walked over to the table, Leilani told me about her job as a virtual assistant. Although the thought of answering emails, updating spreadsheets, and scheduling appointments didn't sound all that appealing, I did like the fact that she didn't have to change out of her pajamas to start work. All she needed was her laptop and an internet connection.

When we got to the table, I saw that Alejandra was surrounded by three young men—Darren was sitting to her right, Liam to her left, and Ben was standing behind her. I noticed that the wannabe pirate had taken my advice and traded in his "booty" T-shirt for one that featured two cute dolphins diving through the water. What girl could resist dolphins?

Liam was leaning back in his chair, his sunburned arms folded behind his head. "Maybe you could teach Ben a thing or two about manicures," he said to Alejandra. "Just look at all that grease on his hands."

"I work for a living, that's why they're greasy," Ben said gruffly, shoving his hands in his pockets.

Liam pulled out his wallet and waved a wad of cash at Ben smugly. "I work for a living too, and I make a lot more money than you do. You haven't changed at all since high school. Still scrounging around, trying to make ends meet." He glanced over at Alejandra, then back at Ben. "And you don't have a clue how to dress to impress the ladies."

Ben's shoulders slumped. He looked down at his shirt, then walked to the other side of the table and sat next to Scooter.

Alejandra gave him a smile. "I think you look great, Ben. Did I ever tell you that dolphins are my favorite animal?"

Ben perked up, but before he could respond, Liam leaned in close to Alejandra. "Did you see my new car? How about you and I take her out for a spin after dinner and go for a moonlight stroll on the beach at Treasure Cove?"

She pulled back. "Sorry, I can't. I told Ned and Nancy I'd help them clean up after the barbecue."

"They don't need your help. Look at them." He pointed at Ned, who was taking hamburgers off the grill and placing them on a big platter that Nancy was holding. "They've got it all under control."

"Leave the girl alone," Darren said, pushing his dreadlocks off his face. "She's not interested." He pulled his chair closer to hers. "I'll stay and help you clean up."

Alejandra shrugged. "Sure, I guess. The more the merrier."

He beamed. "Great. Then you'll be done quicker, and afterward *we* can go out for a stroll."

"Hey, if she's going out with anyone, it'll be with me, not you,"

Liam said.

Alejandra placed her cup on the table. "Stop it! I'm not going out with any of you." She looked firmly at the squabbling duo. "It was bad enough having to put up with you two fighting over me in high school. Aren't you guys ever going to grow up?"

Darren pushed back his chair. He pointed angrily at Liam. "See what you did? We were having a perfectly friendly conversation until you got involved."

Liam rose and advanced toward Darren. "Want to see friendly? What do you say we head down to the beach and talk about this man to man?"

As the two of them lunged toward each other, Scooter pulled Darren back. Ben did the same with the other young man.

"Hey, what's going on here?" Norm strode over to the table. "What did I tell you about getting into fights, Liam? It's bad for business." He gestured at the far side of the patio. "I've got some potential customers lined up over there. What are they going to think if they see their charter boat captain punching some guy's lights out?"

"But—" Liam started to say.

"I don't want to hear your buts. Now, the hamburgers are done," Norm said. "I suggest you go over there, fix yourself a plate, and eat it as far away from here as possible."

Liam looked down at the ground and muttered something. "What was that?" Norm asked.

"Nothing," he spat out, and stormed over to the grill.

Norm turned to Darren. "And you. I should have known *you'd* be involved. You're as bad as your uncle."

"Leave my uncle out of this!"

"Tell that old man to head back to the Bahamas. Things were a lot more peaceful here when he wasn't around."

"Seriously, after all that he's been through, how can you say something like that?" Darren asked, his voice dripping with venom. He grabbed his soda can from the table. "I seem to have lost my appetite." He turned to Alejandra. "Sorry about what happened. I'll make it up to you later."

She nodded. Ben sat down in the chair next to her. "You okay?" he asked.

"I'm fine."

"You know how guys get when there's a pretty girl involved." He reached behind his head and tightened his ponytail. Then he stared at his hands. "Do you really mind the grease? I scrub them after work, but I just can't seem to get it off completely."

Alejandra gave him a gentle smile. "They're fine, Ben. You work hard. It's nothing to be ashamed of."

Ben brightened up. "Cool. Now that they're gone, what do you say to heading over to the Tipsy Pirate later?"

Alejandra shook her head. "Sorry, Ben. Like I said, I'm not really interested in dating anyone at this time. I've got too much going on with waitressing, my business classes, and trying to get my nail salon off the ground."

"How's that going?" I asked.

"Really well," she said, seeming relieved to be talking about something other than her love life. "I'm looking into the licensing requirements and checking out a few potential sites in town. It'll be a while yet before I can quit waitressing, but one of these days."

"You'll do it, sugar," Penny said. "You're determined, hardworking, and smart. Look at me. I'm only in my thirties and I run two businesses now—the sailing school and the boat brokerage. No reason you can't do the same. I bet in ten years' time you'll own half the town."

"Well, I'm not too sure about that. Norm seems to own half the town. I'm surprised he hasn't run for mayor yet."

"Thank goodness he hasn't," Penny said. "I'm not sure Coconut Cove could cope with his style of leadership."

* * *

"Here, kitty, kitty," I called out as we neared the boatyard. "I wonder where she got to," I said to Scooter. "She must be starving. She didn't stick around the patio long enough to get her usual handouts from people."

"Well, with all that commotion going on with the guys fighting, you really can't blame her. It's much more peaceful back here."

The place was deserted. Although a few people lived in the boatyard while they were working on their boats, like Ken and Leilani, Ben had told me that most of the boat owners were locals who went home each night.

We picked our way through the yard, walking around piles of wood, metal jack stands, toolboxes, and a couple of dinghies.

I saw lightning out of the corner of my eye. A few seconds later, a large clap of thunder startled me. As we neared the section where our boat, Norm's boat, and the Chois' boat were located, the overhead lights flickered, then went out.

"Looks like a power outage," I said.

I heard a crashing noise, followed by the sounds of someone in pain.

"Scooter, was that you?"

"Yes, I tripped over something."

I retraced my steps. "Are you okay?"

"I'm fine. Here, help me up," he said, holding out his hand.

"I'm not so sure you're fine. You're favoring your right leg."

"It's okay. I twisted my ankle a little bit. Just need to walk it off." I watched him hobble in the direction of our boat.

"I guess you won't be playing basketball with the guys this week," I said.

"Stop worrying. It's nothing." He glanced up at the sky. "Come on, let's find that cat and get out of here before it starts pouring."

I got a flashlight out of my purse and illuminated our path. When we got to *Marjorie Jane*, the light caught a pair of green eyes staring down at us from the deck. The feline yawned, then stretched her front paws in front of her lazily.

"Are you ready to go home?" I asked.

Scooter climbed partway up the ladder, wincing in pain, and lifted her down to me. "I'm just going to gather a few things off the boat. Why don't you get her ready to go?"

As I tried to hold on to Mrs. Moto while digging in my bag for her harness and leash, a lizard dashed in front of me. The cat squirmed and jumped out of my arms. I sighed as she ran under the boat in pursuit and then into the wooded area at the back of the boatyard.

"Why do you always have to chase things?" I yelled after her. "Just leave that poor lizard alone. It won't be nearly as tasty as one of the cans of Frisky Feline's gourmet delicacies I have waiting for you back at home. Just think, tasty morsels of fish in a savory cream sauce. Sure, it smells disgusting, but the label promises a rich, hearty taste you can't resist."

No response. Maybe I shouldn't have added in that part about how it stunk. I walked carefully toward the edge of the wooded area. I heard a rustling sound to my right. When I pointed my flashlight in that direction, I saw a large object covered in a blue tarp with an overturned paint can lying beside it. Mrs. Moto stood with her back arched next to it, hissing loudly.

"Did that lizard fight back?" I asked her.

She nudged the tarp with one of her paws and yowled.

"What is it, kitty?" I pulled back the tarp, expecting to see a lizard. Instead, I saw Darren, his dreadlocks covered in a mixture of blood and paint. It didn't look like he would be going on any moonlight strolls with a pretty girl on the beach ever again.

CHAPTER 4
THE MOST ANNOYING EYEBROWS EVER

"WHERE IS SHE?" I ASKED impatiently. "She said she would be here at nine and it's already nine thirty."

"Stop pacing, my little panda bear. She'll be here when she gets here. Why don't I make you another mocha while we wait?"

"Fine," I snapped. "I don't even know why she's coming, anyway. I never agreed to sell the cottage and move onto *Marjorie Jane*."

"I told you, I tried to cancel, but she didn't answer her phone, and for some reason it didn't go to voicemail." He ruffled my hair. "You look like you could use some extra chocolate in this one."

I nodded and passed my mug to him. "Sorry I bit your head off. I didn't sleep well. I kept having nightmares about finding Darren underneath that tarp. And if that wasn't bad enough, I also had dreams about cans of paint flying around trying to knock me off the boat."

"Flying paint cans?" Scooter asked as he turned the espresso machine on.

I shuddered. "Like those flying monkeys from *The Wizard of Oz*. They always creeped me out when I was a child." I sat on one of the barstools at the kitchen counter.

"That does sound bad." Scooter foamed up some milk. "You want full-fat milk, right?"

"Is there any other kind?" I asked.

"Not according to Mrs. Moto. She turns up her nose when I try to give her skim," Scooter said. "We're lucky she can tolerate milk, unlike most cats. Can you imagine if we had to tell her no? We'd have to wear earplugs because she'd scream so much."

"Remember when we told her to stop sharpening her claws on the couch?" I asked.

Scooter sighed. "Yep. That's when she added the armchair to her list of feline-approved scratching posts."

I inhaled the smell of coffee and chocolate as Scooter placed my mug on the counter. But even the tantalizing aroma couldn't help me forget my nightmare. "At least the paint cans didn't have bushy eyebrows like Chief Dalton. I don't think I'd ever be able to sleep again if I had a dream about those. I wonder if there's some sort of class about how to read eyebrows. If he ever lost the power of speech, he could communicate solely with them, like some sort of sign language."

Scooter sat on the stool next to me. "He can't help it if his eyebrows resemble...what is it you always compare them to?"

"Caterpillars. Fuzzy caterpillars. I can't keep my eyes off them. They're mesmerizing, but not in a good way." I blew on my mocha to cool it down. "It wouldn't have been so bad if he hadn't kept asking the same questions over and over." I tried to imitate his gruff voice while raising my eyebrows. "What were you doing in the boatyard at that hour? Did you touch anything at the crime scene? Isn't this the third murder victim you've found in Coconut Cove?" I took a cautious sip from my mug. Nope, still too hot. "It's almost like he thinks I deliberately try to find dead bodies."

Scooter frowned. "Well, I don't think it's deliberate, but you do have a knack for it."

"Hang on a minute—"

The ringing of the doorbell interrupted my retort.

"What a charming little cottage," a voice rang out brightly as the door opened before either Scooter or I could answer it.

An overpowering smell of floral perfume wafted around the corner, followed by a woman who looked to be in her midthirties from a distance, but closer to her late forties up close.

"Panda, this is Suzanne. Suzanne, this is my wife, Mollie."

"Panda. That's adorable," she said. "The only pet name my husband calls me is...well...I probably shouldn't mention it in polite company." She giggled, then extended her hand. "Pleased to meet you," she said. "Your husband has been telling me all about you. Isn't that right, Scooter, darling?"

I was fascinated by her elaborate hairdo. Her auburn hair was piled on top of her head in a manner that could only be achieved with an endless supply of bobby pins and at least two cans of hairspray. She wore a formfitting sheath dress of white linen and teetered on impossibly high stiletto heels.

"Here you go, all my details," she said, handing me a business card. "What's that heavenly smell?"

"Do you mean my mocha?" I asked, although I wasn't sure how she could smell anything over her cloying scent.

"Mmm...yes. A skinny latte would be divine before we begin," she said.

"Don't look at me," I said. "Scooter is the resident barista."

"My, you're such a talented man, aren't you? A successful businessman, and you also make coffee. What else should I know about you?" she asked, squeezing his bicep.

Scooter glanced down at the hand on his arm. "Uh, sure. One latte coming right up," he said, escaping from her grasp.

Suzanne flitted around the kitchen while her beverage was being prepared, regaling me with stories about her real estate career and gossiping about her clients.

"Thank you, darling," she said when Scooter set a mug in front of her. She swirled her latte with a spoon, then took a tiny sip. "This isn't skim milk, is it?" She set the mug back down. "Never mind. Let's have a look around, shall we?" she said as she edged past me into the living room. "Now, I believe you said this was a two-bedroom, two-bath, didn't you?"

"One-and-a-half-bath," Scooter said.

"Hmm. Well, that's not ideal, but we'll find some way to spin it," she said breezily. "This is such a lovely space. So light and airy. I bet the view of the sunset over the water is just magnificent." She pulled a notebook out of her bag and jotted something down. "I think that will be a top selling point."

She perched delicately on the edge of the couch and fiddled with the bracelets around her wrist, then delicately stifled a yawn. "Can you believe the police came to our house to question my husband and me last night? They kept us up so late." She leaned forward and said dramatically, "You did hear about what happened at the marina, didn't you? Someone was murdered!"

"Here, why don't you finish this?" I said, handing Scooter my mug, knowing that talk of homicide would be upsetting to him. "The chocolate should help." He gulped it down in one swallow.

"Yes, we know," I said. "I was the one who actually found the body. Poor guy. He was so young."

"You found Darren? Simply ghastly! I can't imagine how I would have reacted if it were me. Fainted, I suppose. It was a good thing you had such a nice strong man there to help you."

Scooter coughed and gave me a look.

"Oh, I'm not the one who fainted. He did. He landed on the ground before I could catch him." Scooter's look turned into more of a glare. I was beginning to think he didn't want me to tell people about what had happened.

"I didn't faint," he said, giving me yet another pointed look. This one I was able to interpret easily. "I had just twisted my ankle. It went out on me, so I stumbled and fell down."

"That makes much more sense," Suzanne said, her faith in male courage and bravery in the face of dead bodies restored.

"Why did the police question you?" I asked.

"Oh, didn't I say? There was some silly fight at the marina earlier that evening, and for some reason, they thought my husband's nephew might have been involved."

"Liam?" She nodded. "So that means that Norm's your husband?"

"That's right. We're coming up on five years. It's a second marriage for both of us."

"So what do you know about Darren?" I asked.

Suzanne sighed. "Well, I know him a bit. He graduated from high school with Liam and my son, Xander. The three of them used to hang out. We would see Darren at school events, football games, that type of thing."

"Didn't Alejandra go to school with them too?"

"Oh yes. Her family moved to Coconut Cove at the start of high school. She's such a nice girl. She and Liam are really sweet on each other. Who knows, maybe wedding bells in the future?"

"Really? It didn't appear that way last night. She didn't seem to want anything to do with him, especially after that fight between the guys."

"Well, just between you and me, Liam can be a bit of a hothead. He was constantly getting into trouble at school. My son would have been a much better match for Alejandra. They went to prom together, you know. But after graduation, Xander decided to move in with his father back in Arizona and go to college out there. I keep hoping he'll come back to Coconut Cove and help Norm with his businesses. He's got such a good head on his shoulders. Liam's great at the grunt work, but what Norm really needs is someone who can take over when he retires." She sighed. "But all Xander can talk about is how much he loves it out west, so I guess I shouldn't get my hopes up."

Scooter showed her the rest of the house while I tidied up the kitchen. As I poured Suzanne's latte down the drain, I thought about what she had said about Liam's temper. Was it possible that jealousy over Alejandra had driven him to murder Darren?

"This is such a charming house," Suzanne said, interrupting my thoughts. "I love how you've decorated it, Mollie. The baskets with seashells on your nightstands are a cute touch. I'm sure I can get you guys a great price for it, assuming you're willing to move quickly." She set her purse on the counter. "Your delectable husband says you're going to move onto your sailboat. That sounds so romantic. Me, I couldn't do it, but you look like a woman with simpler tastes." She eyed me head to toe the way they do on those TV shows that promise to turn someone frumpy into someone fabulous.

"The only person thinking about moving onto the boat is Scooter. Not me. In fact, it was his idea to have you come see the cottage."

"Oh, don't be silly. I don't believe that for a second." Suzanne opened up the patio door and took in the views of the beach, then turned back to me. "Do you know Leilani Choi?"

"You mean Mrs. Diamond?"

Suzanne furrowed her brow. "Who?"

"Sorry, you mean the woman who broke her arm, don't you?"

"Yes, that's the one. You should talk to her. She and her husband sold their house last year and moved onto their catamaran. I bet she could give you lots of tips about downsizing, having garage sales, paring down what you need to a minimum, that sort of thing. She's a lovely young thing. A bit of a hippie, but a sweetheart. I don't think she owns too many clothes, either. Fashion isn't important to everyone, is it?"

"Why exactly is the market so hot?" Scooter asked, trying to change the subject before I said something he thought I might regret. I'm not sure I would have regretted it, but I'm certain he wouldn't have been pleased.

"Oh, you know, just snowbirds who come down here every year, then decide to sell their property up north and make it a full-time thing. Besides, Coconut Cove is a darling town. We've got lovely restaurants, bars, shops..." She reached over and whispered, "You might check that new boutique out, Mollie. They've got some gorgeous dresses in the window. Men like it when we ladies make an effort." Then in a louder voice she added, "And we're close enough to the big city to stock up on things. It's a wonder the town hasn't grown. It's ripe for development."

"But wouldn't that ruin its charm?" Scooter asked. "My uncle used to own this place, and one of the things he loved about Coconut Cove was the fact that it was a small town. If you let large developers come in, it won't be any different than any other place on the coast. Strip malls everywhere, heavy traffic, and no character. I'd hate to think that's what selling this place would bring to the area."

"See, Scooter, we shouldn't sell," I said enthusiastically. "We don't want that to happen here."

"No, no," Suzanne said in a reassuring tone. "We have strict zoning laws. Nothing like that will ever happen here. It's just that a few snowbirds will move down and splash their money around the town. It'll be good for everyone."

As she went to pick up her purse, her wrist jangled against the counter.

"Your bracelets are quite distinctive. That one in particular," I said, pointing at a heavy gold one laden with charms.

"Isn't it? Every time I make a really big sale, I treat myself to a new charm. See, I even have one of a sailboat. Business has been so good lately that I'll probably have to get another bracelet for my other wrist," she said with a laugh.

"Now, I'll let you two get on with the rest of your day. I'm going to run over to the office and type up all the agreements." She yawned. "Although a nap does sound tempting after all that police questioning."

"The chief does like to ask a lot of questions," I said. "I bet he asked where you and Norm were when Darren was murdered."

"Oh, he did."

"And where was that?"

Suzanne seemed annoyed. "At our office, dear. It's in that building right near Penelope's Sugar Shack. We were both there all night catching up on paperwork. You know how it is when you're a successful businessperson, don't you, Scooter, dear?"

As we walked Suzanne to the door, she told us that she'd send the photographer out the next day to take pictures of the cottage.

"Listen, Suzanne, I appreciate your coming out here, but Scooter and I have a lot to talk about before we move forward. *If* we move forward. So, no photographer," I said.

She winked at Scooter. "Everyone gets cold feet, but once you see that big, fat deposit in your bank account and move onto that cute sailboat of yours, you'll be glad you sold this place."

* * *

As the door to the Sailor's Corner Cafe swung open, I could smell the aroma of burgers and fries. It helped clear the stench of Suzanne's perfume out of my nostrils.

Alejandra waved to us as she scooted past with a tray full of ice cream sundaes. "*Hola.* Pick any table. I'll be with you in a sec."

We sat at a booth by the window looking out on Main Street. Scooter twisted around to read off the lunch specials from the board by the kitchen. "Okay, they've got minestrone soup, grilled ham and cheese sandwiches, and something called 'Ocean's

Delight Stew.' Any of those sound good to you?"

I crinkled my nose. "Ocean's Delight? That sounds like the kind of cat food Mrs. Moto would eat. What do you suppose is in it?"

After Alejandra described what was in the stew, we both opted for the grilled cheese.

"What can I get you to drink?" she asked.

"Root beer for me," Scooter said.

"I'll have an iced tea, please," I said.

"Unsweetened, right?"

"Yes, I get enough sugar elsewhere in my life."

"You know, *chica*, if you live down here in the south long enough, you're going to have to start drinking sweet tea."

"That'll be right after I start eating tofu."

Alejandra smiled as she made off with our menus.

Scooter leaned forward. "Well, what did you think of Suzanne?"

"You're going to have to be a bit more specific. Her fashion sense? Her overuse of the word 'darling'? Her admiration of your biceps?"

Scooter flexed his arm. "Well, I do have nice biceps, but I was thinking more along the lines of her selling our house."

"I just don't get why you're so hot on selling the cottage? The one good thing about having her out this morning was that she pointed out all the great features it has, like the ocean view, how light and airy the rooms are, and how nicely I decorated the place. After hearing all that, why would you want to move onto a cramped sailboat?"

"Because—"

"And it has a washer and dryer. Did you know Leilani and Ken have to do their laundry in coin-operated machines at the marina?"

"But—"

"And don't even get me started on what happens if you insert the wrong quarters."

Alejandra set our drinks down on the table.

"Can I say something?" Scooter asked after taking a sip of his root beer.

"Sure."

"Remember that article I showed you the other day in that sailing magazine? The one about that couple who sold everything to move aboard their boat, and how much they loved their new lifestyle?"

"You realize that's just propaganda, don't you?"

"No, it was a real story. You should talk to Leilani like Suzanne suggested. She's not a propaganda machine. She can tell you what it's really like. Besides, if we want to sail to the Caribbean or maybe even to the South Pacific, we're going to have to move aboard the boat one of these days."

"Whoa, big fella. One step at a time. The longest cruise we've done on *Marjorie Jane* was from our slip to the Travelift. And you know how well that went. Why don't we go slowly? First things first—we've got to fix up the boat. Then we can take her out for a day, maybe a weekend, and see what that's like. You don't have to jump into everything headfirst, you know."

Scooter smirked. "Isn't that like the pot calling the kettle black? Remember that time you signed up for skydiving lessons before you remembered you're scared of heights?"

"That was different."

"How exactly?"

Fortunately, Alejandra came by with our meals before I had to explain how jumping out of a plane could come in handy in the future.

While we ate our lunch, I looked out the window and noticed Ben and Liam having an animated discussion across the street. Ben threw his hands up in the air and walked over to the cafe. He saw Alejandra through the window and waved. She nodded and gave him a lukewarm wave in return before going back to taking an order. Undeterred, he came inside and sat down next to me.

"Hey, what's new?" he said as he grabbed a fry off my plate.

"Daring move, Ben," Scooter said.

"Sorry, Mollie," Ben said sheepishly. "I haven't eaten all day."

Alejandra came over to top up my iced tea. "What can I get you, Ben?"

"How about coming to the Tipsy Pirate tomorrow to hear me play?"

"Uh, I can't. I've got to catch up with..." She stared out the window and chewed on her pen, then continued. "With Nancy. We're going to check out some new nail polishes that she ordered." She finished filling up my glass and placed it back in front of me. "Did you want anything to eat, Ben?"

Ben looked downcast. "Nah, I lost my appetite." Alejandra shrugged and bustled over to the kitchen.

"Is this the band you were telling me about?" Scooter asked.

"Yeah. It's me and some high school buddies. We call ourselves Eye Patches and Peg Legs."

"That's an interesting name," I said.

"Do you like it? I had to convince the other guys in the band to go along with it. We play all sorts of stuff, from Jimmy Buffet to Bob Marley. Why don't the two of you come?"

Scooter nodded. "Sure, we'll be there."

Ben smiled, slyly stole another fry, and scooted out of the restaurant.

"Poor Ben," I said. "He just doesn't seem to get a break. First, he was sweet on Penny, and now he's got a thing for Alejandra. There's this girl in FAROUT who might be perfect for him. I think I heard her mention that she likes rum. That's a pirate drink, isn't it?"

"No matchmaking, Mollie. Just stay out of it."

Screams of laughter erupted in the back section of the restaurant. I glanced over and saw Penny surrounded by several young kids banging their spoons on the table. "Ice cream, ice cream, we all want ice cream!" Alejandra rushed over and grabbed spoons from some of the more rambunctious children. It didn't really help matters. They used their hands to beat on the table while they shouted, "Spoons, spoons, we all want spoons!" What they didn't realize was that you could eat ice cream just as easily with a fork, provided you gobbled it up quickly enough. Trust me, it can be done. If I were them, I would have gone back to chanting about ice cream rather than spoons.

"Look, there's Katy," I said.

Scooter laughed. "Can you picture the expression on Nancy's face if she were here and saw what a mess they've all made of the table? I can't imagine she'd approve."

"Well, Katy is her granddaughter. I'm sure she lets her get

away with things no one else would be able to."

I walked over and tugged on one of Katy's braids. "What are you making such a fuss about?"

"Mollie, it's you! Guess what?"

"What?"

"No, you have to guess!"

"You won the lottery?

"No, don't be silly. Guess again!"

"Your grandmother said you could have a kitten at her place?"

Katy giggled. "Of course not. Grandma doesn't like anything covered with fur, not even Grandpa. Once he let his beard grow for a few days, and she made him shave it off."

"Okay, then you have to tell me. I'm out of guesses."

Penny looked at Katy encouragingly. "Go on. Tell her."

"We won the regional competition! I took first place! Penny is treating us all to hot fudge sundaes as a reward!"

"That's fantastic, sweetheart. I'm sure everyone is so proud of you."

Katy held out her wrist. "Look what else I got—a candy bracelet."

"Oh, I'd love one of those," I said.

"You don't need one. You always wear your necklace with the little lighthouse," Katy said before proceeding to eat some of the candy beads.

I glanced over to Penny. "Sure you can handle this by yourself?"

"Well, it'll be worse for the parents when they pick them up, and they're all hyped-up on sugar."

I felt Scooter put his hands on my shoulders. "I paid the bill. We should probably get going and head over to Melvin's to pick up some supplies while the sale is still on." He rubbed his fingers on the back of my neck. "Hey, where's your necklace?"

I put my hands on my neck. "It's gone!"

* * *

After a fruitless search for my necklace at the cafe and many tears on my part, we reluctantly gave up and drove over to the marine store.

"Welcome to Melvin's Marine Emporium," Chad said chirpily. He adjusted the name tag on his blue vest, then held out his hand to Scooter. "Nice to see you back here, Mr. McGhie."

"I'm surprised you aren't on a first-name basis by now, considering my husband is in here practically every day," I said.

"That's what we like to see—satisfied return customers," Chad said with a big grin on his face. "Now, what can I help you with today, sir?"

Well, of course they were fond of return customers. The whole marine industry depended on repeat business. Everything on a boat broke down frequently, almost as if it had been engineered that way. And while you might pop into Melvin's for the sole purpose of getting a replacement fuse, you usually ended up walking out with a number of items all designed to help you lead a more nautical lifestyle—a holder for your fishing rod that doubled as a beer-can dispenser, a tote bag which could be converted into a bathing suit cover-up or beach hat, and a brass plaque reminding landlubbers not to flush anything down the head unless they'd eaten it first.

Despite the fact that he was still in high school, Chad had a flair for sales, talking customers into buying things they didn't really need. "Did you see the new multipurpose tool we just got in?" he asked Scooter. "Not only does it have a knife, scissors, screwdriver, bottle opener, and tweezers but it's also attached to a floating key chain in the shape of a dolphin. Buy two, and you get the third free."

Chad pointed at a colorful display case. Scooter's eyes lit up. He was in danger of thinking he needed three of them when even one would be overkill. And I don't think he had really thought through the fact that the tool itself was so heavy that there was no way the poor foam dolphin key chain could keep it afloat in the water. That's why I carried the credit cards in my purse and why he wasn't allowed to shop at Melvin's unsupervised anymore.

"Remember, we're just here to get supplies to paint the bottom, nothing else," I said.

"I know, but it can't hurt to look," he said over his shoulder as he went to check out the amazing, once-in-a-lifetime opportunity. He held one up to show me. "Don't you think these would make great Christmas presents?"

"You realize it's only February, don't you?"

"Yeah, but they're on sale now."

While Scooter was trying to decide whether his sister would prefer the blue one or the orange one, I glanced out the window and saw Chief Dalton standing outside talking with Officer Moore. Chad followed my gaze. "Did you hear what happened at the marina?" he asked.

I sighed. "Yes, we did. In fact—"

Chad gasped. "Did you find the body?" I nodded. "Wait a minute," he said. "Didn't you find both of the people who were murdered there a few months ago?"

I nodded again.

"So that makes—"

"Three bodies," I snapped. "Yes, I've found three bodies at the marina."

A couple looking at deck shoes turned and stared at me. Chad struggled with his desire to go over and cajole them into purchasing a few dozen pairs and his desire to know more of the gory details about the murder. Gore won out. He lowered his voice. "So what happened?"

"I'm not sure. I found him at the edge of the boatyard over by the wooded area. He had been covered by a tarp. There was an open can of bottom paint next to him, which had spilled everywhere." I checked to make sure Scooter wasn't in earshot. "From what the chief said yesterday, it appears as though someone hit him on the back of the head with the paint can."

Chad took a step backward. "I hope that paint wasn't bought here. It'd be awful if people associated Melvin's with murder. I'm not sure he could take it, especially after all the trouble he had with the previous store manager."

"I'm sure people don't blame Melvin for what happened before, and no one would think any less of him if the paint came from here."

"I hope you're right. It's bad enough that he has to deal with the death of his nephew. Imagine how he'd feel if he knew the murder weapon had been purchased here," Chad said. He pointed at his name tag. "Something good did come out of the last manager getting fired. I got a promotion. You're looking at the new assistant store manager. After I graduate high school this year, I'm sure Melvin is going to promote me to store manager."

I smiled at his enthusiasm. I'm not sure I would have the temperament to deal with all the paperwork that went along with managing a store, let alone try to sell stuff to people, but I could see Chad reveling in it. He began telling me about his ideas for inventory management, but I steered the conversation back to the murder. "I didn't know Darren, but from what everyone says around town, he was a nice young man."

"He was always friendly when he came in," Chad said. "But he spent most of his time running Melvin's fishing charter outfit."

"I know that Coconut Cove is a popular tourist town, but is there really enough business to support two fishing charter companies? I saw Darren and Melvin get into an argument with Norm and Liam about it on Thursday night."

"Wasn't that Valentine's Day?" Chad asked. "Did Mr. McGhie give you a nice present?"

"He played it safe this year and got me chocolates."

Chad frowned. "I asked Tiffany to go out with me, but she said she had to work late at Penelope's that night. She always seems to have to work late." Chad reminded me of a younger version of Ben in a way—no luck with the ladies.

"What do you know about Norm and Liam?" I asked to distract him.

"They get a lot of foreign tourists. Liam likes it because he gets really good tips from them. He makes a big production out of filleting their fish when they get back in port, tossing knives between his hands. Then he drops their fish off at Chez Poisson and they cook it up for the tourists."

"I heard a rumor that there was some poaching going on. Do you think Liam could be involved in that? I heard him bragging about having a new car last night, and I'm not sure just getting good tips is enough to make those kinds of payments."

Chad looked around, then leaned toward me and whispered, "I overheard my dad and his buddies talking about the poaching that's going on."

"What exactly do the poachers do?" I asked.

"They take catch out of season, go after protected species, keep under-sized or over-sized fish." He shrugged. "My dad says it ruins it for the rest of us. Not to mention the environment."

"I'm impressed with your knowledge on the subject," I said.

Chad beamed. "My dad and his buddies are really angry that people are getting away with it. Everyone knows it's going on, but no one has been able to prove it yet."

Melvin stuck his head out of the office door. "Do you have those reports for me, Chad?" He looked at me and walked over. "Oh, I'm sorry, ma'am. I didn't mean to interrupt."

"Oh, it's no problem. Chad was just telling me about his promotion."

Melvin smiled fondly at Chad and patted him on the shoulder. "He's a hard worker. He deserved it." He stuck his hand out. "I'm Melvin Rolle, owner of this establishment."

"Mollie McGhie," I said. "I can't believe we've never met before."

"Well, I've been back in the Bahamas for the past several months," he said, his eyes welling up with tears. He took a handkerchief out of his pocket and dabbed them. "Sorry about that. I still get misty-eyed thinking about the passing of my Velma."

I squeezed his hand. "I'm so sorry about your loss. How long were you married for?"

"Forty-one years. I was a lucky man." He glanced around the store. "She's the reason for all this. She believed in me and my dreams." He dabbed at his eyes again. "As much as I miss her, I'm glad she doesn't have to deal with the loss of Darren. She was so fond of the boy. It would have broken her heart."

"When did you get back to Coconut Cove?" I asked.

"Last week. I decided it was time to come back and face things. The store needs someone looking after it full-time. Chad does a great job working after school and on the weekends along with a couple of other high school kids, but you really need someone managing it day to day." Chad looked crestfallen. "And this young man will be heading off to college next year. He's got a bright future in front of him."

"You must have a lot on your plate with the store and your fishing charter business," I said.

"We used to have four boats, but then...well, we just have the one now, and it's a struggle to keep that going." His voice choked up. "Now that my nephew is gone, I don't know what I'm going to do."

"Mr. Rolle," a deep voice said behind me. "Are you ready for some more questions?"

I didn't have to turn around to know whom that voice belonged to. I was all too familiar with the burly man behind it. "Chief Dalton, what a surprise to see you here," I said.

The chief raised his bushy eyebrows and scowled. "Well, it's not really a surprise to see you here, Mrs. McGhie. Whenever there's a body to be found and a murder to be investigated, you're right there in the thick of things." He turned to Melvin. "Sir, if I could have a minute of your time."

"How many questions can you possibly have?" Melvin said, raising his hands in the air. "I don't have time for this! Darren's parents are flying over from Nassau later today. We've got to organize everything for the funeral, and I've got to cancel the fishing charter I had scheduled for tomorrow."

"It won't take long. Just a couple more questions regarding your whereabouts last night."

"I told you everything already. I was home alone, watching TV, trying not to think too much about Velma." He turned to me. "It was our wedding anniversary yesterday. I watched *Roman Holiday* and made conch fritters with some pigeon peas and rice. I even made a pitcher of *switcha*." He smiled at the quizzical look on my face. "That's what we Bahamians call lemonade, except we make it with limes. That was how we celebrated every year."

"I love that movie, especially the part where Audrey Hepburn drives around the streets of Rome on a Vespa scooter."

"Velma liked that part too," Melvin said. He started sobbing.

The chief coughed. "Mrs. McGhie, you can talk about movies on your own time. Right now, I'm here to speak with Mr. Rolle."

"My own time? What are you talking about?" I said. "It's not like I work for you. But if I did, I would know better than to badger people." I pulled out a pack of tissues from my purse and handed it to Melvin, while the chief gazed on dispassionately. "You should be ashamed of the way you're treating him!"

The burly man's eyebrows twitched. "Fine. Why don't I come by your house later today, Mr. Rolle, and we can discuss matters then?" Melvin nodded. The chief turned to me. "And while I'm in the neighborhood, why don't I come by and have another chat with you?"

"That'd be delightful," I said with a touch of sarcasm. Okay, maybe more than just a touch. "I always look forward to our visits." I watched as he walked toward the door, praying he wouldn't turn back around to have another go at the older man.

"What did he mean by 'in the neighborhood'?" I asked Melvin. "Wait a minute—you don't happen to live in the pink cottage on the beach, do you? We've never seen anyone there. I assumed it was vacant, maybe a rental property. We're right next door in the blue one."

He nodded. "Yes, the pink one's mine. Maybe I should rent it out. It doesn't feel the same without Velma there."

"Have you ever thought of selling?" I asked. "A real estate agent was out at our place. She's desperate to get us to list it."

"I bet that was Suzanne Thomas," he said bitterly. "If I were you, I'd stay clear of her and her husband. The police should be talking to them about Darren's death, not me."

"Do you think they had something to do with it?"

"I wouldn't put it past them," he said darkly. "They've destroyed businesses all over town. I don't think they'd bat an eye at killing someone to get what they want."

CHAPTER 5
MYSTERY INGREDIENT

AFTER ALL OF NANCY'S SNIDE comments about the fact that I rarely cooked, I decided to go all out and make a big Sunday lunch for Scooter and me. While I was in the kitchen mashing up some potatoes, my husband wrapped his arms around my waist and nuzzled my neck.

"I see sour cream, butter, bacon bits, and shredded cheese on the counter," he said. "Does that mean what I think it means?"

"How do twice-baked potatoes sound?"

"That sounds great," he said. "But what did I do to deserve them?"

"By not buying those ridiculous multipurpose tools yesterday. Your self-control was awe-inspiring."

"But that was just because you had the credit card in your purse," he said as he tried to peek in the oven.

"Hey, stay out of there."

"It smells good. What is it?"

"You'll see. It's a new recipe. There's a special ingredient in it that I think you're going to love. Why don't you go wait on the patio? I'll be out in a little bit. I just have to finish up in here." I handed him a bottle of salad dressing. "Here, take this with you."

"Salad?"

"It's good for you."

"All right, just make sure you put extra butter in those spuds to make up for it."

* * *

After reluctantly eating a bowl of salad, Scooter gobbled down everything on his plate in record time. "You've outdone yourself, my little panda bear. This chicken is delicious," he said. "There's something so familiar about the breading, but I can't put my finger on it."

"Well, if you can figure out the mystery ingredient, you can have dessert. I made brownies earlier."

Scooter's eyes lit up. "Well, I'd better have another piece in the interest of research."

I pointed at the cottage next to ours. It was painted a bright shade of pink with lilac trim and shutters. "I can't believe that's Melvin's place. Did your uncle ever mention him?"

"I guess he did say something about a Bahamian guy living next door, but I never put two and two together." Scooter took a sip of water. "You know, he bought this cottage from Alligator Chuck around fifteen years ago. Chuck's family originally owned all the cottages on this stretch of beach. I wonder if Melvin bought his cottage from him at the same time."

I turned and glanced at the purple cottage on the other side of us. "I wonder why he kept that one to live in. They're pretty much all the same inside, aren't they?"

"I think the layout is the same, but Chuck made improvements to the yellow cottage on the other side of his so that it'd have more appeal as a rental property."

"We hardly ever see him around here," I said. "He's probably too busy running his barbecue joint." I watched as Scooter finished off the rest of the chicken. "We haven't been there in a while. I wouldn't mind getting some ribs sometime this week. Besides, it's always fun to listen to him tell tourists his alligator-wrestling stories. It's amazing what they'll believe. Remember the one about the poodle?"

Scooter chuckled. "That was a good one." He leaned back in his chair and rubbed his now-extended belly. "But, to be honest, I'm too full to even think about ribs right now."

I looked at the plates on the table. "We really should have invited Melvin over to lunch. Poor guy, all on his own."

"You were talking to him quite a bit at the store," Scooter said. "He seemed really broken up."

"Of course he was. First, losing his wife, now his nephew. And then the chief started harassing him."

"Harassing seems like a strong way of putting it. He must have some reason for wanting to question Melvin."

"From what Melvin says, it's Norm and Suzanne he should be questioning. He practically accused them of killing Darren."

Scooter took his glasses off and rubbed his eyes. "Maybe I shouldn't tell you this, but…"

"Tell me what?" When he didn't reply right away, I added, "Don't forget that brownies are at stake here."

Scooter smiled. "Okay, but don't turn this into some sort of dark conspiracy that you need to investigate."

"Me? Never."

"Well, Suzanne called to arrange for the photographer to come out, and then she went on about how Darren was involved in all this poaching activity everyone's been talking about."

"Darren? Everyone I talk to says it's Liam. Haven't you heard about that flashy car of his?"

He shrugged. "I have, but it's none of our business. Right?"

"I'd better clear the table," I said, stacking the plates and utensils.

"Right?" Scooter asked as I walked inside. I came back out with a notebook and pen.

"Okay, time to make a list."

Scooter sighed. "Don't you have enough lists already?"

I opened up the notebook to a blank page. "Okay, the first person I need to speak with is Norm. There's obviously no love lost between him and Melvin. Maybe Norm killed Darren in order to drive Melvin out of business? Melvin is already having to cancel fishing charters because he doesn't have anyone to captain the boat."

I underlined Norm's name, then wrote Suzanne's next to it. "I'll also have to talk to his wife, but I'm afraid that's going to be a tricky conversation."

"Why? You think she'll be evasive?"

"Well, that goes without saying. But what I'm really concerned about is that she'll try to turn the conversation into a discussion about my fashion sense, or lack of one. Plus, that perfume she wears is quite overpowering."

"Maybe I should have gotten you a bottle for Valentine's Day," Scooter said with a smile.

I wrinkled my nose. "No, you did just fine. You can never go wrong with chocolate." I tapped my pen on the table. "Okay, next on the list is Liam. He's an interesting suspect. I can think of two motives as to why he would have killed Darren. The first is the same as Norm—to drive Melvin out of business. The second is jealousy. He wanted Darren out of the picture so he could have Alejandra all to himself."

Scooter scoffed. "Jealousy? Who would kill someone because of love? If a relationship doesn't work out, you move on."

"My, how logical you are, Mr. Spock."

"Is he the pointy-eared guy?"

"You know he is. I love how you pretend not to know anything about any of the sci-fi shows I watch, yet you always happen to sit next to me when I have them on and pester me with a million questions. Admit it, you're a sci-fi geek too."

"The only reason I watch those shows is because you hide the remote from me."

"Speaking of hiding things, do you remember that conversation between Darren and Ken in the boatyard the other day? I wonder what they were talking about. It almost seemed like Ken was scared of Darren." I made a note on my list. "That will be easy. I'll go talk with Leilani about downsizing and then slip a few questions into the conversation about Ken."

"So you are seriously thinking about moving onto the boat!" Scooter said triumphantly.

"Calm down. It's just a ruse. I have no interest in selling this cottage."

Scooter grabbed my notebook from me and put it on the other

side of the table. "Okay, enough of that. Let's have dessert."

"But you haven't guessed the secret ingredient yet."

"Oh, come on, I'll never figure it out. It's probably some exotic ingredient. Or a fancy French thing I can't pronounce. In any event, it was delicious. I did eat every last bite." He got a puzzled look on his face. "Hey, wait a minute. *I* ate every last bite. That never happens. Mrs. Moto is always at my feet demanding handouts. I haven't seen her in a while. Where is she?"

"That's a very good question." As we walked into the house, I heard a rustling noise in the hallway and went to investigate. "Scooter, come here. I think I solved the mystery of the disappearing cat."

I pointed at a box on the floor. Mrs. Moto had her head inside of it and was trying to knock it off. Scooter picked her up, pulled the box off, and handed her to me.

"Listen, little kitty, this is my Cap'n Crunch cereal." He stroked the calico's head. "You have very good taste." She meowed in agreement, then tapped the box with her paw. "Yes, it's empty," Scooter said. "We'll have to get some more. Wait a minute, is this —"

"Yep, you guessed it. That's the secret ingredient—I used Cap'n Crunch in the breading on the chicken."

* * *

The Tipsy Pirate was a favorite hangout among both locals and tourists. Visitors to the area loved to have their picture taken with the wooden statue of Coconut Carl, a pirate who'd plied the local waters and had been known for his love of plunder and women, but most of all for his love of rum.

Legend had it that he'd once donned a dress and put a coconut underneath in an attempt to disguise himself as a pregnant woman and evade capture. However, he was more than a little tipsy at the time and forgot to shave off his mustache and beard, which made his story a little less believable.

It was considered good luck to rub Coconut Carl's belly while drinking a shot of rum. Tourists gobbled it up, while the residents politely hid their laughs. After all, they knew the legend was good for the local economy.

Despite differing views on the Tipsy Pirate's kitschy mascot, everyone agreed that happy hour there was the place to be. The owners had converted an abandoned fish-processing plant into the local watering hole. A large wooden deck extended out the back over the water. The inside was decorated with fishing rods and lures hanging from the rafters, mounted fish on the walls, and a long bar made out of two old wooden rowboats.

"Thanks for the ride," Melvin said to us. "After I got home from church, I just wanted to crawl back in bed and try to forget everything that had happened. I'm sure glad you came over and convinced me to get out of the house and do something tonight." He waved at a couple of older men sitting in the corner. "I'm going to go catch up with my pals for a few minutes."

"It's really crowded tonight," I said, glancing around to see if there were any empty tables. "We might have to sit up at the bar, and you know I hate that. Why do they have to make the barstools so high? I can barely climb up on them with my short legs."

"Your little legs are in luck," Scooter said. "Leilani is waving us over. Looks like they have some empty seats."

"Perfect," I said. "I can ask her and Ken about Darren."

Scooter shook his head. "You mean downsizing, right?"

"Darren, downsizing—same thing. They both begin with D."

"Here, sit next to me," Leilani said, patting a seat between her and Alejandra. "We girls can catch up, while the guys get us some drinks."

"I thought you weren't going to come tonight," I said to Alejandra.

"I wasn't, but then I felt bad about making that thing up about looking at nail polish with Nancy. I decided I really should come out and support Ben and Liam. They've been working so hard getting their band together." She toyed with her coaster. "As annoying as they can both be at times, they're still my friends."

A young woman wearing a tie-dyed tank top and purple leggings walked on stage and picked up the microphone. "Hello, everyone, and welcome to the Tipsy Pirate," she said. "I hope you're all having a good time. We're Eye Patches and Peg Legs, and we're delighted to be here this afternoon. So kick back, grab another drink, and we'll play our first set soon."

"What can I get everyone?" Scooter asked. He pointed at me. "Gin and tonic, right, my little panda bear?" I nodded. Leilani and Alejandra both asked for rum and cokes. Ken rose. "I'll come with you and help carry the drinks back."

Alejandra giggled. "Panda bear? I thought he used to call you his little sweet potato?"

I sighed. Scooter always had the most ridiculous pet names for me. He rarely called me Mollie, and when he did it usually meant he had something serious to say, or he was in trouble.

"He started using panda bear after we won a trivia pub game. He was the only person who knew the Chinese call them giant bear cats. Scooter thought it was cute because my mom gave me panda bear pajamas for Christmas, and he claims that I'm always sneaking around like a cat investigating things."

"I think it's cute too," Alejandra said.

"Well, I guess it's better than having someone refer to you as a root vegetable."

I watched as Ben and Liam walked up to the stage. There didn't seem to be any of the tension I had seen the previous night. Ben got his guitar out of its case while Liam sat behind a drum set. A third guy picked up a bass. After conferring for a few minutes with the band, the woman sat down on a barstool at the front of the stage.

"She's got a great voice," Leilani said. "We heard her last week."

"Did you know she lives in a van?" Alejandra asked as Ken passed us our drinks. "I can't imagine living in such a small space."

"Living on a boat can't be much different," I said, squeezing a lime into my drink.

Alejandra considered that. "I guess you're right. Either way, you have to downsize." I tried to ask about my other *D* topic, but before I could utter Darren's name, she shushed me when the band began to play. She was right—the young woman had a great voice, and the band was surprisingly good.

While they took a break between sets, Alejandra told us some more about van living. Then she turned to Leilani. "I have to ask.

Why in the world did you move onto your boat?"

She thought about it for a minute. "A lot of reasons, really. We wanted to lead a simpler life and not get caught up in that whole competing-with-the-Joneses mentality. You know, having a new car, a big house, expensive clothes. When I look at my parents, sure, they have lots of nice things, but I'm not convinced those things make them happy. They actually encouraged us to go simple now, while we're young."

"Did you have a house before you got the boat?" Alejandra asked.

"Yes, a two-bedroom townhouse."

"You must have had to get rid of a lot of stuff," Alejandra said.

Leilani smiled. "Oh yes. Anything you want to know about selling your stuff online and at yard sales, I can fill you in. But at least we didn't have thirty, forty years of stuff to get rid of." She turned to me. "Do you know Louise?"

"Sure, I take sailing lessons with her."

"Well, she and her husband sold their place when they retired. It was so hard for her to get rid of everything. She told me that when she looked through a box of presents her kids had made for her over the years, she broke down in tears. In the end, she couldn't bear to part with everything, so they got a storage unit. She figures after they've been cruising for a while, if she doesn't miss what they've put in storage, then she can get rid of it. But if things don't work out, and they decide to move back on land, she'll still have her prized possessions."

"Sounds sensible," I said.

"Do you think that's what you'll do?" Leilani asked me.

"Huh?"

"When you sell your cottage."

"What, when did this happen?" Alejandra asked.

"It hasn't. It's just another one of Scooter's crazy ideas, like buying a boat. It's never going to happen."

"Well, you did buy a boat," Alejandra pointed out.

"Okay, it's like the time he wanted to...wait, we ended up doing that." I put my head in my hands.

"Would it be so bad?" Leilani asked. "What is it about living on a boat that puts you off? Is it getting rid of your stuff?"

"No, it's not that so much. We did a bit of downsizing before we moved to Coconut Cove. Sure, there's some things I can't imagine living without, like my collection of boots, but it's more the thought of living in such a small, cramped space. For example, I made a nice lunch today, and there were dishes everywhere. I can't imagine making a meal like that in the tiny galley that *Marjorie Jane* has."

"Maybe you need a bigger boat," Alejandra suggested with a smile.

"Don't you dare let Scooter hear you say that," I said.

"To be fair, it does take some getting used to," Leilani said. "But it is possible to live in a relatively small space."

The band started playing again before I had a chance to change the subject away from downsizing and toward the murder investigation. While the singer paused to take a drink of water, the doors to the bar swung open.

"I told you not to trust Liam with the accounts," a shrill voice rang out. I watched as Suzanne stood in the entrance, jabbing her finger in Norm's chest. "He failed algebra in high school. Did you really think he would know the difference between an asset and a liability?"

Norm brushed her hand away. She continued, oblivious to the fact that the room had gone silent and everyone was watching her. "The real liability here is Liam. I really think I should call Xander and persuade him to move back here and help you with the business."

"For the last time, Xander is your son, not mine. Liam is going to be the one who inherits, not Xander."

Suzanne's jaw dropped as she watched him storm off to the bar. Then she looked around the room, her eyes lighting on the band. She waved at the singer, the gold charms on her bracelet flashing in the overhead light. "Can you sing something by Jimmy Buffett, dear?"

After the band resumed playing, she joined Norm at a table next to the one where Melvin was sitting with his buddies. Suzanne waved a waitress over, then whispered something to her husband. Norm scowled and pushed his chair away from hers, bumping into Melvin.

"Oh, I think this is going to get ugly," I muttered.

"What's that?" Alejandra asked.

I pointed at Melvin, who had risen to his feet and was towering over Norm. I couldn't hear what he was saying over the noise of the band, but his meaning seemed quite clear by the way he slammed his fist down on the table.

As the singer belted out the last of the lyrics to "Cheeseburger in Paradise," Norm stood and lunged at Melvin. By the time she got to the final note, the entire audience was staring at the fight breaking out, not at her. Once the music stopped, Melvin's voice could be clearly heard.

"I know it was you, Norm. You killed Darren. And if you think you're going to get away with it, you've got another thing coming. You strut around town like you're the top dog here, but you're nothing but a liar and a cheat. We all know what your nephew really gets up to when he's out on one of your boats. You can be sure that the fish and wildlife warden is going to hear about that!"

Norm threw a punch, landing it on Melvin's right cheek. Melvin staggered backward, his face flushed and his hands balled into fists. Before he could strike, two of Melvin's buddies pulled him away. Suzanne grabbed Norm's arm.

"It's not worth it, darling. Let it go." She added in a stage whisper that everyone could still hear. "This kind of thing won't look good if you want to become mayor."

Norm pulled his arm away. "Fine, let's go."

As they walked toward the door, Melvin yelled out, "And don't think I don't know about your role in that property deal, either. You and your wife are both going to end up in jail."

* * *

Everyone at our table was dumbstruck after watching the drama between Norm and Melvin unfold. Leilani attempted to lighten the mood by telling us about what it was like to grow up in Hawaii, which was fascinating. Scooter tried to impress us with some random trivia about the Aloha State, which was a tad boring. And Alejandra told us the secret to making a great tamale, which made me wonder what we were going to have for dinner.

Finally, we all decided to call it a night. While Scooter went over to see if Melvin wanted a ride back, I took a detour to pay a visit to the statue of Coconut Carl. I waited my turn while a couple of young guys downed shots of rum and rubbed Carl's belly. From the way they were watching a group of attractive young women seated at the bar, I was pretty sure they were trying to enlist Carl's help in successfully chatting them up.

It was times like this that made me so glad I was married. The thought of having to ever dive back into the dating scene made me shudder.

When it was my turn, I put my hand on the pirate's stomach and whispered in his ear. "Coconut Carl, here's the thing. I've got to give a speech at the FAROUT meeting this week, and I'm scared to death. I hate speaking in public. What if they boo me off the stage? What if I forget what I'm supposed to say?"

"Ahem, are you almost through?" I turned and saw a tourist holding up his phone. "I want to get a picture of my wife." A woman stood next to him, grinning from ear to ear and holding two shot glasses in her hands.

"I'll just be a minute," I said. I turned back to Carl. "So, do we have a deal? I'll rub your tummy, and you'll help me out with the speech. I don't really like rum, but I figure that part is just an old wives' tale, right?" I looked Carl in the eye and rubbed my hand on his midsection three times in a clockwise direction. I stepped back. "He's all yours."

As I was about to join Scooter at the car, I saw Ben and Liam standing on the deck, engrossed in conversation. I decided it wouldn't hurt to pop outside and have a quick look at the view over the water. And if I happened to overhear anything that could shed some light on the murder investigation, well, that would just be a bonus.

I leaned over the railing and watched fish searching for the morsels of food that people tossed into the water for them. The guys were so caught up in what they were discussing that they didn't notice me.

"Come on, tell me the truth, man," Ben said. "Did you get Darren involved in poaching?"

"I don't know what you're talking about," Liam said.

"There's no way you can afford that car on what you make, even with tips. And I heard you bragging about how much your new watch cost you." Ben took a sip of beer. "Everyone knows what you're up to. Darren couldn't exactly keep a secret. It's only a matter of time before you're caught."

"Sounds like someone who's jealous. Look at you, Ben. You live on a boat that's a wreck, you don't even own a car, and you bought your watch at the dollar store. No wonder you can't get a girl." Liam lowered his voice. "If you want to change all that, I can help you out. But if I do, you can't go around telling everyone about it."

"Like you helped Darren out? No way, man. I don't worship you the way he did in high school. He would have done anything you told him to. I bet you tried the same spiel on him, and he fell for it, hook, line, and sinker. And see what happened. It cost him his life."

Liam drained his glass. "I didn't have anything to do with that," he said coldly. He stared off into the distance, drumming his fingers on the railing. "Tell you what, Ben. Why don't we forget what you said? You're just upset about Darren. We all are." He punched Ben's arm playfully. "Come on, let's get another beer before our next set."

CHAPTER 6
OOMPA-LOOMPAS VS. SMURFS

"I WOULDN'T DO THAT IF I were you." I glanced up and saw Ben leaning over the side of Ken and Leilani's boat, *Mana Kai.*

I had learned that the name of their boat was Hawaiian for "Spirit of the Ocean," which was a lot prettier than boring old *Marjorie Jane.* They'd also told me that if you reversed the words you got *kaimana,* which could be translated as "diamond." I thought that was quite fitting, considering that I used to refer to the young couple as Mr. and Mrs. Diamond, on account of her diamond necklace.

"You wouldn't do what?" I asked Ben. He pointed behind me. "No, I didn't mean you, I meant him." I turned and saw Scooter grinning as he snapped a picture of me with his phone.

"Tell me you didn't just do that," I demanded. "I look ridiculous in this getup!" I tugged at the white plastic head-to-toe protective suit I was wearing. Well, it had used to be white. Now it was covered in a blue dust that had blown all over me while I was sanding the paint off *Marjorie Jane*'s bottom.

I removed my safety goggles and gloves, then pushed back the hood. "We've talked about this before, Scooter. You're only allowed to take pictures of me when my hair looks good, I don't have spinach caught in my teeth, and I'm wearing something that doesn't make my rear end seem enormous. This hardly qualifies."

I wiped the sweat off my forehead and pushed my frizzy hair behind my ears. Ben and Scooter both chuckled. "What's so funny?"

"It's just that you look like a..." Ben was consumed with laughter before he could finish his thought.

"Like a what?" I demanded.

"A Smurf," Scooter said. He took one look at my face and quickly added, "An *adorable* Smurf." He snapped another photo and smiled as he gazed at the screen. "A really adorable Smurf."

"Give me that," I said, seizing the phone. "Ugh. That is not a good look."

Scooter pointed across the boatyard at a couple who were sanding the bottom of their boat. "It could be worse. If *Marjorie Jane* had reddish-orange bottom paint like that one, you would look like some sort of demented Oompa-Loompa. Although given your love of *Charlie and the Chocolate Factory*, I imagine you'd rather be one of those than a Smurf."

While I was pondering which version of the movie was better—the original with Gene Wilder or the remake with Johnny Depp—my husband grabbed the phone back from me and stuck it in his pocket.

"Are you sure you don't want me to take over sanding?" he offered. "It's hard work."

Part of me desperately wanted to shout out, *Yes! Save me from this torture that's turning me into a small blue creature who lives in a tiny mushroom-shaped house!* Sanding was hard work. My arms were killing me, it was insanely hot outside, and we'd already mentioned that I wasn't going to win any fashion awards wearing my Smurf suit. But I was determined to stick it out and win the bet with Norm.

"No, I've got it," I said. "You keep working on trying to sort out the cause of the leak."

Ben leaned over the side of *Mana Kai* again. "Hey, did you know Mrs. Moto is aboard the Chois' boat?"

"Yeah. They've got air conditioning, and Leilani offered to let her stay there while we're working on our boat. I don't want her running around the boatyard when I'm sanding and Scooter has all the floorboards torn out of *Marjorie Jane*. I'm worried she'll end up getting stuck some place we can't get her out of. Hope that's okay with you."

"Fine by me. She's good company while I'm working." He smiled. "Well, maybe except when she bats screws off the chart table, and I have to get on my hands and knees to pick them up."

"Yes, I know that game well," I said.

As I was readjusting the hood of my Smurf suit, Liam pulled up in his flashy new car, the stereo blaring. He got out and stepped back to admire his baby. Then he glanced up at Ben. "Practice later this week at my place?"

"Sure thing," Ben replied. "Text me the details. How's your head today?"

"I'm fine. Norm's the one with the hangover. That's why I'm here and he's not."

"He and Melvin really got into it, didn't they?" I asked.

"It's always been like that between the two of them," Ben said. He looked at his red-haired friend. "You and Darren always used to be at odds too," he said with a frown.

"We were never as bad as the old guys," Liam said. "Sure, Darren and I had our differences, but we were still buddies." He bit his lip. "Well, enough about that. I've got to get some work done."

Before walking over to his uncle's boat, he examined the progress I had made with *Marjorie Jane*'s hull. "You're tougher than I thought," he said grudgingly. "You might just give my uncle a run for his money."

A black SUV pulled up behind Liam's car, blasting its horn. Ken leaned out the window. "Hey, move your car! The spot by my boat is for my car, not yours. Unless you and your uncle want to buy this part of the boatyard too, just like you're trying to buy up half the town?"

"Take it easy, man," Liam said soothingly. "I'll move, don't worry. You've probably got enough on your mind as it is, don't you? I don't want to add to your troubles."

"What's that supposed to mean?" Ken asked.

"Oh, nothing," he said. "Hey, did you hear that? Sounds like your phone is beeping, Ken. I heard you've been getting interesting texts lately."

Ken pulled out his phone and looked at the screen. "There's nothing on here."

"My mistake. Although you might want to check your old messages. Maybe someone sent you something important that you really should deal with, if you know what I mean."

Ken gave him an icy stare. "I have no idea what you're talking about. Now, get your car out of my spot."

Liam held his hands up. "Sure, no problem."

After the guys got their cars situated, I nudged Scooter. "Why don't you go over there and have a chat with Liam? See if you can find out more about these texts he was talking about. I'll do the same with Ken."

"You're kidding, right?"

"I never kid. This is important. It could be related to what happened between Ken and Darren the night of the murder. I remember Ken reading a text on his phone, and it seemed like Darren had sent it to him." Scooter appeared unconvinced. "Pretty please?"

He smiled. "Fine. I'll go have a chat with him. Not because you asked, but because he's wearing a shirt with my college basketball team's logo on it. I want to see what he thought about the game. Besides, I could use a break."

While Scooter talked about sports and texting with Liam, I approached Ken. "What was that about?" I asked.

"I don't know. I think he's just playing mind games," he said. "He's one of those guys who never grew up. Here, do you mind holding this?" he asked, handing me his briefcase. He pulled a cardboard box out of the back of his vehicle, carried it over to his boat, and set it on the ground by the ladder. "Articles for my research on sea turtle habitat encroachment," he said.

"That looks like a lot of reading. I guess you have to do a lot of that if you have a PhD. You must always have your head in a book."

"Well, I do read a lot of academic journals and research papers, but I also spend a lot of my time doing fieldwork outdoors."

"Do you ever get a chance to relax?"

"Sure. I like to watch movies."

"We do too. What was the last one you saw?"

"Hmm...that's a good question." He glanced down at the box on the ground. "Oh, I saw one on Friday. One of those action, shoot-'em-up flicks."

"That's right. You and Leilani came back to your boat after the barbecue," I said. "I'm surprised neither of you heard anything when Darren was attacked."

"I wish we had," he said ruefully. "Maybe I could have stopped the attack." He shook his head. "No, we had the AC running full blast, and the volume on the TV was up really loud. We couldn't hear a thing happening outside."

"Leilani was watching the movie too?"

"No, she doesn't like that sort of thing," he said. "Rom-coms are more her cup of tea. She was in the aft cabin working." He picked up the box. "I've got to go through this."

"And I guess I've got to get back to sanding *Marjorie Jane*'s bottom," I said reluctantly.

"Listen, if you're interested in the work we do with sea turtles, how about if you take a break this afternoon, and come with me out to the sanctuary? I told Penny I'd show her around, and it'd be great to have you along as well."

I watched as Scooter walked over to us. I wondered if he had obtained any useful information from his conversation with Liam. "Hey, we're going to see turtles this afternoon," I said as I tried to read his face for clues.

"You should come too," Ken said.

"I wish I could, but I've got a conference call this afternoon."

We all turned as Mrs. Moto started meowing on the deck of *Mana Kai*.

"Sorry, Mrs. Moto," Ken said with a chuckle. "No animals allowed. At least, no furry animals."

She batted a screw off the deck, then gracefully bounded down the ladder onto the ground to investigate. "Come on, kitty. You shouldn't be down here," Scooter said. Before he could grab her, she darted across the boatyard toward the wooded area.

"She must have seen another lizard," I said. "I'd better go get her."

"How about if I pick you and Penny up by the marina entrance at two?" Ken asked.

"Sounds good," I said over my shoulder as I chased after the calico.

After acquiring some new scratches from poking between prickly bushes, I spotted my little lizard hunter—smack-dab where Darren's body had been. She apparently didn't believe the police tape cordoning off the murder scene applied to her.

I crouched down and called out softly, "Here, kitty, kitty. Why don't you be a good girl, and come out from there? If I have to go back there to get you, the chief will be furious."

Instead of rushing into my arms, she stared at a small glittery object a couple of feet outside the cordoned-off area. She crouched down, wiggled her rear end, and made a trilling sound. After pouncing on the object and toying with her "prey" for a few minutes, she swatted it toward me. I picked it up and brushed the dirt off, uncovering a small gold charm in the shape of a sailboat.

There was one person I knew in town who sported a charm bracelet—Suzanne. She had made a point of telling me that she wouldn't be caught dead in the boatyard, so how could her charm have ended up here? Could she have been here the night of the murder? Then I brushed that thought aside. Suzanne hoisting a heavy paint can and bashing Darren in the head while wearing those high heels of hers—I just couldn't picture it.

* * *

"Are you ready, ladies?" Ken asked, leaning out the window of his vehicle. "Hop in. Next stop—the Gulf Coast Turtle Sanctuary."

As we drove up the coast, we passed through towns that all looked the same—strip malls, gated retirement communities, chain hotels and restaurants, people driving golf carts on the sidewalks, and bumper-to-bumper traffic. "This is what I'm afraid Coconut Cove is going to turn into if developers have their way," Ken said. "It'll become just another generic-looking town with no character. Places like the Tipsy Pirate and Alligator Chuck's BBQ Joint will be replaced by fast food chains."

While I'd been known to patronize the occasional drive-through for a cheeseburger and chocolate shake, I agreed with Ken's assessment. One of the reasons I liked our newly adopted home was that it was a small community with unique spots that added to its charm.

After about an hour of fighting traffic, I spotted a large sign with two smiling sea turtles. "Here we are," Ken said as he pulled into a gravel parking lot.

As we entered the visitors' center, an elderly woman greeted us. "Hello, Dr. Choi. We haven't seen you here in ages." She patted his hand. "You should have told me that you were coming today. I would have baked you some of those oatmeal cookies you're so fond of."

Ken rubbed his stomach. "That's why I didn't tell you, Mabel. I've been putting on weight ever since you began volunteering here."

"You're too young to be worrying about that sort of thing," she said. "Now, who are these two lovely young ladies you brought with you?"

"This is Penny," Ken said, pointing at the blonde Texas transplant. "She's a boat broker at the Palm Tree Marina, and she also runs the sailing school."

"Oh my. That must keep you busy," the older woman said. "My son has been talking about getting a boat."

"That would be fun, Mabel," Ken said. "He could take you and your husband out on day sails."

"No, not me," she said, clutching her chest. "I'm scared to death of the water."

Penny handed Mabel a business card. "If I can be of help to your son in looking for a boat, tell him to give me a call."

"Are those new?" I asked.

"Yes. Aren't they cute?" she said, passing me one as well.

"It's very pink," I said. I shouldn't have been surprised, considering that was Penny's favorite color. It found its way into every aspect of her life from her clothes to her sailboat, fittingly named *Pretty in Pink*.

"I know. Don't you just love it?" Penny beamed. "Did you see the starfish logo in the corner?"

Mabel placed the card on the front desk. "I'll be sure to give this to him. It must be an interesting job, selling boats. Kind of like a car salesman, I imagine."

Penny stiffened. "It's nothing like selling cars."

"Well, you have to admit that it's a little bit like it," Ken said. "You show people boats, try to find one that suits their lifestyle and budget, take them out for test drives, and do all the paperwork."

"The paperwork is the worst part of the job," Penny said. "It's something the previous owner, Captain Dan, didn't take seriously. Did you know I had a woman call up screaming the other day about how he had messed up the paperwork for a boat he sold her? She hasn't been able to get insurance for it or register it. I've been trying to help her, even though the sale happened before my time."

"There are just some people who are always trying to cheat the system," Ken said. "People who think rules and regulations apply to everyone but themselves."

Mabel turned to me. "Now, what about you, dear? What do you do?"

After I explained to her about my work with FAROUT, she smiled politely. "Investigating aliens. That sounds...um... interesting."

Based on her reaction, I decided she probably wouldn't be interested in signing up for our mailing list.

"Well, ladies, why don't I show you the exhibits in the visitors' center, and then we can go outside to the saltwater lagoon, and you can meet our resident sea turtles?"

"Oh, Dr. Choi. Don't forget to check your office before you leave. You have some mail back there."

"How long did it take you to get your doctorate?" Penny asked.

"It's a long process," he said, trying to usher us into the next room.

"He's such an impressive young man, isn't he?" Mabel gushed. "Imagine all the studying he had to do to become a doctor."

Ken looked impatient. "We should get going."

Mabel grabbed his arm. "My grandson is working on his PhD in marine biology too," she said proudly. "I'd love for him to meet you one day. Imagine...two doctors in the same room. He'd be so inspired by the work you're doing here at the sanctuary. Maybe when he comes to visit this summer, you can give him a tour."

"Sure," Ken said. He tried to pull his arm away from Mabel.

"Summer seems like a bad time of year to visit," I said. "It gets way too hot here."

"You're not from these parts?" Mabel asked.

"No, we moved here from Cleveland."

"Oh, that's where you got your degree, isn't it, Dr. Choi?"

Ken muttered something under his breath.

"What was that, dear?" Mabel asked. Before he could answer, the phone rang, and she walked over to the desk to pick it up while Ken hurried us into the display area.

* * *

After learning about the dangers of toxic algae bloom in the local waterways, that seahorses develop in a kangaroo-like pouch on the male of the species, and how oysters purify water, we left the air-conditioned building to explore the rest of the sanctuary.

"Make sure you put some sunscreen on," Ken said, handing us each a water bottle. "Even though it's winter, the sun is still strong."

"That's a good idea." I pulled a bottle out of my purse and slathered it on before offering it to the others. "I'm trying to take better care of my skin. I don't want to end up with a bad sunburn like Liam has. I guess that comes with the territory when you're a redhead like he is."

Ken pointed at a large pool behind the visitors' center. "We pump in water from the ocean. You'll see all sorts of creatures in here, including sharks, game fish, and, of course, sea turtles. Come on, let's head over to that pavilion, where you can get a better view."

Once we were situated in the shade, Ken told us about the sanctuary's mission. "We aren't able to release these guys back into the wild. That one over there is a loggerhead." He smiled. "His name is Donatello. We ran a contest. You should have seen how excited the kid was whose name we picked. He came out here with his family for a naming ceremony. Mabel baked a huge cake in the shape of a turtle."

He leaned over the railing and sighed. "It's a sad story, really. Donatello was hit by a boat, and the damage resulted in buoyancy issues. Fortunately, he can spend the rest of his natural life here with us."

"It's great that places like this exist," Penny said.

"I just wish we could do more," Ken said. "We're reliant on grant money and donations. In fact, we're hosting a cocktail party here next week to try to raise money to protect nesting grounds."

Ken warmed up to his subject, telling us how population growth and urban development were putting turtle habitats at risk. "If we don't act now, we're in danger of losing these magnificent creatures forever."

He took us on a short walk down to the beach to show us where the turtles nested. "Female turtles come ashore after mating to lay their eggs, usually during the warmest months of the year. They return to the same beach each time they're ready to nest, often just a few hundred feet away from their last nesting grounds. Did you know that the beach by your house is also a popular spot, Mollie?"

"I've seen signs there telling visitors not to disturb turtles and their nests. There was even one warning that it's illegal to shine lights on the beach at night."

"Yes, that's because artificial lights can keep females from nesting and disorient hatchlings. The Florida Turtle Trust helped to fund the signs. We're trying to do more work in the area but keep running into roadblocks from some of the local business owners. They think it will hurt tourism if we block off access to the beach."

Penny frowned. "I would think that would actually be a tourist draw."

"Potentially, but there's a fine line between ecotourism and creating more damage and putting the turtles in jeopardy. We're hoping to set aside land up there as a protected wildlife sanctuary, but some powerful people want to build a big resort there instead."

"Really? Do you know who's involved in that? Suzanne Thomas came by our cottage and said we could get a lot of money for it.

She didn't mention anything about a resort, though."

Ken frowned. "I hope I can persuade you and Scooter not to sell. Especially not to any buyers Suzanne puts forward. She's all about how much commission she can make, not what's in your best interests."

"You don't have to worry about persuading me," I said. "I don't want to sell. It's Scooter you have to talk to. Maybe you'll have more luck than me."

As we walked back into the visitors' center, Mabel called out, "Don't forget about your mail."

While we waited, I examined a display of brochures by the front door. Ken came up behind me holding a stack of mail. He opened up a large manila envelope and chewed his lip as he read the enclosed document. Some photos fluttered onto the ground. I started to pick them up, but he swiped them from me and shoved them back into the envelope. Despite the fact that we were back inside the air-conditioned building, he was perspiring.

"Everything okay, Ken?" I asked.

He glanced at me sharply. "Everything's fine. It's just a bill." He shoved the papers back into the envelope, then pointed at the brochures. "Go ahead and take those if you want," he said with a smile that didn't quite reach his eyes. "There's some good information in that one about the turtles you just saw, and that one has details about how you can contribute to the Gulf Coast Turtle Sanctuary."

While Ken went over and said goodbye to Mabel, I shoved the pamphlets in my purse and wondered what exactly had been in that envelope. Sure, no one liked to get bills, but they didn't usually cause you to break out in a nervous sweat. Nor did they generally come with photos attached.

CHAPTER 7
SUGAR CRAVINGS

"DO YOU MIND DROPPING ME off here?" I asked Ken as we approached Penelope's Sugar Shack. The lavender brick building with its bright purple awning had become a favorite haunt of mine since we moved to Coconut Cove. "I'm not sure why, but all that talk about turtles has given me a serious sugar craving."

"When don't you have a sugar craving?" Penny asked.

I ignored her. "I'm thinking of picking up a pie for dessert, but I'll walk back to the marina with it and burn off some calories as a preventative measure."

"Are you sure?" Ken asked. "I don't mind waiting for you."

"No, it's fine. It's not a long walk."

"I'll tell you what," Penny said. "I'll join you. I have a serious craving for one of Penelope's flax and chia seed carob almond bars. They're so good for you."

"But how do they taste?" I asked.

"Delicious."

"As delicious as that tofu you tried to pass off as potato salad at one of the marina potlucks?" I asked as I got out of the car.

"Before you knew what was in it, you said you liked it."

"I was just being polite. I could detect that something wasn't quite right," I said with a smile.

Penny chuckled. "One of these days, we're going to do a blind taste test. I bet you'll end up picking dishes made with tofu over ones made with mayonnaise."

"Sure, right after I give up sugar. And that'll only be because my taste buds will feel betrayed and decide to punish me with soy products."

She held her hands up. "I give up." While she went inside in search of her healthy treats, I examined the unhealthy ones on display in the window. My taste buds seemed adamant that I should get some red velvet cupcakes in addition to a pie. Who was I to argue with them?

As I opened the front door, I spied a fresh-faced teenager behind the counter. "When did you begin working here, Tiffany?" I asked.

"After the holidays. I needed a part-time job, and I really didn't want to go back to Melvin's. Chad was constantly asking me out, and I was running out of ways to say no without hurting his feelings. Then Penelope said she needed some help, so here I am." She straightened her purple polka-dot apron, then asked, "What can I get for you?"

"How about two of those?" I said, pointing at the cupcakes in the window. "And do you have any chocolate pies left?"

"No, sorry. Someone just bought the last one. But I've got a pecan pie left. Want to give that a try? It's almost as good as chocolate."

"I suppose," I said. While Tiffany went into the back to get the pie, I turned to Penny. "Why are you empty-handed?"

"They ran out," she said. "See, that's how popular they are. They sell out by noon."

Tiffany came back with a purple box, then packed up my cupcakes. As she was ringing up my order, the door burst open. Suzanne barged in, followed by Norm. The stench of her floral perfume trailed after her, overpowering the smell of freshly baked pastries.

"Tiffany, we're running late. Can you grab my catering order?"

"Sure thing, ma'am, just as soon as I ring Mollie up here."

"I'm sure she can wait, can't you, dear? We're in a rush." She pushed me aside and waved at the back of the store. I had to step back quickly before her bracelets made contact with my face and left their mark. Some of her charms had really sharp edges. "Now be a dear, pop in the back, and get my order."

Tiffany apologized to me before going into the back room. Norm leaned up against the display counter and checked his phone.

"Why are you standing there like that?" Suzanne demanded. "Go help Tiffany. After all, that's why you're here—to carry everything."

"I don't know why you had to have this meeting in the first place," Norm protested. "The last thing we need is a bunch of people running around the office. I've got work to do."

"The meeting isn't for me, it's for you. You're the one who wanted to impress these overseas investors."

Norm shook his head and went back to reading texts.

Suzanne plucked the phone out of his hand. "If Xander were here, he could have hosted the event with me. He looks so nice when he's dressed up in a suit. He'd be so charming that they'd be fighting each other to be the first to give us a check."

She tucked his phone in her purse, then waved dramatically toward the back. "Be a good boy, and go help Tiffany."

After he slunk away, Suzanne turned to me. "Now, what time should I come by the cottage tomorrow?"

"Why would you come by?"

"To sign the paperwork, of course. I'll also bring the photographer with me."

"Suzanne, I don't seem to have been able to get my point across clearly before, but let me try again. I have no intention of selling our cottage."

"That's not what your husband says."

"That's because he has this ludicrous dream of living on a boat."

"Oh, is that what you're worried about?" she asked. She put her arm around my shoulders. "Of course you're not going to live on a boat. That sounds dreadful. You'd never catch me on one."

"I live on a boat," Penny said.

"You poor thing." Suzanne pulled a card out of her purse.

"Here, give me a call, and we can set up some viewings and get you off that boat in no time."

Penny pulled out a card from her bag and handed it to Suzanne. "And here are my details so that I can show you some boats."

Suzanne fingered the pink card dubiously, then turned back to me. "There's a darling condo that you absolutely have to see. I just know you're going to love it." She pulled out her phone. "Let me just put this in my calendar. I'll come by the cottage at nine. Then once we're finished there, I'll take you to view the condo."

Before I could tell her exactly what I thought of her plan, Tiffany and Norm came out laden with boxes.

"Penny, be a dear, and get the door for these two," she said as she punched a number into her phone. "See you at nine," she said breezily as she followed after them.

When Tiffany came back in, she shook her head. "I'm so sorry about that. It's just that it can be hard to say no to her, and she spends a lot of money here on catering."

Penny chuckled. "Don't worry about it. Mollie knows how hard it is to say no, don't you? After all, you just agreed to see a condo tomorrow."

"I don't know how Norm puts up with her," I said.

"I do," Penny said. "They're a match made in heaven. They're both bossy and push people around."

"My mom says she remembers when they first started seeing each other," Tiffany said. "No one thought it would last, but Suzanne told my mom that every woman needed a man on her arm. Norm was apparently the best catch in Coconut Cove at the time."

"I'd rather be single than be with a guy like him," Penny said. "I've been burned in the past by men like that."

"What else did your mom say?" I asked.

"That Suzanne felt that Norm needed someone to push him to take more business risks. Suzanne told my mom that behind every successful man is a more successful woman."

"Well, maybe it paid off. She's certainly strong willed, and she sure does seem successful," I said. "Just look at those clothes, all those rings, and her bracelets. She's wearing more money on her than our cottage is worth."

"Maybe it's all an illusion," Penny said. "For some people, appearances are more important than reality. For all we know, they could be up to their ears in debt. Maybe some of those gems she wears are fakes."

"You may have a point. Hmm...maybe they're not as rich as they act like they are," I said.

"Your husband seems successful," Tiffany said as she wiped down the counters.

"He does all right," I said. "But he'd never go around bragging about it or telling everyone how much he's worth."

"That's what I like about the two of you," Penny said. "You're both so unpretentious and down to earth."

"Well, that's how we were raised. Be grateful for what you have, and don't rub people's faces in it. Luck comes and goes. You never know when yours might run out." Tiffany handed me my change, and I picked up my box and my bag of cupcakes. "Come on, we'd better get going before I starve to death and eat a piece on my way back to the marina."

"Is that what you're having for dinner?" Penny asked.

"Well, as tempting as that sounds, we're having real food before our dessert. Scooter's in charge. I think he's planning on a Thai recipe."

"Didn't a Thai restaurant just open up in town?"

"Precisely."

*****

After meeting up with Scooter and Mrs. Moto at the marina and stopping to get takeout, we had a nice meal back at the cottage—pad thai and spring rolls for the humans and liver pâté from a can for the feline. Over dessert, I filled Scooter in on our visit to the turtle sanctuary.

"Mabel, the volunteer there, reminded me of your aunt Ethel. She was fawning over Ken, going on and on about how smart he was and the fact that he's a doctor. Ken looked like he wanted to die. He was so embarrassed."

"But I don't have a doctorate."

"No, but your aunt is always bragging about what a great basketball player you were in college. It's all she ever talks about."

Scooter's face reddened. "That's sweet, but I wasn't that good."

"See, that's what I love about you. You're so self-effacing. Penny and I were talking about that earlier."

"You know I hate it when you talk about me," he said.

"Oh, it really wasn't so much about you as it was about Suzanne and Norm. I guess they have a reputation in town for flaunting their wealth and bragging about how successful they are. You never do that."

"Well, first of all, we're not rich. And second of all, I wouldn't say I was successful. Remember all those issues I had with my last company? You never know when something is going to go south."

I pushed my dessert plate toward him. "Go on, why don't you finish this? You look like you could use it."

After polishing off the piece of pie, he said, "Let's talk about something more cheerful. Tell me more about Mabel. She sounds interesting."

"She seems to enjoy her volunteer work," I said. "I don't really know that much more about her."

"You know, we should do some volunteering."

"Uh, you realize that I already do volunteer work, don't you?"

"You mean with FAROUT? I thought you didn't like it when I referred to that as volunteer work."

"I don't. It's a real job."

"But you don't get paid."

"That's not the point. It's important work. What I'm talking about are all the hours of my life I spend fixing up *Marjorie Jane*. I should get a medal or something for that. She's a lost cause. That's got to be considered charitable work."

"I have to say, I have been impressed with how hard you've been working on her. You might even win this bet you have with Norm. Liam said the same thing."

"Hey, you never did tell me about your conversation with him. What did you find out about what's going on between him and Ken?"

"I didn't ask him about that. We ended up talking about the

game on Friday night. I never did end up getting to see it because of...what you found."

"You mean Darren's body?" Scooter blanched. I squeezed his hand. "I'm sorry. I shouldn't have said that out loud. Maybe we should develop some sort of code when we talk about murder investigations." Scooter started to look faint. At least he was sitting in a chair this time. If he passed out, hopefully he would slump over the table and not on the floor. "Want me to get you some more pie?"

"Please."

"Why don't you tell me about the basketball game?" I said, hoping to distract him while I served him another slice.

After he gave me a play-by-play recap and scraped the last bit of pecans off his plate, his color improved.

"Hmm...it sounds like Liam gave you a really detailed account of the game," I said.

"I guess that means he has an alibi," Scooter said. "The game was on when the you-know-what happened."

I sighed. "I don't know. I really thought he might have done it, especially after that conversation I overheard him having with Ben at the Tipsy Pirate."

"You never told me about that," Scooter said.

"Sure I did."

"Nope. But that's probably because you were eavesdropping, and you knew I would give you a hard time about it."

"I wasn't eavesdropping. I just happened to be standing nearby when they were talking about poaching fish. It sounded like Liam was involved in it, and he got Darren messed up in it too."

Scooter raised his eyebrows. "Uh-huh."

"No, you're the one who always forgets to tell me things. I bet you bought a powerboat and you've forgotten to tell me about it."

Scooter grinned. "Trust me, after what happened when I bought *Marjorie Jane* for you, I'd never buy another boat without talking to you about it first."

"Speaking of boats, I want to show you Penny's new business card." I walked over to the counter and looked through my purse. "Huh, it's not here, and neither is my wallet."

"Where do you think it is?"

I shrugged. "Maybe I left it at Penelope's, or it fell out of my purse on the way back to the marina." I slung my purse over my shoulder and gave Scooter a quick kiss on the forehead. "I'm going to retrace my steps and see if I can find it. That means you're on dish duty," I said quickly over my shoulder as I dashed out the door.

* * *

As I drove past the bakery, I noticed that the lights were off, and the sign on the door said Closed. I parked the car in their lot and began retracing my steps back toward the marina. I halted in my tracks when I reached Suzanne and Norm's office and reviewed the listings displayed on the large window extending from the corner of the building to the entryway. Wow, property really was going for a pretty penny in Coconut Cove.

After reading the details for a condo in town and admiring the large pool that residents had access to, I noticed a picture of a very familiar-looking cottage next to it. I peered through the window and spotted Suzanne sitting at a desk with her back to me, tapping on a keyboard with one hand while holding a phone up to her ear with the other.

When I knocked on the glass to try to get her attention, she turned and gave me a wave before looking back at her computer. I pushed the office door open and marched up to her desk.

"What's the meaning of that?" I demanded, pointing at the window.

She glanced up at me, held up her phone, and motioned for me to sit on a chair. Instead, I strode over to the window and tore the advertisement down. When I turned it over, I realized I had ripped the wrong one off the glass—this was the condo. The views from the balcony overlooking the pool really were nice.

I moved over to the file cabinets running along the wall, where office supplies were stacked. I took some tape and reattached the condo ad to the window, but not before noting that it had a large spa tub in the master bath. I do love a good soak in a big tub. Then I pulled the one featuring our cottage down and slammed it on Suzanne's desk.

"Care to explain this?"

"Just a sec," she said to the person on the other end of the phone. "Mollie, have a seat. I'll be with you as soon as I can."

"Tell them you'll call back," I said forcefully. "I want to talk about this now."

Suzanne frowned, then ended her call.

"Now, what's all this fuss about, dear?"

I pointed at the picture of my cottage.

"Oh, that." She clucked her tongue. "You're right. It isn't a great picture, but it's the best I could do with my phone. When the photographer comes out tomorrow, he'll get much better shots. This one is just a temporary one."

"Suzanne—"

"No, don't say another word. I take full responsibility for not having the photographer come out earlier."

"But—"

She wagged a finger. "Really, it's my fault. Now, you look like you could use a cup of coffee." She pushed back her chair and walked over to the back of the room where there was a small seating area. She picked up an insulated coffee carafe and poured some into a china cup. "How do you take it?"

"I don't really want any—"

"Let me see if I can guess." She looked at me thoughtfully. "You seem like a gal who takes two sugars and plenty of cream. Am I right?"

"Actually—"

"Of course I'm right." I shook my head as she fussed with the coffee. "You know what would go nicely with this? One of the chocolate tarts we have left over from our client event tonight. How does that sound?"

"No, I couldn't..." I started to refuse, but I had given Scooter most of my piece of pecan pie. "Oh, what the heck. Why not?"

"You just have a seat over here," Suzanne said. "I'll go grab them from the kitchen."

As I sank into the comfy chair, she set the box down in front of me. "French provincial?" I asked, pointing at the white coffee table.

"Why, yes, it is." She gave me an appraising look. "I'm

surprised you recognized the style."

"My mom is really into interior design." In an effort to distract Suzanne from the crumbs I'd brushed off my shirt, which had landed on the Persian rug, I pointed at a lamp. "Tiffany?"

"Right again. That's Norm's side of the office," she said. "I had a hard time convincing him that it would add a touch of class to his desk."

The shared office space was a study in contrasts. Suzanne's side was feminine. The furniture was white, the rugs were pastel, and there were needlepoint cushions on the pale blue velvet-upholstered couch in the seating area. Norm's side was full of dark wood, leather seats, and a variety of taxidermy specimens adorning the walls.

"I don't know how he works like that," Suzanne said, waving her hands dramatically. "His desk is tucked back against that wall, and he can't see out the window." She poured some more coffee into my cup. "Now, if my Xander were working here, we'd reconfigure the whole space, maybe knock out that wall there, and—"

"Suzanne, can I interrupt you for a second?" Before she could refuse, I quickly added, "We really need to talk about the cottage." I walked over and picked up the advertisement from her desk, crumpled it up, and tossed it in the garbage can. Or rather, next to the garbage can. I really need to work on my aim.

"When—I mean if—we ever decide to sell, we'll let you know. Right now, the cottage isn't on the market."

"You're being a tad dramatic, don't you think, dear? I promise you, we'll get better pictures." She picked the paper off the ground and smoothed it out on her desk. "We'll make sure to get a shot that shows off those lovely flower beds."

I tried to snatch the paper back and ended up knocking some files onto the ground. I bent down and was shoving the pages that had fallen out back into the folders when I noticed a document labeled "Coconut Cove Tropical Resort."

"Here, give me those," Suzanne said. As she placed them on her desk, her charm bracelet caught my eye. How could I have forgotten Mrs. Moto's discovery earlier today?

I walked back to the seating area and picked my purse up off the coffee table. I pulled the gold charm out and held it up. "Does this look familiar?"

She rushed over. "Oh, you found it! I've been searching for that. Where was it?"

"In the boatyard."

"The boatyard? That doesn't make sense. I never set foot in there." She clutched the charm in her hand. "Thank you so much for bringing it back. I'm so lucky you found it."

"Actually, it wasn't me who found it. Mrs. Moto did."

"I don't think I know her. Is she new to the area?"

"No, she's lived here for a while at the marina."

"Another one of those people who lives on a boat, like your friend Penny. I should have a word with her. I just got a new listing she might be interested in."

"I think she might have a hard time getting a mortgage."

"Oh, bad credit?"

"No, she's a cat."

"A cat?" After she considered this for a moment, she asked, "Is she one of those pets who had a rich owner who left her everything in the will?" She chewed on her lip. "I might just know the perfect place for a well-to-do feline."

"She's happy where she is," I said. "Now, getting back to the charm—Mrs. Moto found it near the murder scene."

Suzanne gasped. "What a grisly thing to find." She dropped the charm on her desk, opened up a drawer, pulled out a disinfectant wipe, and scrubbed her fingers. "Well, I'm just glad it's back safe and sound with me and out of that nasty, dirty boatyard."

"How do you think it ended up there?"

She picked up the charm with a tissue, being careful to avoid touching it directly, and placed it on top of a notepad. "I'll have to take that into the jewelry shop tomorrow and have them clean it properly and reattach it to my bracelet," she said, ignoring my question.

I bit my lip. I was beginning to have second thoughts about giving the charm back to Suzanne. Even though it wasn't exactly found at the murder scene, Mrs. Moto did find it nearby. Perhaps I should have reported the discovery to the authorities.

"Uh, Suzanne, do you think maybe we should tell the police

chief about the charm?"

"Why would they be interested in a silly little charm?"

"Well, because of where it was found."

"Don't you think you're overreacting, dear?" Suzanne said. "I'm sure there's a simple explanation."

"Like…"

She shrugged. "Maybe it fell off in the car, Norm put it in his pocket to give back to me later, and then it fell out of his pocket when he was working on the boat." She fussed with her bracelets. "Why are you so interested, anyway? It's not like we had anything to do with that poor young man's death. Besides, we were both here in the office the night of the murder."

"Well, if it wasn't one of you, who do you think did it?"

She leaned forward in her chair and lowered her voice. "I hate to speak ill of the dead, but apparently Darren was poaching fish. That sort of thing angers a lot of people."

"Do you really think anyone would murder someone for poaching fish? That seems a bit extreme."

"What's this about murder?" Norm asked darkly, standing in the entryway.

"Oh, Mollie and I were just talking about what happened to Darren. Such a sweet young boy." She gave Norm a warning look. "I was telling her how we were both here working late the evening he was killed."

Norm put his hand on the back of his wife's chair and glared at me. "What business is it of yours what we were doing? Do you think aliens were involved? Maybe one of them beamed down and killed Darren because he was going to tell everyone he had been abducted." He gave a humorless laugh.

Suzanne reached up and tugged on his arm. "Norm's just kidding. Isn't that right, darling?" she said.

"Sure, I was just kidding," he said. He walked around to the other side of his wife's desk, picked up the charm, and stared at it thoughtfully. As he set it back down, he grabbed the file folders. "What are these doing here? How many times have I told you to keep these locked up?" He walked over to a file cabinet, placed the folders inside, and shut the drawer.

I picked up my purse and made my way to the exit. As I opened the door, Suzanne took my arm. "Don't mind him. It's just the stress of everything. I'll see you tomorrow morning," she said as she gently pushed me outside. "And don't worry yourself into a tizzy about my charm."

"But—"

"Tell you what, why don't I tell the chief about it? Will that make you feel better?"

Before I could respond, she stepped back inside, shut the door, and flipped the sign in the window over to the Closed side.

I walked toward my car overwhelmed by questions. Was it really plausible that Norm had dropped Suzanne's charm in the boatyard? What exactly was the Coconut Cove Tropical Resort, and why had Norm locked the files up? And more importantly, did Mrs. Moto think she was going to inherit a fortune from us when we died?

CHAPTER 8
THE CASE OF THE MISSING COLLAR

BEN LOOKED UP FROM SANDING the teak rails on *Mana Kai*. "Taking a break again, Mollie? Wasn't your last one five minutes ago?"

"No, it wasn't. It was..." Okay, just between you and me, it was five minutes ago, but I wasn't going to admit that to Ben. "I'm not actually on a break. I'm...uh...oh, never mind."

"Calculating how much paint you'll need to cover the bottom?" Ben offered helpfully.

I gave him a thumbs-up. "Yes, that's it."

"And how much paint do you think you'll need?" he asked.

"Um...I'm not sure yet. I think I'll need to do some more calculations while I have some water. Math problems are always so dehydrating." I plucked a bottle out of a cooler, closed the lid, and sat on it. "Want one?" I asked. "Looks like you're on a break too."

"Yeah, why not? I've been at it for a couple of hours."

I watched as Ben climbed down the ladder attached to the Chois' boat, holding on with one hand while balancing a large toolbox in the other. He lost his balance when his foot slipped on one of the rungs.

"Oh no," he said, looking at the hammers, screwdrivers, and wrenches scattered on the ground.

"Are you okay?" I asked. "You could have broken your arm like Leilani did."

"I'm fine." He put everything back in the toolbox with some help from me, then wiped dust off his tattered shorts. "Do me a favor. Don't tell Nancy what happened. She'll have a fit."

"She has fits all the time," I said. "What's so special about this?"

"We're supposed to hand things down to someone else or use a bucket with a rope attached to it to lower stuff down. 'Two hands on the ladder,' she always says."

"Don't worry, your secret is safe with me. Although, as much as I hate to say it, Nancy probably has a point."

Ben raised his hands in the air. "You're right. It won't happen again. I really don't want to lose this job."

He walked around *Marjorie Jane*'s hull and inspected my work. "How come you and Scooter don't pay the boatyard to take care of your projects?"

"Well, Scooter wants us to do everything ourselves. That way we'll know the systems inside and out."

Ben nodded. "Makes sense. Of course, things end up taking twice as long or more when you're doing them for the first time. I can see how Scooter would think it's an exciting challenge doing all this, but what about you? You don't seem like you're enjoying it."

I laughed. "There are times when I've thought a root canal sounded like a much more pleasant way to spend the day. But I don't want to spend a penny more on this boat than we have to. She's costing us a fortune as it is." I brushed my hand along the keel, noting areas that needed more sanding. "Plus, there's the matter of that bet I have with Norm. I would love to see the look on his face when he has to name his boat *ET*."

"I think there are a lot of people who'd pay to see that," Ben said. "By the time you're finished with this, you're going to be a pro, Mollie. Maybe you should get a job working at the boatyard too."

"I probably should," I said. "At least that way I'd get paid to be tortured instead of paying the marina for the privilege of having our boat here to work on it."

"Are you seriously thinking of getting a real job?" Ben asked.

I scowled. "Why does everyone think my work with FAROUT isn't a real job?"

"Hey, I get it," Ben said. "When I'm not working here, I'm practicing my guitar. I consider it my real job. The boatyard is just what pays the bills." He started strumming an air guitar. "One of these days, I'm going to make it big."

"I admire the fact that you can get up there in public and perform." I unzipped my Smurf suit in an attempt to cool down. "I would get such stage fright."

"You? That surprises me. You seem like you'd be a natural at it."

"Well, we'll find out soon enough. I have to give a speech tonight at a FAROUT meeting." I shaded my eyes and looked up at the sun. I wasn't sure how much longer I could stand to work outside in this heat. I kept reminding myself that I should be grateful I was doing this in winter. Things would be even worse during the summer. Hopefully, we'd be done working on this boat by then.

Ben gulped down the rest of his water. "Is your bottle empty? Give it to me, and I'll toss these in the recycling bin. Then I should probably get back to work. Break time's over."

While I debated whether I should continue sanding or go practice my speech, I noticed that Scooter had left his cell phone on a work table next to the Chois' boat. At last, my opportunity to erase those horrible Smurf photos he'd taken of me. I went over, picked it up, and tapped the screen. For some reason, his phone was unlocked. Not that it was ever hard to crack his passwords. His one for the computer was always the name of his current favorite cereal, and the PIN for his phone was my birthday.

I tapped on the album icon and scrolled through the photos. When had Scooter taken all these pictures of turtles? When had he even had a chance to go to the turtle sanctuary? And what were all these ones of the beach about? I was always the one who took those kinds of shots when we were out for a stroll. Not one single Smurf picture. Had he already deleted them?

His phone beeped, and a text flashed up on the screen.

I've got proof. If you don't do what I say, everyone will know what you did.

Proof of what? What did Scooter do? Who would send him something like this?

"No problem. I'll just head to the house and call you from there. We can walk through the contract then," a familiar voice said behind me.

I turned and saw Scooter holding a phone up to his ear. Then I looked back at the phone in my hand.

He ended his call, walked over, and gave me a quick kiss on the cheek. "Listen, panda, I've got to head back to the cottage for a while. Problems with that deal I'm working on. How about if I bring some fish-and-chips by for lunch?" The phone in his hand rang. "Oh, gotta get this. See you later," he said, dashing off toward the car.

If Scooter was talking on his phone, then whose phone was this? Did he have two phones?

I reread the text and noticed that it had come from Liam. Why would Liam text my husband? They barely knew each other. When I checked the other texts, there was a series of similar threats, but from Darren, not Liam.

As I puzzled over this, Ken pulled up in his vehicle. He leaned out the window and shouted up at Ben, who was back working on the teak rails. "Hey, have you seen my phone anywhere?"

"No, man. Sorry, I haven't," Ben said.

"Is this it?" I asked, holding up the phone. "I found it on the work table."

"That's it! Thanks, Mollie. Got to go. Class starts in thirty minutes."

As he pulled away, I wondered why Liam was threatening him, and Darren before that. What was Ken mixed up in?

* * *

After sanding the bottom for a couple of hours and elevating my Smurfiness to a new level, I took another break. Okay, okay, I'd only been sanding for thirty minutes, but it had felt like hours.

Was this bet with Norm really worth it?

The answer to my question came in the form of a conversation I overheard between Liam and his uncle. The redheaded young man was on his phone, leaning against his car. "I'm telling you, at the rate this chick is going, you'd better plan on changing the name of your boat. On the plus side, *ET* is only two letters, so it won't cost as much to get the vinyl decal printed up."

By the way in which he held the phone away from his ear, I guessed that he was getting chewed out. "Relax. I was just kidding." He listened for a moment. "You want me to do what? Oh, come on, it's just a stupid bet." After another pause, he interjected, "Hey, just wait a minute. I did everything you asked —"

My back was getting stiff from crouching under *Marjorie Jane*. I thought about coming out from underneath the boat, but I didn't want to be seen, especially when the conversation was getting so interesting.

"No way. I'm not going to. I've been asking around town about her, and—just let me finish, will you? Anyway, apparently she's really nosy, always asking questions and getting involved in things that aren't her business. The last thing we want to do is give her a reason to poke around in our affairs."

Norm must not have liked his answer because Liam held the phone away from his ear again. I could hear his uncle's voice, but I couldn't make out what he was saying. I did my best imitation of a limbo dancer and crept under *Marjorie Jane* to get closer. I lay on the ground, grateful for once that I had a protective suit on. The dirt and grime on the tarp underneath the boat was disgusting.

From my new listening post, I could make out about every other word that Norm said. "Paint...send message...scare...crazy... broad...Yoda...fish..." He also mixed in a lot of swear words, which I won't repeat here. And yes, it sure did sound like he said "Yoda." Of course, if Scooter were here, he would have said that perhaps I've watched the *Star Wars* movies one too many times and that Norm probably said something like "you shoulda," and I misheard it.

Liam ended the call after assuring his uncle that he would take care of the matter. I was beginning to worry that I might be the matter in question. I was shimmying backward when a cloud of dust swirled around me, causing me to cough loudly.

"Mollie, what are you doing under there?" Liam asked.

"Uh, just checking the...um..." I tried to remember what could be on the bottom of the boat that I would be looking at. Scooter had given me a book on sailboats for Christmas. Granted, it wasn't one of his best gift-giving ideas, but at least it had been better than presenting me with another *actual* sailboat. One was enough. The book itself was really dry—I hadn't made it past the first chapter—but it did make a handy coaster on my nightstand. It had a diagram on the back cover showing the different parts of a sailboat. I chewed on my lip while I tried to remember what was underneath the boat.

"Checking the what?" Liam asked.

"Um...the running rigging," I said, hoping I had guessed right.

"Do you mean the thru-hulls? Or maybe the sacrificial zinc?" Liam asked.

I climbed out from underneath the boat. I tried to visualize the back of the book again, but drew a blank. I didn't have a clue what a sacrificial zinc was, but thru-hulls sounded vaguely familiar. "Um, yeah, the thru-hulls. That's what I said."

"No, you said 'running rigging.'" He pointed upward. "Those are the lines you use with your sails."

"Don't be silly. I know that. Everyone knows that." I made a mental note to do a bit more studying up on sailboats going forward.

Liam looked at me with a bemused expression on his face while he tapped his phone against his leg.

"Hey, can I borrow your phone?" I asked.

"My phone? Why?"

"I need to call Scooter. You don't mind, do you? I left mine at home."

He handed me his phone reluctantly.

"Let me guess," I said. "Is the password 'YODA' by any chance?"

"What?" He snatched the phone back. "Give me that." After punching in a few numbers, he handed it back.

I clicked the text icon and scrolled through his past messages.

Sure enough, there was the one he'd sent to Ken. There was also a very naughty one to a female friend. Then I saw an interesting series of old messages from Darren.

Found a sweet fishing spot

They're biting! Gonna be a good haul!

Crap! Patrol boat!

Dumped overboard b4 they boarded

"I thought you were making a call?" Liam said.

"No, I said I was going to text him," I said, quickly closing the incriminating texts. "You might want to get your hearing checked. I said 'thru-hulls' before, and you heard 'running rigging.' A minute ago, I said 'text' and you heard 'call.'" I pointed at my ears. "Do you go to a lot of loud concerts? That can destroy your hearing."

"Can you just hurry up?"

I looked at Liam's sunburned arms. "You probably should start wearing sunscreen more often too." I punched in Scooter's number and reminded him to get extra tartar sauce when he picked up our fish-and-chips.

Liam seemed confused. "But you just called him, not texted him."

I tapped my ears. "Really, go see the doctor. I said I was going to call him. Why would I text him? What if he texted back after I gave you back your phone?"

The young guy looked like he needed to sit down and take a few minutes to process everything.

"Hey, speaking of Scooter, he said you guys chatted about the game the other day."

He nodded and rubbed his temples.

"So that's your alibi for the night Darren was murdered, right? Watching a game? Watching it all by yourself?"

He looked at me sharply. "You ask a lot of questions, don't you?"

"It's called making conversation. So you said you watched the game at home, right? Where's that?"

"I'm staying with my uncle and Suzanne."

"Oh yeah, that's right. But you're a young guy. How come you don't have your own place?" I pointed over at his car. "If you can afford that, I bet you could afford a nice apartment. In fact, I bet Suzanne could fix you up with a sweet one."

"Believe me, she's tried," he said. "She keeps saying how cramped it is at their house, and goes on and on about the fact that her precious son doesn't have any place to stay when he comes to visit because I'm there. Not that he would ever come to visit. He can barely stand that witch either."

"She told me that she wants Xander to come back and take over your uncle's business."

"He's welcome to it."

"Really? I thought you liked working for him."

"No way! The man's a tyrant. Always telling me what to do and giving me the crap jobs. He doesn't want to get his hands dirty, but he doesn't mind if I do."

I carefully considered my next question. While I knew that Liam was mixed up in something, I wasn't sure if it was just poaching or if it was something more deadly. I felt safe enough talking to him in the middle of the day in a crowded boatyard, but the snippets of his conversation with Norm were causing knots in my stomach.

"So, what do you mean by getting your hands dirty?" I asked tentatively.

He clenched his fists and stared at me. "Working on boat projects. Cleaning fish. That kind of thing."

I laughed nervously. "I know exactly what you mean. Just look at me. I'm covered in dirt and paint dust and who knows what else. I guess I get stuck with the dirty jobs too."

Liam's posture relaxed. "Yeah, how come Scooter isn't helping you?"

"Good question. I'll be sure to ask him." I put my goggles back on, secured my Smurf suit, and got back to sanding. While *Marjorie Jane*'s old blue paint slowly came off, I thought about what other "dirty jobs" Liam was involved in. I was pretty sure there was more to it than just gutting fish and fixing Norm's boat.

* * *

"I want to thank all of you for coming to the first in a series of lectures on alien abduction," I said. "Tonight, I'm going to talk to you about the checklist we use to identify individuals who may have—"

"Ahem. Mrs. McGhie?" I turned and saw Chief Dalton standing in the doorway.

"May I interrupt your..." He stroked his chin. "Your *performance* for a minute?"

I had given up on sanding the boat and had escaped to the air-conditioned lounge at the marina to rehearse. I felt my face grow warm. Rehearsing in front of a cat was one thing, but having the chief overhear me was another.

"Uh, sure. I was just practicing my speech for the FAROUT meeting tonight."

The burly man raised one of his bushy eyebrows. "FAROUT? Is that the little club you belong to? We had something like that when I was a boy. The meetings took place in our tree house. There was even a secret handshake."

My face grew warmer, but this time it was due to anger, not embarrassment. I was tired of everyone mocking what I did. "It isn't a *club*. It's a nonprofit organization. We even have an accountant."

He raised his other eyebrow. "Oh, an accountant," he said dryly.

"Listen, if it wasn't for the work we do, your phone would be ringing off the hook."

"Is that right?"

"If people want to report alien activities, they can call the FAROUT hotline. We take their calls seriously. When they contact the police, they just get mocked."

"No one in our department would mock anyone, no matter why they were calling," the chief said.

"Are you sure about that?" I asked. "When's the last time anyone reported an alien abduction or UFO sighting?"

The chief scratched his head. "Well, I'm not sure. I don't recall seeing anything like that in the monthly reports."

"That's because people are too afraid to contact you. Either you'll make fun of them, or worse, you'll bully them."

"Hey, hang on there, Mrs. McGhie. We certainly don't bully people."

"Oh yeah? How do you explain your treatment of Melvin Rolle the other day? The man is grieving. First, he lost his wife, then his nephew, and all you could do was grill him as though he was a suspect."

Chief Dalton furrowed his brow. "How would you know if he's a suspect or not? That kind of information is confidential."

"Because he's not on my suspect list, that's why!"

Both his eyebrows shot up. "Your suspect list?"

I pulled out my notebook, opened it, and held it up to him. "See, there it is. Now why don't you have a seat, and I'll take you through it."

The chief smiled. "Why not? I could use a break. This should be entertaining."

As he was lowering himself onto one of the armchairs, Mrs. Moto growled.

"That's her spot," I said. "Come on, Chief, you know the rules when it comes to cats. They get first dibs on all the comfortable spots. You can tell which ones they like by all the hair they leave behind." I pointed at the couch. "Why don't you sit there instead?"

While he eyed Mrs. Moto warily, I sat on a chair opposite him.

"Well, first on the list are Ken and Leilani Choi. They were on their catamaran when the murder took place. He told me that they had the AC running, and the TV was blaring, and that they couldn't hear anything that took place outside over all that noise."

I tapped my pen on my notebook. "On the face of it, their alibi seems solid. They can both vouch for each other. Of course, Leilani couldn't have done it with her broken arm. I would think you would need two hands to lift the paint can up in the air and hit someone on the head with it. But there's something about Ken that makes me wonder."

"Such as?" the chief asked.

"Well, on the day of the murder, I saw him and Darren arguing in the boatyard. Then this morning, I saw a number of texts on

Ken's phone threatening to expose him as a fraud. Most of them were from Darren, but there was also one that Liam had sent."

"Dr. Choi showed them to you?"

"Well, not exactly." There went those eyebrows again. "Look, it was an accident. I thought it was Scooter's phone when I picked it up. But then there were all these pictures of turtles. Totally not what I expected."

"What were you expecting?"

"Smurf photos."

"Smurfs?"

"You know, the little blue people."

"Are they any relation to the little green men that you're so fond of?"

I sighed. "Can we just get back to the topic at hand?"

"Why not?" he said. "Let me try to recap. You took Dr. Choi's phone without his permission. You looked at his pictures and you read his texts, again without his permission."

"You're forgetting the most important thing here."

"No Smurfs?"

I threw my hands up in the air. "No, the threatening texts!"

Mrs. Moto jumped onto the back of the couch and sniffed the side of the chief's face. She pressed her paw on his cheek and meowed loudly before bounding back to her chair.

"See, she's trying to tell you to pay attention." I flipped over a page in my notebook. "Let's just continue, shall we?"

"By all means."

"We should probably talk about the other texts."

"Wait, there were more on Dr. Choi's phone?"

"No, Liam's phone."

"Did you accidentally borrow his too?"

"No, he loaned it to me. He was standing right there when I read the texts."

The chief furrowed his brow. "He knew you were reading his texts?"

"No, of course not. I think he would have been really embarrassed if he knew I saw the one he sent to a girl named Fiona."

"So this is about what, sexting?"

"No, this is about poaching. Pay attention."

"I'm trying, but this conversation is starting to remind me of one of those telenovelas. You know, those Spanish-language soap operas with the overly dramatic, convoluted plots."

"You don't strike me as the kind of guy who watches soap operas."

"I don't. My ex was into them. Is there a point here?"

"Liam and Darren were taking fish illegally. I know that's not your department's responsibility, but you should touch base with the Fish and Wildlife people about it."

"Noted."

"Ready to go on?"

"Sure. This is almost better than TV, even soap operas."

"Next up are Norm and Suzanne Thomas. They're another one of those husband-wife alibis. Suzanne told me that both of them were working in their office the night of the murder."

"I heard that you've listed your cottage with Mrs. Thomas."

"What? Where did you hear that?"

"I'm the chief of police. I hear everything."

"Well, did you hear about all the fights?" I leaned forward in my chair. "Melvin and Norm appear to have a long-standing feud. They nearly got into blows on Valentine's Day, and then they really got into it at the Tipsy Pirate on Sunday night."

The chief perked up. "Hmm. Go on."

I took a deep breath and continued. "And, of course, getting back to Norm's nephew, Liam, he isn't much better. He got into a fight with Darren on the night of the barbecue over Alejandra Lopez. He claims he was watching a basketball game on TV that night, but I'm not sure if he has anyone to back up his alibi."

I scrawled a few notes down on things I wanted to follow up on. I noticed that Chief Dalton had his arms folded over his chest. "How do you keep track of all this, Chief? Don't you have a notebook or anything?"

The chief tapped the side of his head. "It's all here. Carry on. This is most enlightening."

I leaned back in my chair. "Maybe it's your turn to enlighten me. Did Suzanne talk to you about her charm?"

"It would be inappropriate for me to comment on whether a

woman is charming or not. Especially a married one."

"No, I meant the charm that fell off her bracelet."

"I have no idea what you're talking about."

"Didn't she call you about it?" The burly man shook his head. "We found it in the boatyard near the murder scene. I recognized it from Suzanne's charm bracelet. I considered telling you about it, but it wasn't in the cordoned-off area, and when I returned it to Suzanne, she said it wasn't any big deal. She thought maybe her husband had dropped it. But she did say she'd tell you about it."

The chief got a small notebook out of his pocket and scribbled something down. "You said 'we found the charm.' Who was with you?"

"Mrs. Moto. She's actually the one who found it. I just returned it to Suzanne."

"Mrs. Moto found it?"

"Yes, she's a very clever cat."

The calico began purring loudly. The chief watched as she kneaded the cushion.

"She also appears to be a cat in need of a collar and license," he said.

I looked at Mrs. Moto's neck and put my head in my hands. "I can't believe she's managed to lose another one." She rolled onto her back. I walked over, sat on the armrest, and rubbed her belly. "She doesn't like wearing a collar. They're too constrictive."

"If she's going to be an outdoor cat, she's going to have to learn to wear one," he said sternly. "My two Yorkies manage to wear their collars without complaining."

"Maybe we just haven't found the right one yet. She's very particular about what they look like."

The chief arched one of his bushy eyebrows. "Well, I suggest you find one that she'll wear, or keep her indoors." He looked at his watch. "Before I go, what exactly did this charm look like?"

After I described it and answered a few more questions about where it was found, he walked toward the door. He put his hand on the doorknob, then looked back at me. "Mrs. McGhie, can I offer you a piece of advice?"

I nodded reluctantly. When someone asks you if they can offer advice, it's usually not something you want to hear.

"If you really want to be an investigator"—he held his hand up —"and I'm not saying you should pursue that line of work, then you need to be objective. I noticed there were people you didn't have on your suspect list. Now, maybe that's because they're friends of yours or because you think they're too nice to have committed a crime, but you can't rule people out for those reasons."

"Friends of mine? Like who? Do you mean Ben and Penny?"

"I don't mean anyone in particular," he said. "But we can rule them out anyway. They were both playing Mexican dominoes late into the night with a group of people."

I breathed a sigh of relief. It had never occurred to me that they would be involved, but it was good to hear that the police wouldn't be harassing them with questions.

As if he could read my mind, the chief added, "I would also caution you not to characterize the questioning of individuals as *harassment*. There are things you aren't aware of, information you're not privy to."

"Well, you could be a little nicer about how you ask questions," I said.

The chief rubbed his face with his hands. "Maybe you should just stick to this alien stuff. You actually have people in Coconut Cove convinced it's real."

My eyes lit up. "Really? Like who?"

"Well, my ex-wife for one. She reads your newsletters."

"Is she the one who does paintings of fairies?"

He rolled his eyes. "Yep, that's her." He pointed at Mrs. Moto. "Don't forget that collar."

After he left, I sat on the couch and considered what he had said. Was it possible I wasn't as objective in this investigation as I had thought I was? Were there other people I should have on my suspect list?

CHAPTER 9
STAGE FRIGHT

"WELL, HERE GOES NOTHING," I said as I pulled into the parking lot of the community center. "I really wish I hadn't had those cookies before we left. I feel like I'm going to throw up."

"Don't be nervous. You're going to do great," Leilani said, unfastening her seat belt. As we walked toward the building, she added, "I heard about how you handled Norm when he was making fun of you for believing in aliens. You weren't a shrinking violet. You put him in his place."

"But that was in the heat of the moment. There were only a few people there. There are over fifty people signed up for this event." I gulped. "Fifty!"

I pivoted and began walking back to the car. Leilani grabbed my arm. "Wrong way, Mollie. Take a deep breath. You can do this." She steered me toward the entrance while I tried not to hyperventilate.

A young man with spiky orange hair and an alarming number of facial piercings greeted us at the door. He was wearing a bright green T-shirt with a picture of a spaceship beaming a human aboard and the words "Pick Me" printed underneath. I had purchased a shirt just like it at the FAROUT convention last year for Scooter, but for some reason he never wore it.

"Are you here for the talk?" he asked.

"We are," Leilani said. She nudged me. "Well, actually, I'm here for the talk. This lady here is your speaker."

"You're Mollie?" he asked. "I'm Simon." He took my hand and shook it vigorously. "I'm so honored to meet you! I read your recent article in the newsletter about the alien abduction case at that marina in Coconut Cove. Whatever happened to the victim?"

"Oh, it's a long story," I said. "Suffice it to say, other issues came up."

"I want to hear more about that," Simon said. "I hope you're going to cover it in your lecture."

Those cookies were making their presence seriously known in my stomach. "Do you mind if we go inside? I'd like to freshen up before we start."

I pushed the door open and darted for the ladies' room. When I came back out, a small crowd had gathered around the registration desk. Simon was handing out FAROUT brochures and answering questions. He waved me over.

"Can I get you a cup of coffee or tea before we begin?" he asked. "One of the volunteers also brought some chocolate macaroons. I can get you a couple of those too."

Fortunately, I'm not fond of coconut, so it was easy to pass on the macaroons, which my upset tummy thanked me for. I took my cup of coffee and made my way to the front of the room, nodding nervously at the people sitting in folding chairs. I put my purse on the table next to the lectern and pulled out my key chain. I stroked the tiny Wookiee doll attached to it for good luck, just in case rubbing Coconut Carl's belly hadn't been enough to help me get through the evening.

"Everyone, take your seats, please," Simon said. "It gives me great pleasure to introduce our speaker tonight, Mollie McGhie, who's going to talk about alien abduction. Mollie is not only an investigative reporter for FAROUT but also lives on a sailboat and has plans to sail around the world with her husband. Maybe they'll even explore the Bermuda Triangle." Several people oohed and aahed. Simon smiled at me. "I'm sure she'll be happy to answer questions about their planned voyage at the end of her talk."

Leilani smiled at me from the front row and gave me a thumbs-up sign. I narrowed my eyes. Did Scooter have her on his payroll? Was she the one spreading rumors about Scooter and me circumnavigating the globe on our boat?

Fortunately, thoughts about *Marjorie Jane* sinking in the Bermuda Triangle distracted me from speaking to a large crowd. After explaining the signs that indicated that someone had been abducted, giving evasive answers to questions about sailing, and blushing at the loud applause at the end, I joined Simon and Leilani at the refreshment table.

"You did a fantastic job," Leilani said. She fished a tea bag out of her cup and tossed it in the trash. "I didn't realize that sleepwalking and bruises were signs that you had been abducted."

"Sounds like we've got another convert." Simon handed her a membership form. "You should join FAROUT."

"I'll think about it. Right now, I belong to a lot of organizations, mostly to do with sea life conservation. I don't know if I can commit to another one just now."

"Ooh...sea life conservation. My girlfriend's really into that. She leads scuba diving tours and does underwater photography in her spare time. How did you get into it?"

"It's kind of the same for me. My husband got me into it. He's a marine biologist. He works at the Gulf Coast Turtle Sanctuary, and he's an adjunct professor at the community college." Leilani took a sip of her tea and smiled. "Some friends set us up on a blind date. I thought he was really smart and cute, and the next thing you know, I started volunteering at the same organization. I really enjoyed working with the nesting habitat project with him, and in no time at all, we got married."

"How long were you dating before you got engaged?" I asked, wishing they had something to eat other than macaroons. Maybe I could convince Leilani to grab a bite to eat before we headed back to the marina.

Leilani blushed. "Only six months. It was love at first sight. My parents objected to us getting married so quickly. They said we didn't have time to really get to know one another, but they were wrong. I couldn't be happier."

"Did they warm up to him after that?" I asked.

"Oh yes, especially once they found out he had a doctorate. They were very impressed by that."

"Same for me and my girlfriend—love at first sight," Simon said. "So what other organizations do you guys belong to? Maybe we're all part of the same ones."

"Well, there's the Florida Turtle Trust, the Waterways Protection Society, and the Coastal Environment Action Group."

"The Coastal Environment Action Group?" Simon frowned. "Aren't they the ones who were responsible for sabotaging those boats in the Florida Keys last year?"

"Why did they do that?" I asked.

"There was a group of fishermen who were taking lobster out of season. They had already been investigated and fined by the authorities, but apparently that wasn't good enough. These people are really hard-core. The-ends-justify-the-means type of group. They'll do anything to send a message."

Leilani shook her head. "That was all hyped up by the press. It's run by a group of scientists who wouldn't hurt a fly. In fact, they'd go out of their way to save a fly. Well, maybe not a fly, but dolphins and whales and that sort of thing."

Simon pursed his lips. "Well, that's not what my girlfriend says, but—"

My stomach growled loudly, interrupting his thought. "Leilani, do you mind if we get going? I'm starving. I really need to get something to eat."

Leilani shrugged and mumbled goodbye to Simon. As we walked out the door, I remembered that I had left my purse by the lectern. Simon intercepted me as I went up front to get it. "How much do you know about your friend and her husband?" he whispered. "No matter what she says, the people who run the Coastal Environment Action Group are into some scary stuff. I'd be careful if I were you."

Leilani called out, "Are you ready, Mollie? It's starting to rain outside." I pulled the car keys out of my bag and looked at my lucky Wookiee charm. I knew many members of FAROUT were prone to conspiracy theories. Maybe Simon was reading more into the group Ken belonged to than there really was. Or maybe Leilani and Ken were mixed up in something more serious.

* * *

I chowed down on a cheeseburger, fries, and a chocolate shake on our way back to the marina. Leilani swore she wasn't hungry after eating macaroons at the FAROUT meeting, but I did notice that she helped herself to a number of my fries.

"So, what did you think of Simon?" I asked, hoping to maneuver the conversation toward the topic of the Coastal Environment Action Group.

"Nice guy," she said, pilfering another fry. "Although I can't say I liked all those piercings he had on his face. Looks painful."

"It was quite a coincidence that his girlfriend and Ken have so much in common. Maybe you'll run into her and Simon at some conservation meetings in the future."

Leilani angled the air-conditioning vent toward her. "Maybe. Although Ken hasn't been going to as many of those lately as he used to."

"Does that have anything to do with the sabotage Simon was talking about?"

Leilani frowned. "Like I said before, that's just someone trying to stir things up. Look, he cares about poaching and its effect on sea life populations, but he would never stoop to something like that. He's an environmentalist, not an ecoterrorist."

I stopped at an intersection and reached down to grab a fry, only to find that Leilani was holding the bag in her hand.

She popped one in her mouth, then stared at me earnestly. "Ken focuses more on educating the public about the dangers of big companies and developers. Their whole focus is on making money. They don't care what damage they do to the environment. They'll say or do anything to get around zoning laws and regulations, including trying to tarnish the reputation of people like my husband." She crumpled up the french fry container and shoved it into the paper bag forcefully.

As we neared the entrance to the marina, I saw Liam standing on the corner having a heated discussion with a woman. He was leaning forward and jabbing his finger in the air repeatedly. She put her hands on his chest and pushed him backward, then ran across the street, her flowery dress flapping in the breeze behind her.

Liam stared at her retreating back, his face contorted with rage. She tried to open her car but dropped the keys on the pavement. She leaned against the car and put her head in her hands. Liam crossed the street, picked up her keys, and handed them to her. She looked at him tenderly as he wiped away a tear on her face.

"What was that about?" I asked as the light changed. I made a right turn into the marina parking lot and pulled into a spot.

"I don't know," Leilani said. "I think that was Fiona Anderson. She and her husband live in the Tropical Breeze condos."

"She's married?" I adjusted the rearview mirror to have a better look. Liam was holding the door open as she got into the car. "They seem kind of cozy."

Leilani twisted in her seat to have a look. "Maybe there's an innocent explanation."

"Or maybe he's a bit of a player. Did you notice how he was all over Alejandra at the marina potluck?"

Leilani grinned. "He didn't have much luck, did he?" She grabbed her purse and the paper bag with her good arm. "Thanks for the ride. The FAROUT meeting was really interesting."

"So, do you think you're going to join?"

"I'll think about it," she replied. "Maybe when things calm down at work. I picked up a new client this week. He's really demanding, and I've got a huge database project to complete over the next few weeks." She opened the car door. "Hey, Ben should be done with the teak tomorrow. You'll have to stop by and have a look. He's done a great job."

"Will do. I have to be out here anyway. Lots more work to do on the bottom."

I watched as she tossed the bag into the trash, then made her way down the path toward the boatyard. As I backed out of my parking spot a horn sounded. I slammed on the brakes. I glanced in the rearview mirror and saw a dark SUV zip past me toward the back of the parking lot.

After my heart stopped racing, I continued reversing, making sure to keep an eye out behind me. As I put the car into forward, I looked behind me again. Someone wearing a dark hooded top got out of the vehicle and pushed through the brush that separated the parking lot from the boatyard.

I couldn't imagine ever being in such a hurry that I'd walk through there at night. Not only would you get scraped by the thorny bushes, but you could never be sure if a snake or rabid raccoon were lying in wait. Any sensible person would take the well-lit path instead. Unless, of course, you didn't want to be seen. Was that how the murderer had sneaked into the boatyard the night of Darren's death?

CHAPTER 10
HOW NOT TO CLIMB A LADDER

I DECIDED TO GO TO the boatyard early while Scooter slept in. He had been tossing and turning all night, worrying about the latest deal his company was doing. After taking a quick shower, brushing my teeth, and running a comb through my hair, I gave him a kiss on the forehead. He mumbled something that sounded like "more Cap'n Crunch"—probably a reference to the fact that we were still out of his favorite cereal.

Mrs. Moto lifted her head and blinked slowly at me, in that way that felines do to let you know you've been deemed worthy of being allowed to be part of their lives, as long as you keep their litter box clean and food bowl topped up.

She meowed softly, which I took to mean that I should pick up more cat food at the grocery store along with Scooter's box of crunchy nuggets. I scratched her on the head as she nestled back into the crook of her second-favorite human's arm. Of course, I was her number one human. That just went without saying.

Since Scooter wasn't up to make me my morning coffee, I swung by Penelope's. I chose a couple of *pains au chocolat* fresh out of the oven to go with my cinnamon spice mocha. While I waited for my coffee, I noticed a large poster advertising the upcoming annual Coconut Cove Boating Festival. It promised all sorts of exciting activities—sailboat races, concerts, a parade, and a pet-costume competition.

Hmm...I wondered if I could get Mrs. Moto to wear a Sherlock Holmes outfit. Or maybe dress her up as Miss Marple. No, that would probably be a mistake. Miss Marple was always knitting something. I could just imagine the mischief she would get into if one of the props were a ball of yarn. Who was I kidding? We couldn't even get her to keep a collar on. Wearing an adorable detective-themed costume was never going to fly.

Next to the poster was a sign-up form for a cake contest that would be taking place during the festival. I scrawled my name down. I was confident that my fudge chocolate cake was going to win first prize. Then I noticed who was on the panel of judges—Nancy. Knowing her, she'd probably accuse me of trying to poison someone with my home baking.

The sun was just coming up by the time I parked next to *Marjorie Jane*. I decided to sit in the cockpit and watch the sunrise while having my breakfast. I clutched my coffee cup and pastry bag in one hand and slowly climbed up the ladder, holding on with my other hand. When I neared the top, I reached up to grab the railing on deck in order to hoist myself up the final stretch.

Instead of feeling something metal as expected, my fingers encountered a damp and slightly squishy object. I jerked my hand back, then started to fall backward. I quickly seized the ladder with my other hand, causing my cup and pastries to plummet to the ground.

I cautiously peeked over the side of the deck to see what the dampness and squishiness were all about. Three tree frogs stood stock-still staring at me before making their escape via some overhanging branches. I breathed a sigh of relief. Tree frogs were a far better outcome than some of the other scenarios that had played through my head.

Unfortunately, my early morning wildlife encounter had resulted in a tragedy. I gazed down at my coffee cup sitting in a puddle of cinnamon-chocolaty goodness. This was not a great start to the morning. On the plus side, the *pains au chocolat* had come through unscathed, but they definitely needed caffeine to accompany them.

After tossing the empty cup in the trash, I trudged back up the rungs. This time I had learned my lesson—two hands for the ladder. I didn't have a pail and rope to hoist my pastry bag up as Ben had suggested, so I did the next best thing and tucked the bag inside my shirt. Sure, it looked a little strange, but the boatyard was deserted at this hour of the morning.

I decided to hunt in *Marjorie Jane*'s galley for the jar of instant coffee that we had left on board for emergency purposes. If this didn't qualify as an emergency, then I didn't know what did.

The search proved to be a monumental challenge. In his quest to discover the source of our water leak, Scooter had removed all the floorboards, exposing the bilge, in order to gain access to the various hoses, fittings, and tanks that lay underneath. I had studied the sailing book Scooter had given me the previous night, so I now knew the bilge was the compartment below the waterline. Water could collect in this area, something both Scooter and I were now very familiar with. That's why a functioning bilge pump was so important. You wanted to get water out from inside the boat before it sank her.

Scooter had laid down some narrow pieces of lumber over the cavities at the bottom of the boat. I felt like I was walking the plank as I made my way across the cabin. One wrong move and I would fall into the bilge, likely twisting an ankle in the process. The experience reminded me of one of Ben's T-shirts, the one that read "Walk the Plank, Ye Scurvy Dog." I didn't have scurvy, but I was seriously suffering from a case of caffeine withdrawal.

Balancing on a board running the length of the galley, I finally found the instant coffee in the farthest cupboard. It was sitting behind a tub of dehydrated acai berries and a container of turmeric, both left over from one of Scooter's short-lived health kicks. I think that particular one had lasted thirty-eight minutes.

I got the kettle out, put it under the faucet, and turned the water on. Nothing. Then it hit me—our water tanks were empty. I should have realized this earlier. Why would we have water in the tanks if Scooter had the whole system torn up? The lack of coffee was really impacting my ability to think clearly.

I cautiously made my way across the plank and sat on the

couch. I pulled out one of my pastries and took a few bites. The flaky crust and gooey chocolate filling gave me the energy I needed to figure out a solution to my problem. There was a water tap between our boat and *Mana Kai*. I could fill the kettle up there and presto, coffee would be served.

When I sat at the edge of the deck and prepared to twist my body around in order to climb down the ladder, I realized there was a problem. How would I keep both hands on the ladder and carry the kettle down? I remembered Ben's suggestion to pass things down to another person on the ground, but the boatyard was still deserted.

I looked at the kettle. It really wasn't a nice kettle. We had picked it up in a secondhand store, and it was beginning to show its age. So I dropped it overboard. I watched as it bounced off *Marjorie Jane*'s hull, chipping some of her red paint off, then struck the ladder and landed in the puddle of coffee at the bottom that I had never bothered to clean up.

I was beginning to think this was the worst plan I had ever come up with, but then I remembered the time I had tried to teach sign language to raccoons. Boy, had that ever been a disaster.

After washing the kettle off and filling it up with water, I faced my next hurdle—how to get the darn thing back up. It was too big to tuck inside my shirt. My throwing ability wasn't the best and would likely result in more paint being chipped off the boat and water ending up everywhere. I decided to take Ben's advice and hoist it up.

I searched around our boat for a rope to tie to the handle. All I found were a few toy mice that Mrs. Moto had batted off the deck, sandpaper, a chisel, and a large pile of rags. I poked under the stained and smelly scraps of cloth and discovered not one but two cat collars. So that's where she had been hiding them.

This whole enterprise was getting ridiculous. It now dawned on me why they referred to having your boat out of the water propped up on jack stands in the boatyard as being "on the hard." Just trying to make one simple cup of coffee was hard work for sure.

I remembered that Liam had tossed some ropes over the side of his uncle's boat. Surely they wouldn't mind if I borrowed one. I walked around the stern of *The Codfather* and stopped dead in my tracks. I looked on in horror at the scene in front of me—Suzanne, lying on the ground, her legs and arms twisted unnaturally beneath her.

After leaning up against the side of the boat for a moment, struggling to breathe normally, I forced myself to go over and check her pulse. But as I got closer, it was clear that I wouldn't find one.

As I collapsed on the ground in shock, I felt one of her stiletto heels under me. For some reason, all I could think about was how its robin's-egg-blue color matched the pencil skirt she was wearing. As I picked it up, the breeze caught a scrap of green paper and blew it across the boatyard. I spotted the other shoe by the bow of Norm's boat. I'm not sure why, but I felt compelled to take that one as well.

My eyes focused on the matching shoe, I tripped over the metal ladder on the ground next to Suzanne. That's when I noticed the message spray-painted on *The Codfather*'s keel: You've Been Warned, Now You'll Pay.

* * *

The chief found me huddled on the steps of the boatyard workshop. I was shivering despite sitting in the warm sunlight. While finding dead bodies was always unnerving, Suzanne's death had really shaken me. I wondered if it was because she had fallen off the ladder, something that I'd almost done earlier that morning.

"Mrs. McGhie, are you okay?" he asked gently. I think even he realized how upset I was. He held out his hand and helped me up. "I understand you were the one who found Mrs. Thomas. Are you up to answering a few questions?"

"I think so," I said. I reached up to touch my necklace, something I always did when I was feeling stressed or anxious. My eyes welled up when I realized it wasn't hanging around my neck. "I can't believe I lost it," I said, tears dripping down my face.

"Lost what?" The chief searched in his pocket, pulled out a crumpled-up napkin, and handed it to me.

"Thanks." I blew my nose. "The necklace Scooter gave me. I think of it as my good-luck charm, but I lost it a few days ago, around the time I found Darren's body. Do you think there's a correlation? Am I jinxed?"

"No, you're not. Besides, there's no such thing as luck, good or bad."

"Of course there is," I said. "You don't think it's bad luck that I've found *four* bodies now?"

"I'd say it's unfortunate. But it isn't because you're jinxed or because you lost your necklace. You just always happen to be in the wrong place at the wrong time." He reached in his other pocket and handed me another napkin. "What time did you find Mrs. Thomas?"

"About a half hour ago, I think," I said. "Although it could be longer than that. I'm not really sure." I chewed my lip. "It seemed like her body had been there for a while. I took a seminar at the FAROUT convention last year. It was given by a medical examiner. He told us that you can estimate how long someone has been dead by—"

"You don't need to worry about that," the chief said. "Our coroner will determine the time of death."

"But it was before I got to the boatyard, right? I'd hate to think she was lying there dying, and I didn't hear her screaming out in pain."

"Why do you think she screamed?"

"Well, you saw the body and the way she was lying on the ground. She must have been on *The Codfather*'s ladder when she fell off. Landing like that would be incredibly painful. She could have been lying there for hours in agony." I took a deep breath. "I guess we can only hope she was struck unconscious when she hit the ground."

"So, just to be clear, did you or didn't you hear anyone screaming?"

"No, I didn't hear anything. The place was deserted." I glanced over toward where I had found Suzanne. *Marjorie Jane* was right next to *The Codfather*. I should have been able to hear something from there. Next to our boat was *Mana Kai*. "Have you spoken to Ken and Leilani yet? They live on their boat. Maybe they heard something."

"Officer Moore is talking with them now."

"Now that I think about it, they probably didn't. Darren was murdered not too far from their boat, and they didn't hear a peep then."

The chief gazed over at the three boats. "Strange to think people actually live here."

"Strange is right," I said. "The idea of living on a boat is weird enough, but living on one here? That's crazy. Not to mention dangerous."

I looked at the placard on the side of the workshop listing the boatyard's rules and regulations. "I hate to say this, but Nancy is right. Going up and down ladders here is dangerous. I almost fell off ours this morning. I can only imagine what would have happened if it hadn't been tied on. When I had that nasty tree frog encounter and let go of the boat, the ladder could have tipped backward. I could have been lying on the ground like Suzanne."

"So you think it was an accident?"

I glanced at him quizzically. "You don't?"

"I didn't say that."

"Oh my gosh! I just remembered something. The ladder next to Suzanne had some rope attached at the top. It had been tied on." I chewed on my lip while I thought through the implications. "That means that either the rope frayed naturally—although it's pretty unlikely that it happened at the same time on both sides—or someone deliberately untied it or cut it. Maybe they even pushed the ladder when she was on it."

"Hmm."

"That's all you can say—hmm?"

The chief shrugged. "Why exactly were you over by *The Codfather*?"

"I was making a cup of coffee."

The chief raised his eyebrows. "Coffee?"

"It's a long story." I sighed. "I could really use a cup right about now."

"We're almost through here. So, you were making coffee over by *The Codfather*, and…"

"No, I was looking for a rope."

"I've never heard of making coffee with rope. Sounds interesting."

Officer Moore walked over from questioning the Chois, saving me from explaining the whole kettle fiasco. She whispered something in the chief's ear and handed him a piece of green paper.

"All right, just a few more questions, Mrs. McGhie. Did you touch anything over by where you found the body?"

"I touched Suzanne to see if she had a pulse."

"Other than that."

I shook my head. "Nothing."

"Are you sure?"

"Positive."

"You said you were looking for some rope. You didn't pick any up?"

"No, I completely forgot about rope and coffee when I saw Suzanne."

"Let me try phrasing this another way. Did you pick anything up and remove it from the scene?"

"Of course not."

The chief stared at me. I stared back without saying a word. I was convinced I was going to win the stare-down competition, but then he raised both of his bushy eyebrows. I couldn't help but look up at them twitching above his eyes like fuzzy caterpillars making their way across a tree branch, just like the tree frogs had done earlier.

The minute I broke eye contact, he took a step toward me. "I'll ask one more time," he said, enunciating every word. "Did you touch anything, accidentally *borrow* it, put it in your purse or your pocket, and completely *forget* about it?"

His breath smelled like coffee, which caught me off guard. I had figured him for a sweet tea drinker. "Do you know where I can get a cup of coffee around here?" I asked. "I don't want to have to drive all the way back to Penelope's."

"Just answer the question."

"No, I didn't touch, borrow, stash away, or forget to tell you about anything. Are we done?"

"Just one last question. What do you think the message 'You've Been Warned, Now You'll Pay' means?"

I scratched my head. "It could refer to just about anything or anyone. Warning Liam off about poaching. Warning Norm and Suzanne about this property deal they're supposedly mixed up in, or…"

"Or what?" the chief asked.

"Or maybe someone could have left it because they were angry about Norm trying to drive other fishing charter businesses out of operation."

"Someone like whom?"

I took a deep breath. "Someone like Melvin."

* * *

Officer Moore had asked me to wait for her at the patio in case there were any follow-up questions. There was no way I was going to survive a minute longer without some form of caffeine. But here was the conundrum—there was bound to be a Coke or possibly even an iced coffee for sale at the marina office, but could I face dealing with Nancy before I had had any caffeine?

I'd have to try to sneak in, creep stealthily toward the coolers in the back, open them quietly, nab a couple of cans, and get back outside before she spotted me. The sticking point was how to pay for them without talking to Nancy. Perhaps I could tuck some money in between the beer and milk for her to find later.

My plan fell completely apart when Nancy yanked open the door, causing me to fall headfirst into the office, knocking down a display of fishing lures in the process.

As I tried to pick them up without slicing my fingers with the barbs, Nancy barked, "What were you doing skulking outside?"

Rather than tell her about my ingenious caffeine-procurement plan, I said, "Sorry, I was just preoccupied thinking about Suzanne's tragic death."

Nancy put her hands on her mouth, speechless for once.

Ned stepped out from behind the counter, holding a bucket

full of cleaning supplies. "Did you say Suzanne was dead?"

I nodded while sorting the purple lures from the ones with orange spots.

"What are you doing on the floor?" Nancy asked, her power of speech restored.

I stood and placed the lures into color-coded piles on the counter. "Just picking these up."

"Humph. Those ones go over there," she said, pointing at the ones with long green streamers. "And those other ones go over there."

"Nancy, can you forget about the lures for a minute? I want to hear what happened to Suzanne," Ned said.

After I told them about finding her body at the bottom of Norm's boat, my theory about the ladder being deliberately untied, and the message the killer had left behind, they both peppered me with questions.

"Do you think the two murders are connected?" Ned asked.

"Hmm. That is a good question." I pondered the connection between Suzanne's and Darren's deaths while I hung the lures on the display stand. "I can think of people who might have wanted one of them dead but not the other."

Nancy handed me a lure. "Like who?"

"Well, Norm might have killed Darren to drive Melvin out of business, but he wouldn't have killed his own wife." Nancy and Ned exchanged glances. I looked back and forth at them. "Or would he?"

Ned shifted the bucket of cleaning supplies from one hand to the other. "Well, I did hear Norm complain about how much money Suzanne kept spending on furniture for their office. He said she married him for his money and was bleeding him dry."

"Interesting turn of phrase, considering she's the one who ended up covered in blood."

Nancy pursed her lips. "I can't say I like the man, but killing your own wife..."

"Sometimes a woman can be insensitive and stick her nose into things where it doesn't belong," Ned said.

She gave him a sharp look. "Well, sometimes a woman can just be trying to help, and her husband is too pigheaded to realize it."

"I've got a question for you guys," I said, trying to defuse the situation. "What was Suzanne doing there, anyway? She told me she would never set foot on a boat, let alone one on the hard." I thought about her robin's-egg-blue stilettos and skirt. "And she certainly wasn't dressed for climbing up a ladder and onto a grimy boat."

"That's a good point," Ned said. "She always was dressed to the nines."

Nancy pointed at the lures. "You need to redo that section, Mollie."

"What, aren't these organized enough for you?" Ned asked.

"Things can always be better organized." She glanced at the bucket Ned was holding. "And cleaned properly."

When he didn't respond, she turned back to me. "What were you doing in the boatyard at that time in the morning? I didn't think you were such an early bird."

"I couldn't sleep, so I decided to work on sanding the bottom before it got too hot."

"I doubt if you'll get any more work done on it for a while now," Nancy said. "The police will barricade it off while the investigation is under way."

"But it didn't happen by *Marjorie Jane*. It happened on *The Codfather*."

Nancy shrugged. "They're both right next to each other. What were you doing over by Norm's boat, anyway?"

"Trying to get a cup of coffee." Before Nancy could ask any follow-up questions, I said, "It's a complicated story. I don't want to go into it now. And it's been a really long morning, and I still haven't had a single cup of hot, liquid caffeine."

"You know we got a new coffee maker in the lounge, don't you?" Ned asked.

"That's the best news I've had all morning."

"Come on, I'll show you where it is."

Nancy frowned. "Why would you need to show her where it is? She isn't blind. I'm sure she'll have no problem finding it." She pointed at the pile of papers on the counter. "I need you to work on this after you're finished cleaning up over there."

Ned placed the bucket on the counter right on top of the papers. "Do it yourself. I'm on break. Come on, Mollie. Let's go have some coffee."

Nancy scowled. She moved the bucket to the side and shook off imaginary dust from the top sheet of paper. As we walked out the door, she said, "Don't forget to put some money in the donation jar next to the machine. Both of you."

* * *

"What's going on with the two of you?" I asked as I filled up our cups. Ned stirred sugar into his, then motioned over to the sofa. I leaned back against the cushions and took a sip from my cup. There wasn't any milk in the fridge, but I didn't care. Even black, this was the best coffee I'd ever had.

"Let me ask you a question, Mollie. Would you ever take something that was important to Scooter, that he had spent days organizing, and completely undo all the work he had put into it?"

"Well, he's pretty disorganized with laundry. He always leaves his dirty socks on the floor, and I end up having to put them in the hamper. Does that count?"

"Wow, that's brave. If I ever did that, Nancy would kill me." He smiled. "But that really wasn't what I was talking about."

"So tell me. Maybe I can help."

"I don't know if anyone can help," Ned said, wringing his hands together.

"Well, maybe I can't help, but I can listen. It might make you feel better to get it off your chest."

"You know how I like old movies?" I nodded. "I've been collecting DVDs for years and keep them in plastic storage tubs in the spare bedroom. Nancy started complaining about how much space they were taking up. Then our son suggested I transfer them to the computer. It sounded like a good idea. Nancy would be happy that there was more room, and I could play them directly from my laptop."

"That is a good idea. I've heard that lots of people who live on boats do the same thing."

"Right. Same reason that e-readers are so popular. Cruisers

can't afford to carry lots of books, considering how many spare parts they need to stow on board."

"How does Nancy figure into all this?"

"I spent a long time separating them into different piles based on the type of movie they were—westerns, comedies, thrillers, epics, that sort of thing. I even had a stack dedicated to films featuring Peter Lorre."

I smiled, remembering how Ned had been the one to name our cat after Peter Lorre's detective character in his *Mr. Moto* films. Only he hadn't realized at first that it was a she, not a he, which was why she was now known as Mrs. Moto. Her black markings in the shape of eyeglasses and the fact that her breed had Japanese origins had reminded Ned of the lead character in the movies.

Ned took another sip of his coffee. "I had it all planned out. I put the discs in groups to make it easier to save them in separate folders on my computer. That way, if I was in the mood for a World War II movie, for example, I would be able to go straight to that folder and find one easily."

"Sounds like a great system. So what happened?"

"Nancy's what happened. She got a bee in her bonnet that I wasn't doing it right. She said my approach didn't make sense. I told her I had it set up just the way I wanted. Then one day when I was out, she decided to reorganize everything alphabetically. When I came back and saw what she had done, I was furious."

"Maybe she was just trying to help," I said tentatively.

"That's what she said. But I didn't ask her to help, and I certainly didn't want her help." He walked over to the window and stared outside.

While he collected his thoughts, I refilled our coffee, stirring extra sugar into his. After a few moments, he sat back down.

"Thanks," he said when I handed him his cup. "I'm sorry to dump this all on you."

"Don't worry about it. Sometimes you need to get things off your chest."

"When it comes to running the marina, her organizational skills are great, second to none," he said. "She enjoys doing all the paperwork, managing suppliers, and overseeing the staff. I'm happy she takes care of all that. Believe me, I don't want to be in charge of making arrangements for the garbage dumpsters to be emptied. But when it comes to *my* movies, I wanted to be the one in charge of that."

"Have you tried talking to her about it?"

"Lots of times, but she can't or won't admit to what she did."

"I have a feeling that kind of thing doesn't come easily to Nancy."

Ned smiled. "You're probably right."

"I can kind of relate to how she feels. I hate admitting when I'm wrong." I leaned forward and patted his hand. "You guys will work through it."

"You're right, we will. When I think about couples like Norm and Suzanne, I'm grateful that we've got a solid marriage at the core."

"Do you think he could have killed her?"

Ned hesitated, then said, "I can't say for sure."

"What can you say?"

"He has a temper." He shrugged. "Although everyone around town already knows that. But..."

"But what?"

"I saw him put a guy in a choke hold once. We're not talking an ordinary fistfight that sometimes happens when guys have had too much to drink. This fellow was standing outside the Tipsy Pirate having a smoke, and Norm grabbed him from behind, totally unprovoked. I saw him say something to him before letting him go, and then he laughed when the guy collapsed on the ground."

"That's awful!"

Ned chewed on his lip. "The worst part about it was that I was across the street and should have rushed over to stop it, but I just froze. By the time I came to my senses and went over to help, Norm had already taken off."

"Did you mention it to the police?"

"I did, but the guy didn't want to press charges, so nothing came of it."

Ned looked at me grimly. "So yeah, could I see Norm murdering someone? Sure. But his own wife? That I'm not so sure about."

CHAPTER 11
FUN WITH MARKERS

OKAY, SO REMEMBER WHEN I'D told Chief Dalton that I didn't touch anything at the crime scene, or accidentally borrow it, stash it away, and forget about it? Well, that wasn't exactly the truth. But it wasn't a lie either. I actually did forget. You would have, too, if you'd been confronted with a dead body. Finding Suzanne had really thrown me for a loop. It wasn't until later that I remembered the incident with the shoe. Of course, the chief didn't see it that way.

"What do you mean, you forgot?" The burly man leaned forward across his desk. "You picked up a shoe and went in search of another one. You just spent five minutes describing the exact shade of blue it was..." I waited while he referred to his notebook. "Here it is—robin's-egg blue. And you went on in excruciating detail about what type of skirt she was wearing..." He made another check. "A pencil cut skirt. Why would anyone name a style of clothing after a writing implement?"

"Can I go now?"

"No. Back to the shoe. You held it in your hand just minutes before I questioned you, and you *forgot* about it?"

"But I dropped it."

"So when you drop things, you no longer remember them?"

He made a show of dropping a pen on the floor. He bent down and picked it up, then removed the cap in a dramatic fashion. "Good thing I remembered I was holding this just a second ago," he said. "It's one of my favorites."

He jotted down a few notes on a piece of paper while I tried to make myself comfortable on the hard wooden chair in front of his desk. I don't think the townspeople would object if he spent a little bit of our tax money on some cushions.

He raised his head and caught me squirming. "Officer Moore is going to be back in a few minutes with some photos of the crime scene. I'll want you to review them, so you can point out where the evidence was *originally* before you contaminated the crime scene."

While he was scribbling things down—probably specifications for a more uncomfortable chair for visitors to sit on—I looked around his office. There was a stack of file folders on one side of the desk next to a coffee cup crammed full of markers. Maybe he spent his spare time coloring in drawings of jail cells and squad cars.

I watched as he pulled a green marker and an orange one out. After debating between the two, he jammed the orange one back. Good choice—green was much easier on the eyes. Next, he underlined something on his notepad.

"What does green stand for?"

"Things to follow up on," he said without looking up.

"Like the message spray-painted on Norm's boat," I suggested. The chief ignored me and selected a pink marker.

"Okay, since you're not exactly in a talkative mood, how about if I make an educated guess? It has to do with the suspects in the two murders." I pulled the cup closer to me and selected a dignified marker, a fine-tipped black one. I got my notebook out of my bag and opened it up to a list of names.

The chief looked pointedly at the black marker.

"Do you mind if I use this one?" I asked.

"I do." He pulled open the top drawer of his desk and handed me a run-of-the-mill ballpoint pen. He pointed at the container of markers. I replaced the black one, then examined the pen in my hand.

"You don't happen to have a blue one I could use instead of this one, do you?"

"Does this look like Walmart?" He glanced at his watch and muttered something about Officer Moore taking a long time.

I put a star next to a couple of names on my list. The pen left annoying globs of ink on the page. "Okay, why don't we start with people who had motive to kill both Darren and Suzanne? Now, that's the tricky part of this investigation, isn't it? Who would want to murder both of them? Melvin wouldn't have killed Darren —he's his own flesh and blood—and one would think Norm wouldn't have murdered Suzanne—she's his wife. Rather, she was his wife."

I noticed the chief had paused his scribbling. I took that as a sign to continue. "But what about Liam? He and Darren got into a fight over Alejandra at the marina barbecue. He could have killed Darren in a jealous rage." I tapped my pen on my notebook. "Did you know that Scooter doesn't think anyone would kill just for love? But I happen to know for a fact that it's the number one cause of spousal homicide."

"And how do you know that?"

"I read an article on it. A *scholarly* article."

The chief smirked. "You do realize that what you read in the *National Enquirer* isn't exactly written by academics."

I slammed my pen down on his desk. "I'll have you know that I read it in *Extraterrestrial Studies Quarterly*, which is a highly regarded, peer-reviewed journal."

Chief Dalton plucked a purple marker out of the container and went back to his notepad.

"Although there did seem to be some issues between Suzanne and Liam."

I watched as the chief's eyebrows twitched slightly. He was definitely listening. "Suzanne went on and on about her son and how much better he would be as a successor to Norm. She didn't exactly think Liam had a lot going for him in the intellectual department. Maybe he got tired of her attitude?"

Both of his eyebrows shot up on his forehead. He quickly scribbled something down.

"Of course, Norm had his share of enemies. Maybe someone killed his wife to send a message to him."

"You do realize that the murders might not be related," the chief said. He tore off the colorful pages from the pad and stuck them in a file folder.

"I guess," I said. "But what are the chances that two murders happened within days of each other, in a small town, and they aren't related?"

The door to the chief's office opened, and Officer Moore poked her head in. "Do you have a sec, chief?"

"Sure." The burly man rose. As he walked around the desk, he pointed at the markers. "Don't touch anything while I'm gone."

I held out for a minute, but there was this one pen that looked like it might be a nice shade of robin's-egg blue. I couldn't help myself. As I reached across the chief's desk, my foot got caught in my purse strap and I stumbled, knocking the markers to the floor along with the file folders.

Fortunately, the coffee cup didn't break. I set it back on the desk, scooped up the markers, and replaced them in the container. The file folders were a different matter. They had scattered across the room, sending the papers flying out of them into a jumbled mess. I sat on the floor and attempted to sort everything back into the right folder.

Nancy would have had a field day here. I'm sure she could have organized the documents in no time, probably developing a new and improved filing system in the process. I, on the other hand, was struggling to determine whether all the expense reports belonged together or were meant to be placed in separate folders based on date.

As I started to collate the papers, I found an evidence bag stuck between two autopsy reports. Inside was a piece of lined pale-green paper that looked like it had been ripped out of a notebook. The top corner was missing, and there were dark stains scattered on the page. But what really caught my eye was the message, written in block letters.

If you want to get it back, meet me on The Codfather *at 9:00 PM. Bring $5,000 in small bills. Wait for me in the main cabin. Come alone. Don't even think about going to the police. If you do, I'll know about it and then I'll destroy you.*

While I tried to process what I had just read, the door opened. "What's going on here?" the chief demanded. "I thought I told you not to touch anything."

"It was an accident. These fell off your desk, and I was just picking them up."

"Give those to me," he barked. He grabbed the folders and papers, but I held on to the evidence bag.

"Do you want to tell me about this?" I asked.

"I most certainly do not."

"I've seen this before."

"Don't tell me you touched that, too, at the crime scene."

"I wasn't actually sure it was found there, but now you've confirmed it." He snatched the bag from my hand. "But I did recognize the paper. It's an interesting shade of green. I saw what must have been the corner of the page get blown away by the wind."

"So you didn't touch this?" he asked, placing the bag on the center of his desk.

"The shoes, yes. The paper, no." I leaned forward to have another look. "What do you think the message means? What did they have on Suzanne that she was willing to pay five thousand dollars for?"

Officer Moore knocked on the door. "I've got those photos ready."

"Great. Why don't you get set up in the conference room, and I'll bring Mrs. McGhie down there in a minute?"

I picked my purse up off the floor and edged toward the door.

"I'm not finished with you yet," the chief said.

While he paced back and forth behind his desk, I could hear Officer Moore in the hallway telling someone that they found an empty spray-paint can, but that there weren't any prints on it or on anything else at the scene. This was turning out to be a very productive visit to the police station. First, learning about the message the killer had sent Suzanne, and now the spray paint.

And, as a bonus, when I'd picked up Suzanne's autopsy report, I'd noticed that the time of death had been between nine and ten in the evening.

"Are you listening to me?" The chief had stopped pacing and was staring at me.

"Uh, yeah." I tiptoed over to his desk and set the ballpoint pen he had lent me down. "There you go."

He threw his hands up in the air. "Fine. Let's just go look at those photos and be done with it."

* * *

After I had finished reviewing the photographs and explaining in excruciating detail exactly where Suzanne's shoes had been originally, I sat on a bench in the police station lobby and gave Scooter a call. He had left a few messages checking to see if I was all right. I reassured him that I had recovered from the shock of finding Suzanne's body and told him about the new leads I was going to follow up on.

Before he could try to dissuade me from investigating the two murders further and possibly putting myself in danger, I changed the subject and asked what he wanted to do about dinner. Apparently, he and Mrs. Moto had something special planned, provided I agreed to swing by the grocery store and pick up some Cap'n Crunch and half a dozen cans of Frisky Feline Ocean's Delight.

After he promised that cereal and cat food weren't involved in his secret recipe, I ended the call. As I walked down the steps from the police station, I ran into Melvin. He looked terrible. His face was gaunt, he had dark circles under his eyes, and his hands were shaking as they gripped the metal railing on the stairs. When he reached the top step, he stumbled. I rushed over to take his arm.

"Are you okay?" I asked. I pushed the door open, ushered him inside, and held his arm while he slumped on the bench.

"What is with these people?" he demanded angrily. "All I want to do is bury that boy in peace. I was at the funeral parlor with his parents making arrangements when the police chief summoned me here to answer more questions. How many more questions could they have of me? It's their job to figure out what happened and bring his murderer to justice, not mine!"

"Maybe it's not about Darren. Maybe it's about Suzanne," I said.

He cocked his head at me. "Suzanne? Why would the police want to talk to me about her?"

"You haven't heard? She was killed yesterday in the boatyard."

"Killed? How?"

"Someone untied the ladder from Norm's boat. Then when Suzanne was climbing up it, they pushed it, and she fell to her death."

"Are you saying it's murder?"

"Looks like it."

Melvin frowned. "No, I hadn't heard. It's no secret that Norm and I don't get along, but I'd never wish that on him. I know what it's like to lose your wife." He slapped his hands on his thighs. "No, this can't be about Suzanne. I didn't even know about it."

"I think it must have happened sometime between nine and ten. I'm sure you have a good alibi for then."

He rubbed his eyes. "Sure, sure. I was at the Tipsy Pirate then. You can ask anyone." He had a determined look on his face. "I don't have anything to worry about."

"I'm sure you don't."

"The person who should be worried is Norm. And not just about Suzanne. He killed my Darren. And now he's going to pay. He can grieve for his wife from prison."

"So you're sure he did it?"

"Of course he did." Melvin shook his head. "Not that going to jail is enough for what he did to that fine young man. And it sure won't keep me from going out of business."

"I didn't realize things were so bad."

"We were operating on a knife-edge with the charter business. Stealing customers from us was bad enough, but now he's been spreading rumors about how my boat isn't seaworthy. People are scared to charter with us."

"What about the marine store? Is that doing poorly as well?"

"No, it's doing okay. But to tell you the truth, I just don't have the energy to manage it anymore. I'm tired. Maybe I should just sell the store, retire early, move back to the Bahamas, and live out my final days there. I don't have any fight left in me anymore."

While I tried to console him, Officer Moore came out into the hallway. "Mr. Rolle, we're ready for you now."

He got to his feet slowly and squeezed my arm. "You won't tell anyone what I said, will you? I was just letting off a little steam."

As I watched him follow Officer Moore, I wondered if maybe he'd had a little fight left in him after all. Perhaps enough to have killed Suzanne as retribution for Darren's death.

* * *

After the police station, I went to the marina. Scooter had texted me to say that one of us needed to go to the office to deal with some paperwork. Nancy had updated the rules and regulations and was requiring all boat owners to review the changes and initial their acceptance. And since I was already in town, I had drawn the short straw.

"It's right here," she said, pointing at the printout on the counter. "Section 7.2(a). Only American quarters can be used in the washing machines and dryers. Anyone found using a non-American coin will be responsible for paying a fifty-dollar fine and the cost of labor to fix the machine." She handed me a pen. "Initial right there."

"Are you serious, Nancy? Is this because Leilani accidentally put a Bahamian quarter in the washer?"

"Do you know how long it took Ned to get it out?" She didn't wait for my answer. "Three hours! That's three hours he could have spent repairing the dinghy dock." While I considered the potential ramifications of not playing along with her rules and regulations game, Nancy glared at a fly on the counter. She raised the swatter in the air and smacked it down right next to my hand.

"Hey, there wasn't even a fly there," I said. "It had already flown away."

"They're everywhere, dear. The sooner you put your John Hancock on that piece of paper, the sooner you can get out of here. You don't want to get caught in the cross-fire, do you?" she asked as she took aim at another fly.

I scribbled my initials and stepped back quickly, bumping into Ned. "I'm sorry. Here, let me help you pick those up." I bent down and scooped up the screws that had fallen out of his hand.

"Thanks, Mollie," he said. He glanced over at the counter. "I see she's got you in here too."

I shrugged. "It's fine. I wash my clothes at home. No need to use the machines here, so it really doesn't apply to me."

"Are you finished yet, Ned?" Nancy asked as she stapled some papers together. He walked out of the office like he didn't hear her, swinging his toolbox. I guessed he wasn't quite ready to make up.

Nancy slammed down the stapler. "I don't know what's gotten into him. You make one little change, and he totally overreacts." She picked up the flyswatter and began decimating the insect population again, one smack at a time.

While I was debating whether to buy a regular iced coffee or a vanilla-flavored one, the door swung open, and Nancy's grandkids —Katy and her younger brother, Sam—ran in.

"Grandma, tell Katy not to touch my race cars," Sam said.

"What's this about, children?" Nancy asked, tousling their hair.

"They're my cars, not hers!" the little boy said.

"They were in my way," Katy said.

Sam leaned against his grandmother and sniffled. "She took apart my race track, and she hid my cars."

"I didn't hide them. I just put them away." Katy put her arm around her little brother. "I was just trying to help. Mama would have been mad if she came home and found them on the dining room table like that."

"See, Sam? Katy was just trying to help," Nancy said. "Now, why don't the two of you make up? Katy, say you're sorry for touching Sam's cars without his permission, and then you can each pick out a candy bar."

While I walked up to the counter with my iced coffee, I noticed Nancy looking thoughtfully at the two kids as they selected their treats.

* * *

By the time I left the office, it was a little after five o'clock. It's amazing how quickly the day goes by when you find a dead body, and there's a murder investigation going on. I spotted Leilani over at one of the patio tables typing away on her laptop with one hand. Her day had probably been more productive than mine.

"Did you hear about Suzanne?" I asked, pulling up a chair next to her. "It was just awful finding her body like that."

I set my purse on the table. Leilani looked up with a start. "Oh, hey there, Mollie," she said, removing a pair of headphones from her ears. "Did you say something?"

"Oh, I was just talking about the latest body in the boatyard."

She grimaced. "Wasn't that awful?" She wrapped the cord around her headphones and tucked them in her bag. "Sorry, I didn't hear you. I've been listening to an audiobook. I can't wait to find out whodunit."

"I've never really gotten into audiobooks. I like mine the old-fashioned way."

"Oh, they're fantastic. I listen to them all the time when I'm working. It helps the time pass faster, especially when it's a boring task, like updating spreadsheets or working on boat projects. I always turn the volume way up so I can't hear what's going on around me. The fewer distractions I have, the more focused I can be."

"I should probably leave you be so you can work."

"No, stay. I'm done for the day. Have you heard anything more about what happened?"

I told her about finding Suzanne and what Ned had said about Norm's temper. I also told her about the note in the evidence bag, leaving out the part about the markers and papers flying everywhere.

"But if Norm killed his wife, why would he have sent her a note asking her to meet him at the boat? Couldn't he have just asked her to meet him?" Leilani asked.

"That might have been the only way he could have gotten her there. She would never have stepped foot in the boatyard unless she thought that was the only way she could get back what had been taken from her."

"So it was a diversion?"

"Maybe. Same thing with the message that was spray-painted on his boat. It was designed to throw suspicion off him." I opened up my iced coffee and took a sip. "I'm still surprised that you and Ken didn't hear anything. It happened between nine and ten."

"Hmm...between nine and ten? Ken wasn't there at the time. He was at a Florida Turtle Trust meeting. He didn't get back until eleven. And you and I were at the FAROUT meeting. You really were great, by the way."

"Thanks," I said. "I dropped you off around eight thirty, eight forty-five, didn't I?"

"Around then."

"What did you do after that?"

"Headed straight back to our boat." She tapped her ears. "Then I listened to my audiobook while I caught up on email."

"So you didn't hear anything?"

Leilani frowned. "No, I didn't. It's scary to think all that was happening just a few feet away from where I was sitting." She held up her broken arm. "At least I'm not a suspect. Of course, it's not like I had any reason to kill Suzanne. Besides, there's no way I could have pushed a ladder over with just one arm."

"Not to mention your other wrist," I said. "Is it getting any better?"

"A little bit. At least I can do some one-handed typing. Otherwise, I'd be so far behind with work it wouldn't even be funny."

"I'm impressed with how well you manage with just one arm."

"You learn to adapt, don't you?" She pointed at the teenage girl walking across the patio. "Tiffany's here, and it looks like she brought pie." Leilani closed her laptop. "Come on, we should probably get going."

"Going where?" I asked.

"Nancy's, of course. I love these girls' get-togethers of hers— wine, appetizers, dessert, and doing our nails." She stared at her hands, one in a cast and the other still bruised from her fall. "Of course, I think I'll just be sticking to my toes this time."

"Uh, I wasn't invited."

"Oh, I just assumed that's why you were here," she stammered.

"Don't worry about it. I'm not exactly one of Nancy's favorite people. She hates that Mrs. Moto runs around the marina, and I made a stink about one of the regulations a few weeks ago. Besides, I don't paint my fingers or my toes."

Tiffany came over to the table and set the pastry box down. "It's blueberry," she said. "I'm excited to dmy fingernails in our school colors for the basketball game this weekend. It was so nice of Nancy to invite me. Probably because I babysit her grandkids."

"Ah, to be back in high school—those were the days," Leilani said. "What I wouldn't give to not have to worry about working for a living. It'll be nice to chill out this evening, especially with all the commotion in the boatyard."

"I haven't been back there since this morning," I said.

"The place is still crawling with cops. They've got the area around your boat and Norm's completely cordoned off. I was so relieved when they decided we would still be able to access our boat. Guess you're off the hook for a while on painting the bottom."

"I'd almost be happier to be sanding than have to deal with Chief Dalton and his questions." I inched my chair away from the pastry box. The smell of blueberries was tempting me to crash Nancy's party just so I could have a slice of pie.

"I think we lucked out," Leilani said. "Officer Moore questioned us. She's a lot more pleasant to deal with."

Tiffany slid forward in her chair. "Who do you think did it? Everyone's talking about it around town. It's scary to think there's not only one murderer out there on the loose but possibly two."

"That's what makes it tricky—was it the same person?" I thought about the charm that Mrs. Moto had found. "One possibility is that Suzanne killed Darren. Then someone killed her as retribution."

"No, it couldn't have been Suzanne," Tiffany said. "I saw her working in her office that night."

"You did?"

"Well, promise you won't tell anyone, especially my parents," she said.

"I don't think we can make that promise until we hear what you have to say first," Leilani said. "Murder is a serious matter."

Tiffany took a deep breath. "Okay. I was at the park across from her office that night with my boyfriend. My parents don't like him, and they told me I'm not allowed to see him anymore." She made a face. "They keep telling me I should date someone like Chad."

Leilani and I exchanged glances.

"But it's not like anything happened," Tiffany said quickly. "We were just talking."

"Then you don't have anything to worry about," Leilani said. "I think you need to tell your parents and the police what you saw. It could be important."

She reluctantly agreed. While she texted someone—presumably her boyfriend to tell him the cat was out of the bag—Leilani asked me who the prime suspect was.

"I don't know if I have a prime suspect, but I'm leaning toward Liam," I said. "He's the only person I can think of who would have wanted to kill both of them."

"After what you've told me, I can see why he might be responsible for Darren's death," Leilani said. "But Suzanne?"

"There was a lot of animosity on Suzanne's part toward Liam. She resented the fact that Norm was working so closely with him instead of with her son, Xander."

Tiffany looked up from her phone. "I remember Xander," she said. "He used to play on the basketball team with my cousin. I was in elementary school at the time, but we still went to all the games. My dad's the coach. It's kind of weird now that I'm in high school. He knows all the guys in school and makes a point of telling me who I should and shouldn't date."

After describing how he had embarrassed her at the previous week's game, she added, "I heard Darren and Melvin arguing at halftime a couple of weeks back."

"They were at one of the high school games?" I asked.

"Coconut Cove is a small town," Leilani said. "Lots of people go to the games to cheer the team on even if they don't have kids in high school. We do sometimes too."

"The town I grew up in was a lot bigger," I said. "What were they arguing about?"

"Darren's uncle was furious at him because he had caught him poaching. He told him that it could cost him his business and fishing licenses."

"How did Darren react?" I asked.

"He seemed pretty upset, especially after Melvin threatened to call his parents and tell them."

Leilani glanced at her watch. "We should probably get going, Tiffany. Nancy doesn't like it when anyone's late." She looked at me. "You sure you don't want to come? I'm sure Nancy wouldn't mind."

"Thanks, but I'm good. Scooter is making dinner tonight. I'd better scoot off myself."

On the drive home, I thought about what Tiffany had said. As much as I liked Melvin, doubts were creeping into my mind. Could he have killed his own nephew to cover up the poaching activity and protect his fishing charter business?

CHAPTER 12
ANOTHER MYSTERY INGREDIENT

"I'M BACK!" I MANAGED TO close the door with my foot while balancing the grocery bags in my hands. Mrs. Moto ran into the hall, rubbed against my legs, and purred loudly. "All right, I see you. Let me get these into the kitchen, and then I'll say hello properly."

Scooter plucked the bags out of my arms and set them on the counter. "I'd better make sure this doesn't burn," he said as he dashed back to the stove and looked inside a steaming pot.

"It smells delicious. What is it?"

"You'll have to guess."

"Give me a clue."

He removed a wooden spoon from a ceramic holder and gave his concoction a few stirs. "Hey, no peeking," he said as he covered the pot.

"Come on, just one tiny clue."

"What's it worth to you?" I gave him a peck on the cheek. "That works. Okay, are you ready for your clue?" He did a drum roll on the stove. "It doesn't involve cereal."

"Wow, that really narrows it down."

While he continued to stir our mystery dinner, I filled my

husband in on my chat with the chief and my discussions with Melvin, Leilani, and Tiffany. We did have a bit of a digression when he disputed my characterization of my meeting with Chief Dalton as an "interrogation." He was of the opinion that the use of colored markers negated any potential intimidation factor. Then things naturally devolved into a debate about which of the fruit-scented ones that we'd had as kids smelled the best. I voted for orange; Scooter opted for cherry.

"I'm sorry Nancy didn't invite you to her shindig," Scooter said as he put canned goods away in the cupboards.

"I'm not. Why would I want to spend time with that grouchy old lady? Although there was blueberry pie. Which reminds me, did you make dessert?"

"No. I figured we could use a break from all that sugar."

"Really," I said, holding up two boxes of Cap'n Crunch. "Should I return these to the store? I still have the receipt."

"Give me those," he said, grabbing them from me.

Mrs. Moto jumped on the counter and supervised while I pulled out half a dozen cans of Frisky Feline Ocean's Delight. She sniffed at each one, and when she was satisfied I had bought the right brand, she hopped down on the floor and rolled over on her back.

"How am I supposed to put these bags away if you're in the way?"

"She doesn't want you to put them away," Scooter said. "Look." He took one of the reusable tote bags, opened it up, and set it on the floor. Mrs. Moto jumped into it, causing it to slide across the tiles. "See, it's a new toy." We watched for a few minutes as she darted in and out of the bag, then batted her toy mouse inside and wrestled with it.

"I think dinner is almost done. Why don't we eat at the kitchen counter so we can watch the floor show?"

I got out plates and napkins while Scooter dished up chicken with a dark brown sauce served over rice and accompanied by a black bean, cilantro, and mango salad.

I leaned over my plate and inhaled the fragrant odor. "This smells great. Better than any scented marker."

"Take a bite, and tell me what you think."

I sampled a piece of the chicken. "Oh, this is so good." I took another bite. "It tastes so familiar, but I can't put my finger on it."

"Keep eating. Maybe you'll figure it out." He pulled a bottle of Corona beer out of the fridge. "Want one? I think there might even be a lime around here to go with it."

While we sipped our beer and ate our chicken—and yes, I had seconds—Scooter told me about a video he had seen of a couple sailing in the Bahamas. "They were anchored off Staniel Cay. Isn't that where Melvin said his family was from? It'd be fun to take *Marjorie Jane* over there one day. Ned was telling me that some of the boats at the marina go down there every year. They call themselves the Coconut Cove Crew. Wouldn't that be a blast?"

"That sounds like a long way off," I said. "I'm not even sure when we'll be able to get back to working on the boat."

"I hope the chief wraps up the investigation soon."

"Well, if he stopped playing with markers and took me more seriously, he might stand a better chance."

* * *

After dinner, the three of us walked down to the beach. "We really have to do something about getting her a new collar that she'll actually keep on for more than two minutes," I said. We watched Mrs. Moto tap a crab on its back tentatively before retreating to a safe distance.

I breathed in the salt air and enjoyed the cooling breeze coming off the water. "It's so peaceful here. Why would you ever want to sell the cottage? Just think—could you have made a meal like that on board the boat?"

"Maybe you have a point," he conceded. "Hey, you never did guess what the mystery ingredient was. That means I win."

"Win what? I don't recall making a bet."

"Sure you did. Mrs. Moto can back me up. You agreed that if you couldn't guess what I put in the dish, you would be in charge of cleaning the bathrooms for the next month, including her litter box."

"I never agreed to any such thing."

"Mrs. Moto, do you hear that? My little panda bear is trying to get out of a bet." The calico darted up to us and deposited a shell at my feet. Then she meowed loudly. "See, she agrees with me," he said.

"I went to the store and got you cat food. Where's the gratitude?"

We sat on a piece of driftwood and watched Mrs. Moto play with her seashell. "So what was it?"

"Cocoa powder. I thought for sure you could taste the chocolaty flavor. It's a Mexican *mole* sauce. Alejandra gave me her mother's recipe."

"Well, you'll have to make that again. It's a winner."

"She gave me some other recipes I want to try out. How does *pozole* sound?"

"It sounds like something I can't spell, but I'm game." I pointed at a young man with spiky green hair and a clipboard who was approaching us. "He seems familiar," I said. I waved at the green-haired man. "Is that you, Simon?"

He looked in my direction and returned the wave. "Hey, Mollie. Fancy running into you here." There were two other people with him—an older woman with short blonde hair and a young woman wearing a baseball cap. All three of them were sporting fluorescent orange T-shirts that glowed in the moonlight. As they neared us, I noticed that their shirts featured a cheerful sea turtle holding up a sign urging people to keep the sea plastic-free.

Simon put his arm around the younger woman. "This is my girlfriend, Fiona. I told you about her at the FAROUT meeting." I did a double take when I heard her name. Nope, a different Fiona than the one Liam had been seeing behind her husband's back.

Simon pointed at the older woman. "And this is Connie." I shook their hands and introduced Scooter and Mrs. Moto. Scooter extended his hand. Mrs. Moto sniffed their shoes. "Mollie is the foremost expert on alien abduction in the whole state," Simon said.

"Are we talking little green men?" Connie asked dubiously.

"Well, some are green, but not all of them," Simon said.

Fiona smiled. "It's something they're passionate about, just like we're into wildlife conservation."

"Well, to each his own, I guess," Connie said. "But we have more pressing problems here on Planet Earth to be concerned with." She gestured at the sky. "Before we start worrying about what's out there, we need to fix what's broken down here."

"From looking at your T-shirts, I'm guessing you're worried about sea turtles."

"You bet we are," Fiona said. "Did you hear there's a resort being planned for this area? They want to knock down those cottages and build a big hotel, swimming pool, restaurants, and a spa. It's going to destroy the delicate ecosystem here."

The older woman chimed in. "Sea turtles come here every year to lay eggs. It's hard enough to protect their nesting grounds as it is. We don't have enough volunteers to monitor and patrol the area. Imagine all those tourists swarming on the beach, shining bright lights, disrupting nests, and killing baby turtles. It has to be stopped at all costs!"

Fiona touched Connie lightly on her arm. "Hey, you're beginning to sound like Ken Choi."

She took a deep breath. "While I don't agree with his methods, at least he's making a stand. All we're doing is filling out forms."

Simon shook his head. "Some might call his methods ecoterrorism."

Connie folded her arms across her chest. "I don't know where you've heard that, but it's just not true."

"It's not just what I've heard, it's what I've seen," Simon said through clenched teeth. "And I don't want my girlfriend caught up in—"

Fiona seized his arm. "Enough, you two. Let's not lose sight of what's important here—the turtles. We did a great job today talking to people about endangered species and handing out educational materials. So no more talk about Ken, okay?" Fiona stared at both of them until they mumbled their agreement.

"We actually live in one of those cottages," I said, trying to steer the conversation toward more neutral grounds. "What can you tell us about this proposed development?"

"Whatever you do, don't sell, no matter how much they offer you," Connie said. "They'll do anything to con you out of your property."

"Who's 'they'?" Scooter asked.

"Norm and Suzanne Thomas. He's orchestrating the deal through a shell company, and she's buying up the property. It isn't the first time they've done it. Remember what happened last year?"

Simon and Fiona nodded.

"But that doesn't make sense," I said. "She posted a listing of our house on her website and put an advertisement in the window of her office. If she were planning on having a shell company buy it, why would she do all that? Why wouldn't she just present an offer from the shell company?"

"If you just had one offer, you might not accept it," Connie said. "So she pretends to be offering it to other buyers, but if anyone shows any real interest she doesn't return their calls. She's even gone so far as to have people pretend to be potential buyers and go to view the property. Then she tells you that the highest offer came from the shell company. You think she did her best to drive up the price, and you happily accept it."

"Wow, that sounds really complicated."

"She's perfected her scheme over the years," Fiona said. "She goes to a lot of trouble to make it all seem legit. She has professional photographs taken, puts listings on her website—"

Connie interrupted. "Coconut Cove isn't the first place she's done this at, and it probably won't be the last. No matter what it takes, she needs to be stopped."

"But wouldn't people get suspicious if the same company kept making offers on neighboring properties?" I asked.

"She sets up a number of them so it seems like a different one each time," Connie said. "She's also been known to get family members to buy properties, then transfer them to her later. Like I said, you should stay away from her. She's a cold-hearted—"

"You do realize she's dead, don't you?" Scooter asked before she could specify exactly what kind of cold-hearted person she had been.

Fiona frowned. "No, I didn't."

Connie shot her fist up in the air. "That means the resort won't go ahead! Wait until Ken hears about this. He'll be over the moon. Remember how he was saying just last week that the only way we could stop this development would be over her cold, dead body?"

"Connie, come on, show some respect. The woman is dead. And besides, Ken didn't mean it literally," Fiona said. "We should probably head back now. It was nice to meet the two of you." She bent down and stroked Mrs. Moto's back. "Sorry, I meant the three of you."

I scooped the cat up in my arms. "Everyone loves you, don't they?" As we walked back home, I asked Scooter what he thought about Ken.

"He seems like a nice guy. Bright, obviously, and passionate about the work he does."

"Yeah, but do you think he could have killed Suzanne?"

"How could he have? You're the one who told me he had an alibi. Wasn't he at a conservation meeting? Now come on. I'll race you back. Last one there has to wash the dishes."

CHAPTER 13
SNOWBIRDS

THE NEXT DAY, I HEADED over to Melvin's Marine Emporium. It was a weekday morning, so I was spared Chad's cheerful greeting when I entered. He was probably acing some sort of math test at school at this moment and trying to convince Tiffany to go out with him.

I had swung by the marina first to get an update on when we could get back aboard *Marjorie Jane*. I almost hated to admit it, but she looked kind of lonely behind the police barricade.

Ben was working on an outboard engine at the other end of the yard. After wiping grease off his hands onto his T-shirt, he told me that there hadn't been any update as to when we'd be able to access our boat.

According to my aspiring-musician and wannabe-pirate friend, Norm had been there earlier in the morning, enraged that he couldn't get on his boat either. He had complained bitterly about the revenue it was costing him. Each day he couldn't work on the boat meant another day's delay getting her launched again and going out on charter trips. Ben wasn't too impressed that Norm was more focused on making money than on the loss of his wife.

With time on my hands, I decided to swing by Melvin's to look at bottom paint. Scooter was busy with work again, which meant that I could focus entirely on the different color options available without being distracted by the latest three-for-one offer that they were running on something we didn't need. I definitely knew we wouldn't be doing Smurf-colored paint again. Despite my lack of fashion sense, even I knew that a bright blue keel and a red hull wasn't a good color combination.

As I examined paint chip samples, I saw Penny walking past a display of fishing tackle boxes. "Hey there," she cried out cheerfully. As usual, she was dressed head to toe in her favorite color. Today's outfit consisted of bright-pink sandals, a ballerina-pink skirt, and a floral-patterned top in shades of fuchsia and salmon-pink. "Come meet Alan. He just bought a boat from me, and I'm showing him all that Coconut Cove has to offer."

Her client's dress sense was more muted—dark-gray shorts and a light-gray polo shirt with a yacht club insignia on it—which went perfectly with his bland features. He kept his eyes focused on the ground and mumbled hello when Penny introduced us.

Turns out Alan already knew all about me. "So, you're the gal who found the bodies in the boatyard," he said in a quiet, monotone voice. He held up his camera and shyly asked if he could take my picture.

I sensed a glimmer of excitement as he listened to my account of the two murders. For a brief moment he made eye contact, then looked away. He continued to ask questions, inching closer to me as I described the murder scenes while at the same time flinching as the details got gorier. He made me think of a timid little mouse who desperately wanted that piece of cheese despite the fact that it was sitting on a lethal trap.

I had been constantly bombarded with questions everywhere I went in town. Printing up some fliers with all the relevant facts to hand out was starting to seem like a good idea. It got old repeating the same story over and over again. So far, I had managed to stay one step ahead of the reporter from the local newspaper and hoped to keep it that way.

"So, if you had to pick one restaurant for Alan to try, which would it be—the Sailor's Corner Cafe, that new Thai place, or Alligator Chuck's barbecue joint?" Penny asked.

"Oh, that's a tough one. Why pick one? Go to the cafe for breakfast, Alligator Chuck's for lunch, and have some Thai food for dinner," I said diplomatically. "Scooter and I have done that before."

"That's a lot of eating out," Penny said.

"I know, but sometimes we're just too busy or too lazy to cook. We're probably going to have to cut back on going out, considering how much money we seem to be spending here at Melvin's."

Alan chewed on his fingernails and mumbled something.

"What was that?" I asked.

He shuffled toward me. "Do you ever order stuff online? There are some discount sites where you can get good deals, probably better than some of the prices here."

"We have," I said. "But we like supporting local businesses when we can. At least, that's the rationale we use when we eat out."

"As a local business owner, I'd have to echo that sentiment," Penny said. She turned to Alan. "You do get a discount at Melvin's for a limited period of time since you bought a boat from me. Plus, the poor guy has been through so much lately that anything we can do to support him is a good thing."

While Penny filled Alan in on more of the details regarding the loss of Melvin's wife and nephew, I spotted Liam pulling up in front of the store in his sports car. Norm got out of the passenger side and marched toward the door. Liam pulled him back before he could open it. The two of them got into a lively discussion. Norm kept gesticulating wildly at the store while Liam tried to cajole him back to the car.

Alan had crept up to the window and was snapping pictures. Norm caught him out of the corner of his eye, slammed his hand against the window, then pressed his face against the glass and glared at him. The photographer jumped back in surprise.

"I wonder what that's about?" I asked. "Why do you think Liam is trying to keep Norm from coming inside the store?"

"I'm pretty sure I know," Penny said. "Did you hear about Norm's boat? The one at the public docks?"

"What happened?" a quiet voice asked. Alan had managed to

creep back toward us unobserved and was standing next to Penny, clutching his camera.

"Well, someone vandalized it the night that Suzanne was murdered," Penny said. "They slashed seat cushions, overturned coolers, broke fishing rods, used bolt cutters to break the padlocks on the lockers, and then threw everything they found in there into the water."

"Was anyone hurt?" Alan asked.

"Thankfully not."

Alan fidgeted with the strap on his camera bag, then asked, "Do they think that lady's murder and the vandalism are connected?"

Penny shrugged. "I don't know for sure, but there was a can of spray paint on the deck."

"What kind of message did they leave?" Alan asked, his eyes shining with excitement. "Was it like the one left by Suzanne's body?"

Penny shook her head. "No, there wasn't a message."

"Oh, that's disappointing." He chewed on his finger for a moment. "I bet the murderer thought Norm was going to be on the boat and was planning on killing him and leaving a message before he had to flee the scene."

"Or it was just high school kids messing around," Penny said dryly.

While Alan considered this less-than-exciting possibility, the front door swung open and Norm charged toward Melvin's office. "Get out here, you coward!" he yelled. "You're going to pay for what you did!"

Melvin came out of his office clenching his fists. "If you don't leave my store at once, I'm going to call the police." He looked at Liam. "Get your uncle out of here before he causes trouble."

Norm lunged at Melvin, but before he could land a punch, Liam pulled him back. "Don't. You'll just make things worse. There are witnesses."

Norm glared at the small crowd that had gathered to watch.

Melvin crossed his arms. "You should listen to the boy, Norm."

"If anyone is going to listen, it's going to be you," the other man spit out. "How dare you do that to my boat? You're going to pay!"

By this point, Liam had lost all control of his uncle. Norm grabbed Melvin by his shirt. "You vandalized my boat! Do you know how much damage you've done? I've got one boat stuck in the yard, and now the other one is out of commission. Do you know how much business I'm losing?"

Melvin shoved Norm backward. "You? You've got four boats, two of which are still operational. Remember when I used to have four boats? That was until all your dirty tricks caused me to lose all of them except *Nassau Royale*. Finally, you're getting a taste of your own medicine. Whoever did it should get a medal!"

Norm scoffed. "A medal? That's rich." He leaned against one of the display cases. He seemed calmer, but I was worried that it was only a temporary reprieve. "So how'd you do it?" he asked coldly. "Did you kill my wife, then destroy my boat? Or was it the other way around?"

"Do you really think I would have killed Suzanne?" Melvin asked. "She was your wife. I wouldn't wish that on anyone. Besides, I was at the Tipsy Pirate when it happened. I couldn't have done it."

"Got anyone to back you up?"

"Ask anyone," Melvin said. "How about you? Got anyone to back up your alibi the night of Darren's murder?"

"Yeah, my wife. Except now she's dead."

"I wouldn't have believed a word she said." Melvin walked over to Norm, clutched his arm, and slowly said, "You killed that boy."

Norm stared down at the floor for a beat, then punched Melvin in the gut.

"Would someone like to explain to me what's going on here?" a deep voice boomed out.

The crowd scattered at the sight of Chief Dalton. Officer Moore ushered us outside while the chief dealt with Melvin and Norm.

"Can we stop by the public docks, Penny?" Alan asked. "I'd love to get some shots of the boat that was vandalized."

"I thought you were a wedding photographer?" Penny asked.

"Why do you want to take pictures of something like that?"

"Yeah, I do weddings, family portraits, school pictures..." Alan sighed. "It's so boring. I'm really trying to get a break as a photojournalist. But I need to build up my portfolio. I've been trying to take pictures and videos at accidents and crime scenes. I even set up a website to showcase my work." He pulled a phone out of his pocket and showed us shots that he had taken recently. "See, this one is of the big pileup when that truck overturned near here last week. This is one of a fishing boat that was deliberately set on fire in the Keys a couple of weeks ago. And this one is of a—"

"Do you mind going back to that one of the fire?" I asked. "That woman looks familiar." Alan handed me his phone. I zoomed in on the corner of the photo. "Hmm...I wonder if that's Connie?"

"Who's Connie?" Penny asked.

"I met her last night. She's an environmentalist." I squinted at the phone. "But I can't really be sure if that's her."

"I took a video of the fire too," Alan said. "I was there for a wedding reception when it broke out, so I've got it all on tape. If you want, I'll upload it and send you a link to it. You might be able to get a better look at the bystanders."

"That would be great," I said. I remembered what Simon had said about Ken having been involved in sabotaging fishing boats in the Keys previously. Was there any connection between the two incidents?

* * *

Mrs. Moto was waiting at the front door when I got home from Melvin's. She knew that the sound of a car pulling up in the drive meant that one of her servants had returned to attend to her every whim. While I pulled my keys out of the lock, she rolled onto her back across the threshold and batted at my foot.

"What, you want a belly rub now?" I picked up the shopping bags that were sitting on the welcome mat and stepped over her. "I've got to get this stuff inside. Maybe later."

She tore in front of me and was sitting on the kitchen counter before I even had time to close the door and set my purse on the entryway table. I placed the shopping bags next to her and opened the fridge to get a can of soda. When I turned back around, she had flipped both of the bags on their side and was pawing through the contents. She knocked the sanding pads I had picked up at Melvin's on the floor and stared at them. Next came the blue tape, followed by the respirator masks. This was a game I was used to. The rules were simple: (1) cat knocks stuff down; (2) humans pick it up; (3) repeat.

As I bent down to retrieve the items, Scooter came into the kitchen. "Oh, are you playing our fur baby's favorite game?" He scratched the cat behind her ears. "Good, that varnish I wanted was in stock," he said before placing the can on top of a cabinet, out of paw's reach. "Did you get anything good to eat?" he asked. "I'm starving."

"There should still be some chicken *mole* left. Why don't we heat that up for lunch? Then I'm going to head to the marina to finish working on my FAROUT report in the lounge."

"Why don't you work here?" Scooter asked as he took a plastic container out of the fridge. "Mrs. Moto can help you."

"Yeah, right. Her idea of 'helping' is lying on top of my keyboard. I think she'd rather keep you company."

Scooter turned on the microwave and leaned back on the counter. "To be honest, I could do without her company for a while. I'm trying to sort through files and paperwork, and she's making a mess of everything. If I close the door to the office, she yowls until I can't take it anymore. You should take her with you to the marina."

"Nah, she'd rather stay here."

We continued our discussion of who should spend quality time with the cat over lunch but didn't manage to come to an agreement. We did manage to agree that *mole* tastes even better the next day.

While we finished off our meal, I filled Scooter in on what had happened at the marine store after the chief arrived on the scene. "Can you believe he actually arrested Melvin?" I asked.

"On what charge?" Scooter asked.

"It's got to be murder, doesn't it?"

"From what you described about the fight between Melvin and Norm, maybe he arrested him on a charge of vandalism."

I leaned back in my chair. "You could be right. I didn't actually hear what the chief charged him with. Officer Moore made us all leave the store. I could only see what was going on through the window. It looked like he took statements from both men, then led Melvin out in handcuffs while Norm gloated."

"See, that's probably what it was."

"But vandalism? Can you imagine Melvin doing that?"

"Look, the man is in mourning. Grief can do strange things to people. And it does sound like he blames Norm for his nephew's murder."

I pushed back my chair. "Let's talk about more pleasant things, like what we're going to have for dinner?"

He shook his head. "You just finished lunch, and you're already thinking about your next meal?"

"I like to be organized," I said as I cleared the table. "How about if we meet up at Alligator Chuck's around seven?"

"Okay. I'm sure I'll have worked up an appetite by then."

After popping the plates and utensils into the dishwasher, I looked around for Mrs. Moto. "Where is that cat? She usually doesn't go too far away when we're eating."

I checked her favorite napping spots—on top of Scooter's pillow, near the sliding glass doors to the patio, and in the bathroom sink—but didn't see her anywhere.

I peeked into the second bedroom. We had turned it into an office for Scooter to run his business from. Seriously, where did that man think he was going to fit all his work-related stuff on a sailboat? Two file cabinets, a large desk, and a floor-to-ceiling bookshelf. We'd have to buy another boat to tow behind us just to hold the contents of this room.

I picked up the files and papers that were scattered on the floor, brushed cat hair off them, and set them on the desk next to Scooter's boring collection of pens. All black, not a single colorful marker. As I was straightening the stack, I noticed one of the documents had my name on it.

"Scooter, can you come here for a sec?" I said.

"What's up, panda bear?" he asked, walking down the hallway.

"Why did you take a life insurance policy out on me? Should I be worried?" I joked.

"Very worried. Why do you think I made dinner last night? Maybe I poisoned it."

"But you ate it too."

"Ah, but maybe I have the antidote and took it before dinner."

"Did you remember to take it before lunch today? We just had leftovers."

Scooter clutched his chest and said dramatically, "My heart! I think I'm dying!" He leaned on the desk, then starting laughing. He picked up the life insurance policy. "Don't you remember talking about this?" He pulled another document out of the pile. "See, here's the policy on me in case I die first."

"But the big question is, who's the beneficiary—me or *Marjorie Jane*?"

He pretended to think about the answer. "Hmm. That's a tough one." He gave me a kiss. "You, of course. Our lawyer also wants us to come by and review our wills too. Now that we have Mrs. Moto, we have to think about what happens to her if we both should pass away at the same time."

"Wow, for someone who didn't even like cats before we got her, you've certainly grown fond of her." I pointed at our adorable fur ball sprawled on his office chair having her afternoon nap. "I think that's why she's made it clear whom she'd rather keep company this afternoon. You."

"But where am I supposed to sit?" he asked.

I shrugged. "Guess you'll have to find another chair. That one's occupied."

* * *

After making a lot of headway on my report in the marina lounge during the afternoon, I packed up my stuff and headed off to Alligator Chuck's to meet Scooter for dinner. I wondered if he had gotten much work done perched on a wooden dining room chair next to his desk, while the cat rested comfortably on his padded office chair.

As I drove down Main Street, I saw an older couple standing in front of Norm and Suzanne's office pointing at something in the window and having an animated discussion. I sent Scooter a text letting him know I might be a few minutes late, pulled into a spot on the next block, and walked back over to see what was going on.

"What do you think about this one?" I heard the woman say loudly. "It's a cute cottage right on the beach. Perfect for just the two of us. It says it's a two-bedroom. We can use one as a guest room when the grandkids come to visit."

"I don't know," the man said in an equally loud voice. "I still think a condo is the way to go. Then we don't have to worry about yard work and maintenance. I've had enough of that over the years. I want to enjoy my retirement."

"Well, let's look at them both. Here, let me jot down the name and number of the real estate agent, and we can give her a call in the morning." She searched in her purse, handing her companion her wallet, lipstick, and reading glasses. "Hmm. I could have sworn I had a pen in here somewhere."

I peered over her shoulder and looked at the window. A familiar sight greeted me—yet another advertisement for our cottage. Had Suzanne printed another copy out and stuck it up here after I threw the last one in the trash?

"Are you interested in that one too?" the woman asked.

"I'm very interested in it," I said. "But it's not for sale."

"It doesn't say anything about being sold or under offer," she said.

"Trust me, it's not on the market."

She tapped on the glass. "Of course it is. It says so right here." She handed her husband a hairbrush, a crossword-puzzle book, and a bottle of hand sanitizer. "Now, where is that pen?"

I briefly considered telling her that I already owned the cottage, but the last thing I wanted was another person trying to come around and buy it out from under me. "Seriously, it's not for sale," I said. "This is a mistake."

The man gestured at the window. "Now wait a minute here, missy. Just because *you* want to buy this place doesn't mean that you should go around trying to pretend it's not for sale. Whoever makes the best offer wins." As he waved his hands wildly to emphasize his point, the lipstick fell on the sidewalk and rolled into the street. "Gosh darn it!" He handed everything back to his wife unceremoniously and went chasing after it.

She struggled to keep everything in her hands. I watched as the hairbrush made its way into the flower box underneath the window. "Hank, how am I supposed to find that pen when I'm holding all this?"

Hank returned, brandishing the lipstick victoriously in his fingers. "Here, give me that." She piled everything back into his hands and rooted around in her purse again.

"Here it is," she said, triumphantly waving a ballpoint pen. She pointed at the hairbrush. "Honey, do you mind picking that up?"

After the two of them managed to put everything back into her purse, she handed the pen to her husband. "Jot down that number, will you?"

"Do you have any paper, Violet?" They both looked at her purse and sighed.

I decided to put them out of their misery before they went through the whole purse charade again. "If I were you, I wouldn't bother writing the number down. The real estate agent is dead."

"Can you believe the nerve of this gal?" Hank asked his wife. "Some people will stoop to any level to get what they want."

The woman clutched her husband's arm. "You should be ashamed of yourself. Saying that someone has passed away just so you can get your hands on that cottage. Come on, honey, let's get out of here. We'll come back first thing in the morning."

"I'm not making it up. I saw the body," I said.

The woman gave me a horrified expression before walking off.

I gazed at the headshot of Suzanne in the upper corner of the window. "Even in death, you're managing to cause problems," I told her. A passerby looked at me oddly, so I waited until he was out of earshot before continuing my conversation with Suzanne's picture. "Did you know we've had people come by at all hours, knocking on the door and asking to see the cottage? The cottage that we never even put up for sale?"

I didn't expect an answer, but it felt good to get that off my chest. I pressed my face up against the window to see if anyone was inside, lurking in the dark. I needed to get that flier down from the window pronto to prevent any future misunderstandings, as well as any other unannounced visitors.

I tried the front door but it wouldn't open, even after jiggling the handle repeatedly. I wasn't going to be able to gain access through the large plate glass window, so I decided to see if there was a back entrance.

As I walked down the dark alley behind the building, I sent my husband another text.

Still running late. Need to sort out paperwork with Suzanne.

My phone beeped right away.

Huh? Suzanne's dead.

Something cold brushed past me. I startled and dropped my phone. I picked it up, turned on the flashlight, and aimed it up and down the alley. Nothing. Probably just a raccoon. I tapped in a reply.

Yeah, I know. But some people still think she's alive.

Thinking about Suzanne's murder was probably too much for Scooter because he changed the subject.

Should I order nachos while I'm waiting for you?

He knows I love nachos. It was clearly a ploy to get me to hurry up. But first things first. I needed to get that ad out of the window. When I got to the rear of the office, I noticed a light on in the back room. Maybe Norm was in the kitchen, hiding out from people staring into the office window. After knocking on the door and not getting a response, I turned the knob, opened the door a crack, and poked my head inside. "Yoo-hoo, is anyone here?" Still no response. Could he be indisposed in the bathroom? I pushed the door open, walked into the hallway, and called out again. Only silence in response.

Since I was already inside, and the office was technically open —after all, the door was unlocked—surely Norm wouldn't mind if I quickly removed the sign. I would actually be doing him a favor. People wouldn't wander by the window, think the cottage was for sale, and annoy him with calls to set up viewings for it.

I walked over to the window and took down the ad. I crumpled it up and took aim at the trash can near Suzanne's desk...and missed. Two out of three, I told myself. I grabbed it off the floor, popped a chocolate from the candy dish next to the computer in my mouth, and tried again.

At least I got closer this time. I took two chocolates this time as a consolation prize. As I got ready to go for my third attempt, I saw something out of the corner of my eye—Violet and Hank were back, along with another older couple.

They were pointing at the spot where the picture of the cottage used to be displayed. When the woman put her face up against the window to try and see inside, I darted behind Norm's desk and out of sight.

Despite the pane of glass, I could hear their voices. I wondered if they realized that they both needed to replace the batteries in their hearing aids. From their discussion of low-maintenance plants and lawn fertilizers, it sounded like they might be there for a while. Because I had left my purse on the floor next to the window and wouldn't be able to retrieve it without being spotted, it looked like I was going to be there for a while too.

I settled down into Norm's chair while I waited. I swiveled back and forth and pondered my situation. My phone was in my purse, so I couldn't send another message to Scooter letting him know I was further delayed. Plus, I was getting hungry. I really wished he hadn't mentioned nachos in his last text.

Fortunately, Norm also had a candy dish on his desk. Unfortunately, his was full of peppermints. Not nearly as tasty as Suzanne's chocolates, but beggars couldn't be choosers. As I reached across to take one, I accidentally knocked over a cup, spilling tea all over Norm's desk. I quickly wiped up the liquid with tissues, but wasn't fast enough to prevent it from dripping into the top drawer, which was partially open.

I pulled the drawer open. There was a collection of pens, a protein bar, and a handgun on top of a file folder that was sitting in a puddle of tea. I used one of the pens to nudge the handgun to the side—I hate guns and do my best to avoid touching them—and placed the folder on top of the desk. After cleaning up the inside of the drawer, I started to dry off the folder with a fresh tissue. That's when I noticed that it was labeled "Coconut Cove Tropical Resort." It was the same one that had been on Suzanne's desk when I was last in the office, which Norm had complained about because it wasn't locked up.

Curiosity got the better of me, so I leafed through the papers inside. Usually, I find legal documents to be incredibly boring, but these held my interest. The first one was an agreement for the purchase of a house by Sierra Vista Rental Properties. I recognized the address of the property in question immediately. It was right next door to us and owned by our neighbor, Alligator Chuck.

The second document revealed who the owner of Sierra Vista was: Xander Carlton. I didn't know too many men named Xander, so I was pretty sure this Xander was Suzanne's son. It looked like she was using the technique that Connie and Fiona had told us about. She had a shell company, owned by her son, make an offer on Chuck's house. Then the shell company sold the property to the developer of the resort.

I imagine she had planned on taking a similar approach to try to purchase our cottage, as well as Melvin's. We all would have thought they were separate transactions, either bought by individuals or by rental companies. Then once she owned all the cottages on the beach, the construction of the resort could begin, and it would be too late for any of us to protest.

As I flipped over the last page, I noticed an envelope at the back of the folder. Thinking it contained more details about the shady real estate deal, I opened it up. Instead, I found something far more interesting. It seemed that Norm had taken a life insurance policy out on his wife rather recently. And from what I read, it appeared as though he was about to come into a lot of money.

CHAPTER 14
SEEING GHOSTS

AS I WAS PORING OVER the life insurance policy, I heard the front door handle rattling. I froze, hoping Norm wasn't going to come charging in and find me sitting at his desk. I breathed a sigh of relief when I heard a very familiar and very loud voice.

"Someone has to be in there," Violet said. She began banging on the door.

"Honey, no one is there. The lights are off," Hank said.

"Well, how do you explain the fact that the advertisement for the cottage is gone? Someone must have taken it down." She banged on the door some more.

"Violet, stop it. If someone was in there, they would have come to the door by now."

Well, that wasn't exactly true, I thought. I was inside but had no intention of answering the door.

"Where was it exactly, Violet?" another woman asked. I peeked around the corner, making sure to stay hidden in the shadows, and looked at the window. Violet, Hank, and the other couple were staring at the spot where the picture of my cottage used to hang.

"Right there," Violet said, tapping on the glass. "I really

wanted you to see it. It's so cute and it's right by the beach. You and Jim really should think about getting a winter place in Florida as well. Think of how much fun we would have. While the guys are off fishing, we can go to the community center. They've got lots of arts-and-crafts classes. I was thinking we'd use the second bedroom as a combination guest room and crafting studio—"

"Violet, come on, let's go," her husband said impatiently. "Jim and Angela don't want to hear about this."

"And we can go for walks on the beach every morning," Violet said, ignoring his interruption. "I was thinking about going with a tropical jungle decorating scheme in the living room to match the palm trees in front of the house." She turned to her husband. "Honey, go knock on the door again."

He shook his head. "I'm telling you, no one is there. We'll come back tomorrow."

"I just don't want to lose out on this place. It's perfect for us." She turned back to her friend. "I think there's going to be a lot of competition for it. There was this woman here earlier who's also interested in the cottage. She's going around telling prospective buyers that the real estate agent is dead. Can you believe that?"

"Well, that takes the cake," the other woman said. "She really must be desperate to get her hands on it."

Her husband took a couple of steps back and glanced up at the office sign thoughtfully. "You know, she may have been telling the truth. I think I saw something about this in the local newspaper. A local real estate agent was murdered recently."

Violet looked crestfallen. "Dead? How are we going to view the property now?"

Her friend gasped. "Did you say the advertisement was hanging right here?" Violet nodded. "And when the woman told you the real estate agent had been murdered, you didn't believe her?" Violet nodded again. "Well, don't you see what that means?" Violet shook her head. "Her ghost was here. *She* tore down the sign. The recently departed don't like it when people make light of their passing, especially ones who have been murdered!"

The blood drained from Violet's face. "A ghost? Do you think she could haunt the cottage? Maybe this office is haunted too!"

she said, clutching her friend's arm. Their husbands looked at each other and rolled their eyes.

I rolled my eyes right along with them. Ghosts? Haunted houses? Who believed in this kind of nonsense?

I stopped my eye-rolling when I heard Norm's voice. "Can I help you folks? Did you stop by to sign up for a fishing charter?"

"No, we were just looking at the signs in the window," Violet said.

"Oh," Norm said. After a long pause, he added, "My wife was the real estate agent. She recently passed away." The two couples murmured their sympathies. Violet started to ask something about ghosts, but her husband put his finger on her lips.

"Was there a particular property you were interested in?" Norm asked. He sounded awfully businesslike for someone who had just lost his wife. But maybe getting a hefty insurance payout sped the grieving process along.

"Definitely not the cottage on the beach," Violet said. "Right, honey?"

"The cottage on the beach? There's four of them." Norm pursed his lips. "There's already an offer on two of them." I glanced at the file folder in my hand. I knew exactly what he was talking about—Sierra Vista Rental Properties, aka Xander Carlton.

He scratched his head. "We're still in negotiations with the owner of one of the cottages, but I expect he'll be heading back to the Bahamas soon and will put it on the market then." The way Melvin felt about Norm, I couldn't imagine any scenario where he'd list his property with him.

"The Bahamas. How exciting. We went on a cruise there last year," Violet said loudly.

Norm rubbed his ear and took a step back. "There's another one up for sale at the moment, but I think there's already a potential buyer."

Violet nudged her friend. "I bet it was that awful woman who was here earlier."

"What awful woman?" Norm asked.

"We didn't catch her name, but she was short with medium-length brown hair. Nothing really stood out about her."

I breathed a sigh of relief. I was pretty sure Norm wouldn't figure out it was me based on that nondescript description. Then I got slightly miffed. What did they mean that nothing stood out about my appearance? I was wearing some really cute earrings.

"Tell you what, why don't you give me your name and number, and I'll give you a call tomorrow once I've had a chance to go through Suzanne's things?" Norm said.

Thankfully, he entered their details into his phone rather than asking Violet to get a pen and paper out of her purse. They asked him where a good place in town was for breakfast the next morning. While he walked with them a few steps away to point out the Sailor's Corner Cafe, I dashed over to the window, grabbed my purse, and exited through the back door before Norm could catch me in the office.

* * *

I slid into the booth across from Scooter. "Sorry about being late. I got held up with some work stuff." I tucked my purse and the file folder next to me on the bench seat. Yes, before you ask, I took the folder with me. After all, it was evidence that I'm pretty sure Norm forgot to mention to the police. "Did you order already?" I asked.

"No, I thought I'd wait for you. Besides, I can't decide. It's a toss-up between the baby back ribs and the gator."

"Alligator? That's adventurous."

"Well, we've lived in Florida for a while. I figured it might be time we tried it."

"By *we*, I'm going to assume you mean *you*. I have no intention of eating something with that many teeth."

A tall man wearing an apron and chef's hat came up to our table. "Mollie, Scooter, it's nice to see you!" he said.

"You too, Chuck," Scooter said, shaking his hand. "It's hard to believe we're neighbors. The only time we ever see you is when we're here at your restaurant."

"This place sure keeps me busy," Chuck said as he handed us a couple of menus. "If you want to see me going forward, you're going to have to come here more. I'm selling my property."

"Both your cottages?" Scooter asked. "Even the one you're living in?"

"Yep. It's too much of a hassle to manage the one that's a rental property, and I can't keep up with the maintenance on my own cottage, let alone two of them. I'm buying a place at the Tropical Breeze condos."

"That's pretty lucky that you found two buyers," my husband said.

"No, it's just one buyer. It's a company that manages a lot of rental properties in the area. Suzanne told me they liked the idea of the two cottages being next door to each other. Sometimes, large families like to rent two adjacent properties and go back and forth between them."

"Is it Sierra Vista Rental Properties you're dealing with, by any chance?"

"That's the one," Chuck said. "You know them?"

"I've read about them." I leaned against the corner of the booth to hide the file folder from sight. "Are you sure they're going to keep them as rentals? Rumor has it someone wants to develop a resort right where our houses are."

"Oh, I've heard that too. I asked Suzanne about it, but she said it was just that, a rumor." He shrugged. "But to tell you the truth, maybe something like that would be good for business. More visitors to town means more customers."

"I guess there are pros and cons to that sort of thing," Scooter said diplomatically.

I felt my purse begin to slip. I wedged myself against it to keep it on the seat.

"Why are you so fidgety?" Scooter asked.

"Me? I'm not fidgety. Just hungry, I guess. I thought there would be nachos waiting for me."

Scooter pointed at an empty plate. "You snooze, you lose."

"Did you want to go ahead and order dinner? Do you know what you want?" Chuck asked.

"Can you give me a few minutes to look at the menu?" I asked.

"I was thinking about gator," Scooter said. "But my little panda bear turned up her nose at the idea."

"Too many teeth," I said.

Chuck smiled. "Ah, you're a vegetarian. No problem. We just added veggie burgers to the menu."

Scooter snorted. "Trust me, she eats meat. She's just picky about it. Besides, I think she'd make the worst vegetarian ever. She'd probably just subsist on chocolate and cheese."

"Sounds good to me," I said.

"Why don't you take a few minutes, check out the menu, and a waitress will be by to take your order. I'd better head back to the kitchen. Those gators aren't going to cook themselves."

Two couples came into the restaurant, chattering loudly. "There's only one table left. We'd better grab it before someone else does, Hank," I heard a familiar woman say.

"Violet, cool your heels. The hostess will be right back."

"Oh no," I said, scrunching down in my seat.

Scooter turned around. "Who are you hiding from?"

"Hiding? I'm not hiding."

"Yes you are."

"Can you just move a little that way?" I indicated which direction with my hand so that his back would block me from view. "That's better," I said.

"Care to explain?"

"Oh, it's just that I had a little...run-in with one of those couples earlier."

"Run-in?"

Our waitress came over to our table and set down two glasses of water. "I'll be back in a few to take your order," she said.

"Go on," Scooter said.

"It was just something to do with a ghost."

"I thought you didn't believe in ghosts."

"I don't, but they do." I unfolded my napkin and placed it on my lap. Scooter gave me a meaningful look. "They think Suzanne's ghost is haunting her office and our cottage."

"Why do they think that?"

"They were checking out the sign for our cottage in the window. She thought it would be the perfect house for their retirement. Then when they came back to show their friends, the sign had disappeared."

"And they think a ghost was behind it?" I nodded. Scooter leaned forward and stared at me. "I'm going to go out on a limb here and guess that a ghost wasn't involved. Exactly why were you late for dinner?"

"Oh, look, there's Ken and Leilani," I said, pointing at the door. "There aren't any empty tables. Maybe we should ask them to join us." I waved them over enthusiastically. "Come sit with us," I said.

"Thanks," Leilani said as she sat next to me. "We appreciate it. This place is really packed tonight."

Ken snagged one of the menus and handed the other to his wife. "So, what have you two been up to?"

"Oh, my adorable wife was just telling me some ghost stories," Scooter said with a smirk.

"You're kidding, right?" Ken said.

"Of course he's kidding," I said quickly. "I was walking down an alley in the dark earlier tonight, and I felt something cold brush against me. I was just joking, saying that it must have been a ghost."

"Dark alley?" Leilani asked, raising her eyebrows.

"Taking a shortcut. Anyway, it was probably just a raccoon. No big deal."

Scooter leaned back with a big grin on his face. "Why don't you tell them about the time you tried to teach raccoons sign language?"

I put my head in my hands. "You promised not to ever bring that up again." When I glanced up, Leilani and Ken were looking at me quizzically. Scooter was laughing. "Tell you what, why don't we change the subject? Did you know that Chuck is selling his two cottages?"

Ken slammed his fist on the table. "What? That traitor! I've talked to him numerous times about the importance of protecting the turtle nesting grounds." He snatched Leilani's menu from her hands. "Come on, let's get out of here. I refuse to patronize his restaurant."

"No, we're staying here," she said firmly. She took the menu back. "I'm tired and hungry. We're not going to run around town trying to find another place to eat that meets your standards."

Ken folded his arms. "My standards?"

Leilani sighed. "Look, not everyone is as passionate about the environment as you are. But lashing out at everyone isn't going to help. Remember, you can catch more flies with honey than with vinegar."

"Hey, folks," our waitress said as she deposited a basket and small bowl on our table. "Alligator bites and swamp sauce, on the house. I'll be right back."

Leilani pushed the basket toward Ken. "Go on. You know how much you love these."

He pulled a breaded nugget out, dipped it in the sauce, and popped it in his mouth. "They are good."

Before he could grab another one, Leilani placed the basket in front of me. "Better get some now before Ken eats all of them."

"Um...I'll pass. I'm not sure I want to eat anything that comes with something called swamp sauce."

Leilani laughed. "It's just a type of barbecue sauce."

"That might be okay, but maybe with chicken strips instead."

Ken reached across the table and pulled the basket back. "Good. More for the rest of us."

After the three of them had polished off the appetizer, I asked, "Ken, what would happen if there was, say, some proof that Norm and Suzanne were involved in the resort development?"

Ken wiped his mouth with a napkin. "That's the problem. I don't have any proof. I know they're in it up to their necks, but it's all just hearsay. But if there was proof, that would make a huge difference." He looked at me curiously. "Why, do you have some?"

I smiled mysteriously. "You never know. Something might turn up."

* * *

The following evening was the night of the weekly barbecue and potluck at the marina. It was hard to believe so much time had gone by already. In the span of just seven days, two people had been killed, Mrs. Moto had "lost" two more collars, I'd managed to get through my first public speech, and I had uncovered a real estate scam.

What I hadn't managed to do yet was discover who had murdered Darren and Suzanne. The thought of Chief Dalton beating me to the punch was more than I could stomach. As I looked around the patio, I wondered if someone here had done it. Was there some clue I was missing?

I saw Liam at a table with a couple of other young guys laughing, drinking beer, and checking out girls as they walked by. His uncle was over at the barbecue giving Ned unsolicited advice on how to get the chicken skin crispy without burning it. Ken was at the buffet table ladling baked beans and potato salad onto Leilani's plate. Melvin was sitting in the corner by himself, sipping on a soda.

"Penny for your thoughts, Mollie." I glanced up and saw Ben smiling at me. "Can I join you?"

"Of course. Have a seat. I'm just waiting for Scooter to get here."

He set a six-pack of beer on the table. "Want one?" When I passed, he cracked one open, took a swig, then leaned back in his chair. "I'm so glad it's Friday," he said. "It's been such a long week. We've been so busy in the boatyard."

"Is there any word on when we'll be able to get back to our boats?" I asked.

He shrugged. "I haven't heard anything. You should probably ask Nancy. She's been on the phone every day to Chief Dalton, chewing his ear off."

"That sounds like Nancy," I said. "I'd love to see how he reacted to that."

"Not well, I would imagine," Ben said. "There are very few people who will stand up to her."

"Ned seems to have developed a bit of a backbone as of late."

"I heard about that. Something to do with his movie collection." Ben finished his beer and opened another. "Well, it just goes to show you that there's a line everyone has that you don't dare cross."

I looked at him thoughtfully. "It does make you wonder what would cause someone to snap and murder Darren and Suzanne."

"I try not to think about it," Ben said. "I thought when the chief arrested Melvin, that was who did it. But then they released him last night."

"I spoke with him earlier," I said. "He was really cagey about the arrest. He told me he didn't want to talk about it, and then he walked off and sat at that table by himself."

Ben shrugged. "Maybe it was just about vandalizing Norm's boat."

"I hope so. I mean, I don't really hope so. It's just that I hope that's why they arrested him, not because he's a murderer. Does that make any sense?"

"Yeah, makes total sense. Melvin's a nice guy. No one wants to think he killed someone. You want the bad guys to be...well...bad guys. But I guess that's why neither of us is in the police force, Mollie. We can't be objective when it comes to this kind of thing."

"You think Chief Dalton is objective?"

"Sure, why wouldn't he be?"

"It's just that he's such a pain in the you-know-what sometimes." I thought about the colored-marker incident. "Actually, make that all the time."

Ben laughed. "Maybe that's why they have an anonymous tip line. So people don't have to talk directly to him."

"There's an anonymous tip line?"

"Sure." Ben leaned forward. "Why? Do you have a tip for the police?"

"Me? Of course not," I said, thinking about the file folder I had tucked away in the drawer of my nightstand. That might solve the problem of how to get the information about the real estate scam to the police without revealing exactly how it was found.

"Earth to Mollie," Ben said. "You're lost in thought. Come on, you can tell me. What have you found that you want to tip the police off about?"

"Nothing. I was just thinking about dolphins. I see you've got your dolphin T-shirt on again."

Ben's face turned a little pink. "Alejandra said she liked it last week."

"She won't be here tonight. She's at a friend's wedding this weekend."

"Oh," he said glumly.

"But I like your shirt."

"Thanks, I guess."

A loud commotion over by the buffet table interrupted Ben's thoughts about Alejandra and my thoughts about how best to disguise my voice when I called the tip line.

"Get out of here, you mangy cat!" Nancy was waving a broom as a streak of fur bolted past her and hid underneath a table.

"I'd better go see what trouble Mrs. Moto has gotten into now," I said.

I walked over to the table, crouched down, and gave her a stern look. "Nancy is mad at you. You really don't want to get on her bad side."

As I was trying to convince the cat to come sit over at our table, my phone beeped, alerting me to a new email. Alan had sent me a link to the video from the fishing boat fire in the Keys. I held the phone with one hand while scratching Mrs. Moto under her chin with my other. The first part of the video showed the wedding reception that he had been there to film. The happy couple was posing on one of the docks with their bridal party when a boat burst into flames behind them. They screamed and ran back up to the clubhouse while Alan stayed behind and continued to capture footage of the fire.

After watching the video a couple of times, I was convinced that Connie was in the background by the boat that went up in flames. And the man standing next to her looked a lot like Ken.

CHAPTER 15
HARASSING SEAGULLS

"ENOUGH, ALREADY!" I SAID AS the third sanding belt of the day broke. I had spent the past five hours working on *Marjorie Jane*'s bottom, and nothing had been going right. I was exhausted, frustrated, and ready to pay the next person who walked by a hundred dollars to take the boat off our hands. I pulled back the hood of my Smurf suit and knocked on the hull. "Hey, is anyone in there? I'm ready to go home, get something to eat, and wash all this grime off me."

"Wow, are you done sanding the bottom already?" Scooter asked, leaning over the side of the boat.

"No, but I'm through for the day."

Scooter looked down at his watch. "But it's only two."

"I can't take any more torture today." I wiped grit off my lips, which were desperately in need of some sort of industrial-strength lip balm. "Besides, Mrs. Moto needs to be fed."

"Oh, come on, she can hold out for a little while longer. This is the first day we've been able to get back in the boatyard and work on *Marjorie Jane*." He wiped the sweat off his brow. "Did you see Nancy go after Chief Dalton at the barbecue last night? It's thanks to her that we're finally able to catch up on all the work we need to do on the boat."

"Did we sign up for a race that no one told me about?"

"Well, not exactly."

"So there aren't any real deadlines other than the ones you decided to set for us?"

"But the sooner we finish up in here, the sooner we can splash the boat in the water, the sooner we can get her ready to go, and the sooner we can sail off to the Caribbean."

"Wow, there's a lot of 'sooners' in that sentence. If you checked a thesaurus, there would be a lot of helpful alternatives like, 'the more *speedily* we go home and feed Mrs. Moto, the more *quickly* I can have a nice bubble bath, and the more *rapidly* you can give me a foot rub.' See how much better that sentence sounds? It just rolls off the tongue."

Scooter smiled and held his hands up. "Okay, I know when I've been beaten. Why don't you head back home, and I'll give you a call later so you can come back and pick me up? That'll give me time to finish up a few things."

"Okay, sounds like a plan." I unzipped my suit, wadded it up into a ball, and threw it into the trash.

After I walked back to the boat, Scooter said, "Actually, you know what? Why don't I sleep on the boat tonight? That way you can just relax and don't have to worry about coming back here."

"You want to sleep here? It's a mess down below. The floorboards are still torn up. The lights aren't working. Neither is the toilet. Are you some sort of masochist?"

"I don't mind roughing it."

"Fine, I'll tell Mrs. Moto you chose *Marjorie Jane* over her. We can have a quiet girls' night together. I'll have a glass of wine, she'll have some catnip, and we'll watch a movie."

Scooter pointed over at *Mana Kai*. Leilani was sitting in the cockpit of her catamaran working on her computer. "Why don't you ask Leilani to come over? You were saying it would be fun to get together with her again."

"That's a good idea. Maybe she'd like a break from her boat as well." I knocked on their boat and shouted, "Hey, Leilani! Fancy some wine and Thai carryout?"

She didn't respond, so I climbed up a few rungs of their ladder and knocked again. Still no response. I didn't want to go the rest of the way up and hoist myself on deck to get her attention—it's a little like opening someone's front door and walking in uninvited —so I tried knocking one more time, bruising my knuckles on the fiberglass in the process.

"She probably can't hear you." I looked down and saw Ken standing at the bottom of the ladder. "She's always listening to those audiobooks of hers. I can drop an entire toolbox on the floor, and she wouldn't hear a peep. Here, let me try."

I watched as he ascended the ladder, walked across the deck, and tapped her on the shoulder. She lifted up her head and gave him a smile. He removed the headphones she was wearing. "Mollie was trying to get your attention," he said, pointing down at me.

"Oh, she was? I didn't hear her." She leaned over the side of the cockpit and waved at me. "Sorry about that. My book is getting to the good part," she said. "I'm determined to finish it tonight and find out whodunit."

"Ah, I understand. I was going to see if you wanted to come over later for a girls' night, but maybe another time."

After Leilani and I settled on a date for the following week, I asked Ken to tell me more about the volunteer work he did with Connie. I mentioned that I had heard the two of them had worked on a project in the Florida Keys a few weeks ago. Of course, I hadn't heard that so much as possibly seen the two of them on a video next to a boat on fire.

Ken squirmed and looked at me uncomfortably. He told me that he hadn't been down in that part of Florida in months and that the only work he did with Connie was related to public lectures and films. The conversation ended abruptly when he went inside their boat without saying goodbye. Leilani tried to apologize for his behavior, saying that he was under a lot of pressure trying to secure grant money, but I wasn't convinced that was the reason why.

* * *

Mrs. Moto and I enjoyed an early dinner for two, probably better described as "linner"—that meal you have between lunch and dinner. Personally, I could see making this a regular part of my day. Like my feline companion, I function so much better when I have frequent feedings.

We both had tuna, except hers came out of a can, while mine came out of the freezer. Despite what Mrs. Moto would try to lead you to believe, one can is a perfectly adequate serving for a cat of her size and age. I even showed her the label to prove it to her, but she still wasn't having it. I was finally able to appease her, but only after I put a tiny piece of my own tuna on her plate.

Afterward, we went for a walk on the beach. As usual, she dashed off in pursuit of gulls. While she terrorized the birds, I paused and breathed in the salt air. Why would Scooter voluntarily choose to spend the afternoon and evening working on a dilapidated boat when he could be here listening to the gentle lapping of the waves on the shore?

My peace and quiet was interrupted by the loud shrieks of two boys running down the beach chasing Mrs. Moto. The birds had scattered and were watching smugly from a safe distance. The tables had finally turned in their favor. The cat was the one being chased, not them.

"Get over here right this second!" a harried-looking mother screamed. "Leave that poor cat alone."

She seized the boys by their hands and led them back to their beach towels, muttering something about taking away their Xbox privileges. Poor things, I thought as I walked past them. I knew all about maternal threats, except in my case, we didn't have all the electronic gadgets kids had nowadays—although the mention of taking away my collection of Barbie dolls always elicited good behavior. For a while, at least.

I looked around for Mrs. Moto, but there was no sign of her. The seagulls were still enjoying their reprieve from their furry stalker. "Here, kitty, kitty," I shouted as I walked down the beach. "Come on out from where you're hiding, and I'll give you some extra tuna." Still nothing.

The two boys had escaped the clutches of their mother again and were running toward a very impressive-looking sandcastle.

"If you don't get back here this instant, there won't be any ice cream for dessert," she shouted. That did the trick. They galloped back, grabbed their plastic sand buckets and shovels, and obediently made their way up the path toward the parking lot.

As I paused to examine the sandcastle more closely, admiring its four large turrets decorated with seashells and seaweed, I saw two pointed ears and a pair of green eyes peeking over the top of the moat.

"Don't worry, they're gone," I told the feline. She gave a faint meow. I motioned her over to a piece of driftwood. "Come on, let's sit here for a while and make sure there aren't any more small humans waiting to attack you before we head back." She curled up by my feet while I kept a lookout.

"Is that you, Mollie?" a woman called out.

Mrs. Moto gazed at the intruders with a mixture of curiosity and wariness.

"It's okay. This is Fiona and Connie," I said. "You remember them, don't you? We met them the other day when they were with Simon, that nice guy from FAROUT. They're not going to chase you. They're turtle people. They love animals."

She padded over to them and sniffed at them cautiously. Fiona won her over completely when she picked her up and gave her a few scratches under her chin.

"What are you two doing here?" I asked.

"We were passing out these," Connie said. She reached in her backpack and handed me a pamphlet. "Trying to raise awareness about turtle conservation."

"You guys are so dedicated. It's really great that you have a cause you believe so much in."

"Well, we do what we can," Fiona said. "We have to try to reach the public in lots of different ways to get the message across. These work for some people." She pointed at the pamphlet in my hand. "But others throw them away."

"At least people take them from you. Maybe they read them before they toss them. We've got a much harder time trying to hand out stuff for FAROUT. All you have to do is mention alien abduction, and for some reason, people just walk away without hearing what you have to say. Even the offer of a free bumper sticker doesn't do it."

"Yeah, well, talk of little green men will do that," Connie said dismissively. "But when it comes to serious causes, I really think Ken has the right idea—videos."

"Ken Choi?" I asked.

"Yep, him. He's over there right now filming. He's making a video about how the toxic red tide we've been having on the coast is impacting sea life."

I looked over where she was pointing and could just about make out someone standing near the shore holding up a small camera on a selfie stick.

"He makes short videos for his YouTube channel, but he's also been involved in making longer films," Connie said.

"Speaking of films, I think I saw you on a video of a wedding that took place a few weeks ago in the Florida Keys."

"Me?" Connie asked. "Couldn't have been. The last wedding I was at was for my niece last year."

"Are you sure? The lady looked a lot like you. A fishing boat caught on fire during the reception."

Connie frowned. "Must have been someone else. I think I'd remember that. Probably just someone who looked like me. What are you doing watching wedding videos anyway? Unless you're the one getting married, they're so boring. Now, films about protecting wildlife, like the ones Ken makes, are much more interesting."

"Didn't he just show one the other day at the Florida Turtle Trust meeting?" Fiona asked.

"Yeah. He introduced it and then led a Q&A afterward," Connie said. "That turned out to be a huge disaster."

"Why, what happened?" I asked.

"Right after the film started, I saw him take off in his car. We couldn't find him anywhere when it ended, so we improvised by serving refreshments while we waited for him to show up."

"So he wasn't there the whole time?"

"No. I tried to ask him where he was going, but he said he had something urgent to take care of."

"How long was the film?" I asked.

"About two hours."

"And how much longer after it finished before he turned up?"

Connie scratched her head. "I don't know. I guess thirty, forty-five minutes? Why are you so curious about Ken? I was ticked off that he left, but it all worked out okay in the end."

"Just one last question. What time did the movie begin?"

"Eight," Connie said. "Listen, if you're interested in future film showings, I've got another pamphlet that lists them all." She bent down and started to stick her hand in her backpack. A furry paw reached out and swiped at her.

Fiona laughed. "Looks like you have a hitchhiker."

The older woman did not appear to be amused. She coaxed Mrs. Moto out of the bag, zipped it up, and slung it over her shoulder. "Come on, let's get going," she said to Fiona.

"Hey, something fell out," I said, running after them. As I handed Connie her MP3 player and earbuds, it all clicked into place. I knew who had killed Darren and Suzanne.

* * *

I sat there for a while thinking about what Fiona and Connie had said. Ken wasn't at the Florida Turtle Trust event the entire night, which meant that he didn't have an alibi for Suzanne's murder. And his alibi for the night of Darren's murder didn't hold up either. Because Leilani had been working in the aft cabin with her headphones on, drowning out any other noise, he could have easily left his boat and killed the young man without his wife being any the wiser.

"Come on, Mrs. Moto. It's time to go home," I said, scooping her up in my arms. "I think I left my phone on the counter, and we need to call the—"

"Who do you need to call?" I turned and saw Ken standing behind me, holding his camera.

"Just my mom. You know how moms are," I stammered.

"Oh, your mom will be fine. You can call her later. I'm making a video, and I thought you could help me with it. You were so interested earlier today in the work Connie and I did in the Florida Keys that I think you'll like this one."

"Sorry, I really have to go and call her. She gets worried when

I don't check in every night at this time." I laughed nervously. "She might even call the police to check up on me." I backed up a few steps toward the sandcastle and stumbled. Mrs. Moto leaped out of my arms and dived into the sandcastle's moat.

Ken grabbed my arm and pulled me toward him. "I said, I need your help with my video."

"I really need to get back. Scooter is waiting for me at the cottage."

"No, he isn't. I heard him tell you that he's staying on the boat tonight, remember?"

He reached behind his back, pulled a handgun out from the waistband of his shorts, and jammed it into my side. "Now, start filming." He shoved the camera into my hand and stepped back, keeping the gun pointed at me.

I looked behind me at the sandcastle. Mrs. Moto had crawled down into the moat. Her ears were flattened, her back was arched, and she was growling. Ken waved the gun at her. "Go on, get out of here," I yelled. She stood her ground, growling louder.

"Stop staring at that cat," he hissed. "Press the Record button, and aim the camera toward me." While I tried to keep my hands from shaking, Ken coldly recounted why Darren and Suzanne deserved to die and that anyone else who stood in the way of the environment would also suffer retribution.

"You killed them to protect the environment? How is that going to win anyone over to your cause?" I blurted out. "Ecoterrorism is bad enough, but murder?"

Ken took a step toward me, pointing the gun at my chest. "An ecoterrorist? Is that what you think I am? Someone has to protect innocent wildlife from humanity. Handing out pamphlets and giving lectures isn't enough. It doesn't stop the poaching. Everyone knows it's going on, but no one does anything about it. But I'm stepping up to the plate. I'm taking care of it!"

"Is that why you've set fishing boats on fire?"

Ken gave a humorless laugh. "If they don't have a boat, they can't go out poaching, now, can they?"

I flinched as he took another step forward. "Vandalizing property is one thing," I said cautiously. "But killing people?"

Ken lowered the gun and looked over at the sun setting on the water. "I didn't have a choice," he said softly. "Darren had overheard Connie and me talking about setting those fishing boats on fire. He recorded the whole thing on his phone and threatened to go to the police with it unless I paid him off. He even had some pictures that he got off a website of the two of us next to a boat we torched."

"Is that what you got in the mail the other day at the turtle sanctuary? Pictures?" Ken nodded. "But couldn't you have just turned him in for poaching?"

"With what evidence?" Ken asked sharply. "And even if I did have any, all they would do is make him pay a fine. This way, I could keep him from blackmailing me and stop the poaching."

"So why Suzanne?"

Ken waved the gun toward the shoreline. "Because of this. She was going to destroy the turtle habitat with her resort development." He narrowed his eyes and looked intently at me. "Everyone who is complicit with the resort development—people like you and Chuck, agreeing to sell your cottages to her—are in on it!"

"But we don't want to sell," I stammered.

"I've heard Scooter talk about selling." Ken pointed the gun at me again. My legs started trembling. I tried to scream for help, but I couldn't get any words out. "Don't even think about yelling. If you do, I'll shoot you. Besides, the sun has set and the beach is deserted. No one would hear you." He gripped my arm and spun me around, pressing the gun into my side. "Now, here's what we're going to do. We're going to walk over to your house, slowly. Any false moves and...well, you know what will happen."

I stumbled as he pushed me forward. As I tried to regain my balance, I saw a ball of fur flying through the air and heard Ken scream. Then I felt a sharp pain in my leg, collapsed on the sand, and everything went black.

* * *

I felt something scratchy on my face and opened my eyes. Mrs. Moto was standing on my chest. She licked my nose, meowed loudly, then pawed at the side of my head. "Hey, that hurts!" I rubbed my eyes and took in my surroundings. I was on the beach, my head propped up against a piece of driftwood.

How did I get here? I wondered. Then I saw the large sandcastle and remembered. When Mrs. Moto had attacked Ken, he'd dropped the gun and it had gone off. I glanced down at my leg. Blood was dripping down it, and although I was in agony, the bullet appeared to have just grazed it. I slowly got to my feet and looked around in a panic. "Where is he?" Mrs. Moto yowled and tore down the beach toward our cottage. That's when I smelled it —the fire.

I hobbled after her, keeping an eye out for Ken and doing my best to ignore the pain in my leg. My heart was racing, and I was struggling to breathe, but I kept pounding my feet in the sand, trying to catch up with my cat and keep her safe from that madman. Finally, I saw her, sitting quietly on the beach. She stared at me with those green eyes of her, meowed softly, then looked straight ahead of her.

I followed her gaze and saw what was burning. Our cottage. Our home. Our everything.

CHAPTER 16
BLING FOR MRS. MOTO

"MOLLIE AND SCOOTER ARE HERE, everyone!" I heard a voice shout as we walked into the Tipsy Pirate. A crowd swarmed around us, giving us hugs and asking us a million questions.

"Let them breathe, folks," Ned said, gently pushing people aside. "We saved you some seats at our table." He pointed at a spot near the stage where Penny, Ben, Alejandra, and Nancy were sitting. "You two must be so stressed out and exhausted after everything you've gone through. Come on, let's get you a drink."

"Drinks are on me tonight," a nasal voice said behind us. I turned and saw Norm holding his hat in his hands. "It's the least I can do," he said. He lacked his usual bluster, probably because he was now under investigation for his role in the real estate scam. Before we could thank him, he walked over and told the bartender that he would be picking up our tab. I hoped he didn't think that would get him out of our bet. I was still determined to finish the bottom paint on *Marjorie Jane* and then throw a boat renaming party when Norm changed the name of his boat to *ET*.

"You look really good, Mollie," Penny said as I sat in a chair between her and Alejandra. "Is your leg doing okay?"

I glanced down at the bandage wrapped around my calf. "A little sore, but it's fine."

"It's hard to believe it was just yesterday that Ken had you at gunpoint, you got shot, and your cottage burned down," Alejandra said.

"You probably didn't sleep well last night," Ben said. "You have some dark circles under your eyes."

Alejandra gave him a warning look. "No, she doesn't. She looks great. I like your top. Pink's a good color on you. Don't you like her top, too, Ben?"

Ben shrugged. I noticed he was sporting his dolphin T-shirt again, probably hoping Alejandra would notice that instead of what I was wearing.

"Thanks. Penny lent it to me," I said. "We haven't had a chance to go buy new clothes yet. Everyone has been so great helping us out."

Ben leaned forward. "I want to hear all about how you solved the case."

"Well, I wouldn't really say I solved it. I didn't figure out who did it until it was too late." I bit my lip. "Too late to save our cottage."

"But you put all the puzzle pieces together," he said. "Come on, tell us how you did it."

Nancy scowled. "For goodness' sake. She's not a detective. If you want to know what happened, ask Chief Dalton."

Ben rolled his eyes. "Yeah, that'll be the day."

"I'd actually be interested in hearing what Mollie has to say," Alejandra said.

The waitress handed me a gin and tonic. I took a sip, then glanced at Scooter. "Are you okay if I tell them what happened? I promise I'll leave out any gory details." I reached into my purse and handed him a pack of M&M'S. "But just in case, these should help."

"We should probably start buying these in bulk," he said with a smile.

I leaned back in my chair. "Well, at first, when it was a question of just one..." I looked at Scooter and watched him pop some candy in his mouth. "Of just one...um...victim, I thought Liam might have done it. I wasn't sure why, though. It could have been because Darren was involved in poaching with Liam.

Apparently, he had been blabbing about it all over town. Maybe Liam wanted to put a stop to that in a permanent sort of way."

"Did you hear Darren talking about the poaching?" Penny asked.

"Not exactly," I said. I glanced at Ben. "I happened to overhear you talking about it with Liam out there on the deck last week."

Nancy peered at Ben over her reading glasses. "So, you knew about the poaching, and you didn't tell anyone."

Ben squirmed in his seat. "I didn't know for sure. It's not like I had any proof," he said. "Besides, these guys were buddies of mine."

"Leave the boy alone, Nancy," Ned said. "It's hard to rat out your friends. Anyway, it's all out in the open now. Liam is going to pay the price for what he did." He looked at me. "You said you weren't sure why Liam might have done it. What other theory did you have?"

"Well, there was obviously no love lost between Melvin and Norm. Liam told me that he often had to do his uncle's dirty work. What if he killed Darren on his uncle's instructions to drive him out of business? The loss of his nephew was devastating to Melvin. He's even been talking about getting out of the fishing charter business as a result."

"I talked to him earlier," Penny said. "He's decided to sell *Nassau Royale*. It's just too hard for him to manage now that Darren is gone."

"Is he going to go back to the Bahamas?" Alejandra asked.

"No, he's decided to stay and focus on the marine store," Penny said.

"Fortunately, he didn't lose his cottage in the fire," Scooter said. "That probably would have been the last straw. All four of the cottages on the beach are right next to each other. It's really lucky they didn't all go up in flames." He finished off his drink and motioned to the waitress for another one. "Ken Choi," he said, shaking his head. "I can't believe we actually started to become friends with that guy. First, Darren and Suzanne, then setting fire to our place. Not to mention the cold-hearted bastard was responsible for my wife getting shot," he said through gritted teeth.

"That's something I was wondering about. Why did he burn your place down?" Alejandra asked.

"He was convinced we were going to sell our cottage. So he set fire to our and Chuck's properties for what he saw as our role in the resort development."

"But weren't they planning on tearing down the cottages to develop the resort?" Penny asked. "What would it matter if they were burned down?"

"The man was completely unhinged," Scooter said. "He just wanted to make a grand statement about what happens to people he thinks are abetting the destruction of the environment."

"Do you mind going back to the part about Liam?" Alejandra asked. "I thought he had an alibi for the night of Darren's murder."

"Well, it wasn't a really good one. He said he was at home watching a basketball game. But no one was with him."

"He knew everything that happened in the game when I talked to him about it," Scooter said.

"He could have read about it online," Ned said. "I always check out the sports news every day. Sometimes, I even watch replays of games I missed."

"True," I said. "To be honest, even if you have someone to back up your alibi, it doesn't mean the other person is telling the truth. Take Norm, for example. He definitely had motive to kill Darren because of Melvin, but Suzanne said the two of them had been at their office all night." I leaned forward. "Turns out he had actually left during the time Darren was killed, only no one knew about it."

"How did you find out about that?" Alejandra asked.

"Officer Moore might have let it slip when I saw her earlier today at Penelope's. We bonded over our love of cinnamon mochas. Norm was actually meeting with an insurance agent that night. I happen to know that he took out a very hefty life insurance policy on Suzanne."

Penny raised her eyebrows. "That would give him a great motive for her death."

"Hang on," Alejandra said. "Let's focus on Darren's murder first. Who else did you think could have done it?"

"Well, I thought Suzanne might have been a suspect when Mrs. Moto found one of her charms near the crime scene. But when I returned it to her, she seemed really calm about it and genuinely perplexed about how it had ended up there. And besides, I couldn't picture her setting foot in the boatyard in those heels of hers, let alone killing someone and risking getting blood on her clothes."

"It took a threatening note to get her to go into the boatyard the night she was, you know..." Scooter said. He took a deep breath. "It was probably the first time she had ever been there."

"And of course Melvin couldn't have done it," Alejandra said. "He was his nephew."

I looked over where Melvin was sitting in the corner with a few of his friends. "I thought so too. But I found out that he knew Darren was mixed up in poaching, and he was furious about it. Tiffany overheard them arguing about it at a basketball game."

"Fortunately, he wasn't furious enough about it to kill him," Penny said. "He was his own flesh and blood, after all."

"That's what everyone assumed, myself included. But when I think about it objectively, did I assume that because I liked him? After all, I thought Norm might have killed his own wife."

"Okay, tell us about Suzanne's death," Alejandra said. "Who had an alibi for that one?"

"Liam was with a woman that night. She's married and was hesitant to come forward at first to vouch for him."

Nancy frowned. "What was he doing with a married woman?"

I smiled, thinking about the texts I had seen on Liam's phone. "You don't want to know."

Ben shook his head. "That guy just can't keep his hand out of the cookie jar." He glanced at Alejandra. "Aren't you glad you didn't go out with him? You deserve a one-woman kind of guy," he said with a hopeful look on his face.

"So, what about Norm?" Alejandra asked without meeting Ben's eyes.

"He claimed he was at the Tipsy Pirate when the murder took place. Officer Moore said there were a number of people who could vouch for him," I said.

"Melvin told me the same thing," Penny said.

"Yeah, he told me that too, but..." I glanced at Melvin again. He was staring into his beer, oblivious to his friends chatting away around him.

"But what?" Penny asked.

"Melvin wasn't at the Tipsy Pirate. Office Moore told me he was at the waterfront park that night getting some fresh air and thinking through everything."

Penny gasped. "So was he the person who vandalized Norm's boat?"

"No," I said. "But he saw the whole thing and didn't call the police. He honestly believed Norm killed his nephew, and he was so upset about it that he practically cheered the vandals on."

"So, who did do it?"

"A woman named Connie. She shares Ken's views on taking extreme measures to protect the environment, including sabotaging boats involved in poaching." I took a sip of my drink. "Oddly enough, it turns out that both Liam and Melvin ended up vouching for each other at the time of Suzanne's death. Liam was at the park as well with his lady friend."

"But didn't Liam see Melvin?" Penny asked.

"No, Liam was a little too distracted by other things, if you know what I mean," I said. "Did you know that Leilani and I had actually seen Liam and this woman earlier that night when I was dropping her back off at the marina after the FAROUT event? The two of them were having a fight on the street by the marina entrance. He chased after her, and then they went to the park to talk things through. Melvin was sitting on one park bench thinking about the death of his nephew, and they were on another one making up." I shrugged. "Liam did have a good reason to kill Suzanne. He was tired of her lording her son over him, but he didn't do it."

Alejandra swirled the ice around in her drink with a swizzle stick. "So, Liam and Norm had alibis for Suzanne's death. I guess that brings us to Ken."

Scooter reached across the table and squeezed my hand. "The thought of him holding a gun at you and you getting shot." He turned pale and shuddered. I looked at the empty M&M'S bag on the table.

"Why don't we stop off and pick up some chocolate ice cream to take back with us to the hotel tonight?"

He leaned back in his chair and nodded. "Good idea."

Everyone at the table was watching me expectantly. "So, Ken. Well, he had alibis for both murders. Leilani and he were both on their boat the night of Darren's murder. But she was in the back cabin and had her headphones on. Her husband was able to sneak out without her knowing. Darren had been blackmailing Ken about his ecoterrorist activities. The two of them had arranged to meet that night, and Ken was supposed to pay him off. But he did more than that—he killed him."

"All because he was blackmailing him?" Alejandra asked.

"That was just part of it. Ken was enraged that Darren was poaching. Saving the environment was very important to him."

Scooter scowled. "So important that he'd kill for it."

"How did Suzanne's charm end up in the boatyard?" Penny asked.

"Ken went to her office to confront her about the real estate scam they were running. You know, the one where they were secretly buying property up in order to develop a large resort. It must have fallen off her bracelet onto the floor. He picked it up, thinking it might come in handy at some point. So he left it at the murder scene. But when I found it, it was outside of the cordoned-off area, and the police hadn't found it during their initial investigation." I thought about how Mrs. Moto loved to bat objects around. "Ken was probably wondering why Suzanne was never arrested for Darren's murder after he tried to pin it on her."

"So is the property deal what drove him to kill Suzanne?" Penny asked.

I nodded. "It is. When he heard she was still trying to buy property in Coconut Cove, including our cottage, he snapped. He sent her a note threatening to expose her and told her to meet him at Norm's boat. And...well...you know what happened."

"But he didn't stop there," Scooter said. "He held you at gunpoint, you got shot, and he burned our house down."

"Thankfully, you weren't hurt too badly, dear," Nancy said gently.

I felt my eyes well up. "It could have been worse. I was sure he was going to kill me." I took a deep breath. "But Mrs. Moto saved the day. When he kept waving the gun at me, she jumped out from the sandcastle she was hiding in, hurled herself at his leg, and sunk her claws and teeth in. He was so startled that he dropped the gun. That's when it went off, and the bullet grazed my leg. Then he ran off to torch the cottages."

"But you didn't see him set them on fire?" Alejandra asked.

"Uh...no, I didn't."

"That's because my little panda bear fainted from the shock of it all," Scooter said, squeezing my hand.

"Should we talk about the time you fainted?" I asked Scooter with a smile, remembering what had happened when he'd seen Darren's body.

Fortunately for Scooter, Norm came over and handed me an envelope. "Here, we all took up a collection for the two of you. You'll probably need a little help getting back on your feet."

My eyes grew wide when I looked inside the envelope. "We can't possibly accept this," I said as I handed it to Scooter.

"No, we can't," he said. "It's a very thoughtful gesture, but we're fine. We've got insurance and savings." He pointed over to the bar where a couple of off-duty volunteer firefighters were standing. "I've got an idea." He leaned across the table and filled me in on his plan. Then he pointed at the stage. "Go on, tell everyone."

"Oh no, not me. Why don't you do it?"

"You can do it. You're experienced at public speaking now."

I reluctantly got up on stage, picked up the microphone, and thanked everyone for their donations. When I suggested that we give the money to the fire department instead, everyone cheered.

* * *

"You did great, my little panda bear," Scooter said, giving me a big hug. "I have a feeling you're going to be in demand as a public speaker. Next stop, Mollie's World Tour!" He stepped back and gave me an appraising look. "Hey, are you okay?"

"I just need a minute," I said. "I'm going to go get some fresh air. I'll meet you at the car."

"All right, just don't take too long. Mrs. Moto is waiting for us back at the boat."

I walked out onto the deck, leaned up against the railing, and took a few deep breaths. I was feeling overwhelmed by all the love and support everyone had shown us. Coconut Cove really was a special place. People looked out for one another. Sure, they might know a little too much about your personal business—you certainly couldn't hide anything in a town this small for very long —but that also meant that they genuinely cared when something tragic happened in your life.

As I gazed out across the water, I had to admit that Ken had been right about one thing. Big developers coming in would ruin the quirky charm of Coconut Cove. There had to be a way to bring more revenue into the area while retaining our small-town identity and appeal. Next month's boating festival would be a good test of this. It was sure to draw lots of tourists, but it would also highlight locally-owned small businesses, like Penelope's bakery, Chuck's restaurant, the Sailor's Corner Cafe, and the Tipsy Pirate. I hoped nothing would ruin it.

I took a last look at the sun setting over the water. When I turned to head back inside, I noticed Ned and Nancy at the far side of the deck, holding hands. This was a first—I don't think I had ever seen them be affectionate toward each other in that way before. Nancy probably thought it would come across as a sign of weakness.

They walked toward me, whispering to each other. Nancy even giggled at one point. As they passed me, she noticed me watching. She dropped Ned's hand, then fixed her piercing blue eyes on me. "What are you looking at, Mollie?" She pursed her lips and continued to glare at me. "Are you going to stand there all day? You're blocking the entrance." I took a step back and she whisked past me. "Come on, Ned, let's go," she said over her shoulder.

Ned started to follow his wife, then paused and gave me a big smile. "She apologized. Can you believe that?"

"That's terrific," I said. As he walked inside, I muttered under my breath, "Enjoy it while it lasts."

Before I met Scooter at the car, I had one last thing to do—pay a visit to my old friend, Coconut Carl.

"Hey, Carl, remember me? It's Mollie. I just wanted to say thank you for everything you did. My FAROUT speech went great. Now I have another little favor to ask. We could really use some good luck when it comes to finding a new place to live. Do you think you could help out with that?" I rubbed his belly three times, clockwise.

As I was about to give some tourists their chance with Carl, I remembered something. I stepped back and whispered in his ear. "By the way, I wasn't talking about living on *Marjorie Jane*. Just thought I should make that clear." I threw in a few extra belly rubs for good luck.

* * *

"Mrs. Moto, where are you?" I called out. A furry face peeked over the side of the boat and watched me climb up the ladder, her whiskers twitching. Once I clambered onto the deck, she rubbed against my legs and purred loudly. Then she padded back to the side of the boat and watched Scooter make his way upward. As he neared the top rung, she leaned over and quickly licked his forehead before darting into the cockpit.

"Yuck. What was that about?" he asked as he wiped the remnants of her kiss off.

"I think she's worried about us. She's afraid we might fall down and get hurt." I gave her a scratch on the head. "Or worse," I added.

Scooter rolled his eyes. "I think that would only upset her if it meant we couldn't open a can of her favorite cat food at least twice a day."

He sat in the cockpit and stretched his arms behind his head. "It's a nice night out. I love a full moon, don't you?" He put his arm around me and pulled me close. Mrs. Moto climbed onto his lap. "It wouldn't be so bad living on the boat, would it?"

I pulled back and stared at him. "You're joking, aren't you? There's barely enough room to move, the floorboards are torn up, the toilet doesn't work, and I can't even begin to imagine cooking down below." Mrs. Moto yowled loudly. "See, Mrs. Moto agrees with me."

"You're right. It doesn't make sense to move aboard. At least, not yet." I leaned back and gave him a pointed look. He tried again. "At least not for a while?" I raised my eyebrows. "At least, not until it's your idea?"

"That's better," I said.

Scooter smiled. "I thought you'd feel that way. Fortunately, I think I found us a place to live. A place that's on land with a working kitchen and bathroom."

"That's great! Where?"

"There's a unit available for rent at the Tropical Breeze condos. It's fully furnished, so we can move in right away." The calico meowed. "And yes, pets are allowed," Scooter said, giving her a scratch on her head.

He sighed. "I guess it won't be a big deal to move, considering we've lost everything."

"I'm really going to miss my boots."

"I'm going to miss my comic book collection," Scooter said in a strained voice.

I squeezed his hand. "Hey, are you crying?"

Mrs. Moto stood and looked at him curiously. She reached up and put her front paws on his shoulder. He picked her up and rubbed his face against her fur. "I'm fine. I think it's just my allergies acting up."

Mrs. Moto squirmed in his arms and stuck her paw into his shirt pocket.

"Looks like she found another clue," I said jokingly.

The calico kept poking in his pocket insistently.

Scooter smiled. "Actually, she found something better than a clue in the bilge earlier today. Of course, she may have been the one who put it there in the first place." He picked her up and gazed into her eyes sternly. "You're going to have to stop knocking stuff off tables and counters." She leaned forward and licked his face. "Hey, stop that."

He set the cat on the seat next to him, reached into his pocket, and pulled out my diamond necklace. I put it around my neck and gave Scooter a kiss. "Thank goodness. I thought it had been lost in the fire!" Mrs. Moto meowed. "Yes, of course you deserve all the credit. What would we do without you and your uncanny ability to find things?"

Scooter smiled. "I suppose she isn't too bad." He looked at our little fur ball. "But I don't really think that collar suits her, do you? It's just too ordinary for such a clever cat."

I stroked Mrs. Moto's neck and inspected the plain navy collar. "Well, it's not like it's going to last long. She'll mysteriously lose this one soon too."

Scooter pulled a small bag out of the pocket on his cargo shorts and opened it up. "I think the reason she hasn't been happy with her collars is that she's jealous that you get to wear a sparkly necklace with a diamond and she doesn't." He pulled out a glittery silver collar encrusted with rhinestones. "See, now you've got some bling too," he said, fastening it around her neck. Mrs. Moto started purring loudly. I think she approved.

Scooter smiled at her reaction. "You know, it doesn't really matter about the cottage. Things can be replaced, Mollie. What's important is that I've still got my favorite girl." Mrs. Moto meowed. "Sorry. Of course I meant my two favorite girls." Then he rubbed his hand along *Marjorie Jane*'s woodwork. "Make that my three favorite girls."

Poisoned by the Pier

Book #3

THE CREW

MOLLIE MCGHIE—When she isn't investigating murders, Mollie spends her time educating the public about UFOs and alien abduction.

SCOOTER MCGHIE—Mollie's husband. Passionate about boats, he dreams about sailing around the world.

MRS. MOTO—Mollie and Scooter's Japanese bobtail cat who has an uncanny talent for finding clues.

NANCY AND NED SCHNEIDER—Owners of the Palm Tree Marina.

KATY AND SAM—Nancy and Ned's grandchildren.

PENNY CHADWICK—Runs the local sailing school and boat brokerage.

ALEJANDRA LOPEZ—A young waitress at the Sailor's Corner Cafe.

BEN MORETTI—A wannabe pirate who works at the marina.

CHIEF DALTON—Coconut Cove's chief of police.

ANABEL DALTON—The chief of police's ex-wife.

NORM THOMAS—Owner of several local businesses, including a fishing charter business.

MIKE WILSON—Lawyer specializing in wills and estates.

WANDA GROSSMAN—A member of Mollie's weekly sailing class and a food demonstrator at the grocery store.

PENELOPE PRINGLE—Owner of the Sugar Shack, a popular bakery in Coconut Cove.

ALAN SIMPSON—Wedding photographer and aspiring photojournalist.

JEFF MORGAN—Australian who is interested in buying a boat.

EMILY VAN DER BYL—Jeff's fiancée and a resident of Destiny Key.

THE ADORABLE DOGS—Frick and Frack (Yorkies), Chloe (a chocolate Labrador retriever), Bob (a scruffy terrier), and Chica (a German shepherd mix).

CHAPTER 1
DUMPSTER DIVING

WHAT WOULD YOU DO IF your husband announced that he had signed the two of you up for a strict diet program and tossed all your chocolate, cookies, potato chips—even your red wine—into the trash? Would you:

(a) feel his forehead to see if he had a fever;

(b) search your purse to make sure he hadn't thrown out your emergency supply of M&M'S;

(c) start to think living on a dilapidated sailboat wasn't the craziest idea he'd ever had; or

(d) go dumpster diving?

I began with (a)—checking his forehead. The only rational explanation for Scooter's behavior was that he was ill. Seriously, we're talking about a man who's addicted to sugary cereal and steals french fries off my plate. He wouldn't last a minute without regular infusions of junk food.

After determining that he wasn't sick, at least not physically (although thinking a detox was a good idea made me wonder about his mental health), I opted for (b)—rooting through my purse. Thankfully, he hadn't found my stash of M&M'S. I was definitely going to need them to deal with this crazy food regimen of his.

While I munched on my candy, I reflected on (c)—all the other harebrained schemes my husband had come up with over the years. Of course, presenting me with a sailboat named *Marjorie Jane* on our tenth wedding anniversary and thinking I'd be happy about it topped the list. But this ridiculous diet was coming in a strong second.

Just think about it for a minute—what's the first part of the word "diet"? *Die.* Would you really want to go on a "die-it"? I'd much rather be on a "live-it." And living for me involved all the things Scooter had chucked in the trash—chocolate, potato chips, cookies, and wine.

After I finished the last M&M, I looked around my home and sighed. You would have sighed too if you lived where I did—on a rundown sailboat in the noisy, dusty, grimy boatyard at a marina in Florida. The yard was where repairs and maintenance were done while vessels were out of the water, their hulls supported by metal jack stands. Seeing them propped up like nautical tree houses always made me more than a little nervous, especially living in a hurricane zone. Sure, the boats were tied down with straps, but I still wondered how many would remain standing should a serious storm blow through.

We had hauled *Marjorie Jane* out of the water the previous month when we discovered a leak on board. Once she was on land, we'd realized that fixing the leak was the least of our problems. The list of boat projects we needed to tackle was endless. We were in danger of becoming long-term residents of the boatyard—the type of people who spent years working on their boats and ended up running out of money and/or enthusiasm before they ever got to use their vessels.

Yeah, you're probably thinking we're crazy. I don't blame you. I think we're crazy too. Why would anyone live on a boat? Trust me, it certainly wasn't my idea. We used to have an adorable seaside cottage—the ocean views were to die for. Unfortunately, we ended up losing our sweet little place. Please don't ask me what happened. Every time I tell the story, I get teary-eyed. Chocolate was the only thing that helped me feel better, and that, at this point in time, appeared to be in seriously short supply.

After the cottage fiasco, we had sublet a place at the Tropical

Breeze condos. I fell in love with the spa tub and luxury kitchen. The fact that there were a couple of fast-food places around the corner didn't hurt either. Sadly, it was a short-lived love affair, as the owners unexpectedly came back to town, leaving us homeless again.

That's when Scooter had come up with the idea of living on our sailboat as a temporary solution. I did mention that he was the king of harebrained ideas, didn't I? If not the king, at least he had a seat on the royal court.

It was downright depressing thinking about it all. I definitely needed more chocolate. It was time to enact option (d)—dumpster diving.

After carefully climbing down the ladder attached to our boat, I walked over to the trash bin at the far end of the boatyard. Turns out I wasn't the only one with the same idea. Ben Moretti, one of our friends who lived at the marina and made ends meet by working in the boatyard, was standing next to the dumpster holding a very familiar-looking bottle of wine and a bag of Hershey's Kisses.

"Look what I found, Mollie! Major score, don't you think?" he said, grinning from ear to ear. He pointed at the plastic garbage bag by his feet. "There's even more good stuff in there. Come on, I'll share with you. What should we celebrate? That you're finished painting the bottom of your boat?"

I thought about saying we should celebrate the fact that he had rescued my vino and candy before I had to dig through the trash personally, but I didn't want to admit to him that I'd been so desperate for chocolate that I'd been about to resort to dumpster diving myself. So, I did what anyone would do in that situation— told an itty-bitty white lie.

"You don't really think I'd eat something that came from the garbage, do you?"

The young man kicked at the ground. "Well, beggars can't be choosers. Things are a little tight until payday."

I bit my lip. "I'm sorry. I shouldn't have said that."

He shrugged. "It's okay. Besides, I figure it's like the ten-second rule." I stared at him blankly. "You know how when you drop something on the floor, if you pick it up within ten seconds, it's okay to eat? I figure when it comes to fishing something out of the garbage, it's more like a ten-minute rule. And I saw Scooter toss this in here just a few minutes ago, so we're good."

"Food wouldn't last on our floor for even a second," I said. "Mrs. Moto would pounce on it and gobble it down in no time." I smiled at the thought of our Japanese bobtail cat's love of human food. Well, most human food. She did turn her nose up at asparagus. But then again, so did I.

Ben popped a Hershey's Kiss in his mouth. "Sure you don't want one?"

I refused his offer. I know, you must be in awe of my willpower. I was even impressed...for exactly five seconds. Then I grabbed the bag from him and unwrapped the chocolate morsels as quickly as I could. The bag seemed clean—no dirt or stains on it. Maybe there was something to Ben's ten-minute dumpster rule after all.

After a few more Kisses, Ben glanced at the garbage bag, then looked at me before it slowly dawned on him. "Hey, wait a minute. If Scooter threw this out, isn't this your food?"

I sighed. "Yep, it's mine. See that bag of chips right there? They're delicious with some sour cream dip."

"Why did he throw it out?"

"He's got this crazy idea that we should go on a diet."

Ben frowned. "Why? Scooter doesn't really have a beer belly, and you look pretty good for a middle-aged woman."

"Gee, thanks," I said, popping another piece of chocolate in my mouth. "It must be my frizzy hair. People are so entranced by the rat's nest on my head they don't notice the laugh lines by my mouth and the crow's feet around my eyes."

"Your hair looks fine to me." Considering Ben's hair was pulled back in a greasy ponytail, I took this compliment with a grain of salt. He stood and wiped his hands on his tattered khaki shorts, adding to the decorative pattern of stains he had going on. "You should take all this back with you."

"I want to, but I'm afraid Scooter will just throw it out again. I need a place to stash it temporarily until he forgets about this diet and begins eating his Cap'n Crunch cereal for breakfast again like a normal human being."

Ben's eyes grew wide. He shook his head and put his finger up to his lips in a shushing motion. I felt a pair of hands squeeze my shoulders. "What's this about Cap'n Crunch?" Scooter asked after he leaned down and gave me a quick kiss on my cheek.

"Boy, you're stealthy. I didn't hear you sneak up on me," I said. "Ben was just telling me about his favorite cereals. Doesn't a nice bowl of cereal sound good right now?"

"No, that sounds awful," he said. "All that sugar and other processed ingredients—do you have any idea what that does to your body? Like Trixie Tremblay says, 'Live Healthy, Live Long, Live Strong.'"

"Who the heck is Trixie Tremblay?" I asked.

"Is she the lady on TV?" Ben asked. "The one who wears those brightly colored leotards and legwarmers?"

"That's the one," Scooter said. "She used to be overweight and would get out of breath walking from her car to her front door. Now, thanks to science, she's unleashed the power of rutabagas and created a meal plan designed to help everyone 'Live Healthy, Live Long, Live Strong.' These days, she's slim, powerful, and full of energy."

"Did you say 'the power of rutabagas'?" I was gobsmacked. "You realize they're just root vegetables, right?"

"Ah, but that's where science comes in. Turns out rutabagas are more than just root vegetables. They're the secret to a healthy, long, and strong life." Scooter had a dreamy expression in his eyes. "Trixie is so inspiring!"

"What you call inspiring, I call brainwashing," I said. "Why else would you throw perfectly good food away and replace it with rutabagas?"

"She didn't brainwash me. She helped me see the truth—people who love themselves care about what they put in their bodies." He put his arm around my shoulders. "And if you love someone as I love you, then you care what they put in their bodies too. I'm really doing this for you."

I narrowed my eyes. "I know what this is really about. This is because you just turned fifty."

"Ah, so it's like a midlife crisis," Ben said. He cocked his head to one side. "But didn't Mollie tell me that buying *Marjorie Jane* was your midlife crisis?"

"Hah, that's right!" I said. "One midlife crisis per customer." I turned to Ben. "Wanna hand me that bag? I'll be taking my potato chips and chocolate back home with me."

Scooter's shoulders slumped. "Come on, my little Milk Dud. Just give it a chance. It's really important to me." He stared at me with those dark-brown puppy-dog eyes of his that I always had trouble resisting.

"Did he call you his little Milk Dud?" Ben asked.

"Yeah, it's his latest pet name for me," I said.

"There's been so many that it's hard to keep track," Ben said. "Didn't he used to call you his little sweet potato? And before that, what was it—" He tightened the ponytail at the back of his neck while he tried to remember.

"Panda bear. He called me panda bear." I glanced at my husband. "Guess you won't be able to call me Milk Dud anymore. You can hardly refer to me as a chocolate-covered caramel candy while you're on this diet. What's it called, anyway?"

"Rutamentals." Ben and I both broke out laughing. Scooter frowned. "What's so funny? It makes perfect sense. It's all about getting back to the fundamentals of healthy eating, and that begins with embracing the power of the rutabaga. Get it—'Ruta' for 'rutabagas' and 'mentals' for 'fundamentals.' Rutamentals." He wrapped his arms around my waist and gave me a squeeze. "So what do you say, my little... Actually, I'm not sure what to call you now. How about my little ruta—"

I stopped him before he could finish his thought. "Why don't you stick with Milk Dud. It sounds like there are already enough root vegetables in your life."

He shrugged. "Okay. Can you at least try Rutamentals for a week?"

"Fine, I'll give it a week." I crossed my arms and gave Scooter an appraising look. "Although, it's funny how you decided to start your new diet *after* you polished off that entire German chocolate cake I made you for your birthday."

"I love German chocolate cake," Ben said.

Scooter shook his head. "I don't really think you could have called it that. There wasn't any coconut in the frosting, and that's pretty much the hallmark of the cake."

"Coconut is gross," I said. "I did you a favor by leaving it out."

"You did *yourself* a favor." Scooter stared at me pointedly. "You wanted to help yourself to some cake too. If there had been coconut in it, you wouldn't have eaten it."

I decided I didn't like the way this conversation was going, so I steered it in another direction. "I wonder why German chocolate cake isn't the official town cake, considering this place is called Coconut Cove."

"Oh, actually it is," Ben said. "The two of you have lived here for almost a year now—I'm surprised you didn't know that already."

I shrugged. "I'm constantly learning new things about this town. Like, did you know that if you go to Alligator Chuck's BBQ Joint on your birthday, you get free nachos?" I nudged Scooter. "Aren't you glad you weren't on your diet then? And speaking of which, I have a few terms and conditions before we start Rutamentals. First, cake is allowed. Don't forget that I've entered the cake competition at the Coconut Cove Boating Festival. So, I have to bake a cake. And not just any cake, but the winning cake. Second—"

Scooter put his finger on my lips. "Terms and conditions? You sound like a lawyer."

"That reminds me," Ben said. He fished a crumpled-up envelope out of his pocket and handed it to me. "This came for you at the marina office."

I smoothed the envelope out. "It's from a law firm," I said as I ripped it open. As I scanned the letter, my jaw dropped. "You won't believe this. Our old neighbor at the Tropical Breeze condos is threatening to file a restraining order."

"A restraining order against us?" Scooter asked incredulously.

"No, not us. Against Mrs. Moto." I handed him the letter. "How do you file a restraining order against a cat?"

Ben laughed. "Especially a cat like yours. She's always wandering around the place and jumping on people's boats."

"That's because everyone is always giving her cat treats," I said. "They love it when she comes to visit."

Scooter folded up the letter. "Everyone except this lady. I

guess she didn't like it when Mrs. Moto climbed through her window and made herself at home. Let me see that envelope," he said. "Hmm. This came from Mike's firm."

"Mike Wilson, the guy who just bought that new sailboat?" I asked.

"That's the one. Hey, there's something else in this envelope." He pulled a piece of paper out, then scowled. "This is ridiculous—a bill for a cat-hair removal service."

"Want some Hershey's Kisses?" Ben asked. "That might cheer you up."

Scooter reached into the bag, then stopped himself. "No. I think I'll go back to our boat and have a Red Ruta Smoothie instead. It's designed to energize you. It's made out of radishes, radicchio, ginseng, and concentrated rutabaga extract. You guys want one?"

"Yeah, I'm going to pass," I said.

"Uh, I think I'll have to give it a miss too," Ben said. "I've got a bit of a tummy ache."

"You go on ahead. I'll be right there," I said. "I need to catch up with Ben about something."

After Scooter was out of earshot, I playfully punched Ben in the arm. "Tummy ache? Yeah, right. Faker."

Ben rubbed his stomach. "I'm not faking it. Did you see all that chocolate I ate? Not to mention I polished off the potato chips when you weren't looking."

"Lightweight," I said with a smile. "Now, listen, I need you to do me a favor and stash the rest of this stuff on your boat."

"You mean until after you're finished with the diet?"

"Huh? That doesn't make sense. I'm going to need as much wine and junk food as I can get my hands on to make it through Scooter's diet."

"And I suppose you don't want your husband to know about our little arrangement."

I carefully reached into the garbage bag, pulled out a bag of Doritos, and handed them to Ben. "Is this enough to buy your silence?"

"Throw in that Kit Kat bar, and we've got a deal."

CHAPTER 2
UNICORNS IN SPACE

"RISE AND SHINE, MY LITTLE Milk Dud," Scooter said the next morning. He gently pulled back the covers and kissed me on my forehead. I propped myself up on the pillows and yawned. "How did you sleep?" he asked as he handed me my favorite coffee mug, the one with Luke Skywalker saying, "May the froth be with you."

"Fine. But I had the weirdest dream. I had turned into a giant Persian cat with luxuriant long white hair and an adorable pink bow."

"I thought you didn't like the color pink," Scooter said.

"I don't. But it's not like I have control over my dreams. If I did, I'd be dreaming about being the United Nations ambassador to Endor and having diplomatic dinners with the Ewoks, not being a huge cat wearing a bow." I stared at the lump nestled under the covers next to me. "No offense, Mrs. Moto."

"You do realize Endor isn't real, don't you? *Star Wars* was just a movie."

"Are you sure about that?" I asked. "Sure, George Lucas has a good imagination, but come on, nobody could come up with all that unless there was some basis in reality."

"Why don't you get back to your dream," Scooter suggested.

"Okay, there I was, lying on my back and sunning myself in

front of a window, when that crazy neighbor lady grabbed me and shaved all my fur off with an electric razor. By the time she was finished, I resembled one of those Sphynx cats, the bald ones. Believe me—a pink bow does not look good on wrinkly, hairless skin."

Mrs. Moto peeked out from under the covers and meowed plaintively. "Don't worry. We won't let that happen to you." She snuggled against my side while I took a sip from my mug. "Gross! What is that?" I said, spitting out a foul-tasting liquid that bore no resemblance to coffee.

Scooter sat on the edge of the bed. "Remember, you agreed yesterday to do the Rutamentals program. This is the Rise and Shine Smoothie. You drink this in the morning to stimulate your energy follicles, which primes you for a vibrant day."

"My energy follicles? Are those anything like hair follicles? Wait a minute, did I lose my hair while I was sleeping? Is that why I had that dream?" I reached up and felt my head. Nope, same old frizzy rat's nest. Phew. While I may not love my hair, I still loved having hair. "The only thing I want to stimulate are my taste buds. All I want is my regular morning mocha. Chocolate and caffeine. That's the secret to a vibrant day." I handed him back my mug. "Have you actually tried this?"

"Uh, no. I wanted to give you yours first."

"Go on, take a sip."

"No way," he said. "You spit in this one."

"Trust me, that will probably make it taste better." Scooter snorted. "Fine. Go get your own cup and try some." While Scooter went into the galley, Mrs. Moto and I snuggled back under the covers. Just as I was dozing off, I heard a gagging sound. "Are you okay?" I asked.

"I'm fine," Scooter said faintly. "It just went down the wrong way."

"See, I told you, it tastes horrible," I said. Scooter's reply consisted of more gagging, so I crawled out of bed to investigate. I found my husband leaning against the teak cupboards clutching my second-favorite mug—the one with Princess Leia riding a unicorn in space. "You look a bit green. Kind of like the color of that dreadful Rise and Shine Smoothie. Why don't you put that down, and we'll have some normal coffee, like normal people?"

He shook his head. "No, it tastes great. I must just have a stomach bug or something. I probably caught it from Ben. I'm totally committed to Rutamentals."

"Well, if it tastes so great, have another sip."

He put the mug to his mouth, took a cautious drink and then shuddered. He gave me a forced smile. "Yum."

"Very convincing," I said. "Why don't I let you finish that while I go to the grocery store. You threw out all the ingredients for my cake, so I'm going to have to stock up again."

"Okay, but get *just* what's required for the cake. Nothing else," he said. "I've already got everything we need for our meals this week."

Mrs. Moto jumped on the counter and butted her head against my arm. "While I'm away, you better feed this one. You know how she is when she doesn't get her breakfast on time."

Scooter scratched the feline on her head and smiled. "Wait until you see what I have for you, kitty. Trixie Tremblay has a range of pet foods too." Mrs. Moto sniffed the Princess Leia mug, then sat back on her haunches and yowled.

"Wow, you're a brave man to try to feed her anything other than Frisky Feline Ocean's Delight. Good luck with that," I said as I grabbed my shower bag and a change of clothes and darted up on deck.

* * *

After a quick shower in the communal bathrooms at the marina (yes, you heard that right: communal bathrooms—life on a sailboat isn't as glamorous as you'd think), I stopped off at the best bakery in Coconut Cove—Penelope's Sugar Shack.

The lavender brick building with its bright purple awning and colorful flower boxes had beckoned to me as I drove down Main Street. I was going to need fuel before I hit the grocery store, so I picked up an extra-large cinnamon mocha and two muffins. One of the muffins was chocolate chip, because I needed an extra dose of chocolate to get rid of the taste of the Rise and Shine Smoothie. There was only so much toothpaste could do in that department.

The other one was blueberry. I figured if Scooter asked me if I'd stuck to the diet, I could tell him how I'd had fruit for breakfast. Can you believe I came up with such a cunning plan even before I'd had coffee?

When I walked into the grocery store, I was greeted by Wanda Grossman, one of the ladies from my weekly sailing class who also lived aboard her boat at the marina. She was standing behind a food demonstration table underneath a banner that read Rejoice with Rutamentals. "Come get a free sample," she said, holding up a small paper plate.

I pointed at a life-size cutout of a woman standing next to the table. She looked like a cross between Suzanne Somers from her *Three's Company* days and Aquaman himself, Jason Momoa. Yep, just as weird as it sounded. Doubly weird when you took into account the canary-yellow legwarmers, royal-blue leotard, and purple stilettos. "Is that Trixie Tremblay?" I asked.

"Yes," Wanda gushed. "Isn't she fabulous?" She waved the plate in front of me. "This is her latest creation—fermented tofu cubes drizzled with rutabaga dressing and pickled poppy seeds. It's delicious."

The smell promised anything but delicious. I took a step back to get away from the stench and bumped into a short man dressed all in gray. Gray pants, gray short-sleeved button-up shirt, gray baseball hat, and gray sneakers. His socks were probably gray too, but I decided not to investigate too closely. Men's socks always seem to smell bad, even ten seconds out of a brand-new package. But I would have rather smelled a pair of Scooter's socks after one of his basketball matches than what Wanda was serving.

"Sorry, Alan," I said as I untangled myself from the gray-clad man's camera-bag strap. His color choice matched his personality —quiet, mild-mannered, and bland. He stared at the ground and mumbled something. "What was that?" I asked.

"Can I get a picture of you trying some of Wanda's food?" he asked softly.

"Do you mind, Mollie?" Wanda asked. "Alan agreed to do a photo shoot for the company. It would be a big help if he could get photos of people enjoying the samples."

"Sorry, I wish I could help, but I'm afraid all you'd get from me is a grimace if I had to choke that down." I pointed at a woman clad in fuchsia spandex leggings and blue legwarmers. The way she was pushing her shopping cart made me think she was going to break out into an aerobics routine at any minute. "That lady seems like a likely candidate."

After being waylaid, the woman reluctantly took the plate Wanda offered her. She slowly put the fork to her lips while Alan leaned in and snapped pictures. Her face while she chewed and swallowed was expressive to say the least, and not in a good way. For someone who dressed like a Trixie Tremblay-wannabe, she didn't seem to enjoy her food. After handing the half-finished plate back to Wanda, she murmured something about having a stomach bug, then made a rapid exit.

"I'm never going to make any commission at this rate," Wanda said with a sigh. She pointed at a stack of brochures on the table. "For every person I get to sign up for the program, I earn a little bit of money. So far, I've only been able to get a few people to give it a try."

"Let me guess. One of those people was my husband."

Wanda smiled. "Yes, he was my very first customer. He was so excited to tell you all about it. How are you enjoying it so far? You really should try this sample. It's a great recipe the two of you can add to your meal plan."

I cleared my throat. I didn't want to hurt her feelings, but I didn't want to lie either. "I already had blueberries today." There, completely truthful.

"Oh, you must have had the blueberry, rutabaga, and algae breakfast bar. Trixie says they're wonderful for muscle pain. All that climbing up and down a ladder to get on and off your boat must cause a lot of aches and pains."

"It does," I said. What I didn't say was that blueberry muffins, minus any algae, were wonderful for giving you a nutritious sugar high. And nutritious sugar highs also had a way of making you forget about any aches and pains.

When Wanda asked me what I thought about the roasted parsnip swirl in the breakfast bar, I suggested that Alan take some photos of her next to the cutout of Trixie Tremblay. Before she could continue extolling the virtues of Rutamentals, Alan pointed at where she should stand, then mumbled something.

"What was that?" Wanda asked.

"I think he said that you're very photogenic. And he's right. I've always thought your green eyes were very striking with your dark hair."

Wanda smiled and tucked some stray hairs behind her ears. "Well, at my age, it isn't dark like this naturally, but it's close to the color it was when I was younger."

Alan viewed the pictures he had taken, then quietly said, "These remind me of someone I know."

"Who's that?" she asked.

He shook his head. "I can't put my finger on it. It's something about your eyes."

"They are quite distinctive," I said. "Mrs. Moto has emerald-green eyes like yours." I turned to Alan. "Maybe that's who you're thinking of—my cat."

Alan furrowed his brow. "No, not a cat."

"Do you have a sister or a cousin in the area?" I asked. "Maybe that's who Alan knows."

Wanda's lips trembled and her eyes grew moist. "I had a sister." I reached into my purse and pulled out a packet of tissues. She took one gratefully and dabbed her eyes, taking care not to smudge her eyeliner. "Sorry. I still get so choked up every time I think about her. It happened almost twenty-five years ago, but..." Her voice trailed off. She threw the tissue in the trash and took a deep breath.

I gave her a hug. "It's okay. She was your sister. No matter how much time has passed, you're still going to miss her."

"It's not just that I miss her. It's that her death was so tragic." Her expression darkened. "All because of *him*. He betrayed her. I never forgave him. How could I after what he did to her?"

While Alan shuffled his feet and stared at the ground, I racked my brain trying to figure out what to say. I wanted to ask who *he* was and what he did to her sister, but the look on Wanda's face made me think twice about that. Instead, I asked her if she wanted me to take some brochures and pass them out at the marina.

She gave me a weak smile. "That's okay. I already put some up on the bulletin board by the office. Thanks anyway." She pulled a few containers out of a cooler and placed them on the table. "I better get more samples ready."

After saying my goodbyes, I grabbed a grocery cart. As I glanced back at Wanda chopping vegetables, I thought about how lucky Wanda was to have had a sister, even if her life had been cut short. As an only child, I had always wanted siblings. I rolled the cart down the baking aisle, tossing in flour and three kinds of sugar while thinking about whether I could forgive anyone who hurt someone close to me. Betrayal could drive people to a very dark place.

***

Things were not going well. And that was a serious understatement. My attempt at baking a cake for the competition had turned into a disaster. So much of a disaster that I searched through all the nooks and crannies on our boat in search of any chocolate that Scooter might have overlooked in his purge.

"Aha! I found some," I told Mrs. Moto as I plopped on the couch next to her. "It was in the engine compartment. Scooter is always so worried that he's going to electrocute himself or set something on fire that he never looks in there. I think it's going to be up to me to learn about diesel engine mechanics instead of him." The calico sniffed at the plastic storage box I was holding. "See how clever I was? I put bags of chocolate inside so they wouldn't get any oil or fuel on them." I opened the lid and pulled out a bag of miniature Reese's Peanut Butter Cups. "Sure, they might be a little melted, but they'll still taste great."

I popped a few in my mouth and sighed with pleasure. Then I looked at the remnants of my baking efforts in the galley and sighed in disappointment. Dirty dishes were piled in the sink, batter had spilled on the floor, and the trash bag had ripped, causing the contents to be strewn all over the place. There's a reason why they called cooking facilities on boats "galleys"— because they in no way, shape or form resembled a proper kitchen on land. They're not worthy of the designation of "kitchenette," let alone "kitchen."

Cooking on board a boat is no small feat. First, you have to find all the ingredients. Unfortunately, they're not conveniently located in a cupboard next to your Cuisinart. You don't even have a Cuisinart. Who has room on a small sailboat for an appliance that can make your life easier? No, the bottle of vanilla you need will inevitably be squirreled away in a locker in the V-berth—otherwise known as that pointy cabin at the front of your boat—underneath spare fuel filters, bungee cords, and a life jacket. Then, once you find the vanilla, you have to put everything back. But you can't put it all back right away, because the cat has jumped inside the locker and refuses to get out.

As if locating what you need wasn't a big enough problem, counter space will make you want to tear your hair out. *Marjorie Jane*'s galley consisted of one tiny counter, and part of that counter was on top of the fridge. If you need anything out of your fridge, like butter, then you need to move everything off the counter and put it someplace else temporarily. I find that the ladder that leads up from our main cabin to the cockpit is a good place for resting things. Just make sure everyone else knows you have a bowl of cake batter sitting on one of the rungs. I won't make that mistake again.

Just thinking about it all was giving me a headache. I unwrapped another chocolate. "Hey, don't give me that look," I said to Mrs. Moto. "You have your catnip, and I have my chocolate. Let's see you give up your magical kitty-cat stress reliever. Should I dump the catnip in the trash?" She yowled. "Don't worry," I said as I stroked her head and admired the black markings around her eyes that resembled glasses, like those worn by her namesake in the old *Mr. Moto* movies. "I would never do that to you. But Scooter, now, there's someone you need to watch out for."

As she settled on my lap, I tried to figure out how I could manage to bake my cake in the tiny oven we had. It wasn't big enough to hold the special pans that one would normally use for the creation I was making. Forget about even getting a 9x13 inch pan in there, and you certainly couldn't fit two round layer pans at the same time. Not that it mattered—the latch that held the oven in place had broken. Yes, that's right, our oven swayed back and forth unless you fastened it shut. I accidentally knocked the stupid oven as I was reaching for a glass, and it rocked so much that the door swung open and the cake pan flew out onto the floor.

I had asked one of the ladies at the marina why anyone would have a crazy oven setup like that, and she told me it was for when you were out at sea. When the waves tipped your boat from side to side, the oven tilted with the motion of the boat and stayed steady. "Gimbaled" is what she told me it was called. I have another name for it, one I won't repeat here because my mother raised me right.

Goodness. See what it had come to? I had been living on a sailboat for only a short period of time and had now started to cuss like an old, crusty sailor. But at least I reserved my swearing for times when I was alone—and provoked by kitchen appliances.

Mrs. Moto batted at the crumpled-up wrappers on the sofa. One after another, she knocked them all on the floor. When I picked them up, I made the mistake of counting them. Whoa, that was a lot of chocolate. No wonder I had a bit of a tummy ache. Or maybe there really was a stomach flu going around.

After I threw the wrappers in the trash, I scraped the half-baked, half-burned cake out of the pan and into a plastic bag. "I'm going to go toss this in the dumpster," I said to my little calico fur ball. "You be a good girl and hold down the fort."

After dumping the trash, I walked back across the boatyard and spotted my friend, Penny Chadwick, the local boat broker and sailing school instructor. She was easy to pick out of any crowd— an attractive blonde always dressed head-to-toe in shades of her favorite color, pink. Today's outfit consisted of coral-colored skinny-legged jeans and a loose fuchsia blouse. I imagine she would have appreciated the pink bow I wore in my Persian cat nightmare.

Penny was standing by the sailboat next to ours, pointing out its features to a young couple. "I think you can get *Mana Kai* at a bargain price. Her current owners are quite eager to sell. Their circumstances have, um, changed, and the wife has had to move back to Hawaii," she said with her adorable Texan twang. She caught sight of me and waved me over. "Mollie can tell you what a great boat this is. Isn't that right, sugar?"

"My idea of a great boat is one that has a dishwasher, freezer, and plenty of counter space," I said. "Oh, and room for a Cuisinart would be heaven."

Penny laughed. "Okay, maybe Mollie isn't the best person to talk to you about sailboats. They're more her husband's thing. But, admit it, you are beginning to like sailing, aren't you, sugar?" she said as she put her arm around my shoulders. "This here is my star pupil in the weekly ladies' sailing class. Here, let me introduce you. This is my client, Jeff Morgan, and his fiancée, Emily van der Byl."

As Jeff held out his hand to shake mine, I couldn't help but notice his ears. Was it my imagination, or was one considerably smaller than the other? Did people have different-sized ears? I shook my head. What a ridiculous thought—probably the result of coming down from my sugar high. It was affecting my thinking. The rest of him seemed normal. A guy in his late twenties, average height, blond crew-cut hair, and pale-blue eyes. I'm sure his ears were normal too.

Then I noticed Emily's fingers. Not because they were weirdly shaped, but because they were beautifully manicured, and because she had a gorgeous emerald ring on her left hand. She looked normal too—probably also in her late twenties, tall and slender with dark hair in a messy bun on top of her head and sporting an adorable sundress.

Jeff smiled as he saw me admiring her ring. "I surprised her with that on her birthday a few weeks ago. I know it's not a traditional engagement ring, but I love how the color matches her eyes." He put his arm around his fiancée's waist. "It's been a real whirlwind romance, hasn't it, babe?"

While he told me about the steps he had taken to keep his proposal a secret from Emily, I was entranced by his accent. He definitely wasn't from Florida. Australian, maybe? Did they have a problem with mismatched ears down under? *Stop thinking about his ears*, I told myself, which caused me to think even more about his ears. That's when I realized everyone was staring at me.

"Why are you tugging on your earlobe?" Penny asked. "Do you have an ear infection?"

I felt my face grow warm. Did they know what I had been thinking? "Uh, no," I said. "Just noticing that I forgot to put earrings on today." I turned to Emily and Jeff and smiled brightly. "Getting jewelry for a special occasion, like your birthday or an engagement, is so romantic," I said, remembering the decidedly unromantic sailboat Scooter had given me on our wedding anniversary. Fortunately, he'd redeemed himself later by giving me a lovely necklace with a diamond lighthouse pendant.

"So, what are you up to today?" Penny asked.

"I'm trying to bake a cake for the competition tomorrow. Emphasis on *trying*."

Jeff's eyes lit up. "I'm taking part too. Once we finish viewing boats, I've got to get back and finish up my entry."

Emily put her arm through Jeff's. "Wait until you see his creation. The man is a master when it comes to icing and sugar art. His cakes are so gorgeous you almost hate to eat them. Not that it stops me. Cake is my favorite dessert. If I see one, I can't help myself. I have to take a bite."

Jeff laughed. "That's why baking is such a good hobby for me. I have an adoring fan club already built in. She has a real artistic flair—not only does she dress like a fashion plate, she also knows a beautiful cake when she sees one."

I nodded politely. Even though Jeff's cake might be artistic, mine was going to be the showstopper. Jaws were going to drop when folks got a load of my masterpiece.

"I do love fashion and cake," she said. "It drove my father to despair. He had hoped I'd have a head for accounting and go into the family business."

"What about your siblings? Can't one of them take over?"

"I'm an only child," she said with a wistful smile. "I guess you could also say I'm an orphan as well, since both of my parents have passed on. It's a good thing Jeff has a head for money. He's helping me manage my father's estate." She held out her hand and admired her ring. "I still can't believe how lucky I am."

"Oh no," Penny said, glancing toward the entrance of the boatyard. "I can't seem to get rid of him."

"Who's that?" I asked, putting my hand over my eyes to shade them from the bright sun. I saw a familiar gray-clad man walking toward us. "Do you mean Alan Simpson?"

"He's been pestering me for weeks. He wants me to hire him to take photographs of boats I have for sale. At first I humored him because he bought a sailboat from me, but then he ended up selling it a week later. He said his mom worried about him falling overboard and drowning. Lately he's been talking about getting a golf cart instead," Penny said. "I keep telling him that I'm perfectly capable of taking my own photos, but he goes on and on about how he's a professional and that if I want to be taken seriously, I should enlist his help."

"Just because some of your pictures have been featured in a small-town newspaper doesn't make you a great photographer," Jeff said, glancing over at Alan.

"Do you know him?" Penny asked.

Jeff frowned and rubbed the back of his neck. "No, not personally. I've just seen him around town."

Penny turned to his fiancée. "What about you, Emily?"

The young woman suddenly seemed absorbed in polishing her sunglasses. "Me? Why would I know him? I'm not even from Coconut Cove."

"Where are you from?" I asked.

"Do you know Destiny Key?"

"Is that the island north of here?"

Emily nodded. "It's a great location. Close enough to the big cities on the Gulf Coast, yet remote at the same time. The only way on and off the island is by ferry, and that only runs a few times a week." She glanced in Alan's direction and exchanged a look with Jeff before putting her sunglasses back on.

"Didn't you say you had a boat to show us that's in a slip at the marina?" Jeff looked at his watch. "Maybe we should head over there now. I've got to get back and put the final touches on my cake."

Alan waved tentatively as he approached the group. Emily grabbed Jeff's hand. "Why don't we meet Penny at the marina office? I could use a cold soda before we see more boats." They hurried away before Penny could respond, giving Alan the perfect opportunity to try to convince Penny to hire him. Or at least that's what I think he was doing. His mumbling made it hard to understand what he was saying.

As I turned toward my own boat, I thought about Jeff and Emily's reaction to Alan. Although people often avoided Alan when they saw him coming—even I had thought he was a bit odd when I first met him—the young couple had said they didn't know him. If that was the case, what was up with their hasty departure?

CHAPTER 3
MINIATURE CROP CIRCLES

THANKS TO A FRIEND'S GENEROUS offer to let me use her family's spacious, well-equipped kitchen, I had finally managed to finish my entry for the cake competition. I was in a great mood—my cake looked amazing, my friend had fed me pizza before I left (mercifully free of rutabaga extract), and now I was out for an evening stroll with Scooter and Mrs. Moto.

Yes, that's right. Our cat goes for walks with us on a leash just like a dog.

Oops. I probably shouldn't have compared her to a dog. She would be so insulted. Let's keep that between us, okay? If she asks, tell her we were talking about the fact that she's no ordinary cat. After all, how many cats do you know who find important clues that lead to solving murder mysteries?

As the three of us meandered along one of the pathways in the waterfront park, I pointed at a grassy area next to a clump of oak trees. "I think that's where the booth will be."

"Uh-huh," Scooter mumbled without glancing up from his phone.

"Did you hear what I said?"

"Sure...something about your tooth."

"No, not my tooth, my booth! The FAROUT booth."

He continued to stare at the screen. "Uh-huh. Your tooth is far out."

"No, not that kind of 'far out.'" I yanked the phone out of his hand. "FAROUT, as in the Federation for Alien Research, Outreach, and UFO Tracking." I cocked my head. "You know, the organization I work for."

Sometimes, Scooter had to be reminded that I had an important job, just as important as his. He spent his days on conference calls, staring at really boring spreadsheets, and reading all sorts of technical documents. I had to stifle a yawn every time I peeked at his computer. It was possibly even more boring than watching golf on TV.

My job was far more interesting. Investigating UFO sightings, interviewing people about alien abductions, and educating the public about our extraterrestrial neighbors—now, that was fascinating work. Sure, I didn't get paid, but as the saying went, "Volunteering ain't for sissies."

Scooter tried to grab his phone back. "Enough work, already," I said, shoving it into my purse. "We're here to relax and have a good time." I squeezed his hand. "And you definitely need to relax."

"It's hard to relax when you're dealing with a contract dispute. Losing all those business records in that fire didn't help either." He held up his hand. "Don't say it."

"Say what?" I asked.

"You were going to say something about how you can't believe I run my own consulting company and deal with technology every day, yet some of my important documents weren't backed up."

"Nope, I wasn't going to say that. I was going to tell you how adorable you look with those new tortoise-shell glasses of yours."

"You realize they're the same exact frames I had before, just with stronger lenses, right?"

"Of course," I said. "I'm very observant. I noticed the stronger lenses right away."

Scooter smirked. "You noticed that my prescription had changed from looking at the lenses?"

I shrugged. "Sure. After all, I'm an investigative reporter for

FAROUT. Noticing small details is a critical part of my job. Remember how I discovered that miniature crop circle in Mrs. MacDougal's garden? Everyone else thinks crop circles have to be huge, but there are miniature ones out there. However, you have to be observant enough to notice them." I tapped my chest. "That's where I come in."

"I remember. She'll never look at her rose bushes the same way again," he said with a smile. "But I still don't think you can tell that my lenses are different." He took his glasses off, rubbed his eyes, and sighed. "Just one more sign of getting older. My eyes are getting worse. Next thing you know, I'll be wearing hearing aids." Then he patted his imaginary beer belly. "But at least I can do something about this."

I reached up and gave him a hug. "You look great to me. I'm sure Mrs. Moto would agree too." I bent down to scoop her up, but all I saw was the end of a leash without our calico attached to it. "Now where did she go?" I asked. It used to be that she'd mysteriously lose all her collars. Getting her a pretty, rhinestone-encrusted collar had put a stop to that. But lately, she had been doing a regular Houdini and getting off her leash when we weren't paying attention.

I put my hands on my hips. "If she wants to go for walks with us, she's going to have to start playing by the rules, and that means wearing her harness and her leash."

Scooter laughed. "Playing by the rules...you're hardly one to talk."

"Well, sometimes rules are stupid. Those ones you don't have to obey. But I'm worried that if Nancy sees Mrs. Moto running around loose in the park, she'll report her."

"But she lets her run around off-leash at the marina," Scooter said. "I wonder why she's never put a stop to that, considering she and Ned own the place."

"She barely tolerates that," I said. "And that's only because her grandkids love chasing Mrs. Moto around the patio area and playing hide-and-seek with her. She can't say no to them. Tell you what—let's split up and find her. You head that way," I said, pointing toward a long pier, which extended out over the water. "She could be there watching the guys fishing and hoping for a handout. I'll go over and check out the playground. You know how she enjoys going down the slide."

After searching for our elusive cat for a good quarter of an hour, I heard a voice over the loudspeaker. "Over here, my little Milk Dud!" You'd think I'd be embarrassed, but after ten years of marriage, I was used to being called some truly bizarre pet names by my husband in public. He even called me by a pet name during our wedding vows. You should have seen the minister's face.

Scooter was standing on a stage that had been set up next to the waterfront for the festival. The way he was holding the microphone and announcing my arrival reminded me of a game show host. "Here she comes, our next contestant, my little Milk Dud!" People broke out into mock applause as I neared the stage. He could be a real goofball at times. Fortunately, he was an adorable goofball.

After taking a mock bow, I noticed Mrs. Moto in the first row of folding chairs set up in front of the stage. She was cuddled up in Emily's lap and purring loudly while the young woman rubbed her belly.

Jeff was seated next to his fiancée. "I'm not sure you're going to get your cat back," he said. "I should probably get Emily one to keep her company after we're married, given how much I travel for work."

"Or a puppy," I suggested as a terrier streaked past me, closely followed by a chocolate Labrador retriever, a German shepherd, and two Yorkies. Mrs. Moto wasn't the only one flaunting the leash laws.

"What's going on?" Scooter asked. "Nancy just kicked me off the stage."

I glanced at the impeccably dressed older woman standing behind the podium. Despite the breeze, not a strand of her hair was out of place. "Oh, yeah, I forgot to tell you. She's giving a briefing on the festival."

"Quick, let's get out of here before she sees us," he said as he scooped Mrs. Moto off Emily's lap.

"Settle down, everyone, so we can commence on time." Nancy winced at the feedback that came through the speakers. Her husband, Ned, hurried to the control panel, adjusted a few dials, and then gave her a thumbs-up. She peered over her reading glasses at everyone milling about and chatting with one another. "Take your seats," she said firmly. When she didn't get a response, she barked, "Sit!"

Scooter and I quickly planted our butts in the chairs next to Emily and Jeff. The dogs all cowered on the ground.

"Do I have to sit through this?" Scooter whispered to me. "I don't have anything to do with the festival. Why don't I meet you later?"

"It shouldn't take long," I said. "Besides, you can't get up now. Nancy would have a fit if you disturbed her presentation."

"Fine," he said, as he tried to grab my bag. "I'll just get my phone and answer a few emails."

I pulled it back. "You know better than to go through a woman's purse. I'll get it for you." I tilted my bag so he couldn't see the package of M&M'S that his phone was nestled under. I pulled it out and handed it to him, wishing there was a way I could sneak a few chunks of chocolate into my mouth without Scooter noticing.

"Quiet down, people," Nancy said. "You don't want to get a detention slip, do you?" I wasn't entirely sure she was joking. "For those of you who don't know me, my name is Nancy Schneider. I'm the chair of the Coconut Cove Boating Festival Organizing Committee. This evening, I'm going to go through the festival schedule, explain how each event is organized, and detail the rules and regulations that everyone needs to follow."

Mrs. Moto yawned. Rules and regulations bored her. They bored me too, but I had a vested interest in two of the main events at the festival—the cake competition and the pet-costume contest—so I was paying close attention.

"The festival kicks off tomorrow," Nancy said. "It's a Saturday, so we're expecting a lot of people, including plenty of out-of-town visitors. We'll have several food booths, featuring local eateries such as the Sailor's Corner Cafe, Penelope's Sugar Shack, the Tipsy Pirate, and Alligator Chuck's BBQ Joint."

"Don't forget the Rutamentals booth," a woman cried out. I turned and saw Wanda decked out in an oversized canary-yellow T-shirt with Trixie Tremblay's smiling face emblazoned on the front. "I'll be doing cooking demonstrations and handing out free samples."

Nancy clenched her hands on the edge of the podium. "Does anyone else have anything to add?" she snapped. No one said a word, although one of the dogs whimpered. "Good. There will be a seminar on hazardous marine products led by Ned in the morning here at the main stage, followed by live music, courtesy of..." She adjusted her reading glasses and peered at the printout in her hand. "Courtesy of Eye Patches and Peg Legs."

"That's a funny name for a band, isn't it, mate?" Jeff asked Scooter.

Scooter looked up from his phone. "That's our friend Ben's band. He's a bit obsessed with pirates. They're really good. You should stick around tomorrow and watch them."

"Shush," I said. "Nancy's talking about the cake competition."

"We have seven entrants this year." As she rattled off everyone's names, I looked around and eyed up the competition— one bored teenager, identical twins named Gertrude and Gretchen, Wanda, Mike, and Jeff.

The teen seemed like she was there under duress. How good could her cake be? You could tell when something wasn't baked with love. Rumor had it that Gretchen and Gertrude used box mixes for their cakes instead of baking from scratch. Wanda was probably going to make a Rutamentals recipe. Rutabaga-flavored cake? I couldn't imagine that would go down well with the judges. Mike was a wild card. I didn't really know much about him, other than the fact that he was a lawyer and had recently bought a sailboat. He was someone I might have to worry about. And then there was Jeff. He talked a good game, but could he deliver?

"Now, let me introduce you to the other judges who will be on the panel with me." My heart sank when I realized that Nancy was going to be one of the judges. I wasn't exactly on her good side after I had filled out the entry form in purple ink using cursive, rather than regulation black ink with block letters.

"First up is local business owner Norm Thomas," Nancy said. I put my head in my hands. There was no way I was going to win now. He had been annoyed at me ever since I'd won a bet that meant he had to rename his boat *The Codfather* to *ET*. For some reason, the silly man had objected to naming his boat after an alien who ate Reese's Pieces.

Norm grabbed the microphone from Nancy. "Glad to be here, folks. As you know, I take my responsibilities as a citizen of Coconut Cove very seriously, and what could be more important than tasting cake?" he said with a chuckle. "And as your mayor, I promise to take my responsibilities even more seriously."

"Leave it to Norm to turn a cake competition into a campaign speech," I said.

"He does realize it's only March, and the election isn't until November, right?" Scooter asked.

I laughed. "If he had his way, he'd skip the election and proclaim himself mayor."

Nancy wrestled the microphone away from Norm. "Our next judge is Chief Dalton," she said. I groaned. I might as well give up now. The chief and I didn't exactly see eye to eye on a range of subjects, from colored markers to murder investigations. Personally, I think he felt threatened by my investigative skills. Although, maybe his extraordinarily bushy eyebrows had given him some sort of complex, which caused him to be so grumpy.

After introducing the burly man, Nancy pointed at the final judge. "We're honored to have Penelope Pringle as part of the judging panel this year. Not only is she the owner of one of Coconut Cove's most popular bakeries, the Sugar Shack, but she's also an award-winning pastry chef and was the youngest winner ever of this year's coveted Sunshine State Culinary Prize."

Penelope seemed embarrassed by Nancy's praise. "I wasn't that young, actually," she said softly into the microphone as she tucked her curly strawberry-blonde hair behind her ears.

"Trust me, dear, twenty-five is very youthful," Nancy said.

Scooter sighed. "I can barely remember when I was twenty-five. Oh, to be young again."

"Now, let me go through the details for tomorrow," Nancy continued. "Contestants must drop their cakes off at the sports pavilion by the fishing pier by nine sharp. The public will be admitted at noon to view the cakes and watch the first round of judging. During this round, the judges will be considering appearance. The top four cakes will be selected, after which everyone except the judges must leave the pavilion. Next, the judges will complete the tasting round. The final step will be to announce the winner."

While Nancy droned on about the rest of the festival events and activities, such as face painting for the kids, concerts, boat tours, and the sailing race, I played games on my phone. My ears perked up when she mentioned the pet-costume competition.

"There will be fifteen dogs...and, uh, one cat walking the runway this year." She stared at her printout. "That can't be right," she said. "Whoever heard of a cat wearing a costume?" Mrs. Moto sat up in my lap and meowed loudly. Nancy looked in our direction and shook her head. "I should have known," she muttered. She took a deep breath, then continued. "All dog owners, and cat owners, should report to the main stage this Sunday at eleven a.m. sharp. And for goodness' sake, make sure all your pets are on a leash. The last thing we need is animals running around creating chaos."

The pack of dogs sitting next to the stage took this as their cue to show Nancy exactly how chaotic things could get as they streaked past her in pursuit of a squirrel. Empty chairs went flying, the microphone was yanked off the podium when the German shepherd got caught up in the cord, and a banner was knocked to the ground by the Labrador retriever. The older woman threw her hands up in exasperation before wrapping things up.

After ensuring that Mrs. Moto's leash was firmly clipped onto her harness and making sure to hold her tightly in my arms, we wandered over to watch her canine competitors chasing each other around a tree. "They don't stand a chance against you," I whispered to the calico. She blinked slowly at me in agreement.

The terrier skidded to a stop in front of us, dropped a tennis ball in front of Scooter, and wagged his tail. Scooter tossed the ball across the lawn. The terrier bounded after it, then promptly ran back, clutching it in his mouth while the two Yorkies trailed after him. Mrs. Moto gazed down at the three dogs assembled at our feet and purred loudly. She leaped out of my arms and greeted the Yorkies like long-lost friends while Scooter and the terrier continued to play fetch.

"Frick and Frack, get away from that disgusting creature right this minute," a woman yelled sharply.

"Oh no, it's that crazy neighbor lady," I said to Scooter.

I watched as her long red braids snapped in the wind as she marched toward us. She bent down and clipped leashes on the two Yorkies and pulled them away from Mrs. Moto. "Didn't you get my letter?" she hissed. "That cat is supposed to stay away from me and my dogs." I expected Mrs. Moto to hiss back, but instead she rubbed against the woman's legs. "Now see what she's done! There's cat hair all over my new skirt."

I looked at the long patchwork garment she was wearing. It appeared to have been assembled from fabric remnants picked up at a secondhand shop. Although I had to admit the embroidery and beadwork embellishing it were impressive in a weird sort of way.

"But aren't you used to having dog hair on your clothes?" Scooter asked in a far more pleasant tone than I think I could have managed.

"It's hardly the same thing," she huffed. "My dogs go to a professional groomer every week. They don't shed. I daresay your cat has never been professionally groomed." She brushed the bottom of her skirt. "You can tell by all the fur she leaves everywhere."

"She's a cat. She grooms herself," I said.

"Just keep her away from me," she said angrily. She pointed at a middle-aged man with a shaved head and goatee standing next to the stage who was chatting to Ned and Nancy. "My lawyer can explain everything. Mike, get over here," she shouted. Then she stormed off with Frick and Frack in tow.

Mike held his hands up as he approached us. "Sorry, it's just business, guys. Nothing personal against you or Mrs. Moto."

"I thought you specialized in wills and estate planning," Scooter said.

"That's what I mostly do, but when you're a lawyer in a small town like this, you end up dabbling in this and that." He lowered his voice. "I shouldn't say this, but don't worry too much about the letter. You've moved out of the condos, so there shouldn't be an issue anymore. She's just blowing off a little steam. She was mad when the chief wouldn't do anything about her complaint."

"I'm surprised the chief took our side," I said.

Mike smiled. "Well, it was probably less about you and more about her from Chief Dalton's perspective. My advice is to let it go. She's kind of a crackpot. One of those artsy types. No one takes her too seriously." He glanced at his phone. "Is that the time already? I've got to get going, but I'll see you tomorrow at the cake competition."

"I'm surprised he called his client a crackpot," I said to Scooter after Mike left. "Wasn't that a bit unethical?"

Scooter shrugged. "Unethical is probably an overstatement, but I'd worry if he were my lawyer. What would he say about me to other people?"

"I guess it's a good thing you already have a lawyer."

Scooter's shoulders slumped. "Well, about that. It turns out I'm in need of a new one. I just got an email that Tom's laid up in the hospital." He saw the expression on my face. "No, don't worry. He'll be okay, but he will be out of commission for a while. The timing couldn't be worse with this contract dispute I've got going on."

I squeezed his hand. "You poor thing. How about some ice cream to cheer you up?"

"Nice try," he said with a smile. "Remember, if we want to 'Live Healthy, Live Long, and Live Strong,' we have to say no to ice cream."

Well, we might have to say no to ice cream, but I could certainly say yes to the M&M'S in my purse when Scooter wasn't looking. I think better when I'm eating chocolate, and I needed to put my thinking cap on and figure out how I could help my husband. I had a funny feeling in my stomach that things were far more serious than he was letting on.

CHAPTER 4
THE SCIENCE OF LEGWARMERS

THE NEXT MORNING, SCOOTER AND I stopped by the sports pavilion to drop off my cake. My adorable nerd of a husband carried my masterpiece while I kept a tight hold of Mrs. Moto's leash to make sure she didn't go wandering off again.

Nancy was standing by the entryway holding a clipboard. "You're late," she said. "I was just about to lock up."

"You said that everyone had to drop their cakes off by nine. It's nine now. How can I be late?"

"Everyone else has been here already. You're the last."

"Last doesn't mean late," I said. "In fact, last is a good thing. Haven't you ever heard the expression, 'Save the best for last'?"

"In my experience, dear, people who quote that expression have poor time-management skills. You might want to try setting your clock ahead by fifteen minutes. It's a trick I used with my kids when they were growing up. It ensured that they were never late."

"But I'm not late," I said. "I'm right on time."

Nancy looked at her watch. "It's three minutes after nine. You're late."

I narrowed my eyes. "I was here at nine on the dot. You're the one who made me late by spending three minutes talking about punctuality. Now, are you going to let me drop off my cake or what?"

She stared at me with those piercing blue eyes of hers for a moment, then wrote something down on her clipboard. "Fine, you can place your cake on the table with the others." As Scooter began to walk through the entrance, Nancy stopped him. "The only people who are allowed access to the pavilion are the bakers and me. The general public can join later when we commence the first round of judging."

"Oh, come on. It's not like this is Fort Knox. Let Scooter carry the cake in. It's a really awkward shape. I'm such a klutz, and I'm worried I'll end up dropping it."

Nancy shook her head. "Rules are rules. We certainly don't want a repeat of what happened last year, do we?"

"What happened last year?" Scooter asked.

"Some kids thought it would be funny to sneak in and steal one of the cakes. It was *not* funny. So this year, I'm closely monitoring who has access." She pointed at Scooter and Mrs. Moto. "The two of you stay out here." While Scooter and I awkwardly exchanged the cake for Mrs. Moto's leash, Nancy pursed her lips. "What exactly is that supposed to be?"

I looked at her incredulously. "You're kidding, right?"

"I don't kid, dear. I have no idea what that is."

"But it's from *Star Wars*."

"Never seen it." My jaw dropped. Someone who hadn't seen *Star Wars*. I didn't think that was possible. "Hopefully, it tastes better than it appears," Nancy said. "Gray frosting doesn't look very appetizing. Now, hurry up and put your cake on the table. It's already ten after nine."

* * *

"You seem like you're in shock," Scooter said as we walked toward the main stage. "Is it because Nancy has never seen *Star Wars*?"

"No, it's not that," I said. "Though that is hard to believe."

"Then what is it?"

I sighed. "It's Jeff's cake. I didn't think anyone would be able to top mine, but his is…I don't even know how to describe it. I've never seen anything like it before."

"Well, keep in mind that appearance is only fifty percent of the overall score. I'm sure you'll knock the judges' socks off in the tasting round."

"I wish you could have tried my cake. I had some cake scraps left after I cut out the pieces I needed. I turned them into cake pops with the leftover frosting."

"Personally, I'm glad you went to Alejandra's house to bake. As Trixie Tremblay says, 'It's easier to avoid temptation than to resist it.'" He stopped and looked at me. "You didn't eat one of those cake pops, did you?"

"No," I answered truthfully. I'd had three, not one. "It made things so much easier to cook in a real kitchen in a real house," I said. "It was sweet of her to offer after she heard about what I went through trying to bake on *Marjorie Jane*."

As we walked past the food booths, my tummy growled. I had abstained from breakfast that morning, telling Scooter that I was still full from the previous night's dinner. My stomach begged to differ. How was a bowlful of watercress, chia seeds, and Trixie Tremblay's special creamy rutabaga-tofu sauce supposed to have filled me up, especially when I could barely choke it down? Maybe that was the secret to the Rutamentals diet program. The food was so disgusting that you happily skipped meals.

"Stop staring at those hamburgers," Scooter said as he pulled me away from the Sailor's Corner Cafe booth. "I don't want to miss Ned's seminar."

"Oh, goody. A seminar on marine products. How fascinating."

Scooter nodded. "I know. It's going to be really interesting."

"You realize I was being sarcastic, right?"

Scooter looked crestfallen. "But I thought you were really getting into boating."

"There's a difference between sailing on a boat and fixing a boat. A *huge* difference."

"Hopefully, Ned's seminar will change your mind."

"I'm just hoping it takes my mind off Jeff's cake."

When we got to the main stage, there were hardly any chairs left. I was stunned. Maybe Scooter had been right, and marine products really were scintillating stuff. We snagged the last two open seats, sitting next to Wanda in the back row.

I glanced at her Trixie Tremblay–inspired outfit. "Aren't you hot in those legwarmers?" I asked. It was an unseasonably warm day for March, and I was already regretting wearing jeans.

"Well, a little," Wanda admitted. "But you can speed up your metabolism if you keep your ankles warm. It has something to do with the detoxification of your energy follicles. I don't really understand how it all works, but science was never my strong suit."

Wow, the science of legwarmers. And I thought I had heard everything. I was about to ask Wanda why she didn't also wear knitted wristbands, but a high-pitched squeal screeched through the loudspeakers.

"Sorry about that, folks," Ned said, looking flustered as he adjusted the microphone. He tucked his navy-blue Palm Tree Marina polo shirt into his pants, took a deep breath, and greeted the audience. "Welcome to the first in our series of safe-boating seminars. Today, we're going to talk about common marine products, the health and safety hazards they pose, and how to protect ourselves when working with them."

While Ned walked over to a table set up at the front of the stage, Wanda nudged me. "I'm really looking forward to this, aren't you?"

I did my best to appear noncommittal, which was easier than it sounded. While Wanda opened up a notebook on her lap, I noticed sweat dripping onto her flip-flops from the bottom of her legwarmers. It looked like some serious energy-follicle detoxification was going on.

"How many of you own this product?" Ned asked, holding up a large blue container.

Heads bobbed up and down. "We own that?" I asked Scooter.

"Of course," he said. "In fact, we own ten of them. It was on sale at Melvin's last week."

I sighed. Ten containers of whatever that product was. Just what we needed. But it was my own fault. I had made the mistake of letting Scooter go to the local marine store by himself. Somehow, he always ended up maxing out our credit cards buying stuff for *Marjorie Jane* that we didn't need. Rather than worry about having willpower when it came to food, he would be better off learning how to just say no to the temptations at Melvin's.

While Scooter and Wanda focused on what Ned had to say about respirators, safety goggles, and work gloves, I managed to achieve a new high score on the latest game I had downloaded on my phone. I glanced over at Wanda's notebook. Not one single doodle, just pages and pages of extremely boring information written in very precise, compact letters. At least she had jazzed things up with a green gel pen and tiny circles for the dots over her *i*'s and *j*'s.

"Okay, I'll open it up to questions now," Ned said. "Raise your hand, and one of my helpers will make their way over to you with a microphone."

After a few questions on how to keep your pets from ingesting toxic chemicals (that was mine), the legal ramifications if you spilled diesel into a body of water (Mike chimed in on this one), and what to do if you inhaled epoxy fumes (Scooter seemed oddly interested in this topic, which was worrying), Jeff rose to his feet. "Excuse me, mate, but isn't the proper ratio three to one when using that, not two to one like you said?"

"You mean when you're using this?" Ned asked, holding up a bottle with a pump handle. Jeff nodded. "Yes, normally three to one would be correct, but in certain applications, you'll want to go with two to one instead."

"Yeah, I think you might have that backward," Jeff said.

Ned frowned as he peered at the back of the bottle. "Uh...I don't think so. It says right here, two to one when you're..." His voice trailed off as he squinted at the label.

"You're probably reading that wrong," Jeff said as he bounded up the steps to the stage. When he reached Ned, he grabbed the bottle out of his hand and put his arm around his shoulders. "Totally understandable, mate. It's hard to see the fine print when you get to a certain age. No shame in reading glasses."

Jeff proceeded to tell the audience all about ratios for different products. Wanda's ankles continued to sweat profusely while I got a headache from all the math involved. Then he started describing tips and tricks he had learned from watching YouTube videos.

Scooter leaned over. "I've seen that YouTube channel. It's a couple of twenty-something kids who bought a sailboat without ever having been on one before and having virtually no sailing experience."

"Sounds familiar," I said dryly. "Except for the age part. Change that to a middle-aged couple and you'd be on to something."

Scooter stared at me blankly. "Huh?"

"That guy's a bit of a know-it-all," Wanda said as she adjusted her legwarmers. Scooter nodded in agreement.

"I hate know-it-alls," I said. "People always think they know better than the experts. Take Chief Dalton, for example. Just the other day, I was telling him the latest statistics on UFO sightings, and he completely dismissed me out of hand. He should just stick to handing out parking tickets and leave alien investigations to the pros."

Scooter laughed. "Not exactly the same thing, my little Milk Dud."

"I thought you were going to come up with a new pet name for me."

"I'm working on it. But I want to make sure I get it just right."

I was afraid Jeff was going to keep prattling on and on, but fortunately he broke into a coughing fit when he opened up one of the canisters to demonstrate something. I guess Ned was right —some of the fumes from marine products were bad for your health.

Ned took that as his opportunity to wrap things up. "We're out of time, folks. But if you have any more questions, please feel free to come up to the stage and chat. You can also have a look at the various products we talked about today."

Both Wanda and Scooter shifted in their seats, eager to run up front and check everything out in more detail. "And don't forget to enter the drawing for a hundred-dollar gift voucher to Melvin's Marine Emporium," Ned added. "I'll be handing out the entry forms. Just put your name, phone number, and email address down, and we'll draw the lucky winner next weekend."

Scooter whistled appreciatively. "A hundred dollars. Imagine what we could buy with that." I shuddered as I pictured all the bottles of marine products we didn't need that he would want to add to our already extensive collection.

* * *

While Wanda and Scooter hustled up front to enter the drawing, I rummaged in my purse for some pain relievers. I washed a couple of tablets down with some water, then surreptitiously tore open a bag of M&M'S.

"Oh, if you like those, you're going to love the cupcakes I have for sale at our booth." I looked up and saw Penelope. She was wearing one of her trademark Sugar Shack purple polka dot aprons over a white sundress. "They have miniature M&M'S inside, and they're frosted in bright colors like the candy. Want me to set one aside for you?"

Hmm. If you scrape the frosting off a cupcake, it's basically a muffin, and everyone knows muffins are healthy, right? Could I convince Scooter of that logic? Probably not.

"Sure. How about a blue one?" Penelope nodded. "But, if you don't mind, can we keep this between ourselves? Scooter and I are doing that Rutamentals diet."

"I don't think you're allowed to have cupcakes if you're on Rutamentals," Penelope said.

"Well, I'm pretty sure that's a technicality," I replied. "Just set one aside for me, and I'll grab it when Scooter isn't watching."

She chewed her lip. "If he asks me directly, I'll have to tell him the truth. I wouldn't feel right lying to him." She frowned. "And you shouldn't lie to him either."

"Don't worry. It won't come to that."

"Okay," she said. "I can't wait to see your cake."

"You won't even notice it next to Jeff's," I muttered.

She sat in the chair next to me and smiled brightly. "I'm sure that's not true. Besides, you shouldn't compare yourself to everyone else."

"But it's a competition. Comparison—that's the whole point. The judges compare the cakes and decide which one is the best."

"If I had my way, we wouldn't hand out prizes."

"Don't tell me. You're one of those participation-ribbon kind of people, right?"

"Sure. The important thing is trying, don't you think?"

"Trying to win," I said. "Maybe you better save me two cupcakes. I have a feeling I'm going to need more than one after I lose out to Jeff."

Before she could try to convince me that winning wasn't everything, the chocolate Labrador bounded over to us and dropped a coconut at Penelope's feet. The Lab wagged her tail so enthusiastically that I was afraid she would knock a passerby over.

"Hello, Chloe," she said, scratching the dog's head. "Did you bring me another coconut?" She turned to me. "Chloe is crazy for coconuts. She loves husking them. Her owners give me the meat that's inside for my coconut pies."

Penelope bent down and inspected the coconut. "Seems like you need to do a little more work on this one." Chloe nudged her hand out of the way, grabbed it in her mouth, and sat under a nearby tree, holding the coconut between her paws.

"Looks like she's got company," I said, smiling at the pack of dogs surrounding Chloe.

"That one's named Chica," Penelope said, pointing at the German shepherd. "And those two Yorkies are—"

"Frick and Frack," I said. "We're acquainted. Or should I say Mrs. Moto and the two of them are acquainted."

"Do you think your cat would get along with a dog?" Penelope asked. "See that terrier over there? Bob's not crazy about the water, and his humans are heading off to the Bahamas soon on their boat."

"We've barely got enough room on our boat for the three of us. I can't see getting a dog. But I know someone who might be interested. Do you know Jeff? He was talking about getting his fiancée a dog to keep her company when he travels." I spotted the young couple by the stage talking with Scooter. "That's them over there."

"I've seen him at the bakery before, but she doesn't seem familiar."

"She's not a local. She lives on Destiny Key. Ever been there?"

"When I was in elementary school, one of my friends invited me to spend the weekend at her family's cottage on the island, but my mother refused. She got really worked up about it. Funny how that memory has stuck with me. Maybe one of these days I'll get out there. But first, I better head back to our booth and tuck those cupcakes away for you."

* * *

The crowd had thinned out at the main stage. Only the true diehards seemed to be left discussing marine products. Ned, Wanda, Jeff, Mike, and Scooter were clustered around the table debating the merits of different brands of epoxy. Emily was leaning against the podium looking bored. I feared she was going to be marrying into a lifetime of sailboat obsession on Jeff's part. I'd have to invite her out for a girls' night and commiserate.

"Can you clear some room on that table?" Nancy asked as she climbed up the steps holding several large cardboard boxes. "These are heavy." She was followed by our restraining-order crazy neighbor lady, also bearing boxes.

After Ned moved the marine products to the side, the two of them set their boxes down. "Are those for Sofia?" he asked.

"Yes," Nancy said. She lifted the lid off the top box. "Can you believe how many bottles she has in here? This is just a small-town festival. There's no way she'll sell that many." Nancy held up a small brown glass vial and inspected the bottom. "She forgot to put the price stickers on them. That's what happens when you're not organized."

Ned reached into another box and took out an envelope. "Are these the ones?"

Nancy pulled out a sheet of labels. "Yes, those are them. See how she used pink stickers in the shape of a sailboat? She printed these up especially for the festival." While Ned took the bottles out of the box, she affixed the stickers.

"What are these?" Emily asked.

"Herbal remedies," Nancy said. "Our daughter has a business selling them online. She also exhibits at fairs like this one, selling them in person."

"Is she the one who makes ointments and balms from plants in her garden?" I asked. "You gave me one of those to try once. It worked wonders."

"I've tried some of them too," Mike said. "Highly recommended."

Nancy beamed. "I'm glad you liked them. There's some of those in one of the other boxes. But the bottles, like this one, she imports from an overseas supplier. You all should stop by her booth later. She has something for everything that ails you." She held up a bottle. "This one is for chronic snoring. Just two drops in a cup of chamomile tea at night, and your partner will thank you for it. It's made a world of difference since Ned started taking it."

"There's no need to tell everyone about that," Ned muttered.

Scooter looked on in interest as Nancy described a concoction that suppressed your appetite. I wondered if it had rutabagas in it.

"Do you have anything for headaches? I took some pain relievers earlier, but they aren't doing the trick." I asked.

"I think there's something in here for that." She rummaged through a box, then pulled out a clear bottle with a stopper top. "Just a couple of drops on your tongue, and your migraine will be gone in no time."

"Oh, it's not a migraine, just a tension headache," I said.

"You need to be careful with these things," Jeff said. "They aren't regulated."

"Mr. Know-It-All," Wanda said under her breath.

"He's right," Emily said. "I would never touch any of those. Not in a million years."

"They're perfectly safe," our former neighbor said. "You just need to use common sense."

"It's a bunch of pseudoscience," Jeff said. "And some of this stuff is downright dangerous."

"You've been brainwashed by Big Pharma," she retorted. "I could give you all sorts of examples of doctors prescribing medicines their patients don't need just to satisfy the pharmaceutical industry. And half the time they don't even think about drug interactions."

Jeff said. "That's a bit harsh, don't you think? People in the medical field are trying to heal people, not harm them."

"Line their pockets is more like it!"

Emily laid her hand on Jeff's arm, but he yanked it away. "You sure could use some—"

Before he could finish his thought, the pack of dogs ran across the stage—correction, a pack of dogs and one very familiar-looking Japanese bobtail cat—and darted under the table, causing one of the legs to collapse. All the boxes fell onto the ground, spilling their contents everywhere. As we scrambled to pick everything up, I saw a flash out of the corner of my eye.

"Say cheese, everyone," Alan said, holding up his camera. At least I think that's what he said. It was hard to hear over the dogs barking.

"Alan, put down that camera and come over here and help," Nancy ordered. "The organizing committee hired you to take publicity shots of the festival, not pictures of scenes like this!"

CHAPTER 5
MATH-INDUCED HEADACHES

AFTER EVERYTHING HAD BEEN CLEANED up, those of us involved in the cake competition made our way over to the sports pavilion while Ned and the crazy neighbor lady carried the boxes of herbal remedies over to where the booths were set up.

The pavilion consisted of one large room, which was normally used for exercise classes. A poster on the double doors at the entryway advertised an early-morning Trixie Tremblay boot camp. At the rear of the building, near the door leading out to the enclosed courtyard, there was another poster—this one extolling the virtues of wearing legwarmers.

If I had fingernails to chew, I would have devoured them while I watched the judges file into the room with their clipboards in hand. I paced back and forth while I admonished the butterflies in my stomach. *Guys, you're getting out of hand,* I told them. *If you don't knock it off, I'm going to down one of Scooter's rutabaga smoothies. We'll see how you like that.*

Nancy had set up a barrier for members of the general public to stand behind while the judges appraised each cake and asked the contestants questions. My creation was the last on the table—because I had dropped it off right on time as I saw it or late as Nancy saw it—so I got to hear the judges' comments on the other entries before they reached mine.

They began with the twins' cakes. "I see you made German chocolate again this year, Gretchen. It's nice to see the official Coconut Cove cake represented today," Nancy said. She jotted something down, then peered over her reading glasses at Gretchen's sister. "And Gertrude, what do you have for us today? A classic white cake with buttercream frosting. Very nice."

Nancy was awfully generous in her praise of the ordinary, obviously made-from-a-box mix cakes. Had the twins bribed her? If so, what could one possibly bribe Nancy with? The crotchety old lady seemed to love only two things in the world besides her family—organizing people and things and rules and regulations. Wait a minute, was that two things or four things? My math-induced headache was getting worse.

While I rubbed my temples, Norm came up behind the twins and put his arms around their shoulders. "How about a picture of me with these two lovely ladies?" he said to Alan. "Make sure you get my good side. Wait a minute, I don't have a bad side." He laughed, not seeming to notice no one else joined in. "Now, you two ladies are going to vote for me in the election, aren't you?"

"Really, Norm," Nancy said. "We're here to judge cakes, not campaign." She pointed at his clipboard. "Why don't you step aside, and let the chief and Penelope have a look at the entries while you fill out the scoring sheet."

Next up was Wanda. "Let's see, what do we have here? It certainly looks attractive," Nancy said. "Very skillful use of icing, dear. I could almost swear those vegetables on top were real. What are they made of? Marzipan?"

"No, they're real—baby peas, asparagus, and carrots. See how they spell out Rutamentals?"

Nancy adjusted her reading glasses. "Hmm...I've heard of carrots blended into cake batter, but never raw vegetables used as decoration, especially asparagus and peas."

Wanda held up a pamphlet. "This is Trixie Tremblay's newest creation, the RutaButaTooting Gâteau—designed for celebrations of all kinds. Anyone who's interested in 'Living Healthy, Living Long, Living Strong,' let me know, and I'll be happy to give you a brochure that includes the recipe for this cake plus a voucher for twenty percent off the Rutamentals program."

Nancy grabbed the brochure, walked over to the trash can, and threw it in. "Just in case I wasn't clear, this is a cake competition, not a campaign stop or an opportunity to sell the latest diet fad." She glared at two young boys who were tossing a ball back and forth in the back of the room. "Let alone a place to play games."

Scooter walked over to the barrier, leaned down, and removed the brochure from the container. While he eagerly read the recipe, I watched as the judges moved on to Mike's cake. He had gone with a classic chocolate fudge creation. While I'm sure it tasted delicious—it was made with chocolate, how could it not?—his decoration was pretty plain. Chocolate frosting with a few chocolate shavings on top wasn't exactly the stuff of gourmet magazines. Things were looking up. So far, three ordinary cakes and one cake made of vegetables.

Next up was the surly teenager. Her parents were in the audience cheering her on. Her father was holding up a banner while her mother was waving pompoms. The teen mumbled one-word answers to the judges' questions about her cake. "How much cola did you use?" Penelope asked.

"I dunno. Ask my mom. She made it."

The audience gasped. You would have thought it was the scandal of the year. Alan snapped pictures as the girl and her parents left the building in shame after she was disqualified.

Five down—one more to go before they got to my cake. I took a deep breath as the judges gathered around Jeff's masterpiece. He had created an entire ocean scene complete with a sailboat, dolphins, and a tropical island. Intricately decorated fish dotted the side of the cake, giving the illusion that they were swimming underneath the water.

"This is truly impressive," Nancy said. "How long did this take you to make?"

"Not long," Jeff said. "It's all a matter of skill and natural talent, and I have both of them."

"Where did you get the idea?" Penelope asked.

"I saw it on a YouTube video."

"The attention to detail is amazing, son," Norm said. "We'll have to talk later about you catering my mayoral victory party."

The judges spent an extraordinary amount of time examining Jeff's cake and making notes. Finally, they turned to mine. Nobody said a word. It was an unnerving kind of silence. I couldn't tell if they were dumbstruck by the sheer creativity of my cake or if they hated it.

Finally, Penelope broke the silence. "What did you use to get the different shades of gray in your icing?"

"It's a special food dye," I said.

"It certainly is...um, gray," Nancy said as she scribbled notes. "But I still don't know what it's supposed to be. It just looks like a large gray ball."

Norm laughed. "You mean you don't recognize this? It's from *Star Wars*. Leave it to the kooky UFO alien lady to make a cake that resembles the Death Star."

"Nancy's never seen *Star Wars*," I said.

"Really?" Norm and Penelope said in unison.

"Do you know what this is?" Nancy asked the chief.

He raised his dark, bushy eyebrows and after a long pause said, "Yes. My ex-wife is a big *Star Wars* fan. This is the kind of thing she'd like."

"Really?" I said. "I'd love to meet her one day."

Nancy gave me a funny look before collecting the clipboards from each of the judges. She added up the scores while the four of them conferred in a corner of the room. At one point, Nancy pointed at my cake and scowled. After fifteen of the longest minutes of my life, the judges reassembled in front of the audience.

"I will now read the names of the four individuals who are going to advance to the next round, in no particular order," Nancy said. "Please step forward when I call your name." Nobody was surprised when she read Jeff's name off. While the audience clapped, Emily leaned over the barrier and gave him a congratulatory kiss. Mike beamed when his name was announced next.

I took a deep breath. With the disqualification of the teenaged girl, it was down to the twins, Wanda, and me. While I tried to calculate my odds, making my math-induced headache even worse, Nancy called out Wanda's name. I was stunned. How could anyone vote for something that featured raw vegetables?

"And now for the final cake," Nancy said dramatically. The sisters held hands and looked nervously at each other. I reached into my pocket and pulled out my lucky key chain—the one with a tiny Wookiee attached. "The gray"—she paused while she peeked at her notes—"Death Star made by Mollie."

"That's my girl!" Scooter shouted while I jumped up and down with excitement.

"If it were up to me, everyone would advance to the next round," Penelope said as she handed the twins back their cakes and ushered them to the other side of the barrier. "You ladies should be very proud of yourselves."

"Shush, everyone," Nancy said, clapping her hands. "It's time to cut the cakes. Norm, make yourself useful and bring that tray of plates over here."

While Norm tore himself away from schmoozing with the audience, Nancy explained the next stage in the competition. "Four slices will be cut from each cake and placed on different-colored plates, one color for each judge."

"Can I have the purple plates? It's my signature color," Penelope said as she smoothed down her apron.

"Of course, dear. Chief Dalton, you'll have the blue plates. Norm, you'll have the green ones, and I'll take the white ones."

Nancy sliced the cakes while Norm handed her a different-colored plate for each judge. After she set the slices on each plate, Penelope and the chief carried them over to four small tables at the back of the room, one for each judge. When she got to Jeff's cake, she startled when Bob the terrier ran into the pavilion. Her hand slipped, smudging the frosting and knocking one of the fish decorations off the final slice and onto the floor.

"Get that mutt out of here!" she yelled before placing the slice onto a purple plate.

Emily leaned over the barrier. "That slice looks terrible," she said to Nancy. "You should cut another one."

"It's fine, babe," Jeff said. "The judges already know how it's meant to look." He winked at her. "Knowing your sweet tooth, you probably want Nancy to cut another slice so you can eat the one that's missing a fish."

"That's right, dear. We've already completed the appearance round. Now we're onto the tasting round. It will taste exactly the same as another slice." She glanced at her watch. "Besides, we're running behind schedule. The judges will take a twenty-minute break, then reconvene here for the cake tasting. That portion of the competition will be closed to the public."

After ensuring the judges' tables were set up correctly, Nancy shooed everyone out of the pavilion. Emily continued to complain about how Nancy had ruined Jeff's cake. "I'm going to go back in there and cut another slice," she said. But when she tried to reenter the building, Nancy locked the door.

"As I said, young lady, only judges from this point forward."

Jeff put his arm around Emily's shoulders. "Don't worry about it. After all—"

"Fire!" someone yelled. "Fire over by the food booths!"

As gray smoke wafted overhead, cell phones started ringing, and people frantically looked for their loved ones.

"Everyone who's a volunteer firefighter, come with me," Chief Dalton shouted above the din. "The rest of you stay back and out of the way." Norm and the other volunteer firefighters ran after the chief, while everyone else followed more cautiously. Everyone, that was, except Jeff, Emily, Scooter, and me.

Emily rattled the doorknob angrily. "I can't believe she locked the door."

"It's almost like she doesn't trust us," I said dryly.

"Did you leave something in there?" Scooter asked.

"I didn't," the young woman replied. "Nancy did. She left a piece of cake that's all messed up. I need to go fix it."

"Babe, just let it go," Jeff said, pulling her away from the door. "Why don't we go see what the fire's all about, like everyone else at the festival."

"But—"

"No buts," he said. "One little missing decoration isn't going to hurt my chances. You saw the competition. It's pretty amateurish. Of course I'll win first place." He glanced over at me sheepishly. "Sorry, Mollie."

Emily seemed embarrassed. "He didn't mean it like that. I

really liked your *Star Wars* theme. Was it hard to get it into a spherical shape?"

"I used to have a special set of cake pans, but we lost them in the..." I paused to listen to the sound of fire engines pulling into the park.

"Lost them in what?" Emily asked.

"A fire," Scooter said softly. "We lost everything." He took a deep breath. "Why don't you two head over and see what's going on. I think we'll wait here. I don't have any desire to see another fire again any time soon."

Before they left, Emily tried the handle again. I thought about showing her alternative ways of opening doors that didn't involve keys but decided against it. Jeff would have probably jumped in and told me he was a black-belt-level cat burglar, having learned the trade through watching YouTube videos.

After they left, Scooter and I sat at a picnic table by the entrance. We both spent the next hour on our phones. I played my game, and he replied to several emails. While I was massaging my fingers—gaming was hard work—I saw a familiar ball of fur streak past the table toward the water.

"Didn't Ben take Mrs. Moto back to the marina after the boating seminar?" I asked.

"Uh-huh," Scooter said without looking up from his phone.

"Are we sure about that?"

"Uh-huh."

"How sure?"

Scooter put his phone down. "Oh no. I'm afraid to ask."

"I think I just saw her run past. Calico cat, green eyes, with a bobtail. There aren't too many of them around Coconut Cove."

Scooter shook his head. "Don't tell me she hitchhiked again." Mrs. Moto had many talents, one of which was sneaking into the backs of vehicles and going for rides around town. Somehow, she always managed to find her way back to the boat in time for dinner without fail.

"Wait here," I said. "I'll go investigate."

I walked behind the sports pavilion through a gate into the fenced-off courtyard and peeked into the restrooms located in an adjacent outbuilding. Nothing. I poked around in the shrubs, calling out her name and promising treats. No response. I turned to head back out front when I noticed the back door of the pavilion was slightly ajar. As I reached out to push the door open to investigate, Mrs. Moto tore past me toward the waterfront.

"Get back here this instant," I yelled. "There's extra catnip in it for you!"

She ignored my attempted bribe and made her way toward the fishing pier, no doubt to vacuum up scraps of fish and bait. As I started to climb the steps, she darted through the rails and scampered down the rocky embankment under the pier and onto the sand. "We're going to get you an industrial-strength leash and straitjacket for a harness if you keep this up," I yelled after her.

Before I could chase her down the beach, I tripped and landed on the jagged rocks, scraping both of my knees. It hurt like the dickens, but I quickly forgot my pain when I lifted my head.

There was Emily lying on the embankment, convulsing violently. As I rushed over, her convulsions stopped, her head fell to the side, and her eyes turned glassy. I quickly dialed 911, then administered CPR to the unconscious woman until the EMTs arrived and took over.

I watched in horror as they tried to revive her before shaking their heads in regret. As they transferred her body to the ambulance, I wondered what could have caused someone to die at such a young age. I wasn't the only one who was curious. While most people were over gawking at the fire, a few of the guys who had been fishing on the pier were milling about, trying to get a glimpse of the scene and asking me what had happened.

I ignored their questions, slumped down on the beach, and put my head in my hands. Visions of what I had witnessed flashed through my mind—poor Emily lying on the rocks with a shattered plate by her side.

Wait a minute. A shattered plate, just like the ones that had been used for the judges' slices of cake. What had she been doing eating cake by the fishing pier?

CHAPTER 6
DOGS WITH KRAUT

"SCOOTER, ARE YOU OKAY?" I asked, noting his clammy skin and shaking hands.

"Is she..." His voice trailed off as he watched the ambulance pull out of the parking lot.

"I'm sure she'll be fine," I said, telling Scooter what he wanted to hear rather than the truth, for fear he'd go into shock. "They're taking her to the hospital now."

"But the lights and siren aren't on," he pointed out. "Please tell me you didn't find another—"

"You're trembling," I said, interrupting him before he had to say one of his least favorite phrases: "dead body." I knew he worried about my propensity for stumbling across people who weren't...let's see, how should I put this...people who weren't exactly alive. Since we had moved to Coconut Cove, I had found four dead bodies, all murder victims. Sadly, Emily took my total up to five. I didn't know the cause of death, but surely it couldn't be murder. Was I going to have to start keeping two separate scoring systems? One to tally up murder victims and one for people who died accidentally? I tried to figure out the statistical probabilities involved in finding so many dead bodies, but that made the throbbing in my head worse.

People were buzzing around, whispering about what had happened to Emily. Someone said that he'd go in search of Jeff. I didn't envy him that task. With the fire at one end of the festival and the commotion at the other end near the fishing pier, the police were spread thin. One of the officers had asked me a few questions before rushing off to coordinate with her colleagues.

Scooter looked miserable. I guided him toward a picnic table. "Here, sit down before you faint." I pulled a bag of M&M'S out of my purse and handed them to him. "These should help."

He ripped open the bag and began popping some of the colorful candy-coated chocolates in his mouth before he caught himself. "Do you have any healthy snacks instead?" he asked. I shook my head, wondering what had happened to my husband, who had always reached for chocolate when he was stressed. Nobody should stick to a diet in times like this.

"No, that's not something I normally carry." I dug through my purse. "How about a breath mint?"

Scooter raised his eyebrows. "Do you have any idea what's in those? Why not just inject poison straight into your bloodstream instead?" He held out his hand. "Give those to me."

"No way. There's a kosher hot dog piled high with sauerkraut, relish, mustard, and onions with my name on it at Alligator Chuck's food stand. I'll be needing a mint after scarfing one of those babies down."

Before I knew what was happening, Scooter grabbed the mints from my hand and lobbed them into a nearby garbage can. "My, aren't you the feisty one, showing off your college basketball skills," I said. "I guess you are feeling better."

He rubbed his hands on his shorts. "Not really. I can't believe you found Emily like that. Admit it. She didn't make it, did she?"

"No, she didn't," I said simply as I squeezed his hand. I thought back to the sight of Emily lying on the ground beside the broken plate. "I wonder if she had a heart attack. She was awfully young, but some families have a higher risk of heart issues at an early age." I sighed. "Poor Jeff."

"I wonder how long they were engaged for," Scooter said, squeezing my hand back.

I laid my head against his shoulder. "Remember how you proposed to me?"

"Me? You're the one who proposed."

"That's not how I remember it," I said. "Besides, girls don't propose to guys. It's the other way around."

Scooter spluttered, "But you're the one who asked me."

Before we could settle that little disagreement, a voice boomed out from the loudspeakers. "Attention: Scooter and Mollie McGhie, come collect your feline from the information booth immediately." Even if I hadn't recognized Nancy's sharp tone, the disdain when she uttered "your feline" would have given it away. After a beat, she added, "Attention: any felines not collected in the next ten minutes will be turned over to animal control."

I stood and pulled Scooter to his feet. "Come on, we better go collect *our feline* before she disappears again." In the aftermath of finding Emily's body, I had lost sight of her. "After that, what do you say to those dogs? Surely, Trixie Tremblay would understand that in a situation like this, junk food is called for."

"There was a fire at the food stands, remember?"

"It's all okay now. I overheard the police officers saying it was an electrical fire at the Rutamentals stand. Wanda was using the patented Rutamentals high-speed, industrial-strength Rutablender to make fresh rutabaga shakes. Guess what she uses instead of ice cream—tofu. Yuck, right?"

"Is she okay?" Scooter asked.

"She's fine, and everyone is back in business."

"Good. That means we can get something that's Rutamentals-compliant at her stand." He tugged at my hand. "Come on, let's get going before Nancy has a fit."

We found Mrs. Moto sprawled out in front of the information booth surrounded by a bunch of kids who were taking turns scratching her belly. Nancy looked at her watch when she saw us approaching. "You're lucky you got here when you did. Another thirty seconds, and animal control would have taken her away."

A young girl scratched the calico behind her ears, then looked up at Nancy. "You wouldn't have really given Mrs. Moto away, would you have, Grandma?"

Nancy pursed her lips. "People need to be prepared to face the consequences for their actions, Katy. Animals need to be on-leash and supervised, as Scooter and Mollie well know." She looked at us sharply. "Rule 11.3 of the town charter. You do have a copy of the town charter, don't you?"

"No, but I'll be sure to get a copy and place it right next to my copy of the Palm Tree Marina rules and regulations," I said. Of course, what I didn't tell Nancy was that I had turned the marina rules and regulations into origami birds that Mrs. Moto liked to bat around when she wasn't busy chasing lizards.

Katy picked Mrs. Moto up and carried her over to her grandmother. "She says she's sorry, Grandma, and it won't happen again," she said before giving the cat a kiss on her head.

Nancy's expression softened. "All right, but you have to help keep an eye on her, okay?"

"Of course!" Katy said. "Maybe we can bring her over to your apartment after school and keep an eye on her there."

I smiled at Nancy's discomfort. The last thing she wanted was to have *that feline* in her home.

"Thanks for taking care of her," Scooter said to Katy as he plucked our wayward cat from her arms. "We should probably go in search of something to eat. Something healthy, right, my little Milk Dud?"

Before I could try to persuade Scooter about the benefits of junk food, Ben rushed up. "There you are," he said, wagging a finger at Mrs. Moto. "I've been searching for you everywhere." He turned to us. "I'm sorry. I didn't realize she had sneaked into my truck until I got to the park and saw her darting out of the cab. Here's a spare leash and harness. I've been keeping it in my rig ever since she started hitchhiking everywhere with me."

After securing Mrs. Moto, Scooter set her on the ground. She made a beeline for Alligator Chuck's food stand, which was conveniently located next to the information booth. Sitting in front of the stand was the usual gang of dogs, all waiting patiently in turn as the cook fed them each a piece of hot dog.

"Does it seem strange to be feeding hot dogs to dogs?" Ben asked. "Funny, there isn't any dish called hot cat."

"Don't let Nancy hear you. I'm sure she'd be tempted to come up with something."

We watched as Mrs. Moto pushed her way in front of the dogs, stood on her hind legs, and yowled. "Here you go," the young man said with a laugh as he handed her a morsel.

"Frick and Frack, come here," a gruff voice said. I turned and saw Chief Dalton glaring at them, both of his caterpillar-like eyebrows twitching furiously. "Here. Now."

The two Yorkies were torn—should they stay with the nice dispenser of hot dogs or risk the wrath of the burly man? The chief took a step toward them and pointed at the ground in front of him. After the dogs slowly walked toward him, he bent down and scooped them up, one in each arm. Then, to my surprise, he kissed each of them on the head.

"What am I going to do with you? It doesn't do my reputation any favors if the two of you are running around off-leash." He set them on the ground and clipped them to matching leashes adorned with embroidery and beads. "Come on, let's get you fellows home. It's been a long day."

"Huh? You're taking them home? But they belong to our former neighbor," I said.

The chief arched one of his eyebrows. "We have joint custody."

"Joint custody? Wait a minute...does that mean that crazy lady is your ex-wife?" He arched his other eyebrow. "Wow. That explains so many things."

"What exactly does it explain?"

"A lot."

"Could you be more specific?"

"Tell you what, why don't you tell me what happened with Emily first. Was it a heart attack?"

"I don't believe you're the next of kin."

"Oh, that's a good point. Who is the next of kin?"

The chief snorted. "Don't turn this into one of your investigations."

"I'm not investigating anything. I'm just curious. Everyone is curious about what happened."

"Can I give them some more?" the cook interrupted, holding a couple of pieces of hot dog in his hand.

"No, they've had enough," the chief said. He looked down at

the terrier, German shepherd, and chocolate Labrador. "Now, where are your owners?"

The three of them took that as their cue to run off across the park.

"Aren't you going to chase after them?" I asked. "They are breaking Rule 11.3 of the town charter, after all."

I glanced at Nancy. She seemed impressed. Sensing sarcasm was not her strong suit.

The chief suppressed a smile. "I'm surprised to hear you quoting rules and regulations, Mrs. McGhie, considering you usually think they don't apply to you." I was glad he got my sense of humor by now. He didn't always appreciate it, but he got it.

While the Yorkies and Mrs. Moto sniffed each other, tangling up their leashes in the process, the chief's phone rang. His expression sobered as he listened to the person on the other end of the line. "Copy that. Meet me at the information booth. Tell the medical examiner I'll call him shortly." After he hung up, he pointed at me. "You, with me. I've got some questions for you."

"About what?"

The chief raised one of his eyebrows, locked his eyes with mine, and didn't respond.

"Will they be multiple choice?" I prompted.

Then he raised his other eyebrow.

"True or false?" I tried to figure out what he was saying with his eyebrows, but even my phone didn't have a translation app for this. "It's not going to be an essay, is it?"

"The last thing I would ask you to do is write an essay. I can only imagine how creative your answers would be."

"Fine, just let me use the bathroom first." While I walked over to the restroom block, Scooter and the chief worked on untangling our pets.

After I washed my hands, I looked for some paper towels, but the ladies' room was out. I sneaked into the men's room and grabbed a few. As I was throwing them in the trash can, I noticed a small clear bottle with a stopper top. It looked exactly like one of the herbal remedies that Nancy had shown us earlier in the day.

When I rejoined Scooter, I showed him the bottle. "I found this in the men's room."

"What were you doing in the men's room?" he asked. "Was there a long line at the ladies'?"

"No, the place was deserted. I just needed some paper towels. For some reason, the men's always seems to have a good supply. Why don't guys wash their hands after they go to the bathroom?"

"That's not true. I do."

"Well, that's because your mother raised you right."

"What is that, anyway?" Scooter asked.

"It's one of those herbal remedies that Nancy was showing us earlier. This one is supposed to help with migraines." I peered at the back of the bottle. "It says you put two drops on your tongue." I shook the bottle. "It's empty."

"I guess the guy gets a lot of migraines, and he used the whole bottle up."

"But this is one of the ones that Nancy put labels on earlier. You can tell by the sailboat-shaped price sticker. That means someone used this whole bottle today. I wonder if there are side effects to such a big dose?"

Scooter shrugged. "I guess there can be side effects to anything."

"Remember how Jeff was talking about how this stuff isn't regulated? Do you think it's dangerous?"

"I'm sure it's fine. Come on, let's go. The chief has been waiting to talk to you."

"Where is he?"

"Getting a hot dog."

"Lucky guy. What about us? When are we going to eat?" I asked in a slightly whiny tone. Hunger brings out my inner petulance.

"You know what, why don't we eat at home? I already have all the ingredients for a Rutamentals meal in the fridge. It'd be a shame to let it go to waste."

"Mrs. McGhie," the chief said, holding a dog with all the fixings in his hand. "Are you ready?"

"Remind me to ask Nancy about this later," I said to Scooter as I tucked the bottle in my purse. "Let's not make a decision about dinner yet, okay?" I turned to the chief. "I'm all yours."

* * *

"I'm starved," I said as we turned the corner onto Main Street. After answering questions from the chief about Emily's condition when I found her, then discovering that our car wouldn't start and waiting three hours for a tow truck that never showed up, we had decided to walk back to the marina. "I never did get my hot dog. I haven't eaten since breakfast."

"Intermittent fasting is good for you," Scooter said.

"Says who?"

"Scientists."

"You realize they make that stuff up just to get headlines."

"No they don't."

"Sure they do. When's the last time you read about how eating three chocolate bars a day is good for you?"

"Never."

"That's 'cause scientists are spreading fake news. You can't believe everything you read."

"Unless, of course, it says that an obscene amount of chocolate every day is good for you," he said dryly.

"Correct. Those are the kinds of headlines you can believe. Not that you ever see that because of the mainstream media's obsession with fruits and vegetables," I said. Scooter's stomach grumbled. "See, you're hungry too."

"That's not hunger. That's just my digestive system realigning itself."

"How about if we realign it with some Thai food? We can call in an order and pick it up on the way."

"Why would we do that? We've got Trixie Tremblay's rutabaga nut roast back on the boat, my little Milk Dud."

"Hmm…when you call me a little Milk Dud, do you know what that makes me think of? All my other favorite candies—M&M'S, Reese's Peanut Butter Cups, Hershey bars… Hey, is that your stomach growling again?"

"Not growling, realigning," Scooter said. His stomach continued to loudly "realign" itself. After a few moments, he dug his phone out of his pocket. "Fine, let's order Thai."

I grinned. Scooter's stomach and I made a great team. "Pad thai for me, please," I said as he dialed.

"It's not going through. Let me see if I can get better reception across the street."

While Scooter went in search of more bars on his phone, I wandered over to Penelope's Sugar Shack to say hello to a few of my favorite friends in her display window—chocolate chip cookies the size of your head, éclairs crammed full of pastry cream, and apple fritters. It was a shame she was closed; I would have bought everything in sight.

As I eyed a particularly decadent-looking chocolate cream pie, I heard a gate creaking around the corner of the bakery.

Naturally, I decided to investigate. Maybe Penelope was walking toward the back entrance. Surely, she needed to offload those pastries since it was the end of the day, and I could get them at half price. Win-win for everyone. Plus, I never did manage to pick up those M&M cupcakes she had set aside for me.

Before I could walk through the gate, it swung shut. I was beginning to open it when I heard a woman talking. Someone who didn't sound like Penelope.

"You're late," the mystery woman said impatiently.

"What did you expect? I was at the hospital. Did you think I could just say, 'Sorry, mate, I know my fiancée just died, but I need to go meet someone at night in an alley.'"

That Australian accent was a dead giveaway—it belonged to Jeff. But who was he talking to? I pressed my ear against the wooden fence, earning myself a doozy of a splinter in the process.

"Stop pretending," the woman said. "It's not like you cared about her. You were just using her."

"Of course I cared about her. Would I have proposed if I didn't?"

"She was loaded. That was the main attraction. Don't forget, I know all about your last fiancée and what happened to her."

"What happened? Nothing happened."

"That's not what I heard."

What happened to her? I wanted to ask. I felt like I was watching a soap opera in a language I didn't understand.

"It was an accident."

"You mean you convinced everyone it was an accident. It's not going to be so easy this time. They know she was poisoned."

"Why would I have poisoned Emily? Your logic doesn't make any sense. Since we weren't married yet, I wouldn't have inherited anything. It's certainly not in my best interests that she's dead." I stood on my tiptoes and tried unsuccessfully to peek over the fence. Sometimes, it sucked being short.

"Actually, if it's in anyone's interests that she's dead, it's yours," he continued. "I'm sure the chief of police would be very interested to find out more about your connection to Emily and her family."

"You wouldn't dare," the woman said.

"Don't go stirring up any trouble for me, and I won't stir up any for you."

"Hey, where'd you go?" I heard Scooter call out.

"Somebody's here," the woman said. "I'm getting out of here. The last thing I want is to be seen with you."

I flattened myself against the wall and behind a hedge. Thankfully, I was wearing a dark top and jeans, which helped me blend in against the dark-purple siding. The gate creaked open. With the hedge in my way, all I could see were the legs of the person who was leaving. I'd recognize those flip-flops and legwarmers anywhere—it was Wanda, without a doubt. Questions flooded through my head. What was Wanda's relationship to Emily? What had happened to Jeff's first fiancée? And more importantly, who had murdered Emily?

CHAPTER 7
EXTRA-CRISPY HASH BROWNS

AFTER A SLEEPLESS NIGHT—nightmares about Emily being poisoned and monsters wearing brightly colored legwarmers kept waking me up—I was more than ready for an extra-large cup of coffee.

It was easier to convince Scooter to go for breakfast at the Sailor's Corner Cafe than I thought it would be. Maybe that was because he had fallen off the Rutamentals bandwagon the previous night with Thai food. Or maybe it was because my tossing and turning had kept him from getting a good night's sleep, and he knew that a Rise and Shine Smoothie just wasn't going to do the trick.

Even though it was early Sunday morning, there was a long line snaking out the entrance of the cafe. "Looks like it's going to be a bit of a wait," Scooter said. "Maybe we should go back to the boat and have smoothies instead."

The smell of bacon, hash browns, and coffee wafted out the door, causing my mouth to water. I had to act quickly before his willpower resurfaced. "Let me just have a peek inside. Maybe we can share a table with someone."

As I sidled past some tourists waiting to pay their checks, I accidentally knocked a carved wooden lighthouse off the counter.

In addition to serving up tasty food, the Sailor's Corner Cafe also sold nautically themed artwork made by local artists. The walls were covered with paintings of fishermen, sailboats, and whales. The display cabinet by the cash register contained jewelry featuring starfish, dolphins, and sea turtles. I made a note to check out a particularly cute pair of sand-dollar earrings later.

As I was placing the carved lighthouse back on the counter, I spotted Penny sitting in a booth by the window leafing through a sailing magazine. "Are you by yourself?" I asked.

"Yes," she said. "Ben was supposed to meet me, but he just texted to say he's not going to make it. I assume Scooter is around here someplace. Why don't the two of you join me?"

"I was hoping you'd say that." I slid onto the opposite bench and tapped on the window to get Scooter's attention. I pointed at Penny and gave him a thumbs-up. "Have you ordered yet?" I asked as I picked up a menu.

"No. It's crazy in here today, and they seem to be short-staffed." She glanced around the room. "I don't recognize anyone. Guess it's mostly out-of-towners here for the festival."

"I think you spoke too soon," I said. "Looks like Norm over there."

"Whatever you do, don't make eye contact," Penny said. "If I have to listen to him stumping one more time, I'm going to lose it."

"Anyone would be better than him as mayor. Even a dog."

Penny laughed. "Now there's an idea. What if we got a dog to run against him?"

"What are you two ladies giggling about?" Scooter asked as he slid into the booth next to me. After we explained our plan to elect Coconut Cove's first canine mayor and brainstormed ideas for campaign slogans ("Bark for a Better Tomorrow" and "Chihuahuas for Change" were some of my favorites), one of the harried waitresses, Alejandra Lopez, came to take our order.

She wiped down our table, then gave us a tired smile. "Sorry it took me so long to get to you. But don't worry, when I saw you come in, I put orders in for your usual—oatmeal for Penny, Denver omelet, sausage, and extra-crispy hash browns for Scooter, and of course pancakes and bacon for Mollie."

Scooter's eyes grew wide. "Um...actually, I was wondering if I could change—"

I jabbed my elbow into his side. "What I think he means to say is thanks for looking out for us. If you hadn't, it would probably be at least an hour before we got served."

"No problem, *chica*. The three of you are some of my favorite customers," she said.

"Order up," the cook shouted as he placed two plates of waffles on the counter.

"I need to get that," Alejandra said. "I'll be back with some coffee in a jiff, and your meals shouldn't be too far behind."

Scooter leaned back in the booth and put his hand on his stomach. "I think I've gained five pounds just sitting in this place. I was going to be good and order the fruit salad and nothing else."

Penny laughed. "That sounds like something my mother would say."

"Hey, how is your mom?" I asked. "Is she still coming to visit this week to watch the sailboat race?"

"No, she can't come now," Penny said glumly. "I really wanted her to see *Pretty in Pink* in action."

"It would have been great for her to see us cross the finish line when we won," I said.

"Oh, please," Scooter said. "There's no way you ladies are going to beat us. *Naut Guilty* is going home with the trophy."

"I didn't realize you were crewing on Mike's boat," Penny said.

"Yeah, he texted last night to say he needed another guy, so I volunteered."

Penny tapped her fingers on her lips. "Let's see if I have this right. This is the first sailboat that Mike's ever had. He used to be a powerboat guy. This is the first race he's ever entered. His crew is made up of people who don't have much sailing experience—"

Scooter interjected, "But I've sailed before."

"That was a million years ago," I said. "The only experience you've had lately is when we moved *Marjorie Jane* from her slip at the marina to the boatyard. Whereas I've been taking sailing lessons with Penny for a while now. And the other ladies on the crew have been sailing for years. There's no way *Naut Guilty* is going to win."

Penny and I high-fived each other across the table while Alejandra set three steaming mugs of coffee down. "Are you guys talking about the race too?" she asked. "It seems like that's on everyone's mind this morning. Norm is over there taking bets that his boat is going to come in first place."

"No, no, no," Scooter said as he placed his hand on my arm. "I can see what you're thinking. You want to make another bet with Norm."

"I sure do," I said. "I won the last one he made with me. I'd love to see the look on his face when I win this one too. Besides, with Penny as our captain, there's no way I can lose."

Alejandra bustled back with our meals. "Thanks again for letting me use your family's kitchen the other day to bake my cake," I said as I moved my coffee cup out of the way to make room for my pancakes. "It was so nice to have enough space to work in."

"No problem," she said. "Having a big kitchen is one of the benefits of still living at home with my parents. Saving on rent is another plus—gets me that much closer to saving up enough money to open up my own nail salon."

Penny gave Alejandra an encouraging smile. "Don't worry. It'll happen sooner than you think. And Mollie and I will be first in line for a manicure."

I held up my hands, showing off my short, unvarnished fingernails. "Good luck transforming these. Boat work has taken its toll."

"Challenge accepted," Alejandra said over her shoulder as she hurried back to the kitchen.

Scooter frowned while he stared at the mound of potatoes piled on his plate. As I reached for the maple syrup, I said, "Anyway, back to Norm. Care to place a side bet? If *Pretty in Pink* wins, you'll go back to eating normal food."

His eyes lit up. "And if *Naut Guilty* wins, you'll stop cheating. Don't think I don't know about the chocolate you've been carrying around in your purse."

"Deal," I said, shaking his hand. "Now, let's eat."

While Penny gobbled down her oatmeal and I polished off my pancakes and bacon, Scooter picked at his eggs, pushed his hash browns around his plate, and tried his best not to make eye contact with his sausage links.

Penny's phone buzzed. "I barely heard that over your tummy grumbling," she told Scooter.

"That's just his stomach realigning itself," I said. She gave me a quizzical look before checking her messages. I stuck a fork in Scooter's potatoes. "If you're not going to eat these, then I am. Extra crispy, just the way I like them."

Scooter pulled his plate away. "How can you still be hungry?" he asked. I smiled as he scarfed down the hash browns. "I'm just saving you from yourself," he said in between hurried bites.

Penny put her phone down. "That was Jeff. He wants to see some more boats."

"Really?" Scooter crumpled up his napkin and put it on his now-empty plate. "I would have thought he would be too broken up over Emily's death."

"Me too," Penny said. "But he seems more determined than ever. He's even decided to name his new boat *Emily Belle*, after her."

"That's sweet," I said. "Makes me wonder if our boat was named after a real Marjorie Jane."

"Sounds like another investigation for you," Penny said.

"Please don't encourage her." Scooter waved at Alejandra and pointed at his coffee cup.

"Speaking of investigations and Jeff, what do you know about him?" I asked.

Penny smiled. "How did we get from investigating the name of your boat to Jeff?"

While Alejandra refilled our cups, I tried to figure out what to say. On one hand, I didn't want Scooter to know I had accidentally overheard Wanda and Jeff talking about Emily the previous night. Knowing him, he might jump to conclusions and claim I was eavesdropping. But on the other hand, they had talked about how Emily had been poisoned, and each of them seemed to want to pin it on the other.

I needed to know more about Jeff's backstory and his relationship with Wanda. Of course, Scooter would say that I didn't really "need to know" anything about it, that it didn't involve me. But after eavesdropping on their conversation—oops, scratch that—after *accidentally overhearing* their conversation, I was obliged to follow up. You know what they say: "Do unto others as you'd have them do unto you." It's like paying it forward. If something mysterious ever happened to me, I'd want folks to investigate.

"Is it just me, or does Jeff have mismatched ears?" I asked. Okay, I know that seems like a random thing to say, but trust me, I had a plan with my line of questioning.

"You're investigating Jeff's ears?" Penny asked while Scooter rolled his eyes.

"I was just wondering if it's an Australian thing," I said casually. "That's where he's from, right?"

"Yeah, he moved here last year for work," Penny said.

"I heard a rumor that he had been engaged before Emily. Was it when he was back living down under? Has he said anything to you about that? Do you know why it ended?"

"You heard a rumor," Scooter said dryly. "Are you thinking his engagement broke off because of his ears?"

Penny scratched her head. "I've never noticed anything funny about his ears."

"What about his former fiancée?" I asked.

"No, I don't know anything about that," she said. "Our conversations have pretty much just been about boats."

"What kind of work does he do?"

"He's some sort of sales rep. Travels quite a bit for client meetings."

"With all that travel, he might not have had a chance to get to know that many people in Coconut Cove," I said. "Like Ned, Nancy, Ben or...uh, say, Wanda. Do you know if he knows them?"

"Not sure if he knows Ben. I introduced him to Ned and Nancy when he first came to the marina to check out boats."

"And what about Wanda?"

"Wanda met Jeff and Emily for the first time at the festival. I introduced them all at Ned's seminar yesterday."

"So none of them seemed to know each other beforehand?"

"No," Penny said. "Why are you so interested in who he knows?"

"Oh, well, I know how it is when you're new to town. It can be hard to meet people. I thought I could organize some sort of get-together for Jeff so he can get to know folks. It might also help him take his mind off Emily's death."

"That's so sweet of you," Penny said. "I'm sure he'd love that."

While she excused herself to go to the restroom, Scooter turned to look at me. "What exactly are you up to?"

"Me? Nothing," I said innocently.

"I'm guessing it's opposite day," he said. "Because when you say 'nothing,' I'm pretty sure you mean 'something.'"

"Aren't you late for your conference call?"

"Shoot, I am," he said. He stood and picked up the check from the table. "I'll pay this and meet you back at the boat later, okay?" After bending down to give me a kiss, he added, "And try to stay out of trouble."

"Sure thing," I said. Which was true. My next stop was to pay a visit to Chief Dalton and get him up to speed on my investigation. I couldn't exactly get into trouble doing that—could I?

* * *

Rumor had it the chief was at the beach by the Palm Tree Marina watching the kids' sailing races. Rumor also had it that the reason the chief and his ex-wife split up was because of a disagreement about what to name their dogs. Now I had two things to investigate—Emily's mysterious death and whose idea it was to name the Yorkies Frick and Frack.

I heard these rumors at Penelope's Sugar Shack. After the Sailor's Corner Cafe, it was the next best place to catch up on all the gossip and find out what people were up to. The young woman who made my mocha had told me where I could find the chief and the scoop on his marital woes.

Coffee in hand, I walked down the wooden steps leading from the Palm Tree Marina to the sandy beach, which stretched from one end of the cove to the other. "Mind if I join you?" I asked.

The chief was sitting on a piece of driftwood. When he looked up at me, his bushy eyebrows twitched. "I don't suppose you'd ever take no for an answer."

"I think you're going to want to hear what I have to say." I plopped down next to him, taking in his outfit—navy shorts, a crisp short-sleeved shirt, and sandals. "I don't think I've ever seen you out of uniform. I'm surprised you're off duty at a time like this."

He shook his head. "I'm not off duty. The dogs were running circles around me, begging for a treat. I tripped over them and spilled iced tea all over myself. All my other uniforms are in the wash, so I've had to settle for civilian wear." He pursed his lips. "What did you mean by 'at a time like this'?"

"Aren't you investigating Emily's death?"

"Why would I be doing that?"

"She was poisoned."

"Was she?"

"Yes. Everyone knows that."

"They do?"

"Wait a minute. I'm the one who should be asking the questions," I said, pulling a notebook and pen out of my bag.

The chief raised one of his eyebrows. "You should be?"

"See, there you go again." He raised his other eyebrow as he looked at my notebook. "What? You've never seen C-3PO and R2-D2 stickers before?" I asked.

He pointed at the kids who had finished their sailing race and were pulling their Optimist dinghies up on the shore. "I have, but usually with that age bracket, not yours."

"How do you know how old I am?"

He shrugged. "It's on your record."

"What record?"

"Are you denying that you have a record?"

I kicked off my flip-flops and scrunched my toes in the sand. "It was just a misunderstanding."

"A misunderstanding involving bolt cutters?" he asked.

"We have more important things to discuss than bolt cutters." I flipped open my notebook. "First, let's talk about what Emily was poisoned with. I assume you have the toxicology report back."

"No comment."

I scribbled a few notes down. "Okay, item number two—how

she was poisoned. Was it an injection? Was it in something she ate or drank?"

"No comment."

"Fine. We'll move on to item number three. Who would have wanted Emily dead?"

"No comment."

"Did anyone ever tell you that you're not a great conversationalist?"

The burly man frowned. "Yeah. My ex-wife."

"Tell you what—why don't we make this more of an interactive discussion. I'll tell you what intel I've come up with so far, and then you shed a little more light on the investigation."

"Fire away," he said.

"Okay. Jeff and Wanda are the prime suspects so far." That generated a few eyebrow contortions on the chief's part. I pulled a pencil out of my bag and made a quick sketch in my notebook.

"Is that a picture of me?" He pulled the notebook out of my hand and peered at it.

"Uh, maybe. You do know that you have very expressive eyebrows, don't you? It's almost like you communicate with them. Far more effectively than you do with words, I might add."

"Have you been talking to my ex?"

"She's the last person I'd want to speak with after she threatened to file a restraining order against Mrs. Moto."

The corners of his mouth twitched. "Did she really go through with sending a letter?" Then he frowned and tapped the notebook. "Explain this picture, if you please, Mrs. McGhie."

"Just trying to decode the language of your eyebrows. I figure when you move them in certain ways, it must mean different things. Kind of like decoding raccoon sign language."

"I didn't know raccoons had eyebrows."

"They don't. It just reminds me of that time I was studying raccoon—"

The chief held up his hand. "Enough about eyebrows and raccoons. Honestly, I'm surprised you and my ex don't get along. You both have some really kooky ideas. Now, why don't you get back to what you were saying about Jeff and Wanda having a motive to murder Emily."

"Hah! You admit it. It was murder!"

The chief shrugged. "It'll be in the newspaper soon enough. That photojournalist, Alan, managed to get a video recording of one of the clerks at the medical examiner's office talking about it to a friend at the Tipsy Pirate. He keeps pestering me for more details. Remind you of anyone?"

"Nah. I've got a lot more personality than he does."

The chief bit back a smile before folding his arms across his chest. "Jeff and Wanda," he prompted. After I told him about the two of them knowing each other, despite pretending they didn't, Jeff's former fiancée, Wanda accusing Jeff of being a gold digger, and Wanda's mysterious connection to Emily and her family, the chief finally relented and shared a detail about Emily's murder.

"She ate a piece of poisoned cake. It was gelsemium that killed her," he said. "Also known as woodbine. Some people use it to treat certain conditions, but it can be very dangerous, even in small doses."

"So dangerous, it can kill someone," I said soberly, thinking about the convulsions Emily had been having when I found her.

The chief nodded. "That makes us square." He got to his feet. "Now, I better get back and feed and walk Frick and Frack before they tear the place up."

While he walked back down the beach toward the marina, I quickly scrawled down things to follow up on: (1) how did the killer get a hold of the gelsemium; (2) how did they know Emily would eat the cake; and (3) why did gelsemium sound so familiar?

* * *

"Where's Mrs. Moto?" Katy asked as she ran up the beach toward me. She was followed by her younger brother, Sam, who was using his towel as a superhero cape.

"She's back on the boat resting," I said. "She had a long day yesterday."

"Oh. I wanted to see her and tell her my good news," Katy said.

"What's that?"

"I came in first place in the under-ten division!"

"That's great," I said. "I saw the end of your race while I was sitting here. I'm going to be in my first sailing race on Tuesday. Do you have any tips for me?"

She thought about it for a moment, then said with a serious look, "Don't fall off the boat."

"Yeah," Sam echoed. "Don't fall!"

"Sound advice," I said. "I will try to stay on the boat."

"My uncle fell off a sailboat last year," Katy said.

"Oh no, that's terrible! Was he okay?"

The young girl tugged at the towel wrapped around her waist. "Yes, but my aunt was really upset."

"I'll bet she was."

"She told him he wasn't allowed to go racing anymore. He didn't like that."

"I can understand that," I said, closing my notebook. "Is he your father's brother or your mother's?"

The two kids thought about that for a while. "Our dad's," they said in unison.

"He has lots of brothers and sisters," Katy added.

"What's a lot?"

Katy counted on her fingers. "One, two, three, four, five!"

"I wish I had brothers and sisters," I said.

She cocked her head to one side. "You don't have any?"

"No, I'm an only child."

"I wish I had another sister, instead of a stupid brother. It would be just like in the movie *Parent Trap*."

"Oh, I'm sure you don't mean that," I said.

"I do!" Katy glared at Sam. "He put my Elsa doll in the washing machine and ruined her."

Sam looked down at the ground. "I said I was sorry," he said softly.

"Why don't you sit down and tell me about *Parent Trap*," I said, patting the driftwood on either side of me.

"We saw it with Grandpa," Sam said as he nestled against me.

"There were two twins—one lived with her mother and one lived with her father—and they didn't know about each other," Katy said. "They met at summer camp and discovered they were secret sisters!"

"Then what happened?" I asked.

"They trapped their parents into getting back together," she explained.

"We ate popcorn," Sam added.

"And cookies," Katy said. "But Grandpa said we weren't supposed to tell Grandma about the cookies. Promise you won't tell her about the cookies either."

"I promise," I said solemnly. "I'm very good at keeping secrets. Speak of the devil." Nancy was standing on the boardwalk motioning at the kids. "You better scoot along."

I reflected on the upside of being an only child while they raced each other down the beach. My mom and I had fun watching *Parent Trap* together—the original, not the remake. I decided to send her a jokey text.

Remember Parent Trap? What's my secret twin sister's name?

I watched the gulls darting in and out of the surf while I waited for her response.

She sent a one-word text back, which probably took her five minutes to type.

Mary

Not the answer I'd expected. *Who's Mary?* I replied, then waited another five minutes.

Your twin sister

I looked down at my phone in shock. Was it possible I really did have a secret sister? The only response I could manage consisted of question marks. A few minutes later, my mom replied with her own series of question marks.

I tapped on my phone furiously. *How come you never told me I had a sister before?*

Don't be silly. You're the one who told me about her. Gotta go. Late for bridge.

After not getting a response to any of my subsequent texts, which mostly consisted of more question marks interspersed with exclamation points, I put my phone and notebook into my bag and felt something hard at the bottom. I pulled out the small, empty, stopper-topped bottle that I had found in the trash in the men's room the day Emily was killed. I peered at the label on the front. That's why it had seemed so familiar. It was the herbal remedy for migraines, also known as gelsemium, that Nancy had shown me the other day.

CHAPTER 8
RUTABUBBLES

I COULD BARELY DRAG MYSELF out of bed the next morning. Nightmares had continued to plague me. This time they featured C-3PO and R2-D2 chasing after me with bolt cutters while I was running through the Death Star wearing a giant raccoon costume and holding a bottle of gelsemium.

I attributed my bad dreams to the herbal remedy I had found in my bag the previous afternoon. It completely freaked me out to know I had been carrying the possible murder weapon around with me, right next to my bag of M&M'S. The possibility of having a secret twin sister might have also been a factor in sleeping poorly. My mom still hadn't responded to my texts. She'd probably misplaced her phone yet again.

When I had dropped the bottle off at the police station yesterday, Chief Dalton had subjected me to a barrage of questions about when I had found it, what else I knew about herbal remedies, and what I was doing in the men's room. He wasn't amused when I kept replying, "No comment." In the end, I explained everything to him, including the fact that men's rooms never seem to run out of paper towels and that maybe his officers should investigate why some men think washing their hands is optional. He assured me that he practiced good hygiene.

I finally dragged myself out of bed, but only because Scooter was talking about going to Melvin's to pick up a shore power cord adapter. Not only was I reluctant to let Scooter go to the marine store unsupervised but I also wanted to pick up some supplies. Somehow I had volunteered to be in charge of installing a new fuel filter and water separator system for our diesel engine. I blamed sleep deprivation for having agreed to take this project on. It was the only logical explanation. Well, there was also the fact that I had been hiding chocolate in the engine compartment that I didn't want him to find.

As we pulled up in front of the store in our newly repaired car, I noticed a sign in the window advertising for a store manager. Melvin had been through a lot in the past couple of months, and I was glad to see he was finally going to get some help. The high school kids who worked on weekends and after school were great, but it wasn't the same thing as having someone manage the store day in and day out. Maybe Melvin would finally have a chance to relax and be able to go back to the Bahamas to visit his family.

Scooter got sidetracked with a display of boating shoes, so I headed to the back of the store. While I tried to remember what model number I was searching for, I overheard two women talking about Emily's death.

Yes, *overheard*, not eavesdropped. I was in the engine systems aisle before they were. It's not like I was hiding somewhere listening in on their conversation. It's just that my ears perked up when one of them mentioned herbal remedies.

"See, what did I tell you? You shouldn't use anything unless your doctor prescribes it," the older woman said.

"Mom, lighten up. I only rub lavender oil on my temples at night. It helps me sleep better. It's not like I'm ingesting anything." She squeezed her mother's hand. "And I made sure to do my research before I started using it."

"That's the problem. People don't research these things. They just pick up a bottle. It says it'll cure your migraine or whatever else ails you, and they take it without a second thought. Would you have known what gelsemium was before that article in the newspaper? Would you have known what the side effects are and how dangerous it is if you have certain medical conditions?"

The younger woman pursed her lips. "I'm not sure. It did sound kind of familiar. Maybe it was on some sort of TV show?"

"You shouldn't get medical advice from TV." Her mother frowned. "TV or not, I don't think most people would have ever heard about it before. I'm telling you, whoever killed that poor girl knew exactly what they were doing."

When the conversation turned to less interesting matters—like why the young woman didn't come home to visit more often—I grabbed the equipment I needed and headed in search of my husband.

While I watched Scooter try on shoes, I considered what the mother had said. I certainly hadn't known what gelsemium was before yesterday. The killer must have gotten the bottle the day of the murder. Did they buy it from Nancy and Ned's daughter's stand? No, that didn't seem likely. Ned had mentioned that Sofia wasn't going to be setting up her stand until later that afternoon. Then I remembered what had happened after Ned's seminar. When the pack of dogs raced across the stage, the boxes with the herbal remedies had spilled on the ground. Could someone have pocketed one of the bottles?

I sat down on the bench next to Scooter and pulled my notebook out of my bag. Time to make a list. I chewed on my pen as I tried to remember who had been there. I wrote down their names—Ned, Nancy, Wanda, Jeff, Mike, Alan, the chief's ex-wife, and, of course, poor Emily.

Ned and our crazy former neighbor hadn't been at the cake competition, so I crossed them off the list. Besides, Ned didn't have a mean bone in his body, and someone who had been married to a police officer wouldn't be a likely suspect.

Nancy's name was the next to be scratched off. The last thing she would have wanted was for the cake competition to be ruined, not after she had spent so much time organizing it. Besides, what motive would she have had?

That left me with Wanda, Jeff, Alan, and Mike. I put stars next to the first two names. Wanda and Jeff definitely were hiding something, and both had a connection to Emily. Maybe Alan had also had a connection to Emily. She certainly seemed to have been avoiding him at the boatyard when Penny was showing boats to her and Jeff. I put a question mark next to the photographer's name. When I got to the next person on the list, Mike, I chewed my bottom lip. What possible link could there be between a small-town lawyer and a young woman from the remote island of Destiny Key?

***

"What are all these kids doing out of school on a Monday?" Scooter asked as he drove down Main Street.

"It's spring break," I said. "That's why they hold the festival during this part of March, so that families can attend events during the week. Lots of parents take the week off work."

"Smart thinking," he said. "Tourist dollars are important to Coconut Cove's economy."

I adjusted my cardigan. "I'm glad it's not as hot as it was this weekend. Folks won't be rushing back to their hotels to soak up air conditioning instead of spending time at the festival. Hey, do you mind stopping here?" I asked, pointing at one of the gift shops lining the street. "We need to pick up your sister a birthday present, and I think she'd like one of those flamingo aprons they have for sale there."

"I completely forgot about her birthday," Scooter said.

"That's why you have me. Quick, a spot just opened up over there."

After parking the car, we crossed the street, dodging tourists carrying ice cream cones, hot dogs, and funnel cakes. "Hey, isn't that Mike coming out of the gift shop?" I said.

"It is. Perfect timing. I want to talk to him about referrals for contract lawyers."

It certainly was perfect. A perfect opportunity to speak with him about Emily's death.

After Mike gave Scooter a few suggestions of people to contact, he offered to have a look at the contract in question. "It's not my area of specialization, but maybe I can give it a once-over while you try to line someone else up to look at it more in depth. It can take a while to get a hold of these guys."

"That would be great," Scooter said. "I'm under the gun with this thing, and there are a few areas that are really concerning me. You could at least steer me in the right direction."

"No problem."

"You deal with wills and estates, right?" I asked. Mike nodded. "So what happens when a young woman like Emily dies without a will?"

"Well, it depends what state they're a resident of." He gave me a quizzical look. "But why do you assume she didn't have a will?"

"Oh, it's just that when I was her age, I didn't have one. I didn't even think about it."

"But you have them now, don't you?"

"We updated them recently to make a provision for Mrs. Moto," Scooter said.

Mike smiled. "You'd be surprised how many people mention their pets in their wills."

"So, in Emily's case, assuming she didn't have a will, who would her estate go to?"

"Well, her estate would get divided by a set formula determined by the state."

"Okay, so we know she wasn't married, both her parents are dead, and she was an only child. How would it work in that scenario?"

Perspiration began dripping down Mike's face, along his goatee, and onto his shirt collar. Wanda probably would have said his energy follicles were detoxifying. Maybe he needed some sort of neck warmer to soak up the sweat. "She was an only child?" he asked.

"Uh-huh. I thought you knew her?"

Mike shook his head. "No, not really."

"Hmm. Well, I think she was loaded. She mentioned having an estate. So there certainly have to be people interested in what happens to her money, right?"

Mike loosened his tie and unbuttoned his collar. "Listen, even if I knew, I couldn't say anything. You know, attorney-client privilege."

"I'm just asking hypothetically," I said as Mike wiped his brow. "Besides, you said you didn't really know her, so there wouldn't be attorney-client privilege."

"Why are you so interested, my little Milk Dud?" Scooter asked. "It's the guy's lunch break. Maybe he doesn't want to talk shop."

Mike patted Scooter on the back. "Yeah, I should grab something to eat. I'll touch base later, okay?"

"Did you see the way he was sweating? It's not that hot today," I said as Mike hightailed it down Main Street toward the Sailor's Corner Cafe.

"Man, I hope he isn't coming down with something," Scooter said. "We've got the race tomorrow."

I wasn't so sure Mike was getting sick. I had a feeling my line of questioning had hit too close to home. I was pretty sure he knew more about Emily's situation than he wanted to admit to.

* * *

Later that afternoon, I successfully installed our new fuel filter and water separator unit. And I made sure everyone knew about it.

"Whoo-hoo!" I shouted from the deck of our boat. "I did it!"

Ben looked up from the thru-hull he was installing on a neighboring boat. "That's great, Mollie. I keep telling you, you could get a job working at the boatyard if you wanted to."

"Yeah, no," I said as I climbed down the ladder. "My work for FAROUT keeps me busy enough."

"Where's Scooter? He should be here to share in your moment of triumph."

"He went to drop some paperwork off at Mike's office."

"Mike the lawyer?" I nodded. "Is it for a will?"

"No, a work contract." Ben frowned. "Why? What is it?" I asked.

"There's been some talk about Mike around town. Let's just say he operates on the edge when it comes to his law practice. He's known as the guy to go to if you want to do something shady."

"You're kidding," I said. "The last thing Scooter needs now is to have some crooked lawyer working on his stuff."

"It's just rumors," Ben said. "There might be nothing to it. What do I know about lawyers, anyway? Look at me. I'm living paycheck to paycheck. I'll never have enough money to need a lawyer, let alone hire one. I'm sorry I said anything. Let's change the subject, okay?"

"All right," I said. "Why don't you tell me about this latest T-shirt of yours."

"You like it?" he said. "I picked it up at the festival."

I took a closer look at the skull and crossbones and the slogan emblazoned underneath: "I might be the reason the rum is gone."

"It suits you," I said with a smile. "A nice addition to your pirate T-shirt collection."

As I was telling Ben about everything that had gone wrong during the installation and how many things I had to do over, Scooter pulled up in the car. "Why are you grinning from ear to ear?" he asked me.

"I did it!"

"Really, you finished already? That's great!" He stepped out of the car and pulled me into a bear hug before kissing the top of my head. "I'm so proud of my little Milk Dud. This calls for a celebration. I have just the thing." After grabbing a few bags out of the back of the vehicle, he gave me another kiss. "I'll be right back."

I spun around in a circle. "I knew it. He got me some chocolate cupcakes to celebrate!"

"Are you sure?" Ben asked. "I thought he was really serious about his diet."

"I think that particular obsession is over. These things usually last a day or two. Maybe three days tops. But he broke down and had Thai food the other night and hash browns yesterday. I think it's safe to say we can kiss Rutamentals goodbye."

Scooter climbed down the ladder with a tote bag slung over his shoulder. "I've got some good news, bad news. Which do you want first?"

"I want the one that involves chocolate."

Scooter gulped. "Sorry, neither has to do with chocolate."

"Okay, give me the bad news first."

"The fridge isn't working. But now that you're done with the fuel filter and water separator, maybe that can be the next project you tackle."

I sighed. "The good news better be extra good to make up for the fact that one more thing has broken on *Marjorie Jane*."

"I have some bubbles to celebrate. I just picked it up at the store, so it's cold." He pulled a bottle out of the bag, along with three coffee cups. Yes, coffee cups. We sure know how to celebrate in style.

"Ooh, champagne," I said. "You've outdone yourself."

"Well, it's not exactly champagne. To be champagne, it has to be—"

"Yeah, yeah, I know. It has to be made in a certain region in France. That's okay. I'm not fussy. A nice bottle of prosecco from Italy will do just fine."

"Well, it's not exactly prosecco. Here, Ben, grab these." He handed him the coffee cups, then unwrapped the foil from the top of the bottle. I wasn't sure I had heard of prosecco coming with a screw top before. What kind of bubbles were these?

After Scooter poured some into each of our cups, he made a toast. "Here's to being one step closer to sailing off into the sunset and around the world."

I choked on my drink. For two reasons, really. One, there was no way I was going to sail around the world, especially in this boat. And two, whatever was in my glass was disgusting. Even Ben seemed a little green around the gills after he took a sip, and he's the type of guy to guzzle down any kind of booze, particularly if it was free.

"What exactly is this?" I asked.

"Isn't it great?" Scooter said. He turned the bottle around so I could see the label. "It's nonalcoholic sparkling wine made out of rutabagas."

"So, I guess Rutamentals is back on," I said before downing my glass. If you can't fight them, you might as well join them.

* * *

On again, off again. Off, on. On, off. I was so confused as to what was up with Rutamentals. After choking down the Rutabubbles, Scooter announced that he was taking me to Alligator Chuck's for a celebratory dinner. Visions of ribs slathered in tangy barbecue sauce, french fries, creamy coleslaw, and a slice of brownie pie for dessert filled my head. My mouth watered. My tummy growled in anticipation. I put on a pair of shorts with some very forgiving elastic in the waistband, grabbed my purse, and hopped in the car.

Turned out Rutamentals was still on. Very much on.

Wanda had somehow convinced Chuck to serve diet-friendly meals at his restaurant. Scooter eagerly pointed out the options: rutabaga "hummus" with celery sticks, pasta made out of spiralized rutabaga and served with a creamy tofu sauce, and a rutaburger featuring plenty of rutabaga and nothing else you'd associate with a burger, like a bun, meat, or cheese.

I told Scooter to order for me and excused myself to go to the ladies' room. As I walked through the dining room, I noticed no one else had ordered anything from the Rutamentals menu. I said hi to a few people I knew, stealing some fries and nachos along the way.

On my way back from the restroom, I ran into Ned and Nancy in the entryway. "Crowded, isn't it," Ned said. "We've been waiting almost twenty minutes for a table."

"Come join us," I offered. "We've got a booth over by the window."

"Thanks, but we're meeting our daughter, son-in-law, and the grandkids for dinner," Ned said. "Katy and Sam love coming here. I think it's the alligator hats they hand out to the kids."

"Totally understandable," I said. "Those hats are really adorable. I got one last time I was here."

Nancy snorted. "You realize those are for kids, don't you?"

"I'm not so sure about that. The waitress didn't ask to see my ID. Maybe you should get one tonight."

Nancy pursed her lips, then looked at her watch. "They're running late, as usual."

"They're only a few minutes late," Ned said. "You know how hard it is to get two young kids ready and out the door on time."

"I never had any problems with punctuality when I was raising our children." Nancy fixed Ned with a pointed stare. "Our daughter must have inherited the lateness gene from you."

While Ned stared uncomfortably at the ground, I decided to

get out of there before Nancy started to analyze my DNA. I was pretty sure she'd find some unsatisfactory traits like "leaves dirty dishes in the sink overnight" and "doesn't floss regularly."

"I guess I should get back," I said. "I wouldn't want my dinner to get cold." Rutabaga was bad enough—cold rutabaga sounded dreadful.

"Hang on a sec," Ned said. "Have you heard about the funeral arrangements for Emily?"

"No. I hadn't realized the medical examiner released her body already."

"They did earlier today. Jeff stopped by the office and asked if we knew anyone who could arrange for a memorial service on a boat. He wants to scatter her ashes on the water."

"Poor guy, having to organize everything. It's a shame she didn't have any immediate family."

"You should come to the service," Ned said. "Jeff said everyone's invited."

Nancy scowled. "Why would Mollie want to go to a memorial service for someone she just met? Why would anyone?"

"Well, I'm going," Ned said firmly. "Jeff doesn't really know anyone in the area, and he could use the support. A number of people are attending. Penny, Penelope, Mike, Wanda, Norm, Alan —"

"Did you see Alan today?" Nancy asked. "He was supposed to email me the photographs from the opening weekend of the festival. I've been trying to get a hold of him all day."

"Don't worry. I mentioned it to him," Ned said.

"Good. What did he say?"

Ned scratched his head. "Well, to be honest, it was hard to tell. He mumbles at times."

"At times?" I asked. "He mumbles all the time."

"I'm not sure about that," Ned said. "He spoke pretty clearly when he heard Jeff talking about Emily's memorial service. He volunteered to come and take pictures. Jeff said he didn't need to bother, that he could take some with his phone, but Alan was very insistent."

"Well, count Scooter and me in. We'll be there to support Jeff."

"Great," Ned said. "It'll be on Friday. A sunset service. I'll let you know once I have more details."

I said my goodbyes and made my way back across the dining room, saying hello to a few more people and snagging some more fries and nachos.

"You're just in time," Scooter said as I slid into the booth. "I think you're really going to like your rutaburger."

"'Like' is such a strong word," I said before taking a bite. "Hmm. It's crunchy. I have to say, I didn't see that coming." As I placed the "burger"—and I'm using that term loosely—on my plate, I noticed Jeff and Mike sitting at a table across from us. Mike pulled a file folder out of his briefcase and handed it to Jeff. While Jeff leafed through the papers, Mike grabbed his napkin and wiped his brow. Jeff held up a document and pointed at a section, jabbing his finger repeatedly to make his point.

"I'm going to grab some ketchup," I said to Scooter. Mike and Jeff were so absorbed in their conversation that they didn't notice me leaning across the table behind them.

"Trust me," Mike said. "It'll work. All you need is a wedding certificate to take care of Emily's will. And I've got some contacts who can arrange that."

I grabbed a bottle of ketchup, and some hot sauce for good measure, and walked back to my table, keeping my head down so the guys wouldn't notice me.

Whose wedding certificate were they talking about? And what exactly did Emily's will say? Hopefully, I would get some answers at the memorial service, if not before.

CHAPTER 9
UNICORNS VS QUADRICORNS

I WOKE IN THE MORNING with a vague recollection of being on a game show. Normally, dreaming of winning the grand prize would be a pleasant thing to wake up to. But in this case, it was a lifetime supply of rutabagas—the stuff of nightmares. As I rubbed the sleep out of my eyes, I resolved to be more supportive of Scooter and his dieting efforts. So I downed a Rise and Shine Smoothie with a smile on my face.

After giving my husband and Mrs. Moto a kiss goodbye, I hopped in the car to head to the waterfront park. It was my day to staff the FAROUT booth. I was really looking forward to it. It would be a great opportunity to talk to people about other life in the universe and hopefully drum up some new members.

The bright purple awning over the Sugar Shack caught my eye as I drove down Main Street. I decided to stop and have a chat with Penelope and see if I could fill in a few blanks about the cake competition. Emily had died shortly after the first judging round with a shattered plate next to her. How did she get the plate? What kind of cake had been on it?

A cheerful tune from *The Sound of Music* caught my attention as I opened the door. Penelope peeked out from the back room. "Finally, a customer! What can I get you, Mollie?" She walked toward the counter, tucking her strawberry-blonde hair behind her ears and adjusting her purple apron. "I just took some lemon poppy seed muffins out of the oven."

I licked my lips as I gazed at the pastries in the display case. Then I took a step back and said firmly, "Thanks, but I think I'm going to have to pass."

"Wow, that's so unlike you," she said. "You must have had a big breakfast."

"You have no idea."

The door opened and two young girls ran in. "Hello, sweethearts, what can I get you?" Penelope asked.

A woman holding a baby in her arms called to them. "Girls, I told you, no cupcakes today. Come on, let's go." She gave us an apologetic smile as she shooed the kids out of the bakery.

Penelope gave a heavy sigh. "It's been like that for the past few days. People are avoiding baked goods like the plague. At this rate, I'll be out of business by the end of the week."

"But why? Everyone needs a sweet treat from time to time."

She untied her apron and hung it up on a hook before sitting down at one of the white wrought iron tables by the window. "It's because of what happened to Emily." She put her face in her hands.

"But what does that have to do with you?"

Penelope lifted her head. Her gray eyes were damp with tears. "She was poisoned."

"But everyone knows that. It's not like people have stopped eating. There were plenty of people at Alligator Chuck's last night."

"The poison was in one of the slices of cake. And because I was a judge and run a bakery, people suspect I had something to do with it."

I reached my hand across the table and squeezed hers. "I'm sure that's not the case. It's probably that Rutamentals diet everyone is on. That's why they're avoiding sugary treats. Don't worry, it's just a fad. Soon, everyone will be sick of rutabaga and you won't be able to keep up with the demand."

Penelope wiped her eyes and smiled. "I hope you're right."

"Of course I'm right. Tell you what, why don't you get me one of those lemon poppy seed muffins and an extra-large mocha, and then we'll figure out how to get people to just say no to rutabagas and begin saying yes to sugar."

She went into the back and returned a few minutes later with two mugs and two muffins. The lemony aroma was heavenly. I dove right in while Penelope stared blankly out of the window.

After slurping down the last of my coffee and making sure there weren't any crumbs left on my plate, I asked Penelope if she knew any more about how the cake slice was poisoned.

She shook her head. "No. All Chief Dalton told me was that it *had* been poisoned, not how. He was here at the bakery questioning me for a long time yesterday."

"What kinds of questions did he ask?"

Penelope shrugged. "The usual ones, I guess—did I see anyone put anything on the cakes, where was I after Nancy locked the doors to the pavilion, did I know how Emily got back inside, what did I know about her. That kind of thing."

"And what did you say?"

"That I didn't see anything, that I didn't even know Emily, let alone who would want to murder her, and that I had been watching the fire, just like everyone else."

"Did he ask you anything else?"

"He was really interested in the bakery. He wanted to see what kind of security system I had. He even sent one of his officers to my house later to check what security I had there."

"That's odd," I said, staring forlornly at my empty cup and plate. I considered buying another muffin and coffee to support the Sugar Shack. Scooter would understand once he heard what Penelope was going through.

"I thought so too," she said. "But when I asked him about it, he said it was routine. There have been some issues with petty theft in Coconut Cove, and they're simply checking to make sure everyone has the proper precautions in place."

"Hmm. I'll have to ask him about that. There's a lot of expensive equipment at the marina. We don't need people sneaking in at night stealing it off people's boats."

A buzzer went off in the kitchen. "That's a batch of chocolate chip cookies ready to come out of the oven. Of course, no one's going to buy them," she said glumly.

"Not if I have anything to do with it. In fact, give me some of your menus. I'll pass them out at the FAROUT booth today." I looked at my phone. "In fact, I should probably get going before I'm late." No time for an extra muffin and coffee after all.

"They're right there by the cash register," she said over her shoulder as she hurried into the kitchen. "Thanks, Mollie!"

As I walked behind the counter, I noticed a framed picture of Penelope with an older woman. The two of them looked so much alike—strawberry-blonde hair, gray eyes, and cheerful smiles. It had to be a photo with her mother. I paused and took a closer look. The smile on the older woman's face didn't quite reach her eyes. *What had she been thinking about when that picture had been taken*, I wondered.

I grabbed some of the lilac-colored menus, which were wedged between a stack of plates and the cash register. That's when I realized I hadn't asked Penelope for more details about which cake had been poisoned and how Emily had gotten a hold of it. I didn't want to upset her with more questions, so I decided I'd go straight to the source for the information I needed—Chief Dalton.

* * *

"Why won't he return my calls?" I muttered under my breath.

"Who's that?" asked my former neighbor.

I gritted my teeth. Much to my dismay, I had discovered that the FAROUT booth was right next to Mrs. Moto's archenemy's art booth. I had spent the entire morning listening to her list reasons why dogs were superior to cats, why Yorkies were superior to any other breed of dog, and the health benefits of Rutamentals.

Yep, another convert to the wonders of rutabagas. She was a full-on fan of Trixie Tremblay, right down to the legwarmers she was wearing underneath her long batik skirt. She had accessorized them with ankle bracelets, which jingled every time she moved. I sighed. It felt like I had a long day ahead of me.

"Cat got your tongue?" she asked.

"If you must know, it's your ex-husband. I've been trying him all day, but he's refusing to take my call. I'd march down to the police station and demand to see him, but there's no one else available to cover the booth."

"Well, I can relate," she said. "Tiny doesn't return my calls either."

"Did you just call him Tiny?"

She smiled. "It's a nickname. I began calling him that when we first started dating. It's caught on—everyone calls him that now."

"I don't think I've ever heard anyone call him anything other than Chief Dalton."

"I guess that's true. He's not exactly the type of guy to be on a first-name basis with many people." She rubbed her left ring finger absentmindedly. "He likes to keep people at a distance. It's one of the reasons we broke up."

"I heard it was over what you named your dogs."

"You gotta love small towns. You'd think people would have better things to do than gossip about my marriage." She held my gaze. "Or spread gossip."

My face grew warm. "I'm sorry. I shouldn't have said anything." I observed the two Yorkies sleeping in a dog bed, which she had set up for them underneath a tree. "For what it's worth, I think their names are really cute. How did you come up with them?"

"Tiny would kill me if I told you..." She hesitated for a few moments, then continued. "What the heck. It's a cute story, and it serves him right for not calling you or me back."

I leaned forward, eager to hear a hopefully embarrassing story about the chief, but before she could dish the dirt, a couple started asking her questions about one of her paintings. While she talked to them about the techniques she used and what inspired her to depict magical creatures like fairies and leprechauns, I managed to hand out a few FAROUT brochures to college kids and some of Penelope's menus to a group of retirees.

"This calls for a celebration!" she said. "I sold one of my largest paintings. They're going to come back later and pick it up."

"Which one?"

She pointed at the back of her booth. "It's the one with the quadricorns grazing in a meadow."

"Did you say quadricorns?" I peered at the painting. "But aren't those unicorns?"

"Look closely," she said as she assembled a large, flat cardboard box.

I examined the painting in more detail. It was certainly colorful, and the use of glitter really accentuated the wildflowers. I zeroed in on the creatures in the foreground. "One, two, three, four...oh, I get it now!"

"They look like unicorns," she said as she extended a finger on the top of her head to resemble a horn. "But since they have four horns, they're called quadricorns." She giggled as she pointed four fingers upward in a perfect imitation of a four-horned unicorn. "See, a quadricorn. They're far superior to unicorns."

Her laughter was infectious, and before I knew it, I had joined in. "And people think I'm crazy for believing in extraterrestrial life," I said. "But you paint pictures of quadricorns."

"And get paid for it." She grinned. "Actually, you're not as bad as Tiny makes you out to be."

I smiled back. "And you're not as bad as your threat to slap a restraining order on us made you out to be."

"About that—" Her watch beeped. "Time to take my pill."

"Nothing too serious, I hope."

She reached into her woven tote bag, pulled out a bottle, and washed down a pill with some rutabaga juice. "No, just something I have to take every day. I have a rare genetic condition. Runs in my family. Tiny used to remind me to take my pills every day." She held up her wrist. "Now that he's not around anymore, I have to rely on my watch."

"Speak of the devil," I said.

"Good afternoon, Mrs. McGhie," the chief said as he bent down to greet the Yorkies. He beamed as they licked his face. After giving them a good scratching, he stood, all traces of his smile disappearing in a flash as he turned to his ex-wife. "Can you look after the dogs tonight, Anabel?"

"What's come up this time?" she asked.

Remarkably, his eyebrows didn't twitch an iota, although his jaw tightened. "It's a murder investigation, Anabel. That's what's come up. And he or she is still out there, and I think they're going to strike again."

She bit her lip. "Fine. Go on. Go save the world."

He stalked off without another word while she busied herself packing up the quadricorn painting. I sat on the stool behind the FAROUT information desk in shock as I tried to make sense of what the chief had said. Who was going to be the next victim?

CHAPTER 10
LEE HO!

FORTUNATELY, THERE WERE LOTS OF visitors to the FAROUT booth in the afternoon, which kept me from dwelling on the chief's dire pronouncement. I passed out bumper stickers and sold some T-shirts without a care in the world.

Who was I kidding? All I could think about was figuring out who the next victim would be. I felt powerless to stop the next murder. Sure, I had a list of suspects for Emily's murder, but I had more questions than answers. As the person who'd found the poor girl's body, I felt compelled to answer those questions. There was a certain burden that came with something like that. One did have a civic responsibility, after all.

Scooter would probably say I was rationalizing things, that finding a dead body didn't mean I *had* to investigate, and that my nosiness was going to get me in trouble as it had in the past. Maybe he was right. But I couldn't help myself. And besides, my nosiness had helped nab killers in the past. I'd be doing Coconut Cove a disservice if I didn't get involved.

In between handing out brochures, signing people up for the FAROUT newsletter, and explaining the difference between carbon- and silicon-based life forms, I jotted down my "Nab the Killer, Pronto" to-do list.

1 - Find out when the cake was poisoned. Was it during the cake competition itself when the cakes were being sliced, or had someone poisoned the cake after Nancy made everyone leave the pavilion? If it was the former, only the judges and the finalists had access to the cakes when they were being sliced. Everyone else was behind the barricade. And of those people, the only ones who had access to the bottle of gelsemium that was used to poison Emily were Nancy, Jeff, Mike, and Wanda. Alan was also in my line of sight. As the official event photographer, he had been allowed access behind the public barrier.

I still doubted that Nancy was a serious suspect, given how the murder had ruined her carefully organized event. She might kill someone to prevent disorganization, but she certainly wouldn't eliminate someone if it meant a disruption to her meticulously ordered life.

The other thing I had to keep in mind was that when I went around to the rear of the building in search of Mrs. Moto, the back door had been ajar. Had the murderer entered while everyone was distracted with the fire and then poisoned the cake?

2 - Find out how the killer knew Emily would eat the deadly slice of cake. She had been complaining loudly about how Nancy had messed up the decoration on Jeff's cake and that she wanted to fix it. Did the killer encourage her to return and replace that slice of cake, knowing that she would eat the original slice?

3 - Figure out who wanted Emily dead and why. Wanda and Jeff were top of my list, given their conversation about Emily outside Penelope's Sugar Shack. There were a lot of questions swirling about Jeff—what had happened to his former fiancée, his discussion of a wedding certificate and Emily's will with Mike, and what was up with his ears. Okay, that last point didn't have anything to do with the murder, but it was still something I was very curious about.

There was definitely something suspicious about Wanda, besides the fact that she had been brainwashed by Trixie Tremblay. I realized that, although we had been taking sailing classes together for a while, I didn't actually know much about her. It wasn't until that day at the grocery store when she had become upset over the death of her sister that I had first learned something personal about her.

Mike was obviously up to his eyeballs in something dodgy. He had been nervous when I'd asked him about Emily's will, and it appeared he and Jeff were up to no good. Plus, he had written that restraining order letter, which didn't exactly put him in my or Mrs. Moto's good books.

Alan was an interesting suspect. He was so meek and mild that I couldn't see him being the killer, let alone imagine what would drive him to murder a young woman like Emily. But he was a strange little man, and those were often the ones you had to watch out for.

I looked over at Anabel in the booth next to me. Part of me really liked her. She was an incredible artist, she didn't mock my involvement in FAROUT, and she had a good sense of humor. But the other part of me was still annoyed. I flipped over the page in my notebook and began another list of questions:

1 – What did Anabel have against Mrs. Moto?

2 – What was the story behind the chief's nickname, Tiny?

3 – If there were unicorns and quadricorns, were there also unicorns with two or three horns?

After I got that out of my system, I flipped back to my "Nab the Killer, Pronto" list and thought about the most important thing that I needed to investigate—who was the killer going after next? My fear was that the murderer believed someone had seen him or her poison the cake during the competition and wanted to eliminate any witnesses. I knew from watching my favorite television show that was what murderers did—made sure no one was left alive who could identify them.

I had been right there in the thick of things. Could the murderer have thought I had seen something I shouldn't have? Maybe there was something to be said for avoiding sugary treats, which might potentially be laced with poison. Or was it possible this was all Trixie Tremblay's doing somehow? The cake poisoning might have driven people to embrace Rutamentals. You can never be too careful about people who have an unnatural obsession with root vegetables.

I snapped my notebook shut and shoved it in my bag. It was

time to head to the Palm Tree Marina for the sailing race. I was excited and nervous at the same time. Excited to participate in my first sailing race ever and nervous that the killer might think it was the perfect opportunity to go after his or her next victim. Pushing someone overboard might go unnoticed during the excitement of the race. I was planning on staying sharp. No one was going overboard on the ocean on my watch.

* * *

When I got to the marina, everything was in full swing. Crews were busy getting the boats ready for the race—taking off the sail covers, making sure everything was battened down, and checking equipment. As I walked down the creaky dock, I kept a sharp lookout for sea monsters. The last thing I wanted was to trip on one of the loose planks, fall into the water, and get eaten by a kraken.

"There you are!" Penny was standing on the bow of her boat, *Pretty in Pink.*

"Sorry," I said as I climbed on board. "The volunteer who was taking over for me at the FAROUT booth was late."

"Quick, change into the team T-shirt down below," she said, pulling a pale-pink shirt out of a bag.

"These turned out great," I said. "I love how you've got the breast cancer ribbon on the back."

"Well, if we win—and we are going to win—then I've earmarked the money that was raised to be donated to breast cancer research." She pointed at Norm, who was standing on the deck of his boat posing for pictures. "Guess what Norm is going to donate the money to if he wins."

"Himself?"

"Yep, his campaign fund."

"Well, even more reason for us to win," I said, giving her a fist bump.

Wanda tossed a coiled rope into the cockpit. "How come you haven't changed yet?" Penny asked her.

I looked at the teal T-shirt Wanda was wearing. Surprise, surprise. It featured Trixie Tremblay holding a purple plate laden with sliced rutabaga. Yellow legwarmers and deck shoes completed the outfit.

"I wish I could, but I can't. I'm contractually obligated to wear Trixie Tremblay gear."

"Great, now we have an extra T-shirt." Penny threw up her hands. "So much for a matching all-female crew."

After checking that all the preparations were in order, she looked at the checklist that Nancy had given her. "Just one thing left to do—have Alan take an official crew photograph." She turned to me. "Mollie, would you mind getting him so we can get this over with and head out toward the starting line? I see him over by Mike's boat."

"Sure," I said. "That way I can give Scooter a good-luck kiss before the race starts."

As I walked down the dock toward *Naut Guilty*, I noticed Jeff towering over Alan. He attempted to grab Alan's camera, but the mousy man pulled back, almost falling into the water before he caught himself on one of the wooden pilings.

"Delete them," Jeff hissed.

"I'm telling you, I don't have any on this card," Alan said. "They're all saved on the cloud."

"So you admit it, you do have photos of her!"

Alan stepped forward and jabbed his finger in Jeff's chest. "She wanted me to take them. They're all I have left of her, and I'm sure as heck not going to delete them!" he said, clearly enunciating every word. I was stunned—the mouse had turned into a lion.

Jeff shoved Alan's hand down, then put his arm around his shoulders. "Listen, mate. I understand. She was a pretty girl, but you have to admit it's a bit creepy that you've got photos of her."

"She was my girlfriend," Alan said quietly.

Jeff slapped Alan's back. "Hardly, mate. She went on a few pity dates with you, that's all."

"It wasn't pity." His eyes looked flinty as he stared up at Jeff. "Emily was interested in me and my work."

"Your work, maybe, but not you." Jeff shrugged. "Tell you what, go ahead and keep the photos. No skin off my back. After all, I'm the one she was in love with. There was a ring on her finger to prove it." He gave Alan one more hearty slap on the back. "I better get back to the boat. See you around."

As Jeff walked toward me, I tried to remember which of his ears had seemed bigger than the other. The sun was reflecting off the water, making it hard to get a view of the left side of his face.

"You okay, Mollie?" Jeff cocked his head toward me. Ah. It was definitely his left ear that was oddly shaped.

"Me? I'm fine. It's Alan I'm worried about. Is he okay?" I asked, noting how the photographer was digging his fingers into the palms of his hands.

"Just girl problems," Jeff said with a laugh. "Good thing you're married, or he might try to ask you out. Gotta go help get the boat ready. It's going to be sweet when we cross the finish line and win this thing."

"In your dreams," I said over my shoulder. After getting Alan's attention, I explained about needing him to take the *Pretty in Pink* crew picture. He avoided eye contact with me and mumbled a response. "Do you mind speaking up a little?" I asked gently.

"I'll be right there," he said more clearly. "I'm also going to take a video."

"Oh my gosh, a video! I completely forgot that you videoed the cake competition." Alan nodded. "Can I see a copy of the footage you took? Is it on this camera?" This could be the key to finding out who put the poison on the cake. It wouldn't be the first time that a video of Alan's had provided an important clue in one of my investigations.

"The police seized the camera I used that day," he said. Darn. Not much chance that the chief was going to let me see the key piece of evidence. Then he added, "But it automatically backs up to the cloud."

"Ooh. Would I be able to access it?" I asked, rubbing my hands together. Thank goodness for the magical cloud.

"I suppose, if..." His voice trailed off as he shuffled his feet on the dock.

"If what?"

"If you convince Penny to let me come on her boat during the race and take pictures."

"Well, it's supposed to be an all-female crew." Alan surprised me by making eye contact with me for a few seconds. It was unnerving. I quickly looked away. "But I guess I could persuade her." As we walked toward *Pretty in Pink*, I remembered the extra T-shirt. "How do you feel about wearing pink?"

* * *

As *Pretty in Pink* tacked along on the starting line waiting for the race to begin, I looked nervously at the boat Scooter was crewing on, *Naut Guilty*. Mike and Jeff were aboard that boat, and one of them might be the murderer. Then I glanced around the boat I was on, my eyes resting on Wanda in her Trixie Tremblay getup and Alan clad in the spare pink shirt. The killer could potentially be here as well. I wrapped my arms around me, shivering despite the warm weather.

The starting gun sounded, jarring me out of my thoughts. "Come on, people, let's go!" Penny cheered from the helm. She steered the boat toward the first mark while the crew focused on trimming the sails. At that moment, we were all seated on the port side, our weight helping to balance the boat.

"Ready about," Penny said.

Two of the women shifted to the starboard side, while Wanda and I stayed on the port side. "Ready," we all said in unison.

As Penny turned the boat, we pulled and released the lines, causing the headsail to shift effortlessly from one side of the boat to the other. We executed a flawless tack, putting *Pretty in Pink* in the lead.

Hang on. I should probably stop here and point something out. Did you notice all that technical babble I uttered? It sounded like I actually knew what I was doing when it came to sailing, didn't it? And like we were a superb crew? Well, let's just say that's not exactly how it happened. Here's how it really went down.

"Ready about," Penny said.

The woman on my right looked at me and frowned. "I forgot what we're supposed to do."

"What's going on, ladies?" Penny asked. She tapped her fingers on the steering wheel. "Come on, get it together. You've done this a million times in practice. Mollie, Wanda, over to the starboard side. Now!"

As Wanda and I rose, a wave crashed into the side of the boat, jostling us. "Ouch," Wanda said. "You hit my head."

"You hit my shoulder."

"Ladies," Penny said. "If we don't tack soon, we're going to hit that reef over there." She took a deep breath. "Ready about?"

"Ready," we all said in unison.

"Meow," someone else said.

I looked at the companionway. Alan was standing on the ladder, which led down to the cabin below, taking photos of us in all our incompetent glory. Perched next to him was Mrs. Moto.

"How did that cat get on board?" Penny said. "Never mind, we'll deal with that in a minute. Lee ho!"

While she turned the boat into the wind, we pulled and released the lines, shifting the sail awkwardly from one side of the boat to the other. In the process, Wanda tangled her foot up in a line on the cockpit floor. As I tried to unwrap it from her legwarmer, I fell off the bench. Mrs. Moto ran over to me, meowed loudly, then licked my face.

"Mollie, get that cat down below. Lock her in the V-berth."

"She's not going to like that," I said.

"I don't care what she likes. She's going to get herself killed running around loose."

I grabbed the cat and hustled down below. "How exactly did you get onto Penny's boat?" Mrs. Moto responded with a loud purr. I smiled. She looked adorable snuggled up in my arms. "You're going to have to stop getting into places where people don't want you. You don't want another restraining order, do you?"

I set her on one of the cushions in the V-berth and quickly closed the door. Not a second later, the yowling started. "Shush," I said. "If you're quiet, I'll give you some extra catnip when we get home." I paused for a minute and listened. No yowling, just a soft meow.

"All right, ladies, we're going to tack again in a few minutes," Penny said. "We can do this. Just remember your training. And don't forget that it's for a good cause—fighting breast cancer and beating the guys."

I'm pleased to report that after that disastrous first tack, we got our act together and took the lead. The two boats trailing us—*Naut Guilty* and Norm's boat *The Codfather II*—didn't have a chance of catching up to us. After making it around the last mark, we headed into the home stretch. I couldn't believe it—we were going to win this thing!

"What is he doing?" Wanda yelled. We all turned and looked behind us. *The Codfather II* was on a collision course with *Naut Guilty*.

"Turn, turn," Penny said, staring at *The Codfather II* as it closed in on the other boat. "Norm, for goodness' sake, turn!"

Norm turned, but it was too late. I flinched as the bow of his boat slammed into the side of *Naut Guilty*.

"Scooter!" I yelled. Mrs. Moto joined in with a piercing cry, which could be heard all the way up in the cockpit. I gripped Penny's arm. "Are they going to be okay?"

"They'll be fine. See that boat over there?" She pointed at a small powerboat speeding toward the accident scene. "They're trained to handle situations like this. The best thing we can do is hold our position here until they give the all clear. If we try to go and help, we'll just get in the way and make things worse."

She comforted me while we waited for news. "Do you want Mrs. Moto to come up here so you can give her a cuddle?" Penny asked. I nodded. "Will one of you ladies go get her?"

Wanda volunteered. When she handed me the upset calico, I noticed that Mrs. Moto had shed a lot of hair on Trixie Tremblay's face. Then it hit me. I knew who the murderer's next victim was going to be.

CHAPTER 11
COCONUT CARL

"HEY, TAKE IT EASY," Scooter said as I embraced him. "You're squeezing the stuffing out of me."

I stepped back and stared into his dark-brown puppy-dog eyes. "Sorry, you're not going to get off that easy. I thought I had lost you when the boats collided. I need at least one more hug."

He chuckled as he pulled me into his arms. "I'm okay," he whispered into my ear before giving me a kiss. A piercing yowl interrupted our tender moment.

"I'm not the only one who needs some reassurance," I said.

Scooter scooped up Mrs. Moto and gave her a cuddle. "I heard you went racing," he said to the calico. "The first feline member of the *Pretty in Pink* crew. I hope you got a T-shirt."

I smiled at the thought of her sporting a cat-sized pink top. After stroking her head, I gave Scooter an appraising look. "Are you sure you're okay?"

"Absolutely fine. Not even a scratch." Unfortunately, the same couldn't be said for everyone else. One of the crew members on *The Codfather II* had broken an arm, and a couple of guys on *Naut Guilty* had some pretty serious cuts, bumps, and bruises.

Both boats had limped back to the marina after the injured men had been taken off by the rescue boat. The paint on *Naut*

Guilty's hull was scraped off where *The Codfather II* had smashed into her, and the fiberglass underneath was in bad shape. The deck was even worse. *The Codfather II* had suffered serious damage as well—her bowsprit had been torn off, her forestay had been detached, and her mast was hanging at a precarious angle. Even if you didn't know what a bowsprit and forestay were, one look at the sailboat would have been enough to convince you that there was going to be a hefty repair bill.

The uninjured crew members and race spectators had gathered at the marina patio. Everyone was buzzing about what had happened and who was to blame. The crowd was divided into two camps—those who thought Norm was a reckless skipper and those who thought he had just done what it took to win the race and admired him for it. Norm, of course, was basking in the attention, posing for photographs and signing people up for his campaign mailing list.

In contrast, Mike was pacing back and forth along the boardwalk, his phone pressed against his ear. "I wonder what's going on," I said.

"I think he's talking to his insurance agent," Scooter said. "It's going to cost a pretty penny to fix his boat." He set Mrs. Moto on the ground. "Everyone is heading over to the Tipsy Pirate for the awards ceremony."

"Is that still on? They halted the race when the accident happened." I rubbed my temples. I could feel a headache coming on. My lack of sleep was catching up with me. "Did you know that some folks are actually complaining that the race was stopped? Apparently, *real* racers don't stop for anything."

"I guess they do things differently in Coconut Cove." He shrugged. "In any case, the skippers and the judges talked it over, and they decided to go ahead with the event. Although there won't be prizes for the race, they don't want the catering to go to waste." He looked around the patio. "Besides, I have a feeling people are going to want to keep dissecting what happened over a few drinks. To be honest, I could use a gin and tonic."

"Tell you what—why don't you take Mrs. Moto back to the boat and meet me back here. I've got something I need to take care of first."

"I'm afraid to ask."

"Don't worry, I'll fill you in later. I think you're going to want to have that drink first."

* * *

After Scooter and Mrs. Moto headed toward the boatyard, our wandering feline firmly clipped into her harness and leash, I made a beeline for Chief Dalton. He was sitting at one of the patio tables, his back toward me, intently focused on something in front of him. As I approached, I caught a glimpse of a certificate of some kind. Perhaps a birth certificate? It was too hard to see over the burly man's shoulder. He flipped the piece of paper over.

"What can I do for you, Mrs. McGhie?" he asked without turning around.

"How did you know it was me?"

"You have a distinctive walk."

I looked down at my feet. "I'm wearing flip-flops. Everyone wears flip-flops in Florida. They all make the same sound—flip, flop. How is my 'flip, flop' any different from anyone else's?"

"No comment."

Great. We were back to his non-response responses. I pulled out a chair and sat next to him. I drummed my fingers on the table.

"Is there something you wanted to say?"

I took a deep breath. "Yes, but only if you promise me something first."

He raised one of his bushy eyebrows. "That isn't how this works."

"Fine. We'll play your little game," I said. "This is too important." I paused for a few moments to collect my thoughts.

"Well?" he prompted.

"I know who the murderer is going to go after next." There was absolutely no response, not even a 'no comment.' I leaned across the table. "Aren't you even the slightest bit curious?"

"I'm always interested to hear your theories." There was a distinct lack of conviction in his voice.

I had hoped for some sort of drum roll. Instead, there was just the sound of coconuts falling from the palm trees onto the patio. "It's Penelope. The killer was after her, not Emily."

"And why do you think that?"

"Remember how there was a broken plate by Emily's body? It was purple. I had completely forgotten until this afternoon on *Pretty in Pink*. Wanda was wearing one of those awful Trixie Tremblay T-shirts. You're not one of those wackos on the Rutamentals diet, are you?"

"This has something to do with rutabagas?"

"Yes. I mean, no. I mean, yes." I put my head in my hands. Everything was getting so jumbled up. It was probably the stress from the accident coupled with the fact that I hadn't had any real food in hours. Scooter had mentioned catering at the Tipsy Pirate. I wondered what they were going to serve. The chef there made these amazing egg rolls with a pineapple dipping sauce.

"Earth to Mrs. McGhie. So which is it—yes or no?"

I popped a breath mint in my mouth to quiet my stomach. "No, the murder doesn't have anything to do with rutabagas. At least I don't think it did. Although, that is an interesting idea—"

"I don't have all day."

"On Wanda's T-shirt, Trixie Tremblay was holding a purple plate with sliced rutabaga. That's how I made the connection. Each of the judges had a different-colored plate at the cake competition. Nancy announced what color each judge was assigned. Penelope was purple. I think the killer was trying to poison Penelope, and somehow, by mistake, Emily ended up eating the slice of cake instead. That means I've been going about my investigation all wrong."

"Your investigation?" the chief asked dryly.

"Okay, fine. Our investigation."

He smiled faintly. "Ours?"

"You know, this would work so much better if you were more of a team player. If it wasn't for my help in the other murder investigations, the killers would have gotten off scot-free."

"I see."

I shook my head. "This isn't getting us anywhere. What you really need to do is make sure that Penelope is okay. Who knows when the murderer is going to strike again."

"You don't need to worry about Miss Pringle."

I leaned back in my chair. Something was off. It was almost like... "Wait a minute. You already knew about Penelope, didn't you?"

"No co—"

I held up my hands. "Yeah, yeah. I know what you're going to say—'No comment.' Just at least promise me that she's okay."

After a beat, he said gently, "She'll be fine. My officers are watching her around the clock." Then he placed the papers in front of him in a folder, pushed back his chair, and stood. "This is why you should leave murder investigations to the professionals. We have the training and the resources required. You have a vivid imagination and a...um...cat."

I tucked my frizzy hair behind my ears. Maybe I should just keep out of it. After all, I'd had it all wrong. Emily hadn't been the intended victim. My suspect list was useless. The investigation had been a waste of time. I chewed on my lip. Maybe the chief was right. But he didn't have to make me feel so stupid about it.

"By the way, what was it you wanted me to promise?" he asked.

I gave him a calculating look. "To tell me how you got the nickname Tiny."

His face reddened while his eyebrows did the most amazing contortions. He spluttered. "What exactly did my wife—I mean my ex-wife—say to you?"

"No comment," I said, smiling sweetly.

* * *

After my disastrous conversation with the chief, I checked my messages. Scooter had texted to say that he'd been delayed. Apparently, one can of Frisky Feline Ocean's Delight hadn't been enough to satisfy our princess, and he was hunting in the cupboards trying to find some more.

My mom had also finally texted back. *Do you still see Mary?* I was even more confused than ever. How could I still see a twin sister I hadn't known about until recently? I didn't even bother to text back. This was probably best handled in a phone conversation. But after everything that had happened, I wasn't up to dealing with it at the moment.

I looked over at Mike. He kept pacing back and forth, talking on his phone. Except for the two of us, the patio was deserted. The crowd had moved the party to the Tipsy Pirate. I was eager to get there as well. Given my run of luck lately, I wanted to pay a visit to my buddy, Coconut Carl, and see if he had any advice for me.

Mike's call must have ended badly. He uttered some very imaginative expletives, then looked like he was going to hurl his phone across the patio before he stopped himself.

"Everything okay?" I asked.

"No, everything is *not* okay!" He ran his fingers through his hair. "I'm sorry. I shouldn't be taking it out on you."

"What's going on?"

"It turns out my boat wasn't insured for racing. That's something extra you have to add on to your policy."

"What about Norm? He hit your boat. Doesn't he have to pay to repair yours?"

"That's how it should work, but Norm is claiming that I was at fault. By now, I bet he's bribed everyone to tell his version of the story."

"Can't you fight it? Maybe sue him? Being a lawyer has got to count for something."

He clenched his fists. "Suing him would take time. And I don't have time. I need that money now. I need to get it from him one way or another." He slowly uncurled his fingers, then stuck his hands in his pockets. "How could I have been so stupid about the insurance?"

"I know what you mean about feeling stupid," I said.

"Do you and Scooter have problems with your boat insurance too?"

"No. At least I don't think we do." I mentally added 'check insurance' to my *Marjorie Jane* to-do list. I would say that our boat's to-do list was growing longer by the day, but it seemed more like by the hour.

"So what do you feel stupid about?"

I weighed up whether to tell him about Penelope having been the murderer's real target. Mike had been nervous when I'd questioned him about Emily's will, but, in hindsight, that didn't have anything to do with her death, since she wasn't the person who was supposed to have been killed. Maybe he had been nervous for another reason. Given his odd conversation with Jeff about a wedding certificate, I still wondered if he was engaging in some less-than-legitimate activities, but that really wasn't my business.

Since the chief had admitted that Penelope was under police protection, I figured it was already common knowledge—or would be soon—so I decided to fill Mike in. After I had explained about the purple plate, Mike frowned. "That changes everything." He pulled his phone out of his pocket. "Hang on a sec. I need to send a quick text."

"Who do you think would want to kill Penelope?" I asked. "I can't imagine anyone having it in for her. She owns a bakery, after all."

"You're right. It wouldn't make sense to eliminate Coconut Cove's source of cupcakes and cookies," Mike said with a teasing tone to his voice.

I smiled. "I like a man who thinks logically."

"I have to admit to having a certain fondness for her vanilla spice cupcakes. My waistline hasn't been the same since she opened the Sugar Shack."

"When was that?"

"Hmm, let me think." Mike leaned against the railing and gazed out at the water for a few moments. "About four years ago? It was after she graduated from college and moved back to Coconut Cove."

"You must know her pretty well," I said. "You've lived in Coconut Cove all your life, haven't you?"

He shrugged. "I don't know about pretty well. But it is a small town, so we do keep tabs on one another. It's both a blessing and a curse." He glanced at his phone when it beeped, then turned to me with a thoughtful look on his face. "You were asking who might have it in for Penelope. There's one person I can think of that the police should be talking to."

"Who's that?"

"Wanda. She and Penelope's mom didn't speak to each other.

In fact, they'd go out of their way to cross the street if they saw the other one on the same side. Wanda used to say some horrible things about Penelope's mom. Really horrible things. Maybe the bad blood extended toward her daughter."

"You think she would have killed Penelope because she didn't like her mother?"

He wiped his brow. "It's just a theory. But there's always been some questions about the circumstances surrounding the death of Penelope's mom." His phone beeped again. "Listen, I've got to go."

Wow. That left me with a lot to think about. Could Wanda be a killer? Then I shook my head. It wasn't my business. I made a vow to leave things to the police and instead focus on more important things like dinner.

*   *   *

"Come on, just do it. Rub his belly," I said. "We could use some good luck."

"What? Rub whose belly?" Scooter asked.

"Duh. Carl's."

"I'm not rubbing any strange guy's belly."

"But you know Carl."

"I do? Are you sure? I can't think of anybody named Carl that I know. Unless you're talking about Carl Kowalski, but he's back in Cleveland."

"No, not that Carl. *That* Carl." I pointed at the wooden statue of Coconut Carl that graced the entryway of the Tipsy Pirate. Coconut Carl was a legend in these parts. A pirate by trade and a womanizer in his spare time, Carl was known for his love of rum and coconuts. Locals and tourists alike believed it was good luck to drink a shot of rum, then rub the statue's belly three times.

Scooter shook his head. "Do you know how many people have had their hands on there?" We watched as a couple of the guys who had been on Mike's boat demonstrated the ritual. One of the guys even kissed Carl's belly. I suspected that more than one shot of rum might have been involved. "I've got enough to worry about without catching a cold or the flu by touching that."

"I've got disinfectant wipes in my bag."

"I'm sure my little Milk Dud does." He grabbed my elbow and steered me into the bar. "You've got everything in there—your phone, wallet, at least three notebooks, a ridiculous number of pens, chocolate—"

"I'm actually out of chocolate."

Scooter smiled. "I'm stunned."

"Me too. It's almost like someone went into my bag and threw it out." I gave him a playful punch in the arm.

"The nerve of some people." He rubbed his arm. "Now, where should we sit—at the *Pretty in Pink* table or the *Naut Guilty* table?"

"It's not a very good turnout at the *Naut Guilty* table," I said. Mike was conspicuously absent, and the folks with injuries were home recuperating. "Why don't we get the guys who are here to join the girls at the *Pretty in Pink* table?"

"Good idea."

While Scooter organized moving tables and chairs, I sat next to Wanda and placed an order. Thankfully, she had changed her outfit since the race. I don't think I could have managed to look at Trixie Tremblay holding a purple plate all night.

"So, what did we miss?" I asked.

"Norm just gave a speech," Wanda said.

"Can't say I'm sorry about missing that."

"I don't blame you." She took a sip of her drink. "Any word on the injured guys?"

"They're all going to be fine, even the one with the broken arm. It was a clean break."

"I broke my leg once," Wanda said wistfully. "My sister was pregnant at the time, really far along. We used to joke about who took longer to get up off the couch. I was such a klutz with my crutches, and she struggled to hoist herself up unaided. It was easier to ring a bell and have my brother-in-law fetch things for us when we needed them."

"That was sweet of him."

"Sweet...no, he wasn't sweet. Manipulative, yes. Sweet, no." She twisted the bracelet on her wrist while she stared out the large windows that overlooked the bay. "You know, I'm actually really tired. It's been a long day, and I've got food demonstrations early tomorrow at the grocery store. I'm going to call it a night."

"Where's Wanda dashing off to?"

I looked up. Nancy was standing next to the empty chair holding a clipboard. "I'm not sure. One minute she was talking about her sister and brother-in-law, the next minute she was gone."

"She talked to you about her family?" She peered at me over her reading glasses. "Wanda never talks about her past. Her life before Coconut Cove is a mystery. All we know is that she was originally from Destiny Key."

"Destiny Key? Isn't that where Emily was from?"

"I believe so." Nancy sat down. "It's a strange place. The folks who live there are a tight-knit group who have a lot of money. They don't like outsiders visiting their island."

"But it's not a private island, is it?"

"No, but the locals resent visitors. There's a beautiful anchorage there that people from Coconut Cove sail up to. Folks take their dinghies to the beach, but if you walk anywhere else on the island, you're made to feel unwelcome pretty quickly."

"I wonder how Jeff met Emily," I said as the waitress set my drink down, along with some egg rolls. Nancy snatched one up, dipping it into the pineapple sauce and into her mouth before I had a chance to pull the plate toward me. "If they don't like outsiders, I wonder what they thought about her being engaged to one."

"I guess it will have to remain an unsolved mystery, now that the poor girl is dead." She grabbed another egg roll, along with her clipboard. "I better get back to my rounds. You're all set for the pet-costume competition, aren't you? You've read the rules and regulations, correct?"

I nodded while I savored my egg roll.

"Your costume is fully compliant?"

I dabbed my mouth with a napkin. "Um...compliant?"

She frowned while jotting down a note. "Noncompliant costumes will be automatically disqualified. You might want to reread those rules and regulations."

"I'll do that." While I ate another egg roll, I tried to remember if I had turned those particular rules and regulations into origami birds. Then I noticed Jeff and Mike at the bar looking thick as thieves. They both glanced over in my direction. Mike held up his glass and toasted me before leaning toward Jeff and whispering something in his ear. I had a feeling my investigation was back on.

CHAPTER 12
RUTABAGA POISONING

"I'M PRETTY SURE RUTABAGAS GO bad if they're not refrigerated," I said to Ben. "Since our fridge is broken, that means I should probably throw away all the Rutamentals diet food Scooter has on board our boat, right?"

Ben scratched his head. "Uh, aren't rutabagas a root vegetable like potatoes and yams? You don't need to keep those chilled, so you shouldn't need to worry about your rutabagas going bad."

"I thought I could count on you for support," I said. "Now repeat after me: you can get food poisoning from eating rutabagas that haven't been kept below forty degrees Fahrenheit. That's what we're going to tell Scooter, okay?"

After Ben managed to recite the food-safety mantra correctly without breaking into laughter, we sat in the folding chairs underneath *Marjorie Jane* to take a break from boat work. Ben had been helping take the mast off *The Codfather II* with the aid of a crane, while I had been trying to troubleshoot why our fridge wasn't working. After the accident at the sailing race the previous day, I was having a hard time focusing on that particular project.

I scooched my chair back a few inches to try to get in the shade, then grimaced as I took a sip of warm water. What I wouldn't have given for a cold drink. I had just about gotten used to not having a freezer since we moved onto our boat, but not having a fridge was quickly getting very tiresome.

"Isn't that Scooter pulling in now?" Ben asked. "There goes your opportunity to throw out the rutabaga food items before he got back."

"Great. It was going to be the most productive thing I did today. I might as well give up now and take a nap."

"Come on, it can't be that bad," he said after taking a sip of his icy-cold soda. I was tempted to see if he'd sell the rest of it to me, but I was feeling too lazy to climb up the ladder onto my boat and dig through my purse to find some money. Warm water it was.

Scooter pulled up one of the other chairs and sat next to me. "Did you get the fridge working?" he asked.

"No," I said. "Either something's wrong with the compressor, or we need to add more magic gas to it."

"Magic gas?" Scooter asked with a puzzled look on his face. "What's that?"

Ben grinned like a five-year-old boy. "Sounds like unicorn farts. It probably has glitter in it."

"Hmm. I'll have to ask Anabel Dalton about that," I said. "She's the town expert on unicorns and quadricorns."

"Uh, quadricorns," Scooter said. "Let's get back to that in a minute. First, can you tell me what this 'magic gas' is all about? Is fixing our fridge going to be expensive?"

"It's a substance that starts off as a gas, then goes through the compressor, turns into a liquid, then finally goes through the evaporator and turns back to a gas, and, in the process, magically keeps everything in your fridge cool."

Scooter smiled. "I have no idea what you just said, but you're awfully cute when you talk about marine technical stuff."

"I think she's talking about adding some refrigerant to your system," Ben said. "Kind of like topping up your car's air-conditioning system. It comes in a can. You can pick it up at Melvin's."

"Bingo," I said. "One of the guys a couple of boats over told me about it. He offered to help if that turns out to be the issue."

"I still can't get over how you know this," Scooter said. "For someone who didn't want to own a sailboat, let alone work on fixing one up, you've sure become pretty knowledgeable about it all. I think you know more than I do."

"I'm just as surprised as you are," I said. "It does make me wonder if I've been abducted by aliens and if they did something funny to my brain. Do you realize I actually read a whole chapter on fixing marine refrigeration systems in that boring boat-repair book we have?"

"Is that the one Mrs. Moto likes sleeping on?" Scooter asked.

"Yep, that's the one. She's really taken to napping on books these days. Doesn't matter what kind of book it is, she just curls up on top and begins snoozing away."

"Not just on closed books," Scooter said. "I saw her nudge one open yesterday with her nose. She flipped the pages over until she found just the right section, then settled down on top of the open book."

"Where is Mrs. Moto?" Ben asked.

"She's napping inside in the air conditioning. Unlike us foolish humans sitting outside sweltering in the heat."

"Why don't you go take a nap?" Scooter asked.

"I'd like to, but what I really need to do is finish the alterations to Mrs. Moto's costume."

"What's she dressing up as?" Ben asked.

"It's a surprise. You'll have to wait until Sunday to see." With the cake contest having ended on a disastrous note, I was pinning all my hopes on winning the pet-costume competition. I already had a place picked out on the boat to put the trophy—on a shelf above the chart table. Of course, I'd have to move Scooter's new collection of Rutamentals cookbooks to make room, but I was sure he would understand.

"What is today, anyway?" Ben asked. "I've lost track of what day of the week it is."

"Did you have one too many at the Tipsy Pirate last night?" Scooter asked.

"Well, maybe," Ben said sheepishly. "There was this really cute girl sitting at the bar watching my band play. I was trying to get up the nerve to go talk to her during a break, but then this other guy swooped in, started chatting her up, and I lost the opportunity. My buddy bought a few rounds of shots to try to cheer me up."

Poor Ben. He never seemed to have any luck with the ladies. I tried to think of any women I knew who would be interested in a sweet guy who lived on a sailboat. The problem was that there weren't many of them out there. It seemed like unattached male sailors outnumbered female ones by leaps and bounds.

"I know what you're doing," Scooter whispered to me. "You're trying to think about who you can fix him up with. I think you should stay out of it. Remember the last time you tried to set someone up?" In a louder voice, he said to Ben, "It's Wednesday."

"Yeah, that makes sense," Ben said. "Another week whizzing by."

"That's probably because so much has happened. The festival opened on Saturday and..." My voice trailed off as I thought about the drama that had ensued on Saturday with Emily's death and all that had transpired since then. I couldn't believe it was only Wednesday. Hopefully, we could make it through to the close of the festival on Sunday without another murder.

"What were you going to say?" Ben prompted.

"I don't know. Just thinking about Emily, I guess. Has anyone heard anything about her memorial service?"

"Ned emailed the marina staff," Ben said, pulling his phone out of his pocket. "Here it is. The service is going to be on Friday evening. Jeff's chartered a boat so he can scatter her ashes at sea while the sun is setting."

"I like that idea," Scooter said. "That's what I want you to do—take *Marjorie Jane* out at sunset and scatter my ashes."

"Don't talk like that," I said. "I don't want to think about you dying."

"I don't want to think about it either for a long, long time. That's the point of Rutamentals. Eating better so we can live longer."

"Speaking of Rutamentals, Ben was telling me that you can get food poisoning from eating rutabagas that haven't been refrigerated. Isn't that right, Ben?"

"I'm not sure I'm the best person to ask. I can barely remember what day of the week it is," he replied.

"Nicely dodged," I said, punching him in the arm.

"I thought so too." Ben smiled. "Ned also attached a copy of Emily's obituary. Want me to read it out loud?"

"Sure," I said, taking a swig of my very warm water before passing the bottle to Scooter.

"Emily van der Byl, aged twenty-nine, lifelong resident of Destiny Key, passed away in Coconut Cove on—"

Scooter leaned forward. "Did you say Emily van der Byl?"

"Didn't I pronounce it correctly?" Ben asked.

"I think so," Scooter said. "It's not a very common name. I only know one other person with that name, or rather *knew* one other person—Maarten van der Byl."

"Who's that?" I asked.

"You know that contract dispute I have going on? It's with his company."

"That's odd," I said. "What are the chances of knowing two people with an unusual last name like that?" I turned to Ben. "Does it say anything about her family in the obituary?"

Ben scrolled down. "Yes. It says that she was predeceased by her mother, Laura van der Byl, and her father, Maarten van der Byl. No mention of any other relatives."

Scooter rubbed his temples. "I wish I had known who she was. Maybe I could have spoken with her directly about the contract issues."

"You're assuming she had inherited her father's business," I said.

"That's my understanding. My lawyer mentioned that Maarten van der Byl's daughter took over after his death. That's when we started having issues. They're trying to change all the terms and conditions, payment schedules, intellectual property agreements —everything. They've got so much money that I'm afraid they'll tie us up in court for years, and I'll end up broke in the process."

I tried to reconcile the Emily I had met—a sweet young woman who seemed more interested in fashion than accounting—with a cutthroat business owner out to destroy my husband's livelihood. It was like there had been two different personalities inside her. I thought about this for a moment. Had there been two different personalities or two different people? Had someone else been calling the shots when it came to the Van der Byl business?

***

After the revelations about Emily van der Byl and her father, Scooter got a headache. I gave him a couple of pain relievers and suggested he lie down for a while. Mrs. Moto was in a feisty mood, running back and forth across the boat batting her origami birds, which wasn't doing Scooter's headache much good. So I grabbed my cat and her costume and headed to the marina lounge to work on the alterations in order to give my husband some peace and quiet.

"Stop wiggling," I said to the squirming ball of fur on the couch. "I just need to put this one pin in, and I don't want to stick you with it." After aligning the zipper against the seam and fastening it in place, I pulled the costume over her head and freed her from my grasp. She darted across the room and leaped onto the bookshelf, perching next to a stack of books.

"Don't give me that look. You're the one who wanted to wear this particular outfit. I gave you two options—you coughed up a hairball on the other one and started kneading this one while purring. Your choice was clear. If you want to look your best, then we need to make sure the bottom part fits just right."

Mrs. Moto's response was to knock one of the books onto the floor, then begin washing behind her ears. After folding her costume and setting it on the coffee table, I picked the book up. "Oh, good choice," I said. "I've read this one. Do you want to know whodunit?" I took her loud yowl to be an affirmative. "It was the butler. I know that's a cliché, but in this case, it really was the butler."

After I placed the mystery back on the shelf, she knocked another one down. "This one was trickier," I said as I leafed through the pages. "I thought I knew who the murderer was, but the author had a huge twist at the end. I didn't see it coming."

Another book landed at my feet. "You're really enjoying this game, aren't you?" I asked. A pair of green eyes stared down at me innocently. "Okay, I have to admit, I didn't love this one. The characters were really boring, and unless the characters grab you right away, it doesn't matter how good the plot is. I'm sure you'd agree."

Mrs. Moto meowed loudly, then jumped onto my shoulders. I pulled her into my arms and snuggled her against my neck. "You'd be a great character in a book, wouldn't you? There wouldn't even have to be a plot. Just a bunch of scenes of you doing cute things. If you kept a journal of what you did every day, we could publish that. It'd be a bestseller."

The door burst open, startling Mrs. Moto and causing her to dig her claws into my chest. But when she saw who had entered the lounge, she meowed, then jumped onto the floor to greet her admirers.

"Here, kitty, kitty," Katy called. She sat on the floor and coaxed the cat into her lap. Her little brother, Sam, plopped down next to her, and they took turns petting Mrs. Moto. While the three of them were occupied, I sat back down on the couch and pulled a sewing kit out of my bag. I picked the cat costume up and started to stitch the zipper in place.

"Ouch!" I said as I pricked my finger with the needle.

"Are you okay?" Katy asked.

"I'll be fine." I walked over to the kitchenette, which ran along one side of the lounge, and grabbed a paper towel. Pressing down on my wound, I sat at the small table by the window and stared outside. There was nothing quite like people-watching at a marina. The types of folks who were drawn to living on boats were often quirky and had fascinating backstories. Some of them were trying to reinvent themselves, escaping from the day-to-day grind of working in a corporate job. Others were drawn to the sea and wanted to enjoy a simple life off the grid. And then there were those whose backstories remained a mystery, like Wanda. How had she ended up in Coconut Cove at the Palm Tree Marina?

"What's this?" Katy asked, pointing at Mrs. Moto's costume.

"Yeah, what's this?" Sam echoed as he put part of the costume on his head.

"It's for the pet-costume competition," I said.

"Cats don't wear costumes," Katy said. "Only dogs do."

"This cat does." I removed the piece from Sam's head and smoothed it out. "Don't you think she's going to look adorable in it?"

"What is it?" Sam asked.

"Don't you recognize it?" They both shook their heads. "We really need to do something about the educational system in our country."

"I don't like school," Sam said.

"You're only five," I said. "What's not to like about school? Aren't there crayons involved?"

Katy tugged on my arm. "I like school. My teacher puts stickers on my worksheets."

"Stickers are good," I said. "We could all use more stickers in our lives."

While the three of us were talking about our favorite stickers—Katy was partial to dinosaurs while Sam liked the ones from the latest Pixar movie—Ned came into the lounge. "There the two of you are," he said. "Your mom is here to pick you up. She's in a rush, so you better hurry up. Give your grandpa a kiss goodbye first though."

After both Ned and Mrs. Moto got kisses goodbye, he walked over to the coffee machine. "Want a cup, Mollie?"

"That would be great. Extra cream if you have it."

Ned brought two mugs over and set them on the coffee table. As he settled into the couch, the pile of books on the floor caught his eye. "What's that about?"

"Mrs. Moto was trying to pick something out to read. She likes a good bedtime story. Don't worry. I'll put everything back later." I took a sip of my coffee. It was delicious—pure caffeine and half-and-half. Not a rutabaga to be found. "Ben was telling us about Emily's memorial service earlier."

"It sounds like it will be a nice tribute to her," Ned said. "You guys are still coming, aren't you?"

"Of course...although now it might be a little weird."

"Weird?" After I explained the connection between Emily's father and Scooter's business dealings, Ned frowned. "That is strange. But I hope you'll still attend the service. Jeff doesn't have anything to do with Van der Byl's company, and the memorial is really about supporting Jeff during his time of grief."

"You're right. I'm sure Scooter will see it that way." I went to the fridge and added some more cream to my cup to cool it down. As I stirred my coffee, I said, "Thinking about it, the memorial service might also be a good opportunity to talk to some of Emily's family and friends. Maybe they can shed some light on what this contract dispute is all about."

"She doesn't have any family, remember?"

I sat back down on the couch next to Mrs. Moto and scratched her belly. "That's right. But her friends will be there."

"I'm not sure about that either. According to Jeff, Emily led a pretty sheltered life. I don't think she had too many friends, and any that she had live on Destiny Key."

"So, why wouldn't they come? There's a ferry from the island to the mainland."

"You haven't lived here long enough to know much about Destiny Key. The inhabitants are a pretty reclusive bunch. They rarely leave the island."

"Makes you wonder how Jeff met Emily," I said.

Ned smiled. "Sometimes, I think you have more curiosity than a cat."

"Hopefully I have as many lives," I said.

"I think you must have, considering the dangerous situations you've found yourself in. How many bodies is it that you've found in Coconut Cove?"

I sighed. Tallying up my murder victim count seemed to be a popular pastime among local residents. I think they liked to keep their math skills sharp. "Five," I said. "But getting back to Jeff, you've got to be curious about how he met Emily too. We'll have to ask him about it at the memorial."

"That would probably be the perfect opportunity. He'll want to reminisce about his time with her. And it might also be your only opportunity, as he's leaving on a business trip next week."

"What kind of business is he in?" I asked.

"He's a pharmaceutical sales rep," Ned said. "He's got a lot of big clients all over the country. Internationally too."

I thought back to the disagreement that Jeff and Chief Dalton's ex-wife had had over herbal remedies versus drugs that doctors prescribed. Jeff had certainly seemed to know a lot about the subject and had warned us of the dangers of medicines that weren't regulated. If only we had known at the time that his warnings would turn out to be prescient. Emily did end up dying as a result of being poisoned by an overdose of an herbal remedy.

* * *

After Ned left, I picked the books up off the floor and set them back on the shelf. All except one—a cozy mystery that featured a corgi—which I decided to borrow. Although Mrs. Moto would have preferred a book that had a cat as a central character, I thought it would be fun to read about how a dog helped solve a murder investigation. Plus, it might give us some insight into the canine mind and get a leg up on the pet-costume competition.

Next, I washed the mugs in the sink and put them in the drying rack. After wiping down the counter, I tried to shoo Mrs. Moto off the table by the window so I could clean it as well. She wasn't having it. Instead, she pawed at a brown leather notebook, which was sitting next to a set of salt and pepper shakers and a napkin dispenser. She poked her nose in between the pages and pushed the front cover open.

"We have our own book," I said, showing her the corgi mystery. "Why don't you sleep on that instead of someone else's?" Mrs. Moto rolled on her back and stretched out all four of her legs, obscuring the pages. I lifted her off and set her on the chair. She hopped back on the table and made a beeline for the notebook. This time, I used more common sense. I pulled a napkin out of the dispenser, crumpled it up, and tossed it across the room. While she bounded after it, I picked the notebook up to close it. That's when I recognized the distinctive green ink, precise, compact letters, and dots over the *i*'s and *j*'s as Wanda's handiwork.

She must have forgotten it. Maybe it was a journal of some kind. I decided to stop by her boat to return it to her. But before I could get up to collect my bag and the pet costume, Mrs. Moto jumped back on the table and butted her head against my arm, jostling the book out of my hand. She used her nose again to push several of the pages over. Then she sat on top of the open notebook and yowled.

"What is going on with you?" I plucked the cat off and placed her in my lap. She continued to yowl. "I wish you'd use your words," I said. "Although, I guess you are. Your feline equivalent of words. What are you trying to say?"

Mrs. Moto reached out and pressed her paw on the notebook before staring intently at me. "Do you want me to read this? Don't you think that would be nosy, reading someone's journal?"

When it comes to stare-downs, my cat always wins. I finally relented and pulled the notebook toward me. It was a journal. The page that Mrs. Moto had opened the notebook to was dated a couple of weeks prior. I shivered as I read what Wanda had written:

I made a vow on my sister's grave that I would avenge her death. But I was a coward. I could never bring myself to do what needed to be done. To destroy the person who had destroyed my sister. Year after year went by and I did nothing. I just waited and watched. No action, no vengeance, just waiting and watching. An exile without any purpose.

I can't wait and watch anymore. Not with her flaunting it in my face. Her success, her happiness, her youth. All of that should have been my sister's. She doesn't deserve it. She doesn't deserve anything.

This time it's going to be different. This time I'm going to be strong. This time I'm going to do what needs to be done.

I felt my skin go clammy. I put the journal down on the table, then scooped Mrs. Moto up and hugged her, burrowing my face in her fur. She licked my cheek before wriggling out of my arms. She flipped a few more pages over with her paw and meowed quietly. I took a deep breath, then bent over the book. This entry was from Monday.

How could the wrong girl have been taken? How could this have happened? How am I supposed to mourn while I'm in exile?

I can hear my sister from her grave, calling to me. Don't worry, dear sister, this time, she will die.

CHAPTER 13
THE WISDOM OF YODA

HOLY BUCKETS! WHAT WOULD YOU do if you had read something like that? Wanda seemed like such an ordinary woman—she lived on a sailboat, made money doing food demonstrations at the grocery store, wore legwarmers, and led a quiet life—but I guess she wasn't ordinary after all. Unless scribbling homicidal journal entries was normal. I'm pretty sure it wasn't.

One of my favorite quotes from *The Empire Strikes Back* popped into my head: "Once you start down the dark path, forever will it dominate your destiny." I had always liked how Yoda uttered that phrase with that cute speech pattern and accent of his, but now it had taken on a new meaning. Wanda's grief over her sister's death had caused her to take a very, very dark path toward murder. And not just one murder, but two murders. Penelope's life was in danger.

"Come on, Mrs. Moto," I said. "We've got to get out of here!"

I grabbed the journal and stuck it in my bag along with the corgi mystery and the pet costume. Mrs. Moto must have sensed the urgency of our mission, because she sat quietly while I put her harness and leash on.

We dashed out the door while I dialed the chief. "What do you mean he isn't at the police station?" I demanded of the woman who answered the phone. "He's at the festival? Doesn't he know there's a murderer on the loose?"

I hung up and quickly texted Penelope, warning her to avoid Wanda. Then I sped toward the waterfront park. After asking around, I heard that the chief was where I least expected him to be—at his ex-wife's art booth.

Anabel was busy with some potential customers, helping them to decide which painting would look better displayed over their mantel. My vote would have been for the one of fairies dancing around a toadstool, but they seemed partial to one of an elf family picnicking on a beach. The chief was sitting on a stool underneath a nearby tree feeding Frick and Frack treats.

"There you are!" I said after I caught my breath. "I've been searching for you everywhere!"

The burly man stood, then pointed at the doggie bed in the corner of Anabel's stand. "Lie down." After the Yorkies were convinced to settle down, he turned to me and raised both of his eyebrows. "Looks like you've found me."

I reached into my bag and thrust the evidence into his hands. "Read this."

"I'm not sure this is my cup of tea," the chief said. "Now, if it was about Yorkies instead of a corgi, then maybe."

"Oops. Sorry, wrong one," I said, exchanging the cozy mystery for the journal.

"It's nicely bound," he said, turning it over in his hands. "I like the decorative pattern on the leather."

"I'm not showing you this because of how it looks. It's proof that Wanda is the murderer." I grabbed the journal out of his hands, flipped the pages to the relevant entries, and passed it back to him. "Start here."

The chief's eyebrows were eerily still while he was reading. "Where did you find this?" he asked when he was finished.

"I didn't find it. Mrs. Moto did."

"Of course she did."

"Really, she did. It was sitting on the table in the marina lounge. I didn't pay any attention to it until Mrs. Moto pointed out its significance."

"I see. Will you excuse me for a moment?" The chief walked

toward the waterfront while he talked to someone on his phone. I desperately wanted to follow him and listen in, but Anabel had finished up with her customers and wanted to know what was going on.

"I've just given your ex-husband an important clue that's going to crack open the murder investigation and save someone's life. He's probably on his way to arrest the culprit now."

She put her hands over her mouth and gasped. "I hope Tiny takes backup. I always get so worried." Frick and Frack, no doubt sensing their mom's distress, rushed over and began barking. She bent down and gave them a cuddle. "It's okay. Your daddy is going to be okay."

Mrs. Moto decided to get in on the cuddling. She barged in between the two dogs and butted Anabel's hand, catching her by surprise. I held my breath, waiting to see how she would react. "Okay, but just this once," Anabel said as she tentatively scratched the top of Mrs. Moto's head.

"Can I get you anything?" I asked. "You seem a little shaky."

"Can you grab me a rutabaga juice? Feel free to get one for yourself too."

"I think I'll pass," I said. "Why don't you go sit on that stool and I'll bring it over."

While I dug through the assortment of bottles in the cooler—who knew there were so many varieties of rutabaga juice available—Frick and Frack crawled into their doggie bed. Mrs. Moto followed, her leash dragging behind her. The three of them looked pretty adorable snuggled up together.

"I used to find her in my condo like that," Anabel said. "When she wasn't napping with Frick and Frack, I'd find her eating their dog food."

I sat on the ground next to Anabel and ran my fingers through the cool grass, trying to figure out how to broach the subject of the letter she had sent us. After a few moments, I went for the direct approach. "Listen, I'm really sorry she kept getting into your place, but why didn't you just talk to us about it and let us know it was a problem?"

"I don't know." She fiddled with the lid on her juice bottle while she stared at the people wandering through the booths, hunting for that perfect souvenir from the Coconut Cove Boating Festival. "I guess, if I'm honest, it's because it gave me an excuse to talk with Tiny. He came over one afternoon and listened to me complain about the cat hair. It was nice having a conversation with him about something other than joint custody of our dogs. I went to the station the next day to talk with him about it some more, and he told me he didn't have time. Then I think things just escalated from there. I guess I took out my anger at Tiny on you guys."

"I get it," I said. "Scooter tells me that sometimes I let things get out of hand."

"Do you think we could just forget about everything that's happened and move on?"

"Sure," I said. "Water under the bridge." Mrs. Moto looked at us and meowed softly. "I think she forgives you too. Either that or she wants one of those dog treats."

* * *

I had another sleepless night. If Chief Dalton thought I had an overactive imagination during my waking hours, he'd be amazed at what my mind came up with while I was sleeping. My nightmares were getting stranger and stranger. The latest one featured giant rutabagas wearing Trixie Tremblay T-shirts and polka-dotted legwarmers and chasing after me on stilts. I wasn't sure what I found more disturbing—the fact that the rutabagas had somehow grown legs and could move around unaided or the fact that I thought their legwarmers were cute.

While Scooter made our morning smoothies, I checked my phone. Despite having sent Penelope several texts warning her about Wanda the previous day, she hadn't replied. My stomach churned. I really hoped that meant that Wanda hadn't gotten to her first. I dialed the police station and asked to be connected to the chief. After the receptionist asked who was calling, she told me that the chief had left a message for me: "No comment."

I choked down my smoothie while drawing some unflattering pictures of the chief's eyebrows in my notebook. It was a therapeutic way to deal with my annoyance. They actually looked very realistic. Maybe I was more artistic than I realized. I'd have to show my drawings to Anabel and ask her what she thought. Art classes might be in my future.

I finally dragged myself out of bed and headed to the waterfront park. I was scheduled to man the FAROUT booth that morning. If I hadn't been running late, I would have stopped by the Sugar Shack to check on Penelope beforehand. Fortunately, I didn't have plans for the afternoon, which would give me time to visit her, as well as finish Mrs. Moto's costume.

Anabel was setting up her artwork when I got there. I helped her hang a large painting of a leprechaun riding on the back of the Loch Ness monster while it swam through the water. I have to confess that I was a little confused by it at first—leprechauns were indigenous to Ireland and the Loch Ness monster lived in Scotland —but then she explained that the Loch Ness monster had actually spread worldwide. There was even one living in Lake Okeechobee in the middle of Florida. It was quite reclusive, so most people weren't aware that it was there.

Then she confided to me that if she sold that painting, it would cover her mortgage payments for several months. After hearing that, I definitely decided to look into art classes. Perhaps I could make a small fortune selling watercolor paintings of the chief's eyebrows.

When I asked Anabel if she had heard from her ex-husband, she got a little teary-eyed, so I dropped the subject. I tried to reassure myself that he had everything under control. Surely, Wanda was locked up in a cell. Penelope's cell phone battery had died, and she was safe and sound at the Sugar Shack whipping up a batch of muffins. At least, that's what I told myself.

I was organizing T-shirts when I heard a cheery voice call out, "Get your free Rutamentals sample here!" My jaw dropped when I saw Wanda standing only a few feet away holding a large tray and trying to convince people about the health benefits of carob-covered rutabagas. My hands started shaking, and the T-shirts tumbled to the ground. As I bent down to pick them up, I bumped my head against the table. When I looked up, I found myself staring into a pair of homicidal green eyes.

"What are you doing here?" I spluttered. I reached into my bag and tried to pull out something to protect myself with. The best I could come up with was my trusty roll of breath mints. If only I had stuck with those karate classes. Fresh breath wasn't really going to be an effective self-defense strategy. Bad breath maybe, but not fresh, minty breath.

"One of the other gals is watching the Rutamentals booth, so I decided to stroll through the park and hand out samples." She waved a gooey brown lump in front of my face. "One taste of these and people will be flocking to our booth to sign up for the program. Go on, try it. You'll be surprised how much carob tastes like chocolate."

I took a step backward. "Surprised? I'll tell you what I'm surprised about, that you're walking around free."

Wanda set the tray on the table and wagged her finger at me. "You know, I should be mad at you. That was very naughty what you did—giving the chief my journal. It was private."

I glanced over at Anabel and frantically tried to make eye contact. Fortunately for her, she was busy making a sale. Unfortunately for me, she didn't notice I was alone with a homicidal maniac.

"Cat got your tongue?" Wanda asked. "Speaking of, where is that cat of yours? Chief Dalton said she found my journal."

For once I was glad Mrs. Moto had decided to stay on the boat with Scooter rather than keep me company. "Don't you dare hurt her!"

Wanda pursed her lips. "Why would I hurt her? Don't you think you're overreacting?" She smiled. "Kind of like how you overreacted when you read my journal. Like I told the chief, it didn't mean anything. It's just an exercise my therapist has me do. By writing about things that anger or frustrate us on a daily basis, we can process our feelings and let go of our negative emotions."

"The things you wrote about were pretty out there. These weren't everyday frustrations you were talking about," I said. "You wrote about murder, for goodness' sake."

"You're right, Mollie. I wrote about some serious things." She sighed. "I've experienced some very painful things in my past. I'm still angry to this day about what happened to my sister. But you have to believe me. I would never actually hurt anyone."

"What exactly happened to your sister?"

Her eyes welled up with tears. "My therapist says I should confide in other people. I've never told anyone other than him what happened, but since you've read my journal, I might as well tell you." She pointed at the chairs set up behind the table. "Mind if I sit down?"

"Uh, sure," I said. There were enough people milling around that I didn't think she'd try anything. Still, to be on the safe side, I didn't plan on eating anything that she had prepared. Not even poison could enhance the taste of rutabaga.

Wanda ran her fingers through her long dark hair and took a deep breath. "Okay, here goes. My brother-in-law killed my sister."

"That's awful! He murdered her?"

"She committed suicide, but he drove her to it. Although it wasn't murder in the technical sense, she wouldn't be dead if it wasn't for him. He betrayed her in the worst possible way." Tears flowed down her cheeks. "She was only twenty-five. She left behind a..." I handed her a tissue. After blowing her nose, she continued. "She left behind a beautiful four-year-old girl. I couldn't bear it. My sister and I had been so close. We did everything together. We were best friends."

Wanda started sobbing uncontrollably. I shifted uneasily in my chair. People were staring at us. Anabel mouthed, "Are you okay?"

I nodded, then gently patted the distraught woman on her back. "There, there," I said, which was such a stupid thing to say. What do people mean when they say that while consoling someone? It's not like you're pointing at something when you say it—There, there, look at that there. Over there. There, there. *Get a grip, Mollie,* I told myself. *You're starting to channel Dr. Seuss.*

"Can I get you something to drink?" I asked. Another pretty banal thing to say, but it got Dr. Seuss out of my head.

"Do you have any rutabaga juice?" she asked.

"You're sure you don't want something with some sugar and caffeine instead? That's what I turn to when I'm stressed."

Wanda glanced down at her Trixie Tremblay T-shirt. "No, I'll stick with the juice. Live Healthy, Live Long, Live Strong.”

“Okay, coming right up.” I scooted over to Anabel’s booth. “Can I snag a juice from you?”

“Sure.” She scratched her head. “Didn’t you tell me that she’s a murderer?”

“Uh-huh.”

“Um, far be it from me to judge, but do you think it’s a good idea to be having a drink with her?”

I held up my hands. “Honestly, I don’t know what to think right now. When I read her journal yesterday, I was convinced she was a killer. But now, I’m not so sure. She said her therapist told her to write that stuff down. You wouldn’t believe the horrifying story she told me about her sister. I think she might just be a messed-up lady.”

“Hmm. Maybe you’re right. Besides, if she was a killer, Tiny would have locked her up.”

A sense of relief washed over me. “That’s true. She isn’t in custody, so her story must have checked out.” I squeezed Anabel’s hand. “Thanks for that and for the juice.”

After I handed Wanda the bottle, I apologized for reading her journal and giving it to the police.

“That’s okay. I probably would have done the same thing in your shoes,” she said. While she sipped her juice, I noticed a slight grimace on her face. Was it possible that the Trixie Tremblay spokesperson didn’t like the taste of the products she was selling? “You sure you don’t want some?” Wanda asked.

“Oh, I’m sure. I think I’ll stick to water.” I tapped my finger on my lips. “I hope you don’t mind me asking, but who were you talking about in your journal? Were the women you wrote about Emily and Penelope?”

Wanda’s eyes grew wide, and she started coughing. She set her bottle on the table. “Sorry, it must have gone down the wrong way. Why would I have written about Emily and Penelope? I didn’t really know either of them.”

“But you wrote about the wrong girl dying. I assumed that referred to Emily. Then you talked about another girl who didn’t deserve to live. Wasn’t that a reference to Penelope?”

“Goodness, no. It doesn’t have anything to do with present-day. I was writing about what happened in the past. The wrong girl was my sister. She didn't deserve to die."

"Then who was the other girl?"

Wanda bit her lip. "My brother-in-law had an affair. It referred to his mistress. It's what drove my sister to…"

I squeezed her hands. "It's okay. I didn't mean to dig up painful memories."

She pulled her hands back and folded them in her lap. "The chief did say that you fancy yourself an amateur investigator. If you're really interested in who's after Penelope, then you might want to talk to Alan."

"Alan?" I asked in disbelief. "Why would he want to kill her?"

"He was in love with Penelope, but she refused to go out with him. He got really angry."

"Angry enough to kill?"

"Emily's death is proof of that," she said.

I thought about this for a minute. If you had asked me a few weeks ago if mild-mannered, meek-as-a-mouse Alan could fly into a jealous rage and murder someone, I would have laughed. But I remembered the confrontation he'd had with Jeff before the sailing race. There had been a look in Alan's eyes that had frightened me. Maybe he was capable of violence.

Wanda patted my hand. "The chief and I had a long talk about it. You don't need to worry. He has everything under control. They're conducting some lab tests. Once he gets the results back, he'll arrest Alan, and Coconut Cove can go back to being the pleasant, sleepy tourist town that it is."

* * *

"Are you ready to go, my little Milk Dud?" Scooter asked.

"Well, that depends on where we're going," I said. "Is there going to be lunch involved?"

"I think that could be arranged."

"Then I'll be ready in five minutes." After I explained to the volunteer who had arrived at the FAROUT booth for the afternoon shift which T-shirts were on sale, I grabbed my bag and put my arm through Scooter's. "Where do you want to eat at?"

"I would say the Rutamentals booth, but after you told me about Wanda's journal, I'm hesitant to go there."

I was torn. Scooter was on the cusp of being persuaded to have hot dogs instead of rutabagas. If I let him continue to believe that Wanda had a deft touch with using poison as a seasoning, that would be unfair to her. But the price of telling him about her therapy and her tragic past was that he'd probably opt for the "healthy" choice.

My big mistake was glancing up at him. One look at those dark-brown puppy-dog eyes of his and I sang like a canary. I waited nervously while he thought about what I had said. For the record, it turned out that telling the truth worked in my favor this time.

"Hmm. I suppose that means we could eat something that has Trixie Tremblay's blessing on it," Scooter said. "But maybe we deserve a treat. We've been doing really well on our diet. I'm sure having one hot dog wouldn't do any harm."

Falling off the wagon never tasted so good, I thought to myself as I piled extra sauerkraut on my dog. Scooter moaned with pleasure as he took a bite of his. After handing him an extra napkin, I went in for the kill. "Wanna get some ice cream after this?"

Scooter took a swallow of his soda. "I'm not sure we should."

"We don't have to get sundaes," I said. "They sell small cones. Surely, one little scoop of ice cream would be okay. Even Trixie Tremblay must have a treat from time to time."

"I guess..."

"Good. I'm glad we're in agreement." I wiped some mustard off Scooter's cheek. "You won't regret this."

After we got our dessert—double chocolate chip for me and raspberry swirl for Scooter—we walked toward the waterfront and sat at one of the picnic tables next to the public docks. Fishing and charter boats tied up there to offload their catch and pick up passengers. One of Norm's boats, the newly christened *ET*, was coming into port. A bunch of college-aged kids on spring break disembarked. A good-natured argument broke out about who had caught the biggest fish.

"It seems like Norm's charter business is benefiting from

visitors to the festival," I said.

Scooter licked the ice cream that was dripping down the side of his cone. "Do you think he'll be able to juggle his business with being mayor?"

"Bite your tongue," I said. "Let's pray he doesn't get elected."

"Isn't that Mike over there?" Scooter smiled. "Hopefully, he's not making a campaign contribution."

"Maybe it's time that you got into politics," I mused. "I think you'd make a fine mayor. You tick all the boxes—you're honest, trustworthy, reliable, and you look good in green."

"What does green have to do with running for office?"

"Isn't it obvious? Green has—"

"Hey there," Mike said. He slapped Scooter on his back, jostling his elbow. I looked on in dismay as his ice cream toppled off his cone and onto the table. "Oh, man, I'm sorry about that. Let me get you another one."

"No, it's okay," Scooter said glumly. "It was probably a sign that I shouldn't be eating it."

I hurriedly finished my ice cream before he decided that the sign also applied to me. "What were you doing talking to Norm?" I asked as I licked the last of the double chocolate chip off my fingers. "I'm surprised to see the two of you so chummy after the sailboat accident."

Mike stroked his goatee. "We came to an agreement."

"You mean he paid you off?" I asked.

"Something like that. Let's just say we've put our differences aside for the moment to focus on something more important— making the arrangements for Emily's memorial service tomorrow. Jeff asked if I could help out."

"He chartered Norm's boat?" Scooter asked.

"Yeah. He gave him a good rate."

"Norm must want something from him," I said.

Scooter laughed. "His vote." He turned to Mike. "It's nice of you to help Jeff out."

"That's what friends are for," he said. "And I have an idea of what she would have wanted. Plenty of yellow roses and the soundtrack to *Mamma Mia!*"

"I thought you didn't know Emily," I said. "How would you

know about the flowers and music?"

"It's hot today, isn't it," Mike said. He grabbed one of the napkins on the table and wiped his brow.

"Not really," I said. "It's actually quite pleasant. I don't think the temperature is why you're breaking out in a sweat." I patted the seat next to me. "Why don't you take a load off."

"Um, I should probably get going," Mike said with a slight stammer.

"Sit," I said, doing my best imitation of Nancy. It worked. Mike planted his butt on the bench next to me. "What I don't understand is why you've been pretending not to know Emily. I already know you drew up her will."

Mike's jaw dropped. "You do?"

"I do now." By this point, his napkin was soaking wet. I passed him another. "Why have you been keeping it a secret? Wouldn't it impress potential clients if they knew you were doing work for such a big estate?"

"It wasn't my idea," he said. "Her family is very secretive. They don't like outsiders knowing about their business. When I first started working for her father—"

"Maarten van der Byl, right?" Scooter asked.

Mike nodded slowly, then leaned forward. "You might want to keep that name to yourself," he said softly.

Scooter banged his fist on the table. "Why should I do that? He's putting the screws into me from the grave. Don't pretend like you didn't know it was his company that I've been having contract disputes with."

Stunned by my husband's uncharacteristic outburst, I found myself at a loss as to what to say next. I watched as Scooter drummed his fingers on the table while Mike tried his best to avoid eye contact. "How about some more ice cream?" I suggested. Unsurprisingly, that fell flat.

"How about some answers, Mike," Scooter said.

"The Van der Byls are one of the families who founded Destiny Key. They have a lot of money, and they use that to buy people's silence." He gulped. "Including mine. I've done some things I'm not proud of."

"Like trying to destroy my company."

"No," Mike said. "I didn't have anything to do with Mr. Van der Byl's business interests. The only thing I dealt with was the family's estate planning."

"Then you can tell us about Emily's will," I said.

Mike blanched. "No. I can't."

"You're going to tell us something," Scooter said.

"Listen, I know the firm that represents the Van der Byl's business side of things. Maybe I can try to find out what's going on with the contract."

"And you can tell us about Emily," I said.

"I've already told everything I know to the police," Mike said.

I furrowed my brow. "Does that mean you're a suspect?" At the rate sweat was dripping down his face, Mike was in danger of becoming dehydrated. I offered him some of my water.

"Me? Why would I be a suspect? I don't stand to gain anything from Emily's death. But if you want to know who I think the police have in their sights, I can—"

Before Mike could spill the beans, he was interrupted by the screams of a young girl. She had her hands over her mouth and was staring at something lying on the ground next to the dock.

The three of us leaped up and raced toward her. It turned out it wasn't a something lying on the ground. It was a someone, and her name was Wanda.

I leaned down to check on her while Scooter dialed 911. She was breathing shallowly, her eyelids fluttering as she fought to stay conscious. As I stroked her forehead and told her that help was on the way, she whispered my name.

"Ssh. Don't say anything. Save your breath, Wanda," I said.

"Mollie," she said weakly. I put my ear against her mouth to hear her better. "Alan. It was Alan. He poisoned me."

CHAPTER 14
MICE IN TUTUS

THE COCONUT COVE GRAPEVINE WAS working overtime. I woke up to several texts updating me on Wanda's status. She was going to be fine, but the doctor wanted to keep her in the hospital for another day for observation. With any luck, she'd be discharged on Saturday morning.

The grapevine was silent on two key issues: (1) what Wanda had been poisoned with and (2) what the story with Alan was. I didn't even bother calling the police station for an update, as I was sure I'd get a two-word response: "No comment." So I fired up my laptop to do my own research.

After being distracted for a few minutes by cat videos on YouTube (could Mrs. Moto be the next internet sensation?), I typed Alan's name into the search bar, pressed Enter, and held my breath. Fortunately, Google searches took less than a second to pull up a list of results, so I didn't really have to hold my breath, something I was never very good at. I always ended up hiccoughing, which wasn't great when you were trying to rescue the sunglasses your cat had batted into the deep end of the pool.

While Alan didn't make a huge impression in real life, preferring to blend into the background, he had a big presence online. I found three websites—one for his photography business, one for his nonfiction books (apparently his DIY guide on how to winterize composting toilets hit the bestseller list in Mongolia), and a blog where he posted articles on a number of fascinating topics, including...wait for it...yep, you guessed it—poisonous substances.

Our mild-mannered photographer wasn't as mild-mannered as he seemed. His descriptions of what different poisons could do to the human body were pretty gruesome. I was particularly interested in his series of posts on the use of poisons in different television shows. He rated each one on how difficult it was for the murderer to obtain the poison in question and how realistic the depiction of the poisoning was. In his introduction, he stated that he wanted to provide this information as a resource for mystery writers. Then he added a disclaimer: "Don't try any of these at home, unless you can be sure you won't get caught. LOL!"

LOL indeed. It was time to find out more about Alan's background. I clicked on his bio. Turns out he had an advanced degree in biology and had worked in a research lab for many years. After becoming a little too attached to the test mice (he kept sneaking them into his briefcase and taking them home), he had an epiphany—by "epiphany," I think he meant he had been fired for mice-napping—and he made a career change, becoming a photographer.

Alan also had a YouTube channel, which featured a number of videos of mice doing adorable things. Mrs. Moto was entranced by the tiny outfits they wore while they walked across a miniature balance beam. I was entranced by the beadwork on their tutus. Alan apparently was handy not just with winterizing composting toilets but also with needlework.

As I watched a mouse swinging on a trapeze, I realized that Alan had never shown me the video he had taken the day of the cake competition. Was that because it revealed him doing something suspicious like poisoning Penelope's slice of cake? Nah, that couldn't be it. If that had been captured on video, the chief would have arrested him for the murder at the outset. Still, I wondered if there was something the police had missed that Alan didn't want me to see.

I checked my phone again. Still no helpful messages about

what was going on with Wanda and Alan. It was time to go directly to the ultimate source of information in Coconut Cove—the Sailor's Corner Cafe.

* * *

"*Hola.* What can I get you, *chica*?" Alejandra asked as she set a cup of coffee down in front of me.

"Nothing, just the coffee," I said in an admirable display of willpower.

"Are you sure? The chef's got a new special—smothered fries."

"What are they smothered in?" I asked. "Not that I want any. It's just professional curiosity."

"Gravy, cheese, bacon, onions, bell peppers, sour cream, grated rutabaga—"

"Did you say rutabaga?"

"It's the latest craze," she said. "People are requesting it on everything. Even if they're not hardcore into Rutamentals, they're adding small amounts of rutabaga to other dishes to get the health benefits. So, one order of fries for you?"

I shuddered. "Thanks, but I think I'll stick to coffee."

A few minutes later, I was chowing down on smothered fries, minus the rutabaga. Willpower is so overrated.

When Alejandra came back to refill my coffee, I asked her if she had overheard any juicy tidbits during the morning rush. She looked around the cafe. The few people who were there had been served, and no one was waiting to be seated. She slid into the chair opposite me and rolled her shoulders back and forth. "I'm so stiff," she said.

"Waitressing is hard work," I said.

"Nah, that's a piece of cake compared to the Trixie Tremblay boot camp I enrolled in." She twisted her head from side to side, then stretched her arms over her head.

"Don't tell me you're a convert too."

"I sure am, *chica*. I have so much more energy now. You should try it."

I glanced under the table. Sure enough, Alejandra was wearing legwarmers. How had I missed them earlier? Please tell me that

Scooter hadn't begun sporting legwarmers, and I had failed to notice.

"I get enough exercise working on our boat," I said.

"Fair enough, but remember how you were asking me if I'd heard any good gossip about the poisonings?" I nodded. "Well, the place to hear what's really going on isn't here at the cafe, it's at the boot camp. You won't believe what I heard this morning."

I leaned forward, eager for her to spill the beans. She glanced around to make sure that no one needed anything. "Penelope told me that—"

"Wait a minute. This is huge news!"

"But I haven't told you any news yet."

"Yes, you have. You said Penelope was at the Trixie Tremblay boot camp. Do you know what that means?" Alejandra shook her head. "It means the end of the Sugar Shack as we know it. She's going to stop serving cookies, pies, cakes, basically everything that makes life worth living."

"Relax. It was the first time Penelope had attended. A friend invited her. She's been going a bit stir crazy—the police have tried to limit her movements to the bakery and her home, and she has protection around the clock. But she was able to convince them to let her attend an exercise class, provided one of the officers went with her."

"So she's not wearing legwarmers yet?"

Alejandra smiled. "Nope, I think you're safe for now. Although she was talking about creating a special line of Trixie Tremblay-inspired muffins."

"That's a relief. So what was your news?"

"Between you and me, Penelope told me about Alan asking her out."

"Ooh, that's interesting. Wanda mentioned something about that." I used a spoon to scoop up the last of the gravy from my plate. "What happened?"

"He came to the Sugar Shack to do an interview with her. At first, the questions seemed pretty normal. He asked how she got into baking, about the culinary awards she had won, the challenges in starting your own business, that kind of thing. Then he began asking her some really odd questions. Originally, she thought the interview was for the local newspaper, but when the article never got published, she checked and found out he had made that up."

"What kinds of questions did he ask?"

"About her family. He had some information on her mother, but he asked her what she knew regarding her father." Alejandra did a few more stretches. "The thing is, she doesn't know anything about her father. Her mom raised her on her own, and she clammed up whenever Penelope would ask her about her father. Alan's questions made her feel really uncomfortable."

"I hope she told him that he was asking inappropriate things."

"You know what she's like. She's so sweet. She never tells anyone when she doesn't like something. She can't stand hurting people's feelings."

I remembered how Penelope hadn't wanted to award prizes at the cake competition. I didn't recall her saying anything negative about anyone's cake. Nancy could probably learn a thing or two from her about diplomacy. "So what happened next?" I asked.

"He switched over to the topic of genetic diseases. He asked her if she had any medical conditions."

"Surely she slugged him by this point."

"Nope. She kept smiling and offering him cookies."

"She's too sweet for her own good," I said.

"Good thing she owns a bakery. A sweet lady selling sweet things. It's the perfect fit for her." Alejandra did a few more neck stretches, then reluctantly got up from the table. "The lunchtime crowd is going to start coming in soon, and those tables aren't going to clean themselves."

As I finished sipping my coffee, I thought about Alan's devious behavior. Faking a newspaper interview to try to pry information out of Penelope was pretty low. Why in the world was he so interested in her family and her medical history?

While I pondered this, I sent my mom a text.

Any genetic diseases in our family I should know about?

I had come to the conclusion that I didn't have a secret twin sister named Mary. It had probably been my mom's idea of a joke. She rolled on the floor in laughter over knock-knock jokes, which gives you an idea of the sophistication of her humor. I was ninety-nine percent sure there was no way she'd forget to tell me that I had a sibling. But she might have forgotten to tell me something important about my medical history.

A few minutes later, she replied.

Do you mean like Mary's large ears?

Great. We were back to this whole Mary business. I reached up and felt my ears. Were they misshapen too, like Jeff's and Mary's?

* * *

I ran into Alan at the place I least expected—the hairdresser's. I'm one of those people who puts off getting their hair cut until it's so out of control that even Mrs. Moto encourages me to wear a hat in public. Each time I visit the salon, I have renewed hope that it will be the time my frizzy hair is finally tamed once and for all. Instead, I squeal with delight at how sleek and shiny the stylist makes my hair, eagerly buy the latest miracle product, and step outside with a huge grin, only to find the unruly frizz resurfaces within ten minutes' time in the humidity.

Alan was in the back having his hair shampooed. I sat in the chair next to him while I waited for the hairdresser to get an industrial-size container of deep conditioner from the back. I was already convinced that the "Frizz Banishment Gel, Now with Extra Moisturizing Pearls of Liquid Gold and Imported from Siberia for Discerning Ladies" was going to be the answer to my dreams. Intellectually, I knew that it didn't contain any gold and that Siberia probably wasn't where you wanted your beauty products imported from. But I was happy to suspend disbelief. After all, I was certainly a discerning lady.

"Mollie, what are you doing here?" Alan whispered as a towel was wrapped around his head.

I pointed at my frizzy mane. "Turning this into a work of beauty. What about you?"

"I wanted to make an effort for Emily's memorial service," he said.

"Exactly how long did you two date?" I asked.

"Long enough."

"And how long is that?"

"A week," he said as he fiddled with his smock. "But it was enough to know we were meant to be together. If only Jeff hadn't gotten in the way."

Before I could hear more about his ill-fated love affair with Emily, his hairdresser whisked him away to one of the stations. For the next ten minutes, I oohed and aahed during my shampoo. My body felt like it was melting into a puddle of happiness as my head was massaged with the Siberian miracle mix.

As luck would have it, I was shown to the station right next to Alan. I picked up where we left off. "I heard you asked Penelope out. Was that before or after you dated Emily?"

Alan spun his head toward me, causing his stylist to narrowly avoid nicking his ear with the scissors. "Where did you hear that?"

"Oh, you know how small towns are. Nothing stays secret for very long." Alan's hairdresser gently turned his head back toward the mirror and started snipping the hair on his neck. "You know what else isn't a secret," I added. "The fact that Wanda accused you of poisoning her."

Both of our stylists gasped. They were torn between wanting to keep a distance from a potential murderer and wanting to hear all the juicy tidbits so they could pass them on to their other clients. I did notice that Alan's hairdresser kept a firm grip on her scissors.

"That's not true," Alan said emphatically, staring at my reflection in the mirror. "I wasn't even at the festival yesterday. I was photographing a wedding seventy-five miles away from here."

"Can you prove that?" I asked.

He clenched his hands in his lap. "I've already been through this with the chief. There are plenty of witnesses, starting from the bride and groom down to the flower girl and ring bearer. Do you want to talk to them too?"

By this point, Alan's hairdresser had given up all pretense of cutting his hair. He set down his brush and scissors, sat in the chair next to Alan's, and eagerly listened to our exchange. Mine was still combing and sectioning my hair but in a very halfhearted way.

"Why do you think she tried to pin the blame on you? And more importantly, if you didn't do it, who did?"

"Wanda is vindictive," he said. "She doesn't understand what's involved in investigative journalism. She claimed I was sticking my nose in where it didn't belong, and she's been out to get me ever since."

"Well, were you?"

"Was I what?"

"Asking nosy questions?"

"It seems like you're the one asking nosy questions," Alan said with a surprisingly firm tone. It stunned me into silence for a few moments.

"You know, Alan, maybe we're going about this all wrong. You're not just a wedding photographer. You're also an investigative reporter and photojournalist, right?"

"That's correct. I'm in discussions with the local newspaper about a permanent role with them."

I had a feeling his dialogue with the newspaper might be a little one-sided, but I plowed on. "Well, I'm an investigative reporter for FAROUT. We should join forces. Between the two of us, we'd get to the bottom of what's going on a lot faster. You did help me out with my last case, after all."

He grinned from ear to ear. "That's a great idea! We'll be a detective team, like Nick and Nora from the *Thin Man* movies."

"No, they had a dog, Asta, and I'm a cat person."

"Sherlock Holmes and Dr. Watson?"

I shook my head. "I look funny in hats."

"The Hardy Boys?"

"Nope. Nancy Drew all the way for me," I said.

One of the stylists chimed in. "How about the guys from *CHiPs*? They had good hair."

Alan frowned. "That won't work. My mom won't let me ride a motorcycle."

"I've got it," I said. "Shawn Spencer and Burton Guster from *Psych*. You're Gus and I'm Shawn. Shawn pretends to be a psychic in the show. I've met a lot of psychics in my time, so I can pull that off."

"What does Gus do?"

"He has a really good sense of smell," I said. "You can smell things, right?"

Alan furrowed his brow. "Sure."

"What's your favorite scent?"

"I have a candle that smells like cotton candy. I also have a peanut butter scented one. It's—"

"Perfect. Burton Guster it is. Okay, now that that's settled, let's get down to business." I reached down, picked my bag off the floor, and whipped out my notebook. "Here's what I need to know..."

While the stylists worked on our hair, I managed to get Alan to tell me why he had asked Penelope all those strange questions about her family and genetic conditions. It turned out that Emily had put him up to it. On their first date—Alan took her to the video arcade—she suggested that he do a series of profiles on some of Coconut Cove's residents. He was excited about the idea and thought he could pitch it to the local newspaper. Before he could draw up a list of prominent citizens to interview, she handed him her own list. It had only three names on it: Wanda, Penelope, and one of Penelope's mother's old friends.

Penelope's name made some sense. She was a young, local, award-winning business owner, but the other two names didn't. Wanda led a relatively quiet life. She wasn't involved in community activities or the town council and didn't own a business. And speaking with an old friend of Penelope's mom and asking questions about her was just plain odd. Sure, Penelope's mom had worked at the library up until her death—and everyone loved library people—but even that, from Alan's point of view, didn't merit a profile in the paper.

Emily had given him a very specific set of questions to ask. While he rattled them off, I jotted down the highlights in my notebook:

<u>Wanda</u>

1 – When did she move from Destiny Key to Coconut Cove?

At first Wanda denied being from Destiny Key, but after Alan showed her a copy of old property records, she said that she moved to Coconut Cove following the death of her sister twenty-five years ago.

2 - Does she have any family back on Destiny Key?

She stated that she was the only one left in her family. When pressed on the issue, she clammed up.

3 - Why did she leave Destiny Key?

At this point in the interview, she burst into tears. Alan felt terrible. He offered to take publicity shots of her Rutamentals food demonstrations for free to make it up to her.

<u>Penelope</u>

1 - What does she know about her family history? Where did her father come from?

She said she didn't know her father. He had died before she was born. Her mother didn't like to talk about him. Her mom became moody whenever Penelope asked questions about him, so she learned to stop bringing it up. She changed the subject and brought Alan a selection of pastries to try. His favorite was the chocolate éclair.

2 - Does she have any genetic conditions that she inherited from her parents?

Penelope was surprised by Alan's question, but after a while she told him about having a congenital heart condition. She was able to manage it with medications, but had to be careful with certain activities. She didn't know which side of the family she inherited it from. At this point in the interview, Penelope made Alan a latte.

3 - What's the secret to her puff pastry?

Penelope wouldn't share her secret recipe no matter how many times Alan asked.

<u>Cindy, Penelope's Mom's Friend</u>

1 - What was the family history of Penelope's mom? Where did she grow up?

Cindy didn't know anything about her background. They had children the same age. Cindy divorced when her daughter was quite young, so the two of them bonded as fellow single moms. But despite doing so much together, Cindy never learned anything about her life prior to Coconut Cove.

2 - When did she move to Coconut Cove?

A few months before Penelope was born.

3 – How did she support herself with a young baby?

She seemed to be financially independent. She wasn't rich, but she didn't have to worry about putting food on the table and was able to stay home with Penelope when she was young. Later, she got a job working at the local library, but that seemed like it was more for something to do while her daughter was in school, not because she needed the money.

I asked Alan if by any chance Emily had broken up with him after he'd finished the interviews. He admitted that was the case, but was still convinced Jeff was the reason why Emily had ended things.

Eventually, we had to halt our conversation so that my hair could be blown out. It looked amazing! I asked Alan to take a picture of me so I could remember what I looked like before the humidity destroyed my sleek coiffure. As he showed me the photo, I remembered the video from the cake competition. In the spirit of our newfound partnership, he was more than happy to pull it up on my tablet.

"But you can't really tell what happened," I complained. "All I see is a bunch of people milling around. What we need is a clear shot of who put the poison on the cake slice."

Alan replayed the video at a slower speed. We watched as Nancy cut four slices from each cake—one for each judge—and placed them on the different-colored plates that Norm handed her. Penelope and Chief Dalton then carried the plates over to the small tables set up at the back for the judges. All the blue ones were placed on the chief's table, the green ones on Norm's table, the white ones on Nancy's table, and the ill-fated purple ones on Penelope's table.

"Okay, so it didn't happen then," I said. "You can clearly see Nancy's and Norm's hands as they plated up the cake slices. Neither of them got out a bottle and doused one of the slices with gelsemium. And it couldn't have been when Penelope and the chief carried the plates over. There's no way Penelope would poison herself, and if Chief Dalton did it, then we've got bigger things to worry about."

"Have a look here," Alan said. "After they set the cake slices on the tables, all the contestants and judges gathered around to check out the display."

"What's Scooter doing there?" I watched as he walked over to Penelope's table and looked from side to side for a few moments. "I thought Nancy forbade the general public from that side of the barrier."

"Look there," Alan said as he pointed at the screen. Scooter bent down and picked up a ball from the floor, then walked out of the frame. "I think he was retrieving it for those kids."

"And isn't that you?" I asked, pointing at a short man wearing a gray shirt.

"Uh-huh," he said. "I had my camera on a tripod at that point."

I watched as Alan stood with his back to the camera right in front of Penelope's table all by himself. My earlier doubts about the newly christened "Burton Guster" resurfaced. Maybe he'd had an alibi for when Wanda was poisoned, but he could have still been responsible for what had happened to Emily.

"Hey, you don't think I did it, do you?" He fast-forwarded and then froze the picture. "See, that's you all by yourself by the cake. It could have been you too. In fact, it could have been any of us."

As we watched the rest of the video, my heart sank. He was right. Everyone had been by themselves in front of Penelope's table at one point or the other, and with the angle of the camera, there was no way of knowing if they had taken that opportunity to poison the cake.

"Ugh. We're no closer to finding out who did it." I tapped my fingers on the armrests of my chair. "Hey, wait a minute. What if someone came in the back door?"

"Easy enough to find out," Alan said. He tapped on my tablet for a few minutes, then passed it to me. "Here you go. The security footage from the camera in the courtyard."

"How did you get this?"

Alan shrugged. "Don't ask."

My estimation of him shot up. A man with hacking skills. That could come in handy in the future. It never pays to underestimate mild-mannered people. They often surprise you.

"So what does it show?" Alan asked.

"Only two people entered through the back—Emily and Mrs.

Moto. I guess we're back to the drawing board."

Alan ran his fingers through his hair, studying his reflection in the mirror. "Mollie, can I ask you a serious question?"

"Sure."

"Do you think I should color my hair? Maybe go for dark brown like Scooter? Women like tall, dark, and handsome men, don't they?"

"Um...it's what's on the inside that counts, not the outside," I said diplomatically.

Alan picked at his fingernails. "If that's the case, why did Emily break up with me?"

I didn't have the heart to tell him that it might have had something to do with his taste in scented candles or the fact that he had a YouTube channel featuring mice in tiny costumes. But I am convinced that there's someone out there for everyone. Once we nabbed the murderer, I planned to turn my attention to finding Alan the perfect woman. Provided, of course, that he didn't turn out to be the murderer himself. My skills at fixing people up on blind dates only went so far.

CHAPTER 15
WRINKLE-FREE CLOTHES

ONCE I GOT BACK FROM the hair salon, it was time to get ready for Emily's memorial service. I wasn't sure what to wear. Normally, I'd select a black dress and heels, but the service was being held on a boat. My typical boat wear consisted of shorts, T-shirts, and flip-flops, but that seemed disrespectful. And my hair wasn't helping matters either. The sleek beauty-salon look was gone, replaced by the usual frizz. Sure, the frizz had a better shape to it, but it was still frizz.

I ended up opting for a navy-blue sundress, a cotton pashmina draped over my shoulders, and my dressy flip-flops. Yes, there really is such a thing as dressy flip-flops, at least here in Florida. Scooter scrubbed up nicely—he had freshly ironed khaki pants on, which were paired with a dark-green button-up shirt and his deck shoes.

Confession time—we didn't own an iron or an ironing board. Given the lack of space we had on board our boat, they were luxury items that didn't make the cut, much like a Cuisinart. We didn't even have a place to hang clothes. Everything was stacked on shelves in a cupboard. Fortunately, we didn't have a full-length mirror either, so when we got dressed in the morning, we had no idea how bad we looked. It was a blessing in disguise. When you ate as many sugary treats as I did, it was nice not knowing exactly how big your behind really appeared in your shorts.

The only reason that Scooter was wrinkle-free for the memorial service was that Nancy took pity on him and offered to iron his outfit. That was the thing about her—she had these moments of thoughtfulness that made you forget all those other moments of crankiness, at least for a little while.

We headed to the public docks at the waterfront park to board the boat that would be taking the group out into the bay for the ceremony. I was impressed with how Norm had transformed his run-of-the-mill charter boat into a charming setting to celebrate Emily's short life. Ropes of greenery were tied around the railings with bows, yellow rose petals were scattered on the deck, and there was a framed picture of the young woman displayed in the main cabin flanked by those flameless candles that wouldn't burn the boat down if they fell over.

Jeff stood at the top of the boarding ramp, greeting everyone as they came on board. He looked terrible—dark circles under his eyes, ashen skin, and trembling hands. Even his misshapen ear seemed larger than normal.

In addition to Norm and his nephew, Liam, who was helping crew the boat, approximately fifteen people were in attendance. I looked around and saw Ned and Nancy sitting on a bench in the stern, their clothes ironed to perfection. I was pleased to see Penelope carrying trays laden with hors d'oeuvres and miniature cupcakes down below. Ever since the residents of Coconut Cove realized that Penelope had been the intended murder victim, business at her bakery had picked back up. Jeff had arranged for her to cater the memorial service, which I thought was touching, considering the circumstances of Emily's death.

I heard Penny's Texan twang before I saw her. She was at the bow chatting with Ben. I was impressed with how well he had cleaned up. Tidy shorts and a shirt with a collar. Even his normally greasy hair was freshly washed, and there was a noticeable absence of grease stains on his hands.

Mike was standing on the dock, pacing back and forth and talking on his phone. After a few moments, he ended the call and gave Jeff a thumbs-up before he hoisted himself on deck. I groaned as I saw Chief Dalton shaking his hand. Just what we needed, Mr. No Comment on board. Then I saw him go over to Penelope and whisper something in her ear. That's when it hit me —the burly man was here to protect her. A sober reminder that the murderer was still on the loose.

"Did you see Alan?" Scooter asked as he handed me a glass of white wine. "He looks, um..."

I caught the photographer out of the corner of my eye. "I can't believe he went through with it." The mild-mannered man waved before snapping a picture of us. Despite the fact that he was wearing his usual ensemble of gray clothes, which normally caused him to blend into the background, today he stood out for the wrong reasons. His formerly gray hair was now chestnut.

"Is that one of those DIY men's hair dyes?" Scooter asked.

"No, I think he paid good money at the salon for his new look." I watched as Alan flitted around the deck, chatting with people. He was exuding confidence, and every word he said could be heard clearly. No more mumbling. I shrugged. "Maybe it was a wise investment. He certainly seems to be feeling good about himself."

Scooter ran his fingers through his hair. "Do you think I need to color mine? Between the gray hairs and my beer belly, I'm beginning to look like my father."

"First of all, you don't have a beer belly. You're just a little bloated, and that's from all the rutabaga. And second, you only have a few gray hairs on your temples, and it makes you very distinguished looking. I always thought your father was a handsome man, and you are too."

"All right, folks," Norm said. "We're going to get under way."

Liam was untying the dock lines when a woman came rushing up. "Wait for me!"

"Is that Wanda?" I asked. "Shouldn't she still be in the hospital recovering?"

After the woman had clambered on board, Alan made a beeline for her. "How dare you blame me for what happened to you!" Wanda shrank back against the railing. "I was out of town at a wedding when you were poisoned. Ask the chief. He can back me up."

Penelope came to Wanda's rescue. "Why don't you come down below and sign the memorial book?"

As the two ladies walked away, Alan shouted, "You haven't heard the last of this!" Who knew that hair dye could completely transform someone's personality.

* * *

The conditions were perfect—no wind and calm seas. Norm motored the boat across Sunshine Bay and dropped anchor in a quiet cove. Jeff stood at the bow while everyone gathered on deck. "I want to thank you all for coming this evening. It means a lot to me. One of the things that's impressed me ever since I moved to Coconut Cove is how kind, caring, and supportive everyone is. I know that Emily would be touched to see this turnout." He pressed his hand to his lips, gazed up at the sky, and blew a kiss. "I know that she's up there looking down at us…"

His voice cracked as tears formed in the corners of his eyes. Mike clasped his shoulder before handing him a napkin. "Thanks, mate," he said. After dabbing at his eyes, he took a deep breath. "I was so lucky to have been married to Emily, even if it was for a short time."

The crowd started murmuring. "Did he say married?" I whispered to Penny. "I thought they were engaged. He introduced her to me as his fiancée, not his wife, when you were showing them boats."

"It's news to me," she said. "Do you think they eloped?"

"When would they have had time to do that before her death?"

Scooter nudged me. "Shush. He's still talking."

Jeff was holding up the framed picture of Emily. "Would anyone like to come up and say a few words about my beloved wife?"

There was an uncomfortable silence as everyone looked at each other. Truth be told, no one had really known her.

Ned came to the rescue. "I suppose I could say a few words. I first met Emily when Penny brought her into the marina office to introduce her. She was a sweet young woman, always very polite.

She seemed very interested in Coconut Cove, asking questions about what it was like to live in a small town on the mainland. And, um...she was, um—"

Nancy chimed in. "She was punctual."

"She was?" Ned asked.

"Yes. One day she said she'd be by the office at three in the afternoon to pick up some papers, and she was there at three on the dot." Nancy frowned. "Oh, wait a minute. I think that was another young woman. Never mind."

Ned looked flummoxed. Then he raised his glass. "Here's to Emily."

"I knew Emily better than anyone here," Alan said as he pushed his way forward to the front of the boat. "In fact, I took the photograph that Jeff's holding. See that smile on her face? She was smiling at me."

"Listen, mate," Jeff said, fury burning in his eyes. "She married me, not you. Understand?"

The rest of their conversation was drowned out when Norm started up the engine. "The sun is going to go down soon," he said while Liam pulled up the anchor. "We're going to head out to sea now so Jeff can scatter Emily's ashes as the sun sets."

While everyone stayed on deck sipping wine and gossiping about Jeff and Alan's altercation, I went down below to use the head. As I was washing my hands, I heard the door to the adjacent cabin creak open.

"Where did you put them, mate?" That was definitely Jeff.

"The urn is in that bag in the corner," the other man replied. He sounded like Mike.

"Okay, I see it now. What about the paperwork?"

"My guy is going to deliver it when the boat docks," Mike said.

"And it looks legit?" Jeff asked.

"That's why you paid extra. No one will ever be able to tell it apart from the real thing."

"It better work or I'm taking you down with me."

"No need to threaten me. I had enough of that from old man Van der Byl."

"Fine, you're right," Jeff replied. "It must be the stress of it all. Why don't you give me a few minutes to get myself together, and

I'll join you back on deck?"

By this point, I was getting very uncomfortable. Bathrooms on boats can be very cramped, and the one on Norm's boat was no exception. I had wedged myself in between the tiny sink and a towel rack, but my right leg was beginning to fall asleep. Hopefully, Jeff would leave soon so I could sneak out without him seeing me.

"There you are," a woman said. "We need to talk."

Great, just what I needed. Another tête-à-tête with Jeff while I stayed in hiding, wondering what it was about marine toilets that made them smell so bad.

"What are you doing here, Wanda?" Jeff asked.

"You didn't think I'd miss out on saying goodbye to her, did you? I've known her for longer than you have." She began sobbing.

"Give me a break. You haven't spoken with her since she was a child."

Wanda blew her nose. "That doesn't mean she still wasn't special to me." The tone of her voice turned steely. "It's awfully convenient that you and Emily were married, isn't it? Especially as it means you've inherited everything. No need to eliminate any other...um, what's the best way to describe it...competition?"

"Just keep your mouth shut, do you hear me?" Jeff hissed.

"Sure, just as long as the monthly payments from the estate continue."

"You greedy little—"

Before Jeff could finish his thought, Liam came down to tell him that the sun was about to set. After a discreet interval, I opened the door and sneaked up onto deck. When I got there, Jeff was leaning over the stern rail, scattering Emily's ashes while the soundtrack to *Mamma Mia!* played in the background.

"Where have you been?" Scooter whispered as he handed me a memorial program. The front featured a picture of Emily, the same as the framed one that Jeff had been holding earlier. She really had been an attractive girl, I thought. Long dark hair, striking green eyes, flawless bone structure...wait a minute, something was so familiar. What was it? Then it hit me—Emily was a younger version of Wanda. The similarities were unmistakable. They must have been related, but how?

Wanda had roots on Destiny Key before she had moved to Coconut Cove twenty-five years prior. Emily had lived on Destiny Key. Wanda had mentioned how her sister had committed suicide after she found out that her husband had had an affair, leaving a four-year-old daughter behind. Could Emily have been Wanda's niece? Could what she had written in her journal have been about the present-day death of Emily and not about what had happened in the past as she had previously told me? If so, and Emily had been killed by mistake, did that mean Wanda had meant to kill Penelope? What was the connection between the three women? And who had poisoned Wanda, and why?

CHAPTER 16
POISONING IS SO EXHAUSTING

I TRIED TO GET A FEW quiet moments with Chief Dalton as the boat made its way back to Coconut Cove, but he rebuffed me. "Now's not the time or the place, Mrs. McGhie," he said. "But I promise you, I'll speak with you and your husband once we're back on shore."

"Scooter? Why do you want to speak with him?" I asked.

The burly man's reply was what you would have expected: "No comment."

Since he was being so uncooperative, I decided to tackle Wanda instead. She was the key to it all. I had a hunch that if I could figure out exactly what her relationship to Emily had been and how Penelope factored into things, then I'd be able to solve the case.

Of my four original suspects, I had more or less ruled Alan out. While there certainly was a dark side to him that one rarely saw, I wasn't convinced that he would have attempted to kill Penelope merely because she didn't want to date him. He was also in the clear when it came to the poisoning of Wanda. If his wedding photography alibi hadn't been watertight, the chief wouldn't be letting him run around loose.

Mike was obviously a sleazy lawyer, but he didn't appear to

have any reason to want Penelope dead. However, he did know the details of the Van der Byl estate, which could shed light on things. I made a mental note to try to worm that information out of him later. He had seemed ready to share some juicy details while Scooter and I were eating ice cream, but the discovery of Wanda collapsed on the ground had proved to be an untimely interruption.

That left me with Jeff and Wanda. In my gut, I knew that one of them had done it.

Here's the problem with my gut. It's very good at telling me when I'm hungry, and it's very good at nudging my intuition in the right direction. What it's bad at is follow-through. It sparks ideas in my head, but then it stops providing me with useful information and instead goes back to whining about the lack of potato chips and Hershey's Kisses in its life.

I'd say things like, *Gut, how could Wanda be the killer, as she herself was poisoned?* And it would reply in a low, gravelly voice, *Hungry! Very, very hungry!* Then I'd try something like, *Gut, why would Jeff want to kill Penelope? What's in it for him?* And then I'd get another unhelpful reply: *Feed me! Feed me now!*

Darn it. I was going to have to sort this out by myself, no thanks to my annoying gut. I needed to get the killer to confess. It was that simple. I'd start with Wanda, see if I could get her to break. If not, then I'd move on to Jeff.

* * *

People are more likely to confess if they've had some wine, right? Makes sense to me. So I brought a glass of a lovely zinfandel, filled almost to the brim, over to Wanda. She was sitting by herself up at the bow.

"How are you holding up?" I asked. "You must be exhausted. Poisoning would do that to a person, wouldn't it? Exhaust them, right?"

Wanda took a healthy slug of her wine. "Poisoning is a little more serious than that. I could have died."

I felt my face grow warm. *Poisoning was exhausting*—what a stupid thing to say. "You were lucky that little girl found you when she did." There, that sounded better, didn't it?

"I really was," she replied, guzzling down more wine.

"Poor Emily. If only I had found her sooner." Wanda gave me a pained stare. "You were related, weren't you?" I asked gently.

She emptied her glass. "How did you know?"

"I didn't until I saw you next to her picture. The resemblance is uncanny."

"You should have seen her mother." She wrapped her arms around herself. "We looked so much alike. There were times people couldn't tell us apart."

"So Emily was your niece?"

Wanda twisted her body and rested her head on the rail, staring vacantly out at the water. "Yes, she was."

"Why did you pretend like you didn't know her?"

"I didn't have a choice." She glanced at her empty glass, then leaned toward me. "That's not entirely true. I did have a choice. A choice between money and family. I chose money."

"What do you mean?" I asked.

"After my sister killed herself, I threatened to expose him. To tell everyone about his affair. It would have ruined his social standing on Destiny Key." Her eyes narrowed as she spat out her words. "And he couldn't have that. No, not him. He wrote me a check, put me on the next ferry to the mainland, told me never to return and never to contact Emily, otherwise I'd be penniless. The checks kept coming and I kept silent."

The night had turned cool after the sun had set. I shivered in the light breeze. Wrapping my pashmina tightly around my body, I considered what Wanda had said. Had the money she'd accepted from her brother-in-law been worth being separated from her niece?

Scooter poked his head out of the pilot house. "Are you two ladies okay out there? Why don't you come inside with the rest of us? Penelope's serving cupcakes and coffee."

"You're having a cupcake?" I asked.

"Jeff's been telling us about Emily's sweet tooth," Scooter said. "The cupcakes are in her memory. I couldn't really refuse, could I?"

Wanda's eyes welled up with tears. "Think of all the birthday cakes I missed as she was growing up," she said quietly.

I squeezed her hand, then turned to my husband. "I think we're going to stay out here. Save me a cupcake, though."

"Okay. Norm says we'll be docking in about twenty minutes."

"It's ironic that Penelope provided the cupcakes for Emily's memorial," Wanda said between sniffles.

"How exactly does she fit into all this?" I asked.

"I'm surprised you haven't figured it out," Wanda said. "You seem to have figured everything else out."

"Hmm, let's see. Your sister was twenty-five when she, um, passed away. And Emily was four at the time." Wanda nodded. "Her death would have been shortly after she found out that her husband's mistress was pregnant, right?"

"That's correct. She suspected he had been cheating on her for a while, but it wasn't until one of the nurses at the local clinic let it slip that the young woman who ran the bookmobile was expecting a child that the penny dropped. That's when she realized he was the child's father. He had been the one to set up the bookmobile program. Living on a small, out-of-the-way island meant that many of the residents didn't have access to a library. So he donated money to buy an old bus, had it refitted for use as a mobile library, and hired a young woman from the mainland to run it. He spent most of his free time helping her out, and one thing led to another."

"And that young woman was Penelope's mother," I said.

Wanda took a deep breath, then exhaled slowly. "Yes, she was."

"So that means Penelope and Emily were half sisters." Wanda nodded. "Did they know they were sisters?"

"As far as I know, Penelope never knew. Her mother did the same thing I did, accepted his blood money. She got checks every month, just like me."

"You must have resented her," I said. "Blamed her for your sister's death."

Wanda pursed her lips. "If it hadn't been for her, everything would have been fine!" she snapped. "I would have stayed on Destiny Key, watching my niece grow up and spending time with my sister. Instead, I spent the past twenty-five years stuck in

Coconut Cove."

"That doesn't make sense," I said. "Why would you move to the same town as the woman you despised?"

"It was part of the terms he set me. I had to stay and keep an eye on Penelope and her mother. My brother-in-law figured if the two of us saw each other on a regular basis around town, we'd be reminded to keep our silence so we could keep our checks coming."

I considered my next words carefully. "It must have galled you to see Penelope grow up into a successful young woman when you were separated from your own niece. Perhaps enough to want to kill her?"

"I can see why you'd think that, but it wasn't me. I'm color-blind. The killer would have to be sure he poisoned the right slice of cake, and he would only be able to do that if he could be sure the plate was purple."

"I thought color-blindness only affected men," I said.

"Usually, but there's a small percentage of women who are affected. It has to do with genetics."

I felt another headache coming on. Instead of a math-induced one, this one felt science-related. I tried to remember what I had learned in my genetics class in high school, but all that came to mind were the letters X and Y and something to do with pea plants. Ugh. Peas. Such an overrated vegetable, much like rutabagas. As I mentally ranked vegetables in my head by order of tastiness (potatoes topped the list, especially in the form of french fries), I realized that there was something different about Wanda tonight.

"How come you're not wearing anything with Trixie Tremblay's face on it?" I asked.

"Let's just say we've parted ways."

"No more Rutamentals?"

"If I never see another rutabaga again in my life, it won't be soon enough," she said with a shudder.

"Wow," I said. "That's quite a turnaround. Do you mind having a word with Scooter and convincing him that rutabagas aren't all they're cracked up to be?"

"All you have to tell him is that if he keeps up with

Rutamentals, he'll end up in the hospital like me."

I sat up straight. "Wait a minute, you mean you weren't poisoned?"

"No, it was a side effect of the rutabagas. Apparently, if you eat too many, you can develop some nasty symptoms, like a severe stomachache. It exacerbated my heart condition, which made it hard to breathe, causing me to lose consciousness."

"But why did you tell me that Alan had poisoned you?"

She bit her lip. "He'd been digging into my background, and I was afraid he'd expose our family history."

"So you would have sent an innocent man to jail just to keep your dirty laundry from being aired?"

"I regret what I did," she said. "When you've spent your whole life lying and covering up lies, it becomes easy—all too easy—to keep lying."

"Did you tell the chief that you accused Alan falsely?"

"No, but what does it matter, anyway? He had an alibi for that day, and it turns out it wasn't poison, just too many rutabagas."

"It does matter. The poor man was dragged into the police station, questioned, and made to feel like a common criminal. Actually, worse than a common criminal. You implied he was a murderer." Wanda stared at the deck silently. "You knew he wasn't the murderer, didn't you?" She nodded. "You know who the murderer is, don't you?" She nodded again. "And before you found out it was the rutabagas that made you sick, you actually believed someone had tried to poison you, didn't you? You thought it was Jeff, right?"

Before she could answer, Norm called out, "Liam, get those dock lines ready. We're almost there."

While Norm maneuvered the boat toward the dock, Wanda grabbed my hands and stared at me intently. "I've said all I can," she said softly. "The chief knows Emily and I were related and he knows about Penelope, but he doesn't know everything. Talk to Mike. He can fill in the missing pieces. Talk to him before someone ends up taking the fall for Emily's murder."

* * *

Once the boat was secured, Wanda rushed off, pushing others out of her way in her haste.

"Is she feeling sick again?" Scooter asked. "She probably shouldn't have been discharged from the hospital so soon."

"She's sick because of rutabagas. And guilt..." my voice trailed off as I watched Mike help Penelope down to the dock.

"Guilt?" Scooter asked. "She feels guilty about rutabagas?"

"It's a long story. But I need to speak with Mike first. In the meantime, stay away from rutabagas. They really are bad for your health." I started to walk toward the lawyer when Scooter grabbed my arm. "Hey, you can't just run off like that without filling me in on what's going on."

"I'll be fine. Mike isn't the murderer."

"Right," Scooter said slowly. "So Mike isn't the murderer, and that makes it okay? Let me hazard a guess—you're planning on talking to him about murder, though."

"Of course. From what Wanda said, he's the key to it all."

"Okay, no. Just no," Scooter said emphatically. "You're not going off to talk with someone about murder late at night by yourself. I'm coming with you."

"I'm afraid you aren't going anywhere, sir," an officious voice said, a voice that could belong to only one person—Chief Dalton. "I need to speak with you about some developments in the case," the burly man said.

"Don't you mean you need to speak with me?" I asked. "I'm the one who knows about the case."

"No, I need to speak with Mr. McGhie."

"Who you need to speak with is Jeff. He's the one who killed Emily."

"Emily wasn't the target," the chief said.

"I know that. We all know that," I said. "He meant to kill her sister, Penelope."

Scooter furrowed his brow. "Her sister? Penelope and Emily were sisters? How come I didn't know that?"

"As I told you, I have a lot to fill you in on." I turned to the chief. "But you knew they were related, didn't you?" His only reply consisted of raising one of his eyebrows. "Jeff thought he was killing Penelope. I just haven't figured out why yet, but I'm sure it has something to do with their father's estate."

"Maarten van der Byl's estate?" Scooter asked. "So this is all about money?"

"So you're admitting you knew Mr. Van der Byl?" the chief asked.

"I never met him personally. Everything was done through lawyers," Scooter said.

"But your company had dealings with him, isn't that correct?"

Scooter ran his fingers through his hair. "What does that have to do with anything?"

"That's exactly what we're going to find out. Now, if you wouldn't mind, I'll give you a ride to the police station."

"What?" I stepped forward and jabbed my finger at the chief. "Listen here, Tiny. You need to back off right now, and go arrest Jeff Morgan this instant!"

Scooter gently pulled me back. "Did you just call him Tiny?" he whispered in my ear.

The chief's face remained impassive. He pointed at his squad car. "Shall we, Mr. McGhie?"

"You can't question him without a lawyer," I said.

"I'm so tired of lawyers," Scooter said. "It seems like we can't do anything anymore without involving lawyers. And you can't trust any of them."

"That's not true. Some of them are trustworthy, like your lawyer, Tom. You've been working with him for years."

He sighed. "Fair enough. If only he wasn't laid up at the moment." He shook his head. "Listen, we're making a bigger deal out of this than we need to. I'm sure I can clear things up with Chief Dalton in no time. Nothing to worry about. I just want to get this over with as soon as possible. Why don't you go back to the boat, feed Mrs. Moto her supper, then come pick me up in our car." He turned to the chief. "It shouldn't take more than twenty minutes, a half hour tops, right?"

The chief shrugged.

"I can interpret his silence for you," I said to Scooter. "What he meant to say was 'no comment.'"

As the squad car sped away, I sank down on one of the park benches next to the public docks. Thoughts raced through my head—why did the chief want to question Scooter? He didn't really think he had anything to do with Emily's death, did he?

"Good night, Mollie," someone said behind me. I turned and saw Alan walking across the grass holding his camera. *Oh, no, the camera! That's what caused this all!* Scooter had been caught on tape near Penelope's table retrieving that kid's ball on the day of the cake competition. The chief would have taken one look at that and determined that Scooter had an opportunity to kill Emily. But the big question was, what motive did he think he had?

Mrs. Moto's dinner was going to have to wait. I had some investigating to do, starting with Mike.

CHAPTER 17
A BOX OF KITTENS

"HEY, WAIT A MINUTE!" I stepped in front of Mike's car before he could pull out of the parking lot.

He rolled down the window and leaned out. "You could have been killed. I almost didn't see you."

"Killed. That's a good choice of words." I walked around to the passenger side, opened the door, and slid into the seat.

"Uh, what are you doing?" Mike asked.

"We're going to have a little chat."

He glanced at his watch. "Can this wait until tomorrow? I'm beat."

"No, it most certainly cannot. Scooter needs our help. He's at the police station. And you're going to get him out of that place."

"I can't represent him," he said, gripping the steering wheel. "But I can refer him to a criminal lawyer."

"He does need a lawyer, but it won't be one that you recommend. No, what I need from you is to know all the details of the Van der Byls' estate." Mike's phone buzzed. He reached for it, but I grabbed it from the dashboard before he could. "Hmm. Looks like a text from Jeff. Want me to read it out loud?"

"Give me that!" We tussled for a few moments, and then Mike gave up after I threatened to throw his phone out the window. He leaned back in his seat and groaned. "Has anyone ever told you how annoying you are?"

"Sure," I said with a shrug. "But the people who usually say that are people who have something to hide. Like you. Look, I already know most of it. I just need you to fill in some of the details."

"What is it that you think you know?"

"One—Penelope is Maarten van der Byl's illegitimate daughter. Two—Emily and Penelope were half sisters," I said, ticking items off with my fingers. "Three—Wanda was Emily's aunt. Four—Maarten van der Byl bought Wanda's, as well as Penelope's mother's, silence. And five—Jeff is the murderer."

Mike ran his fingers through his hair. "If I tell you about the estate, will you leave me alone? Deal?"

"Let's hear what you have to say first, before I make any promises."

He shook his head and sighed. "Fine. Upon Maarten van der Byl's death, his estate was to be divided equally between his children."

I furrowed my brow. "If that's the case, how come Penelope doesn't know she was his daughter? Wouldn't you have had to inform her of her inheritance?"

"It's not that cut-and-dried. He didn't mention Penelope by name. The only way she would inherit was if she came forward with proof that she was his daughter."

"But she didn't know he was her father."

"Correct. And—"

"Oh, wait, I think I know what you're going to say next," I said. "Emily wanted to make sure that Penelope didn't know about her parentage. And with Penelope's mother having passed away, she would have never known unless someone else told her."

"That's right. And—"

"I know this one too!" I said, bouncing up and down in the car seat. It was like being on a game show, albeit one where the grand prize was saving your husband from incarceration. "The only people who knew about Penelope this whole time were Wanda and Emily."

"You're half-right," Mike said. "As you said before, Wanda had been paid off by Maarten van der Byl to keep quiet, but Emily didn't know about her sister until recently."

"Ah, that explains the interviews that Alan did with Wanda, Penelope, and Penelope's mom's friend."

Mike cocked his head to one side. "So you know about that."

I nodded. "Emily put Alan up to it, didn't she? She pretended to like him, going out on dates with him, but all she really wanted was for him to dig into Penelope's background."

"That's right. She ran across some old letters in her father's study and realized her father had another child. She just needed proof of who that child was, and then..." his voice trailed off when his phone buzzed again.

"Once she had the proof, she decided to eliminate her rival heir." I glanced at Mike's phone. It was another text from Jeff: *When are you dropping off the papers?* I tapped my fingers on the screen. "No, that's not quite right. Emily didn't want to kill Penelope, did she? It was Jeff."

Mike stared out the windscreen and stroked his goatee. "I don't want to talk about Jeff."

"Why? Are you afraid he'll kill you too?"

"Kill me? No, he doesn't have any reason to. He has other ways of getting what he wants."

"But you are saying he's a murderer."

He shook his head. "I'm not saying any such thing. But if we're talking hypothetically, Jeff isn't a violent person by nature. He doesn't even own a gun."

"You don't need a gun to kill someone. Turns out poison is pretty effective."

"Let's just say that was a one-off." He held up his hands. "Hypothetically, of course. People like Jeff and the Van der Byls are more sophisticated when it comes to getting what they want. Blackmail, forged documents, less-than-legitimate legal transactions, financial fraud—those are their tools of the trade."

"He has something on you, doesn't he?" The lawyer nodded. "But he didn't have anything on Penelope, so he had to resort to poison, right?"

Mike drummed his fingers on the steering wheel. "I've said all that I'm going to say. We had a deal. Once I told you about the estate, you promised to leave me alone." He leaned across me and opened the passenger door. "You should probably go see what's happened to your husband."

I reluctantly exited the car. As I walked toward my own car, Mike pulled up alongside me, leaned out the window and held out his hand. "You've still got my phone."

"Just one more question," I said. "Wouldn't Jeff still want Penelope dead? Otherwise, he only inherits the half of the estate that belonged to Emily."

"But Emily and Jeff were married," Mike said. "That changes everything. In the event that Emily married within a year after her father's death, she stood to inherit the entire estate. Don't worry, Penelope is safe now. So are you and everyone else. Jeff has all his ducks in a row."

I dropped the phone into his hand and watched him speed away. While Mike had answered a lot of questions, he hadn't answered all of them. And I needed answers, not only to put a killer behind bars but also to save my husband from being falsely accused.

* * *

I didn't have time to get answers to my questions, not with Scooter at the police station. I rushed over there, breaking speed limits willy-nilly, only to end up waiting on the hard wooden bench in the lobby for hours.

The receptionist was pleasant the first twenty times I asked her how much longer my husband would be. After that, her only response was "no comment." She even had the nerve to pretend to be on the phone when I asked her if I could have one of the donuts she had in the box next to her computer.

I tried to forget about my hunger pangs by texting my mom.

You were joking about Mary, right?

No response. I tried again.

Do I need to worry about my ears becoming unnaturally large?

Crickets. Maybe she was playing bridge. I spent the next thirty minutes reorganizing the contents of my purse. I really did have a lot of pens. Finally, my phone buzzed.

I would never make fun of you. It's so cute when kids have imaginary friends. Or a twin sister, in your case.

I ran my fingers through my hair, then tapped a reply.

OMG. Did you mean Veronica this whole time?

Wasn't her name Mary?

No. Veronica. Not even close.

Oops. Gotta go. Got brownies in the oven.

I could really have used a brownie by this point. Texting with my mom always drove me nuts and straight into sugar's open arms. I stared up at the ceiling and smiled, remembering Veronica. Sometimes, it had been lonely being an only child when I was younger. Making up an imaginary sister had helped.

I slapped my thighs. Shoot. While the mystery of Mary was solved, my mom hadn't answered the really important question. I sent her one last text.

What about my ears?

Not surprisingly, I didn't hear back. Like me, when my mom is focused on brownies, everything else fades into the background, including the sound of a phone buzzing.

My stomach churned as I watched the hours tick by on the large clock mounted on the wall. I paced back and forth, stopping periodically to reread the wanted posters, reward notices, and takeout menus tacked to the bulletin board. I had tried in vain to have Thai food delivered to the station, but the restaurant had already closed.

The reward notices were typical of crime in Coconut Cove—information was sought about the theft of a golf cart from the Tropical Breeze condos, the identity of the person who had left a box of ten-week-old kittens outside the Tipsy Pirate (they had all since been adopted), who was passing counterfeit ten-dollar bills around town, and who had stolen roses from Mrs. MacDougal's garden.

While I was staring at the wanted posters and wondering what would compel someone to get a tattoo on their face, the door to the interior of the station swung open. Scooter stood there in a daze. He looked awful. His previously freshly ironed clothes were now wrinkled, his face was drawn, and his eyes were bloodshot.

"What did they do to you?" I asked as I hugged him.

"They asked me a lot of questions, over and over." He pulled back and brushed my hair behind my ears. "Mollie, it doesn't look good. I think I'm in real trouble."

My heart sank. The only time Scooter ever called me by my first name instead of by a pet name was when things were serious. "What's going on?"

"They think I murdered Emily."

I gasped. "The chief said that?"

"Not in so many words."

"Well, what words did he use? I know Chief Dalton isn't prone to verbosity, but he must have said something."

Scooter tucked his shirt into his pants. "He kept asking me about Emily and Penelope, about the Van der Byl estate, and about my business ties to them. Then he mentioned a cousin of Maarten van der Byl, some guy named Andreas."

"Who's that?"

"I met him once at a telecommunications conference. We had a drink together. He has a different last name, so I didn't connect him with the Van der Byl family. But apparently, if both Emily and Penelope are out of the picture, then Andreas is next in line to inherit the bulk of the estate."

"So what does that have to do with you?"

"The chief thinks I want Andreas to be running the Van der Byl business, because he would make all the contract disputes go away. Can you believe he thinks I would murder an innocent young woman to save my business?" He pulled me into a bear hug. "I'm so glad I have you by my side."

I squeezed him back. "Always," I said. "I'll always be by your side."

"Now, how about something to eat?" Scooter asked. "I'm starved."

"I think everything is going to be closed by now except a fast food place."

"That sounds good to me. The greasier the better." He opened up his wallet. "I think I might even have a coupon in here." He pulled out a stack of bills and shuffled through them. "There it is. A free chocolate milkshake with the purchase of a burger."

As he started to shove the cash back in his wallet, I stopped him. "Let me see those ten-dollar bills." I pointed at the notice on the bulletin board. "There's some counterfeit money being passed around. We should get these checked."

Then it hit me—people who counterfeited money needed to make it look as genuine as possible so they didn't get caught. The same thing went for forged documents. If you wanted something to pass scrutiny, you had to pay extra, and you had to know someone who could arrange for that sort of thing. Someone like Mike. Ten to one, Jeff's wedding certificate to Emily was a fake. Now, I just had to prove it.

* * *

The next morning, I let Scooter sleep in. He had tossed and turned for hours before finally falling into a deep slumber. I hadn't slept well either. My nightmares had taken on new proportions. How I longed for the day when only rutabagas and raccoons haunted my dreams, instead of visions of my husband languishing in a jail cell.

Mrs. Moto knew something was amiss. She didn't yowl as usual for her breakfast when the sun came up. Instead, she stayed perched on top of Scooter's pillow, keeping watch over him.

After leaving a note saying I'd be back soon with breakfast, I grabbed my bag and sneaked off the boat. I made a couple of phone calls to ensure everything was set up, and then I headed to the waterfront park for my meeting. You'll notice I didn't say I stopped off for a coffee or pastry beforehand. That's how serious things were—stopping for caffeine or sugar wasn't an option.

After parking my car, I walked over to the sports pavilion. The place was deserted, something I was counting on. I pushed the door open and walked inside. The room looked exactly like it had on the day of the cake competition. The cakes, plates, and tablecloths had been removed, but the setup was the same, even down to the barrier dividing the place into two and the Trixie Tremblay posters on the walls.

I sat behind one of the tables in the back and waited. After a few minutes, the door opened and Jeff walked in.

"Thank you for coming here," I said, my voice shaking slightly.

I knew I was taking a calculated risk meeting Jeff, but, based on what Mike had told me, I didn't think the Aussie would try to kill me. The lawyer had said everyone was safe from Jeff, including me. My assumption was that this meant that if he did try anything, it would involve something nonlethal, like blackmail.

Jeff sat in the chair across from me. "My pleasure, mate. I figure we should clear a few things up."

"I know about the wedding certificate. It's a fake. Mike arranged for it to be forged so you could pretend that you and Emily had been married all along."

"You're a clever girl, aren't you?" he said with a sneer.

"Not clever enough," I said. "If I was, then Scooter wouldn't have been questioned by the police. You'd be in jail instead."

Jeff leaned back in his chair and put his arms behind his head. "About that. I think your husband is going to have to spend some more time in jail."

I leaned forward. "I don't think so. You're the one going to jail. Once the chief finds out about your fake wedding, it will all be over."

"Well, here's the thing. He isn't going to find out. It's your word against mine. Besides, Mike's guy is an expert in what he does. No one is going to think my wedding certificate is fake."

"That piece of paper might work at first, but all they have to do is check the state records. There's no way you could have hacked into the government systems too."

"Ah, you're not as clever as you think, are you? The wedding certificate isn't from Florida. It's from a small Caribbean island, one where government officials are more than happy to look the other way with the right enticement."

"You mean a bribe?"

He put his finger on his nose. "Bingo!"

"Bribe or not, people are still going to question it. All this time, you've been saying that you were just engaged. Now, you've changed your story, and you're claiming she married you."

"That's easily explained. You see, Emily flew down to the islands with me to a pharmaceutical conference a couple of weeks ago. We got swept away with the romance of it all and were secretly married. It was a beautiful ceremony. It took place at sunset on the beach. Emily had flowers in her hair and wore a white sundress. I wore a white shirt and Bermuda shorts. We were both barefoot. After the justice of the peace pronounced us husband and wife, I drew a heart in the sand with our initials inside of it." He smirked. "Romantic, huh? People are going to lap that story up when I tell them."

I had to admit, it did sound romantic. Except for the part about it being a total fake. "How are you going to explain the fact that neither of you told anyone about it?"

He shrugged. "Easy. She wanted to have a formal reception on Destiny Key. That's when we'd announce we were already married. She thought it would be a fun surprise."

I chewed my lip. It did sound convincing. This man could talk anyone into anything. It probably explained his success as a sales rep. I steeled myself and got to the heart of the matter. "Couldn't you have been happy with half of the Van der Byl estate?" I asked. "Was it really worth murdering someone to get all of it? You killed your own fiancée, for goodness' sake."

Jeff frowned. "That was an unfortunate accident. I was fond of Emily. She rarely left the island, except for business. So when I met her at her lawyer's office in Miami, I figured it was meant to be. I was looking forward to marrying her. It was Penelope I wanted out of the way."

"Because you were afraid she would find out that she was Maarten van der Byl's daughter?" He nodded. "And you didn't have any way to blackmail her to keep her from claiming her share of the estate?"

"Correct." He leaned forward. "That girl's reputation is spotless. I couldn't find any leverage on her."

"So you admit it. You meant to kill Penelope."

"Sure, I admit it," he said. "I didn't have a choice. Sometimes, people get in the way."

"People like your former fiancée?"

Jeff furrowed his brow. "How do you know about her?"

"It's not important. What happened to her? Did you poison her too?"

"Let's just say she drank something she shouldn't have." He looked up at the ceiling for a few moments. "She really shouldn't have tried to make me sign a prenuptial agreement," he said softly.

I shifted in my seat. Jeff certainly wasn't holding anything back. I'd suspected that his arrogance would drive him to want to tell someone about how clever he had been. About how he managed to get exactly what he wanted, no matter what the cost to anyone else. My palms were clammy. Jeff's confession was coming a little too easily.

Never mind. Things had already gone this far. I had to press on. "Wanda knew about your former fiancée, didn't she? You were ensuring she still got regular payment from the estate, right?"

Jeff's eyes grew cold. "Hmm. Maybe I've underestimated you."

"Perhaps you should check to make sure no one is around when you have secret conversations."

He nodded slowly. "Fair enough."

"Maybe you can clear something up for me," I said. "When you and Wanda were talking outside the Sugar Shack the night Emily died, you said something about her having a vested interest in her death. What did you mean by that?"

"It all comes down to money. If Emily had been unmarried at the time of her death, Wanda would have inherited a modest sum, more than she's getting now with her monthly payments. But as we know, Emily was married to me, so Wanda gets nothing."

"Fake married, you mean."

"Like I said, it's your word against mine, and, well, my word is backed up with some very authentic looking paperwork." He leaned forward and placed his hands on the table. "Not that it matters, because here's what's going to happen. Your husband is going to confess to killing Emily."

I sat back in my chair. "Huh? Why would he do that?"

"To protect you, of course. You see, Mike's guy does an excellent job forging not only wedding certificates but also other things, like emails and letters. I have a file folder full of some very convincing evidence that you plotted to kill Penelope. You stole the bottle of gelsemium and poured it on Penelope's slice of cake, knowing that it would kill her. You'd do anything to save your husband's business." He smirked. "At least, that's what all the documents I have in my possession would lead anyone to believe."

"So just to be clear, you killed Emily, you faked your marriage to her, and you forged documents implicating me in Emily's death."

"That about sums it up. I've seen how the two of you are together. Your husband loves you very much. He'll do anything to keep you from going to jail. The police already think he did it, so it's just a simple matter of his confession." Jeff pushed back his chair and stood. "I'll expect Scooter to turn himself in to the police by the end of the day."

As he sauntered out the front entrance, I took a deep breath and put my head in my hands. Then I walked to the back door and pushed it open. "Did you get all that?" I asked.

Alan held up his tablet. "It's all on here, saved to the cloud, and I just emailed a link to Chief Dalton."

"Okay, let's grab the camera, and then I'll treat you to a coffee."

I watched as Alan walked over to the Trixie Tremblay poster by the rear door, peeled it back, and pulled out a camera that had been wedged on a small ledge hidden behind Trixie's face. As he pressed the poster back in place, I smiled at how her right eye had been discreetly cut out with just enough room for the camera lens to peek through. For once in my life, I was grateful for Rutamentals.

CHAPTER 18
THE NEWEST YOUTUBE SENSATION

"WISH US LUCK," I SAID. Mrs. Moto squirmed in my arms as I adjusted her costume.

Scooter scratched her head. "You don't need luck. The two of you look adorable. I think this is going to be the year that the first feline ever wins the Coconut Cove pet-costume competition."

Nancy's voice boomed over the loudspeaker. "Attention: all dog owners, and, ahem, cat owner, please bring your pets to the main stage immediately for the costume inspection."

"Costume inspection?" Scooter asked.

"She said something the other day about all costumes needing to be compliant. If they aren't, your pet is automatically disqualified."

Scooter examined the metallic belt wrapped around her middle. "You did an amazing job with this," he said. "Are you going to have her wear the hood up or down?"

"I think up when we first walk across the stage, then I'll pull it down to reveal what's underneath."

The loudspeaker boomed again. "Attention: this is your three-minute warning. All pet-costume competition entrants to the main stage immediately."

"You better get going," Scooter said, kissing us both on the top of our heads. "I need to go get set up with Alan."

"Set up for what?"

"He's going to film the competition. I want to watch and learn how he does it. He was telling me about his YouTube channel, and I was thinking we should start one for Mrs. Moto." Our calico meowed loudly. "See, I think she agrees."

"Well, the man to learn about making great videos from is definitely Alan."

"Isn't that the truth," Scooter said. "If it hadn't been for him taping Jeff's confession yesterday and sending it to Chief Dalton, I'd be in jail."

"Attention: Mollie McGhie. Please bring your feline to the stage immediately. This is your final warning."

"We better scoot," I said.

After barely passing the costume inspection—Ned intervened when Nancy wanted to eliminate us on the basis that she didn't know what Mrs. Moto was dressed as—we took our place backstage.

While our soon-to-be YouTube sensation sat calmly in my arms purring, the dogs were running around sniffing each other and tangling up their leashes in the process. Their barking drowned out what Nancy was saying over the loudspeaker. Eventually, she poked her head behind the curtain and glared at humans and dogs alike. "Quiet!" Everyone obeyed immediately. "That's better. Now, I'm going to call you up one by one. Walk your dog or"—she paused and peered at me over her reading glasses—"your *feline* across the stage toward the podium. Stop for a moment while I read out the description of your pet's costume. Then promptly exit to the other side of the stage. Is that clear?"

The humans nodded, the dogs barked in unison, and Mrs. Moto meowed.

The first dog up was a chihuahua dressed as Superman. He was a fierce little thing. If attitude was one of the judging criteria, he would have won hands down. After a few more dogs took their turn, the German shepherd, Chica, made an appearance wearing a shark costume. An extremely energetic dog, she tore across the stage without pausing at the podium. Then she raced back to the other side, her human desperately trying to keep up.

"If you can't control your dog, it will be disqualified," Nancy said. Chica did what any dog would do in a situation like that. She walked over to Nancy, gazed at her with soulful eyes, then held out her paw. Nancy surprised everyone by shaking her paw. Hmm. Maybe she was a dog person after all.

Next up was Bob, the terrier who we all thought should run for mayor against Norm. He strutted across the stage in a Sherlock Holmes outfit. He appeared utterly dignified until someone in the audience threw a tennis ball on stage. There was nothing Bob liked more than chasing tennis balls, and there was nothing Nancy liked less than dogs dropping balls at her feet and expecting her to play fetch. After kicking the ball to the side and admonishing Bob's owners, she called out the next dog's name. Maybe she wasn't a dog person after all.

I wondered what she was going to make of the next contestant—Chloe, the chocolate Labrador retriever. She was dressed in a hula skirt and lei and carried a coconut in her mouth. When she got to the podium, she laid down on the ground and started husking the coconut. Her tail wagged from side to side as shredded coconut husk flew everywhere. I stifled a smile when I saw Nancy pluck some out of her hair with disdain. After a few minutes, Chloe picked the husked coconut up in her mouth, carried it to the edge of the stage, and deposited it in Penelope's hands. I had a feeling coconut pie was going to be on the menu at the Sugar Shack later that day.

"And now, join me in welcoming the winners of the pet-costume competition for three years in a row, Frick and Frack." I wished Anabel luck as she herded the Yorkies onto the stage. "Don't they look adorable dressed up as fairies?" Nancy asked the audience.

Finally, it was our turn. You know what they say—you save the best for last. Mrs. Moto walked confidently toward the middle of the stage. When we got to the podium, I picked her up and pulled back her hood. The audience gasped in delight when they saw what she had on her head.

"This is our feline entry," Nancy said with zero enthusiasm. "She's owned by Mollie and Scooter McGhie and—"

"Actually, it's the other way around," I interjected. "When it comes to cats, they own their humans."

Nancy tapped her perfectly manicured fingernails on the podium. "Are you done? Good. As I was saying, Mrs. Moto is a Japanese bobtail cat who is modeling a"—she paused to adjust her reading glasses—"a Princess Leia costume. Who is Princess Leia? I've never heard of her before. I've heard of Princess Grace and Princess Diana, but Leia is new to me."

I turned to Nancy, holding my cat up. "Of course you know Princess Leia. Everyone knows who she is. This long white senatorial gown is the outfit from the original *Star Wars*. Surely, you recognize the earmuff hairstyle?"

The older woman shook her head, then straightened her papers on the podium. "You may exit the stage now. We'll begin our deliberations."

While the judges added up their scores, Mrs. Moto and I were surrounded by members of the audience, all eager to see the Princess Leia costume up close and take pictures. Alan and Scooter filmed the crowd, while our calico basked in the adoration.

"Attention: will all pet-costume competitors and their owners please return to the stage."

After Nancy made sure we were all neatly lined up, she opened the envelope that the judges had handed her. "In third place is Bob, the terrier who was dressed as Sherlock Holmes. In second place is Chloe, the chocolate Lab who was dressed up as a Hawaiian hula dancer."

"And now for the grand prize winner." While Nancy paused for dramatic effect, Anabel reached out and squeezed my hand. "No matter how it turns out, I just wanted to say I'm glad we've become friends." I squeezed her hand back and wished her and the Yorkies luck.

"The dog taking home this year's crown is...this can't be right." Nancy walked over to the judges and pointed at the results. After a lengthy consultation, she shook her head and returned to the podium. "This year's winner of the Coconut Cove pet-costume competition isn't a dog, it's the *feline*, Mrs. Moto."

"Way to go!" Scooter shouted. Mrs. Moto leaped out of my arms and darted to the front of the stage. The kids in the audience ran up and took turns congratulating her and scratching her belly. I sighed in relief. After everything we had been through over the past week, beginning with Emily's murder and ending with Scooter practically being accused of killing her, it was nice to have something finally go our way.

* * *

"Cupcakes for everyone," Penelope said as she set three large purple boxes on the table. An impromptu gathering had broken out after the pet-costume competition. The group had laid out blankets on the grass and commandeered the picnic tables and grill by the waterfront. Ned was dishing up hamburgers and hot dogs, while Nancy scooped potato salad and coleslaw on plates. To everyone's relief, there wasn't a single rutabaga in sight.

"Hey, those are for dessert," Scooter said when I tried to peek into the pastry boxes.

"So, what I hear you saying is that dessert is back on," I said as I slid onto the bench next to him.

"It is," he said as he squeezed some ketchup onto his burger. After he took a bite, he added, "But in moderation. It's possible I might have gone overboard with Rutamentals, but I still think my motivation was worthwhile. We really need to take better care of ourselves so we can Live Healthy, Live Long—"

"Yeah, yeah, I know—Live Strong." I ate some potato salad. It had the perfect mix of mayo and mustard. "Why don't we try to come up with an eating plan that works for both of us." I waved my fork at him. "But I have two rules. One—we have to be able to eat dessert and french fries at least twice a week." Scooter nodded. "And two—no rutabagas."

"What was the deal with all those rutabagas?" Penny asked as she sat down next to me.

"I think you were one of the few people in Coconut Cove who didn't get suckered into the Rutamentals diet," I said.

"There were some good aspects to it," Scooter said.

I smiled. "Wanda got sick from eating too many rutabagas. That certainly wasn't good."

"I thought she had been poisoned," Penny said.

"She thought she had been too, but it turned out not to be the case," I said. "You missed a lot while you were out of town."

"Where were you, anyway?" Ben asked.

"In Miami looking at some boats," she replied. "What else happened?" After I explained about how Jeff had plotted to kill Penelope so Emily would inherit all her father's estate, she shook her head. "I always thought there was something off about him."

"I know," I said. "His ears gave it away."

Penny laughed so hard that she almost choked on her hot dog. "His ears? Since when can you tell if someone is a murderer by their ears?"

"What was wrong with his ears?" Ben asked.

"Didn't you notice how one was misshapen and much larger than the other one? I couldn't take my eyes off it."

Ben shrugged. "Sounds like cauliflower ear."

"Huh? Do you get that from eating too much cauliflower? Oh my gosh, what are the side effects of eating too many rutabagas? What's going to happen to Scooter? He ate a lot of them. Is one of his ears going to start growing?"

"Well, they do say your ears keep growing as you get older, like your nose, feet, and hands," Ben said. "But cauliflower ear comes from getting hit. Rugby's big down under. The guys get knocked around, and their ears get damaged."

Scooter sighed. "So, in addition to turning fifty and getting a beer belly and gray hair, now I have to worry about my nose, feet, and hands getting bigger?"

"Don't forget about the hair that will start growing uncontrollably from your ears," Penny added with a chuckle. "On a more serious note, how did you get Jeff to admit to what he had done?"

"That was easy. He was really full of himself, a real Mr. Know-It-All. I knew he would want to brag about how clever he was. Alan was happy to help. He set up a hidden camera in the sports pavilion and monitored everything from outside. I called Jeff and told him that I wanted to meet, set a time, then just sat back and listened to him confess."

"I still think you should have told me what you were up to," Scooter said. "Things might not have gone as smoothly as you planned. He could have turned on you."

"But he didn't," I said, giving Scooter a quick kiss on the cheek. "Everything worked out okay."

Penelope walked over to the table and opened the boxes. "Are you guys ready for a cupcake?"

"Me! Me! Can I have one of the chocolate ones?" I asked. After she passed me one on a napkin, I thanked her. Then I looked back and forth between the baker and the Texan sitting to my right. "What are the odds that the two of you would have the same name?"

Penny's brow furrowed. "What do you mean? Hers is Penelope and mine is Penny."

"Isn't Penny short for Penelope?" Scooter asked.

"Nope. It's just plain Penny. My mom found a penny on the sidewalk after the doctor told her that she was pregnant with me. You know the saying—'Find a penny, pick it up, and all the day, you'll have good luck.' She had been trying for years, so she took it as a sign that her luck had finally changed. When I was born, she named me Penny."

"That's sweet," I said. "Although it is a bit confusing at times having a Penelope and a Penny in the same town."

Ben wadded up his napkin on his plate and held out his hand for a cupcake. After Penelope doled out a few more to us (yes, I nabbed a second chocolate one), she walked over to the other table before we ate more than our share.

"What else did I miss?" Penny asked.

"A lot of family drama," Ben said as he wiped frosting off his mouth. "Turns out Penelope and Emily were sisters, and Wanda was Emily's aunt. There's some bad blood there."

"I'm not so sure about that." I watched as Penelope sat down on the picnic blanket next to Wanda and offered her a cupcake. "Penelope is too sweet of a person. I don't think she can stay angry with anyone for long or hold a grudge. Who knows, maybe the two of them might become friends over time."

"Penelope sure did dodge a bullet when Emily ate that cake instead of her," Ben said. "What was that stuff he put on it called again?"

"Gelsemium," I said. "Because Jeff was a pharmaceutical sales rep, he knew about the dangers of herbal medicines, especially if someone had a preexisting health condition. Thanks to the interviews Alan did on behalf of Emily, he knew Penelope had a heart condition. When he saw that bottle of gelsemium, he grabbed it and waited for the right opportunity to use it."

"And that was at the cake competition," Penny said.

"That's right. Unfortunately, Emily sneaked back to the sports pavilion to cut another slice of Jeff's cake while he was occupied watching the fire. Then she took the other slice out to the fishing pier and ate it. She had the same heart condition as her half sister, and the gelsemium ended up killing her."

Everyone was silent for a few minutes, lost in their thoughts.

"I've got more hot dogs and burgers," Ned called out from the grill. "Come and get 'em." Penny and Ben grabbed their plates and excused themselves. Scooter convinced me to skip seconds as part of our new approach to eating in moderation.

"Do you think she's bothering him?" my husband asked, pointing at Chief Dalton, who was sitting under a tree next to Anabel. The two Yorkies were sleeping in their doggie bed, and, much to my surprise, Mrs. Moto was dozing in the chief's lap while he stroked her.

"Can you pass me that hot dog you didn't finish?" I asked. "She's probably hungry. I'll go take her a snack."

All three of the critters woke up when I approached. The smell of grilled meat will do that to you. I knelt on the grass and handed out the treats. "One at a time," I said. "Frack, you're first. Now Frick. Okay, Mrs. Moto, now it's your turn." After the last piece was given out and my hands had been thoroughly licked clean by their tongues, I scratched the calico's head. "Are you bothering the chief and Anabel?"

"She's fine," the burly man said gruffly. "For some reason, Frick and Frack have taken a liking to her."

"Admit it, Tiny, you have too," Anabel said.

"Why exactly is your nickname Tiny?" I asked.

The chief raised one of his bushy eyebrows. "No comment." Then he turned to Anabel. "It's our little secret, right?"

"No comment," she replied with a smile. As she adjusted Frick's and Frack's fairy wings, she congratulated me on Mrs.

Moto's costume and taking the top prize. Then she wagged her finger at me playfully. "But wait until you see what I have lined up for next year's costumes. We're going to take back the crown."

Alan walked toward us, his chestnut hair glimmering in the sunlight. "Can you all sit next to each other with the dogs and cat in the front?" he asked, holding up his camera.

After he was finished, the chief cleared his throat. "Good job," he said. "Both of you."

Anabel leaned over and whispered in my ear, "Tiny rarely offers any praise. You two must have really impressed him."

I knew I should have left when the going was good, but I couldn't help myself. "It was actually the three of us. If Mrs. Moto hadn't found Wanda's journal, then I never would have followed the clues that led to discovering the tragic Van der Byl family history and uncovering Jeff's role in trying to make sure Emily inherited everything."

Mrs. Moto meowed in agreement while the chief scowled.

* * *

After the picnic, both Scooter and I were stuffed, despite not having seconds. Mrs. Moto, on the other hand, yowled until her dinner was served. After she gobbled down all her Frisky Feline Ocean's Delight, the three of us sat in the cockpit and watched the sun go down over the boatyard.

"I've got a surprise for you," I said to Scooter. "I signed us up for the Fourth of July regatta with the Coconut Crew. It's going to be great. We'll race up to Destiny Key and anchor overnight. Then there are shorter races and activities during the weekend, followed by a race back to Coconut Cove."

Scooter's mouth fell open. "Really, that's something you want to do? Even after *Naut Guilty* and *The Codfather II* crashed into each other?"

"What are the chances something like that could happen again? Statistically, it's not possible."

"I don't think I've ever heard you use mathematically based logic before," he said with a chuckle. "If you want to talk statistics, what are the chances you would have found five dead bodies since we've moved to Coconut Cove?"

"Okay, you may have a point." I toyed with my necklace while I considered what he said. After a few moments, I slapped my hands on my thighs. "You know what, math gives me a headache. Let's not think about statistics. Let's just go for it. Owning a boat has been your dream, and I loved racing on *Pretty in Pink*. It'll be fun to do some more sailing."

"The Fourth of July." Scooter chewed on his lip. "That's a little over three months away. Do you think we'll be ready by then? We've got a lot of boat projects left on our list."

"We'll have to be. The deposit was nonrefundable. Anyway, I've already checked one thing off the list—I sorted out our insurance policy. After what happened to Mike, I want to make sure that we're covered for racing." I held up my hands. "Not that we're going to crash into anyone, of course."

He nodded. "Okay, let's buckle down and get it done."

Mrs. Moto crawled into my lap and curled up in a ball. "I was thinking I should make her a little sailor's costume, complete with a captain's hat."

Scooter smiled. "Why don't you make three? That way the crew of *Marjorie Jane* can have matching outfits."

"Oh, I almost forgot. I have another surprise for you." I reached into a bag sitting on the bench next to me and pulled out a box. "Ta-da!"

"What is it? Is that cereal?"

"Yep. Since you're off Rutamentals, I figured it was time you got back to your regular diet. I know you used to eat Cap'n Crunch, but I got you Lucky Charms this time. After everything that happened with your business, I figured you could use a little luck."

Scooter sighed. "About that. I was thinking it might be time for a career change. I've got a few ideas in mind."

"Whatever you want to do, I'm behind you one hundred percent." I leaned against Scooter's chest and looked out at the boats in the yard. Soon we'd be leaving this place, putting *Marjorie Jane* back into the water where she belonged and taking her out sailing. What could possibly go wrong?

Mollie's Sailing Tips

MOLLIE'S SAILING TIPS
SAILING TERMINOLOGY

I asked Mollie if she wouldn't mind sharing a few sailing tips with us. She thought about it for a few minutes while scratching Mrs. Moto behind the ears, then said, "Here's my tip—don't buy a boat."

After I explained that our readers were probably hoping for a bit more than that, she finally relented and offered up the following advice on sailing terminology.

Sailing Terminology as Explained by Mollie

Sailors have some sort of secret language which I have a hard time understanding. To help you out, here are some common boat terms and definitions.

Starboard & Port—It would be far too easy to use "right" and "left," so sailors say "starboard" and "port" instead. Sheesh. I've got enough problems telling my right from my left as it is.

Bow & Stern—"Bow" refers to the front of the boat, "stern" to the back. Anything near the bow is referred to as "forward," anything near the stern is referred to as "aft." Personally, I prefer "bows" on presents, not boats.

Aft Cabin—When I think of "cabins," the image of a log house in the middle of the woods comes to mind. But, on a boat, a "cabin" is basically a room. We have an "aft cabin" on our boat which we use as our bedroom.

V-Berth—The cabin at the front of the boat. It's named after the pointy part of the boat which is shaped like the letter *V*. Some people sleep in their V-berths. I don't think Scooter would want to do that after what happened on our boat.

Winch—To be honest, I still haven't figured out exactly how these work. Scooter says that it will make sense once we take our boat out sailing. All I know is that it's used to pull ropes in or out so that you can adjust the sails.

Lines—Scooter just read what I wrote and said that there's only one rope on a boat and it's the one attached to the ship's bell. All other ropes are referred to as "lines."

Companionway—Entryway that leads from the cockpit down below to the main cabin. I'm not sure why they're called "companionways." These things are narrow. It's hard enough to fit one person through them let alone you and a companion.

Washboards—Wooden slats that you use to board up the companionway. Some people secure them with a padlock, which unfortunately isn't a match for a determined thief with bolt-cutters.

Lifelines—A wire or cable that runs alongside the deck and is supported by stanchions. It's kind of like a guardrail that is supposed to keep you from falling overboard. My personal experience would say otherwise.

Stanchion—A pole that sticks up from the deck. When you're trying to get around on deck in the dark, it's quite possible you'll run into one of these and get yourself a "boat bite."

Boat Bites—This is what sailors call bruises. If you're going to spend any amount of time on a boat, you're bound to get a few boat bites. There are tons of things to trip over and stumble into.

PFD (personal flotation device)—These give you buoyancy so that you can float in the water. They're sometimes called "life jackets" or "life vests." Some have a CO_2 cartridge inside which allows the

PFD to automatically inflate when you hit the water. At least that's the theory.

VHF Radio—VHF stands for "very high frequency." This is basically some sort of walkie-talkie that you use to communicate with other boats and call for help. If a murderer is on the loose, having a working one of these sure would be handy.

Galley—A ridiculously small space that you're supposed to cook meals in. Thankfully, we can always grab a bite to eat at the Sailor's Corner Cafe or Alligator Chuck's BBQ Joint instead.

Sundowner—This is one of the few sailing terms that makes sense to me. It refers to a drink that you have when the sun goes down. It doesn't matter what you drink—although we're partial to gin and tonics—just sit back in the cockpit of your boat with your sundowner in hand and enjoy the sunset.

MOLLIE'S SAILING TIPS
DOWNSIZING & MOVING ONTO A SAILBOAT

I asked Mollie if she wouldn't mind sharing her thoughts about downsizing and moving onto a sailboat. "Living on a boat is Scooter's dream, not mine," she said while petting Mrs. Moto. The Japanese bobtail cat meowed loudly in agreement. "It's not her dream either," Mollie said with a smile. "She likes to have plenty of room to play with her catnip mice."

When I explained that some of our readers might be interested in a liveaboard lifestyle, she agreed to share some downsizing tips that she had picked up from people at the marina.

After taking a sip of coffee and nibbling on a brownie, she sighed. "Of course, if you are going to downsize, don't do it the way we did it. Losing everything in a fire was absolutely devastating."

Mollie's Thoughts on Downsizing & Moving onto a Sailboat

1—Think Small

Our cottage was so spacious in comparison to *Marjorie Jane*. To be honest, it was quite a shock to the system to find myself living in such a tiny space. Only one person can be in the kitchen (aka galley) at a time, Scooter can't stand up in our bedroom (aka aft cabin), and there's a distinct lack of closet space. If you're going to move onto a sailboat the size of ours, you'll have to do some serious downsizing.

2—Multi-Function Items

Since you won't have much room, look for items that can serve more than one purpose. For example, when we lived in our cottage, we used to have different glasses for red wine, white wine, and champagne. Now we have one set of glasses and we use them for everything—water, soda, juice, wine, beer etc. Oh, and they're not even made of glass, they're plastic because when your sailboat gets tippy (aka heeling to one side), things get broken.

3—Scan Photos and Documents

Some of the ladies in my sailing class told me that they scanned their photos and important documents and saved them on a hard drive or up in the cloud. It saves a ton of space on board, plus if you have water leaking into your boat, your papers won't get all soggy.

4—Do You Really Need It?

Some of the cruisers we've talked to told us that they found that there were lots of things that they had on land that they ended up not needing once they moved aboard. One of the guys tried to tell me that I could get by with just one pair of shoes and two pairs of underwear on-board. Yeah, like that's ever going to happen. This girl likes her shoes and underwear isn't something you should ever skimp on in my opinion.

5—E-readers

One of the things I was most upset about losing in the fire was my collection of books. While I like my e-reader, there's something special about holding a real book in your hands and turning the pages. But, if you live on a boat, storage space for books is at a premium, so it makes sense to switch to e-books.

6—Storage Units

One couple we know decided to rent a storage unit for the first couple of years they lived aboard their boat. They weren't sure if the cruising lifestyle was going to work for them and they hated the idea of getting rid of precious keepsakes and family heirlooms in case they decided to move back on land.

7—Save Space for Cat Stuff

Mrs. Moto wanted me to make sure to remind everyone that the most important thing to do when downsizing is to remember that you need to leave plenty of room on your boat for cat food, toys, and litter. In her opinion, humans can get by just fine with one pair of shoes and two pairs of underwear which leaves more space for catnip mice.

MOLLIE'S SAILING TIPS
COOKING ON A SAILBOAT

I asked Mollie if she would share some tips on how to cook aboard a sailboat. "Sure," she said with a smile. "That's simple. My number one tip is to go out to eat instead. There are lots of great places in Coconut Cove that will cook or bake for you—Alligator Chuck's BBQ Joint, the Sailor's Corner Cafe, the Tipsy Pirate, the Thai place, or Penelope's Sugar Shack."

After explaining that our readers might not always be anchored near Coconut Cove or another town and might have to cook on board their boats at least some of the time, she offered this tip: "Avoid any recipes that include rutabagas." Then she laughed so hard that she snorted her coffee through her nose.

"Sorry," she said after she composed herself. "Every time I think about rutabagas I get a serious case of the giggles. Can you believe everyone was so crazy about that Rutamentals diet?"

At this point, Mrs. Moto crawled onto Mollie's lap and demanded attention. After rubbing her belly for a few minutes, she said, "In all seriousness, cooking on a boat has its challenges. I've been fortunate enough to be connected to shore power while we've been living aboard *Marjorie Jane* which means I don't have to worry about having enough energy to use our appliances. I'm also have a grocery store nearby, so I can stock up on supplies whenever I need to."

She took a cautious sip of coffee, then continued, "But we're planning to go sailing for the first time during the Coconut Cove regatta which means I'll have to learn how to cook while at anchor. And if that goes well, we may go on longer trips. The ladies at the marina have been fantastic sharing their cooking tips and tricks which I'll be happy to pass on to you."

Mollie's Tips for Cooking on a Sailboat

<u>1 – Limited Power</u>

Once you're disconnected from shore power and leave the marina, you have to monitor your energy consumption. You won't be able to run the electrical appliances that you did on shore without an inverter. And you also have to be careful that you don't drain your batteries. Instead of running a coffee maker, you might use French press. Rather than using your Cuisinart to mix and knead dough, you do it by hand. Grill bread under the broiler or brown it in a skillet rather than using a toaster. Reheat leftovers in a pot on the stove, not a microwave. You get the idea.

Some boats can produce their own electricity with solar panels and wind generators, but we're not so lucky on *Marjorie Jane*. Just one more thing to add to the never-ending boat project list. Sigh.

<u>2 – Limited Water</u>

The same constraints apply to water. Even if you have a watermaker—a sort of magical contraption that turns salt water into fresh water—you still need to keep an eye on your water consumption. The tanks on your boat can only hold so much water, they could end up leaking, the water could go bad, and watermakers tend to break at the most inconvenient times.

We'll have to think differently about how we use water on board our boat. No more letting the faucet run mindlessly. Some tips the ladies gave me included minimizing how much water you use to cook pasta or boil potatoes, using canned beans rather than dried (no need to pre-soak them in water), and using salt water to rinse your dishes.

3 – Limited Space

Unless you're living on a mega-yacht, chances are the kitchen on board your boat will be a lot smaller than the one in your house on land. Limited space means you're going to have to be creative when it comes to cooking. Remember how I balanced a bowl of cake batter on the ladder leading up to the cockpit? Be prepared to use every inch of space you can find and to move everything to get into the fridge if yours is under the counter like ours is.

4 – Be Creative

Although there are limitations, cooking aboard a boat is also a chance to be innovative. One of the ladies was telling me how much she enjoys having to create something out of the ingredients she has on board. One night, she wanted to make chili, but she didn't have any onions or ground beef. So she used some onion soup mix instead of fresh onions and opted for a vegetarian version with kidney beans and canned potatoes instead of meat. Her kids loved it.

5 – Things Can Go Flying

While we've been living in the boatyard, I haven't had to worry about the boat moving. But when we're cooking out at sea or at anchor, things will be different. I'm going to have to remember to be careful about where I set down things. The thought of a knife or a glass flying across the cabin if the boat is rocked by the wake of a powerboat is a little scary. Our gimbaled stove will come in handy. It will swing back and forth with the motion of the boat, keeping the pans and pots level.

6 – It's Going To Get Hot

It's always hot where we live in Florida, but while we're connected to shore power, we can use our portable air conditioning unit. This won't be possible when we're out sailing.

Everyone has warned me that cooking will heat up the inside of the boat and make it uncomfortable. Using the grill on our deck, eating cold dishes (like pasta salad), or making things that cook quickly will be important when it's insanely hot.

Although cooking on a boat is different and has its own challenges, I am looking forward to trying out the tips, tricks, and recipes the ladies have shared with me. Provided, there aren't any rutabagas involved.

AUTHOR'S NOTE

Thank you so much for reading my book! If you enjoyed it, I'd be grateful if you would consider leaving a short review on the site where you purchased it and/or on Goodreads. Reviews help other readers find my books while also encouraging me to keep writing.

My experiences buying our first sailboat with my husband in New Zealand (followed by our second sailboat in the States), learning how to sail, and living aboard our boats inspired me to write the Mollie McGhie Sailing Mysteries. You could say that there's a little bit of Mollie in me.

I want to thank my wonderful beta readers who were so generous with their time, graciously reading earlier drafts and providing insightful and thoughtful feedback, my husband, Scott Jacobson, for
his encouragement throughout the writing process, and my editor,
Chris Brogden at EnglishGeek Editing for his keen eye, thoughtful edits, and support.

And many, many thanks to all of my readers. Your support and encouragement means everything.

ABOUT THE AUTHOR

Ellen Jacobson is a chocolate obsessed cat lover who writes cozy mysteries and romantic comedies. After working in Scotland and New Zealand for several years, she returned to the States, lived aboard a sailboat, traveled around in a tiny camper, and is now settled in a small town in northern Oregon with her husband and an imaginary cat named Simon.

Find out more at ellenjacobsonauthor.com

ALSO BY ELLEN JACOBSON

Mollie McGhie Cozy Sailing Mysteries

Robbery at the Roller Derby
Murder at the Marina
Bodies in the Boatyard
Poisoned by the Pier
Buried by the Beach
Dead in the Dinghy
Shooting by the Sea
Overboard on the Ocean
Murder aboard the Mistletoe

Smitten with Travel Romantic Comedies

Smitten with Ravioli
Smitten with Croissants
Smitten with Strudel
Smitten with Candy Canes
Smitten with Baklava

North Dakota Library Mysteries

Planning for Murder